Six lawyers—three men, three women—
all sworn to uphold truth and justice.
Three couples with three ties binding them: the law,
lust and love.

But what happens when the truth hurts?

What happens when life isn't fair?

And what happens when love doesn't
listen to reason?

A higher power decides.

VERDICT:
Matrimony

Relive the romance...

by Request™

*Three complete novels by your
favorite authors!*

JoANN ROSS—Named the Best New Romance Writer of 1984 by *Romantic Times* magazine, JoAnn has gone on to write over 50 novels that have been published in 28 countries. She wrote her first story—a romance about two star-crossed mallard ducks—when she was just seven years old. JoAnn married her high school sweetheart—twice—and makes her home in Arizona.

SANDRA CANFIELD—Award-winning author Sandra Canfield, who has been recognized by *Romantic Times, Affaire de Coeur* and Romance Writers of America for her contribution to her craft, is also a popular keynote speaker at conferences. Although born in Texas, she has spent most of her life in Shreveport, Louisiana, where she lives with her husband, Charles, creating the warmly emotional love stories her fans so appreciate.

BOBBY HUTCHINSON—Bobby gleaned some of her ideas about legal issues from her daughter-in-law, a lawyer. Her family is all grown now, affording her the time to indulge in creating the stories she loves. When not writing romance fiction, Bobby teaches romance writing and is a dedicated runner, gourmet vegetarian and reader—often of books on parapsychology. Bobby and her husband, Al, live in her native province of British Columbia.

VERDICT: *Matrimony*

JoAnn Ross
Sandra Canfield
Bobby Hutchinson

Harlequin Books

TORONTO • NEW YORK • LONDON
AMSTERDAM • PARIS • SYDNEY • HAMBURG
STOCKHOLM • ATHENS • TOKYO • MILAN
MADRID • WARSAW • BUDAPEST • AUCKLAND

HARLEQUIN BOOKS

by Request—Verdict: Matrimony

Copyright © 1996 by Harlequin Books S.A.

ISBN 0-373-20127-3

The publisher acknowledges the copyright holders of the individual works as follows:
WITHOUT PRECEDENT
Copyright © 1986 by JoAnn Ross
VOICES ON THE WIND
Copyright © 1987 by Sandra Canfield
A LEGAL AFFAIR
Copyright © 1991 by Bobby Hutchinson

CONTENTS

She told him there was no such thing
as a happy marriage.
He put it to a jury of her kids.

WITHOUT PRECEDENT

JoAnn Ross

1

FORCING HERSELF TO IGNORE the thousands of hot needles pricking her legs, Jessica O'Neill reminded herself that pain was all in the mind. The fact that her thighs felt as if they were on fire was merely a temporary mental aberration. While Jessica had been repeating that axiom for the last four blocks, the words were beginning to ring false, even to her own ears.

Only a fool took up jogging on San Francisco's hilly streets, she considered, urging her weary body back to her Haight Ashbury town house. Or a masochist. Jessica decided she was probably a little of both. She dragged herself up the concrete steps and leaned against the bright blue siding, gasping for breath. Just then she heard the telephone ring. And ring. And ring.

"For Pete's sake," she muttered, flinging open the screen door, "you'd think someone could answer the damn phone."

Her rubbery legs proved scant support, and intent on reaching the telephone, Jessica failed to notice the matching set of Louis Vuitton luggage in the foyer. She tripped, sprawling ignominiously over the oak flooring. The strident demand of the telephone was unceasing, and giving up on walking for the moment, Jessica crawled the rest of the way into the front parlor of her Victorian home.

"Jill," she shouted upstairs to her eldest daughter, "turn down that music! Hello?" she got out, lying on her back, gasping like a grounded trout, her breath stirring her unruly auburn bangs. The room was suddenly bathed in a brilliant light as an eleven-year-old girl aimed a video camera at her.

"Knock it off," Jessica snapped, scowling into the camera lens.

There was a stunned silence on the other end of the phone. "Are you talking to me?" a hesitant female voice finally asked.

Jessica was still waving her hand at the whirring camera. "No, not at all.... Mallory Anne O'Neill, get out of here," she hissed at the aspiring cinematographer.

The caller's voice was a frantic combination of a screech and a sob. "You have to do something!"

Now what? Jessica sighed as she struggled to a sitting position. "Jill!" she shouted again, covering the mouthpiece with her palm before returning to her hysterical client. "Mrs. Thacker? What's the problem?"

"It's Keith!" the woman wailed.

Vowing never to handle divorce cases once her law career was established, Jessica closed her eyes, garnering strength to continue this conversation. "What's he done now?"

"I can't believe it! Mrs. O'Neill, I want that man arrested. Right now!"

"Mrs. Thacker," Jessica crooned in a calm, authoritative voice, "why don't you take a deep breath and start at the beginning?"

A sound like a steam engine came across the line as the woman obviously followed Jessica's advice. "It's my Mercedes," she said finally in a voice that cracked slightly, but was at least understandable.

"He had it stolen," Jessica guessed.

She was at her wit's end with the antics of Mr. and Mrs. Thacker. Jessica empathized with her client—what discarded ex-wife wouldn't—but the term "civilized divorce" was obviously not in the Thackers' vocabulary.

"I only wish he had," Sylvia Thacker wailed, her voice high enough to shatter glass. "Then at least it would still be in one piece.... The bastard cut it in half. With a hacksaw!"

"A hacksaw?" Jessica arched an auburn brow. "Is that even possible?"

"He left the saw behind. Shall I call the police?"

"Let me handle it," Jessica suggested. "I'm certain if I contact your husband's attorney, we can settle this without pressing charges."

"I'd rather see the creep in jail," the woman muttered.

"I'm certain you would. But if we press charges for this act of vandalism, you may end up behind bars yourself. He could always countersue for your little display of temper last week."

The tears stopped abruptly as Jessica's client recovered her poise. "I thought you were supposed to be on my side, Mrs. O'Neill. Mr. Bennington assured me that you were quite capable of handling my divorce."

The threat was sheathed in silk, but Jessica recognized it for what it was. Mrs. Sylvia Thacker née Montgomery, came from one of San Francisco's oldest families. One suggestion to the head of Bennington, Marston, White and Lowell that the newest member of the firm was not treating a valued client with due respect and Jessica would be lucky to end up working in the public defender's office.

"Of course I'm on your side," she said quickly. "And if you're certain you'll be all right, I'll hang up now and contact your husband's attorney immediately."

"Tell him that if I catch that worm of an ex-husband on my property, I'm going to shoot first and ask questions later," Sylvia Thacker warned.

"Please don't do that, Mrs. Thacker. I'm sure we can all come to an amicable settlement."

"Terrific. Now I've got Pollyanna representing me," the woman muttered as she hung up the phone.

Jessica went onto her knees, riffling through her Roledex on the cluttered desk top. "Marston...Martin... Masterson. Quinn Masterson, you'd better still be in your office," she mumbled, knowing it to be a long shot. It was past seven o'clock, and if the man's reputation was halfway warranted, he usually spent his evenings in far more pleasurable pursuits than working on legal briefs.

His answering service confirmed Jessica's suspicions. The woman agreed to try to get a message to Mr. Masterson, but her bored tone didn't give Jessica a great deal of confidence. She was debating what to do next when her eye caught an invitation she'd glanced at and dismissed several weeks ago. The San Francisco Committee for the Preservation of the Arts was having a fund raising ball at the Fairmont Hotel. The chairman of the ball was none other than Quinn Masterson. As Jessica read the date on the invitation, she decided her luck was looking up.

"Mrs. Thacker's having trouble with her husband again, right?" The youthful voice cut through her musings.

In the midst of her client's problem, Jessica had forgotten all about the video camera still trained on her. "Put that thing down," she instructed firmly. "I'm getting sick and tired of living in a goldfish bowl."

Blue eyes as wide and vivid as Jessica's held her mother's stern gaze with implacable purpose. "It's my class project. Do you want me to fail?"

"I want you to find another project," Jessica snapped. "Whatever happened to rock collections? Or Styrofoam models of the moon?"

"I'm doing a sociological study of a family in transition," Mallory O'Neill stated resolutely. "You'll love it."

"I doubt that, since I already hate it," Jessica countered, raising her voice to be heard over the throbbing beat of rock music. "Jill," she called, going in search of her eldest daughter. "I'm going out."

Jessica followed the sound to the upstairs bedroom shared by two of her three daughters where she found her thirteen-year-old lipsyncing to the latest Cyndi Lauper record.

"Hey!" Jill protested as Jessica lifted the needle. "I'm rehearsing for Mallory's movie!"

"That shows how much you know about cinema vérité," Mallory sniffed, still filming the confrontation. "It's true life, dummy. You're not supposed to rehearse. Boy, are some people dumb!"

"Mallory, if you don't put that camera down right now, you're going to have your first experience with censorship," Jessica warned. "And, Jill, from now on, when I'm conducting business at home, I'd prefer to forego the background music, okay?"

Her daughter shrugged, irritating Jessica unreasonably as she blew an enormous pink bubble through pursed lips.

"Sure, Mom," she agreed nonchalantly. "But I didn't hear the phone ring."

"I'm not surprised since the noise level in this room was somewhere between a jackhammer and the Concorde. Where's Sara?" she asked belatedly, realizing that she hadn't seen the youngest O'Neill daughter.

"Sara's out shopping with Gran."

"Gran?"

"Yeah. Gran says everything in our refrigerator is loaded with additives."

"I don't see where my additives are any of your grandmother's concern. Mallory, turn that camera off!"

"I don't want to miss your expression when you hear the news," Mallory argued.

"News? What news?"

"Gran's moving in with us," Jill answered her mother.

Jessica blinked, forgetting the whirring camera capturing her stunned reaction. "In here? In this house?"

Mallory bobbed her strawberry blond head in the affirmative. "Isn't that neat? She's bound to get me an A on my project. Just think, three generations of women living in the same house, all experiencing the slings and arrows of divorce."

"That's ridiculous," Jessica returned instantly. "Your grandmother has been married forty-six years. She'd never get a divorce."

"That's not what she said," Mallory put in. "Tell her, Jill."

"She says she's left Gramps," Jill confirmed.

Before Jessica could answer, the phone began to ring again. "That's going to be Mrs. Thacker," Jessica said with a sigh. "Jill, tell her I've gone to meet with Mr. Masterson." She spun around, fixing her middle daughter with a stern glare. "And turn that thing off!"

"All right," Mallory muttered, reluctantly lowering the camera. She spoke quietly in deference to Jill's conversation. "But I would have loved to show how adults make their kids lie for them."

"It was her," Jill acknowledged, hanging up the phone. "Are you really going out?"

"I've got to," Jessica said reluctantly, the idea not on her hit parade of things to do with a rare free evening. "But there's plenty of stuff in the freezer for you to heat up in the microwave for dinner. I shouldn't be long."

"Are you going out like that?"

Jill's voice was laced with teenage scorn as she eyed Jessica's pink sweat suit. Jessica, in turn, fixed her daughter with a slow, appraising look, taking in the dark hair slicked back with styling gel, the neon orange sweatshirt, kelly green vinyl pants and suede boots.

"You're a fine one to talk, kiddo," she said. "I figure if I can put up with the punk look, you can survive a mother who has more important priorities than looking like a fashion plate." Jessica grinned over her shoulder as she left the room. "Tell your grandmother I won't be late. She's got some heavy explaining to do."

"Radical!" Mallory clapped her hands. "I just know I'm going to get an A this year."

"Off the record," Jessica warned, wagging her finger. "I don't want this family's private lives dragged through your junior high school."

"We've already had our lives dragged through the press," Mallory pointed out with deadly accuracy. "This at least will be the truth."

From the mouths of babes, Jessica considered as she took the bus to the Fairmont Hotel atop Nob Hill. She'd done her best to protect the girls when the news of her divorce had hit the papers, but, after all, Brian O'Neill had been in the public eye for some time, including his unsuccessful campaign for governor of California. When the word got out that he'd left his family for another woman, the spotlight had shifted to Jessica and her three daughters. Fortunately, a story about graft payments to certain members of the city council had drawn the attention away from them, allowing a fairly normal existence the past three years. Although it certainly wasn't the luxurious Marin County life they were used to, Jessica privately thought the changes had done them all good.

She smiled at the liveried doorman, ignoring his arched brow at her attire as she entered the elegant hotel. Looking neither right nor left, Jessica crossed the thick black-and-red lobby carpeting to the desk.

"May I help you?" The young man looked doubtful, but his polite, professional smile didn't waver.

"I'm looking for the Arts ball," Jessica explained.

"It's in the main ballroom, but—"

Jessica gave him a dazzling smile. "Thank you very much," she said, heading off in the direction he'd just indicated.

QUINN MASTERSON was bored stiff. He'd always hated these things and, at age forty, was beginning to lose patience with the pretence that he found them at all enjoyable. While he understood the need for charitable organizations, and the necessity of well-meaning individuals to direct them, he'd never gotten to the point that he felt comfortable. As he nodded at the clutch of women around him, hoping that he was answering with the proper phrases at the appropriate times, he wondered if they ever suspected he felt totally out of place in the luxurious ballroom, surrounded by all these glittering people.

Face it, Masterson, he told himself. *Deep down, you're still that Missouri farm boy struggling to learn the two-step.* His bored gaze circled the room, looking for someone, anyone, he could carry on an interesting conversation with.

His green eyes locked on the slender woman standing in the doorway. She certainly didn't belong here, he mused, eyeing her pink running suit, which stood out like a sore thumb amid the sequined and beaded gowns of the other women in the room. Her auburn hair had sprung free of the ribbon at the back of her neck, creating a brilliant halo around her head that he found far more enticing than the stiff, well-coiffed hairdos of the women surrounding him. Some distant memory tried to make itself known in his mind, but Quinn had no time to dwell on it now.

She was obviously arguing with the man taking tickets at the door, but while she appeared determined, Quinn had the impression that this was not a lady used to making a scene. What was she doing here? While no answer came immediately to mind, Quinn had every intention of finding out. She'd piqued his interest, and it had been a very long time since a woman had done that. His mind went into gear as he tried to come up with some way to escape this inane conversation before she got away.

"No, I don't have a ticket," Jessica told the guardian of the door for the third time. "I've no intention of attending the ball. I only want to speak with Mr. Masterson."

"I can't let you in without a ticket, ma'am," the elderly man stated firmly. "Those are the rules."

"Oh, for heaven's sake," Jessica huffed, her breath feathering her curly bangs. "This is ridiculous!" She watched as three more couples handed over their five-hundred-dollar tickets and achieved immediate access. Then an outrageous idea occurred to her.

"Excuse me," she stated sweetly, "but it is very important that I speak with Mr. Masterson."

"I've already explained—"

Jessica's blue eyes were absolutely guileless. "I know—the rules. But would it be breaking those rules if I asked you to take a message to Mr. Masterson for me?"

He rubbed his jaw. "I don't know."

"It's a very short message," she coaxed.

"I don't see where any harm would be done by that," he allowed.

"Thank you." Jessica rewarded him with her prettiest smile. Leaning forward, she placed her palm on his arm and lowered her voice slightly. "Would you please tell Mr. Masterson that Trixie is here with her cheerleader outfit and needs to know if he wants her to wait up in his room, as usual."

Jessica's expression was absolutely bland as she ignored the gasp of a couple who had just arrived. The ticket taker's face blossomed to a hue rivaling a lobster's, and his eyes widened as they took a jerky tour of her body, clad in the soft cotton jersey.

"Why don't I just get Mr. Masterson for you and let you deliver the message in person," he suggested.

Jessica nodded. "Thank you," she agreed sweetly.

Quinn had just about decided to forego social tenets and walk away from the quintet of babbling women when he was rescued by the doorman.

"Excuse me, Mr. Masterson, but there's someone here who insists on speaking with you."

Quinn's eyes cut to the doorway where the woman still waited. Her blue eyes were directed his way and for a long, timeless interval their gazes held, exchanging any number of messages, each one more personal than the previous. He couldn't believe his luck.

Jessica recognized the man instantly. Quinn Masterson's picture had appeared on the cover of innumerable magazines. He also showed up regularly in newspapers and on television. But none of those mediums had captured the essence of the man.

He was gorgeous, she admitted reluctantly. Thick, sun-gilt gold hair fell over a broad forehead. His eyes were bright green and seemed to light with something akin to recognition as he came toward her.

"You must be a genie," he stated immediately, his emerald eyes warming provocatively.

Jessica hadn't missed the gleam of appreciation in his gaze as he'd stared at her from across the room. While she knew she was no beauty, she still received her share of appreciative glances from men, even if Jill did consider her thirty-five-year-old mother "over the hill." Under normal situations, Jessica liked being found attractive. What had shaken her to her toes was the fact Quinn Masterson had stirred something long forgotten within her.

"A genie?" she asked blankly, ignoring his outstretched hand.

"There I was, wishing for you, when you popped up. Just like that." He snapped his fingers.

"Not exactly just like that," she countered, unreasonably irritated by his boyish smile. "I'm here to find out what you're going to do about your client sawing a brand-new Mercedes in half with a hacksaw."

Quinn arched a blond brow. "A hacksaw?"

"A hacksaw."

"I assume you're talking about Keith Thacker."

This was the woman Keith Thacker consistently described as an ill-tempered harridan? While Quinn had known Keith for years and knew of his wife's social status in the city, this was the first time he'd actually met Sylvia Thacker. Lord, he considered, staring down at her, while Keith could admittedly be accused of irrational behavior from time to time, letting this woman get away proved he was downright certifiable.

Jessica nodded, causing a few additional strands of unruly auburn hair to spring loose. "That's exactly who I'm talking about. You have to do something about your crazy client, Mr. Masterson. The man is literally driving me up a wall!"

Two red flags waved in her cheeks, revealing a barely restrained inner passion, and Quinn decided Keith was indeed crazy to leave this woman for that twenty-year-old art student. Although he usually attempted to convince his clients to try marriage counseling, Quinn knew he wasn't going to recommend that option this time. In fact, tomorrow morning he was going to call his old college buddy and inform him he couldn't handle the case. There would be a definite conflict of interest, since Quinn had every intention of winning Thacker's wife.

"Let's go somewhere quiet and talk about it," he suggested, cupping her elbow with his palm.

Jessica shook off his hand. "We can talk about it right here," she insisted. "Besides, aren't you needed in there?"

He waved off her concern. "Don't worry about it—they'll carry on without me just fine. Are you hungry? I know a little place in Chinatown that the tourists haven't discovered."

"Are you asking me to dinner?"

"Have you eaten?"

"No," Jessica admitted.

He grinned down at her. "Then I guess I am."

"I'm not dressed," she protested, suddenly feeling out of place in the glittering crowd. She'd been so angry when she'd come down here that the contrast in attire hadn't disturbed her. Now, seeing herself through Quinn Masterson's attractive green eyes, Jessica felt hopelessly disheveled.

"I think you look great," he argued. "I don't know many women with your hair color who'd dare to wear hot pink, but it sure works on you."

Instructing herself not to blush, Jessica dragged her mind back to business. "I'm here to discuss your client," she stated firmly, rocking back on the heels of her running shoes.

"And we will," he agreed, his palm pressed against her back as he urged her down the mirrored hallway. "Just as we'll discuss that little trick you pulled."

Jessica stopped in her tracks. "Trick?"

"Emptying the house while the poor guy was at work. That was playing dirty pool, Mrs. Thacker."

She stared up at him uncomprehendingly. "I'm not Mrs. Thacker."

Now Quinn was confused. "Then who are you?"

"Jessica O'Neill. Mrs. Thacker's attorney."

"I thought George Bennington was handling the divorce for her."

"He assigned it to me last week. Didn't you get my letter?"

"I've been out of town," he answered distractedly, as he attempted to remember exactly where he'd seen this woman before. "Jessica O'Neill," he mused aloud. "The name rings a bell."

"I'm not surprised," Jessica said dryly, waiting for the recognition to hit.

She didn't have to wait long. "You're Brian O'Neill's wife."

"Ex-wife," she corrected.

"Ex-wife," Quinn repeated, telling himself he shouldn't sound so damn happy about her marital status.

But he felt as if he'd been waiting for Jessica O'Neill all his life, and it was a distinct relief to discover she was available.

Not that it would have mattered, of course. It only would have made things a bit messier if she'd had a husband out there somewhere.

"I suppose I should tell you I'm sorry," he said slowly.

Jessica merely shrugged in response.

"But I'm not going to," Quinn decided. "Because I've always had one firm rule in life."

"And that is?"

He reached out, tugging on a bright russet curl that kissed her cheek. "Never look a gift genie in the mouth."

It was only a few blocks from the Nob Hill hotel to the Chinatown restaurant and since the early spring night was unseasonably balmy, Quinn and Jessica decided to walk.

"What did you tell Ernie, anyway?" Quinn asked. "I've never seen the old guy's feathers as ruffled as they were when he came over with the good news that you'd come to the hotel tonight to see me."

Knowing that it wasn't going to do a lot for her professional image, Jessica nevertheless confessed, drawing a deep, appreciative laugh from Quinn, who proceeded to imitate the stuffy doorman perfectly. He continued to disprove the theory about lawyers being as dry as their documents by treating Jessica to a series of impersonations, spoofing some of the city's more illustrious individuals.

"You're terrible!" Jessica's blue eyes were gleaming with tears of laughter as Quinn portrayed an eccentric, left-wing councilman with uncanny accuracy.

"Hey," he complained with a grin. "I thought it was pretty good."

"It was," she admitted, forgetting for the time being that she had every reason to be furious with Quinn Masterson. His client's behavior had been unconscionable. "If you ever give up the law, you can always have a career in show business."

"A few clients like Keith Thacker and I'll consider it," he agreed. "A hacksaw?"

"That's what Sylvia claims." She gave him her sternest expression. "Now I suppose you're going to claim you had nothing to do with it."

The look had as little effect on Quinn as it did when she used it on the girls. Instead of being intimidated, he appeared wounded by her words.

"Me?" Quinn flung a hand innocently against his chest. "Are you really accusing me of using such tactics?"

Jessica honestly had her doubts, but although she had just taken on the case a few days ago, the couple had been driving her crazy. She couldn't help taking some of that frustration out on Quinn.

"What if I am?"

"Then, Ms O'Neill, I'd be forced to point out that what we have here is a case of the pot calling the kettle black. I suppose you didn't have anything to do with your client absconding with every last thing in their house the day before she filed for divorce?"

Jessica rose to her full height in an attempt to look him straight in the eye. Just under five foot six, she'd always considered herself reasonably tall, but Quinn was at least two inches over six feet. That, plus the fact she was wearing running shoes, put him at a distinct physical advantage.

"Of course I didn't. Besides Sylvia didn't take everything. She left his clothes."

"Which she cut to shreds."

"Touché," Jessica murmured. "Whatever happened to civilized divorces, anyway? Those two are driving me up the wall."

"You're not alone," Quinn muttered. "Do you think that's possible?" he asked suddenly.

"What?"

"Civilized divorces. Do you really believe a man or woman can give up someone they love without a lot of anger?"

"I did."

He stopped, looking down at her with a thoughtful expression. "If that was actually the case, perhaps you didn't really love your husband," he suggested.

"That's ridiculous," Jessica snapped, drawing her arms about herself in an unconscious gesture of self-protection.

How had they gotten on the topic of her ill-fated marriage, anyway? She didn't like discussing it with anyone; she damn well wasn't going to discuss it with a man who'd been voted San Francisco's most eligible bachelor so many times that he'd been elevated to the Hall of Fame.

"Besides," she said tightly, "what do you know about marriage?"

"Not much," he remarked. "But after fifteen years of practicing law, I know a hell of a lot about divorce. And it's rare when the parties involved don't end up at each other's throat."

"I didn't have any choice," Jessica found herself admitting softly. "I had three daughters I wanted to protect from being hurt any more than they were. Speaking of which, I need to let them know I'm not going to be home for dinner."

"You can phone from the restaurant," he assured her, his hand lightly on her back once again. Jessica tried to ignore how right his touch felt, how much she was enjoying his company.

Just then she made the mistake of glancing in a darkened store window, and her heart sank at her reflection. She looked at least ten pounds heavier in the jogging suit and her hair was a wild, unruly cloud springing out in all directions from her head. She looked as if she'd just gone ten rounds with Larry Holmes and felt like groaning at the contrast between her disheveled appearance and the formally dressed man beside her.

"Look," she stated suddenly, "this is a bad idea. I'm sorry I went off the deep end about the Mercedes—I believe you didn't know anything about it. Why don't I call you at your office tomorrow and we can work out a fair settlement?"

"What's the matter?" Quinn asked, his heart sinking as he viewed Jessica's determined expression. She was going to get away, after all. He vowed not to let that happen."

"I have to get home."

"Are your daughters alone?"

Jessica had always been a lousy liar and knew better than to try now with a man renowned for his ability to read a jury. "No," she admitted. "My mother's with them."

His grin practically split his tanned face. "Terrific. Then you don't have anything to worry about."

That's what you think, Jessica thought, trying to make sense of these errant feelings she'd been having since she and Quinn Masterson had exchanged that long look across the ballroom. It was too corny to be believed, but it was true. Something indefinable had passed between them, and Jessica was unwilling to pursue its cause.

"Jessie," he murmured, two long fingers cupping her chin to raise her eyes to his coaxing smile. "You wouldn't really leave me to eat alone, would you?"

"You weren't alone back there," she argued, tossing her head in the direction of the Fairmont.

"I felt alone."

"Oh." Jessica thought about that for a minute, understanding the feeling. She'd always felt like that on the campaign trail, even though she'd been continually surrounded by members of Brian's staff. "How do you feel now?" she asked softly.

Jessica was entranced by his broad, boyish grin. "I feel terrific." Then his expression suddenly turned unnervingly sober. "Please have dinner with me, Jessica. I can't remember when I've wanted anyone's company quite so much."

If it was a line, Jessica considered, it was certainly working. She didn't think she could have turned Quinn Masterson down if her life depended on it.

"I have to get home early," she warned.

"Don't worry, Cinderella," he stated with a bold, satisfied smile. "I promise to get you home before you turn into a pumpkin."

2

JESSICA WAS SURPRISED as Quinn led her up a set of back stairs to a small, intimate restaurant over a store filled with tourist paraphernalia. She'd grown up in San Francisco, but had never run across the Empress Pavilion.

"Is this place new?" she asked as they settled into a high-backed, private booth.

"No. Bruce Tso took over the management about five years ago when his mother retired. She ran the place for fifteen years before that."

"I've never heard of it."

Quinn grinned. "Once you taste the food, you'll see why Bruce doesn't have to advertise. Actually, it's off the beaten track for the tourists and lacks the celebrity status a lot of the natives require." He seemed to be studying her, waiting for her reaction.

Jessica silently compared his attitude toward dining with that of her ex-husband's. Eating with Brian O'Neill had been an occasion to be in the public eye; he'd never select a quiet, out-of-the-way spot like this. Which was one of the reasons they seldom went out together in the later years of their marriage. She'd disliked having her meal constantly interrupted by other diners who shared Brian's compulsion for table-hopping.

"I like it," she murmured.

Quinn visibly relaxed. "I thought you might. How adventuresome are you feeling tonight?"

Did he have to even ask? Here she was, practically picking up a strange man, agreeing to share an intimate meal while dressed like Little Orphan Annie. For a woman known to plan every waking hour of her day, she was definitely throwing caution to the winds.

"What did you have in mind?" she asked in a low, throaty voice. Good Lord, Jessica considered, was she actually flirting?

Quinn decided that if he was perfectly honest with her, she'd probably think he was certifiably crazy. She didn't look like a woman who'd believe in love at first sight. He had a vague feeling Jessica O'Neill was extremely practical and down-to-earth, under ordinary circumstances. But this was no ordinary night.

"The house specialty is Szechwan, but some of it is admittedly a little spicy for American palates."

Jessica laughed delightedly. "Does the chef know how to cook *la chiso ch'ao chi?* It's my favorite."

Quinn was not surprised to discover that Jessica shared his enjoyment of the spicy chicken sautéed with peppers. Accustomed to acting on instinct, he had known at first glance Jessica was precisely the person he'd been seeking.

Quinn had set a master plan for his life back in college. After law school he'd sign on with a prestigious firm, concentrating his energies on becoming one of the best legal brains in the country. And though he had no intention of living like a Trappist monk, neither was he going to allow himself to get involved while learning his craft. He would become a senior partner by the time he was forty; then, and only then, would he turn his energies to creating a family.

Well, he'd turned forty last month, he was a senior partner as planned, and it was time to concentrate on finding a wife. Quinn was pleased but not overly surprised by the fact that Jessica had shown up exactly on schedule. He'd always been lucky.

"You're going to love it here," he promised.

Jessica's gaze swept the room, taking in the enchanting Oriental atmosphere before settling on Quinn's handsome face. "I already do," she said.

Jessica was vaguely aware that the dinner Quinn had ordered was superb, but if anyone had asked her what she was eating, she wouldn't have been able to answer. All her attention was focused on Quinn Masterson—even on the smallest of details. She observed the unruly lock of blond hair that seemed destined to fall over his forehead, noted the way little lines fanned out attractively from the corners of his green eyes when he smiled at her, which was often. His deep baritone voice, she decided, seemed to be coming from inside a velvet-lined drum. Everything about him fascinated her, and Jessica was amazed when the waiter took their empty plates, bringing them a fresh pot of hot tea.

Taking a sip of the fragrant brew, Jessica lifted her eyes and was unnerved to find Quinn staring at her intently.

"I keep trying to remember where we've met," he admitted.

"We haven't."

"Of course we have," he corrected amiably. "I never forget a face. Especially not one as lovely as yours. Just give me a minute and I'll come up with it."

"You're wasting your time," she said firmly. "Watch my lips, Quinn. We've never—I repeat, never—met. You're undoubtedly remembering me from the news coverage of the campaign."

"Nice," he murmured.

"What?"

"Watching your lips. I think that could easily become my second favorite thing to do."

He didn't have to mention his favorite pastime—the innuendo hung there like a living, breathing thing in the close confines of the booth. Just when she thought she was going to scream into the thick, swirling silence, Quinn tried a new tack.

"Have you lived here all your life?"

"Yes. Although I spent the last few years of my marriage in Mill Valley."

He appeared not to have heard the bitterness in her voice that came from all those years of playing the dutiful little suburban housewife for a man who had belatedly decided career women were more stimulating.

"That's not it," he mused aloud, more to himself than to her.

Jessica realized it was useless to argue with this man once he'd made up his mind about something. Oh well, she thought, he'd eventually have to realize they'd never met. Because if there was one thing Jessica knew with an ironclad certainty, it was that this was not the type of man a woman could meet and forget.

Possessing an eidetic memory, Quinn knew he'd met Jessica O'Neill before. The idea was disconcerting, because this was not the type of woman a man could easily forget. Her hair was a gleaming sunlit auburn, laced with strands of dark gold. Her blue eyes, fringed with lush, dark lashes, were beautiful. His gaze moved down her slender nose and came to rest on voluptuously full lips.

"Jessica O'Neill . . . Maybe I'm going by the wrong name. Aren't you Judge Terrance MacLaughlin's daughter?"

"That's right. But I haven't been Jessica MacLaughlin for fifteen years," she protested.

Quinn's lips tightened into a firm line. Then he shook his head and gave her a devastatingly attractive grin. "Don't worry about it, I'll get it eventually," he assured her. "Ready to go?"

While Jessica would have loved to stay until the studiously polite waiter threw her out, she suddenly realized she and Quinn were the only patrons left in the small restaurant. She agreed, smiling an apology to the patient staff clustered in a far corner of the room, obviously waiting to go home to their own families.

"Did you leave your car at the hotel?" Quinn asked as they exited the restaurant.

"I don't have a car."

He looked down at her with interest.

"It's expensive to keep a car in the city," she pointed out somewhat defensively. "Besides, San Francisco is an ideal walking city."

"I agree. But why do I feel that your decision to rely on public transportation goes a little deeper than locating an affordable parking garage?"

"That station wagon seemed to symbolize my entire worth as a wife," Jessica admitted. "I left it back in Marin County with the hot tub, the tennis court and my former spouse."

"And now that you've eschewed suburbia, you feel reborn into a modern career woman of the eighties."

"Precisely." Her tone challenged him to disagree. Something Quinn had no intention of doing.

"My car's back at the hotel," he said instead. "If you don't mind walking off some of those Szechwan prawns, we'll retrieve it and I'll drive you home."

"That's not necessary. I can take a taxi."

"Hey, I may be unfamiliar with the logistics of courting a genie, but the least you can let me do is see you home to your bottle."

"You're crazy."

He grinned down at her. "About you," he agreed.

The warmth in his deep tone and the lambent flame in his eyes caused a shiver to skim up Jessica's spine. She tried to suppress the slight sensation, which did not go unnoticed.

"You're cold. I should have noticed the fog's come in." He immediately slid out of his jacket, holding it out to her. "Put this on."

"I don't need it," she protested.

"Don't be so stubborn," he argued. "Wearing my jacket is not agreeing to a lifetime commitment." His tone was firm, but his eyes were still smiling. "Unless there's an old Irish custom I'm unaware of that states when a man lends his coat to a lovely woman, he's actually proposing marriage."

"Of course there's not." Jessica gave up, accepting the warmth of the superbly cut tuxedo jacket. "Besides, this woman definitely isn't in the market for a husband."

Quinn refrained from answering as he heard the unmistakable clanging bell. "Want to take a cable car back?"

"I'd love it," Jessica agreed, taking his hand as they ran to board the clattering, clanging national monument.

They chose an outer bench and as they made the turn at Grant and California, Jessica slid against Quinn. When she attempted to move away, his arm went around her shoulder, keeping her close. All too soon they reached the hotel.

"Want to stay on and ride for a while?" His green eyes sparked encouragement.

Jessica was feeling amazingly like Rip Van Winkle awakening after a long sleep. She couldn't remember feeling so young, so carefree. She wanted the night to go on forever. She also knew it couldn't.

"I have to get home," she said, her flat tone revealing that it wasn't her first choice.

"I thought you said your mother was with your daughters."

Jessica sighed as she jumped down from the cable car. "She is. But I don't know what she's doing there."

Quinn's arched brow invited elaboration.

"Jill said something about her leaving Dad. I haven't the foggiest idea what's going on, and to be honest, I never should have stayed out this long."

Jessica expected an argument, but Quinn surprised her. "Then we'd better get you home right away," he said, handing his parking stub to the valet. "You seem to have your hands filled with domestic spats these days."

"You know, life would probably be a great deal simpler if Congress simply passed a law abolishing matrimony."

It was impossible to miss the trace of bitterness in her tone, but Quinn was saved from answering by the arrival of his Maserati. Jessica gave him directions to her home and for a time both seemed content to allow the easy silence.

"How long have you been divorced?" he asked, knowing the answer already.

"A little over three years," Jessica said, eyeing him curiously. "Why?"

"Don't you ever consider remarrying?"

Her laugh was short and harsh. "Never."

"Never?"

"I wouldn't get married again for all the tea in China," she professed firmly. "Looking back on it now, I realize that my entire worth as a wife was as cheerleader for my husband. All Brian wanted was an avid and eager audience who'd sit spellbound while he talked about his real estate deals and recited his latest achievements."

"Didn't you have your own goals and aspirations?"

Jessica thought back on Brian's insistence that she drop out of law school. "Of course I did," she responded curtly. "But Brian was always too busy, or too tired after a long day at work to listen to what he considered the petty events of my life."

She shook her head as if to clear it of unhappy memories. "Now, for the first time in my life, I'm doing what I want to do. Not what someone expects me to do."

It wasn't at all what he wanted to hear, but Quinn was undaunted. "What about your daughters?"

Jessica gave him a puzzled glance. "What about them?"

"Don't you want them to have a father?"

She folded her arms across her chest. "They have a father. They spend two weekends a month with Brian and Deirdre, every other Christmas and six weeks every summer. In fact, they probably see more of their father than they did when we were married. Spending time with his family was not one of my former husband's highest priorities."

"So you really did get a civilized divorce?"

"It was extremely civilized," she said dryly. "In that respect it was precisely like my marriage. Utterly predictable and devoid of any honest emotion."

What on earth had possessed her to admit that? To outsiders, the O'Neill marriage had seemed idyllic. For political reasons, Brian had wanted it to appear so, and Jessica had never seen any reason to set the record straight. That had been one of the reasons their divorce had garnered such interest. That and the fact that the handsome candidate for governor had left his wife and three children for another woman.

"Weren't you upset when he . . ."

Quinn's voice trailed off as he realized he'd been about to ask a highly indelicate question. Not that he wasn't curious; he just didn't know if Jessica would be willing to discuss her husband's well-publicized infidelity with him.

"Of course I was," she admitted. A slow, reluctant grin curved her lips. "I broke every dish in the house."

Quinn returned the smile. "Good for you." He reached over and squeezed her hand.

Jessica realized that aside from work, this was the first time in ages she'd been alone with another adult. Enjoying the camaraderie, she allowed her hand to remain in Quinn's larger one the rest of the way home.

"Nice house," he observed, pulling up to the curb outside her quaint Victorian town house.

"It will be. There's still tons of work to do on it, though," Jessica told him. "The first year, while I was in law school, all we could manage was a coat of paint. The next year I had the plumbing replaced. Last year I sprang for a new roof and next month we're having the entire place rewired."

"Sounds as if you've got a lifetime project going."

"I think I do." She grinned. "But it keeps me out of pool halls."

Quinn smiled at the incongruous image. Then, unable to help himself, he leaned toward her, tucking a thick russet curl behind one ear.

"Thank you."

Jessica was more than a little shaken by his suddenly solemn tone. "For what?"

"Rescuing me tonight." Quinn's hand was stroking her cheek, leaving sparks wherever he touched.

"You certainly didn't look like a man in need of rescuing. That blonde was practically eating you alive with her eyes."

Those attractive lines crinkled out from his eyes. "You noticed."

"It was hard to miss," Jessica whispered, struggling to remain indifferent to the fingers lightly spanning her throat. Quinn felt her swallow and knew Jessica was not unaffected by what was happening here.

"It was even harder to get away gracefully. I was wishing for someone—anyone—to save me. And you came. My lovely genie."

Jessica wondered if Quinn could feel the rapid rise in her pulse rate as his husky tone stirred something deep and long forgotten within her.

"You're very fanciful." She laughed unsteadily, backing away both physically and emotionally from the provocative moment.

Stifling a slight sigh, Quinn allowed her to inch toward the passenger door. "I'd better get you in before your mother decides to investigate whether we're necking out here."

His tone was far steadier than his emotions at the moment, and it was only all those years practicing trial law that allowed Quinn to pull off this nonchalant air. What he really wanted to do was pull Jessica into his arms and never let her go.

"That's a good idea," she agreed with matching casualness.

As Quinn opened his door, the dome light came on, flooding the interior of the Maserati with light. The raw desire on Jessica's face was sufficient compensation for tonight, he decided. It was enough to know that at this moment she wanted him as much as he wanted her.

"Are you free for lunch tomorrow?" he asked as he walked her to the front door.

"I've got a lunch date," Jessica stated, refraining from mentioning that it was with Vanessa Parker, the only other woman attorney employed at Bennington, Marston, White and Lowell.

"How about a drink after work?"

"Sorry."

"Another date?" he inquired grittily, not bothering to hide his irritation.

"Something like that."

Jessica knew Quinn was suspecting the worst, but what business of his was it if she wanted to date every man in San Francisco? Deciding it would do him good to discover that not every woman in the city was swooning at his feet, she didn't admit she had to pick up Sara's ballet slippers before the shoe repair shop closed at five-thirty.

"Dinner?"

She had to give him an A for tenacity. "I'm sorry, Quinn, but—"

"I know," he muttered, shoving his hands into his pockets. "You've got another date."

"Not exactly," she found herself admitting.

His expression brightened slightly. "Washing your hair?"

"No."

"Washing your mother's hair?"

She laughed at that one. "No."

"Your daughters'?"

"Close. Sara, my youngest, has a dance recital at the War Memorial Opera House. She's been practicing her pirouettes for weeks. It's like living with a human top."

Quinn laughed. "Well," he stated on an exaggerated sigh, "I suppose I'll have to settle for seeing you in court."

"Speaking of which..." Jessica suddenly realized she'd been so entranced with Quinn's company that she hadn't even insisted he make his client replace Sylvia's Mercedes.

"I know, there's still the little matter of a severed Mercedes."

"It's not a little matter," she pointed out briskly.

"Since California is a community property state, why don't we let them each take a half?"

"That isn't funny!"

"Come on, Jess," Quinn coaxed. "Can't you see the humor in the situation? By the time the two of them are finished, there won't be anything left to divide."

"You may find the entire situation humorous, but I'm not fortunate enough to be a senior partner in one of the city's most prestigious law firms," she retorted. "Your horrible client has put my job in jeopardy, and you'll have to excuse me if I can't see my way clear to laugh about it!"

From the way her voice faltered, Quinn realized Jessica was not as self-confident as she led one to believe. While that could work in his favor, he'd have to proceed cautiously.

"I'll talk to Keith," he assured her, his hands shaping her stiffened shoulders. "I promise he'll be on his best behavior from now on."

"He'd better be," Jessica grumbled. "Because Sylvia is threatening to shoot the minute she sees the whites of his eyes."

"Then the guy's safe."

"What does that mean?"

"You've heard of the three-martini lunch?"

She nodded.

"Keith Thacker is a proponent of the five-martini breakfast. On a good day the whites of his eyes look like a map of the Los Angeles freeway system." Quinn winked, earning a crooked smile from Jessica.

"You're not at all what I expected," she murmured, more to herself than to Quinn as she turned away to unlock her door. She took off his jacket, feeling oddly deprived of its woodsy, masculine scent as she returned it to him. "Thanks for dinner."

"It was my pleasure," he said, nodding his head.

Jessica had to thrust her hands behind her back to keep from reaching up and brushing back that curl that had fallen over his forehead once again.

"Well, good night," she murmured.

"Good night, Jess." He reached out, feathering a light path up her cheek with his knuckles. "Sweet dreams."

Jessica closed her eyes momentarily at the tender touch, half afraid Quinn was intending to kiss her, half terrified he might not.

Not immune to the desire he'd seen in those soft blue eyes before her lush lashes fluttered down, Quinn forced himself to back away from the sensual moment. Jessica was obviously a strong, independent woman, but when it came to relationships, the lady was as skittish as a doe. One false move and she'd take off running.

As much as he wanted to taste those lushly pink lips, he couldn't risk it. Not yet. He ruffled her hair in a friendly, almost fraternal gesture.

"See you in court, counselor," he said in a casual tone.

Jessica's eyes flew open. "In court," she echoed, watching him take the steps two at a time.

She experienced the oddest feeling of sadness as he drove away, and wondered what it was about Quinn Masterson that could make her respond so uncharacteristically. She couldn't remember the last time she'd laughed so freely. Or allowed an evening to pass without phoning home to make certain the girls were in bed on time. It was as if she had been a different person tonight. Jessica glanced up at the gleaming white moon hanging over the city, wondering if there was any truth to the notion that people behaved differently under the influence of a full moon.

The question of her uncharacteristic feelings was a complex one, and Jessica suddenly realized exactly how exhausted she was. It had been a long and tiring day, and if she knew Keith and Sylvia Thacker, tomorrow wasn't going to be one iota easier. She went into the darkened house, unerringly locating the couch, and sank down. Leaning her head back against the cushions, she shut her eyes.

"Jessica?" a voice inquired from the hallway. "Is that you?"

Jessica stifled a groan. "It's me, Mom. I'm sorry I woke you."

"I was awake." The censure in Elizabeth MacLaughlin's tone was unmistakable. "I couldn't sleep until my little girl was back home, safe and sound."

Jessica reined in the temptation to remind her mother that as the mother of three daughters, one a teenager, she was far from infancy. "I'm safe enough," she assured Elizabeth as the older woman entered the living room, tying the sash of her silk robe. "But as for sound . . ." Jessica's voice drifted off as she rubbed the back of her neck.

"You work too hard."

"Please, let's not get into that again. I certainly didn't plan for things to go so wrong today. Speaking of which, what on earth is going on? Jill told me you've left Dad."

Elizabeth MacLaughlin smoothly ignored Jessica's question. "What you need is a cup of tea and something to eat. I'll bet you didn't have dinner, did you?"

"I ate downtown," she hedged, not wanting her mother to know she'd gone to dinner with Quinn Masterson.

"Where?"

Jessica shrugged. "A little Chinese place. I forget the name."

"The food was probably loaded with monosodium glutamate," Elizabeth said with blatant disapproval.

"Probably," Jessica agreed. "That's what makes it taste so good."

Her mother shook her head. "Now you're teasing me. You're as bad as your father."

"Speaking of Dad . . ." Jessica inserted quickly, hoping her mother would explain why after forty-six years of marriage, she'd suddenly shown up on her daughter's doorstep.

"Tell me about the Thackers' latest escapade," Elizabeth said, sidestepping the issue. "Did you see his cartoon in the *Star* today? He's very talented." Elizabeth's brow furrowed. "You know, your father and I used to be very good friends with Keith's parents. It's too bad he ended up an alcoholic. However, I have to admit I'm not that surprised. Mary spoiled the boy rotten."

Jessica refrained from answering that San Francisco's most controversial political cartoonist had problems that went far deeper than an indulgent mother.

"I'd better be getting to bed," she said, rising from the couch. "I've got a hectic day tomorrow."

"What you need is a husband," Elizabeth advised, not for the first time. "Someone to take care of you and the girls for a change."

Jessica decided not to fall back into the old argument that she was quite capable of taking care of her family all by herself. She was more interested in finding out the reason behind Elizabeth MacLaughlin's recent actions.

"Speaking of husbands—"

"Good night, dear," her mother stated firmly.

Shaking her head in frustration, Jessica bent and kissed the top of her mother's head. The natural auburn hair was still as vibrant as Jessica's, without a hint of gray.

"Good night, Mom." Jessica suddenly wanted nothing more than to fall into bed and sleep around the clock.

But sleep was not that easily found, she discovered much, much later. She couldn't get Quinn Masterson out of her thoughts. It was as if his smiling green eyes and handsome face had been indelibly printed onto her mind's eye. It had been over three years since she'd had a casual evening alone with a man. In the beginning, she'd been hurting too badly to even consider the idea.

Later on, trying to juggle law school with the bringing up of three spirited children precluded anything that remotely resembled a social life. Now, while her life was going a little more smoothly, it was still a simple matter to beg off any invitations from the men she'd meet in the course of her workday. Not many men could remain undaunted by Jessica's ready-made family.

But tonight had been different. There had been such an inevitability to it. If she were a more fanciful person, Jessica might have thought her meeting with Quinn was preordained. But she prided herself on being an extremely practical woman and did not believe in kismet, fate or anything to do with stars, horoscopes or numerology. Or full moons, either, she reminded herself briskly. Those ideas she willingly left to the romantics of the world.

Yet, Jessica considered, lying in bed, her head pillowed by her arms, she'd almost felt romantic tonight. She'd forgotten how nice it was to feel a man's firm hand on her back. Or what a pleasant experience it could be to linger over dinner, sharing conversation that had nothing to do with orthodontist appointments, permission slips for seventh-grade field trips or Girl Scout cookie sales.

It was odd. She'd grown used to all the labels. Divorcée, single head of household, ex-wife, mother, attorney. Any one of those terms could accurately describe Jessica O'Neill. But until this evening, she'd forgotten the most intriguing one of all. Woman.

For a few fleeting wonderful hours Quinn had made Jessica feel like a woman. He'd managed to transport her to a magical realm where she was alive, desirable, utterly fascinating. For that, she was grateful. She'd always remember it as a special evening with a very nice man. Of that Jessica was certain. Just as she was certain it would never happen again.

3

THE SMELL OF BURNING BACON wafted into Jessica's subconscious the following morning and she groaned, pulling the rose-hued comforter over her head. Muffled conversation drifted up the stairs, the steady drone punctuated at intervals by a raised voice or grievous shout.

"Mom! You have got to do something about Mallory and that damn camera of hers."

The insistent tone refused to be ignored and Jessica threw off the comforter, eyeing her daughter standing in the doorway. Smoke practically poured from Jill's ears.

"Don't cuss," Jessica answered automatically. "What has Mallory done now?"

"She invaded my privacy!"

Stifling a sigh, Jessica climbed out of bed, reaching for her robe. "She's been doing that all week and I haven't heard a word of complaint," she pointed out. "In fact, if I recall, you were rehearsing for a starring role last night."

"That was before I knew she was going to hide in the closet and tape my telephone conversations. Mom, she filmed me telling Lori what a hunk Tommy Drew is!"

"Sounds like the end of the world to me," Jessica agreed calmly.

"Mother! This is serious!"

Remembering her own teenage traumas, Jessica forced herself to remain patient. "I'll talk with her," she promised. "After I have a cup of coffee."

"Good." Jill nodded with a vast amount of youthful satisfaction as she left the room and headed back downstairs. "Hey, Mallory," she hollered, "are you ever in trouble now!"

Jessica shook her head, going over to her closet. A list of possible choices was posted on the back of the closet door, and she wryly decided that since Brian had forced her to join the ranks of career women, it had been nice of him to arrange her wardrobe beforehand.

It had been her inherent lack of clothes sense that had provided the impetus for the breakup of their marriage in the first place. Although after the first pain had passed, Jessica was forced to admit the writing had been on the wall for a very long time before Deirdre Hanson had entered the picture.

The entire O'Neill-for-governor campaign staff had unanimously decided that Jessica didn't project the proper image for the wife of an up-and-coming politician. Her jeans and paint-spattered sweatshirts might possess a certain cachet in the artists' communities of North Beach and Sausalito, but they were a definite liability when seeking the yuppie vote. It was the general consensus of opinion that Jessica O'Neill was decidedly lacking in style.

An interior decorator, Elizabeth MacLaughlin was as different from her daughter as night from day, and it was only natural Jessica would turn to her mother for advice. When Elizabeth suggested a visit to The Emporium-Capwell, little did Jessica realize what a difference that shopping trip would make in her life. She was introduced to the store's career dressing coordinator, a tall, striking woman in her thirties, who promised to coordinate her mismatched pieces of clothing into a workable, stylish wardrobe. Since Jessica spent most of her days in Mill Valley, it fell to Brian to stop by the fashionable department store at frequent intervals to take home the chic clothing Deirdre had accumulated.

Now Jessica's closet boasted a treasure trove of Ultrasuede suits, silk blouses, linen blazers and Italian pumps fashioned out of buttery-soft leather. And Deirdre, in turn, had Jessica's husband. Jessica had decided long ago that she'd gotten the better of the trade.

She showered and dressed quickly, then followed the billowing black cloud and the blare of the smoke detector's siren downstairs.

"Mother!" Mallory jumped up from the table. "Would you please explain the First Amendment to Jill? She's threatening to break my camera."

Jessica smiled benignly at her family, going over to pour a cup of coffee. "Good morning. Did everyone sleep well?"

"Mother, did you hear me?"

"Of course I did, dear," she murmured, pulling a pad of paper and a pen from a drawer. "But if you expect a treatise on the First Amendment before I've had my coffee, I'm afraid you're going to be disappointed."

"I told you she wouldn't back you up," Jill said, her hands clenched into tight fists at the hips of her crimson parachute pants.

"She didn't say that," Mallory retorted. "She only said we'd have to wait for a decision until after she had her coffee. So there."

"Mallory O'Neill," Elizabeth stated firmly, "don't stick your tongue out at your sister."

"She's not my sister," Mallory countered. "Gypsies stole my sister from the hospital nursery and left Jill in the bassinet in her place. By the time Mom and Dad discovered the mistake, the Gypsies were long gone and they were stuck."

Jill turned her back, going to the refrigerator to take out a pitcher of orange juice. "You're a riot, Mallory. In fact, you could probably go on the stage with that routine. It's just too bad you've got railroad tracks for teeth."

Knowing her middle daughter's sensitivity about her braces, Jessica prepared herself for the impending storm. When it didn't occur, Elizabeth and Jessica exchanged a long, curious look.

"Jill, you owe your sister an apology," Jessica said sternly.

To her further amazement, Mallory only shrugged. "That's okay," she stated blandly. Then she grinned. "I'm selling outtakes of Jill trying out Gran's mudpack. If the advance orders are any indication, they're going to go like hotcakes all over school." She picked up her camera and escaped the room, a wild-eyed Jill close behind.

Jessica shook her head. "Why did I have three children?"

"Because you didn't want four," Elizabeth offered. "Here, I thought you might enjoy a home-cooked breakfast."

Jessica stared down at the charred strips of bacon and something she vaguely recognized from her youth as scrambled eggs. "You didn't have to go to so much trouble."

Elizabeth smiled with the air of a woman who had never possessed a single insecurity. "It's the least I can do. Especially since I'll be staying here until I get settled."

"About that—"

Jessica's question was cut off as a whirling dervish spun into the room, twirling her way into a chair. "How's that, Mom?" she asked breathlessly.

Jessica grinned at her youngest across the table. "Dynamite. Dame Margot Fonteyn couldn't have done it better."

The freckled face was wreathed in a smile. "Thanks. I'm really nervous about tonight."

"Your mother used to worry, too," Elizabeth said, placing an identical plate of food in front of Sara, who looked at it with suspicion. "With good cause," she murmured under her breath.

Busy scrutinizing the morning meal, Sara missed her grandmother's qualifying statement. "Isn't this the same thing we had for dinner last night?"

"Of course not," Elizabeth scoffed.

"It looks the same."

"Well, it's not."

"It's the same color," Sara persisted with a nine-year-old's tenacity. She sniffed the air, as if noticing the smoke for the first time. "And it's burned."

"It's well done," her grandmother countered, joining them at the table.

Sara pushed the plate away. "Well, I'm not going to eat anything today, anyway. Ballerinas never eat before a performance," she stated, tossing her head regally. Then a frown furrowed her freckled forehead. "Mom, you won't forget to pick up my shoes, will you?"

"It's at the top of the list," Jessica answered, tapping her pencil on the pad.

Sara's grin blossomed. "Thanks, Mom—you're the best." She jumped up from the table.

"Sara, you have to eat something," Jessica insisted, nevertheless understanding her daughter's reluctance to sample the breakfast that had been placed in front of her.

"Don't worry, I'll stop at the deli and pick up a bagel," she promised, blowing a kiss as she executed a grand jeté out the door.

Elizabeth frowned as she watched Sara leave the house. "Your daughters have atrocious eating habits. They only picked at their food last night."

Jessica wondered how such an intelligent woman as her mother had never caught on to the fact that she was a horrendous cook. "They're all at a difficult age," she replied instead, pushing her own food unenthusiastically around the plate. "They think they need to diet."

"I still don't approve," Elizabeth said firmly. "But far be it from me to interfere with the way you rear your children. What are you doing for lunch today?"

"I'm going out," Jessica murmured, writing down her engagement with Vanessa as she answered. It wasn't that she would forget their weekly luncheon; Jessica was an incurable list maker. It always gave her a feeling of accomplishment at the end of the day when she could draw a bold, black line through the final item.

"Why?" she asked, eyeing Elizabeth suspiciously. "What's the matter now?"

"Why should anything be the matter? Can't a mother drop by to have lunch with her daughter without everyone suspecting the worst?"

Jessica sighed. "Don't play coy, Mother. What's up? Is it something to do with Dad?"

"In a way."

Jessica ground her teeth, making mental apologies to the orthodontist who'd spent years correcting her overbite. "Mother, could you simply tell me what you're up to, without making me drag it out of you, bit by agonizing bit?"

"I wanted you to come with me to look at that vacant office down the hall from yours."

"Why?"

"Why do you think? I'm thinking of leasing it."

"Why?" Jessica repeated.

"For my business, of course."

"But you've always worked out of the house," Jessica protested, having grown up surrounded by the bolts of fabric and rolls of wallpaper that were part and parcel of her mother's successful interior design business.

"I don't live there any longer, dear," Elizabeth reminded her patiently. "So, since I had to find a new location, I thought it would be nice if I leased an office close to yours. That way we could have lunch together more often. What do you think?"

Out of a deep-seated sense of parental respect, Jessica refrained from telling her mother exactly what she thought of the scheme.

"Does Dad know what you're up to?"

Elizabeth expelled a frustrated breath as she rose from the table. "Honestly, Jessica," she said stiffly. "Whose side are you on, anyway?"

"It's a little difficult to choose sides when neither of you will tell me what's going on," Jessica pointed out.

Elizabeth busied herself by scraping the uneaten breakfasts into the garbage disposal. "Since your father's retirement, he's become an entirely different man," she answered finally. "He's dictatorial, unbelievably stubborn, and believe it or not, he's behaving like the world's champion male chauvinist."

"But Dad's always been that way."

Elizabeth glanced back at Jessica over her shoulder. "Really?" Her tone displayed honest surprise.

"Really."

"I wonder why I never noticed that before," she said thoughtfully. "Isn't it odd how you can live with a man for years and never see his faults?"

Jessica thought back on her parents' marriage—one she'd always viewed as idyllic. "Mom, don't you love him anymore?"

"Of course I do. But that has nothing to do with it. I simply can't live with the man any longer." With a slight sigh, Elizabeth changed the subject. "What would you like me to fix for dinner?"

"You don't have to cook," Jessica hurried to assure her.

"Nonsense. I want to earn my keep around here."

Jessica's mind went into overdrive as she tried to come up with a way to forestall her mother's culinary efforts. "Why don't we all go out after the recital? I'm sure Sara will be too nervous to eat beforehand. We can make it a celebration."

"All right, dear," her mother agreed cheerily. "That will give me more time to look for office space."

Jessica murmured an agreement, then, eyeing the copper clock on the wall, she jumped up, kissing her mother on the cheek.

"Gotta run," she explained. "I've got exactly two minutes to catch the bus."

With that she raced out the door, arriving at the bus stop just as the doors closed. The driver reopened them with obvious irritation, his mood not improved as Jessica dug through her purse, searching for the proper change. As she finally sank onto a seat at the back of the bus, she said a small, silent prayer that the remainder of her day would go more smoothly.

IF JESSICA NEEDED FURTHER PROOF that the gods were not on her side, the constant stream of emergencies she was forced to deal with once she arrived at her office would have convinced her once and for all. Sylvia Thacker called every ten minutes, wanting to know exactly when her husband would be behind bars.

Another client, a real estate developer suing a local television station for libel, belatedly admitted that there might be "a glimmer of truth" in the reports of several thousand dollars in kickbacks being given to members of the zoning commission, after all. Since the case had been highly publicized, Jessica knew it would be impossible to keep the firm's name out of the papers now that the man was withdrawing his suit.

When called on the carpet for not discovering the truth before filing, she couldn't resist pointing out to George Bennington that he'd been the one to file the damn suit, leaving her to figure out how to prove their case. In turn, the founder of Bennington, Marston, White and Lowell coolly reminded Jessica that she had only been invited to join the firm in the first place as a favor to her father. He, for one, had never approved of women attorneys. They were too emotional, he alleged, his steely gaze indicating that he found Jessica's irritation nothing more than feminine pique.

After that less than successful meeting, she was forced to cancel her lunch date in order to accompany a prominent neurosurgeon across town while he gave a deposition to the IRS concerning his financial interests in several Bahamian banks.

By three-thirty that afternoon, Jessica's head was aching, her stomach was growling, and she'd yet to cross a single thing off her list. When the intercom buzzed, signaling another call that undoubtedly meant more bad news, she felt like throwing the telephone across the room.

"Yes?" she bit out.

"Uh-oh. You're having a bad day." Quinn Masterson's deep voice came across the line, a welcome respite from the constant stream of petty irritations.

"I've had better," she admitted, glancing up at the mirror on the far wall, relieved that her caller couldn't see her.

Her unruly auburn hair, responding to the high humidity in the air, had sprung in a wild tangle of curls. She'd spilled a cup of coffee earlier in the day that had left a large brown splotch on her gray flannel suit. Jessica couldn't help comparing her appearance with that sleek blonde who'd seemed so fascinated with Quinn at the ball last night.

"Would you like some good news?"

"I'd love some," she answered immediately. "Please tell me that Keith Thacker delivered a new Mercedes to his wife today."

"Can't do that," he replied cheerfully. "But I'm prepared to offer a compromise."

"Let's hear it," Jessica agreed on a sigh.

"He'll give her the BMW if she returns his Nautilus exerciser and gives him custody of Maximilian."

"Maximilian?"

"The Lhasa apso," he reminded her with a deep chuckle that had her smiling in spite of herself. "Remember, the little guy that was named stud of the year by the Bay Area Kennel Society?"

"How could I forget?" Jessica answered dryly. "It sounds reasonable to me. Let me call Sylvia and get back to you."

"Fair enough," he agreed amiably. "Want to discuss it over drinks?"

"I'm sorry, but—"

"I know. You've got another date." His tone deepened. "I was hoping you'd changed your mind."

The invitation in his voice was unmistakable and Jessica glanced down at the list she'd made this morning, grateful for an honest excuse to turn him down. She was too tempted to see Quinn again, she admitted to herself. Too drawn to him.

"I can't," she murmured.

There was a slight pause before Quinn answered. "I see. Well, I'm going to be tied up in conferences the rest of the afternoon, but you can leave a message with my secretary when you get an answer from Mrs. Thacker."

"I will," she said softly, unreasonably disappointed by the fact that she'd have no further reason to talk with him today. "Oh, thanks again for dinner last night."

"I enjoyed it," he said simply. "Do you like Indian food? I know a place that serves dynamite curried lamb."

"I don't think so."

"Curry takes some getting used to," he agreed cheerfully. "How about Greek food?"

Jessica shook her head. "It's not that," she said, her tone hesitant.

Quinn wondered why he just didn't hang up and write Jessica O'Neill off as an impossible quest. He was certainly not used to courting rejection, nor was he in the habit of chasing after a woman. But then again, he reminded himself, Jessica was no ordinary woman.

"Why don't I call you later this week?"

It took every ounce of willpower Jessica possessed to refuse that enticing invitation. "I don't think so."

Quinn made an impatient sound. "May I ask a question?"

Jessica swallowed hard and nodded.

"Jessica? Are you still there?"

"I'm still here."

"Good. Are you involved with someone?"

"No," she answered honestly, preparing to tell him that was just the point.

Jessica had no plans to become romantically involved with any man. Her independence had not come easily, and she wasn't willing to give it up for anyone. No matter how warm his green eyes or enticing his smile.

Quinn didn't give her the chance to make her carefully rehearsed speech. "Now that's the best news I've heard all day," he said on a husky chuckle that stirred her even as she fought against it.

"Quinn . . ." Jessica felt obliged to explain.

"Just a minute," he stated in a brusque, businesslike tone, giving Jessica the impression he was no longer alone in his office. His next words confirmed that feeling. "I've got to run. But I'll see you soon, okay?"

"It's not okay at all," she protested. "I'm trying to tell you that I'm too busy for any involvements right now. You're a nice man, and I like you, but—"

"Jessica," he interjected firmly, "I'm already late to my meeting, so we'll have to discuss this at some other time. But believe me, sweetheart, you're going to find the entire experience absolutely painless."

With that he hung up, leaving Jessica to stare at the telephone receiver. What experience? Her reverie was cut short as her intercom buzzed, announcing yet another call.

"Yes, Paula," she said on a sigh, answering her secretary's page.

"Mrs. Thacker on line two." The brisk tone displayed no sign of irritation and as Jessica pushed the button with unnecessary force, she wished she could remain as cool and composed as her efficient secretary.

"Mrs. Thacker," Jessica enthused as she greeted the woman for the hundredth time today, "do I have good news for you!"

JESSICA LEFT THE OFFICE LATE, arriving at the shoe repair store just as the elderly manager was drawing the shade on the door. His expression mirrored the one the bus driver had given her this morning, but Jessica was not about to let it deter her from accomplishing the most important thing on her list.

She smiled sweetly at the man, earning a reluctant smile from him as she complimented him effusively on the marvelous job he'd done replacing the worn sole. Jessica had warned her daughter that a new pair of ballet slippers was in order, but Sara had proven stubbornly superstitious, insisting that she absolutely *had* to have her "lucky shoes."

Fortunately, everyone was dressed and ready to go when Jessica burst in the front door. "Here, Sara," she said, tossing the shopping bag toward her youngest. "I've got to change my clothes."

"We're going to be late," Sara complained, her blue eyes appearing even wider because of her unnaturally pale complexion.

"I'll be down in five minutes," Jessica promised.

"They'll take me off the program," the youngster groaned.

"Three minutes and counting," Jessica called down, flinging pieces of her wrinkled suit onto the stairs as she ran.

She grabbed the first thing she came to, a high-necked, Victorian lace blouse paired with a softly gathered flowered cotton skirt that hit her legs at midcalf. It was one of the few outfits that Deirdre hadn't chosen, and although it had been declared far too whimsical for a candidate's wife, Jessica had fallen in love with the look at first sight.

"Laura Ashley," Elizabeth said as Jessica descended the stairs two at a time.

"Laura Ashley?" Jessica repeated blankly, struggling to pin a cameo at her throat without a mirror. With the way her luck was going today, she'd probably puncture a major artery.

Elizabeth stepped in to help. "The designer," she said on an exasperated breath. "Surely even you have heard of her."

"Afraid not," Jessica admitted. "I just liked it. I didn't know it was designed by anyone famous."

Elizabeth secured the catch, stepping back to eye her daughter judiciously. "Well, the look suits you far better than those tailored things *that woman* put you in."

Jessica stifled a smile. Elizabeth had never forgiven Deirdre for breaking up her daughter's home, despite Jessica's avowal that the divorce had been inevitable. It had put a crimp in Elizabeth's wardrobe for a time, since she'd steadfastly boycotted The Emporium-Capwell. Recently Deirdre had opened a boutique in trendy Cow Hollow, that newly restored area downtown where cash registers rang more briskly than cowbells ever had, allowing Elizabeth to return to her favorite department store.

Jessica turned to her daughters with a smile. "Ready?"

"Ready," they chorused, marching out the door single file. It was times like this, when they were sweet and cooperative, that she remembered why she had wanted a large family.

They were barely settled in the taxi when Mallory managed to destroy the peaceful mood. "It would really be neat if you'd fall into the orchestra pit or something, Sara," she declared casually. "It'd make for some really dramatic film footage."

"I think I'm going to be sick," Sara moaned, turning white as newly driven snow. Her freckles stood out even more vividly against her pallor.

While Sara had performed in recitals before, the cast had always consisted of students. This time, after months of auditions, she had gained a small part dancing with members of the San Francisco Ballet Company.

Giving Mallory a warning glare, Jessica managed an encouraging tone. "Of course you're not," she stated blithely. "Those are simply butterflies. All great performers have them."

"Really?" Sara looked doubtful.

"Really," Jessica insisted. "I read just last week that Alexander Godunov got them before every performance."

"Did they go away?"

Jessica kissed her daughter's clammy forehead. "The minute he began to dance."

"I read the very same article," Elizabeth professed firmly.

Jessica could have kissed her eldest daughter as Jill added her two cents to the fictional account. "I read it, too, Sara. Don't worry, you'll be terrific!"

Breathing a sigh of relief, Jessica decided things might go smoothly tonight, after all. She changed her mind when they took their seats in the theater and she discovered Quinn Masterson seated next to her.

"What are you doing here?"

He grinned, appearing unperturbed by her impolite tone. "Didn't you know? I'm a supporter of the arts." Before she could comment, he looked past her at the avidly interested trio of females.

Elizabeth was already sizing him up as future son-in-law material; the appraising gaze was unmistakable. Jill was staring as if Rick Springfield had suddenly appeared in their midst, and even Mallory looked as if she might consider giving Quinn a starring role in her latest epic.

"Quinn Masterson," he said, holding out his hand. "I believe we've met before, Mrs. MacLaughlin."

"Of course," she agreed with an answering smile. "Several times." Her blue gaze narrowed. "However, I had no idea you and my daughter were acquainted."

"We're very old friends," he stated, ignoring Jessica's intake of breath at his outrageous lie. His gaze slid to Jessica's daughters. "You two are every bit as lovely as your mother. I feel sorry for all the men whose hearts are going to be broken."

Jill and Mallory both appeared to melt on the spot, leaving it up to Jessica to introduce the two girls who had suddenly gone mute. A moment later the orchestra began to warm up, drawing everyone's attention to the stage.

"I remembered where we met," he murmured.

"I told you, Quinn," she insisted, "we haven't met."

"Yes, we have. Tonight brought it all back."

She shook her head, keeping her eyes directed to the stage, waiting for the performance to begin. "You're mistaken."

"I couldn't possibly be mistaken about the worst day of my life."

"Terrific," she grumbled, still refusing to believe him. "It's nice to know I made such a wonderful impression."

"It wasn't you. It was the damn dance class."

Jessica turned her head, eyeing him with renewed curiosity. "Dance class? Don't tell me that you attended Madame Sorenson's Academy of Ballroom Dancing, too?"

"Didn't everyone? At least that's what my grandmother alleged when she dragged me there."

At her questioning expression, Quinn elaborated. "My parents died when a tornado hit our farm that summer and I was sent out here to live with my grandparents."

"I'm sorry."

"It was a rough year," he confessed. "Grandmother was shocked to discover that her only living heir was a wet-behind-the-ears Missouri farm kid without what she referred to as *social graces*." Quinn winced, giving Jessica the feeling that the memories were still slightly painful, years later.

"Anyway," he continued, his tone low, his words intended for her ears only, "she talked Madame Sorenson into taking me into that class, even though I was a head taller and five years older than everyone else."

Jessica tried to recall a tall, handsome boy—a younger version of Quinn Masterson—and came up blank.

"The first class I was paired with a skinny little kid who had flaming red pigtails and a ski-jump nose sprinkled with an amazing array of freckles."

Comprehension suddenly dawned. "I remember you!" Jessica exclaimed, drawing irritated glances from the people sitting around her. She lowered her voice. "You scared me to death, Quinn Masterson. You spent the entire two hours scowling at me and cussed every time I stepped on your foot."

He gave her a lopsided grin. "I probably did," he admitted. "Although you were less than graceful, sweetheart. Next to me, you were the worst dancer in the room."

"I'm left-handed," she said defensively. "As well as left-footed. I have trouble following because everything's backward."

Quinn shrugged. "Hey, Ginger Rogers probably couldn't have followed my clumsy steps. Anyway, that was such a humiliating evening, I went back home and told my grandmother that I refused to ever go back again."

His eyes suddenly gleamed with an unmistakable desire. "However, if I'd known what a beauty that freckle-faced little kid was going to grow up to be, you couldn't have kept me away from that class."

Jessica was saved from answering as the houselights dimmed. She was grateful for the darkness; Quinn wouldn't see the color heating her cheeks at his huskily stated words.

She kept her eyes directed toward the stage, but she was unaware of the dancers as she wondered idly if Quinn had ever learned to dance. She'd certainly seen his picture in the paper enough times, squiring a steady stream of glamorous, sophisticated women to society balls.

"We'll have to try it some night soon," he said, his lips suddenly unnervingly close to her ear.

Every instinct Jessica possessed warned her not to turn her head, but it was as if she were merely a puppet, with Quinn Masterson expertly pulling the strings.

"Try what?" she asked softly, staring at the firm lips only a whisper away from her own.

His broad white teeth flashed in a knowing grin, acknowledging that she was not alone in having these moments of odd, sensual yearning.

"Dancing. We're going to have to give it a whirl and see if either of us has improved."

"Quinn, really, this is impossible," Jessica protested, drawing a chorus of loud shushing sounds from the people seated around them.

She could feel the self-satisfaction practically oozing from him as he patted her cheek and returned his attention to the stage. Jessica didn't dare open her mouth to protest when he took her hand under the cover of darkness, his fingers linking perfectly with hers. Gradually, as the dancers whirled across the stage in the bright costumes and the music swelled, it seemed entirely natural for Quinn's thumb to softly stroke her palm.

Later, in the final scene, when Sara finally pirouetted onto the stage with a group of other young dancers, Jessica's blood ran icy cold with maternal anxiety. It was only when the lights came on again that Jessica realized how tightly she'd been gripping Quinn's hand.

"My God," she murmured, staring at the deep gouges in his skin caused by her fingernails, "why didn't you say something?"

Quinn shrugged. "It was nice to feel needed," he said simply.

Then he turned his attention to Mallory and Jill. "Does anyone else around here feel like a double bacon cheeseburger with fries?" he asked, earning an enthusiastic acceptance from Jessica's daughters, who seemed eager to avoid another evening of their grandmother's cooking.

"There's no way all of us will fit into your car," Jessica pointed out, still unwilling to encourage Quinn's company.

He gave her a slow, patient smile. "I've already thought of that," he assured her. "As we speak, a limousine is circling the block."

He certainly didn't lack self-confidence, Jessica considered, trying to think of another reason that his suggestion was impossible. Before she could come up with one, they were joined by Sara, who came running up the aisle, still dressed in the frothy pink net tutu.

"Mom, look at what someone sent me!"

Her wide eyes, exaggerated by the heavy stage makeup, appeared like two blue saucers in her flushed face. In her hand was a slender crystal bud vase, which held a pair of sweetheart roses and a spray of baby's breath.

"It's from an admirer," she stated proudly.

"An admirer?" Mallory's tone was skeptical.

Sara thrust the card toward her. "See. That's what it says." Her youthful expression grew dreamy. "I've never gotten flowers after a performance before," she said on a sigh. "I feel just like a real prima ballerina."

Jessica had a suspicion exactly who had sent the flowers, but when she caught Quinn's eye over Sara's bright auburn head, his gaze was absolutely guileless.

"How would the prima ballerina like to go get a hamburger?" he asked with a smile Jessica was sure worked wonders on women from eight to eighty.

Sara, however, was imbued with a new importance and was not to be taken lightly. "With fries?"

"Of course."

"And onion rings?"

"Can you imagine a hamburger without onion rings?"

She pinned him with a particularly sagacious gaze. "And a double hot fudge sundae for dessert?"

"With nuts," he agreed.

"Is he with us?" Sara asked her mother.

Giving up, Jessica nodded with resignation. "It appears so."

Her youngest daughter's eyes went from Jessica to Quinn, then back again. "It's about time you brought a man home." She turned to Mallory. "I hope you got my *tour jeté* right before the finale."

Mallory nodded. "Mom wouldn't let me use the floodlight, but I think we got enough illumination from the stage lights."

"Good. It was probably my best one ever. Don't you think so, Gran?"

"It was breathtaking," Elizabeth agreed. "Now why don't you go change so your sisters can go ruin their systems with chemicals? We'll meet you out in the lobby."

She'd obviously read one of the latest pop nutrition books, Jessica decided. Her mother was given to embracing short-lived whims and she could only hope that her worries about food additives, as well as this latest decision concerning her marriage were simply the newest in a long line.

"I want to go out like this," Sara complained. "How will anyone know I'm special if I have to change?"

Jessica's stomach suddenly growled, reminding her that she hadn't eaten all day. She was in no mood to argue. "You can't run around San Francisco in that costume," she said firmly, causing Sara's expression to resemble a depressed bloodhound's.

"However," she added with a smile, "you don't have to wash all that makeup off your face until you go to bed."

Sara's smile could have brightened the entire city with its wattage. Shoving the flowers into Jessica's hands, she raced back down the aisle, disappearing through a curtain.

"A decision worthy of Solomon," Quinn murmured. "Just one more facet in the increasingly complex puzzle of Jessica O'Neill."

Jessica had been following Elizabeth, Jill and Mallory to the lobby, but at Quinn's words, she stopped to look up at him.

"I'm not all that complex."

"Of course you are," he argued lightly, reaching out to gently tug one of her curls. "You're the most aggravating, enticing, incomprehensible woman I've ever met. Just when I think I know what's going on in that gorgeous head of yours, you switch gears and leave me behind."

His green eyes gleamed as they roamed her face. "But I've always been fond of puzzles, Jessica. And you're the most fascinating one I've come across in a long time."

Jessica suddenly felt light-headed, a condition she was determined to ascribe to hunger and not the warm gaze directed her way.

"We'd better catch up with the others. That is, if you were serious about eating with us."

"I've never been more serious in my life." Quinn's tone assured Jessica that they were talking about a lot more than cheeseburgers, and her fingers unconsciously tightened about the crystal stem of the bud vase.

Her heart quickened, making her wonder if Quinn could see its wild beating under the ivory lace of her blouse. Something she recognized as desire thickened her blood, curling its way through her body, red and hot, leaving her trembling in its wake. Not even Brian, with the impetuous lovemaking she'd enjoyed in the early days of their marriage, had made her tremble. Jessica was stunned by her response to Quinn, unable to understand it, unwilling to accept it.

"You'd better let me take this," he said, prying her fingers from the slender stem before she snapped it in half. His smile was gently indulgent. "Don't worry, Jess—" his fingertips brushed a feathery path along her fragile jawline "—I won't push." Then he cupped her chin, lifting her hesitant gaze to his. "But I won't give up, either," he warned, his expression tender, but determined.

Then he winked, his grin boyishly attractive. "Come on, sweetheart," he encouraged, his hand resting lightly on her back as he directed her up the aisle. "We've got a hungry crew to feed."

4

LATER AS THEY ALL SAT around a table at a downtown restaurant, Jessica was forced to give Quinn credit. For a lifelong bachelor, he seemed totally at ease with the disjointed conversation jumping around the table. She had grown so used to her daughters cutting one another off, addressing several varied and dissimilar topics at once, that she had come to accept it as a matter of course. Now, viewing it through Quinn's eyes, Jessica was amazed he was able to keep track of what was going on. He even appeared unperturbed by Mallory's camera whirring away, capturing the evening on videotape.

He answered Elizabeth's questions about a case he'd tried last year before Judge Terrance MacLaughlin, and Jessica was not at all surprised that her mother remembered it as a superb presentation. One did not become a partner in such a prestigious law firm as Quinn's without being an excellent attorney. She also couldn't help noticing how attractive he was, his enthusiasm for his profession brightening his tanned face.

At the same time, he fielded questions from Sara, who was vastly interested in this man who'd suddenly shown up in their midst.

"Are you married?"

"No."

Sara nodded understandingly. "Mom's divorced, too," she offered.

"I've never been married," Quinn responded, correcting Jessica's youngest daughter's mistaken comprehension.

"Why not?" she persisted.

"Sara," Jessica warned, "that's a very personal question and absolutely none of your business."

"I don't mind," Quinn replied. He leaned back in his chair, crossing his arms over his chest. "You see, Sara, when I was in college, I came up with a plan for my life."

"Mom does stuff like that," Mallory interjected. "She's the world's greatest list maker."

Quinn gave Jessica a thoughtful glance, then returned to answering Sara's initial question. "Well, it wasn't that I didn't want a wife and children," he assured his avidly interested audience. "I just didn't think I could concentrate my energies on my career and a family, so I decided that I'd go to law school, join a good firm and work to become a partner by the time I was forty. By then I figured I'd have the time to devote to my personal life."

"How old are you, Quinn?" Jill asked, ignoring the blistering warning glare from her mother.

Quinn's eyes twinkled as he slid a meaningful glance Jessica's way. "I turned forty three weeks ago."

The significance of that statement swirled about them, causing Jessica to grow extremely uncomfortable under the watchful gazes of her mother and daughters. She was distinctly relieved when Sara spoke up, continuing her cross-examination of Quinn with the tenacity of a terrier worrying a particularly succulent bone.

"So you don't have any kids, huh?"

"Not yet." He grinned unrepentently at Jessica, who began fiddling nervously with her silverware.

"Then you probably don't go to many recitals like this," Sara continued to probe.

"This was the first," Quinn agreed cheerfully. "And believe me, I thoroughly enjoyed it. You're quite talented, you know."

Sara bobbed her bright russet head. "I know."

"Are you thinking of making it a career?"

She straightened her slim shoulders. "I *am* going to be a professional ballerina," she said firmly. "I plan on studying for five more years, then I'm going to get an apprenticeship at the San Francisco Ballet Company. Then, before I'm twenty I'll be dancing with the New York City Ballet."

"As a soloist?" he queried, a ghost of a smile hovering at the corner of his lips.

"Of course not," Sara said with youthful disdain. "You don't start out as a soloist. I probably won't get that far until I'm twenty-two or twenty-three."

The smile broke free. "You seem to have your life all planned out."

"Of course."

Elizabeth broke in. "Sara's just like Jessica in that regard. My daughter never begins a day without making a detailed list."

"There's nothing wrong with organization," Jessica snapped, annoyed by the way her mother made her sound like some boring, staid individual. Just because Elizabeth flitted her way through life like a lovely, free-spirited butterfly didn't mean everyone had to follow suit.

Her sharp tone was at odds with the carefree celebratory mood, and five heads swiveled at once to study her curiously.

"I'm going to be a cinematographer," Mallory stated into the uncomfortable lingering silence.

Quinn dragged his attention from Jessica, deciding this was no time to attempt to discern what was bothering her. "I figured as much," he said cheerfully. Then he looked across the table at Jill. "And what about you?" he asked, his gaze taking in her spiky hair and bright, neon apple-green minidress. "Are you going to be a famous rock star? Or an actress?"

Jill shook her head as she slurped the last of her cola making a loud, unmannerly sound. "No. This is just a stage I'm going through," she answered calmly. "I'm going to get married and live in a big house and have lots of children."

Jessica's expression could have been carved in granite. "I think it's time we went home," she announced, pushing her chair back from the table and standing up abruptly. "Tomorrow's a school day."

A chorus of dissent echoed around the table. "I haven't finished my sundae," Sara complained.

"Tough," Jessica retorted. "You should have spent more time eating and less time talking." Her icy gaze rose to Quinn. "Thank you very much, but we have to be going."

"Fine. I'll drive you."

"We can get a taxi."

Quinn's smile didn't waver, but his tone was firm. "I think we exhausted that suggestion last night, Jess. I don't invite people out to dinner, then send them home in a taxi."

Jessica felt as if she were being examined under a microscope as four pairs of female eyes suddenly riveted on her.

"You went out to dinner with Quinn last night?" Mallory asked incredulously.

"In that horrid old running suit?" Jill tacked on, her youthful expression displaying what she thought of her mother's casual apparel.

"That explains it," Elizabeth murmured thoughtfully.

Sara simply stared.

Jessica's eyes shot daggers at Quinn, who appeared totally unperturbed by the sudden interest in their relationship.

"Come on, girls," he said, his grin breaking free. "We'd better get you home before your mother lays down the law and grounds us all."

That earned a laugh Jessica refused to acknowledge as she marched out of the restaurant, head held high, her back as rigid as if someone had dropped a rod of steel down her lacy blouse.

If she thought she was going to get away without inviting Quinn in, Jessica was sadly mistaken. As the limousine pulled up in front of the house, she was outnumbered four to one, and her irritation rose to new heights as Quinn cheerfully complied with the majority.

Sara insisted on showing him her scrapbook, and Mallory proudly displayed the certificate won for a short animated film she'd made using space creatures fashioned from modeling clay. Jill, not to be outdone, treated him to a performance of her lipsyncing the latest rock hit.

Finally the three girls had been convinced it was well past their bedtime, and as the adults drank espresso in the living room, only the giggles drifting down the stairs revealed the level of excitement the unusual evening had created.

Jessica was annoyed, but not particularly surprised, when Elizabeth used the opportunity to do a little motherly detective work.

"My husband has always spoken very highly of you, Quinn," she said with a smile. "But I didn't realize you and my daughter were acquainted."

"We're old friends." Quinn's deep voice invested the outrageous statement with a masculine intimacy, causing Jessica to glare at him.

Elizabeth's eyes gleamed with interest, and Jessica could practically see the wheels turning inside her mother's head.

"We're simply business acquaintances," Jessica corrected firmly. "Quinn is representing Keith in the Thackers' divorce case."

Elizabeth had deftly manuevered the seating arrangements so that she had possession of the only chair in the small, intimate parlor, forcing Jessica to share the love seat with Quinn. At her prickly tone, he put his arm around her shoulder and grinned wickedly.

"Don't forget that memorable evening we spent dancing, Jessie."

Elizabeth suddenly popped up, a brilliant smile on her face. "I'm so exhausted," she claimed, her hand covering her mouth to stifle a yawn Jessica suspected was feigned. Her mother had always been a night owl. "I think I'll head up to bed now. Good night, Jessica. Quinn. It was a pleasure seeing you again."

Quinn's eyes danced with amusement at Elizabeth's less than subtle matchmaking. He rose immediately from the couch. "The pleasure was all mine, Mrs. MacLaughlin," he stated. While his words were directed at her mother, his eyes remained on Jessica.

With a throaty chuckle, Elizabeth made herself scarce, leaving Jessica and Quinn alone in the dimly lit room.

Jessica jumped up and turned on him, her hands on her hips. "Why did you do that?"

He arched a gold eyebrow. "Do what?"

"Make my mother think there's something going on between us."

"Isn't there?"

"No." Jessica held her breath, irrationally waiting for a bolt of lightning to strike her down for telling such a blatant lie. She couldn't remember either of them moving, yet a moment later she was standing in the circle of his arms.

"Jessie," he murmured, "didn't your mother ever teach you it's not nice to tell a lie?"

She couldn't think with those warm green eyes moving so slowly over her face. She stared down at the floor.

"Jess." It was only her name, but his husky voice made it a caress. And a command. She slowly lifted her eyes, shaken as she reluctantly met his desirous gaze.

He reached down, taking one of her hands in his, uncurling the fingers from the tight, nervous fist she'd made. Her fingernails had left little gouges in her palm and as he stroked her skin, Jessica could only stare, entranced by the sensual movement of his dark fingertips. When those devastating fingers curled lightly around her wrist, Jessica knew he could feel her pulse racing.

"Do you know the last time I held hands with a girl while her mother was upstairs in bed?" Quinn's tone was conversational, but his eyes were handing her an increasingly sensual message.

"No," she managed, her voice as shaky as her body.

"Neither do I," he admitted with a crooked grin. "But it's been a very long time."

He'd laced their fingers together, bringing her hand to his chest, allowing her to feel his own erratic heartbeat. His eyes were still focused on hers, and Jessica felt as if she was drowning in pools of molten emeralds. Every nerve ending in her body was alive, reaching for his touch.

"Once we settle the Thackers' problems, perhaps we should do a little matchmaking of our own," he suggested. "See if we can do anything to get your parents back together. It would be a shame to stand by and watch a marriage of that long a duration go down the drain."

"My parents are pretty stubborn," Jessica said. "I'm not certain how they'd take to any outside interference." She hesitated. "I'm sorry she behaved that way."

Jessica could feel the rise and fall of his chest under her hand and had a sudden urge to touch his skin, to see if he was beginning to burn with the same intensity that had her body glowing with a lambent heat. She stifled a gasp as he lifted her hand to his lips, pressing a kiss against her wrist, causing her pulse to leap in response.

"That's okay—it was rather endearing. Besides, I think she had a great idea." Quinn breathed in the fragrance of her skin, needing to know if she tasted as sweet. His tongue teased the inside of her wrist.

"Idea?" Jessica's free hand moved up to his shoulder, to support herself against the desire sweeping through her.

"She's expecting me to kiss you good-night."

"I don't think that's a very good idea," she protested weakly. "Besides, you let her think we were romantically involved. 'Very old friends,' you said."

"I *have* known you since you were eight."

"Not since," she countered. "Except for those two hours, we only met yesterday."

"Isn't there an old Chinese proverb that states once you've broken a man's toes, he's yours for life?"

Jessica's heart pounded in her throat. "Not that I've heard."

"Then you obviously haven't been spending enough time in Chinatown," Quinn said with a smile. "I'm certain I heard it only last week." His eyes darkened to a deep, swirling sea, enveloping her in his gaze. "I don't think you should disregard your mother's wishes, Jessica. She has enough problems right now without worrying about a willful daughter."

Jessica watched, transfixed, as his head lowered, his lips approaching hers with sensual intent. *Too fast*, she told herself, even as her own lips parted. *This is happening too fast.*

She pressed her hands against his chest. "No," she whispered, knowing that her eyes were giving him an entirely different answer.

Quinn was unmoved by her weak protest. "Don't fight it, Jessie," he murmured, his lips altering their course, moving along her jaw. As he put his hand on her cheek, coaxing her mouth toward his, Jessica turned her head away in sudden panic.

"I said no, Quinn!" She would have moved away, to safer territory, but his hands were on her shoulders.

"Why not?" The words came out harsher than he intended. But he'd never met a woman capable of making him feel this way, and it was all he could do not to drag her by that long auburn hair to bed right now. Caveman tactics, he considered bleakly, knowing that primitive method would never work with Jessica O'Neill. But damn, how he wanted her!

His angry tone only served to fuel her irritation. Jessica felt her temper rising, but reminded herself that if she lost it, she would give Quinn even more of an advantage than he possessed at the moment.

"I don't think I owe you an explanation," she stated coolly, backing out of his arms.

Quinn bit down a frustrated response, allowing her to move away. "Perhaps you don't owe me one," he admitted. "But it would be nice to know why you suddenly changed your mind. Face it, Jess—a minute ago you wanted me as much as I wanted you."

She tossed back her head. "Even if that were the case, which it's not," she quickly added as she saw the victorious flash in his eyes, "I'm not in the market for an affair, Quinn."

"Scared?" he taunted lightly.

Quinn knew he hadn't misread those soft gazes she kept giving him; he knew Jessica had experienced the same elemental jolt he had when they'd first seen each other last night at the Fairmont. So why did she insist on playing these ridiculous games?

She turned her back, wrapping her arms around herself, as if in self-protection. "That's ridiculous," she said softly, her slight trembling giving her away.

Quinn shoved his hands into his pockets to keep from reaching out and touching her. She *was* frightened, he realized suddenly.

"Is this the same Jessica O'Neill who put her life back together all by herself and who prides herself on her independence? Is this the same woman who has gained the reputation of an *iron lady* around the municipal courthouse this past year?"

She looked back over her shoulder. "You're making that up."

"No, I'm not. In fact, that's one of the more charitable descriptions, if you want to know the truth. You've got a reputation for being a loner, Jess. A woman with ice water for blood and a stone-cold heart."

She was not going to admit how that uncomplimentary description stung. "Why is it that no one questions a man if he chooses not to marry, but if a woman values her freedom, there's something wrong with her?"

"Perhaps it's because you wear your bitterness like a chip on that lovely shoulder," he suggested softly, coming over to stand behind her. "I like this blouse," he murmured. "You look different tonight. Softer." His palms shaped her shoulders, warming her skin under the fragile ivory lace.

"I don't want to look soft," she argued. "I don't want to *be* soft."

Despite her words, Jessica didn't resist as he turned her slowly in his arms. His green eyes as they studied her thoughtfully, were gently censorious.

"I know you've been hurt, Jess," he said quietly. "But don't let your feelings ruin your daughters' chances for happiness."

Jessica knew immediately which particular daughter Quinn was referring to. "Jill," she muttered, shaking her head sadly.

"Jill," he agreed. "She's got a lot of love to give. Don't teach her to bottle it all up, just because you've found that's the safest way to deal with life."

Jessica shook her head, her distress eloquent in her blue eyes. "You don't understand," she whispered. "I was just like Jill at her age. I don't want her to be hurt."

"Of course you don't," he said, his palms rubbing lightly on her back. "But just because Jill wants a family doesn't mean she's going to be hurt. Fifty percent of marriages *don't* break up."

"And fifty percent do," she reminded him.

"Ah, sweetheart, I never would have figured you for a woman who looks at the glass and sees it half-empty," he chided.

She didn't used to be, Jessica admitted secretly. There was a time when she could have been described as an eternal optimist, always expecting the best from life. But she'd learned the hard way what happens to women who wear blinders.

When she didn't answer, Quinn heaved a deep sigh. "I'd better be going."

She slowly lifted her head, trying to remain unaffected by the lingering desire in his eyes. "Thank you for dinner," she murmured. "It was you who sent Sara the flowers, wasn't it?"

He managed a crooked grin. "Guilty as charged, counselor."

Jessica tried to smile and failed miserably. "It was a very nice thing to do. And I'm sorry if I gave you the wrong impression about . . ." Her voice failed her momentarily. "You know."

He shrugged. "There'll be another time."

"No, there won't."

Quinn surprised her by smiling, a slow, devastating smile. "Don't bet the farm on that, sweetheart," he warned softly, brushing his knuckles against her cheek. The dazzling smile didn't quite reach his strangely hard green eyes. "Because you'd lose." With that he was gone, leaving Jessica to stare after him.

JESSICA REFUSED TO ANSWER any questions about Quinn the next morning, her stern tone assuring everyone that she was in no mood to discuss her personal life. Even Sara remained silent, although her steady blue gaze was unnervingly knowing for a nine-year-old. Although Sara was the youngest, in some ways she was far more mature than her sisters. Jessica had often thought the child had mistakenly been born with an adult mind.

Jessica managed to reschedule her lunch with Vanessa and after a noneventful morning's work was seated in a white wicker gazebo, in a veritable arboretum, surrounded by blooming plants and live banana palms. The soothing sound of splashing fountains could be heard over the murmurs of the luncheon crowd.

"So," Vanessa said, eyeing Jessica over the rim of her glass, "I hear you and Quinn Masterson are an item."

Jessica slowly lowered her menu, staring across the table at the other woman. They weren't particularly close, but being the only two women working in the decidedly male bastion of Bennington, Marston, White and Lowell had created a certain bond. Lunch discussions, however, seldom included personal topics.

"Where on earth did you hear that?"

"I was at a party last night and Pamela Stuart was sulking because you'd managed to spirit San Franciso's most eligible bachelor away from the Arts' Ball."

"Pamela Stuart?" Jessica's brow furrowed as she tried to place the woman.

"You know," Vanessa said, "Fletcher Stuart's wife."

Jessica knew Fletcher Stuart was one of the city's most successful real estate developers, on a par with her own former husband. She struggled for a mental image of his wife.

"Tall, willowy, blond," Vanessa added, to help out.

Jessica suddenly remembered the sleek woman whose hand had been resting so possessively on Quinn's arm. A jolt of something dangerously akin to jealousy forked through her and it was all she could do to keep a placid, inscrutable expression on her face.

"Are they still married?" she asked with far more aplomb than she was feeling at the moment.

The waiter chose that inopportune time to arrive to take their order, and Jessica was forced to wait for an answer. "Well?" she asked once they were alone again.

Vanessa was crunching on a stalk of celery from her Bloody Mary. "Well, what?"

"Are Pamela and Fletcher Stuart still married?"

Her friend's brown eyes narrowed. "So there is something going on between you two?" Her tone displayed her incredulity. "I figured it was just party gossip. Or a case of mistaken identity. I mean, let's face it, kiddo, you're not really in the same league with Quinn Masterson."

"What exactly do you mean by that?" Jessica asked frostily.

"Hey," Vanessa said quickly, "I didn't mean to hurt your feelings, Jessica. It's just that you don't even date, and Quinn, well . . ."

"I know," Jessica muttered. "Quinn Masterson has elevated the dating game to Olympian heights."

"The man does have quite a reputation," Vanessa stated cautiously. "I don't think he's ever shown up two nights in a row with the same woman."

"So why was Pamela Stuart making such a big deal about it?" Jessica asked, wondering how the idea of Quinn and all his women could hurt this way. "And you never answered my question. Is she still married?"

"She's married, but to my knowledge that has never slowed her down. As for her relationship with Quinn, I think she has her sights set on him for husband number three. At least she was dropping plenty of hints that the golf-ball-size aquamarine ring she was sporting was an engagement gift from the man."

Jessica suddenly realized she was tearing her paper napkin to shreds and lowered her hands to her lap. "Look, I don't want to talk about him, okay? I did meet with him the night of the Arts' Ball, but only to insist that he control the behavior of one of his clients."

"You're on opposite sides of a case?"

"Yes. And that's all it is."

"Wow," Vanessa murmured, taking a sip of her drink. "If there's one thing more dangerous than getting involved personally with that man, it's probably going up against him professionally."

Her dark eyes surveyed Jessica with renewed interest. "How on earth did you get anything that important? Usually one of the partners handle things in Masterson's league."

Jessica shrugged. "It's not that big a case. It's a divorce. I'm representing Sylvia Thacker."

At that Vanessa laughed. "Now I understand. That woman is an absolute menace and her husband's even worse. As long as her grandfather's estate represents one of Bennington, Marston, White and Lowell's major accounts, none of the guys on the top floor will touch that divorce with a ten-foot pole." She shook her head. "I don't envy you," she said cheerily, before turning her attention to the waiter who'd arrived with their lunch.

Try as she might, Jessica could not get the vision of Quinn and Pamela Stuart out of her mind. It was ridiculous to feel this jealous about a man she had no intention of getting involved with, she knew. She told herself that over and over again as the day wore on, but her heart seemed to have a mind of its own as it steadfastly refused to listen to her head.

When her secretary announced a call from her mother, Jessica stifled a sigh, hoping Elizabeth wasn't going to start in again on her incessant matchmaking.

"Hi. How's the hunt for an office going?" She hoped that starting the conversation out with her mother's life would forestall any mention of Quinn's name.

"Fine, I suppose." Her mother sounded less enthusiastic than she had yesterday. "Although I'll admit I've been having second thoughts about taking space in some impersonal office building."

Hallelujah, Jessica sang out inwardly. Elizabeth was ready to return home. "Oh?" she inquired with feigned casualness.

"I've been thinking about joining the peace corps." Elizabeth dropped her latest bombshell casually.

"Peace corps? At your age?"

She could practically see her mother's spine stiffen. "Lillian Carter was older than I am when she joined."

Deciding that her mother would definitely not appreciate her only daughter pointing out there was a vast difference in the need for nurses and the need for interior decorators in the peace corps, Jessica remained silent.

"What do you think about Alaska?" Elizabeth asked suddenly.

"I don't think the peace corps works in the United States, Mom," Jessica answered, picturing an igloo with Levolor blinds and art deco posters on the ice-block walls.

"Not for me, I was thinking about Africa.... Your father's the one talking about moving to Alaska. Can you imagine the old fool?"

"Alaska? Dad? Why?"

"He's bought a gold mine. Honestly, Jessica, can you picture your father as a prospector?"

Jessica could picture that about as well as she could her mother off in the African bush decorating huts.

"Do you want me to talk to him?" she asked.

"Don't waste your time," Elizabeth snapped. "There's no reasoning with the man lately. Well, if he thinks he's the only one who can have an adventure, he's going to find himself sadly mistaken."

That explained the peace corps notion, Jessica realized, wondering if her parents were going through some sort of delayed adolescence. They'd always been so stable—the rocks that had formed the foundation of the MacLaughlin family. She sighed. Maybe some substance had been dumped into San Francisco's water system, causing all the city's inhabitants to behave totally out of character. The way she'd been acting with Quinn certainly hadn't been normal.

That thought brought to mind Pamela Stuart and her alleged engagement ring. "Look, Mom," Jessica said swiftly, "I've got a call on the other line, but I'll be home for dinner."

"Fine, dear," Elizabeth answered cheerfully. "And don't worry about cooking. I've got everything under control."

Envisioning the mutiny the girls were going to stage if Jessica couldn't figure out some way to keep her mother out of the kitchen, she closed her eyes wearily. "I've got to hang up now," she said. "Oh, and Mom?"

"Yes, dear?"

"Please don't do anything rash until I get home and we can talk about it."

"Honestly, Jessica," Elizabeth huffed with very real indignation. "I don't know where you get these crazy ideas. Sometimes I think you must take after your father. Of course I won't do anything rash. I'm the sensible one in the family, after all."

Jessica shook her head, smiling as she hung up the phone. Her parents were driving her crazy, but she loved them both and only hoped they could work out their difficulties.

Moments later the intercom buzzed again. "Mr. Masterson on line one," Paula's disembodied voice announced.

Jessica fought down the flush of pleasure, reminding herself that to get involved with a man who in earlier times could only be described as a *rake* would be pure folly.

"Hello," she said stiffly. "What can I do for you?"

His answering chuckle was low and deep. "Ah, Jess," he teased. "You should know better than to give me a straight line like that."

His intimate tones caused a warmth to begin deep in her middle regions, spiraling outward until she could feel the tips of her fingers tingling. Her toes literally curled in her tan pumps.

"I assume you're calling to discuss Mr. Thacker," she said briskly, fighting down the unwelcome surge of desire that threatened to be her undoing.

"So it's going to be strictly business where you and I are concerned?"

Jessica tried to read an undertone of regret in Quinn's deep voice, but failed. "I've already told you that," she pointed out briskly. "Several times, in fact."

"That's right, you have," he agreed amiably. "Mr. Thacker extends his appreciation to Mrs. Thacker for having Maximilian delivered so promptly."

"I'm pleased that he's pleased," Jessica murmured, secretly admitting it had come as a surprise when Sylvia had agreed without a word of complaint to her husband's latest proposal.

"Oh, he's not exactly pleased," Quinn added casually. "In fact, I'm giving official notice that he intends to bring a civil suit against Mrs. Thacker for the destruction of private property."

"What?" Jessica's voice rose at least an octave.

As she dragged a hand wearily across her eyes, Jessica reminded herself that she was the one who'd insisted on keeping things on a professional level. Quinn's tone was silky smooth, but as dangerously sharp as a well-honed stiletto, and she suddenly understood Vanessa's comment at lunch concerning his ruthless reputation as an adversary.

"She shaved him, Jess. Right down to the skin."

"Oh, no," Jessica groaned. "She didn't?"

It was a rhetorical question and Quinn didn't bother to answer. "As we speak, Maximilian looks more like a very fat rat than the city's most valuable stud," he informed her.

"I'm sorry."

He surprised her by chuckling, his cold attitude dissolving as quickly as it had appeared. "You probably will be," he agreed cheerfully. "I advised the guy against retaliation, but if you'll take a little professional advice, counselor, I'd warn Mrs. Thacker to take a long vacation out of town."

"I'll talk to her," Jessica said flatly.

"You do that," Quinn replied. "And Jess?"

Here it comes, she thought, a ripple of exhilaration skimming up her spine. *He's going to ask me out and I'm not going to be able to refuse.*

"Yes?" she asked, unable to keep the expectation from her tone.

"See you in court," he said, leaving her feeling slightly annoyed as he hung up.

"The least he could have done was tell me to have a nice day," she muttered as she placed a call to Sylvia Thacker, vowing that this time she wouldn't allow herself to be intimidated by the woman's veiled threats.

It was Sylvia's fault Jessica was mixed up with Quinn Masterson in the first place, and if the Thackers couldn't get their act together, Jessica was simply going to remove herself from the case. She refused to admit that her irritation had anything to do with Quinn's sudden dismissive attitude.

5

IF JESSICA THOUGHT she'd experienced the worst her day could offer, she was in for a surprise as things went from bleak to miserable. Sylvia Thacker showed no remorse about her act of vandalism, stating briskly that a BMW was no fair trade for a Mercedes.

"Then why did you agree to accept your husband's offer in the first place?" Jessica asked wearily.

"Because, my dear, a BMW is still a far sight better than public transportation. Besides—" the woman chuckled wickedly "—I couldn't resist driving Keith's blood pressure up. I only wish I could have been there to see his face when Max was delivered."

Privately Jessica considered that Sylvia's absence from the scene was probably the only reason Keith Thacker wasn't in jail at this very minute, charged with murder.

"He has every intention of suing you," she felt obliged to point out.

"Let him." The woman's voice held a careless shrug. "And we'll sue for the Mercedes, of course."

"Of course," Jessica agreed faintly, mentally ringing up the costs of the continual charges and countercharges made by the Thackers.

While both law firms' coffers were growing the longer the couple fought their marriage out to the bitter end, she hated to consider the way she and Quinn were going to be tying up the already crowded court calendar.

"I've got to go," Sylvia said suddenly. "Keith just drove up."

"Mrs. Thacker, you wouldn't . . ." Jessica left the sentence unfinished, afraid to remind Sylvia Thacker of her earlier threat. Perhaps the woman didn't even own a gun, Jessica considered hopefully.

"Don't worry about a thing, Mrs. O'Neill," her client assured her. "I have everything under control."

As the dial tone echoed in her ear, Jessica could only hope so. She debated phoning the police, then decided that she was probably only borrowing trouble.

She had returned to preparing a brief for an environmental group attempting to gain funds from the EPA Superfund when her intercom buzzed again. Experiencing a fleeting wish for the good old days before telephones, Jessica answered the page.

"Yes? And if you tell me it's Sylvia Thacker, I'm going to slit my wrists."

Paula laughed. "No, it's the judge. You'd better talk to him before he explodes."

Jessica groaned. "Is he that upset?"

"The usually unflappable Judge MacLaughlin could give Mount St. Helen's a run for its money right now," she stated. "What on earth is happening in your family, Jessica? You've gotten more phone calls in the past three days than you have in the past year."

"I don't know," she said on a deep sigh, casting a quick glance at her watch. "Look, I've got a meeting with Mr. Bennington in two and a half minutes. Will you do me a favor and tell Dad that I'll get back to him as soon as possible?"

"Sure. But if you look to the north and see smoke billowing into the sky, don't say I didn't warn you."

Jessica rubbed her fingertips against her temples, gathering strength for the upcoming meeting with the head of the firm. It was her monthly review, a procedure suffered by all first-year attorneys, and though she never found it the least bit enjoyable, she was thankful she no longer broke out in hives when summoned to the executive offices.

Compared to some of the others Jessica had suffered through, this month's review was relatively painless. As she returned to her office, Paula's grave face displayed her concern. The secretary's worried expression broke into a congratulatory grin as Jessica gave her a thumbs-up sign.

"Your father called three more times," she said pointedly, single-handedly managing to burst Jessica's little bubble of pleasure.

Realizing she couldn't keep avoiding the issue, Jessica assured Paula that she'd take care of it immediately. She went into her office and dialed the MacLaughlin residence.

"That better be you, Jessie MacLaughlin O'Neill," her father said abruptly.

"It's me," she acknowledged. "What's up?"

"What's up?" Her father's deep voice vibrated with incredulity. "What's up?" he repeated. "I expected you to tell me. Do you know what fool stunt your mother has come up with now?"

"The peace corps?"

"So you do know."

He jumped on Jessica's words instantly, reminding her of Judge Terrance MacLaughlin's forceful presence on the bench. He'd been strong and tough, but fair, she conceded. She could only hope his sense of fair play extended to his own wife.

"Well, after all, Dad, you're taking off to Alaska to work that gold mine you bought. Surely you can't deny Mom a little adventure of her own."

"Leased," he corrected gruffly.

"Leased?"

"You don't *buy* a gold mine, Jessica. You lease it from the government."

"Lease, buy, what's the difference? You're heading off to Alaska, what do you expect Mom to do? Stay home and knit you some warm clothes for prospecting?"

"She could be more supportive," he grumbled.

"So could you," Jessica risked pointing out.

"You think I should endorse this peace corps thing?" Jessica could practically see her father's silvery brows climbing his wide forehead.

"Did you invite her to Alaska?"

"Why the hell should I do that? If she can't stand to live with me in that huge mausoleum of a house she's always re-decorating, how long do you think we'd survive together in a prospector's shack?"

Try as she might, Jessica couldn't see either of her parents living happily in such circumstances. "Dad, why don't you at least ask her?"

"And give her the opportunity to turn me down?"

"Would that be so bad?"

"The man is supposed to be the head of the family, Jessica. It's time Elizabeth realized that."

Jessica was rapidly reaching the end of her patience. "If you don't do something soon, Dad," she told him briskly, "there won't be any family for you to be the head of."

She heard his spluttered protests as she firmly replaced the receiver.

Jessica was more than a little relieved when her excruci-atingly long workday came to an end. Despite a continual dosage of aspirin all day, she had a throbbing headache and was feeling ill-tempered and out of sorts. It didn't take a Rhodes Scholar to pinpoint the cause of her discomfort. She'd been feeling rotten ever since Vanessa had told her about Quinn and Pamela Stuart at lunch. If Jessica was distressed by the idea of Quinn involved with another woman, espe-cially a married one at that, she was aghast at how much she cared.

Deciding it would be unfair to submit her family to her bad mood, she chose to walk home, using the time to calm down and dismiss the handsome attorney from her mind once and for all.

She tried strolling through a few art galleries, pretending interest in the collections of paintings and etchings. But when Quinn Masterson's handsome features appeared to be painted on every canvas, printed on every lithograph, Jes-sica gave up that idea, opting instead for the peaceful respite of Golden Gate Park.

In a city renowned for its economy of space, the park was a vast oasis of open air, the once-desolate wasteland of shifting sand dunes having been transformed into a magnificent, yet seemingly natural, park. Strolling past the manicured lawns and pristine flower beds, Jessica settled down on a bench outside the Conservatory of Flowers, the park's Victorian gem. She breathed in the fresh scent of spring, the sweet perfume of the brilliant blossoms, the heady scent of newly mown grass and slowly began to relax.

With her usual careful, methodical way of tackling a problem, Jessica considered her reaction to Quinn, even conceding that she was undeniably attracted to him. What woman wouldn't be? He was handsome, successful, and although she hated to admit it, his reputation did give him a certain aura that would appeal to many women. Rhett Butler had been a rake, too, and he certainly hadn't fared too badly.

Jessica had to acknowledge that so far Quinn had been a complete gentleman. And he'd certainly managed to charm both her mother and her daughters. She shook her head, wondering at the appeal of a man who had three generations of women responding to his magnetism.

"It's nothing but a silly, schoolgirl crush," she told herself firmly as the setting sun turned the windows of the pyramid shaped Transamerica building to a gleaming bronze. "That's all."

Jessica rose, and leaving the park, headed for home. "Well, maybe it's a little bit more than that," she admitted under her breath, unaware she was talking out loud. "It's also physical. But that's all. Simply sex."

"Hey, lady," a teenage boy drawled from a nearby bench, "that ain't all bad."

Lowering her head to hide her unwilling blush, Jessica walked a little faster, inwardly damning Quinn for this latest display of atypical behavior. She never talked to herself. Certainly never in public!

As she lifted her gaze once more, Jessica's breath suddenly caught in her throat. A tall man was walking a few feet in front of her, his golden hair gleaming with sun-gilt strands in the last light of day. He had broad shoulders, lean hips and the long legs clad in gray flannel slacks were achingly familiar. She was trying to decide whether to say anything when he snapped his fingers, as if he'd just remembered something, and turned around.

Jessica's heart crashed to the sidewalk underfoot as she realized the man's eyes were hazel, not green, and his lips were fringed by a thin mustache. His features were not unattractive, but neither did they cause her pulse to race. As the stranger passed, headed back in the opposite direction, he caught a glimpse of her disappointed face and frowned slightly, as if wondering what he'd done to cause her displeasure. Then he was gone and Jessica was left with the unhappy realization that somehow, when she hadn't been looking, Quinn Masterson had laid claim to her heart.

ELIZABETH MET JESSICA at the door of her town house. "Your father called me this afternoon."

"That's nice," Jessica replied blandly.

"Nice? How can you say that, Jessica O'Neill, after the way you betrayed me. Your own mother!"

Jessica sighed, kicking off her shoes. She should have known better than to walk home wearing a pair of new pumps. She'd be lucky not to get a blister.

"I didn't betray you," she protested, hanging her spring jacket on the brass coatrack.

"Oh, no? I suppose you didn't insist that your father take me to that godforsaken wilderness with him? Honestly, Jessica, if you want me out of your house, just say so. You don't have to ship me off to Alaska like some white slaver!"

"I didn't insist, I suggested," Jessica corrected, trying not to smile at her mother's imaginative description.

"Insist, suggested, what's the difference? The fact remains that you told your father I needed someone to look out for me. So he generously offered his services. The old goat. I know exactly what services he had in mind, too!"

"Mother, you're being unreasonable," Jessica remonstrated, making her way to the back of the narrow house to the kitchen.

Elizabeth was on her heels. "*I'm* being unreasonable? What about your father? Do you know I've read they go in for wife-swapping up there? He probably just wants me along so he'll have someone to hand over to his male guests!" Elizabeth's voice trembled with righteous indignation.

Jessica opened the refrigerator, taking out a half-empty bottle of white wine. "Want some?" she offered.

"Not now," her mother said firmly. "I want to get this settled once and for all, Jessica."

Jessica shrugged, taking down a glass and filling it to within an inch of the top with the crisp white Chablis. "Look Mother, I've had a rough day and I don't need to come home to this. Now I've told Dad, and you're going to hear it, too. If you two don't start behaving like rational adults, you're going to both end up alone. Is that what you really want?"

"Better alone than being handed over to some fur trapper for those long winter nights they have up there," Elizabeth muttered.

"You know," Jessica said suddenly, losing the last remaining vestiges of patience, "you two deserve each other!" She flung open the screen door, escaping to the small brick terrace out back.

"Bad day?" a deep voice inquired blandly.

Jessica stopped in her tracks, staring down at Quinn, who appeared perfectly at home in a white wrought-iron chair. "What are you doing here?"

"I brought Mallory a book on film editing."

"You went out and bought my daughter a book?"

"No, it was one I already owned. I took a few film classes at USC," he revealed. "In LA, it's de rigueur to graduate with at least one cinema class on your transcript."

His green eyes swept over her, from the top of her auburn head down to her stocking-clad feet. "Why don't you sit down?" he suggested amiably, as if it was his backyard and not hers. "You look beat."

"Thanks," Jessica muttered. "It's nice to know I'm so appealing. However, I doubt if I'd ever come up to Pamela Stuart, even on the best of days."

Quinn's jaw hardened and a strange look came into his eyes as he took a long swallow of the Scotch Elizabeth had obviously served him. "Now I understand why you were so abrupt on the phone today. The gossipmongers don't waste any time, do they?"

Jessica was suddenly unbearably exhausted and sank into a chair, stretching her legs out in front of her. She sipped her wine slowly, pretending to have great interest in the ivy climbing the fence.

"Is it true?" she asked finally.

"Would it matter?"

"I don't know. . . . I think so," she admitted softly.

Quinn twirled the ice cubes absently in the glass, his attention directed into the dark amber depths. "If our relationship is strictly business, why would it make any difference who I'm sleeping or not sleeping with?"

"It doesn't," she retorted, rising abruptly. "Forget I even brought it up. Where are the girls?"

"I sent them out for pizza," he answered. "Sit down, Jess. Let's get this out in the open."

"There's nothing to discuss." Despite her argumentative tone, Jessica sat back down in the chair, unaware that her pale face was a study in vulnerability.

Quinn sighed heavily. "What am I going to do with you? You keep protesting that you don't want anything to do with me, but every time you look at me with those blue eyes as wide and deep as the sea, I know you're lying through your teeth. You want me, Jess. Every bit as much as I want you."

"How much does Pamela Stuart want you, Quinn?" she asked acidly.

He arched a blond brow. "Jealous?"

She shook her head vigorously. "Not at all. I just don't consider a man who gets himself engaged to a married woman to be a very good influence on my daughters."

Quinn looked inclined to say something, but refrained, instead throwing back his head and tossing off the rest of the Scotch. "You're driving me crazy," he muttered. Then he leaned forward, his elbows braced on his thighs, his hands holding the glass between his legs.

"Pam and I grew up together," he began. "It's an old pattern with her. Every time she breaks up with a guy, she fancies herself in love with me. It gives her the confidence to carry on.... Not everyone can put their lives back together all by themselves the way you managed to do, Jessica."

Jessica fought down the flush created by his openly tender and admiring gaze. "Why does she pick you?" she asked quietly.

Quinn shrugged. "Like I said, it's an old habit. When she got dumped the night before her junior prom, I agreed to fly back to the city from LA and act as her escort, though I always felt more like her big brother. She showed me off that night, pretending I was her college boyfriend from USC."

"That's sad," Jessica murmured, thinking that for all her wealth and beauty, it didn't sound as if Pamela had an overabundance of self-esteem. Jessica remembered the feeling all too well.

"I thought so at the time," Quinn agreed. "That's why I didn't complain." His somber, level gaze held hers. "And that's why I still play along with the charade every few years, hoping that this will be the time she takes my advice and seeks professional help."

Jessica didn't know what to say to that, so she only nodded, feeling as if she was being drawn into the deep green pools caressing her face.

"Am I forgiven?" he asked.

His warm gaze and slow smile were creating havoc with her senses. Jessica felt as if she was suddenly floating out of her depth, and she struggled to maintain her equilibrium.

"How can I stay angry at a man who'd rescue me from home cooking?" She managed a light, slightly ragged laugh.

"Jill assured me she'd quite literally die if forced to eat another one of your mother's meals," Quinn agreed cheerfully, sitting back in the chair.

Jessica breathed a sigh of relief as the sensual mood was effectively broken. "Jill tends to exaggerate. But your chivalry is noted and appreciated."

"Oh, I'm just getting started," he professed, reaching down with a swift movement and taking her foot in his hand.

"Quinn!"

"You're getting a blister," he observed. "Don't you think you ought to get out of these nylons and put on a Band-Aid? I want you in tip-top condition for Saturday night."

"Saturday night?"

His massaging fingers were doing wonderful things to her aching feet as he grinned at her. "How do you ever expect to rise to the exalted ranks of partner and have your name painted on the door of Bennington, Marston, White and Lowell, if you forget such important things like your boss's wedding anniversary party?"

"Oh, God," Jessica groaned. "I did forget all about it. I suppose I have to go."

"You should at least put in an appearance," he concurred.

"I hate things like that," Jessica muttered, knowing that was one more thing she and Quinn Masterson didn't have in common.

He was obviously in his element at formal society affairs. Affairs. That double entendre brought to mind Pamela Stuart, and although Jessica was willing to accept Quinn's story about the unstable heiress, she didn't believe he dated all those other women for altruistic reasons.

"I suppose you have an invitation, too."

Quinn didn't know what had caused Jessica's eyes to darken with that unwelcome pain, but he had a pretty good idea. In her own way, this strong, self-sufficient woman was as fragile as Pam, he realized. She'd been badly hurt and still carried the scars. He'd never bothered to dispute his exaggerated reputation, never caring what people thought about his personal life. Until now.

"I do," he said, standing up.

As Jessica looked up at him, the setting sun sparked her hair with a warm, fiery glow and Quinn had to restrain himself from reaching down and combing his fingers through the thick waves. He couldn't help wondering how those lush strands would feel spread over his chest after making love and the idea caused an aching yearning deep inside him.

Jessica would've had to been blind to miss the blatant desire suddenly flaming in Quinn's green eyes and she remained transfixed, stunned by an answering need. Her eyes darkened to gleaming sapphire and her blood warmed her skin, imbuing her complexion with the hue of a late summer rose.

"Come here." Quinn's voice was unusually husky as he extended his hand toward her.

As if in a trance, Jessica reached out, allowing her hand to be swallowed up by the one so much larger and stronger. Quinn brought her to her feet, into his arms, fitting her intimately against him as he gave in to impulse and buried his lips in the fragrant softness of her fiery hair. The scent reminded him of springtime—of flower-strewn meadows, fruit trees in full blossom, the rich warmth of sunshine returning after a long gray winter.

"Ah, Jess," he said on a sigh. "I promised myself I wouldn't push, but I think I'm going to go crazy if I can't kiss you."

She lifted her head, a slight, unmistakable smile teasing at her lips. "What's stopping you?" she asked softly.

"Sweetheart," he groaned, "I thought you'd never ask."

Jessica's head reeled as she breathed in a scent reminiscent of the forest after a rain—a rich, earthy aroma laced with the sharper tang of redwoods. Her arms went around his waist as she allowed herself to lean against his rugged strength.

Then he was kissing her, his lips hard and hungry, his tightly leashed control disintegrating into a mindless passion. Jessica had been expecting something gentler, something more cautious. She opened her mouth to object, but at her shuddering soft cry, his tongue slipped past the barrier of her teeth, into the velvet vault beyond, creating havoc with her senses as it swept the moist, dark interior.

Jessica's initial shock disintegrated, replaced by an emotion more vital, more electric than anything she'd ever known. Enticed by the expert sensuality of his kiss, she grew more intrepid, allowing her own tongue to venture forth, at first tentatively, then with increasing boldness, discovering the brisk taste of cinnamon mingling enticingly with a darker, stronger taste of the imported Scotch.

He was a wonderful kisser, she considered through her whirling senses. She could stay here in his arms for the rest of her life. His breath was warm and oh, so seductive as his lips scorched a path from one ravished corner of her mouth to the other. Jessica went up on her toes to run her fingers through his sun-gilt hair.

The movement fitted her feminine frame more closely to his body and as Quinn's hands roamed down her back, they caused little sparks to dance between each vertebra. She could feel the warmth emanating from his body, creating a glow that spread outward from her middle regions, flowing through her blood, warming her fingers, making her breasts ache with unaccustomed heaviness, spiraling downward to her toes.

"You feel good," he murmured, dragging his lips away to blaze a heated trail down the slender column of her neck. "So good..."

Jessica's pulse trebled its rhythm as Quinn's palms cupped her breasts, his thumbs creating an evocative pattern that brought the tight crests surging against the amber silk of her blouse.

Jessica struggled to maintain some slim vestige of sanity, telling herself that if she didn't regain control, not only her mother but her daughters, as well, would soon witness Jessica and Quinn making love on the tiny brick terrace. Even as her body clamored for release, her mind tried to make itself heard, reminding her that she and Quinn were not alone. She had no business behaving like an absolute wanton with this man.

She buried her head in his shoulder, taking deep, calming breaths of air. "Another minute of that and I would have suffocated," she complained on what she hoped was a light note. She failed miserably.

Quinn knew Jessica had been affected as intensely as he by the ardent kiss. Probably even more so. He had talked to Pamela today, seeking information about Jessica, and although his longtime friend had pouted prettily, she had assured him that as far as anyone knew, Jessica had been living the life of a nun since her divorce. She was a remarkably passionate woman; Quinn was surprised she'd been able to keep the floodgates closed for as long as she had.

Quinn felt Jessica gathering up her self-control, wrapping it about herself like a heavy protective cloak. Deciding she had enough problems for now, he opted to match her casual attitude, but was slightly more successful.

"You're supposed to breathe through your nose. But don't worry, a little more practice and you're bound to get the knack of it."

"I don't need any more practice." Her eyes gave him a warning he chose to ignore.

"You're right," he agreed. "You're perfect just the way you are."

His dark gaze made Jessica's legs weaken, and she couldn't muster up the sharp response she knew he deserved. The slam of the front door signaled the return of her daughters, and Jessica heaved a huge sigh of relief as she extricated herself from his arms.

"The girls are back," she stated unnecessarily.

"It appears so." Quinn reached out and looped an auburn strand of hair behind her ear before tilting her chin toward him in a way that effectively captured her gaze.

"I've waited a long time for you," he said suddenly, his husky voice fracturing the silence. "I suppose I can wait until after the pizza."

"You've only known me three days, Quinn," Jessica answered dryly. "So if you think you're going to impress me with your self-restraint, you're sadly mistaken."

"That's where you're way off base," he countered in a serious tone. "I've waited my entire life for you, Jessie O'Neill. And if you think I'm going to let you walk away, now that I've found you, you're dead wrong."

He bent his head, planting a quick, hard kiss on her lips. "Let's eat." Quinn's eyes were laughing as he suddenly noticed her disheveled appearance. "You'd better tuck in your blouse," he warned, "or we'll have some heavy explaining to do to the troops."

Jessica's fingers shook as she tried to shove the amber silk back into her waistband. She finally managed the task, then, pasting a composed expression onto her face, returned to the kitchen, refusing to allow anyone to see that Quinn's statement had shaken her to her toes.

6

EXCUSING HERSELF Jessica ran upstairs to change. When she returned to the kitchen and found Elizabeth sharing the thick, gooey pizza, she was unable to resist a slight gibe.

"I see you're willing to risk a few additives, Mother."

"Quinn is very persuasive," Elizabeth replied serenely. "He assured me that pizza is actually very nutritious."

Jessica wasn't surprised; she'd already witnessed how persuasive the man could be when he put his mind to it. Which was precisely her problem, she considered ruefully. She had no intention of becoming involved with any man; at this point in her life all her energies had to be directed toward her family and building a career.

Shrugging off the problem for the moment, she went over to the refrigerator, taking out a diet cola.

"If you keep feeding me this way," she complained, "I'm going to have to roll down the hill to work in the morning."

He grinned. "I'd say you've got a few pounds to go before we have to ship you off to a fat farm."

"Mom's taken up jogging," Mallory informed him. "She says sitting around an office all day is giving her middle-aged spread."

Jessica could have cheerfully strangled her middle daughter for revealing that little bit of information, but Quinn's gaze, as he submitted her to a slow appraisal, was sparked with masculine approval.

"She hides it admirably," he stated, his eyes lingering on the curves displayed by the snug, well-worn jeans.

"Would you all stop talking about me as if I wasn't here?" she protested, feeling as if she was on public display.

There was a murmured chorus of apologies as she sat down at the table, and Jessica knew she was being overly sensitive. But she didn't retract her complaint.

The conversation turned to the day's events, and Jessica was honestly surprised at how interested Quinn appeared as her daughters related their individual triumphs and small failures. Jill was particularly despondent over the grade on her latest math test, insisting that she never would understand plane geometry.

"Give me one good reason why I will ever need to know the area of an isosceles triangle," she grumbled.

"You've got me," Jessica admitted. "I nearly failed geometry myself. I think the teacher finally felt sorry for me and gave me a passing grade just to get me out of his class."

"I've got a makeup test tomorrow and I know I'm going to fail."

"I can help you memorize theorems again," Mallory suggested, picking up a piece of pepperoni that had slid onto the table.

Despite their differences, her daughters could be very supportive of one another when the chips were down, Jessica observed with an inward smile.

"I know them all by heart," Jill complained. "I just don't know what to *do* with them." Her expression was absolutely bleak.

"Don't look at me," Sara said. "I've just figured out mixed fractions."

The mood around the table was decidedly gloomy when Quinn cleared his throat. "I always liked geometry," he offered almost tentatively.

"You would," Jessica muttered, wishing the man wasn't so damn perfect.

Jill's expression was that of a drowning man suddenly offered a life preserver. "Do you think you could help me study?" she asked hopefully.

Jessica broke in before Quinn had a chance to respond. "I'm sure Mr. Masterson has better things to do with his evening than spend it studying plane geometry," she stated firmly.

"No, actually I don't," he countered calmly. "If you'd like, Jill, I'd enjoy spending the evening here. With all of you."

Jill looked as if she'd just gotten her Christmas present eight months early. Elizabeth's expression reminded Jessica of a very fat cat sitting there with feathers sticking out of its mouth. Mallory and Sara exchanged a long, knowing glance, then eyed their mother, their bright eyes offering congratulations.

They'd obviously all ganged up on her and Jessica knew she'd appear like the Wicked Witch of the West if she offered a single objection. She reluctantly kept her mouth shut, wondering how she was going to keep Quinn Masterson out of her life, when she couldn't even keep him out of her house.

Lost in the problem, she allowed the conversation to continue on around her, no longer pretending an interest. The shrill demand of the phone jolted her out of her troubled musings.

"Jessica," the deep voice said as she picked up the receiver, "how are you?"

"I'm fine, Brian," she replied, drawing interested gazes from the other occupants of the room. "How are you?"

"Fine, fine. Deirdre's fine, too."

As if she cared, Jessica considered with concealed irritation.

"How are the girls?"

"They're fine, too. Do you want to talk to them?"

"I'd love to," her former husband said, "but I'm on my way out the door. I just wanted to see if you'd be willing to change weekends with me."

Jessica shrugged. "I don't see why not."

"Terrific. Thanks a lot, Jess. You're a lifesaver. I'll pick them up tomorrow after school, all right?"

"I'll have everything packed," she agreed absently, uncomfortable with Quinn's thoughtful gaze locked onto her face. She turned her back, fiddling with the telephone cord.

"Great, just great," Brian enthused. "You sound a little tired. Is everything all right? How's work?"

"Everything's fine," she murmured. "Look, Brian, we're eating dinner. The girls will see you tomorrow, okay?"

"Tomorrow," he agreed. "Will you be at the house when I pick them up?"

"I don't know," she hedged. While Jessica had done her best to maintain a friendly relationship with Brian for the girls' sake, she continued to feel uncomfortable in his presence. It brought back too many painful memories. "I may have to work late."

"Oh." He sounded vaguely disappointed. "Well, don't overdo it. You know what they say about all work and no play."

"They say it pays the bills," she countered briskly. "I've got an electrician coming next month who doesn't do charity work."

"I still don't understand why you didn't just keep the house, Jessica. It wasn't that I didn't offer to let you have it."

"I wanted a change," she replied. "We like living in the city."

"I'm not so sure it's good for the girls."

"Was there anything else you wanted?" she asked, firmly closing the door on the argument they'd had far too many times in the past three years.

"Stubborn as always, aren't you?" He didn't bother to hide his irritation.

"That's what I'm told," she agreed. "I'll see the girls are ready."

"Yeah, you do that," he muttered. "Goodbye, Jessica."

"Goodbye." She hung up the phone, forcing down the aggravation she knew was etched onto every taut line in her face.

"You're spending this weekend with your father," she announced, returning to the table.

"This weekend! I can't," Mallory wailed. "You'll have to call him back."

"I won't do any such thing," Jessica said firmly. "Besides, he said he was on the way out the door when he called."

"I'm not going." She folded her arms across her chest.

Jessica knew that of all her daughters, Mallory was the only one who still held a grudge against her father for leaving his family for another woman. She'd done her best never to say anything derogatory about him in her daughters' presence, but the relationship between Brian and his middle daughter was strained, at best. Which was especially unfortunate when she considered that Mallory had always been Brian's favorite. Although Jessica suspected Mallory was suffering her own feelings of personal rejection, she'd never gotten her daughter to discuss it openly.

"Honey," she coaxed, "you always have a good time once you get there."

A mutinous expression hardened the young face. "I had plans for this weekend."

"Plans?"

"The Charlie Chaplin film festival at the Orpheum," she reminded her mother.

She'd talked about little else all month, Jessica recalled belatedly, knowing how excited Mallory had been about the chance to view the comedian's old films.

"I forgot," she admitted. "But as it turns out, I have to work Saturday morning, anyway."

"Gran can take me," Mallory suggested, her gaze as appealing as a cocker spaniel puppy.

"I'm sorry, dear," Elizabeth said. "But I have to go down to Monterey this weekend. I'm decorating a new resort hotel and the owners are flying in from Houston to see what I've planned."

Tears welled up in Mallory's eyes, and the legs of her chair scraped on the oak floor as she pushed it away from the table.

"Terrific," she ground out harshly. "Everyone has their important plans. Why should I expect anyone to care what I want to do?"

Jessica shook her head, knowing that while Mallory was overreacting, her feelings were genuine. "I'm sorry, honey," she apologized. "I promise we'll go next time."

Mallory burst into tears, running from the room. "There won't be any next time," she wailed.

An uncomfortable silence settled over the room and Jessica sighed, pushing back her own chair. "Excuse me," she murmured, following her daughter from the kitchen.

Mallory was lying on her bed, sobs pouring forth from deep in her chest. As Jessica tried to soothe her, it crossed her mind that her daughter's dramatic performance had undoubtedly solved the problem with Quinn. He was probably on his way out the door about now, thankful that he hadn't gotten involved with a middle-aged woman and her three volatile children.

As usual, he surprised her. Jessica heard a slight sound and looked up to see him standing in the doorway.

"May I make a suggestion?"

"It's not necessary," Jessica said quickly, guessing what he had in mind."

Mallory looked up, rubbing at her wet cheeks with the backs of her hands. "What suggestion?" she asked hopefully.

Oh, God, Jessica thought, *don't let her start counting on Quinn. She's already been hurt enough.*

He entered the small bedroom, sitting down on the edge of the bunk bed. "Why don't you and I go to the film festival while your mother's working?"

"Mom?" Mallory's expression begged acquiescence.

"I've already promised your father you'd spend the weekend with him," she protested weakly.

"That's no problem," Quinn assured her. "Let her go to her father's tomorrow night and I'll pick her up and take her into town Saturday morning, then deliver her back to Mill Valley in the afternoon."

Mallory's wobbly smile was beatific. "That's a wonderful idea," she enthused. "Please, Mom."

Jessica shook her head. "I can't allow you to go out of your way for us like that," she said firmly.

"Mom!"

"It's a practical solution, Jess," he argued. "Besides, I can't think of anything I'd rather do than date two gorgeous women in the same day."

"Two?" Mallory asked, sniffling inelegantly.

Quinn handed her a white handkerchief from his pocket. "Two," he agreed. "I'm taking your mother out dancing Saturday night."

Suddenly they were no longer alone. Jill entered the room, followed by Sara. Elizabeth remained in the doorway.

"Mom never goes dancing," Sara offered.

Quinn grinned. "That's where you're wrong, sweetheart," he argued lightly. "Your mother and I danced together once before."

"Really?" Mallory asked, sitting up cross-legged on the mattress, her curiosity getting the better of her self-pity. "After she and Dad got divorced?"

"Before they were even married," Quinn answered. "My big mistake was not grabbing on to a good thing when I saw it. I never should have let your father get first dibs."

"Wow," Jill breathed, her eyes wide. "That's the most romantic thing I've ever heard!"

"At your age, everything is the most romantic thing you've ever heard," Jessica said dryly. "And for your information, I was all of eight years old."

"That was years and years ago," Sara piped up, making Jessica feel absolutely ancient. "And you still remember?"

"Every minute," Quinn asserted, treating Jessica to a particularly warm gaze, which did not go unnoticed by their audience.

"That's because he probably still hasn't recovered," Jessica insisted, rising from the bed to get a little farther away from Quinn. "I spent the entire time crushing his toes."

"You were left-footed," Elizabeth remembered. "Madame Sorenson never could teach you to follow properly."

"See," Jessica said to Quinn, her look saying *I told you so.* "Why on earth would you want to subject yourself to another evening of being stepped on?"

His slow smile made her blood simmer. "I'll buy a pair of steel-toed shoes," he promised. His gaze returned to Mallory. "So is it a date?"

"Mom?"

Unable to resist Mallory's blatant pleading, Jessica merely shrugged. "Since I seem to be outvoted once again, I suppose it's all right," she agreed reluctantly.

Quinn stood up, rubbing his hands together as if he'd never expected any other outcome. "Terrific. Now, Jill, what do you say we get started on that homework?"

"All right!" she said instantly, picking up the thick textbook from the floor where she'd obviously flung it in a fit of desperation. "We can work in the den, okay?"

"Fine with me," he replied amiably, following her out the door.

A moment later, Jill was back, flinging her arms enthusiastically around Jessica's waist. "I don't know where you found him, Mom. But I'm sure glad you did."

Then she was gone, her face wreathed in a brilliant smile. "It's not what you think," Jessica insisted, uncomfortable with her two remaining daughters' and her mother's knowing smiles. "There's absolutely nothing going on between Quinn and me. So don't anyone go jumping to conclusions!"

"I wouldn't think of it, dear," Elizabeth murmured, a secretive light flickering in her blue eyes.

Jessica couldn't stand any more of the silent scrutiny. "I've got work to do," she stated briskly, marching from the room.

She spent the remainder of the evening locked in her bedroom, attempting to work on the environmental group's brief. She didn't even come out when Elizabeth knocked on the door, informing her that Jill had managed to unravel the secrets of the Pythagorean theorem and Quinn was leaving.

"I'm sure he can find his way out by now," Jessica muttered under her breath, earning an exasperated sigh from her mother as Elizabeth returned downstairs to join in the chorus of good-nights.

TO JESSICA'S RELIEF, the following morning flew by, remaining blissfully uneventful. She experienced a sense of satisfaction as she crossed one item after another off her lengthy list. A few minutes before noon, she was staring down at the paper, debating whether or not to skip over the errand she'd capriciously scribbled down this morning.

The one thing Jessica had always hated most in the world, with the understandable exception of a trip to the dentist, was clothes shopping. That initial dislike had been amplified by the fiasco with Deirdre Hanson. More than three years later, Jessica was still relying solely on the clothing her husband's second wife had selected for the campaign. The last time Elizabeth had managed to coax Jessica into a department store was eighteen months ago. She'd suffered a horribly embarrassing anxiety attack and had no interest in repeating the experience.

Still, she considered, tapping her pen thoughtfully on the paper, Quinn's appreciation of her appearance the other night was etched onto her mind, making her smile whenever she remembered the sensual gleam in his green eyes. It had been a long time since a man had looked at her in that way, even longer since she'd experienced an answering response. As long as both of them understood that nothing could come of their relationship but a brief, enjoyable affair, could it be so wrong to see him from time to time on a social basis?

And, she mused, continuing along that train of thought, if she was going to have an affair with Quinn, wasn't it only natural to want to look her best? To feel desirable?

She took a brief mental inventory of her closet, knowing that the evening dresses encased in clear plastic were expensive, chic and timeless in design. Deirdre had seen to that. But those clothes belonged to another time. Another Jessica O'Neill. If she was going to do something as uncharacteristic as have a fling with a man whose reputation made Casanova's seem tame by comparison, Jessica wanted something new. Something of her own choosing.

Telling Paula she was taking a long lunch, Jessica left her office, taking the bus to Macy's Union Square. While many cities had experienced a deterioration of their downtown area, the four-block hub surrounding Union Square housed an abundance of elegant stores and richly decorated shops. The names of many prestigious New York stores appeared over several doors, especially along Post Street.

But as the bus approached Union Square, Jessica began to experience a creeping sense of anxiety. Her breathing quickened and suddenly the half-filled bus seemed horribly claustrophobic. She reached up, pulling the cord to direct the driver to stop. Once outside on the sidewalk, she took in deep gulps of air, willing her body to relax.

She told herself that she was a strong, independent woman who should certainly be able to go shopping on her lunch hour without falling apart. But as she walked down Post Street, the street became too narrow, the sidewalks too crowded, the buildings tall and menacing as they towered over her. People jostled her as they walked by in the hurried stride demonstrative of San Franciscans. Everyone seemed to have a purpose, a destination, as they strode past, speaking in a wide variety of native tongues.

Jessica wanted desperately to return to the safety of her office, where she was able to remain in control, where she wouldn't feel as if she'd go spinning off the globe at any moment. But something kept her from turning back.

By the time Jessica reached Macy's, her scalp was beginning to burn as if she had hot coals under her hair. Dizziness, chills, shakiness—all the classic symptoms of an anxiety attack returned and she closed her eyes for a moment, leaning against a wall just inside the door. Her distressed state drew the attention of a young salesclerk.

"Are you all right, ma'am?"

The woman's voice seemed to be coming from the bottom of the sea, but Jessica forced herself to concentrate, to carefully watch the full red lips move as she attempted to decipher the words.

Embarrassment threatened to overcome anxiety as she nodded slowly, taking a deep, calming breath. "Yes," she mumbled. "I'm fine," she said a bit more firmly.

"Are you certain?" Lovely slanted dark eyes viewed Jessica with a very real concern.

"Positive," Jessica assured her, standing up a little straighter. "Could you tell me where I can find the Laura Ashley section?"

"Laura Ashley?" The woman's gaze moved over Jessica's severely tailored suit.

"That's right," Jessica said, managing a smile. "I'm in the mood for something romantic."

An hour and a half later, Jessica was watching the salesclerk ring up the results of her uncharacteristic shopping spree. Handing over her charge card, she experienced a sense of pride that could have only come with scaling Mount Everest. Without any help from the ultrachic saleswoman, she'd chosen a glorious selection of clothing that captured the romantic spirit of a bygone era. More important, she'd overcome the ridiculous anxiety that had been the final lingering result of her marriage breaking up. Instructing the store to have the purchases delivered to her home, she was practically floating on air as she returned to the office.

"It must have been one terrific lunch," Paula observed, taking in Jessica's bright eyes and flushed face. "Anyone I know?"

"I was shopping," Jessica said on a laugh.

"You must have found some real bargains."

"There wasn't a bargain in the bunch. In fact, I'm going to be in debt for the next two years. Lucky for me the girls love hot dogs."

Her secretary shrugged. "Well, whatever turns you on, that's what I always say. Your calls are on your desk."

"Anything important?"

"Sylvia Thacker called four times, your mother called once, asking if you'd be home for dinner. Your ex called, reminding you he was picking up the girls at six-thirty, and Mr. Masterson called, but didn't leave a message."

"Would you get Mr. Masterson on the phone?" Jessica asked, her color rising a little higher with her pleasure.

Paula's eyes narrowed, but she refrained from commenting. "Sure."

Jessica slipped off her shoes, tucking her feet under her as she waited for Paula to ring, announcing Quinn was on the line.

"Hi," she said on a slightly breathless tone.

"Hi. You sound in a better mood than you were last night."

"I am," she agreed. "I'm in an absolutely marvelous, wonderful mood."

"Then you probably don't want to hear my news," Quinn warned almost tentatively.

For a fleeting moment, Jessica experienced the very real fear that Quinn was canceling their date. Not that she could blame him; she'd behaved childishly last evening, displaying about as much maturity as she might have expected from Jill.

"Fire away," she said, unaware she was holding her breath.

"Keith Thacker is on the warpath again."

Jessica's relief caused a silvery laugh to bubble forth. "Is that all? What's the problem now?"

"You *are* feeling good today, aren't you?" She could hear the smile in his voice.

"I am," she said. "Not even the Thackers can burst my bubble."

"I've got an idea. Why don't we both take off and go sailing," he suggested suddenly. "Spring is in the air and you know what they say about a man's fantasies."

"I thought that was a man's fancy."

"Fantasies, fancy, what's the difference? I fancy you, Jessie O'Neill. And let me tell you, sweetheart, you definitely improve a man's fantasy life."

Jessica's body warmed to volcanic proportions. "Don't be such a chauvinist," she chided teasingly. "We women have a few fantasies of our own, you know."

Quinn's pleasure was evident. "I suppose it would be asking too much to know that I was featured in any of yours?"

Jessica realized that she was actually flirting with Quinn. Not only that, she was enjoying every minute of it. "Oh, you've got the starring role," she admitted, her tone throaty and inviting.

He groaned. "Do you have any idea what you're doing to me?"

"I can only hope."

"Let's skip the sailing. I've got a better idea."

Jessica smiled, marveling at the way she was able to create that unmistakable desire in Quinn's tone. For the first time in her life, she suddenly felt like Jezebel, Delilah, Salome— all the sensual, alluring femmes fatales who'd known those mysterious tricks that could drive a man insane.

"Save that thought," she purred seductively.

This time Quinn's groan revealed a deep masculine pain. "I suppose that means you're not coming out to play with me today."

"I can't," she confirmed, her own voice displaying her disappointment. "But there's still tomorrow night."

"Tomorrow night," he echoed flatly, as if it was eons away. "I suppose we have to go to that damn party."

"You're the one who pointed out that my appearance is mandatory," Jessica teased. "I remember your instructing me on the politics of getting my name on the door."

"How long do we have to hang around, do you think?"

Jessica chewed thoughtfully on a fingernail, enjoying the idea of Quinn suffering as he waited for her answer. She'd never felt this sense of feminine power with Brian.

In truth, Jessica's self-confidence had been as hard to come by as her independence, but over the past three years, she'd decided she liked the woman she'd become. And apparently, Jessica considered with an inward smile, Quinn did, too.

"I'd say just long enough to put in an appearance," she finally said.

"And the girls are going to be in Mill Valley?"

"With their father," Jessica agreed.

"And your mother's going to Monterey?"

"For the entire weekend."

"So you've got the entire house all to yourself?"

"*We've* got the house all to *ourselves*," she corrected silkily.

"I'm going to die waiting for tomorrow night," he complained.

Jessica laughed lightly. "You can't. I'm counting on you to keep your word and take Mallory to that film festival she has her heart set on."

"Are you sure you can't come?" he asked hopefully. "We could neck in the back row."

"I really do have to work. Sorry."

Quinn heaved an exaggerated sigh. "Well, I guess I'll see you tomorrow night."

He started to hang up when Jessica suddenly remembered he'd called about Keith Thacker's latest complaint. "Quinn, wait a minute," she said quickly.

"Change your mind?"

"Mr. Thacker," she reminded him.

"Oh." His downcast tone indicated it was not his favorite topic of conversation, either. "He's ready to kill Sylvia for shaving that damn dog."

"He was ready to do that yesterday," Jessica said with a shrug.

"He was ready to wring her neck yesterday," Quinn corrected. "Today I think he'd receive a great deal of pleasure in cutting his spiteful wife into little pieces and feeding her to the sharks out in the bay.... It turns out the little guy is suddenly worthless as a stud."

"Why?" Jessica asked curiously. Then she sucked in her breath. "Don't tell me Sylvia had him neutered?"

"Nothing that drastic. But it seems a certain sexy lady Lhasa apso finds bald suitors less than appealing. She refused to have anything to do with him."

Jessica laughed at that, tears welling up in her eyes.

"Hey, it isn't that funny," Quinn complained. "Poor Maximilian is one frustrated male right now." His voice deepened, sounding like ebony velvet. "A state I can empathize with completely."

"He'll just have to suffer until his hair grows back, I suppose," Jessica stated blithely.

"What about me?"

"You have lovely hair, Quinn. Thick and wavy, like spun gold. It's one of those things I like best about you."

"What else do you like?"

The sensuality in Quinn's voice was so palpable that it practically reached through the telephone line to touch her. "I'll tell you tomorrow night," she whispered, suddenly shaken by what she was agreeing to. What she had, in all honesty, invited.

"I'm going to hold you to that, sweetheart," he warned huskily.

"I certainly hope so.... Oh, do you know how to get to the house to pick up Mallory?"

"She gave me directions last night," he answered absently. "So," he said on a sigh, "are you really working late tonight or hiding from your ex?"

"A little of both," Jessica admitted, not overly surprised by Quinn's accurate perception. There had been more than one occasion when he'd seemed to possess the ability to read her mind.

"I don't suppose you'd like to go out for a late supper?"

"I've got to be at the office early tomorrow morning."

"You realize, of course, you're condemning me to another night spent in a cold, lonely shower."

"I'm sorry."

"She's sorry," he muttered. "I suppose I'd better let you get back to work. Unless you want to talk dirty for a while?"

"Goodbye, Quinn," Jessica said, her smile belying her firm tone.

"Goodbye, Jess." His voice reached out to her like a caress. "I want you to know I'm going to spend the next thirty hours thinking about tomorrow night."

Jessica swallowed. "Me too," she agreed before finally breaking the connection.

Well, she'd done it. Jessica O'Neill, known for her careful, planned life-style, had just agreed to have an affair. As she spent the rest of the day attempting to concentrate on her work, Jessica wondered why, despite the undeniable sense of expectation, that idea made her feel just a little bit sad.

7

JESSICA GREW INCREASINGLY NERVOUS as she prepared for George Bennington's anniversary party. She told herself that at her age, it was ridiculous to be so rattled by the prospect of going out with a man. But it had been a very long time since she'd been out on a date. Fifteen years to be precise.

The term itself was ridiculous. Grown women didn't go out on "dates." There must be another word for what she was about to do. There were several, Jessica thought reluctantly, but she didn't like the sound of any of them. She knew times had changed, knew that there was nothing wrong with exploring the physical desire she'd been experiencing for Quinn Masterson. Yet some nagging little vestige of her upbringing was threatening to take the pleasure from the act.

Nice girls did not go to bed with men they weren't married to, Jessica told herself firmly. All right, she admitted as an afterthought, even in her day, that was not an unknown occurrence. She certainly hadn't been a virgin when she'd married Brian. But she'd loved him—or at least she'd thought she had—and the first time they'd made love had been the result of an unexpected flare of passion. It was certainly not as coldly planned as what she intended to do with Quinn tonight.

As she lay in the tub, surrounded by fragrant bubbles, sipping a calming glass of white wine, Jessica considered that she had spent her entire life seeking other people's approval. She'd been an obedient, studious child, eager for a word of praise or a smile from her larger-than-life father. Terrance MacLaughlin had not spent a great deal of time at home during her childhood; his career had always taken precedence. On those rare occasions that her father was willing to spend time with her, Jessica had never wanted to do anything that might possibly displease him.

She'd continued that same self-destructive behavior in her marriage, dropping out in her second year of law school when Brian insisted that he be the sole breadwinner of his family. He viewed her desire for a career of her own as a threat to his masculine self-esteem. Her place, he had instructed firmly, was home taking care of his house and his children. He'd never be able to love a woman hard-boiled enough to survive the corporate battles found in the real world.

So Jessica, eager to be loved, had acquiesced, creating a comfortable realm where Brian ruled as king, everything revolving around his wishes, his desires. If Jessica experienced resentment from time to time, she assured herself it was a small price to pay to be loved. It was only much later that she discovered what her behavior had cost her in terms of self-esteem and wasted years.

As she sipped the wine slowly, Jessica reminded herself there had been no award ceremonies for wife of the year. No plaques or trophies handed out to "nice girls." When forced out into the high-pressure world that was so different from the peaceful suburban existence she'd known in Mill Valley, she had at first felt like a foreigner in an alien land. She didn't know how to speak the language, play the games.

Jessica had had no idea how one measured accomplishments, judged the constant stream of petty mishaps. For too many years she had measured her success by sparkling windows and pristinely white shirt collars, while a sunken soufflé represented failure. The only things that had remained constant during that time of change were the girls.

Even now, each night before falling asleep, Jessica whispered a short prayer of thanksgiving that they'd avoided the pitfalls so many of her friends' children had fallen prey to. Although her daughters were certainly not the mythical darlings she'd pictured children to be in that romanticized time before motherhood, neither had they ever given her any real cause for concern. In that respect, Jessica figured, she was very lucky.

And she was fortunate to have met a man like Quinn Masterson, she decided, the wine going a little to her head in the warm, humid air of the bathroom. Every woman was entitled to one reckless fling in her life; she'd earned it. Determined to make the most of this weekend, Jessica rose from the tub, her body perfumed with the velvet cling of the bathwater.

She smoothed lotion over every pore, following up with a dusting of talcum powder that left her skin smooth and satiny. She took an unusually long time with her makeup, wanting to appear as feminine as possible, as attractive as she imagined Quinn's usual women to be.

By the time the doorbell rang, Jessica had regained her self-confidence and forced herself to walk slowly downstairs, unwilling to admit her eagerness to see him once again.

Her reward came as Quinn's eyes widened, sweeping over her from the top of her Gibson girl hairstyle, past her slender curves enhanced by the Victorian-style ivory lace gown that swirled about her calves, down to her feet, which were clad in sandals so delicate that they brought to mind Cinderella's glass slippers.

"This," he said, his voice uneven as he moved into the foyer, "was definitely worth the wait."

She smiled, twirling around in the soft glow of the antique wall light. "I'm glad you approve," she murmured, her cheeks flushed with feminine satisfaction that he found her desirable.

"I approved of you in that cute pink running suit," he countered, drawing her into his arms. "I thought you were delightful in that feminine little outfit the other night, and found you sexy as hell in those tight jeans. But this . . ."

He tilted his head back, gazing down at her, his eyes burning. "This is every fantasy I've ever had, come to life."

Jessica's lips curved in a teasing, provocative smile. There was a heady element of power in this situation as she realized how much Quinn wanted her. How much he needed her.

She pressed her palm against his chest, thrilled by the strong beat of his heart beneath her fingertips. "You're not so bad yourself," she murmured, her fingers stroking the front of his pleated white dress shirt.

She could feel his low chuckle. "I'm glad to know I pass inspection."

"Oh, you do," she agreed. "I've always thought men in tuxedos were very sexy."

"Men?" He arched a brow, revealing an unexpected jealous streak that Jessica found absolutely thrilling.

"Don't worry, Quinn," she said, her hands going up to curl about his neck. "Not only do you pass, you set the standard."

They were touching from their chests to their thighs, generating a heat that belied the cool evening temperature.

"You know that you're making it extremely difficult for me to think about your career advancement," he murmured, punctuating his words with light kisses against her lips.

"I know."

"Do you also know that if you keep moving against me that way we'll never get out of here?"

Her fingers were playing in the gilt strands of hair at the back of his neck, her hips moving in seductive little circles against his.

"I know that, too."

"Ah, Jess," he sighed, his breath a warm breeze against her mouth. "You sure picked one hell of a time to pull out the stops."

He kissed her then, a long, lingering kiss that seemed to go on forever. Through her dazed senses, Jessica felt his body trembling with unsatiated desire. His hands moved over her, molding her shape under the lacy dress as if she were malleable clay, and as she dissolved under his touch, Jessica realized that the soft, desperate moans were coming from her own ravaged lips.

All too soon those wonderful, seductive hands moved to her shoulders, putting her a little away from him. "We'd better go," he suggested flatly.

She nodded, her trembling fingers stroking his freshly shaven cheek. "I suppose so," she agreed without a great deal of enthusiasm.

"We won't stay long."

"Just put in an appearance."

"Offer our congratulations."

Her liquid gaze held vast feminine promises. "And then we'll come home."

"Home," he echoed, giving her a short, hard kiss on her pink lips.

"Do me one favor," he said, his voice still far from steady as they drove toward the Benningtons' penthouse apartment.

"Anything," Jessica agreed promptly.

He looked over at her, shaking his head as he gave her a lopsided smile. "Don't look at me that way while we're at the party. Or my resultant behavior may end up getting you canned."

Jessica grinned. "I'll try," she murmured. "But you know, it just might be worth it."

Quinn reached out, taking her hand and lifting it to his lips. "I knew you were a wanton at heart," he professed happily, lowering her hand to his thigh.

Jessica felt light-headed, filled with a strange happiness she'd never known before. "Is that so bad?" she asked, batting her lashes flirtatiously, her fingers stroking the firm muscle under the black dress slacks.

"Honey, I wouldn't have you any other way.... However, if you don't behave yourself, you're going to be forced to walk into that party with a blatantly indecent escort."

"Oh?"

He moved her hand to demonstrate the effect she was having on him. "Any more questions?"

With a forwardness that at any other time would have shocked her, Jessica was in no hurry to retrieve her hand.

"Just one," she said, as he brought the Maserati to a screeching halt in the subterranean parking garage of the building.

"What's that?" he asked raggedly, closing his eyes to her intimate caress.

"Is it time to leave yet?"

Quinn chuckled and picked up her hand, placing it on her own lap. "Behave yourself, wanton," he instructed firmly. Then he leaned his head back, closing his eyes. "Give me a little time," he muttered. "This isn't that easy a task."

Jessica studied the handsome face only inches from hers, watching his smooth brow furrow with concentration, his dark lashes resting against his cheeks, his full lips still curved in a little half smile. A warmth infused her body that went far beyond physical desire, and for a fleeting moment, she thought it might actually be love she was experiencing.

Then she forced that errant, romantic notion to the back of her mind. It was only natural that she was looking for an excuse to justify her uncharacteristic behavior. She had admittedly come a long way in the past three years, but her early socialization went deep. There was obviously still a part of her that needed to feel she was in love before going to bed with a man. That's all it was, the pragmatic side of her nature decided. So long as she recognized this odd feeling for what it was, everything would be all right.

The Benningtons' apartment took up the entire floor of the glittering glass monolith towering above the city, offering a spectacular view of sparkling lights and the darkened waters of San Francisco Bay. The party was in full swing when Jessica and Quinn arrived, and as she viewed the number of people crowding the room, Jessica knew no one would notice if she and Quinn escaped the anniversary celebration early.

"Ms O'Neill!" George Bennington greeted her enthusiastically, as if the unpleasant scene in his office earlier in the week had never occurred. "How nice you were able to attend our little party."

Jessica smiled and shook the outstretched hand of the senior partner and founder of Bennington, Marston, White and Lowell.

"Thank you for inviting me," she answered politely. "I hope my gift arrived."

"I'm sure it did," he replied absently. "Gloria takes care of that type of thing." His gaze moved to Jessica's escort, his eyes narrowing slightly. "Quinn, it's good to see you again."

"Always a pleasure to be invited," Quinn responded. "Congratulations."

"Yes, well, the party was Gloria's idea. To be perfectly honest, I've lost track of the years. It still amazes me we've managed to stay together so long."

"It's an admirable accomplishment in this day and age," Quinn agreed.

"Speaking of which," George stated, "aren't you handling Keith Thacker's divorce?"

"Unfortunately, yes."

"And you, Ms O'Neill, are representing Mrs. Thacker, if I'm not mistaken."

Jessica was not fooled by his casual tone. "That's right."

"Not that I'm questioning your integrity," he qualified his next statement, "but don't you think your, uh, relationship with Quinn might be considered a conflict of interest?"

"Relationship?" Jessica inquired blandly, not willing to help the man out.

Once again she got the distinct impression her employer was not an admirer of women attorneys. How dare he imply that she'd compromise her client because of any feelings she might have for Quinn!

"Ms O'Neill has been representing Sylvia with annoying persistence," Quinn interjected smoothly. "In fact, she's probably the finest champion the woman has found. You don't have a thing to worry about, George." His tone hardened just enough to close the door on that particular subject without being impolite.

George Bennington's smile was irritatingly unctuous and once again Jessica was reminded of Quinn's prowess as an attorney. Obviously, while not caring about her feelings, the older man was reluctant to offend Quinn.

"I'm pleased to hear that," he stated, looking past them to another couple who'd just arrived. "Why don't you two get something to drink?"

"That's a terrific idea," Quinn said, putting his hand lightly on Jessica's back and leading her in the direction of the bar, which had been set up at one end of the vast room.

"The nerve of that man," Jessica spluttered as they walked away. "To even suggest that I'd allow my personal life to interfere with my work!"

"Don't let him get to you," Quinn suggested calmly. "He's always that way with first-year attorneys."

"Women first-year attorneys," she muttered under her breath.

"*All* first-year attorneys," he corrected.

She looked up at him. "How would you know?"

"I spent my first year out of law school at Bennington, Marston and White. Lowell wasn't a partner yet."

"Oh." She was silent for a moment, considering that. "And he was that rough even way back then?"

Quinn chuckled. "You don't have to make it sound like the olden days, you know. Back before dinosaurs roamed the earth. I'm only forty, Jess."

Her irritation melted away and she grinned up at him. "That old?" she asked sweetly. "My goodness you've held your age remarkably well, Quinn." He scowled, causing Jessica to laugh lightly in return. Then her expression turned serious again. "Really, was he so frustratingly unbending when you were there?"

"We called it hell year," he revealed. "And if anything, I think he was even rougher on me." His handsome face turned thoughtful for a moment. "No, I take that back. I know he was rougher on me."

"Why?"

Quinn shrugged. "I suppose it had something to do with bending over backward to demonstrate that family didn't receive preferential treatment."

"Family?" Jessica stared at him blankly.

Quinn arched an incredulous brow. "You didn't know?"

"Know what?"

"That George Bennington is my uncle? I didn't think there was anyone in the legal community who wasn't aware of that little fact."

His words only served to remind Jessica that while Quinn was building his career, she'd been home folding diapers. Now, although she was trying her best to catch up, she secretly wondered if Quinn wouldn't have more in common with someone like Vanessa. Or Pamela Stuart.

Quinn misread her dour expression. "Believe me, honey, it'll get better."

"I certainly hope so," she muttered. "Because to tell you the truth, I've gotten an offer from the D.A.'s office that I'm seriously considering."

"Really?" He looked down at her with renewed interest. "I wouldn't have thought that any woman who starts her day with a detailed list would enjoy the chaos oftentimes found in the D.A.'s office."

"You have to be just as thorough in your work if you want to prosecute," Jessica objected. "Otherwise there'd be no convictions."

"That's true," he agreed amiably. "However, you also have to admit that the ability to punt, when necessary, is a decided asset."

"I'm working on that," Jessica said with a slight smile. "The way I look at it, the Thackers, if nothing else, are a good proving ground."

Quinn chuckled, his eyes warm as he gazed down at her. "You are just one surprise after another, pretty lady."

Jessica's eyes met his, and there was an instant of heat. "Thank you, sir," she said lightly. Then she smiled. "I thought you'd promised me a drink."

"I'd rather ravish your delectable body."

"Your uncle would love that," Jessica said with a musical, happy laugh. As they continued to weave their way through the throng of party guests to the bar, something occurred to her. "If it gets so much better," she challenged, "why did you leave?"

Quinn laughed heartily. "Be truthful, Jess. Can you see George and me working together?"

No, she considered thoughtfully, not at all. They were both incredibly strong-willed men. "I suppose not," she decided aloud.

"You're not the only one who's experienced a need to establish a sense of independence," he stated quietly.

Jessica could read the understanding in his gaze and was trying to think of something to say that would break this silken web that was settling down around them. Then she heard a familiar voice calling her name.

"Dad," she replied with surprise, turning around to view the tall, silver-haired man forging his way through the crowd. "What are you doing here?"

"One of the disadvantages of being an august magistrate in this town is that I get invited to all these bashes," he replied with a grimace. "Hello, Quinn. It's nice to see my daughter's finally latched onto someone who's almost good enough for her."

"Spoken like a properly adoring father," Quinn answered with a broad smile. "How's retirement treating you, Mac?"

"It's the pits," Terrance MacLaughlin confided. "Don't ever retire, Quinn. If I'd known how it was going to change my life, they'd have had to drag me screaming and kicking from the bench."

"It must be quite an adjustment," he agreed sympathetically.

"That's the understatement of the year." Jessica's father took a long swallow of bourbon. "Where's your mother?" he asked suddenly.

"In Monterey."

Terrance "Mac" MacLaughlin muttered a low oath. "I figured she'd be here. That's the only reason I showed up." He ran his finger inside his starched collar. "I've always hated these monkey suits."

"Why did you think Mother would be here?" Jessica inquired curiously.

"She and Gloria Bennington are old friends."

"Perhaps she didn't feel like celebrating a wedding anniversary when you two are having problems," Jessica offered, hoping that her father would admit he'd come here to convince his wife to return home.

"She always was as stubborn as a Missouri mule," Mac grumbled. "And she's gotten a lot worse lately."

"That's the same thing she says about you."

"Sure, take your mother's side, Jessica. You women always stick together, don't you?"

Jessica sighed, putting her hand on her father's arm. "I'm not taking anyone's side," she stated firmly. "I just wish you two would get together and discuss whatever's bothering you."

"I've tried. She won't listen to reason.... Do you know she told me that I drove her crazy? The woman waited forty-six years to let me know I was in her way. Told me to get out of the house and leave her alone." His oath was short and impatient. "Well, I figure Alaska's far enough away that I won't be a nuisance any longer."

"I can't believe Mother said exactly that," Jessica argued. "What were you doing?"

Her father arched a silvery brow. "Are you judging me guilty without a fair hearing, Jessie? Your own father?"

Jessica exchanged a frustrated glance with Quinn who'd wisely remained silent during the interchange. At her silent request, he spoke up.

"Why don't we get you a refill, Mac," he suggested smoothly. "It'll give us a chance to talk man to man." He looked down at Jessica, his green eyes smiling. "You won't mind fending for yourself for a few minutes, will you, sweetheart?"

"Not at all," she answered gratefully. Going up on her toes, she kissed her father's cheek. "It was nice seeing you, Dad. We should get together more often."

"If you're ever in Alaska, look me up," he muttered, allowing himself to be led away by Quinn, who gave Jessica a wink over his shoulder.

"Sweetheart, is it?"

Jessica's shoulders stiffened at the unveiled sarcasm in the deep voice behind her. She slowly turned, eyeing Brian O'Neill. This party was definitely turning into a family reunion, she thought grimly. And this was one former family member she could go all evening without meeting.

"I didn't know you were going to be here."

"Gracious as always, I see."

Jessica refused to respond to her former husband's baiting. "I thought you wanted to be with the girls this weekend. Who's taking care of them? Deirdre?" Despite her best intentions not to show her irritation, Jessica's tone indicated the improbability of that particular scenario.

"Deirdre's in New York on another one of those blasted buying trips of hers. The girls wanted a slumber party with the Franklin kids and I didn't think they needed me around for that. Mrs. Wilson's staying at the house."

"They've missed Bonnie and Lori," Jessica agreed. "So, what are you doing here?"

"You know Bennington handles O'Neill Development's legal work," Brian reminded her. "I received an invitation at the office last week. I wasn't planning to attend until I spent last night and today hearing all about Mr. Wonderful. I decided I'd better warn you about the big mistake you're making."

"I'm not making any mistake," Jessica argued coolly. "But even if I were, Brian, you're in no position to offer advice about my life. You were the one who said I needed to become more independent." She held out her arms. "Meet Jessica O'Neill, modern career woman."

"Modern enough to sleep with a man with my daughters in the next room?" he sneered.

Jessica felt her color rise. "Not that it's any of your business, but I haven't been doing anything that could harm the girls in any way."

"You let Masterson turn their heads with his slick charm. What are they going to do when he dumps you and moves on to his next conquest?"

Jessica pressed her lips together, her blue eyes circling the room, looking for Quinn. She was definitely in need of a drink. Unfortunately he seemed to have disappeared, along with her father. She schooled her tone to appear calm, uncaring.

"I imagine they'll do the same as they did when you dumped me. Carry on."

His dark eyes narrowed. "You never used to be this strong," Brian mused aloud. "A few years ago you would have been running from the room in tears."

"A few years ago, you would have been able to hurt me," she countered.

"And now?"

She shrugged, surprised to find that although Brian admittedly irritated her, she didn't feel any lingering pain. Or any emotion of any kind, for that matter.

"I've grown up."

His gaze darkened as it moved over her, taking in her thick auburn hair, the stylish yet romantic dress, her long legs clad in sheer stockings. Jessica remained still, submitting to his lengthy study, confident that she looked uniquely attractive.

"I can see you have," he murmured. "Since it seems Masterson has deserted you, why don't you let me get you a drink and we'll talk about old times."

The invitation in his deep voice was unmistakable, and rather than being pleased by the fact that her former husband suddenly found her desirable, Jessica was stunned to discover that she felt absolutely nothing.

"This is supposed to be a party, Brian. Not a wake." Glancing around the room, she spotted Quinn headed their way. "Have a good evening," she suggested with a smile, leaving him staring after her as she went to meet Quinn.

"I see you weren't lonely." He didn't bother to hide his annoyance.

She looked up at him curiously. "Are you by any chance jealous?"

"You're damn right I am. I leave you alone for a few minutes and return to find your ex practically eating you up with those beady little eyes. How am I supposed to feel?"

She took his arm and maneuvered through the crowd of guests to the French doors leading out to the balcony. "I think I could use some fresh air."

"The fog's in; it's going to be cool out there," he warned.

Her smile was unmistakably inviting. "Then you'll just have to keep me warm."

The fog had indeed rolled in like a thick blanket, a few stars valiantly managing to make themselves seen as they sparkled in the night sky. A waning moon cast a shadowy, silver light against the top of the Golden Gate Bridge as it thrust its way above the veiled entrance to San Francisco Bay. The sounds of the party drifted away and despite the steady hum of traffic several stories below, Jessica and Quinn could have been the only two people in the world.

"I'm glad Brian was here tonight," Jessica said softly.

"You don't know what that does to my ego," Quinn muttered.

She turned, her back against the railing as she placed her palms on either side of his stern face. "You don't understand," she protested, holding his frustrated gaze with eyes as soft and blue as a tropical lagoon.

"All these years, while I've been building a life for myself, in some little corner of my mind, I've been wanting to become the kind of woman that could compete with the Deirdre Hansons of the world. The type of modern woman who could interest a man, meet him on an equal basis."

"So now you've discovered you've made it. Congratulations. You can steal your husband back from his new wife and it'll be just one happy family again."

Jessica refused to be intimidated by Quinn's icy tone. "Brian did seem honestly interested in me," she admitted. "But the surprising thing was that I didn't care." She shook her head regretfully, her voice quavering ever so slightly. "All these years I'd dreamed of that moment, imagined how I'd feel when I finally earned his approval. Not that I ever thought about going back to him," she stated firmly. "I just wanted him to realize what he'd thrown away without a backward glance."

Quinn was silent for a long time, staring past Jessica out into the billowy mist wrapping itself around the city. "I think I can understand that," he said finally. "So how did it feel?"

Jessica's laugh was rich and full-bodied. "That's the amazing thing. Nothing happened. I kept waiting to feel something—pleasure, vindication, satisfaction. But all I could think about was getting away to find you."

"Oh, Jess." One hand cupped her cheek, while the long fingers of the other splayed against her throat, causing her blood to beat against the delicate ivory cameo. "I was ready to kill that bastard when I saw the way he was looking at you. After what he did, he doesn't deserve a second chance.

"You're mine now, Jess," he professed fiercely. "I've waited too long for you to give you up now."

The possessive statement tolled a warning in the back of Jessica's mind, but she was given no time to consider Quinn's huskily stated words as his mouth fused with hers, scorching away all reason.

The night breeze was creating havoc to Jessica's carefully coiffed hair, fingers of damp fog brushed against her cheeks, but all she was aware of was the heat of Quinn's mouth, the hardness of his body pressing against hers, arousing the most primitive of womanly instincts as she molded her softness to his rigid strength. She was soaring, flying free and high, meeting Quinn's own desperate desire and surpassing it as a shock of need rocketed through her.

She was beyond thought, beyond reason, crying out softly as Quinn dragged his lips away, breathing heavily as he rested his chin atop her disheveled hair.

"I think we're having an earthquake," he managed to gasp between gulps of air.

Jessica's own breathing was unsteady as she turned her head to press a kiss against his neck. "I don't care," she whispered, her lips plucking at the warm, slightly scratchy skin. "I want to make love with you, Quinn."

"Here? That'd be a bit dangerous, darlin', even discounting the earthquake."

"I feel like being reckless tonight. Let's live dangerously, Quinn." Her fingers were toying with the onyx studs on his shirt.

"You are living recklessly, Jess," he murmured, lifting her hand to his lips and eyeing her seriously over the top of their linked fingers. "I don't think you begin to realize what you're starting here."

Her soft smile was provocative and definitely enticing. "Why don't we go home and put your theory to the test, counselor?"

Quinn suddenly realized how Adam must have felt when Eve waved that bright red apple under his nose. She still didn't understand. He wanted her—he wasn't about to deny that. But he wanted more than Jessica's body, as lovely and desirable as it was. He wanted her heart. And yes, dammit, he considered almost fiercely, he wanted her soul.

He understood that she'd suffered with the breakup of her marriage. He realized that she'd undergone a significant metamorphosis in order to become the self-sufficient attorney she was today. He ached for her loss, just as he was pained by her apparent inability to realize that love didn't equal weakness, marriage didn't have to mean subjugation.

Quinn wanted to spend the rest of his life with Jessica. He wanted it for himself, but he wanted it for her, as well. And her daughters. He knew they could be a family, if she'd only let things take their natural course. If she'd only open her eyes to the love he had to offer.

If he gave in to temptation and took Jessica to bed tonight, he'd only be muddying the waters, allowing her to confuse sex with love. If he wanted to play this thing the smart way, he'd wait until she was ready to admit the feeling she had for him couldn't be anything else but love. But God, how he wanted her!

What the hell, Quinn considered with an accepting, inward shrug as he took Jessica's hand and let her lead him back into the room to the front door. He never claimed to be bucking for sainthood.

8

As Quinn guided the Maserati through the fogbound streets, Jessica experienced a sense of anticipation like nothing she'd ever known. She was actually going to do it, she realized. She was going to have a cold-blooded, casual affair.

Not that there was anything cold-blooded about Quinn, she mused, surreptitiously studying him as he drove. He radiated a masculinity so strong, so powerful, so heated that there had been times it had threatened to overwhelm her. She trembled just thinking about the way his touch could bring her blood to flame.

"Cold?"

Those sharp green eyes didn't miss a thing, she thought. Jessica shook her head, meeting his questioning gaze. "No," she admitted on a whisper. "I think I'm burning up."

He treated her to a slow, sensual smile. "Don't feel like the Lone Ranger."

Her hand had been resting on his knee and now he covered it with his, entwining their fingers, his thumb stroking little circles against the sensitive skin of her palm. Jessica felt herself melting into the glove-soft leather seat.

"Your dad's having a hard time adjusting to retirement," he revealed, as if he found it necessary to turn the conversation to something more casual in order to survive the short drive to Jessica's town house.

"Is that what you two were talking about?"

"That. And other things. He thinks quite highly of you, by the way. I had to promise my intentions were honorable."

Jessica felt the embarrassed flush staining her cheeks and was grateful for the cover of darkness. "I hate to have you lie to him," she murmured. "But it's probably for the best."

He slanted her an appraising glance. "What makes you think I was lying?"

Jessica was horrified by the way those simple words managed to pierce her self-protective armor. No, she warned herself, she couldn't allow her desire for the man to cloud her resolve. This was a fleeting, transitory relationship. A night, a weekend, a month at the very most. Surely in thirty long days this attraction would run its course. Little habits would begin to grate on nerves, passions would cool, irritations would set in. Jessica was a realist; she knew that happily ever after was a myth originated in fairy tales, perpetuated by romantic storytellers.

"Did he say anything about the reason for Mother leaving their house?" she asked, changing the subject.

Quinn stifled the urge to shake her until those lovely teeth rattled. He'd always thought of himself as being single-minded, but Jessica's stubbornness surpassed anything he'd ever known.

"It seems that in an effort to make himself useful, he rearranged her office."

"Oh, no," Jessica groaned, recalling the cluttered chaos that Elizabeth had always worked in. Although others might wonder how she ever found anything in the muddle of wallpaper samples, paint chips and bolts of fabric, her mother had always possessed the ability to locate a desired swatch of material without a moment's hesitation.

"While she was in Houston last week, meeting with those developers, he installed shelves on all four walls and, as he so succinctly put it, 'tidied things up a bit for her.'"

"I imagine she was thrilled," Jessica said dryly.

"According to Mac, she stared at his remodeling for about ten minutes, then, telling him exactly what he could do with his handiwork, left the house without even bothering to unpack."

"I can't believe she'd throw away forty-six years of marriage just because of a few shelves. No matter how angry she was."

Quinn shrugged. "I think it was just the last straw. Apparently they've been arguing about what she calls his interference for the past six months since his retirement. Mac, of course, only sees himself as trying to help. I think he's at loose ends these days."

"Poor Dad," she murmured. "I know how it is to feel useless."

Quinn didn't comment on that, instead squeezing her fingers reassuringly. "Give them time to work it out," he advised. "If I tell you something in confidence, promise you won't warn Elizabeth?"

"I promise."

"He's on his way to Monterey."

Well, Jessica considered, that was something. "I hope he uses a little more finesse when he tries to convince her to return home," she stated thoughtfully. "I don't think Mother will respond to his usual steamroller tactics."

"Like mother, like daughter," Quinn murmured, pulling up to the curb in front of her house. He sat still for a long, silent moment, leaning his forearms on the steering wheel, staring out into the well of darkness beyond the windshield. When he finally turned to look at Jessica, his gaze was unnervingly somber.

"I don't want to push you into anything tonight, Jess," he said quietly, his green eyes locked onto her face. "If we make love, I need to know that you want me as much as I want you."

She leaned forward, brushing his lips with her own. "Let me show you exactly how much I want you, Quinn," she whispered, her warm breath fanning his face as she rained kisses over his stern features.

Muffling a groan, Quinn needed no further invitation.

Jessica was suddenly unreasonably nervous as they entered the house. "Would you like a drink?" she offered.

"Sounds nice," Quinn agreed amiably.

"I think there's some white wine in the refrigerator," she said. "But if you'd rather have Scotch, or brandy, or something else . . ." Her voice drifted off.

"Whatever you're having is fine."

She turned in the direction of the kitchen, then stopped. "I don't want anything to drink," she said softly.

"I don't, either," he admitted, taking her hand as they climbed the stairs.

The house was too quiet, and Jessica found herself longing for some of Jill's pulsating rock music to break the thick silence.

"I never thanked you for taking Mallory to that film festival today," she said.

"I had a good time," Quinn replied easily. "Mallory did, too, I think. Although your mother would have definitely disapproved of our behavior."

"Oh? Why?"

He grinned down at her. "Do you have any idea how much popcorn and candy an eleven-year-old can consume? Just imagine the additives."

Jessica laughed, as she was supposed to. She was grateful to Quinn for lightening the mood.

His eyes widened as he entered Jessica's bedroom, although he wondered why he was surprised by the brilliant canvases hanging on her walls.

"You painted those, didn't you?" he asked, already knowing the answer as he studied the bright, abstract swirls of color.

"When I was married," she agreed, unreasonably anxious for his opinion. "Mother cringes every time she walks into the room. She says they clash horribly with the Victorian floral wallpaper."

"It suits you," he replied, his gaze circling the decidedly feminine room, then returning to Jessica's softly flushed face. "You've got a lot of unbridled passion lurking under that enticingly delicate exterior, Jessie."

So thrilled was she by the desire burning in Quinn's dark gaze that Jessica forgot her usual assertion that she was a strong, independent woman. At this moment, she only wanted him to find her desirable.

"I'm glad it's you," she said quietly, moving into his arms.

Quinn looked down at her questioningly.

"It's been a very long time," she explained, faltering a bit as she succumbed to the lambent desire she viewed in those green eyes. "I didn't want to do this with just anybody. It seemed important that it was someone I . . ."

Her voice drifted off as she tried to come up with the proper word. *Not love,* she told herself firmly. Love implied commitment, demands, weakness. She couldn't allow herself to yield to its false, ethereal promises.

Quinn waited patiently, feeling Jessica's inner struggle as she tried to sort out her feelings. One part of him wanted to kill Brian O'Neill for leaving Jessica so wounded, so afraid to trust. Another part of him was thankful that the guy hadn't realized a terrific thing when he had it. If Jessica's idiot of a husband hadn't left her, she and Quinn might never had met. What a void that would have left in his life!

"Care for," she finished weakly, resting her forehead against the firm line of his shoulder.

Well, it wasn't precisely what he'd wanted to hear. But it was enough. For now.

His hands moved to her hair, pulling out the mother-of-pearl combs that held it in precarious order, his fingers sifting through the fiery waves as they tumbled down over her shoulders.

"I love your hair down," he murmured, grazing the fragrant softness with his lips. "You remind me of something from an eighteenth-century novel."

Her full lips curved in a slight smile as she tilted her head back to look up at him. "Ah," she said on a slight sigh, "we're going to play lusty aristocrat and naughty milkmaid."

His fingers toyed with the cameo at her throat, finding the catch and releasing it. "Uh-uh," he argued, opening the lacy frill at her neck to press his lips against her skin. Jessica's pulse leaped in response. "You're every inch an aristocrat, sweetheart. The kind of woman who instilled all that passion in pirates and gamekeepers."

Jessica felt her legs weakening as he slowly began to unbutton her dress, his lips grazing each new bit of freed skin, tasting her warming flesh, drinking in a sweet scent that re-minded him of lilacs in April. He took his time manipulating the pearl buttons through the silk loops, like a man unwrapping the most special of gifts.

"This was a bad idea," she whispered, her fingers digging into his shoulders as she clung to him for support.

For a brief, horrible moment, Quinn thought Jessica was about to change her mind. But as her body swayed against him, he decided he might be wrong.

"What was a bad idea?" His tongue was cutting moist swaths down the slope of her breasts, causing an ache that reached to her very core.

"This dress," she complained, flinging her head back, granting him further access to her creamy skin. "I should have found one with a zipper."

He chuckled as the dress finally fell open to her waist. "Anticipation is half the fun," he murmured, taking one pebbled bud between his lips.

Jessica's head was spinning and she was certain she'd faint at any moment. A dizzying excitement raced through her and she thrust her hands into his thick, crisp hair, pressing him against her suddenly moist skin.

The heat seeping into her body was consuming her, licking through her veins, spiraling outward until she thought she'd explode. But still Quinn took his time, moving his head to the other breast, treating it to a torture just as sweet, just as prolonged.

"Quinn, please," she begged, her fingers fumbling with the studs of his dress shirt, anxious for a feel of the hard chest hidden by the crisp white material. She'd never wanted a man like this—never needed a man as much as she needed Quinn at this moment.

He pushed the dress off her shoulders, going down on his knees as he continued to bring it over the soft swell of her hips, down her trembling thighs, to where it finally lay in a lacy puddle at her feet. As if in a trance, Jessica stepped out of the expensive dress, closing her eyes to the sensual torment as Quinn repeated the motion with her silk half-slip. His eyes seemed to burst into flame at what he found waiting for him.

Jessica had allowed her sensuality to run rampant while shopping for this evening, and if she'd been worried that Quinn might find her purchases too contrived, too costumey, that fear dissolved as he viewed the lacy white garter belt, bikini panties and ivory silk stockings that clung to her legs.

"That outfit definitely invites ravishing," he said huskily.

"Oh, yes," she breathed, shaking like a leaf under gale-force winds.

Quinn slipped the sandals from her feet, then began kissing every inch of her long, slender leg, stopping just short of the lacy confection that framed her femininity. He forged a similar trail back down her other thigh, nibbling at the back of her knee, his tongue dampening the silk covering her ankle. A blood-red passion whipped through her and just when she knew she could no longer stand, he slowly lowered her to the bed.

"You're exquisite." His lips trailed over her soft stomach, his voice echoing against her heated flesh. "Everything I've ever imagined." He untied the ribbons at her hips, easily ridding her of the lacy bikini, his fingers forging tantalizing paths on the satin skin at the inside of her thighs.

As Jessica writhed on the bed, her hips arching into his increasingly intimate touch, she realized that she'd completely thrown away her carefully acquired restraint. But as Quinn's lips caressed her sensitive flesh, she knew that whatever she was giving away, she was receiving tenfold.

"Please," she whispered, her voice ragged. "Please make love to me."

Lifting his head, Quinn knew he had never seen anything as beautiful as Jessica's liquid blue eyes, filled with a desire that equaled his own. He held her gaze, his fingers causing havoc to her body as his hand moved up her leg, tracing beguiling patterns on her silk-covered thigh.

"I am," he said simply, lowering his head once again, his lips exploring the skin of her midriff, leaving a raging heat behind. "I knew it."

"Knew what?" she asked weakly, melting under his expert caresses. Jessica was not inexperienced—she'd been married, after all. But she had never known anything like the sweet, aching passion Quinn's hands and lips were releasing from deep within her.

"That your skin would be even silkier than that lacy confection you were wearing." His fingers drew one stocking down the long length of her leg, his lips returning up the trail his hands had blazed. "And you taste so very, very good."

"Quinn," she complained, lifting her hips invitingly off the mattress, "I don't want to wait any longer. I want to make love to you now."

Through the fog clouding her senses, Jessica was stunned to hear herself issuing such a demand. But Quinn had turned her body to flame, and she knew only he could quench the fires threatening to consume her.

"It's not that simple, sweetheart," he murmured as he slowly stripped off the other stocking. "There are certain stages one must go through before reaching the final destination."

Under normal circumstances, Jessica would have agreed. She preferred her life to run in an orderly fashion, but this was ridiculous. She sucked in her breath as he reached under her, his deft fingers manipulating the catch on the lacy garter belt.

"Can't you skip a few steps?" she suggested, quivering under his touch as the passion he'd evoked escalated to exquisite heights.

Quinn could feel Jessica's surrender as she trembled beneath him. Her body was his for the taking, but he had discovered over the past few days that he was a selfish man. He was determined to have all of Jessica O'Neill.

"That would be cheating," he stated with a breezy attitude he was far from feeling, as his lips explored every inch of satiny skin.

Quinn could feel the heat rising from her body in waves as his lips continued their erotic journey. He found himself being irrevocably drawn into his own sensual snare. His blood was pounding in his ears as he explored her welcoming warmth, and as she cried out, he vowed that she'd never forget this night.

Suddenly she was twisting in his arms, practically tearing his clothes from his body as she displayed a hunger and a power just as vital, just as desperate as his own. Her lips and hands moved over Quinn as his had moved over her, tasting, touching, creating exquisite sensations that were just this side of pain as they sought to give him pleasure.

With a vast effort, Quinn forced himself to remember one final, vital detail. "Jess," he murmured, poised over her. "Is this all right? I don't want you to think I'm the kind of guy who's always prepared, hoping to get lucky, but you did kind of imply..."

He was suddenly unreasonably uncomfortable with this entire situation. But the one thing Quinn didn't want to do was give Jessica any reason to be sorry for this in the morning.

It was at that moment, viewing the atypical uncertainty on Quinn's handsome features that Jessica fell totally, irrevocably in love with him. She reached up, running her fingers over his hair, her eyes smiling at him through a sheen of glistening moisture.

"It's all right," she assured him softly.

Knowing how the evening was going to end, she'd seen to that. As much as she wanted Quinn, one thing she didn't need was another child. Especially one born out of wedlock.

"Please, Quinn," she whispered. "Make love to me."

Quinn ceased to think and so did Jessica as they concentrated only on their feelings of shimmering, golden desire. Then he was deep inside her, moving with a fiery strength that fueled their passion until the earth seemed to tilt on its axis, spinning wildly out of control.

AN IMMEASURABLE TIME LATER, Jessica lay in Quinn's arms, content to let the slow, lingering warmth suffuse her languid body. She'd never behaved like that—flinging herself at a man, teasing him, insisting he make love to her—yet she felt not one shred of remorse. Their lovemaking had been the most beautiful thing she'd ever experienced. And although she knew nothing permanent could ever come of it, Jessica refused to allow herself a single regret.

Quinn pressed a light kiss against her temple. "Well, what do you think? Was it the earthquake? Or us?"

"I don't know," she murmured, sighing with sheer pleasure as his fingers trailed down her side. "But I'll bet it registered at least a ten on Richter scales all over the state."

"At least . . . God, you're beautiful."

Her eyes danced as she lifted herself up on one elbow and glanced down at his magnificent, spent body. "So are you."

She watched him laugh, enthralled by the rippling of the muscles of his abdomen. "Men aren't beautiful."

"You are," she insisted. "The most beautiful man I've ever known."

"Known a great many, have you?"

"Jealous?" She grinned down at him. "I'm not asking about the legions of women in your life," she pointed out, not willing to admit he'd only been the second man she'd ever gone to bed with. Why point out her inexperience?

"Ask away," Quinn invited, rolling over, covering her body with his. Jessica thrilled at the feel of his lightly haired legs between hers and gasped as he lowered his head, capturing an ultrasensitive nipple between his lips. "It wouldn't matter, because you're the only one who's ever counted, Jess."

His eyes met hers, and Jessica could not mistake the message she read in their emerald depths. She knew that any other woman would be in seventh heaven to be in her position right now. Figuratively and, she admitted, as his hips rubbed intimately against hers, literally. Quinn hadn't promised her forever, but it was there, gleaming in his tender gaze. Instead of thrilling her, as it once might have, Jessica found the idea of permanency unreasonably frightening.

Conflicting emotions tore at her, drawing her into a vortex of feelings so deep, so overwhelming, that she did not want to think about them any longer. Not tonight.

She nodded, moved beyond words at the love shining in Quinn's wonderful eyes and gave herself up to his tender, intoxicating kiss.

IF JESSICA EXPECTED the magic to disappear with the morning light, she was to be proved wrong. Quinn had infiltrated all the little pockets of her life, and although a part of her remained convinced that this golden-tinged pleasure would soon fade as the following days melted into weeks, Jessica found herself unable to consider a life before him.

They celebrated the Cherry Blossom Festival together, Mallory's camera never ceasing as she filmed the colorfully costumed dancers and floats winding their way through the streets to the graceful Peace Pagoda. Jessica had been attending the annual spring fete since its inception, but never had she enjoyed herself as she did this year.

A San Francisco native, Jessica could be faulted for foregoing the tourist attractions of her beloved city. But as she shared the warm, yellow sunshine of spring with Quinn, she wondered why she had never realized how romantic it could be to walk along Fisherman's Wharf, the pungent aroma of fresh crab and shrimp cooking in sidewalk caldrons mixing enticingly with the tangy sea breezes.

One mellow Sunday afternoon she bought everyone bright, fanciful kites at Ghirardelli Square, and at the end of the day whimsically released hers, watching it disappear into the ruby-and-gold sky over the bay. When Quinn came out of one of the gift shops with a delicate hand-scrolled Victorian locket, Jessica protested at the price, but he refused to listen.

"It's the perfect adornment for a lady aristocrat who possesses the heart of a naughty milkmaid," he murmured for her ears alone, fastening the sterling silver heart about her neck.

Jill decided that it was the most romantic present she'd ever seen. Sara, ever practical, pointed out that the silver was going to need regular polishing. Mallory's camera just whirred away, going in for a tight shot as Quinn's lips grazed Jessica's earlobe.

Quinn was aghast that Jessica had never taken her daughters on a bay tour, insisting they hadn't seen the city until they'd viewed the towering skyline from the water. In order to remedy that situation, he showed up one Saturday morning with tickets for the Blue and Gold cruise. Jill spent the better part of the afternoon seasick from the choppy water, Mallory and Sara argued incessantly over whose fault it was that the bag containing extra videotape cassettes fell overboard into the icy water off the shores of Alcatraz. Jessica ended the day windblown, cold, but unreasonably happy.

Mother Nature seemed determined to bestow upon San Francisco the warmest spring on record, and one balmy day on her lunch hour, Quinn took Jessica to a "brown bag" opera under the branches of the gnarled olive trees in the courtyard of the Cannery. It didn't matter that she couldn't understand the Italian lyrics and was unable to follow the complex drama being played out before her. Because all her attention remained riveted on Quinn, on his every word, his every movement.

Jessica was still floating on a rosy cloud when she returned to the office, and when her intercom buzzed late in the afternoon, she answered it with a feeling of optimism. That feeling quickly disintegrated when a noncommittal Paula stated that Sylvia Thacker was waiting in the reception area.

"Send her in," Jessica instructed, taking a deep breath.

A moment later, a tall, expensively dressed woman marched into the room, settling regally into a chair across from Jessica's desk. Her ash-blond hair was professionally streaked, her makeup impeccable. Only the fire raging in her hazel eyes and the red spots high on her cheeks displayed her aggravation.

"He's done it this time! First, I want him fired. Then we're going to put that bastard in jail. For the rest of his natural life!"

"What did Mr. Thacker do this time?" Jessica asked calmly.

Sylvia reached into her alligator purse, pulling out a handful of newspaper scraps that she dumped unceremoniously on Jessica's desk.

"Look at that!" she instructed.

Jessica smoothed the pieces of newsprint with her hands, fitting the torn scraps into what was obviously the editorial page of the *San Francisco Star*. Her attention was drawn to a skillfully crafted cartoon depicting the incarceration of a local politician for graft.

"I'm afraid I don't understand," Jessica stated, unable to see what it was about the cartoon that had Sylvia so distraught.

A perfectly manicured nail jabbed at the number printed across the politician's striped prison suit. "Does that number ring a bell?" Sylvia inquired caustically.

Jessica stared, then couldn't stop a slight laugh from breaking free. "Oh, my God, that's your phone number!"

Sylvia was on her feet, glaring down at the shredded cartoon with such fire in her eyes that Jessica was surprised it didn't burst into flames.

"Do you have any idea how many weirdos have called me today because of that cartoon? I never realized so many perverts read the editorial pages!" Sylvia wrung her hands and began to pace the floor. "The phone hasn't stopped ringing! You have to do something!" she insisted on a wail that was in direct contrast to her sleek, sophisticated appearance.

"I'll contact Mr. Masterson right away," Jessica promised. "In the meantime, I suppose you should call the telephone company and have your number changed."

"I've already done that. But do you have any idea how many notes I'm going to have to send out letting all my friends know my new number?"

"A Herculean task, at best," Jessica replied dryly.

The slight sarcasm flew right over Sylvia Thacker's head. "It'll take the entire weekend," she agreed. "I want Keith billed for my time that he's wasted," she decided. "After all, I had plans to go to Big Sur. Now I'm going to be stuck at home."

"That is a shame," Jessica said, pressing her luck a bit further. "I take it you don't want to press charges?"

Sylvia looked at Jessica as if she'd just grown an extra head. "Of course I do!"

"May I point out that it will be a bit difficult for Mr. Thacker to pay you restitution if he's locked away in a jail cell? We've already frozen all his liquid assets."

"You have a point," Sylvia agreed thoughtfully. Then her face lit up. "So we'll get him fired. Then we'll take the bastard for all his unemployment!"

Her mood lifted by that idea, Sylvia left the office, chuckling wickedly to herself.

Paula suddenly appeared in the doorway. "Ain't love grand?" she asked with a laugh.

Jessica returned her grin, shaking her head with good-humored frustration. "Would you get me Mr. Masterson?"

"He's on hold now," Paula informed her, reminding Jessica once again how fortunate she was to have such a level-headed secretary. There were times when the woman seemed to read her mind.

"Quinn, we've got a problem," Jessica said as she picked up the receiver.

"I know," he answered immediately. "After such a delightful lunch hour, I can't keep my mind on my work, either. The sun is shining, the birds are singing and I have this irresistible urge to be with my lady.... Let's go sailing," he coaxed. "Then we'll spend the rest of the afternoon and evening making love."

"Quinn," Jessica stated firmly. "This is serious."

"So are my feelings about you, Jess."

There was a suddenly solemn note in his voice that Jessica decided would be best ignored for now. "Sylvia Thacker just left my office and believe me, the woman is looking for blood."

Jessica could hear Quinn's loud sigh. "What happened now?"

"Do you have a copy of this morning's *Star*?"

"Yeah, but it was such a madhouse around here this morning I didn't get a chance to read it. Why?"

"Check out the editorial cartoon," Jessica suggested.

"Just a minute." She could hear Quinn riffling through the newspaper. His roar of laughter indicated he'd just found Keith's latest artistic effort.

"It's not that funny," Jessica insisted sternly, a rebellious chuckle slipping out despite her efforts to remain totally professional.

"No," he agreed, his voice strained as he made a valiant attempt to match her serious tone. "Keith should be ashamed of himself. I suppose she's gotten a few calls."

"The phone hasn't stopped ringing," Jessica informed him.

"I'd better talk with him," Quinn said without a great deal of enthusiasm.

"You do that," Jessica advised dryly. Then she asked a question that had been bothering her from the beginning. "I know why I was stuck with Sylvia's case," she said, remembering Vanessa's explanation. "But for the life of me, I can't figure out why you're putting up with this circus."

"Keith and I were fraternity brothers at USC," Quinn revealed. "One semester I made the mistake of taking an art history class. Since I seem to lack the ability to tell a Rembrandt from a Matisse, I was in real trouble. Then to top it all off, I got mono.

"Keith showed up at the infirmary every day, drilling me on paintings until I knew enough to get a respectable C on the makeup final."

"So you're paying him back by handling his divorce?"

"He's not such a bad guy when he's off the booze. And you can't deny the fact that he's a genius at what he does."

"If he doesn't stop drinking," Jessica suggested, "he's going to be submitting those cartoons from a jail cell."

"I'll talk to him," Quinn promised. "And, Jess?" His tone suddenly deepened.

"Yes?"

"Have a good day."

Such simple words, she considered. She heard them continually from salesclerks, bus drivers, strangers. So why did they cause her heartbeat to quicken?

"Thank you," she murmured. "You too."

"I intend to," he agreed on a thick, sensual rumble. "I'm going to spend the day thinking of you."

The smile remained on Jessica's face long after she'd hung up. What a difference Quinn had made in her life, she thought as she returned to work.

AS SPRING BLOSSOMED, every day seemed unnaturally special, every moment delightfully memorable, and if Jessica ever suffered doubts about the fragile foundations of their affair, she pushed them to a far corner of her mind.

Her daughters took Quinn's presence in stride, and although they'd dropped more than one heavy hint that Jessica wasn't getting any younger, they wisely refrained from mentioning marriage. It was obvious, however, that they adored him.

Based on what Elizabeth was willing to state about Mac's impetuous trip to Monterey, Jessica determined that her father had made the mistake of demanding that his wife return with him. Now Elizabeth seemed bent on teaching him a lesson, and after forty-six years of marriage, Mac was forced to court his wife all over again. From those nights that Elizabeth didn't return home after a theater date, Jessica could only surmise that things were looking up on the MacLaughlin home front.

They'd been together six weeks when Quinn's patience ground to a halt. Except for those times that Elizabeth was out of town, or staying with Mac, and Jessica's daughters were in Marin County with Brian O'Neill, he and Jessica would make love at his apartment, forcing him to drive her home in the cold, lonely predawn hours.

"I want to stay with you all night," he complained as the car idled outside her house. "I want to hold you in my arms when we go to sleep and wake up with you in the morning."

"We will," she promised. "This weekend."

"Dammit, Jess," he argued, banging his fist on the steering wheel, "it's not enough! I'm tired of receiving bits and pieces of you. I want to be an integral part of your life. I want to know I'm important to you."

She framed his face with her hands, pressing a soft kiss against his tight lips. "You are important to me, Quinn," she murmured.

"Then let's live together," he suggested, as if the thought had just occurred to him. In truth, he'd been waiting days for the right moment. It was now or never, he decided.

She dropped her hands, shaking her head sadly. "You know I can't do that, darling. Not with the girls. It wouldn't be a good influence."

"What if you didn't have the girls?" he pressed, believing Jessica's objections to deepening their relationship went further than she was willing to admit.

"Are you suggesting I send them to live with Brian?"

Quinn hastened to dispel her misconception. "Of course not. It was just a hypothetical question. If it were only the two of us involved, would you live with me?"

Jessica wanted to say yes, that were it not for their situation, she would open her house, her heart, her life to him unconditionally. But in all honesty, she knew that wasn't entirely true. She was happy enough with the way things were right now. Granted, her bed seemed unreasonably lonely when she crawled between the cold sheets while the world still lay shrouded in darkness. And there were times when she'd look up to say something to Quinn, only to realize he wasn't there. He was across town, in his own apartment.

But those were only minor inconveniences compared to the problems they'd have if they were living together. Separate but equal. That was the new Jessica O'Neill motto.

"That's a moot point," she said, finally answering Quinn's question. "I'm the mother of three impressionable daughters. You knew that when you entered into this affair, Quinn."

It was at that moment Quinn decided he'd better leave before he said something he'd regret.

"You're right," he agreed without a great deal of enthusiasm, getting out of the car to walk her to the door. "I'll just have to work around the barriers."

Jessica didn't know exactly what Quinn meant by that vague statement, but she didn't like the glint of determination in his green eyes or the firm thrust of his jaw as he gave her an unusually circumspect good-night kiss. His odd behavior created a sense of foreboding that stayed with her the remainder of the night, making sleep an impossibility.

9

JESSICA'S FEARS WERE REALIZED as she entered the kitchen the next morning to find Quinn seated comfortably at the breakfast table, his long fingers wrapped around a mug of steaming coffee. At any other time, the sight of him would have given her a lift, but she was still unnerved by the intensity of his demands last night. Also, the expectant expressions on the faces of her mother and daughters made Jessica immediately suspicious. She couldn't forget his softly veiled threat about working around the barriers.

"What are you doing here?"

"Good morning to you, too," he stated with a smile.

Jessica let out an annoyed breath. She was due in court in two hours, she was exhausted before the day had even begun thanks to worrying about Quinn all night, and some maniac with a jackhammer was banging away in her head. She was in no mood to be gracious.

"Dammit, I asked you a question, Quinn."

"Jessica!" Elizabeth MacLaughlin turned from the stove, staring in disbelief at her daughter's blatant rudeness.

"Don't worry about it." Quinn sent her mother a broad grin. "I've already discovered our Jessie's not a morning person."

"That's for sure," Mallory offered helpfully, her camera directed toward the action being played out before her. "Mom won't talk to anyone until she's had her coffee."

"Well, we can't expect her to be perfect," Quinn remarked casually, rising from the table to pour some coffee into a bright mug.

"Here you go, darling," he said, leaning down to give her a peck on the cheek. "Drink up." He pulled out a chair for her.

"What are you doing here?" she tried for a third time, taking the chair he offered. She turned to her middle daughter. "Mallory, I'm in no mood for your project this morning!"

"You're going to want this saved for posterity," Mallory answered, zooming in for a close-up.

"I don't like the sound of this," Jessica groaned. "What am I going to want saved?"

"We've been planning your wedding," Quinn announced blandly.

Jessica choked on her coffee at the casual way he'd just dropped his bombshell. "Wedding?" she managed to gasp finally.

Quinn handed her a paper napkin. "Wedding," he repeated.

"It's going to be the most romantic wedding ever," Jill said on a deep sigh.

"You're going to love it," Sara agreed, bobbing her bright head. "Even Gran is all for it."

Quinn nodded. "Your mother had an elaborate church wedding in mind, but knowing how you're really a romantic at heart, I thought you might prefer the Japanese Tea Gardens.... I can picture you in that ivory lace dress you wore to George and Gloria's anniversary party, cherry blossoms woven through your lush auburn waves."

He glanced disparagingly at the elaborate twist he'd made at the back of her neck. "You'll wear your hair down, of course, instead of tying it up like some old maid schoolteacher.

Elizabeth forestalled Jessica's furious response as she set a plate of scorched bacon and runny eggs before Quinn, then placed an identical breakfast in front of Jessica, her stern look indicating she expected her daughter to eat it.

Jessica ignored the food. "Exactly who am I supposed to be marrying?"

"Why, Quinn, of course." Elizabeth laughed. "We should be hurt that you didn't tell us about all this sooner, Jessica. But he explained that you'd wanted to give the girls a chance to get used to him before breaking the news."

"We think it's terrific, Mom," Mallory enthused.

"Absolutely awesome," Jill agreed.

"And about time," Sara said, adding her two cents. "It's not healthy for a woman your age to be living alone."

Jessica shot her daughters a warning glance. "If I want any remarks from the peanut gallery, I'll ask for them," she snapped. "And, Mallory, for the last time, put that camera down or you won't get any allowance for the next twenty years!"

Then, if looks could kill, the one Jessica gave Quinn would have put him six feet under. The girls shifted nervously in their seats, and Mallory reluctantly lowered her camera. Only Elizabeth remained blissfully unaware of Jessica's exacerbation.

"I have to admit, dear," she trilled merrily, "that when Quinn first brought up the subject of having the wedding at the gardens, I found it rather avant-garde. But once he started describing the flowers, your dress and the strolling minstrels, I decided it was a delightful idea."

"Thank you, Lizzie." Quinn grinned up at Elizabeth, who smiled back.

"Lizzie?" Jessica arched a tawny brow. Her mother was a stickler for formality, she couldn't imagine anyone daring to use that nickname on Elizabeth MacLaughlin.

"Quinn decided that calling Gran Elizabeth would be too stuffy, once you were married," Mallory explained.

"And I'd feel absolutely ancient having a handsome man like Quinn call me Mother," Elizabeth interjected.

"Especially since no one would ever believe you were old enough," Quinn said smoothly, directing an appreciative smile Elizabeth's way.

Jessica stared as he mother giggled like an adolescent schoolgirl. "Quinn came up with Lizzie, and after trying it out a few times, I think I like it."

"We have to talk," Jessica said sternly, glaring across the table at the irritatingly smug man.

"Uh-oh," Jill said. "I think I'm going to be late for school."

"Me too!" Mallory exclaimed, jumping up from the table.

"Wait for me!" Sara appeared as eager as her sisters to escape from the room. "Have a good day, Mom," she called back over her shoulder. "Good luck, Quinn!"

"Of course we'll discuss everything in detail, darling," Quinn agreed readily, waving goodbye to Jessica's daughters as they scurried out the door. "Have you chosen a spot for our honeymoon yet?"

"There's not going to be any honeymoon!"

"Sure there is," he corrected smoothly, eyeing her wickedly over the rim of his mug. "You don't think I'd forego that pleasure, do you? I know we both have our work, Jess, but all it'll take is a little juggling of schedules."

"I'm not juggling my schedule for you, Quinn Masterson, so get that idea out of your head. And I'm not going on a honeymoon with you, because I'm not marrying you. We had an agreement and you've no right to go changing the rules!" She was on her feet, glaring down at him, her eyes ablaze.

"If you young people are going to argue," Elizabeth murmured calmly, "I think I'll go upstairs to watch 'Wheel of Fortune' on the bedroom television." She turned in the doorway. "Speaking of bedrooms, dear, if you both decide to live here, I'd better bring home some new fabric swatches. That floral print is far too feminine for a man like Quinn."

Jessica watched her mother leave, then spun toward Quinn. "You had absolutely no right to do that!"

Quinn took his time answering, biting off a piece of black bacon. "You know, this stuff isn't so bad once you get used to it. I just realized we've been eating out so much that I never asked if you inherited your mother's culinary skills. Not that I mind continuing to eat in restaurants," he assured her with a broad smile. "Home cooking is highly overrated."

A wry glance down at his plate seconded that opinion. "Of course, there's something to be said for being greeted at the door by an adoring wife, clad in a frilly little pink apron," he mused aloud. "Have I ever told you my fantasy about—"

"Why did you do that?" she interrupted sharply.

His expression was blissfully innocent. "Do what?"

"Let my family think we're getting married. What do you suggest we do when they find out it's a lie?"

"What makes you think it's a lie?" He rose abruptly, carrying his plate to the sink where he rinsed it and placed it in the dishwasher. Then he looked back over his shoulder. "Are you going to eat that?"

"You know I don't eat breakfast."

He shook his head. "For an intelligent woman, you sure do have a lot of bad habits. You're stubborn, you steal the blankets on the rare occasion we do manage to spend an entire night together, you're a washout at plane geometry and you've got lousy nutritional habits, as well.... It's amazing that you were able to land yourself such a terrific catch." His grin only served to irritate Jessica further.

"It damn well *is* a lie and you know it!"

Quinn didn't answer immediately. Instead he dumped her untouched food into the disposal and finished clearing the table. Jessica's irritation rose even higher as he filled the dishwasher with detergent and turned it on, wiping the counter off with a wet sponge.

She marched over to him, grabbing his arm to turn him toward her. "Would you have the common courtesy to discuss this rationally? I love my children and I'm not going to let some louse hurt them!"

"That's a rotten thing to call your fiancé, Jessica," he said, shaking his head sadly.

"Knock it off, Quinn," she snapped. "This isn't funny."

To her amazement, his expression was suddenly unnervingly solemn. "I never meant it to be. I've been thinking about us a lot lately, Jess, and I've come to the conclusion that I'm sick and tired of this damn affair you've got us locked into."

"Oh."

Jessica turned around, struggling for composure, damned if she was going to let him see her cry. Well, here it was, the goodbye she'd been waiting for. So why did she suddenly feel as if he'd knocked every bit of breath from her body?

Quinn reached out, shaping her shoulders with his hands, the gesture both soothing and possessive. "It isn't what you think," he murmured, his lips grazing the soft skin of her neck. "This arrangement is ridiculous. I love you. I want to marry you. This afternoon couldn't be fast enough, but I'm willing to wait until you can make whatever arrangements women make at a time like this."

She shook her head. "I'm not marrying you, Quinn. I told you that from the beginning."

"*In* the beginning," he corrected calmly. "Before you knew how perfect I was for you. How perfect we were for each other."

"Why are you doing this?" she asked weakly, moving out of his grasp, turning to face him.

"Why do you think?"

Her mind whirled into gear, latching on to the first possible answer. Although she was inclined to disregard the outrageous idea, she couldn't forget the fact that Quinn could not be taken lightly as an adversary.

"We're not going to drop the suit against Keith for printing that cartoon," she warned. "I'm honestly sorry he was fired from the paper, but you have to admit he deserved it."

A nerve twitched along his tight jaw. "Dammit, Jessica, if you think I give two hoots in hell about that crazy couple, you're mistaken. Besides, there isn't going to be any divorce."

"What do you know that I don't?" she asked archly.

"Nothing, really. But this is the fifth time in the past four years Sylvia has sued Keith for divorce. She didn't go through with it any of the other times."

"But she seems to hate him."

"That's right," he agreed. "And at the moment, the guy isn't too fond of her, either. But what we have here is a couple of fruitcakes who can't live with each other, or without each other, either."

"This could always be the time she sticks to her guns," Jessica argued.

"Could be," he said. "But I don't want to talk about them, Jess. It's time we discussed us. We've been sidestepping this issue for weeks. Give me one good reason why we shouldn't get married."

"I don't love you," she lied through her teeth.

Keep it light, Quinn tried to warn himself, realizing that he'd misjudged Jessica's aversion to marriage. The one thing he hadn't wanted to do was box her into a corner. But he'd used up his store of patience; he didn't want to continue living in this limbo she'd made of their relationship.

Jessica didn't like the way Quinn just stood there, eyeing her thoughtfully.

"What now?" she asked finally, unable to hear the stifling silence any longer.

"Your nose," he murmured.

"I was wondering if it grew when you told these big whoppers." He paused, his gaze intent. "I guess not," he said a second later. "It's just as well. I'm particularly fond of the cute little ski-jump effect at the end." He ran his finger along the slightly upward tilt. "It's downright adorable."

Jessica scowled up at him, refusing to answer that ridiculous statement.

"You know," he went on, "Lizzie's a real nice lady, and I've always respected and admired the judge, but I think your parents spoiled you. They probably should have spanked you from time to time. To keep you more manageable."

Jessica could read the gleam in his eyes as easily as a child's primer. "Don't even suggest it," she warned.

He flung his hand over his chest, looking astonished and a little hurt. "Me? Why, Jessie, I'd never dare suggest such a thing." Then he grinned. "The idea does have a few intriguing aspects, though."

It was the smile more than anything that broke the last fragile thread of her self-restraint. She couldn't bear the thought that Quinn considered this, the most important conversation she'd ever had in her life, nothing but a joke.

"I don't love you," she repeated firmly.

Her softly spoken words tore at Quinn and he tried to think of something, anything, to say that would change the course of events.

"You don't mean that."

It was the hardest thing Jessica had ever done, but the pain she thought she'd overcome returned from the past, reminding her that if she gave in to Quinn on this, she'd find herself right back where she'd started. Quinn was a wonderful man. But he was strong willed, as well. How long would he allow her the freedom to make her own choices? To be her own woman?

His behavior today, springing this news on her family, was proof that if she married him, she'd end up living her life under his rules. He hadn't asked her to marry him—he'd insisted as if it were a foregone conclusion.

She swallowed, having to push the words past the lump in her throat. "I do," she whispered.

Quinn flinched visibly. "Well," he said, "I guess since I don't want an affair and you don't want marriage, we've just reached an impasse."

She turned away, unable to bear the pain she viewed darkening his gentle green eyes. "I suppose so."

A stifling silence settled over them, like a morning fog that had yet to burn off.

"Then this is goodbye?"

She nodded, unable to answer.

Quinn didn't want to accept the fact that this was happening. He didn't want to believe Jessica could throw everything away, just to stick to her ridiculous principles that no longer had any bearing on who they were. Or what they had together.

"You're going to end it, aren't you? After all we've had." His ragged tone displayed his own grief and disbelief at the way things had turned out.

Tears welled up in her eyes, but she didn't dare turn around, knowing that if she looked at him, she'd recant her earlier statement. She wanted him. She wanted to be with him. Why couldn't he just leave things as they were?

His frustration finally reaching the boiling point, Quinn turned on his heel, marching out the door before he gave in to instinct and drove his fist through the sunshine yellow wall. The screen door broke off its hinges as he slammed it behind him, causing Jessica's copper gelatin molds to fall off the wall. She stared out into the slanting rain, watching him drive away. And then she cried.

THE DAYS DRAGGED BY without a word from Quinn. Ten very long days and even longer sleepless nights. Jessica attempted to keep her mind on her work, but she felt like a walking zombie as she made a series of foolish, unthinking mistakes that had her spending an uncomfortable amount of time in George Bennington's office.

She had finally made it through her first year at the firm, but Jessica knew she still was on probation. Despite his friendship with her father, the head of the law firm believed in trial by fire. Jessica decided if George Bennington told her one more time that if she couldn't stand the heat, she had better get out of the kitchen, she would save him the trouble of firing her and quit. She'd had several meetings with the District Attorney, and his offer was looking better every day.

Keith Thacker seemed to have dropped off the face of the earth, and Sylvia called several times each day, distraught that Jessica could not locate her missing husband. Continual telephone calls to Quinn's office to inquire about his errant client proved fruitless. His secretary steadfastly insisted that Quinn was out of town on business and although she dutifully accepted Jessica's messages, Quinn seemed determined to ignore her calls.

Things were no better at home. While she was in the throes of editing her project, Mallory's unusual displays of temper flared out of control at the slightest provocation. Every evening Jessica was forced to watch the latest version, her heart aching as she viewed flashbacks of those happy, seemingly carefree days she'd spent with Quinn.

Sara was unusually quiet, but had brought home a note from her teacher, stating that the straight A student was in danger of failing both English composition and math and might be held back unless her grades showed a marked improvement in the next month.

Jill, whose punk rock style had always left a great deal to be desired, came home from spending the night with a new friend, her hair dyed a brilliant fluorescent green and a trio of holes pierced in each earlobe.

Jessica knew her daughters blamed her for Quinn's disappearance from their lives, a fact she could not deny. She also suspected that their uncharacteristic behavior was a direct result of her break with him, but there was little she could do to change things, even if she wanted to. Like his client, Quinn appeared to have vanished.

The only bright spot in her life came when Elizabeth returned to the house late one afternoon, Mac in tow.

"Jessica," her father's booming voice greeted her, "I'm glad you're home. Your mother and I have some good news!"

"I could use some," Jessica muttered, looking up from the brief she was preparing. Then her glance sharpened. Were her parents actually holding hands? "Mother's moved back home," she guessed.

"Nope. Well, that, too." Her father's blue eyes danced with merriment. "But we've even something more exciting to tell you."

"What's going on?"

"We've just put a down payment on a lovely sailboat, dear," her mother broke in.

"A sailboat?"

"A sailboat," Mac confirmed. "We're sailing around the world together. Just the two of us." He smiled down at Elizabeth, whose own gaze was brimming with affection as she grinned back.

"That's the most ridiculous idea you've come up with yet," Jessica snapped waspishly, feeling unreasonably irritated by the warm and loving looks her parents were exchanging.

She had wanted her parents to work out their problems, really she did. So why did their news make her feel even worse? There was only one answer, and Jessica hated to even consider it. She was jealous! Of her own parents.

"We used to sail every weekend, before we both got too wrapped up in our work to take the time," Elizabeth countered. "We know what we're doing."

"I don't remember sailing," Jessica muttered.

"Of course not, Jessica," her father said with the tone of consummate logic he'd used for years on the bench. "Since we gave it up before you were born, you couldn't possibly recall the fun we used to have."

"Well, I only hope you both know what you're doing," she stated on a resigned sigh.

Her parents exchanged a long look. Then Mac nodded at Elizabeth, who took a deep breath and delicately brought up the subject everyone had been tiptoeing around lately.

"We do," she agreed. "But we have to wonder if you know what you're doing, dear."

"I suppose you're talking about Quinn," she said heavily. Jessica had no desire to discuss the topic of her breakup with anyone. Even her parents. Especially her parents.

"Hell's bells, Jessie," Mac broke in. "Anyone could tell the man was head over heels in love with you. And your mother said you felt the same way about him. So what's the problem?"

"It's too complicated to explain," Jessica said, neatly sidestepping the issue, returning her attention to her work.

"You should have been firmer with Jessica when she was young, Mac," Elizabeth pointed out. "This is all your fault."

"My fault?" Mac blustered. "You were the one in charge of discipline, my dear. Besides, she certainly didn't inherit this stubborn trait from me!"

Elizabeth stiffened. "Well, don't blame me. Everyone knows the MacLaughlins have a stubborn streak a mile wide."

"And the Cunninghams don't?" he asked incredulously. "You haven't exactly been a model of compliancy all these years, yourself, Elizabeth. You're every bit as ornery as your mother!"

Elizabeth bristled. "I thought you liked my mother!"

"I never said I didn't like her," he countered brusquely. "I simply pointed out that Marion Cunningham was every bit as unbending as her daughter." His accusing glare shifted from Elizabeth to Jessica. "And her granddaughter."

"You two are going to be alone together on a boat for months and months?" Jessica questioned dryly. "It'll be interesting to see who throws who overboard first."

"Your mother and I understand each other," Mac stated firmly. "Which is more than I can say for you and Quinn."

"I don't want to talk about him," Jessica insisted.

"Just like a Cunningham," Mac muttered, raking his fingers through his silver hair.

"Just like a MacLaughlin," Elizabeth commented at the same time.

They both looked at each other and laughed.

"Look, honey," Elizabeth began again, trying reason. "It's only going to take a month to get the boat seaworthy—"

"Don't forget repainted," Mac cut in.

Elizabeth's smile was beatific. "She's named the *Sea Hawk*, right now," she explained to Jessica. "Mac's rechristening her the *Elizabeth*."

"That's nice," Jessica admitted.

"Isn't it?" Elizabeth agreed, momentarily sidetracked.

"So you see, Jessie—" Mac picked up the conversational ball "—we're only going to be in town another month, but there's still plenty of time to have that wedding in the Japanese Tea Gardens."

"How did you know about that?"

"I told him," Elizabeth stated. "And I still think it's a lovely idea, Jessica."

"There isn't going to be any wedding," Jessica insisted firmly. "Besides, even if I changed my mind, I haven't heard a word from Quinn in almost two weeks. He's obviously lost interest."

Frustration was etched onto every line of both her parents' faces, but knowing their daughter as well as they did, both shook their heads, giving up for the time being on convincing her of her folly.

THREE WEEKS AFTER HER FIGHT with Quinn, Jessica was doodling idly on a yellow legal pad one morning, her mind wandering as she attempted to come up with one good reason why she should stay in her office. She was unreasonably restless. At one time, her work at Bennington, Marston, White and Lowell had been the most important thing in her life—next to her daughters, of course.

But she was slowly discovering that the world of corporate law was as dry as the legal briefs she slaved over all day. The only truly interesting case she'd had in months had been the Thackers' divorce case. While Sylvia and Keith Thacker's behavior had been admittedly frustrating, at least it offered some drama. Unfortunately, she mused, gazing absently out the window, with Keith apparently out of the city, the marital wars had settled into a period of cease-fire, so she didn't even have the battling Thackers to take her mind off Quinn.

"I hope that look isn't directed at anyone I know."

Jessica glanced up to see Vanessa standing in the doorway. "No. Just the world in general."

"Bad day?"

"Bad year."

"The only thing I know that'll put me in the dumps as low as you seem to be is man trouble."

Jessica merely shrugged, covering the paper with lopsided stars.

Vanessa came into the room, taking a chair opposite Jessica's desk. "Have you seen Quinn Masterson lately?" she asked with studied carelessness.

Jessica switched to squares. "No." At Vanessa's continuing silence, she glanced up. "Why?"

The woman's gaze circled the room as she suddenly appeared unwilling to meet Jessica's eyes. "Just wondering . . . Pamela Stuart just returned from Mexico."

"That's nice," Jessica murmured, her fingers tightening around the slim gold pen.

"She came back with a nice tan."

Jessica dropped the pen, placed her elbows on the desk and rested her chin on her linked fingers. "You didn't come all the way down the hall to tell me Pamela Stuart has a tan," she accused. "So, what's up?"

Vanessa fiddled nervously with her ring. "She got a divorce down there, Jessica."

"Good for her. There seems to be a lot of that going around these days," Jessica responded dryly.

"There's something else."

"I figured there would be," Jessica agreed on a slight sigh. "Here's where you tell me she was out with Quinn, right?"

"I'm afraid so." Vanessa's brown eyes were filled with consolation.

So that's where he'd been. In Mexico, holding Pamela's hand while she'd gotten her divorce. The thought caused pain to fork through Jessica.

"Not that it matters," Jessica asserted on a feigned, casual note, "but they're just old friends."

"They looked pretty friendly last night, all right," Vanessa stated, her meaning readily apparent.

"I don't want to talk about Pamela Stuart, or Quinn," Jessica said firmly.

Vanessa rose from her chair with a fluid, graceful motion. "Okay," she said companionably. "I just felt you should know. I'd hate to see you hurt, Jessica."

As she left the room, Jessica considered that Vanessa's warning had come too late. She was already hurting more than she'd ever deemed possible. If she'd thought she'd gone through hell when her marriage had broken up, Jessica was discovering she'd been sadly mistaken.

As if conjured up by some fiendish genie of her thought process, Paula announced a few minutes later that Quinn Masterson was holding on the line.

Jessica stared mutely at the blinking red button, eyeing it with the uneasiness one might view a diamondback rattlesnake, poised to strike. *This is ridiculous,* she mentally lashed out at herself, punching the button.

"Hello?" Damn. She'd planned on sounding brisk, efficient. Instead a revealing, soft note had crept into her voice.

Quinn, on the other hand, seemed to have no difficulty in maintaining a curt, professional tone.

"Jessica," he stated without preamble. "I need to know if Sylvia Thacker will agree to a meeting."

"Where on earth has Keith been? Sylvia's been driving me crazy."

"He checked into a detox center in Phoenix."

"Oh. How is he?"

"Better. He's a long way from being a recovered alcoholic, but at least he isn't at rock bottom any longer."

Jessica wished she could say the same for herself. "I'll check with Sylvia and get back to you," she agreed, struggling to match his impersonal tone. "Will you be in your office all afternoon?"

"I've got a lunch appointment that may run a little long. But you can leave a message with my secretary."

Jessica couldn't help wondering if his lunch date was with the newly divorced Pamela Stuart. "Fine," she agreed curtly. "Well, have a good day."

"If I thought you meant that," he muttered, "we just might have something to talk about."

With that inscrutable statement he hung up, leaving the dial tone buzzing in her ear. Shaking her head with frustration, Jessica dialed Sylvia Thacker's number.

"So the little worm wants to crawl back, does he?" the woman asked gleefully.

"I don't really know," Jessica answered. "Mr. Masterson called and informed me that your husband was requesting a meeting. He didn't go into details."

"Well, he's going to have a lot of apologizing to do if he thinks he's getting back in this house!"

"Mrs. Thacker," Jessica pleaded, running out of patience, "shall I set a time or not?"

"I suppose that's okay," the woman stated thoughtfully. "But don't make it right away. Let the squirt squirm for a while, that's what I always say."

"I know," Jessica murmured, wondering what kind of marriage Sylvia and Keith Thacker had that they could fight so furiously, say such terrible things about each other, then put everything aside and reconcile again. Remembering what Quinn had alleged about their past record, she had the feeling that was what was about to happen.

"By the way, what gutter did Masterson find him in this time?" Sylvia asked, as if on an afterthought.

"Your husband was in a detoxification center in Phoenix," Jessica answered briskly.

There was a long silence on the other end of the line. "Are you telling me that Keith managed to dry himself out?"

"Quinn, uh, Mr. Masterson, said he's doing better," Jessica replied noncommittally.

Again, there was a thoughtful pause. "I'll be damned," Sylvia murmured. "See if you can make that appointment for tomorrow," she instructed. "This I have to see."

Jessica agreed, then waited until late in the afternoon to return Quinn's call, unreasonably anxious for another opportunity to speak with him. But his irritatingly professional secretary informed her that Mr. Masterson was still out. However, according to his calendar, tomorrow morning at ten would be fine, the woman confirmed, promising to pass the message on to her employer.

"Burning the midnight oil?" Vanessa paused in the office doorway, regarding Jessica curiously. "Come on, kiddo. It's time to go home."

"I've got some work to finish up," Jessica stated, unwilling to admit she was hoping Quinn might call to confirm the meeting. She hadn't realized until that unsatisfactory conversation this morning how desperately she'd been needing to hear his voice.

"I thought your mother moved back home."

Jessica made a notation in the margin of a study of Marin County demographics she'd been compiling for George Bennington. "She did," she answered absently.

"So who's with the kids?"

"They don't have school tomorrow—a teachers' meeting or something—so they've gone up to Mill Valley to spend the weekend with their father. Mallory finished her movie about the family and wanted to show it to Brian."

"How did it turn out?"

"Terrific," Jessica admitted, hoping that she wasn't revealing how painful it had been to watch the final version of Mallory's ninety-minute videotape last evening. Quinn had been all too evident, and it had been incredibly distressful, watching her life played out before her eyes, a horrible flashback of her latest failure. "She's really very talented."

"You're on your own tonight?"

"I guess so," Jessica agreed glumly.

"Want to go get a drink? The Cosmic Kitten has a dynamite happy hour."

Jessica grimaced. "I've never liked singles' bars. Besides, I've heard that place is a meat market."

"Of course it is," Vanessa concurred. "But at least the meat is prime. And heterosexual, which in this town is a decided plus."

"I think I'll pass."

"You can't sit around here moping over the great Quinn Masterson forever," she advised.

"I'm not moping, I'm working."

Vanessa came into the office, perching on the corner of Jessica's desk, crossing long legs clad in a patterned navy blue hose that exactly matched her silk suit. Jessica wondered idly if other women were born with the ability for coordinating their wardrobes—possessing an extra gene, or chromosome, or something. Whatever, she decided on an audible sigh, she'd obviously been out to lunch when that particular talent was handed out.

"Jessica," Vanessa said firmly, "surviving a broken love affair is like riding a horse. Sure you fall off, but you have to get right back on again."

"I've always been allergic to horses."

"You know what I'm talking about," Vanessa snapped. "The way you've been acting, it's like you're allergic to men. Believe me, honey, it'll do you a world of good to go out and have a little fun. It wouldn't hurt your reputation any, either."

"What does that mean?" Jessica demanded.

Vanessa's perfect white teeth worried her lower lip as she appeared to be making a decision. "Look," she said, "I want you to know I never believed a single word, but people have been talking about you."

"About me?" Jessica couldn't imagine people so bored with their own lives that they'd find her an interesting topic of conversation.

"Well, until that little fling with the Casanova of San Francisco's legal world, you didn't date. Not that anyone could tell."

"I'm amazed that *anyone* bothered to notice," Jessica snapped.

"You have to admit it *is* unusual. After all, you're an attractive woman who happens to be at an age when your sexuality should be at its peak. And you're a divorcée to boot."

Jessica didn't miss the implication. She shook her head with very real irritation. "And therefore I should be hot to trot, right?"

The other woman appeared unperturbed by Jessica's prickly tone. "Well, to be perfectly honest, it's common knowledge that you've turned down dates with just about every single male in the office. And a few of the married ones, as well." Her voice dropped conspiratorially. "Some of the men don't think that's quite natural, if you get my drift."

Jessica got it all right. Loud and clear. Her blue eyes hardened. "My life is my own business, Vanessa. And I intend to keep it that way."

The woman shrugged elegantly, sliding off the desk. "Well," she murmured, "don't say I didn't try to warn you." She turned in the doorway. "Are you sure you won't change your mind about that drink?"

"I'm sure."

"Don't work too hard," she advised, her fingers fluttering goodbye as she turned and left the office.

As Jessica watched Vanessa leave, she couldn't help recalling Quinn's accusation that Jessica O'Neill was rumored to be an iron lady with ice water for blood and a stone heart. A lot they all knew. Jessica considered how lucky she'd be if that was only true. After all, stone hearts were probably incapable of breaking.

Much later, Jessica stood at her office window. Even through the thick glass she could hear the lonely whine of a siren and glanced down toward the street, where the car lights glowed like stars that had fallen to the ground.

"Excuse me?"

She turned to look at the woman who stood hesitantly in the doorway, a vacuum in one hand and a tray filled with cans of spray polish, dust rags and Windex in the other.

"Is it all right if I clean in here now?"

Jessica took one last look at the telephone, willing it to ring. Then, admitting that Quinn had no intention of calling, she gave the waiting woman an apologetic smile.

"I'm on my way out," she said, taking her purse from a bottom drawer. "I'm sorry I held you up."

"No bother. Have a nice night," the woman called after her.

"You too," she answered automatically.

As Jessica sat gazing out the window on the bus home, she decided that everyone in San Francisco was out taking Vanessa's advice. The sidewalks were crowded with throngs of happy couples, holding hands, laughing, seemingly having a wonderful time. When the bus halted at a stoplight, a couple in a convertible beside her exchanged a brief, but unmistakedly heated kiss. San Francisco might be the city for lovers, but this evening Jessica found all that romance most depressing.

When she finally arrived home, Jessica decided that she deserved a little pampering. She filled the tub to the rim with hot water, dumping in an outrageously expensive amount of bath oil. Then she dug out a novel she'd been intending to read for months and poured a glass of wine. Reconsidering, she retrieved the bottle from the refrigerator, taking it into the bathroom with her.

Although Jessica's mind wandered, as it did continually these days to Quinn, she forced her attention back to the story, letting some of the cool water out of the tub, refilling it as needed. She'd managed to make it to the third chapter when the lights flickered once. Then twice. Then went out altogether.

"Damn," she muttered, rising from the tub and grabbing for a towel in the dark. Wrapping it about herself she went into the kitchen, taking a candle from the cache she kept for just this reason.

"I'll be glad when that electrician is finished," she said under her breath, digging around in the drawer where she stored the spare fuses.

Jessica made her way by the flickering, dim candlelight to the fuse box located on the back porch. She replaced one, but nothing happened. Muttering a series of low oaths that would have drawn an arched eyebrow even from the often colorful Judge MacLaughlin, she returned to the kitchen, taking her last replacement fuse from the drawer.

"This better do the trick," Jessica grumbled. "Because I'm in no mood to spend the night reading by candlelight."

She held her breath, and was rewarded as the house once again glowed with light. "Bingo," she stated, pleased that something, at least, had worked out well for her today. Even though Jessica didn't believe in omens, a little corner of her mind latched on to this good fortune as a hopeful sign.

That slim vestige of hope began to dissolve as she awoke the next morning twenty minutes late, having forgetten to reset her clock radio after the power had gone out. Her hair dryer blew yet another fuse before she'd finished, and as she viewed her wild tangle of wet auburn hair in the mirror, Jessica considered how on the one day she wanted to look her best, she was going to show up for her meeting with Quinn looking like a drowned rat.

Her day continued its downhill slide on the way to the office. The bus driver slammed on his brakes, narrowly avoiding hitting a child who'd run into the street, chasing a baseball thrown to him by a companion. The violent motion sent coffee splashing out of the paper cup held by the passenger next to Jessica, and she watched fatalistically as the dark liquid spread all over the skirt of her blue shirtwaist dress.

"I'm sorry," the distraught commuter moaned, dabbing ineffectually at her skirt with his handkerchief.

"Don't worry about it," Jessica said on a slight sigh. "You couldn't help it."

"But your dress. Look, send me the bill and I'll pay for the cleaning, all right?"

"Really—"

"It's the least I can do," he insisted.

Jessica took the business card he offered, slipping it into her purse. She had no intention of contacting the man again. It wasn't his fault. She was rapidly coming to the conclusion that some fiendishly evil being had taken control of the universe, manipulating events so that anything that might possibly go wrong would. This individual was simply a pawn in the game being played with her life.

The Thackers were waiting for her, as was Quinn, and all heads turned expectantly to the door as she entered. Jessica's heart sank as Quinn's eyes narrowed, taking in her disheveled appearance, but she straightened her shoulders determinedly and entered the room with a false, professional smile.

"I'm sorry I'm late," she stated, taking a seat beside Sylvia Thacker at the conference table. "My alarm clock went off late. You see, I blew two fuses last night, and another this morning, and . . . Well, you don't care about that." She managed another brilliant smile. "Shall we get started? Who wants to go first?"

I'm babbling, Jessica groaned inwardly. *They're all going to think I'm an absolute idiot.* She risked a glance at Quinn, her heart sinking further as she viewed his incredulous gaze.

But Quinn was not listening to Jessica's breathless statement; indeed, her words were a distant hum, hardly audible over the blood roaring in his ears. She'd changed amazingly in the past few weeks. Her face was thinner, paler. A sprinkling of freckles that hadn't been visible before stood out on her cheekbones. Her eyes were bright with nervousness, but it would be impossible to miss the deep purple shadows underneath them. And while he was no authority on women's bodies, he knew Jessica's intimately. How many pounds had she lost? Five? Ten? She looked, in all honesty, as bad as he felt. But she still looked wonderful.

Jessica had been hoping that they could get right down to business, but it appeared the Thackers had their own ideas. Each proceeded to voice a litany of complaints against the other, point and counterpoint, back to the early days of their marriage.

Jessica risked a glance at Quinn, who was viewing the drama with resignation. When he caught her eye, he surprised her by winking. Realizing this was standard operating procedure for the couple, Jessica allowed her mind to wander as Sylvia began berating Keith for showing up a half hour late to their wedding.

Quinn looked tired, Jessica considered, surreptitiously eyeing his drawn expression. He was sporting a dark tan, obviously a souvenir from his trip to Mexico with Pamela Stuart, but his skin seemed more tightly drawn over his bones. His green eyes were devoid of that sparkling gleam she had often thought of during their time apart, and lines bracketed his lips. Those wonderful, seductive lips . . .

A sudden knock on the door captured Jessica's attention and a moment later her secretary entered, the heretofore unflappable Paula obviously distressed.

"There's a telephone call for you, Ms O'Neill."

"Please take a message, Paula," Jessica requested.

"It's an emergency," Paula stated. Her voice cracked, causing Jessica's blood to freeze in her veins. "Oh God, Jessica, I'm sorry."

The girls, Jessica thought dazedly as she made her way over to the phone in the corner of the room. Her heart was pounding in her throat and she screamed a silent prayer that they were all right. The image of that little boy this morning swam before her eyes. What if that had been Sara? Oh, dear God, she begged. Please don't let it be that!

Quinn was on his feet, staring helplessly at Jessica as he watched her face go ashen, her eyes close. "I understand," she managed to respond, her voice not much above a whisper. "I'll be right there."

But she remained frozen, her eyes staring at some unseen location out the window. Quinn was by her side in two long strides, taking the telephone receiver from her icy hands.

"Jess?" he asked, his hands cupping her shoulders as he shook her gently, dragging her attention toward him. "What is it? Not the girls?"

She could have wept at the wealth of concern in his eyes, and managed to shake her head. "No," she said on a deep, ragged breath. "Not the girls."

"Thank God!" He exhaled a deep, relieved breath of his own. "Then what?"

Her hands clasped his upper arm, her fingernails digging into the flesh covered by his gray suit. "Oh, Quinn," she said on a weak, broken sob, "it's my home. There was a fire." Tears welled up in her eyes. "Everything's gone, Quinn. Everything."

Knowing how much the house had meant to Jessica, understanding how it had symbolized her hard-won independence, Quinn drew her into his arms, holding her tight, his hands stroking her hair, her back.

"Listen to me," he said gently, putting her a little away. "It's going to be okay. Do you hear me?"

She stared at him uncomprehendingly.

"Listen to me, Jess," he repeated, his voice firmer, his tone more self-assured. "We're going to go there. Together. And I promise everything is going to turn out fine. You've got to believe me, honey."

She leaned into him, resting her forehead against his chest, taking deep breaths as she drew from his strength. When she lifted her head, her eyes glistened with tears.

"I'm so glad you're here, Quinn," she whispered.

He gave her a long, hard kiss on the lips. "Me too, babe," he murmured huskily. "Me too."

Then he led her to the door, turning back toward an avidly interested pair of onlookers.

"You two work something out," he ordered. "We've got more important things to do than watch you idiots fight."

Ignoring their shocked expressions, he left the conference room. "Ms O'Neill won't be in for a few days," he instructed Paula firmly, preparing for an argument from Jessica. Quinn was disturbed when she failed to offer the slightest protest and realized she was obviously in a state of shock. "Would you reschedule her appointments?"

"Of course," Paula answered immediately, reaching for her appointment calendar.

"Oh," Quinn added on an afterthought, "would you please call my office and tell them I won't be back today?"

"I already did."

Quinn managed to reward Paula with a weak smile, wondering why it was that everyone else saw what Jessica appeared blind to. That however loudly she wanted to protest the fact, they belonged together. Permanently.

And he was going to make her see that if it was the last thing he did.

THE SIDEWALK WAS CROWDED with onlookers as Quinn pulled up in front of the smoldering ruins of what had once been Jessica's beloved home.

The outer walls of the Victorian house were still standing, but the windowpanes had been blown out by the intense heat. Through the gaping holes, Quinn could view the charred interior.

"What do they all want?" she asked weakly. "Why are they here?"

"I suppose it's curiosity. And a certain sense of relief that it didn't happen to them."

"Oh, Quinn," she half sobbed, "I think I just discovered that I'm a terrible person."

He took both her hands in his, his heart torn at her despairing expression. "Nonsense," he objected firmly. "What on earth gave you that idea?"

Her eyes were bleak as they turned to the crowd of gaping bystanders. "I wish it had been one of them," she whispered harshly. "I wish it had been anyone but me." She shook her head and covered her face with her hands.

Quinn drew her into his arms, stroking her back. "That's only natural, sweetheart," he assured her. "There isn't anything wrong with you." He gazed down into her stricken face. "Let me take you to my place," he suggested. "There isn't anything you can do here."

Jessica shook her head. "No. I want to see everything, Quinn."

"Are you sure? Look, honey, we can call your insurance company from my apartment. It's going to take them a while to start the claims process, anyway. You should be resting."

A thought suddenly occurred to Quinn. "We need to do something about the girls. They shouldn't be coming home to this."

At the idea of her daughters, safe with Brian in Marin County, Jessica experienced a cool wave of relief. It was only a house, she reminded herself. Boards and shingles. It could be replaced. Her children couldn't.

"They're all right," she managed through tight lips. "They didn't have school today. Mallory wanted to show Brian her movie, so they're spending the weekend with him."

"Then her tapes didn't burn?"

At the honest relief in his voice, Jessica was once again reminded of what a very nice man Quinn could be. "No, thank God. She's too young to realize that this isn't the end of the world."

"How about you? Can you realize that?"

Jessica took a deep breath. "I've been through worse," she admitted. "I can probably survive this, as well."

"I've no doubt of that," he agreed, wiping away the moisture on her cheeks with his handkerchief. "But are you sure you want to go in there right now?"

"I have to. I have to see if there's anything left."

Quinn looked over her shoulder, doubting that anything had survived the inferno that had gutted Jessica's home. *God,* he thought, his stomach clenching, *if this had happened last night, with Jessica asleep upstairs . . .* The idea was too unpalatable to consider further.

"Let's get it over with," he suggested grimly, opening the car door.

Jessica held tight to his hand as they walked toward the still smoldering house. As they approached, the crowd parted like the waters of the Red Sea, allowing them to pass. Jessica was numbly aware of Quinn speaking to the firemen who were cleaning up the destruction, but she didn't know what they were saying. Neither did she care.

The front door, with its lovely stained glass window, had been hacked to splinters by the firefighters' axes, Jessica noted dully. She stood in the open doorway, her eyes bleak as she viewed the devastation. It was all gone—Jill's wild clothes, Sara's scrapbook, her paintings. Everything. She moaned.

The soft sound drew Quinn's attention. "Are you sure you're all right?"

"I don't know," Jessica said, swaying slightly as her head began to swim.

Black dots appeared before her eyes and she prayed that she wouldn't disgrace herself by fainting in public. She'd never fainted before in her life. But neither had she had the misfortune to witness her life gone up in flames.

"I'm taking you home," Quinn stated brusquely, his firm tone assuring Jessica that he wasn't listening to any further objections.

"I don't have a home."

Her face was an unhealthy shade of gray, and her eyes appeared wider than usual. The shadows beneath them, which had been so evident only an hour ago were even darker and deeper.

"My home."

"Oh."

Jessica remembered little else after that. She was vaguely aware of Quinn leading her to his car, where she was able to lean her head against the back of the seat, closing her eyes against the swirling vertigo that threatened to overcome her. She offered no objection as he took her directly to his bedroom, sitting her down on the edge of the bed before proceeding to undress her.

He knelt on the lush burnt umber carpeting, slipping her pumps from her feet. His fingers made quick work of the buttons on the front of the blue silk dress, and she shrugged her shoulders, allowing him to push the material down to her waist. He laid her gently on the mattress, pulling the dress down over her hips. Her nylons followed, then her half-slip, until she was clad only in her lacy bra and panties.

When Quinn slid her under the chocolate-brown sheets, Jessica closed her eyes as her head sank into the pillow. She couldn't remember being so tired, so wrung out. Then she felt him moving away and her eyes flew open.

"Where are you going?"

"Just into the other room. I'm calling a doctor."

She shook her head. "I don't need a doctor."

"You're in shock," he said. "When it settles in, you're going to be upset. I want to get you something."

"I don't take tranquilizers," she argued weakly, finding speech a major effort. "They're habit-forming."

"One damn pill isn't going to turn you into an addict, Jess," Quinn shot back. "Dammit, for once in your life would you stop being so stubborn and let someone help you?" His concern for her made his voice gravelly, his words harsh.

"I don't need any pills," she repeated. "I need you, Quinn."

Quinn was aware that Jessica was not herself. She never would have admitted that under normal conditions. And certainly not on such a soft, pleading tone. Shaking his head, he sat down beside her, pushing her hair back from her face with unsteady fingers.

"I worry about you, babe."

Her hand reached out for him, then fell to the sheet, as if the movement required more strength than she possessed.

"I know," she whispered. "Please don't leave me, Quinn." Her blue eyes were eloquent pools of need, pulling him into their swirling depths.

Quinn suddenly felt as if he were drowning. "At least let me call the insurance company for you," he suggested, wanting to spare Jessica that initial piece of bureaucratic red tape.

"All right. I got a renewal notice yesterday," she said flatly. "It's still in my purse. I think the number's on that."

"I'll call them and be right back."

"Quinn?"

He turned in the doorway. "What is it, sweetheart?"

"Please don't be gone long."

He returned to the side of the bed, bending down to brush a light, reassuring kiss against her lips. "Don't worry," he vowed. "I won't leave you alone."

She nodded, closing her eyes, crying silently as she viewed the horrid images emblazoned on her mind. It was only a short time later that Jessica felt Quinn lie down beside her. She didn't have the strength to open her eyes, but her fingers inched across the sheet, unerringly locating his hand.

"You came back."

He linked their fingers together, bringing her hand to his lips. "Of course."

"I'm glad," she murmured drowsily. She was so tired! How could she want so badly to sleep in the middle of the day? "I don't know what I would have done if you hadn't been with me today, Quinn."

"I'll always be there for you, Jess. That's a promise."

"Ummm." Her breathing was deeper, and a soft pink color was returning gradually to her complexion.

Quinn drew her into his arms, fitting her comfortably, safely against him. Then his gaze grew thoughtful as he watched her sleep.

WHEN JESSICA AWOKE several hours later, the sun was just setting, filling the room with an orange glow. Momentarily disoriented, she glanced around her. Then her gaze lifted to collide with Quinn's.

"Oh, my God," she groaned, seeing the concern etched onto his harshly set features. "It wasn't a nightmare, was it?"

"No. I'm so very sorry, Jess."

"The girls," she remembered suddenly, struggling to sit up. "I have to talk to them."

"I already did. They're fine. Worried about you, of course, but I assured them that their mother is a trooper. The insurance investigator also called. It was the wiring," he stated, confirming what Jessica had already guessed.

She put her arms around him, pressing her cheek against his shirt. "I feel so empty, Quinn. I keep thinking that I should be crying my eyes out. Or screaming at the top of my lungs about the injustice of it all. But I can't feel anything."

"That's understandable. You're bound to be a little numb right now," he assured her, his long fingers combing through the strands of her tousled hair. The auburn waves smelled of smoke.

"Want a shower?" he suggested. "You'd probably feel a little better."

Jessica nodded slowly. "That might help," she agreed.

"I'll fix you something to eat."

"I don't think I could keep anything down," she protested softly.

He lowered his head, kissing her lightly on the forehead. "Just some soup and maybe a sandwich. I've got some chicken. How does that sound?"

She lifted her shoulders in a weary shrug. "You don't have to go to any trouble for me, Quinn."

"I like to do things for you," he argued. "You never let me do enough as it is. At least let me feed you." His judicious gaze skimmed her body, which appeared unusually slender under the crisp dark sheet. "Besides, you've lost weight. Obviously you need someone to take care of you."

She sighed, unable to work up the strength to argue further. "All right."

Quinn smiled down at her. Then he went into the adjoining bathroom and soon Jessica could hear the sound of running water.

"Can you make it into the bathroom yourself?" he asked with concern as he returned. "Do you need help washing your hair?"

"I'll be fine." Her voice was unsteady, but her eyes offered Quinn assurance.

"I never had a single doubt about that," he agreed. "I left my robe in the bathroom for you. It'll be too big, but your clothes smell of smoke, and you've got that stain on your dress."

Was it only this morning that her worst problem had been spilled coffee? It seemed like a lifetime ago.

"Thank you, Quinn. You're very nice."

As he left the room to fix Jessica something to eat, Quinn considered that "nice" was not how he wanted her to see him. Teddy bears were nice; television weathermen were nice; Quinn wanted to be Jessica's overwhelming passion. He wanted her to be as obsessed with him as he was with her.

He'd gone crazy while he'd been in Phoenix with Keith. It had taken every ounce of his willpower not to pick up the phone and call Jessica, agreeing to whatever she was willing to offer. The knife blade flashed dangerously as he hacked away at the cold roast chicken with angry strokes.

Quinn's irritation disintegrated when Jessica appeared in the kitchen doorway a while later, offering him a slightly wobbly smile.

"That was a good idea. I feel better."

"You look marvelous," he said, gazing at the lovely woman wrapped in the voluminous folds of his navy robe.

Her hair fell wetly over her shoulders, and her skin, what little of it was visible, shone pinkly, as if she'd attempted to scrub away not only the smoke, but the memory of the fire, as well. She looked soft and vulnerable, and although he knew this was a hell of a time to be having such thoughts, deliciously desirable.

"Hungry?" he asked with studied casualness, turning away so Jessica couldn't view his body's reaction to her pleasantly disheveled state.

"Yes."

Her tone was soft, inviting sensual fantasies, and Quinn wondered what kind of man he was to be experiencing sexual hunger at a time like this. Jessica needed someone to take care of her right now. To comfort her.

"Good. I've made sandwiches and the soup's warming. I hope you like cream of asparagus. It's canned. But it's good."

Jessica stared at his back, wondering what to do next. She'd seen the way his eyes had darkened with unmasked desire when he'd looked at her. She knew that whatever had happened to their affair, the attraction between them was as strong and viable as ever.

"I am hungry, Quinn," she agreed, moving quietly across the room on bare feet and putting her arms around his waist. "But not for food." She pressed her cheek against his back, fitting her body intimately against his.

"Jess," Quinn warned raggedly, "do you have any idea what you're doing?"

"Yes," she answered simply.

He spun around propelling her soft curves against him with harsh, unforgiving strength. "Damn you, Jessie," he groaned, his fingers tangling painfully in the wet strands of her hair. "Damn you for making me need you like this!"

Then his mouth came down hard and demanding on hers, his tongue thrusting deeply with a greedy passion that threatened to devour her. His strong fingers splayed against the back of her head as he held her to the blazing kiss.

Her soft cry against his lips only served to fuel Quinn's spiraling passion. He scooped her up, his lips fused to hers as he carried her back into the bedroom. The soft velour robe was no obstacle as his hands moved over her breasts, his fingers kneading the flesh, creating a pleasure that was just this side of pain. In turn, Jessica's fingers tore at the buttons of his shirt, her palms pressing against the warm, moist skin of his chest.

When she dragged her mouth away from his to trail a series of stinging kisses from the base of his throat to his navel, Quinn thought he'd explode. A groan rumbled in his throat as he felt her soft breath against the wool of his pants and then he was tearing them off, Jessica helping him, her own need every bit as desperate.

Tenderness gave way to hunger, both of them giving and taking pleasure as they drove each other mad with passion. Quinn's hot moist breath burned her skin, creating an ache deep inside her as he relentlessly drove her closer and closer to the very brink of sanity. His lips and hands were everywhere, tasting, touching, creating havoc with her senses.

In turn, Jessica explored the hard lines of his body, thrilled by the way he trembled under her touch. Then his fingers dug into her waist and she gasped as he lowered her onto him, filling her with his rigid strength.

"Oh, Quinn," she cried out, leaning forward, the pebbled tips of her breasts brushing his chest. "I think I'm burning up!"

"That's right," he growled, his fingers clutching her hips, thrusting more deeply into her. "Flame for me, Jess. Let me feel your fire!"

Her body was a torch, alive with a heated passion that threatened to consume her. Jessica could only wonder what it was about Quinn that made her go so wildly, primitively out of control.

His tongue explored the moistness of her mouth, thrusting into all the warm dark corners as his movements became faster, deeper. Jessica's entire body was trembling with ecstasy. Finally, she could contain herself no longer and cried out, calling his name from the very depths of her soul.

Her unrestrained response had a shattering effect on Quinn. His mouth clamped over hers with a harsh moan and his body stiffened as he arched against her. His last coherent thought was that despite her continual assertions to the contrary, Jessica O'Neill was his woman. His and his alone.

Jessica's cheek rested on Quinn's warm chest, her hair spread in damp auburn tangles across his body. Her legs were still wrapped around his and the feel of his strong, hair-roughened thighs against hers was intensely satisfying. His heart had slowed to a more reasonable rhythm, and as her lips pressed against his moist skin, Jessica felt his quick intake of breath.

"You are a wanton," he said, his voice rumbling from deep within his body. "I think you've killed me."

Jessica's cheeks grew pink as she considered her wild, primitive response to Quinn's lovemaking. And she understood why he'd chosen to display such passion, rather than a solicitous tenderness.

He had known exactly what was necessary to take her mind from the fire and her troubles. He'd known precisely what to do. As it seemed he always did. She breathed a sad, rippling little sigh.

"Don't," he requested softly, his fingers playing with her hair. "Don't have any regrets."

She lifted her head, her blue eyes solemn. "I don't," she murmured truthfully. "At least not about what we just did. I love making love to you, Quinn."

She gave him a faint smile. "In fact, I can't think of anything else I'd rather be doing." Her fingers toyed nervously with the dark hair covering his chest. "I think I've become a Quinn Masterson junkie."

"Is that so bad?" he inquired with what he considered amazing calmness. He certainly didn't feel that way inside.

Jessica sighed, rolling over onto her back to stare thoughtfully at the ceiling. Not knowing what he could say to forestall her probable answer, Quinn remained silent.

"When I was younger," she said finally, her gaze still directed upward, "my entire life revolved around my family. I was Elizabeth and Mac's daughter, then I was Brian's wife. We weren't married a year before I was Jill's mother, then Mallory's, then Sara's. I only viewed myself in relation to others."

When Quinn failed to comment, Jessica turned her head on the pillow. "I know you can't possibly understand that. But after Brian left me, I realized I had absolutely no idea who Jessica O'Neill was. Who she really was."

"I think I can empathize with that," he argued.

She shook her head. "No, Quinn, you can't," she insisted quietly. "You can sympathize, but you can't empathize." Her somber blue eyes held a certain fondness. "I've the impression you sprang from the womb knowing who you were, what you wanted to do, where you were going in life."

He sat up now, the muscles in his jaw firming as he looked down at her. "You're wrong there," he pointed out brusquely. "Do you know how many times I still feel like I'm playing a role? That I'm still just some dirt poor Missouri farm kid?"

His green eyes turned hard. "Hell, yes, I can empathize with you, but I don't want to play word games, Jess! Sympathize, empathize, what difference does it make? I love you, damn it! That's all that matters."

"If it were only that simple," she said softly, gazing bleakly up at the ceiling once more.

"Do you love me?" he asked suddenly.

"Why do you insist on asking that?" she whispered. "It wouldn't really matter."

Quinn hit the sheet with his fist. "It would to me. I need to know, Jessica. Do you love me or not?"

When she slowly, regretfully turned her glistening eyes back to his, Jessica's face was a portrait of despair. She wept silently, unaware of the tears streaming down her cheeks.

"Oh, Quinn," she said on a sigh that was part moan, turning her head toward the wall, unable to view the need swirling in his stormy green eyes.

What did the man want, Jessica asked herself desperately. She'd given him her body; she'd shared her most intimate feelings, told him of doubts and fears that she'd never revealed to another living soul. She'd even let him into her daughters' lives, something she had always sworn never to do with any man she might date.

But still he wanted more. In that respect, she considered ruefully, Quinn was no different from any other man. He wanted too much. Because he wanted everything. He wanted more than she could possibly ever give.

His fingers cupped her downcast chin and turned her head back toward him. When she would have turned away again, he wouldn't permit it.

"I asked you a question, Jess," he reminded her softly. "And I'm still waiting for an answer."

"Why are you doing this?" she shouted, swiping at her tears. "Haven't I had enough grief today without you making things worse?" The last was flung at him on a wail, and Quinn closed his eyes, unable to view the misery etching ugly lines on her face.

Jessica had to press her hands together to keep from reaching up to stroke the rigid line of his jaw. If this was what love did, she thought miserably, if it could destroy two people like this, then she wished she'd never experienced its treachery.

But then, she considered honestly, she'd have never known the heights of passion and the sheer joy found in being with the man she loved. Why couldn't it have stayed that way, she agonized. Why did he have to ruin everything?

She watched Quinn's chest rise and fall as he sighed soundlessly. Then he opened his eyes and she was shocked at the raw pain she saw there.

"Oh, Jess," he groaned. "I never wanted to hurt you like this. I never wanted to hurt *us* like this."

Quinn knew Jessica was aching as badly as he was at the moment and wanted nothing more than to pull her into his arms, to bury his head between her soft breasts and drink in her sweet scent. He wanted her soothing hands to stroke his flesh, to quiet this pain.

He wanted to make love to her forever; he wanted to immerse himself in her flesh, in her love. He wanted to beg her to stay, to assure her that whatever their problems, they could work them out. But Quinn knew that although Jessica was willing to turn to him in moments of desperation and need, she wasn't ready to make a lasting commitment.

She wanted to be strong, he thought angrily. The ironic thing was that he'd never met a woman capable of turning him inside out like this. He wondered what it would take to make Jessica realize that she was far more self-sufficient than she secretly believed. Enough so that marrying him wouldn't cost her her hard-earned independence.

"The soup will have evaporated down to nothing," he said flatly, his feet hitting the floor as he turned away from her.

Jessica longed to run her hands across the hard lines of his shoulders, but resisted, knowing that it would be unfair to give Quinn contradictory messages.

"I'm not that hungry," she protested softly. "If you'll just call a cab, I'll go to a hotel."

Quinn ground his teeth, suddenly understanding those crimes of passion that were always cropping up on the six o'clock news. He rose from the bed and glared down at her.

"Don't be an idiot, you don't even have any clothes. You're staying here tonight. Tomorrow we'll have Elizabeth bring over some clothes, then we'll—excuse me—*you*," he corrected harshly, "can decide what you're going to do."

"That makes sense," she murmured in a subdued voice. "Thank you, Quinn. This is very kind of you."

He slammed his fist into his palm. One of these days, Quinn decided, after he and Jessica were married, he was going to have a long talk with Mac and find out how the man managed to live all those years with Jessica's mother. Because from what he'd been able to tell, Jessica didn't fall far from the genetic tree when it came to an extra helping of pigheaded stubbornness.

"I'm not doing this out of kindness," he roared, losing patience entirely. "And if I were you, Jess, I'd shut up before you find out exactly how low I am on that particular commodity right now.

"In fact, I'm about ready to double bolt that door and keep you in that bed while I make love to you until you can't move. That might be as effective a method of keeping you here where you belong as any others I might try!"

Jessica was not immune to the anger blazing in his eyes, but neither could she remain unaffected by the sudden flare of desire she viewed there, either. She chewed nervously at her bottom lip, inciting a muffled groan from Quinn. His fingers, as they thrust through his hair, were far from steady.

There was so much he wanted to say. So many things he needed to tell her. Beginning with how much he loved her. And ending with the fact that he always would.

"I'd better check on your dinner," he said instead. Then he left the room.

12

IF JESSICA HAD TO PICK one word to describe the mood the next morning, it would have been "cautious." Both she and Quinn seemed to be walking on eggs, neither anxious to renew the argument that had threatened to blaze out of control last night.

She'd called Elizabeth, who agreed to bring her something to wear; fortunately, her mother had kept her youthful figure and both women wore the same size. Then Jessica had called her daughters, relieved to find that they were amazingly unconcerned about the fire. Staying in Marin County for a few more days gave them a holiday from school, and a chance to swim in their father's new pool.

"I have to admit that surprises me," Jessica said, as she shared a Spartan breakfast of cold cereal and coffee with Quinn. She hadn't wanted to eat even that, but Quinn had insisted, and she didn't have the strength to argue this morning. "I expected them to be in tears."

"Kids are pretty resilient," he replied, slicing a banana atop the cornflakes.

"Fortunately," she agreed.

"How are you feeling?"

She shrugged. "Like I've been run over by a Mack truck," she admitted.

His gaze fell to her arm, which bore a lingering bruise from last night's lovemaking.

"I'm sorry."

Her eyes held a spark of humor, the first he'd seen since the day he'd stormed out of her house. "I'm not. I wasn't referring to that, Quinn."

"Oh."

They both fell quiet again and an uncomfortable silence settled over the room.

"Want a section of the morning paper?" Quinn asked politely.

Following his cue, Jessica nodded. "Thank you."

"Which part? Fashion? You can check out the sales."

"Business, I think," she decided. "The idea of all that clothes shopping is too depressing.... Unless you want the business section," she tacked on with consummate politeness.

"No, it's yours," he offered, handing her the pages, hating this conversation that could have been taking place between two strangers.

"Thank you," she repeated.

"You're welcome."

Jessica hoped Elizabeth would hurry. She couldn't take much more of Quinn's studiously proper manners. She eyed her coffee cup, wondering what he'd do if she suddenly dumped the cooling contents into his lap.

Quinn caught Jessica's thoughtful study of her cup. "Would you like some more coffee?"

"No, thank you."

"Would you like it warmed up?"

She smiled a stiff little smile. "Thanks, but it's fine."

"You're sure?"

"Positive."

"All right. If you want anything, just ask."

"Do you mean that?" she said suddenly.

Quinn's spoon stopped on the way to his mouth and he slowly lowered it back to the bowl. "Of course. What can I get for you? Some toast? An omelet?"

Jessica shook her head firmly. "I don't want anything else to eat."

He arched an inquiring brow. "Then what?"

"Could you stop treating me like I'm visiting royalty? I'm starting to get very nervous, Quinn."

His level gaze met hers. "I was only trying to keep things on an even keel."

"Do you think that's honestly possible?" Jessica asked shakily.

There was a lengthy silence from across the table. "Between us?" he finally inquired.

Jessica knew it to be a rhetorical question and didn't bother to answer. As she watched warily, his eyes seemed to harden and something flickered in their depths. She flinched as he reached across the table, his fingers braceleting her wrist.

"Between us?" he repeated, turning her hand over, tracing thoughtful little circles on her palm with his index finger.

There was nothing overtly sexual in the gesture, but Jessica felt a heat building deep within her feminine core, sending little eddies of flaming current spiraling outward to warm her entire body.

Quinn's emerald eyes gleamed with beguiling satisfaction as he felt the pulse rate under his fingers increase. Jessica unconsciously licked her lips, and as he watched, her expression softened and a soft pink hue darkened her cheeks. When she dragged her gaze away from his stroking finger to meet his, her eyes were melted sapphires, dark, lustrous, shining with shared desire.

"No, Jess," he assured her in a rough voice. "Nothing between us could ever remain on an even keel. When we fight, I suppose we'll fight tooth and nail," he grated. "But when we love, Jessie—ah, there's nothing that equals the storm we make. You can't deny that, sweetheart."

Jessica tugged, retrieving her hand, lowering it to her lap where Quinn couldn't view her fingers twisting nervously together.

"No," she admitted softly. "I've never felt the way I do when I make love with you, Quinn. It's indescribable. But we can't spend the rest of our lives in bed."

"I don't know," he drawled. "The idea is rather intriguing, now that you mention it. Although we'd probably have to plan ahead and stock the freezer." His eyes gleamed with a wicked light, enticing her to give up the battle. "I wouldn't want you wasting away to nothing."

"Dammit, Quinn," Jessica snapped. "This isn't a time for you to pull out your well-honed seduction techniques!"

"Correct me if I'm mistaken," he said with a silkiness that didn't mask the gravelly note in his voice, "but you were the one doing most of the seducing last night." He allowed a wry smile. "Not that I'm complaining, you understand. I just want to get that little fact down on the record."

He was right, Jessica admitted secretly. But even then it had been an act of surrender. She'd given in to the primitive hunger he was able to instill in her with a single word, a single glance or touch. Whenever she was with Quinn, tides of emotion lapped away at her willpower, dissolving it like a sandcastle at high tide.

Quinn hated the way her face suddenly closed, denying him access to her thoughts. "Jessica?"

When she slowly, reluctantly lifted her gaze to his, her eyes were filled with self-loathing that tore at some delicate fiber deep inside him.

"I was just thinking of a line from T. S. Eliot," she murmured. "And how it seemed to fit me lately."

"Are you going to let me in on it?" he asked quietly.

Jessica braced her elbows on the table, rubbing wearily at her temples. "He wrote of the awful daring that's involved in a moment's surrender," she said tightly.

Quinn swore softly. "Why in hell do you insist on putting up these artificial barriers between us?"

"Because they're real," she retorted harshly. "What we have in there—" she tossed her head in the direction of the bedroom "—is one thing. But it isn't enough to base a lifetime relationship on."

"What do you know about lifetime relationships?" he blazed. "You went into this with the intention of having a nice, brief little affair. No strings. No commitment on either side!"

With a swift movement Jessica had been totally unprepared for, Quinn was suddenly standing over her, closing his hands over her shoulders, hauling her unceremoniously to her feet.

"You're a fine one to talk, sweetheart. All you ever wanted from me was sex. I'd say if anyone should be feeling used right about now, it's me." His green gaze raked her scornfully. "Admit it—you used me for stud service. Sexual relief for the frustrated divorcée, right?"

The sound rang out like a gunshot and Jessica stared at the hand still resting on his cheek.

"Feel better?" he drawled dangerously.

Jessica's eyes remained riveted on the red mark disfiguring his harsh features as she slowly lowered her hand to her side. Then she shrugged free, turning away. "I hate what you do to me," she whispered. "I hate the way you make me lose control."

Quinn studied the slump to her slender shoulders, telling himself that he'd gone about that all wrong. He hadn't meant to get into an argument with her. He damn well hadn't intended to say those things. He and Jessica were like a flammable vapor meeting fire; the explosion was inevitable.

"Jess—" he tried what he hoped was a consoling tone "—I'm sorry. You made me angry and I said some things I didn't mean."

Her response was muffled, but he wasn't encouraged as she shook her head, refusing to turn around.

He moved to her, putting his arms around her. Jessica tensed at the intimate touch. "Honey, you frustrated me. You keep confusing what you feel is surrender in bed, to surrender in life."

"Isn't it?" she whispered.

He rested his chin on her auburn hair. "If it is, then we're both in the same boat because I can't keep away from you any more than you can keep away from me."

"You did a damn good job of it the past three weeks," she complained. "How was Mexico, by the way?"

"Mexico?" he asked, sounding confused. "What gave you the idea I was in Mexico?"

Perhaps he hadn't been with Pamela Stuart, after all. Although Jessica experienced a fleeting sense of relief, she reminded herself that it changed nothing. She merely shrugged.

"I was in Phoenix with Keith."

"You didn't return my calls."

"I wanted to. I must have picked up the phone a hundred times a day, but I was afraid you wouldn't want to hear anything I had to say. . . .

"I was going crazy from missing you, Jess." Quinn's voice held a rough, masculine plea. "Doesn't that mean anything?"

"Only that we're just like the Thackers. We can't live with each other, and we can't live without each other." She turned, lifting her distressed gaze to his. "Well, I don't know about you, but I can't go on this way. I'm not going to see you again, Quinn."

A flicker of pain flashed in his eyes, but his voice was steady. His appraising gaze surveyed her tense face.

"This conversation is all too familiar," he grated. "Be certain this is what you really want this time, Jessica," he warned softly. "Because I'm not going to keep setting myself up to be dumped like this."

Jessica stared at Quinn as his words slowly sank in. Is that what she'd done to him? Was she no better than Brian? Had she just taken what he had to offer, then turned her back and walked away, rather than offering a commitment? Oh God, she groaned inwardly, how had things gotten so confused?

Quinn watched the waves of emotion washing over Jessica's face. First confusion, then doubt, then a blinding comprehension so powerful that it caused her to tremble in his arms. He released her, allowing her to slump wearily into her chair as he waited for her to retract her incautious words.

The sound of the doorbell fractured the thick silence. Quinn's oath was brief and harsh. Refusing to leave this matter unsettled, he remained standing over Jessica, his mouth a hard, grim line. The doorbell rang again. Then, when he continued to ignore it, one more time.

"You'd better answer your door," Jessica suggested on a flat, defeated note. "I don't think whoever is out there is going to go away." The strident demand of the bell proved her correct.

He looked over his shoulder to the foyer with a withering glance. Then his gaze returned to Jessica. "This is more important."

When the chimes pealed again, Jessica exhaled a deep sigh. "We're not going to be able to discuss anything with all that racket," she pointed out. "Go open the door, Quinn."

Muttering a particularly violent series of expletives, Quinn marched to the door, flinging it open with ill-concealed anger. He had to swallow his planned response as he viewed Elizabeth, standing in the hallway, a red suitcase in her hand.

"I was beginning to think you weren't home," she said, her smile wavering as she viewed Quinn's harshly set features. "Perhaps I'd better just give you this and leave," Elizabeth suggested, shoving the overnight case at him.

Jessica experienced a mixture of regret and relief when she heard her mother's voice. "Mom?" she called out, getting up from the chair. "You don't have to go."

"Quinn?" Elizabeth asked sympathetically.

He shrugged with feigned carelessness, taking the suitcase from her hand. "What the hell," he muttered, "we're not getting anywhere, anyway. You might as well come in."

Elizabeth embraced her daughter, her judicial gaze deciding that as bad as Jessica looked, Quinn appeared even worse, if that were possible.

"I brought your clothes," she explained needlessly. "How are you feeling?"

"I've felt better," Jessica admitted.

Elizabeth glanced around the apartment. "I talked with Brian this morning. He has to go out of town for a couple of weeks, but Deirdre said the girls could stay with her."

"No way," Jessica said firmly, crossing her arms over her chest.

Elizabeth nodded understandingly. "I told him that you'd probably want to pick them up this afternoon," she agreed. "Since it doesn't look as if Quinn has room for them here, why don't you let them stay with your father and me?"

Jessica could feel Quinn's hard green eyes impaling her as if they were shafts of cold steel. She had never seen him as angry as he had been this morning. She forced her attention back to her mother.

"Thanks, but they have to finish up these last weeks of school and you and Dad live across town. The insurance will pay for us to move into a hotel while the house is being rebuilt."

Her mother's expression remained smooth, but her voice demonstrated confusion. "But I thought you were staying here."

"I was only a convenient port in the storm," Quinn offered sarcastically. "Jessica never had any intention of staying with me." His tone made it clear that he was talking about more than living arrangements.

Elizabeth's gaze moved first from Jessica, then to Quinn, then back to her daughter. "I see," she said quietly. "Well, dear, why don't you change and I'll drive you up to Mill Valley."

"Thank you," Jessica said, eager to escape Quinn's gaze as she took the suitcase he handed her. There was a spark and an instant of heat when their fingers touched, but his eyes displayed no emotion. As Jessica left the room, she felt unreasonably like a crab scuttling away in the sand.

Ten minutes later she was standing in the doorway, trying to come up with appropriate words to say goodbye. Quinn's expression was unreadable, but she thought she could see a weary depression in his eyes. Jessica's throat tightened.

"Uh, thank you," she said softly. "For everything."

"You're welcome," he answered politely. Then an acid tone slid into his voice. "For everything."

Jessica and Quinn studied each other, each waiting the other out. Then, unable to stand the pain another moment, Jessica spun on her heel, leaving the apartment.

Elizabeth remained quiet on the drive north to Marin County, a fact for which Jessica was exceedingly grateful. She stared out at the rugged coastline, unable to forget Quinn standing there in the foyer, his hands thrust deeply into his front pockets, a raw expression of pain on his face. Jessica knew that image would remain with her for the rest of her life.

13

THE GIRLS FOUND life in a hotel an absolute lark for the first five days. Then they began to complain incessantly about the lack of privacy, the tiny portable refrigerator and the fact that their music had to be kept to a reasonable volume. Jessica was grateful that school would be out in another week. Then, since her parents were taking off to sail the high seas, she might take them up on their offer to use their home.

One advantage to living in a hotel, Jessica decided, was room service. Of course, anything would be an improvement over the meals Elizabeth had prepared during her stay in the house. She was sipping on her morning coffee when Jill approached, a tentative expression on her face.

"Mom?"

Jessica looked up and smiled. The punk look had disappeared; in its place was a lovely young girl with glossy hair and a full-skirted cotton sundress.

"Yes, dear?"

"You haven't forgotten next Wednesday, have you?"

"Forget my daughter's junior high school graduation? Don't be silly. Of course I haven't forgotten."

"Gran and Gramps are coming, too." Jill offered.

"I know," Jessica murmured. She had the distinct feeling that something was being left unsaid.

"I want to invite Quinn," Jill blurted out, confirming Jessica's suspicions.

Jessica slowly lowered her cup to its gilt rimmed saucer. "I don't think that would be a very good idea, sweetheart."

Jill's cheeks flamed scarlet. "Well, I don't think it's fair. Just because you were stupid enough to break up with him, I don't think that's any reason for us to suffer."

"Jill, my relationship with Quinn is really none of your business," Jessica stated firmly, rising from the table.

"It is, too!"

Jessica stared at her daughter. Before she could answer, Mallory entered the living room of the two-bedroom suite and offered her opinion.

"Jill's right," she argued. "Even if you don't love Quinn, we do. And we're definitely getting the short end of the stick. He hasn't been to see us for ages."

Jessica's back stiffened at the accusation in her daughter's tone. She slanted a glance at Sara, who was standing in the doorway, watching quietly.

"What's the matter?" Jessica asked dryly. "Don't you have anything to say about all this?"

Her youngest daughter's voice was soft, but firm. "We miss him, Mom."

"We miss him a lot," Mallory seconded.

"A whole bunch," Jill confirmed. "I really want him to come to my graduation, Mom. Please?"

"What makes you think he'll come?"

"He will if you ask him," Jill said, her expression brightening as she took Jessica's question to be a surrender.

"What makes you think I have any influence over him?" Jessica inquired baldly.

"He loves you," Sara said.

"And I suppose you're an expert?" Jessica couldn't resist asking. She was finding this conversation far more painful than she ever could have imagined.

"He asked you to marry him," Jill reminded her.

"That was several weeks ago," Jessica countered. She began gathering up the scattered breakfast dishes and putting them on the serving cart.

"So?" Mallory wasn't going to let her get away that easily.

Jessica managed a careless shrug. "So things change. People change."

"Like you and Dad changed?" Sara asked, her smooth young forehead drawn together into deep, thoughtful frown lines.

Jessica couldn't lie. She'd always tried to be honest with her daughters and she wasn't about to jeopardize their relationship now.

"No, it's different with Quinn," she admitted. "I still care for him very deeply, but..." Jessica drew in a breath. "Things are complicated," she said slowly. "Quinn and I want different things from life."

She managed a weak smile. "That's enough depressing conversation for one morning," she stated firmly. "Now, if you don't hurry, you'll miss your bus and be late for school."

"We're going," Jill said on a resigned note.

Jessica was not that surprised when Sara turned in the doorway. "Mom?" she whispered, her blue eyes grave.

"Yes?"

"Do you love Quinn?"

"Yes, I do," Jessica answered without hesitation.

Puzzlement shadowed her daughter's clear blue eyes. "Then why don't you just tell him that? I'll bet he still wants to marry you."

Jessica shook her head. "It's not that simple, sweetheart," she replied quietly. "Marriage is more complicated than two people simply loving each other."

They all turned and left the suite, but Jessica couldn't miss Mallory's heartfelt words as they made their way to the elevator.

"Boy, if that's what it's like to be an adult, I'm not ever going to grow up!"

"Don't be a dope," Jill argued. "You can't stay a kid forever."

"Peter Pan did," Sara interjected.

"Peter Pan is just a dumb story," Jill scoffed. "Boy, you two are as dopey as Mom."

While that description wasn't the least bit flattering, Jessica experienced an odd sense of relief at the fact that the girls were bickering. That, at least, was normal behavior.

They made it sound so simple, Jessica mused, as she gathered up her purse and briefcase. Two people fall in love, get married and live happily ever after. How nice it would be if that was the way it really was. However, she was living, breathing proof that not all marriages were made in heaven. Then there was always Keith and Sylvia Thacker.

Jessica had not been surprised when the Thackers reconciled, although she wondered how long they'd manage to stay together this time. She was, however, nonplussed when her former client claimed she'd been the very best attorney she'd ever hired, and promised to call her the next time the couple split.

It was at that point Jessica decided that if she needed an additional excuse to quit her job, avoiding the Thackers was probably reason enough. She had accepted the offer from the District Attorney and was honestly amazed when George Bennington not only asked her to stay with the firm, but offered a generous raise as an incentive.

While Jessica was flattered by the knowledge that despite his demanding attitude, George Bennington found her a bright, capable attorney, she remained firm in her decision. She was looking for new frontiers in her work and the District Attorney's office was nothing if not challenging.

For the first time in ages, Jessica found herself looking forward to her future as she prepared to leave for the office. Today she'd clean out her desk, take a month off, then start her life anew. If she was lucky, she might even begin to get over Quinn Masterson, she told herself, brimming over with self-confidence this final Friday at Bennington, Marston, White and Lowell.

A newspaper was lying on her desk as she walked into her office, already open to the society page. As she sat down, Jessica's gaze was arrested by a strikingly familiar face.

"Socialite snares longtime matrimonial holdout," the headline on the gossip column screamed out at her. As Jessica stared at Pamela Stuart's elegant features, an icy fear skimmed its way up her spine. The accompanying story confirmed her worst fears. Pamela had not only announced her engagement to Quinn, they'd set the date for a week from today.

"He's making an enormous mistake," Jessica said aloud. "She's not right for him. She'll only end up hurting him."

And what do you think you did? a little voice inquired from the depths of her mind.

"I did what I had to do for both of us."

You were afraid, the little voice pressed. *You only thought about yourself.*

"I'm entitled," Jessica argued. "After all, look what happened when I spent my life thinking about everyone else *but* me."

Can you honestly compare Quinn with Brian?

"That's not the point," Jessica said heatedly, embarrassed as Vanessa suddenly appeared in the office doorway.

"Jessica?" she asked hesitantly. "Are you alone? I thought I heard you talking to someone."

"Just myself," Jessica explained with feigned cheeriness. "Which means, I suppose, that I'm getting out of here just in time. Don't they say that's the first sign of insanity?"

"Speaking of getting out, I just dropped by to wish you good luck in your new career. It should prove quite a change."

"That's what I'm hoping," Jessica agreed.

The woman's eyes moved to the paper. "I see you've read the news."

Jessica suddenly realized exactly how the newspaper had arrived on her desk. "About Pamela and Quinn?" she asked casually.

"I tried to warn you, Jessica. But you refused to listen."

Vanessa's conciliatory tone couldn't conceal the oddly victorious note, and Jessica wondered why she'd ever thought this woman was her friend. From the beginning, Vanessa had done nothing but offer damning little innuendos concerning Quinn. Professionally, personally, she'd continued to warn Jessica the man was poison.

She looked at Vanessa curiously. "How long have you worked here?"

"Ages. Sometimes it seems like forever. On a good day it only seems like half my life."

Half her life. Vanessa was slightly older than Jessica. And as far as she knew, the woman had never worked for any other firm. All of a sudden, the pieces began to fall into place.

"Did you and Quinn work together?"

Something flickered in the depths of the woman's eyes for a brief instant, so fleeting that if Jessica hadn't been watching carefully, it would have escaped her attention.

"Now that you mention it," Vanessa stated, brushing at some nonexistent wrinkles on her silk suit, "I believe we might have."

It still hurts, Jessica considered, hearing the bitter edge in the woman's voice. She's been carrying around all that pain for years and years, refusing to allow herself a genuine relationship with a man. Jessica couldn't help comparing Vanessa's behavior with her own and found them uncomfortably similar.

"Quinn once told me that he had planned his life very carefully," Jessica ventured.

"He was going to be a partner by age forty," Vanessa agreed bitterly. "Then and only then was he going to get married."

"Knowing Quinn, I imagine he was up front about his plans."

The woman's eyes hardened. "Oh, I'll give him credit for that," she agreed. "But we all hope that we're the one who can change a man's mind, don't we? That he'll love us more than anything else." Her laugh was short and bitter. "Quinn Masterson's first priority has always been himself."

She tossed her head toward the damning newspaper. "As you'll see, he stuck to his master plan."

He certainly had done that, Jessica thought. But he was wrong. So very wrong.

"If you don't mind, Vanessa, I've got a lot of packing to do."

Vanessa shrugged her silk-clad shoulders. "Sure. Good luck in the D.A.'s office—you're going to need it."

Her words were a distant buzz in Jessica's ear, but she managed to slowly decode them. "Thanks," she answered absently. She stared thoughtfully out the window as she considered Quinn's forthcoming marriage.

"Keep in touch," Vanessa stated with a cheery little wave as she left the office.

"I'll do that," Jessica replied automatically, knowing that if she never saw Vanessa again it would be too soon. She finished cleaning out her desk, anxious to leave.

When she returned to the hotel, Jessica tried to put Quinn from her mind, but found it to be an impossible task. The girls were spending the night with Elizabeth and Mac, leaving Jessica alone with her memories.

She went into one of the bedrooms, locating Mallory's award-winning videotape. It took a while to figure out how to hook up the portable VCR to the hotel television, but soon Jessica was sitting in the darkened room, watching selected scenes from her life flickering on the screen in front of her.

In spite of parental prompting, Mallory had not edited out the scene in which Jessica had fallen over Elizabeth's luggage in an attempt to answer the telephone. Little had she known how that single phone call from Sylvia Thacker would change her life.

Despite Mallory's goal of creating a film of the family, Quinn appeared with heartbreaking frequency. And why not, Jessica asked herself, experiencing a jolt of pain as she watched Quinn fasten the silver locket around her neck. In their short time together, he had infiltrated the household of women with amazing ease. There had been times, Jessica recalled, when his presence had seemed more natural than Brian's ever had.

Her heart stopped as she viewed the scene in the kitchen the morning Quinn had casually dropped the bombshell about their marriage. Now, eyeing him more closely, Jessica noted that although his expression was bland enough, his fingers were curved tightly around the handle of his coffee cup, his knuckles white with tension.

As she viewed her own expression, Jessica was stunned to see not the aggravation she had thought she was feeling that morning, but pure, unadulterated fear.

Was she afraid of marriage? Of commitment? Was her demand for total autonomy simply a mask for lingering feelings of insecurity? Had she sent Quinn away because she doubted her ability to hold him? If so, she had done him an injustice. Quinn Masterson would be incapable of cheating on his wife, just as Brian O'Neill was incapable of fidelity.

The screen went blank, but Jessica didn't notice. She rose, pacing the floor as she considered her behavior over the past few months. She had been worried about Quinn's gaining the upper hand in their relationship. But the truth was, she realized belatedly, she had always been the one in control. She had insisted on setting limits, on establishing boundaries, creating obstacles to any deep involvement.

Yet somehow love had blossomed despite her machinations. Somehow she had fallen in love with Quinn, and amazingly enough, he had fallen in love with her. But what had she done to return that love? Nothing. Oh, she'd been more than willing to make love with him, Jessica admitted grimly. But on her terms. And when Quinn finally objected, when he insisted on more—on marriage—she'd sent him away.

In spite of that, the minute she had needed him, Quinn had been there for her. Opening his apartment and his heart, demanding nothing in return. And what had she done in return? Slammed the door in his face again.

"Oh, God," Jessica groaned. "Jill was right. I acted like an absolute dope."

Everything Quinn had done proved that he was not a man to force his will on anyone. Least of all someone he loved. A marriage to him would be one of equals. Two people sharing a life based on common respect. And love. It was, Jessica realized, what she wanted more than anything else in the world. But now, thanks to her blindness, she might have lost her chance.

One thing was clear. Quinn wasn't going to set himself up to be hurt again. If she wanted to resolve things between them, she would have to make the first move.

Picking up the telephone, she dialed Quinn's apartment. She was forced to wait, her nerves screaming as she allowed the number to ring ten times. Then ten more. Finally, an additional ten. When there was still no answer, she slowly replaced the receiver to its cradle.

Jessica paced the floor long into the night, redialing Quinn's number at regular intervals. At two o'clock in the morning she was forced to admit he wasn't coming home. Where was he? With Pamela? Was he at this very moment lying in her arms on satin sheets in some luxuriously decorated penthouse bedroom? That thought was too abominable to even consider.

"It's just as well," Jessica decided aloud as she fell into her own lonely bed. "It'll be better in person, anyway. Telephones are so horribly impersonal."

Refusing to give up hope, she finally fell asleep.

JESSICA AWOKE EARLY the following morning, her resolve intact. After ordering coffee from room service, she called the MacLaughlin home.

Elizabeth answered the phone in a muffled, sleepy voice. "H'llo?"

"Mother," Jessica said, "I need your help."

Elizabeth was instantly awake. "Of course, dear. What can I do for you?"

"Would you mind keeping the girls another night?"

"You know your father and I love having them visit," Elizabeth replied without hesitation. Her voice took on a tone of motherly concern. "You're not ill, are you?"

"No," Jessica answered. "I'm fine. I just have something important to do and if everything works out all right, I won't be home this evening."

"You're going to Quinn."

Jessica was not surprised by Elizabeth's insight. After all, she'd undoubtedly seen that gossip item, as well.

"Yes."

A cheer rang in Jessica's ear. "All right, Mom!" Jill shouted. "It's about time!"

"Jill," Elizabeth scolded, her stern tone giving way to a low chuckle, "it's impolite to listen in on the extension."

"Sorry, Gran. But I just won five dollars in the pool."

"Pool? What pool?" Jessica asked.

"I said you'd get back with Quinn today. Sara bet last night, and Mallory had the weird idea you were going to crash his wedding, like Dustin Hoffman did to Katherine Ross in *The Graduate*."

Despite the fact that her daughter had displayed atrocious manners by eavesdropping on a private conversation, not to mention that all three girls had actually been betting on her love life, Jessica laughed.

"Tell Sara that she would have won if Quinn had been home last night," Jessica revealed.

"Jessie?" Mac's voice came on the line.

"Yes, Dad?"

"Don't worry about a thing. If Quinn doesn't take you back, we'll sue for breach of promise."

"You wouldn't!"

Her father's laugh was rich and deep. "Take your pick, daughter. It's either that or showing up at his office with my shotgun."

"You've never even owned a gun," Jessica protested.

"You know that and I know that. But Quinn Masterson doesn't. I have every intention of seeing my daughter safely married off before I go sailing into the sunset." Mac paused, as if carefully choosing his words.

"What the hell," he continued gruffly. "You may scream bloody murder, but I have to admit I'll feel a lot better knowing that you've got a good man taking care of you while I'm away."

Jessica had no intention of screaming. Because she knew that Quinn would take care of her. Just as she had every intention of taking care of him.

"I love you, Dad," she said softly before hanging up.

Jessica showered and dressed in record time. While she had no idea how Quinn would react to her interference in his life, she refused to allow her determination to falter. As she took a taxi to his office, she hoped it wasn't too late to change things.

The young woman at the desk outside Quinn's office rose as Jessica marched by. "Excuse me, ma'am, but you can't go in without an appointment!"

"D.A.'s office," Jessica announced blithely, ignoring the secretary's protest. "Official business."

Quinn's back was to the door, his gaze directed out the window as he dictated a letter to an elderly stenographer.

"In closing, I believe that Lamberson Electronics can only benefit by the proposed merger and recommend moving to file as quickly as possible. If you have any questions or comments, please don't hesitate to contact me. Sincerely yours, et cetera, et cetera. Could you please read that back to me, Mrs. Young?"

The woman was staring up at Jessica, who'd suddenly appeared beside her, and didn't answer.

"Mrs. Young?" Quinn repeated, turning around in his chair.

When he saw Jessica, an inscrutable mask settled over his features. "Thank you, Mrs. Young," he said, his eyes not leaving Jessica's. "That will be all for today. And please tell Susan to hold all my calls."

"Yes, sir." The woman rose quickly, departing from the room.

Quinn braced his elbows on the arms of his chair, making a tent with his fingers.

"Well, well," he said smoothly. "It's not often I have a visitor from the D.A.'s office. Don't tell me that there's a bench warrant out for my overdue parking tickets?"

He wasn't going to make it easy on her, Jessica thought. Then she gave a mental shrug. Why should he? Since he'd yet to offer her a chair, Jessica remained standing.

"I'm surprised you know about my move," she admitted, wondering when Quinn could have had time to keep tabs on her while courting Pamela Stuart.

"Mac told me. Congratulations, by the way."

"You've been talking to my father?"

Quinn gestured at a chair on the other side of the desk. "Sit down, Jess," he suggested patiently. "And to answer your question, Mac and I were friends long before you and I had our little affair. I'm not going to stop seeing the man just because his daughter walked out on me."

That stung. Jessica looked down at her hands, pretending a sudden interest in her fingernails.

"Jessica?"

She lifted her gaze, looking for something, anything in his smooth green eyes. Some sign that he still cared. Jessica could find nothing there, but she hadn't come here to turn tail and run at the first obstacle.

"Yes?" she asked, managing to match his casual tone.

"You still haven't told me what you're doing here," he reminded her.

Jessica gazed out at the sparkling waters of the bay. The orange expanse of Golden Gate Bridge gleamed copper in the bright sunlight of early June.

She decided to ease into it. "I called you last night, but you weren't home."

"I had a meeting in Sacramento that ran late," he answered easily. "I spent the night there."

"Oh."

The silence settled down between them again. Jessica took a deep breath. It was now or never.

"I've come to save you," she blurted out.

He arched a brow. "Save me?"

She nodded and her tone was a little firmer as she elaborated. "From making the biggest mistake of your life."

"I see." He swiveled back and forth in the chair, eyeing her impassively. "I don't suppose you'd care to explain that a little further," he prompted.

"You can't marry Pamela Stuart," she insisted, leaning forward in her own chair, her body a stiff, tense line. "I know you had this big master plan for your life. But you can't get married just because you've turned forty, Quinn! That's not a good enough reason."

"What *is* a good reason to get married, Jess?" he asked softly.

"Love," she answered without hesitation.

He picked up a gold fountain pen, toying with it absently. Every one of Jessica's nerve endings were screaming with impatience, waiting for Quinn to say something.

"What makes you think I don't love Pam?"

"Because you love me," she stated firmly, her blue eyes daring him to deny that statement.

"You know, Jess, a torch is a damned burdensome thing to carry around forever," he advised her evenly. "After a while it burns down and you end up scorching your fingers."

"And I love you."

Quinn's expression didn't waver. Jessica thought she saw something flash in his eyes, but it was gone too quickly for her to be certain.

"I see . . . When did you come to that momentous conclusion?"

"I think I fell in love with you that first night we met," Jessica admitted softly. "But I knew for certain when we made love the first time."

While Jessica had not known what reaction she was going to receive by coming here today, laying her heart on the line, she'd secretly hoped Quinn would be thrilled by her confession. Instead, he flung the pen furiously onto the top of the desk and they both watched as it skidded across the wide, polished surface, finally coming to land silently on the thick carpet.

When Quinn returned his gaze to Jessica's, his eyes had hardened to stone. Jessica was forced to consider the unpleasant fact that she might be too late.

"Damn you, Jessie O'Neill," he growled on a harsh breath. "Why didn't you tell me? Why did you drive me crazy all these past weeks?"

She shook her head, feeling duly chastised. "I was afraid."

"Of me?" His tone was incredulous. "I told you from the beginning how I felt about you. How in blue blazes could you think I'd do anything to hurt you?"

"You were going to marry Pamela Stuart," Jessica felt obliged to point out, lifting her chin bravely. "You didn't think that would hurt me?"

He muttered a soft oath. "For an intelligent woman, you sure can be some dumb female." As he dragged his fingers through his hair, Jessica noticed his hands were shaking. "What in the hell am I going to do with you?"

It was now or never. Putting her feelings for Quinn before her pride, Jessica slowly rose from the chair, moving around the vast expanse of oak separating them and settled herself boldly onto his lap. Encouraged by the fact that he didn't toss her to the floor, she twined her arms around his neck.

"If you're open to suggestions," she said softly, nuzzling his ear, "I've got one or two to offer."

The muscles in his shoulders began to relax. He put his arms around her waist. "Doing a little plea bargaining, counselor?"

"Could be," she agreed with a tantalizing smile that faded as her expression turned inordinately serious. "Quinn, will you marry me?"

He paused, as if the decision were a particularly difficult one.

Her heart was beating too fast. Jessica felt as if she'd run up a steep flight of stairs. She waved her hand in front of his face.

"Quinn?"

He shook his head slightly, as if to clear it. "Sorry, Jess. It's just that I've never had a woman propose to me before."

The waiting was driving her crazy. If this was what men went through when they proposed, it was amazing that the institution of matrimony had survived all these generations.

"Well?" she asked, unwilling to wait a moment longer for Quinn's answer.

A broad grin split his face. "Sweetheart, I thought you'd never ask!"

His lips covered hers in a long, lingering kiss that neither participant was eager to end. Finally Quinn broke the intimate contact, resting his chin atop Jessica's head.

"Thank you, Pam," he murmured, unaware he'd spoken out loud until Jessica's head suddenly jerked up.

"It's not what you're thinking," Quinn said instantly, soothingly.

"How do you know what I'm thinking?"

"I can venture a guess."

"Try."

Quinn shifted Jessica on his lap, eyeing her warily. "You're thinking that I've got a helluva nerve saying some other woman's name after I've just accepted your proposal."

"I'm sure you've got a marvelous explanation," Jessica responded calmly, secure in the knowledge that it was she Quinn loved and not Pamela.

"I do want to marry you, Jessica. It's all I've wanted from that first moment I saw you standing in the doorway of the ballroom, looking as delectable as a strawberry ice-cream cone in that pink running suit."

Quinn saw Jessica's eyes soften at the memory of that night. Encouraged, he continued. "You have to understand, I was desperate. I was going crazy without you in my arms, in my bed . . . But most of all, I needed you in my life."

Comprehension slowly dawned, and Jessica stared at Quinn in amazement. "Pamela planted that story, didn't she? She played the same role for you that you've always played for her. It was all a hoax!"

"I'm afraid so," he admitted. "I didn't want to hurt you, Jess. I only wanted you to realize how right we were for each other. How we belonged together."

His tanned face appeared heartbreakingly vulnerable. Jessica didn't know whether to kiss him or hit him over the head with the nearest blunt object.

"How did you know I'd see the paper? I normally don't even read the society page."

"I didn't think Vanessa would miss an opportunity to show it to you. I've never been one of her favorite people."

"You were once," Jessica felt obliged to point out.

Quinn shook his head. "Vanessa made more of that than I expected. I never promised her anything, Jessica. I told her from the start about my goals. And at that point in time they never included marriage."

"I suppose I'm lucky I met you after your fortieth birthday," Jessica murmured, a sad little note creeping into her voice.

His eyes darkened with a loving gleam. "Believe me, Jess, if I'd been fortunate enough to have run into you during those days, all my good intentions would have gone flying out the window."

"Really?" she asked, tracing the hard line of his jaw.

"Really," he confirmed, turning his head to press a kiss against her fingertips. "We were made for each other, sweetheart. Timing had nothing to do with it."

Her misgivings dissolved, Jessica snuggled against him. "Quinn?"

"Mmm?"

"What would you have done if I hadn't come to your office today?"

"I was going to give you twenty-four hours, then kidnap you and keep you hostage in my bed until you agreed to marry me," he replied promptly.

"I've already agreed to marry you," she told him. "In fact, for the record, I did the proposing."

Quinn knew what an effort it had taken for Jessica to put aside her pride and come to his office today. He couldn't remember loving her more than he did at this moment.

His eyes brightened with a seductive gleam. "It's still not such a bad idea. I especially like the part about keeping you hostage in my bed."

"Kidnapping's a capital offense."

"Ah, but I was hoping I could convince a certain sexy assistant D.A. not to press charges."

"I couldn't neglect my duties, Quinn. Even for you." She gave him a sensual little smile. "Of course, if you're willing to plead guilty, I could probably get you released to my custody."

"How long a sentence are they handing out for kidnapping these days?"

"It's a very serious charge, Quinn. I'd say fifty years to life, at the very least."

Quinn's answering grin wreathed his handsome face and lines fanned out from those brilliant emerald eyes she had not been able to put from her mind during their time apart.

"Fifty years to life," he agreed between kisses. "At the very least."

He'd buried himself after burying his wife,
but his old friend and courtroom colleague
was determined to resurrect him.

VOICES ON THE WIND

Sandra Canfield

CHAPTER ONE

JILL MCCLAIN FIRST HEARD THE NEWS as she passed by the office alcove housing the soft-drink machine.

"Hey Jill, know what?" the receptionist asked, pounding the Coke machine with her fist and ritually reinserting the change the metal beast coughed up. "Burke's coming back."

"Did you hear about Burke?" Charles Evans, the newest person to join the law firm of Rawlins, Rawlins, Nugent and Carson, asked before Jill had a chance to reply to the first inquiry. Both he and Jill passed like course-charted ships, he in the direction of his office, Jill toward the senior Rawlins's office.

"Yeah, Cindy just..." she called over her shoulder only to be interrupted once again.

"Guess what?" Ellen, the bright-eyed, buxom law clerk, said breathlessly.

"Burke's coming back," Jill answered, a devilish grin on her lips and no hesitation in her clipped steps.

"Ahh, someone's already told you," the woman groaned, pouting prettily as she balanced a stack of old law books and current briefs.

High heels clicking to a halt, Jill paused only long enough to push open the frosted-glass door inscribed with the name Andrew Rawlins. She immediately encountered the woman who'd been the senior partner's secretary for what everyone affectionately said had been a thousand years. Ida Tumbrello would always reply that actually she'd been there only a little over nine hundred years, but that it had been long enough for her to remember Rawlins, Rawlins, Nugent and Carson, when it was nothing more than Rawlins and raw.

"Mr. R. sent for me," Jill announced when Ida's heart-shaped face glanced up from the typewriter.

The secretary smiled. "He said to send you right in." Her smiled widened, sending wrinkleless cheeks upward and causing lights to jump into ageless eyes. "Did you hear that Burke's coming back?"

Jill returned the smile in full measure and added a dollop of teasing. "There is a mild rumor to that effect. In fact, I heard the news four times in three yards." Then, in keeping with the gravity of the announcement, Jill asked softly, "When?"

"He's already in Boston and plans to be in the office in the morning." For the briefest of moments, the older woman looked as if she might cry. Ida's fawn-brown eyes glistened, and a suspicious pink rosed the end of her fair-skinned nose. "Needless to say, Andrew is beside himself. He said it's like a thousand Christmases rolled into one." The statement needed no comment, and both women savored the sweetness of it. Finally, the secretary sniffed and inclined her gray-haired head toward the door behind her. "Better get in there before the old coot has my hide for detaining you."

"Right," Jill said, "and mine for letting you detain me." She tapped once on the door, turned the knob and entered the plush, red-carpeted office of Andrew Rawlins. "You wanted to see me, sir?"

The tall, thin man who stood staring out the wide wall of glass turned, presenting Jill with a face and figure that she never failed to mentally categorize as distinguished. A healthy and full cap of snow-white hair framed a lean, angular face, while silver-green eyes shone brightly and wisely. Jill always fancifully imagined that her boss had been told at least part of the secret of life. A white mustache, neatly manicured, lay atop sensitive and pleasing lips. Those lips were presently smiling with a sincerity that had been absent for the past eighteen months. It was a sincerity that came straight from the man's heart.

"Are you aware of how pretty Boston can be in the spring?" Andrew Rawlins asked.

Jill's lips curved upward at the unexpected question. "You're right, sir. Boston is spectacular in the spring. But with all due respect to the city, I suspect anyplace on earth would seem pretty to you right now."

His eyes made no pretense of hiding a diamond-bright sparkle. "Then you've heard?"

"I don't think there's anyone left in the northern hemisphere who hasn't." As she had moments before with the secretary, she sobered. "I'm very pleased, sir. For him and for you."

"Thank you."

"How is he?"

An image of Burke Rawlins as she'd last seen him flashed through Jill's mind. He'd been dressed in somber black, standing beside his wife's newly turned grave. There had been a blandness to his features, a stark deadness in his eyes, that had said without a doubt that Nicole Rawlins was taking a part of him into eternity with her. Maybe the best part of him.

"He's..." Andrew Rawlins sought out the phrase to best describe his son. "He's all right. It's been a rough year and a half, but I think he's finally learned that there is some truth to that old cliché about life going on." The man before her sighed, and Jill suspected he was thinking of his own wife's death more than ten years before. "It's something we all learn," he added, confirming Jill's suspicion.

"It'll be good to work with Burke again," she said, bringing the conversation from the past and back to the present. She couldn't help but wonder if all the rumors she'd heard over the last eighteen months were true. Like the rumor that Burke refused to get behind the wheel of a car. Like the rumor that he'd fled Boston and become a beach bum down on Cape Cod. Like the rumor that he'd grown a beard and long hair, and that he could now race like the wind with legs athletically at their best from long hours of running along the Atlantic shoreline.

"And that's the very reason I've sent for you," Andrew Rawlins said. "How do you feel about you and Burke working together on the *Stroker* case?"

Jill McClain was known for three things: her petite size— Burke Rawlins had once called her "an elf in search of a fairy tale"—her aggressive zeal for her law career and her bold-faced honesty. It was the latter quality that formed her next words. "You know very well that every lawyer in this office, probably every lawyer in the city, would kill for that case. Me included. And I'd love to work on it with Burke."

"Good. Very good." The man turned toward a wall-unit liquor cabinet of gold-and-black-swirled mirror glass. The late-afternoon sun glinted faintly in its marbled depths, casting a warmth about the elegant office. "Let's have a drink to finalize it then. What can I get for you? Chablis, gin and tonic, amaretto and soda..."

"Chablis will be fine," Jill interrupted, trying to hold in civilized check the whirlwind emotions swarming over her body.

The Stroker *case!* How many nights had she fallen asleep dreaming about arguing in court what was fast becoming Boston's most famous case? Precedents were going to be set that would be quoted for a long time to come, and any lawyer doing a good job had a prominent career signed, sealed and delivered at case's end—regardless of the verdict. But more than that, the case fascinated her, fascinated all sixty inches of her, from the top of her strawberry-blond-haired head right down to her rose-polished toenails. She didn't really know why; it just did. But then, the case had captured the attention of a lot of people, particularly people in the media. The case had all the ingredients guaranteed to sell papers—an elite Bostonian family whose members were fighting one another for control of its riches, plus the added and irresistible complication of an illegitimate child stepping out of the shadows for her share of the wealth. *The*

Stroker *case!* Jill thought, resisting the urge to jump up and down and shout. Just wait until she told her sister . . .

". . . your sister's getting married."

Jill dragged her attention back to duty and tried to piece together what her boss had just said.

"I hear it's sometime this spring."

"Yes, sir," she replied, hoping she hadn't missed anything important. "My sister's getting married in May."

"You two are close, aren't you?" Andrew Rawlins asked, as he handed Jill a tulip-shaped Waterford wineglass.

His comment didn't surprise her. He took the time to know about everyone who worked for him. "Yes, we are," she answered, reaching for the Chablis and wondering if his investigation had revealed just how close she and Mary were. "It's just the two of us. Has been for a long time."

"I'll expect an invitation to the wedding."

"I'll see that you get it."

"May I propose a toast?" the man asked, raising his glass of Canadian whiskey. "To sons and sisters and the *Stroker* case."

"I'll drink to that," Jill McClain said, bringing the glass to her rose-glossed lips.

ON THE OTHER SIDE OF TOWN, in a furnished apartment he'd signed a lease on, sight unseen, Burke Rawlins lifted a glass to his lips and took a long, slow swallow of bourbon and water. The amber liquid slid down his throat comfortably. He felt as if he were greeting an old, familiar friend, but then his life for much of the first six months of the past year and a half could be summed up in one word: bourbon. Bourbon on the rocks, bourbon off the rocks, bourbon shallow and deep. Bourbon morning, noon and night— sometimes all night. But the interesting, and frustrating, thing, Burke had come to realize, was that no matter how much bourbon he consumed, it was never enough. No matter how dense the stupor, he could still remember. He could still remember the accident. He could still remember Nicole limp and lifeless in his arms. He could still remember how the earth-grave had swallowed her up, mounding itself over her in a way that suggested suffocation. He could still remember fighting the urge to fall to his knees and claw the thickly clotted brown dirt off her, as if it were the burial killing her and not the accident that already had. And most of all, no matter how much he drank, he could still remember the guilt—that overwhelming feeling that if justice were truly served, as he'd been taught to hope in the end that it was, he would be dead instead of her. Or, at the very least, dead along with her.

Once he'd realized that no amount of bourbon would give him the peace he sought, Burke had dried himself out and looked for some other way to cope. He'd turned to running and could now truthfully say that he'd left more footprints on the beach of Cape Cod than any other human being. For long hours every day, and sometimes on sleepless nights, he'd run, just run, until his mind would empty of everything, until the only thing in his head was the sound of his feet pounding the earth and the salt sea pounding the shore.

He brought the glass once more to his lips. This drink was the first he'd had since swearing off, and it was the only one he'd allow himself. But, God, he had to have this one! He couldn't face coming back without at least one friend. And how in hell could he run at breakneck speed down the congested streets of Boston?

As if to prove his point, he edged back the sliding-glass door leading to the balcony and stepped out into the brisk March air. A breeze rushed toward him, tumbling a lock of brown hair across his forehead and swaying the nest of darker-brown hair that peeped from the vee of his knit shirt. Five stories below, people milled about absorbed in late-afternoon activities. A woman pushed a stroller with a crying baby in it, a man carried a sack full of groceries into the apartment building across the street and a group of kids, laughing in the probable planning of mischief, ambled by. An occasional car horn honked. A siren wailed way off in the distance—a dismal sound that Burke tried hard not to think about because it, too, was something he was all too

familiar with. That and the hollow sounds of hospital
halls . . . and the even hollower sounds of grief.

*I'm sorry, Mr. Rawlins, your wife was dead on arrival . . .
dead on arrival . . . dead on arrival . . .*

Now, as then, Burke had an overwhelming need to deny
that death, to simply say, "Hey, there must be some mistake here. Nicole and I were just on our way home. If you'll
let her off that table, we can make it back before the rain
gets heavy." Yet, in his heart, despite the shadows of shock,
he had known she was dead the moment the car hit them.
Without a doubt, he'd known it the moment he'd dragged
her into his arms. But he'd prayed all the way to the hospital for a miracle, a miracle that he'd railed against God for
withholding.

Somehow, for a reason that made no sense at all to him,
her death was harder to take because he himself had walked
away totally unscathed. He was almost—no, dammit, he
thought, raking fingers through his wind-tossed hair, he was
more than almost—he was downright angry with her for not
walking away uninjured, too. This anger was just one more
thing to feel guilty about.

Then, of course, there was the "if" guilt. If his reflexes
had been just a shade quicker, could he have avoided the
collision? If he'd been paying just the slightest bit more attention, would Nicole be beside him now? If he hadn't been
laughing and teasing her, telling her what he was going to do
to her when he got her home, would he have gotten her
home?

Burke shoved the devil-owned "if" from his mind,
knowing that the power of the hateful word lay in the fact
that it always posed a question that could never be re-
solved. He heaved a deep breath and emptied the glass to the
tune of clattering ice cubes. It was now time to resolve this
tragedy in some way if he was to go on living. A man could
hurt only so much. Beyond that point, the body went numb
and closed down all pain receptors. Which was where he
presently was emotionally. He felt nothing—except some
basic human instinct to survive. To do that he had to get

back to work. Tomorrow he'd be back at his desk, briefs
and documents before him. Tomorrow the beard would be
gone, like the long hair he'd shorn days ago. Tomorrow he'd
be dressed in a suit and tie and a clumsy awkwardness. Tomorrow he'd try to find the rhythm of life again. But right
now, he thought, once more entering the small apartment,
he had to get rid of this beard and get settled in.

Twenty minutes later, he stood before the bathroom mirror and made one final sweep of the sharp razor. It left a
smooth-cheeked stranger staring back at him. It also left
him feeling peculiarly vulnerable, as naked emotionally as
he now appeared physically. Suddenly, and with a force that
surprised and frightened, a sense of panic hit him. Maybe
he shouldn't have come back just yet. Maybe he needed
more time. Maybe...

The walls of the apartment closed in, tight, tighter, and
it suddenly became imperative that he get out. Out where he
could breathe, out where he could feel the freedom of the
wind, out where he could feel the mind-oblivion that came
from exhausting fatigue. Ramming down the zipper of his
jeans, he shed them and yanked the knit shirt over his head.
His recently cut hair fell in forgotten disarray. A worn gray
sweat suit and running shoes later, he bolted out of the
apartment, took the stairs in favor of the elevator and hit the
front door of the apartment complex at a run. Nearly colliding with someone entering the building, Burke apologized without ever looking up or back.

He just ran.

He ran, dodging in and out of startled passersby. He ran
by shops closed and closing. He ran against red lights and
with green. He ran until the wind chaffed at his newly
shaved and tender face. On and on he chased himself until
his lungs stung with the need to burst, until his breath was
a prickling, reedy gasp in his pressured chest, until his legs
ached with their lead weight. And when he thought that to
run one more step would be instant death, he ran on... and
on... and on. Because the demon behind him would not let
him stop.

THE SOUND OF RUNNING WATER filled the bathroom as Jill washed away the day's makeup. Shutting off the faucet, she patted her oval, freckle-dusted face dry, then spent seconds removing her contact lenses and storing them in their case— a floral-designed, Limoges porcelain confection that Mary had given her for her thirty-fourth birthday two months before. Jill blinked, then blinked again. That felt better, she thought, standing on tiptoe and studying her red-veined eyes in the mirror. Even without the contacts, which were tinted a pale blue, her eyes were an aquamarine, a shade somewhere between high sky and deep sea. Right now, however, those aquamarine eyes were tired from reading too many law books and from too many hours of wearing the sometimes irritating contacts. Reaching for a pair of glasses, she slid them on, through strawberry-blond curls that wisped about her ears and fell in riotous play down her back. She grabbed a robe from its hook and eased the butterfly-yellow satin over her shoulders. She turned off the bathroom light and headed her bare, size-four feet for the kitchen.

There, she tossed a got-everything-on-it-except-the-kitchen-sink pizza into the oven, poured herself a fizzing cola and dragged the receiver from the wall phone. She dialed her sister's number. As she did so, a fresh burst of excitement flooded her. *The* Stroker *case! Just wait until Mary hears!*

The phone began to ring. It rang and rang and rang. Jill frowned and checked the kitchen clock. Ten till seven. She'd stayed at the office later than she'd realized. Again. Mary and Rob had probably already gone out for the evening. Was this the night they had tickets to the theater? The number rang once more. Jill sighed and hooked the instrument back on the wall.

She checked the pizza through the oven door, saw that the cheese was beginning to bubble, and leaned back against the edge of the cabinet. She was hungry. And tired. She started to bring the glass to her lips but stopped midway. Tired, and something else. She was...something else. A niggling something she'd felt often of late, but it was a something she couldn't quite identify. She intuitively knew, however, that it had to do with her sister's upcoming marriage. No, more truthfully, it had to do with the relationship Mary McClain had with Rob Sheffield.

Not that she coveted the happiness her sister had. She didn't. Not for a moment. Heaven only knew, it was more than time that her elder sister found someone to share her life with. In fact, Jill had begun to think that she never would. And for one very good reason: Mary didn't seem to be looking. Sixteen years older than Jill, she had always seemed content to play the role of older sister and old-maid schoolteacher, and when their parents, Margaret and Edward McClain, had died in a plane crash the summer Jill was fifteen, it had just seemed natural that Mary became more mother than sister. It was a role she took to as if she'd been made for it. But it was a role that narrowed her already narrow personal life even more. Not that she seemed to mind, but Jill minded for her. No, she was thrilled that Rob Sheffield had come along. It was just . . .

Just what?

The oven timer pinged, saving Jill from searching for an answer she wasn't sure she could have found anyway.

Ten thousand calories later—Jill consoled herself that at least her cola was diet—she tidied up the kitchen, showered and slipped into bed with a law book almost half her weight. She read until a quarter to twelve, at which time she shut off the light and slid beneath the cool layers of fresh sheets. She wriggled. She stretched. She stretched again over mile after mile of percale. Her feet, her hands, her body touching nothing, she suddenly frowned. Was it possible that she'd just discovered the answer to the question "Just what is the matter with me?" Might the answer be found in all the spacious room she had in her king-size bed? In all the room she had in her life?

Despite a successful career she loved, some part of her, some woman's part, still felt empty. Was it possible that she needed, wanted, to have someone to share her life with—the good, the bad and all that came in between? She'd spent all of her time and energy pursuing a career, to the exclusion of love. Oh, she'd had relationships. Even meaningful relationships. But no relationship had ever matured into a "forever" commitment. It hadn't mattered then. It was only now, as she was getting older—she *was* thirty-four, she reminded herself—that it mattered. She sighed. She wanted someone who would look at her the way Rob looked at Mary. She wanted someone who would love her to distraction the way...

She stopped, surprised by the name that came to mind. She wanted someone who would love her to distraction the way Burke Rawlins had loved his wife.

Burke Rawlins.

She wondered if he'd changed all that much. She hoped not. She and Burke had worked hard and well together the three years she'd been at Rawlins, Rawlins, Nugent and Carson, and furthermore, they'd managed to like and respect each other in the process. They'd been able to make each other laugh at that uncomfortable moment when one always took oneself, and life, too seriously. What if he no longer smiled, laughed, teased? Jill couldn't imagine such a tragedy. But then, she couldn't imagine the hell he must have been through. Which brought her full circle in her thinking. Would any man ever care enough about her to walk through the same hell?

She turned to her side, cozied her cheek into the pillow and forced herself to at least give sleep a chance. Right before it washed its soothing waves over her, though, two thoughts flitted through her mind. The next to the last was in the form of a statement: She had been assigned to the *Stroker* case! The last was a question: Where were all the men like Burke Rawlins hiding?

"HE'S BACK," Cindy commented.

"Have you seen Burke?" Charles Evans asked.

"He looks good enough to eat," buxom Ellen whispered conspiratorially.

Balancing the contents of two Styrofoam cups, Jill smiled at the last remark and walked down the hall. She paused before the door that had been closed for the past year and a half. It presently stood ajar.

"Knock, knock," she called out in deference to the steaming coffee she carried. When she heard no reply, she eased through the slit and into the room. "Burke?" she said softly.

The man staring out the window didn't turn, didn't flinch a muscle. In fact, he wasn't even aware of her presence. Jill's first reaction was that she should respect his privacy and slip unnoticed out the door, but she didn't because of a stronger, second reaction. That reaction had everything to do with the captivating way the morning sun was streaming through the window and solar-skipping in yellow-brown hair until it looked as if it had been sprinkled with glitter. The same bold sun fell across the wide shoulders straining against the navy suit jacket that hung open over a salmon-hued shirt; the sun stripe ended in a diagonal slit of gold across one perfectly pressed, blue pant leg. Into both pockets were jammed hands that were as immobile as the man.

A fish out of water, Jill thought. Something in his stance screamed, "I'm out of my element." Something in his stillness cried, "I'm scared."

She must have made some telling sound because he pivoted toward her. Moss-green eyes immediately meshed with blue. Curiously, at least it seemed so to Jill, neither said a word, but, oh, her mind ran rampant with thoughts.

He *had* been through hell. It was burned in his eyes. Yet there was a strength in those eyes, too. Maybe even a strength he didn't know he possessed. He looked older. Thinner. And his face was bronzed with the darkness that only long hours in the sun can achieve. There were wrinkles in his brow, from worry and from weather. There were also shadows, strangely becoming shadows, hidden in his cheeks. The thighs contained within the pants looked trim and taut, with superb muscular delineation. The part about his running must be true. She'd bet her law career on it. And one other thing was true as well: Ellen had been right when she'd said that Burke looked good enough to eat. Jill admitted this with no undue significance and nothing personal attached to it. It was all part of the honesty of her personality.

"Hi," she heard herself say.

"I wondered where you were."

"I've been out of the office. Interviewing a client who's suing his landlord because a bee in the landlord's geranium stung him. Claims he almost died. Claims also that the bee falls under the heading of a concealed weapon."

His response wasn't a smile, but it was the nearest thing to one that had crossed Burke Rawlins's face in a long time. "How are you going to plead the case, counselor?"

"I'm going to *bee* clever."

Burke groaned. "With a stinging, venomous attack against your opposition?"

"Naturally. I want a honey of a verdict."

Burke's lips twitched just an infinitesimal fraction. And so did Jill's. Privately, she was just shy of being elated. He might have walked with the devil, but the demon hadn't stolen his sense of humor. That fact pleased her.

"Is one of those for me?" Burke asked, nodding toward the cups she was still holding.

Jill glanced down at the forgotten coffee. "Oh, yeah," she said, thrusting a cup toward him. He withdrew his hands from his pockets and took it. She noticed that he was still wearing a slender gold wedding band.

Unasked, she eased into the leather chair across from his desk, he onto the desk's edge, where his legs spread in a slight vee. It was a pose they had assumed a thousand times, just as the comfortable silence that followed had been lived through countless times. Both took slow sips of their coffee. Both acted as though they'd seen each other only hours before.

"How are you?" she asked finally when she intuitively sensed the moment was right.

It never occurred to Burke to lie or sugarcoat the truth. Not with Jill McClain.

"I don't know," he answered with a shrug. Setting down the cup, he slipped from the edge of the desk and resumed his stance at the window. Several seconds rolled by, seconds in which the sun again noticeably sparkled in his hair.

"Take a guess," Jill urged.

He turned, his eyes finding those of the woman before him. "I guess I'm better. Or I wouldn't be standing here."

"Sounds reasonable."

"But I'm still . . . scared to be standing here."

"Sounds normal."

"Of course, I may be back only because I need money. A year and a half of bumming around leaves little in the coffers."

"Sounds prudent."

Both pairs of lips flirted with a grin. Burke's faded before ever being anything more than an essence.

"I'm all right," he said seriously. "Or at some point I will be."

"Sounds like the Burke Rawlins I know."

Something in his eyes said, "Thanks for the vote of confidence." Something in hers said, "You're welcome."

"So how are you?" he asked suddenly changing the subject.

She shrugged, much the same way he had, except that with her petite shoulders, it looked more as if she were dancing. "You know me. I'm always the same."

"Like the sun and the moon?"

"Nah," she said, as if insulted to be compared with such a shabby duo. "They wax and wane. I'm constant. Constantly confused, constantly overworked, constantly . . . whatever."

Burke's lips semigrinned again. "How's everything around here?"

"Well, let's see," Jill said, settling back into the chair. She crossed one sheer-stockinged leg over the other. For all her diminutive size, Jill McClain was proportioned in a way that immediately caught a man's attention, though she herself was totally oblivious to that fact. Burke Rawlins lowered his eyes to the shapely curves of her legs, then instantly shifted his gaze back to her face. "The Coke machine still doesn't work, Charles Evans is still complaining that he gets only the runt of the cases, Ellen's boobs are still out to here—" she made the appropriate gesture "—Ida is still in love with your dad and your dad still has absolutely no idea that she is."

Burke frowned. "You're kidding. Ida in love with Dad?"

Jill rolled her eyes heavenward. "Men! Blind as bats!"

"Well, I'll be damned," Burke said softly, pursing his lips and letting the idea sink in. "Speaking of the man who's as blind as a bat, did Dad tell you we're handling the *Stroker* case?"

Jill smiled. "Yeah."

"Does the smile mean you're pleased?"

"What do you think?"

"I think you're going to be working with someone who's rusty. You still pleased?"

Jill sensed a real vulnerability in the question. "Even rusty, you're one of the best lawyers in Boston. And you know it."

"We'll see," he added. "I am eager to get started." He laughed mirthlessly. "It's funny, but for the last year I haven't wanted to do anything, couldn't do anything, and now all of a sudden I feel that my only salvation lies in work."

"Sounds like a more positive approach."

"Yeah, I guess it does at that."

He took a slow step toward her, at the same time ramming a hand back into a pocket. Pant fabric splayed provocatively across his manhood. Jill couldn't help but notice, though she quickly glanced away.

"What does your schedule look like?" he asked.

She deliberately kept her eyes on his face. "Let me have today to rearrange some appointments and we can start in the morning."

"Good. Are you averse to working overtime?"

"Have I ever been?"

"No. I just keep thinking that one of these days there's going to be a man in your life who's going to resent the hell out of Rawlins, Rawlins, Nugent and Carson." He stopped. "Or is there already? I mean, a year and a half is a long..."

"No man," Jill interrupted, feeling peculiarly bereft by the truth of the statement. To cover that fact, she asked quickly, "Have you been following the case?"

"A little. But I'll need a lot of briefing. In fact, that's what I'm going to do this afternoon."

"Well," Jill said, finishing the coffee, rising and starting for the door, "let me get to work so you can get to work so we can get to work."

"Jill?"

She stopped and turned.

"Thanks for the coffee." The tenor of his voice suggested that he was thanking her for more than the caffeine.

"You're welcome," she answered, adding in a shades-softer tone, "I'm glad you're back." Their eyes held for a moment before Jill started for the door once more. Her hand was just wrapping around the knob when Burke spoke again.

"I see you're still not eating your Wheaties."

She hesitated. Turned. And tried to appear highly offended at his remark about her height—or lack thereof. She couldn't keep back a smile, though. "We've had this discussion before, Rawlins, but I see that I'm going to have to remind you that quality is better than quantity."

Burke said nothing; he simply fought his own smile. Slowly, though, each lost the battle. Mutual smiles emerged despite all attempts to the contrary. They were full smiles, smiles that showed not an inch of compromise. Burke thought how really pretty Jill's smile was and how his own felt really good. He also wondered just when the last time was he'd smiled. A year and a half ago?

Jill wondered why she'd never noticed before how really handsome Burke was when he smiled. He looked exactly as if he'd stolen some of the sun's beams and forced them to shine from his face and eyes.

Suddenly, Burke felt a little guilty standing there smiling. And more than a little guilty at enjoying the smile on Jill's face.

Jill suddenly felt a little awkward, as if she'd said what she came to say and was now wondering why she was still hanging around.

"Well, I'll . . . I'll see you later," she stammered.

"Yeah," Burke replied.

In a flash she was out the door and walking down the hall.

"Doesn't he look yummy?" Ellen whispered dreamily, a law book clutched to her ponderous chest in schoolgirl fashion.

Jill glanced up. "What?"

"Burke. Doesn't he look good enough to eat?"

"Yes," she replied, but her mind was not on the edibility of Burke Rawlins. Instead, she was thinking of Nicole Rawlins—model-tall, model-thin, gorgeous Nicole Rawlins. Nicole Rawlins who had been physically everything she was not. Jill made the honest assessment that petite women in need of Wheaties were not Burke Rawlins's type. She refused, however, to carry honesty a step further and ask why that fact carried with it the pricking sting of disappointment.

CHAPTER TWO

THE NEXT DAY dawned blue and beautiful, the perfect prelude to the weekend that was to follow. In the offices of Rawlins, Rawlins, Nugent and Carson, everyone worked with a thank-God-it's-Friday zeal, including Burke and Jill, whose work reflected the added fervor that only the *Stroker* case could inspire. Burke, in true workaholic fashion, was already ensconced in his office when Jill arrived; she simply moved into his, where they remained without interruption until lunch. That proved to be sandwiches from the nearby deli, which they consumed in record time. Then they went back to work, which they continued until a quarter to four when Jill took time out to take her sister's call. Mary McClain issued an invitation to dinner for the following evening, which Jill happily accepted, opting to wait until then to share her news regarding the *Stroker* case. She had simply told her sister that she had a surprise. Following the call, she and Burke did what they had done all day: they worked.

"Hungry?"

Jill glanced up from the script that was beginning to blur before her tired eyes. "What time is it?" she asked.

Burke angled his wrist and checked the gold watch nestled amid brown hair. The sleeves of his white shirt had been rolled up, his tie loosened to a benign noose, and his beige suit jacket abandoned. "Five till seven. You want to call down to the deli again, or you want to call it quits for the day?"

"What do you want to do?"

"I'll probably work on, but..."

"Pastrami on rye," Jill interrupted.

Burke half smiled and reached for the phone. Jill took the opportunity to ease her feet from the confining patent-leather heels she'd worn all day. Flexing her toes, she tucked her feet beneath her and leaned lazily back in the corner of the leather chair. With her black linen dress, its square, biblike collar of white brocaded lace, and her reddish-blond hair, which was swept back from her face with black combs and allowed to sprawl freely about her shoulders, she looked a little like a calico kitten at the end of a long day of chase-the-mouse.

"You look tired," Burke commented as he hung up the phone and ran his hand around the back of his neck where he kneaded kinked muscles.

"So do you." She blinked against the gritty, dry feel of her contact lenses.

He shrugged. "I am a little. But it feels good to be back at work. And to be honest, it's been easier falling back into step than I thought it would be. Sorta like slipping back into a pair of old jeans."

The latter comment brought a smile to his eyes, if not to his lips. It also brought the realization to Jill that she'd never seen Burke in jeans. She absently made the mental notation that he probably looked sensational in denim, especially since his leg muscles were now so perfectly honed. She instantly had the feeling that maybe she shouldn't have thought that, that maybe it was a little too personal for their impersonal relationship. She covered up the thought by telling herself she was just being honest and by asking, "Is the deli going to deliver our order or do we have to go after it?"

"They deliver until nine." Burke's brow suddenly wrinkled in question. "The building still has a security guard to let them in, doesn't it?"

Jill nodded. The twenty-six-story building, of which all of the twelfth floor belonged to Rawlins, Rawlins, Nugent and Carson, was usually vacated each weekday evening between the hours of six and seven, at which time a security guard went on duty in the main lobby.

"Good," Burke replied. Then, thinking of some other point he wanted to check about the upcoming trial, he launched into another discussion of *Stroker* versus *Stroker*. Suddenly, he stopped in midsentence. "You're not wearing glasses."

The statement took Jill, who was checking a deposition, by complete surprise. She glanced up.

"I've been trying to figure out since yesterday what was different about you." The question had occurred to him at numerous odd times; some of those odd times had been in the middle of work.

"Contacts."

His look was vague.

"I'm wearing contacts."

"Oh."

"I got them about a year ago."

There was a brief silence before he asked, "Why?"

"Why?"

"Yeah. Why?"

"In a word, Rawlins, vanity."

"Vanity?"

"V-a-n-i-t-y. You know—that thing that women are supposed to possess in abundance."

"But you always looked so...intelligent in glasses."

"There you have it," Jill answered. "Don't you know that all women my age are trying to trap a man? I'm thirty-four and getting desperate. Men don't want intelligent looking. They want glamorous, sexy. They want knockout in the looks department. Glasses just don't hack it. And heaven only knows that with my in-need-of-Wheaties size and my little-girl freckles I need all the help I can get." She was teasing. Or was she? she thought, as she remembered the feel of her empty bed. Had she had some subliminal realization a year before that she was only now confronting openly? Had she hoped that contacts would improve her chances of finding a man?

Burke smiled. "You have every right to be desperate. My God, thirty-four!" He said the number as if it were closely akin to the bubonic plague. "And you're so right. Men want looks, sex, glamour. And you look like a dog in glasses. A small, freckle-faced dog."

"Thanks, friend," Jill said, flipping the pencil in her hand across the desk in playful retaliation. Burke caught it in midmotion.

"Some men are turned on by intelligence, McClain." Burke Rawlins had been the only person to whom she'd ever made the statement that she'd love to shave off some of her IQ—which she knew to be above average—and add the figures to her height. "However it's packaged," he added meaningfully.

His remark made Jill uncomfortable. Her uncomfortableness stemmed entirely from the fact that she had the strong urge to ask if he was one of those men. It was an inappropriate question for their relationship. Or was what was inappropriate the fact that she wanted his answer to be yes?

Silence stretched into silence. Conjecture into confusion. At least in Jill's mind.

Suddenly the phone rang.

Jill glanced toward it as if it were her savior incarnate.

The call was the security guard checking out the deli messenger, and within minutes Jill and Burke were eating what everyone called the best sandwiches in town and drinking the last of the office coffee, which conversely had a reputation for being the worst in town. It was so bad that no one at the office would admit to making it. It just seemed to appear from nowhere.

Somewhere in the middle of pastrami on rye, Jill convinced herself that the discomfort she'd felt before the call had been the result of a long, tiring day. So what if she'd been tempted to ask him if he personally admired intelligence in a woman? Such speculation meant nothing. Absolutely nothing. They were simply friends talking.

Following the meal, they once more immersed themselves in work. It was just minutes shy of nine o'clock when

Jill announced defeat. "Uncle," she called out, slapping the papers in her lap onto Burke's desk and reaching for her purse. "I've got to get these contacts out or go crazy. Or blind." Her eyes looked like a red-charted road map.

"They hurt?"

"When you wear them this long without a break, they become less than friendly."

As she fumbled in her purse for the case, Burke mumbled something unsavory about vanity. He also pushed back his chair, rose and walked toward the window. He rammed one hand into a pant pocket, while the other again rubbed weary neck muscles. He stared down at the city below. Car headlights bounced and bobbed as if transmitting silent signals of a secret code. They reminded him of other headlights that had come out of nowhere and changed his life. He could still hear the squealing of his brakes, could still smell the rubbery scent in the air. He could still feel the car skidding out of control and the panic that had rushed through him like some sinister drug. He could still hear the sickening sound of metal crashing with metal.

Jill watched Burke from behind tortoiseshell-framed glasses. She intuitively knew the darkness that had just claimed him. "I never told you how sorry I was about..." Her soft voice trailed off to a thin whisper.

He glanced back over his shoulder. Their eyes connected, and he made the silent acknowledgement that Jill had probably known what he was thinking. He also noted that she did, indeed, look intelligent in glasses. And pretty. But this latter was only a borderline realization, one that was forced out of prominence by what she had just said.

"Nicole?" he supplied. It had been the first time he'd spoken his wife's name aloud in months—eighteen months. He was surprised to find that saying it hadn't been as difficult as he'd thought it would be.

Jill nodded. "Yes." Leaving her shoes where she'd kicked them off earlier, she slowly rose from the chair and walked toward Burke. "In the beginning there was such chaos, and then you left Boston..." She again allowed the thought to go unfinished. "I started to write...later...but the time never seemed right. I guess I just didn't know what to say."

"You should have. Written, I mean. I would have liked hearing from you." He smiled slightly, and, Jill thought, sadly. "You could always cheer me up."

"Then I should have written. I'm sorry." What he'd said touched her. And pleased her, so that her heart glowed with a little bit of warmth. In that moment, she also realized just what a lucky lady Nicole Rawlins had been. For Burke's sake, she hoped his wife had realized that, too.

They were now standing side by side, both staring out the window and into the ebony night. Jill had eased her hands into the deep pockets of her black dress, and with both Burke's hands now bedded in his own pockets, they looked like an artist's rendition of man and woman in contemplation.

"I went a little crazy in the beginning," he said, speaking to her, himself, no one. "I thought I was going to die. And then, when I didn't, and I realized that I wasn't going to, that it just wasn't going to be that easy, I really did go crazy. That's when I started drinking." He took a deep breath and slowly exhaled. "But I couldn't get drunk enough to forget."

She angled her head toward him, admitting that the love he'd just spoken of was the kind she wanted in her life. "Is that when you started running?"

His eyes coasted to hers. It never crossed his mind to question how she knew of this athletic release. "Yeah."

"And did it help?"

"I've survived with reasonable sanity. I probably have the running to thank for that." He then offered her a glimpse of his soul and, had he been asked why he was doing so, he could only have said that it seemed right. "The nights were the worst. There's something about the night and grief that can bring the strongest man to his knees."

The words tore at Jill's heart. "I'm sorry," she whispered. It was a blanket apology, covering everything from the unfairness of Nicole Rawlins's death to the fact that life could be harsh enough to bring a man, a strong man like Burke Rawlins, a deserving man like Burke Rawlins, to his knees.

Their eyes lingered with not even a hint of awkwardness.

Her eyes were full of sympathy, Burke thought. Not pity, the way some people's were. But sympathy and understanding. Caring. And they were a shade of blue, a robin's egg, sky blue, that quite took one's breath away.

Burke's eyes were full of suffering, Jill thought. As though he had battled with too many warrior nights. But there was also a steely suggestion somewhere in the moss-green depths that the nights had not been the final victor.

Small. The word scurried through Burke's mind. He hadn't realized just how short she was. But maybe she seemed so short now because she wasn't wearing her shoes.

He was so tall, Jill thought. Why had she never realized how tall he was? Or was it because she stood only in her stocking feet?

She looked tired, he thought. As if she needed someone, some man, to take her in his arms and hold her.

He looked tired, she thought. Body tired. Soul tired. Suddenly, she had the urge to slip her arms around his waist, lay her cheek to his chest and tell him that everything was going to be all right.

The spell broke for each of them at nearly the same instant. Jill actually took a step back from Burke. And wondered what in the world had provoked her last crazy thought.

"I think I'll call it quits for the day," she said, the words superimposed on his, "Let's wrap it up."

They both smiled. He pulled his hands from his pockets; she pulled hers from her pockets. Crossing the room, she slipped into her shoes. Burke rolled down the sleeves of his shirt and drew on his jacket. In seconds they were walking down the hall toward the elevator. A quick ride downward and they were crossing the main lobby, their footsteps a hollow tattoo in the empty building.

"This is my first weekend back in civilization," Burke said, his voice cutting through the silence that had existed since leaving the office.

Jill heard the uncertainty, maybe the touch of fear, that tinged the statement. "Listen," she said, "my sister is having me over for dinner tomorrow night. If you'd like to come, you're welcome to. She wouldn't mind at all."

Burke didn't hesitate. "No, thanks. I think the beast is still too savage to take out."

"My sister teaches first grade," Jill said with a twinkle in her blue eyes. "She could have you tamed in two minutes."

Burke smiled, and there was a gentle crescenting of his full lips. "She probably could, but I'm going to pass anyway. But thanks. I appreciate the offer."

"Any time," Jill replied.

They reached the front door and exchanged good nights with the security guard, who let them out of the building. Once on the sidewalk, the March-night wind, still cold from its recent acquaintance with winter, sent them a chill welcome. Burke turned up the collar of his jacket; Jill huddled deeper into the light coat she'd thrown on over her dress.

"Could I give you a lift?" she asked, nodding in the direction of the car parked only a few feet away at the curb. She always left the car in the underground garage, but the attendant, who went off duty at seven, insisted on bringing hers out front if she was working late. It was a safety precaution and convenience she appreciated greatly.

"No, thanks. I have an apartment in the Prudential Center."

Jill suspected that the apartment, which was only blocks away, had been carefully selected because of its nearness. The rumor about his refusing to drive was obviously true.

"I need the walk," he added.

"Or run?"

He held up his briefcase. "With this? Are you kidding?" The running would probably come later, he thought. If the walls of the apartment insisted once more on closing in on him. If the past insisted on closing in.

"Well, good night," she said.

"Good night."

"See you Monday."

"Yeah."

He waited until she had unlocked the car door before starting off down the street. He had gone but a short distance when he turned and called, "Hey, McClain?"

She hesitated in her descent into the car. And looked up.

"I like your glasses."

Seconds passed. Jill's heart beat a strange rhythm. Which she ignored. "Yeah, I know," she finally called back. "They make me look intelligent." She knew that he was smiling because there was a wave of warmth undulating in the cool air. Then, just as suddenly as he'd spoken, he turned and moved off into the night. Jill watched as step after step took him farther and farther away. Burke was a solitary man intent on the solitary mission of surviving. She started to call after him, but stopped herself because she had absolutely no idea what she wanted to say. Instead, she crawled in behind the wheel, started the engine and pulled away from the curb.

In a very real sense, she felt as solitary as Burke and, though she was grieving over the loss of no one, the fact that she'd never had a beloved someone to grieve over was grief enough. Curiously, she suddenly felt as if she were on the same lonely mission of survival.

"WHAT'S THE SURPRISE?"

"Well, hello to you, too," Jill teased the next evening as she stepped through the screen door her sister held open and into the living room of a small, modest, yellow frame house. "Speaking of surprises," she added, ditching her purse on the blue, pink and yellow floral sofa and setting a bottle of white wine on the nearby kitchen cabinet, "I see you have one of your own." At Mary McClain's blank look, Jill jerked her head in the direction of the front yard. "The For Sale sign has a Sold plastered across it."

"Oh, yeah," Mary said in a voice that her fiancé proclaimed sounded like a husky June Allyson with a cold. Invariably when he said it, more-youthful Jill feigned ignorance and teased, "Who's June Allyson?" "The realtor came by yesterday afternoon and said it looked as if we had a buyer. A couple from Ballard Vale."

"That's appropriate," Jill said, thinking of the small upstate town of Shawsheen, only miles from Ballard Vale. Shawsheen had been their home until their parents' death. Only weeks afterward, Mary had moved the two of them to Boston. It was only as an adult that Jill had realized what courage it must have taken for Mary, who'd lived all of her life in a small town, to make that decision.

Mary smiled. "Yeah, I guess it is appropriate, isn't it?"

"Why did you move us from Shawsheen to Boston?" Jill asked as if she'd only this moment thought to pose the question.

The other woman's smile edged away, and she slipped into the kitchen and busied herself at the sink scraping carrots under running water. "Because I didn't want you growing up with a small-town heart."

Jill followed, plucked up a coin-shaped piece of carrot and plopped it into her mouth. She crunched down. "What's a small-town heart?"

"An unforgiving heart. A self-righteous heart. The result of a narrow worldview. I wanted you to see more of life, more of people. I didn't want you inhibited, constricted."

Jill frowned at the intensity of her sister's tone, and at the severity of the remark. Both seemed out of character. "Were you so inhibited and constricted in Shawsheen?"

Mary looked back over her shoulder and laughed, quickly, brittlely. "Of course not. You just asked why we moved and I told you. Besides," she added with a let's-change-tack hastiness, "I wanted to get you into a more progressive school system. With your IQ, I wanted the best education you could get." Mary McClain's bright brown eyes danced with a sudden teasing light that negated the seriousness of moments before. "I wanted you to go to law school, to be a rich and famous lawyer, so I could borrow lots of your money. Will you stay out of those carrots?'' she fussed, swatting at the hand pilfering yet another.

"When you borrow money is the day pigs fly, and I guess I don't have to ask what's for dinner," Jill replied, knowing without any doubt that the meal would be her favorite—pot roast with potatoes and carrots, followed by a banana-nut cake.

"I guess you don't."

"So when are you moving out?" Jill asked, rummaging through a kitchen drawer in search of a corkscrew.

"I told the realtor that I couldn't possibly move out until the wedding."

"Antiquated, Victorian—these are just two words that come to mind. Did it ever occur to you, Miss Misfit of the twentieth century, to just shack up with Rob until the wedding? Where's the corkscrew?" she added, then tailgated that request with, "And for goodness' sake, stop blushing."

"I am not antiquated—two drawers over—and I'll blush if I want to." And indeed that was just what she was doing. Just what Jill knew that she would be doing. A faint rosiness had seeped into a complexion that wore only the most minimal of makeup. With her sable-brown hair cut in a short blow-dry style, her big brown eyes practically filling her oval face and embarrassment splotching her cheeks, she, at fifty, looked in many ways younger than Jill. Jill often thought it was her sister's innate naïveté that made her appear so youthful, made her appear as if she were a throwback to a time that was simpler, a time less sophisticated and more pure. Then again, it might have been the hundreds of freckles sprinkled across her face. While Jill had a smattering of the tiny dark dots, Mary had a spill of them.

The two women were grinning at each other, as they spent most of their time together doing. Suddenly, Mary hurled a dishcloth at her. "You! You deliberately try to shock me."

"You wanted me to be uninhibited," Jill pointed out as she dodged the airborne cloth. It landed on the meticulously clean, but old, fruit bowl that had been their mother's. "Even moved me from Shawsheen so I would be."

"Maybe we should have stayed a little longer."

Sighting the corkscrew, Jill eased to one of four tall stools lining the wooden kitchen bar. She began to uncork the wine. "So where is this guy you won't move in with without benefit of ceremony?"

"Grocery store. I didn't have lettuce for the salad. Or more to the point, I had some, but was past its peak. Way past." The carrots were arranged by heaping handfuls into the broth simmering around the pot roast and the lid returned to the cooker. Mary slid to the stool beside Jill. Her jean-clad knee scraped against Jill's jean-clad knee. Both wore blue-trimmed sneakers that could have been identical. "He should be back any minute. So tell me, what's your surprise?"

Jill poured white wine into two glasses. "It's a doozy."

"Let me be the judge of that. You were the one who told me the new hairdresser was a doozy."

"Well, he was . . . is."

"He's a maniac with scissors. Would you just look at this?" Mary ran her fingers through her short hair in a way guaranteed to muss, had not the style been so short. This was a conversation that had transpired more than once in the past two weeks, and each player knew her part.

"It looks wonderful, Mary. Very chic. Very today."

"Very short," Mary supplied.

"Rob loves it," Jill pointed out in her favor.

"Why I let a woman who never gets her hair cut recommend . . ."

"I get it trimmed," Jill said, hand-tossing a russet-blond strand back over her shoulder as she spoke. Tonight, her hair fell somewhere between straight and curly, and one side was bunched back from her face with a currently fashionable clip.

". . . a hairdresser defies all logic," Mary mumbled to the end.

"Do you want to hear my surprise?"

"Of course I do. I'm just warning you that it better be a better doozy than the last."

"It is. Trust me." The self-satisfied smile that always seemed the forerunner of the statement appeared on Jill's lips. "I've been assigned to the *Stroker* case."

There was a pause as the words registered. Mary's hand tightened around the bowl of the glass. "The *Stroker* case? Isn't that the one where there's . . . an illegitimate child?"

"It's a lot more complex than that, but yes, there is an illegitimacy." As invariably happened, Jill's enthusiasm took over and her blue eyes began to sparkle. "Oh, Mary, every lawyer in town would love to sink his teeth into this one. There's going to be new ground covered, precedents set and possibly some restructuring of women's rights. Basically, it's a divorce case between a rich couple. We're talking mega-megabucks here. We're talking the old money of Louisburg Square," she said with the proper Bostonian grandeur to her voice.

"The fascinating part is that Mrs. Stroker is suing for damages that she claims are the result of the emotional and physical abuse she suffered at the hands of Mr. Stroker. She claims that he pressured her, even by rape, to get pregnant five times in the six years of their marriage. She miscarried each time. She claims he was obsessed with the idea of having an heir—which she never produced. And now, in walks a servant who claims he fathered her four-year-old child. I'm telling you, Mary, the case is fascinating. Absolutely fas—" She stopped, aware that Mary McClain was not displaying the delight she'd expected. In fact, Mary looked only shades away from grim. "I thought you'd be pleased."

The disappointment-drenched words sobered like coffee administered to a drunk. "Oh, honey, I am pleased," Mary said, covering Jill's hand with her own. "Of course I'm pleased. Why wouldn't I be pleased?"

"I don't know, but you seemed . . ." Jill couldn't find the right word. Nothing as strong as upset would suffice, yet there was some negative emotion there. Troubled? Yes,

Mary had seemed troubled at the mention of the *Stroker* case.

"What I seemed is outlandishly proud of you," she said in an effusive voice. "And not one thing less or more. I was just surprised that a case I've read so much about was yours. Usually I don't know anything about your work."

The brown eyes staring at Jill so honestly persuaded her in a matter of blinks that she had imagined Mary's reaction. What sense did it make, anyway, for Mary to be uncomfortable with a case that in no way concerned her? And surely she did have a right to be surprised at her little sister being assigned to it. After all, the little sister had been.

"I'm working on the case with Burke Rawlins," Jill announced, her enthusiasm back.

"Burke? Is he back?"

Jill smiled. "Yeah. Came in day before yesterday."

"How is he?"

"Better than he thinks he is. And he looks wonderful. Tanned, trim. He's been running a lot." Jill brought the glass to her lips and drank. "I tried to get him to come with me tonight."

"He should have." There was all the sincerity in the world in the remark. Though Mary had never met Burke, his tragedy had touched her the way it had many others.

Jill shrugged in that kind of nebulous way that really meant nothing. "I don't think he's ready to start socializing." Drawing the glass once more to her lips, she considered the subject of Burke. The result was she wondered what he was doing at that very moment. Eating? Running? Or maybe just staring at the four walls of a lonely apartment? The last thought appealed to some crazy urge in her to comfort. She quickly told herself that Burke did not need her comfort. Some part of her argued that maybe the need was hers. Maybe she'd reached the point in her life where she needed to comfort someone. Maybe she just needed to be needed. Not as a client needed a lawyer, but as a man needed a woman.

A sudden rattling sound at the front door shattered Jill's subtly disturbing thoughts. "There he is," she said at the sight of her future brother-in-law.

Rob Sheffield stood exactly one-quarter inch above six feet, had a head of sun-bleached blond hair that insisted on curling no matter how short it was cut and had coffee-brown eyes that were always smiling. At fifty-one, he had been divorced for ten years, a chemical engineer for twenty-three and for thirteen months on Jill's list of the most likable men she'd ever met. She had placed him on the list within thirty seconds of meeting him—and for lots of reasons, the most specific being that he was wildly, madly, unequivocally in love with Mary McClain.

"Hey, whatcha know, Blue Eyes?" As he passed Mary, a sack in his arms, he brushed a kiss to her lips. "Hi, babe."

"Hi," Mary returned, slipping from the stool and heading for the ringing phone.

"How are you?" Rob asked, scooping a now-standing Jill into his arms for a quick bear hug.

"Great," she answered, banding her arms about his waist. As she did so, she thought that Rob was tall, but not as tall as Burke. If she were to hug Burke this way, her head would rest whole inches from his chin. And Burke's shoulders seemed just a little wider. Maybe a lot wider. Maybe... Prudently, she let her speculations be corralled by Rob's next words.

"How's the law?"

"Never better. I'm working on the *Stroker* case."

Rob's eyes lit up. "Isn't that the one getting all the publicity?"

Jill's lips peaked as expected. "The same."

"Congratulations."

"Thanks." Rob's reaction was confirmation to Jill that she had been mistaken about Mary's initial response to the same news.

Rob Sheffield's attention was suddenly diverted from Jill to her sister, who was resetting an earring as she walked back to the kitchen. "Who was it, babe?"

Mary shrugged. "They hung up. Wrong number, I guess." As she passed by the grocery sack, she peeked in. "Do you two know anything about making a salad?"

Rob looked over at Jill with a feelings-crushed expression. "Do you have the feeling our culinary reputations have just been besmirched?"

"I do," Jill answered in a voice deeply aggrieved.

Rob turned back to his fiancée. "Do we know anything about making a salad? Do we know anything about making a salad?" He glanced once more toward Jill and, with a questioning expression that caused her lips to dance, asked, "Do we know anything about making a salad?"

Jill forced her lips into a stern line. "Of course we do."

"Of course we do," he repeated confidently as he started to rummage through the sack. He produced a couple of avocados, which he tossed in rapid-fire succession to Jill. She caught both. He then pulled out the lettuce. This he clumsily held in his right hand as one might a football. He raised his arm and took aim. He also began a sportscaster's coverage of the event. "It's Sheffield at the fifty-eight, positioning for a long, high-flying pass to McClain. And there it goes." The lettuce went sailing through the air in a high arc. "It's high. It's inside. It's aimed straight for McClain's talented hands, which are reportedly insured for $1.95. Sports fans, it looks like it's going to be a..." Jill caught the lettuce right before it struck a glass of wine; both Jill and Rob scrunched up their faces. "Touchdown!"

"All right!" Jill cried, made a few crazy steps of a victory dance and raised the lettuce in preparation for spiking the "football."

Mary cleared her throat.

Both Rob and his accomplice looked toward the sound. Jill slowly lowered her arm, while Rob uttered the words that produced a round of giggles from both women. "Oh, hi, coach," he said. "You know how to make a salad?"

Twenty minutes later, the salad was finished. It was at that point that the phone again rang.

"I'll get it while you two ogle your creation," Mary said, starting for the phone and automatically removing her earring.

"I think the composition is interesting," Rob commented, having now assumed the pompous role of art critic.

"Very definitely," Jill agreed, gazing down at the colorful bowl of sliced, diced and torn vegetables. "Don't you feel that the artist's statement is a pungent retort to those who would ask, 'Can you make a salad?'"

"I quite agree, Doctor of Art McClain. It's a subtle, yet unmistakably bold, statement of confidence. It says not only that I can make a salad, but that I can make a damned good one."

"I couldn't agree more. I..." Jill's eyes had strayed to her sister, the suddenly, pale-as-chalk face of her sister. "Mary?"

Rob Sheffield swiveled toward his fiancée.

"Mary?" Jill repeated.

The sound of her name seemed to drag Mary McClain from some dark planet. She was still clutching the phone to her ear with both hands. "What?" she murmured, her eyes vacantly meeting those of her sister.

"What's the matter?" Jill asked, taking instinctive steps forward. Rob did the same.

Their motion seemed to bring the room back into focus. "Nothing. Nothing," Mary repeated, dropping the receiver back into its cradle as if the plastic had suddenly grown hot. Her hand trembled slightly. "It was another wrong number. Just someone trying to sell aluminum siding." She appeared unaware of the contradiction in the two statements. "Well, if you two are through admiring your work, let's eat." She moved into the kitchen with all the zeal of an advancing freight train.

Rob caught her arm and turned her around. Their eyes met. "You sure you're all right?"

"Certainly I'm all right," Mary replied, her eyes never wavering, though she quickly pulled away and yanked the lid off the pot roast. "Jill, you put the salad on the table and Rob, you pour the wine."

Rob and Jill exchanged momentary puzzled looks before complying with Mary's orders.

The meal couldn't have been a more normal experience. Mary ate, talked, even laughed at all the appropriate times. They toasted Jill's involvement in the *Stroker* case, an involvement Mary seemed genuinely pleased with, and even made plans to have dinner together the following Saturday night. Once or twice, Jill caught Rob looking at Mary as if he were trying to decide if he'd only imagined her reaction earlier. It was an exercise in looking and judging that Jill could relate to, for she was doing the same thing. She concluded, as once before that night, that she'd simply misread her sister.

"I've gotta go," Jill announced a little before ten. She uncoiled herself from the sofa and reached for her handbag. "I know you two want to neck."

Mary did not give her usual groan and blush.

"Thought you never were going to leave," Rob teased, squeezing his bride-to-be's shoulders.

Still Mary didn't groan or blush—a fact Jill noted, just as she had noted her sister's quiet preoccupation all during the program they'd watched on TV.

"Are you sure you're all right?" Jill asked once more at the door.

"I'm positive," Mary replied with a weak smile. "I think I'm coming down with a cold, is all. We've had a rash of them this week at school."

The two sisters stared at one another, Jill searching for truth, Mary challenging contradiction.

"You take care of yourself," Jill said at last, then looked up at the man who stood behind Mary, his arms curling around her waist and drawing her back against him. "Better yet, you take care of her."

"You bet. Good night."

A few more words and kisses to cheeks and Jill was crunching down the cool grass and pulling open the car door.

"Bye," she called over the vehicle's closed sunroof.

"Bye," Mary returned and waved.

Seconds later, the couple watched as the car disappeared down the street.

Rob's arms tightened and his lips brushed Mary's ear with a worried, whispered question. "You okay, babe?"

Mary nodded, and nestled the back of her head deeper into his chest. It was only the night that saw the lone tear escape from the corner of her eye.

SIGHING DEEPLY, BURKE rested the back of his hand across his closed eyes. He should have taken Jill up on her offer of dinner at her sister's house, he thought for at least the dozenth time. If he had known how long and lonely his first Saturday back in civilization was going to be, he'd have jumped at the chance to protect his sanity. As it was, that thread-thin item seemed about to snap.

Burke rolled to his side and allowed the covers to slip to his waist. Absently, he trailed his fingers through the dark hair matting his chest and adjusted his hips to a more comfortable position. The feel of the soft clean sheets should have been lulling to his tired bare body, but instead, they curiously teased at his senses, reminding him that he was a man, a man who'd been a very long time without a woman. Increasingly, this fact was forcing its way into his consciousness and each time that it did, he rejected it—with guilt for having let it intrude at all, and with desperation because he knew that there was really no way, short of contradicting nature's design, that he could stop its intrusion.

With his usual dosage of guilt and desperation, he rejected the thought once more, replacing it with thoughts of how miserable the day had been. He'd wakened to a deafening silence and the threat of the eternally long day that loomed before him. After forcing himself to finish unpacking, he met his father for lunch, then stopped at the supermarket on the way back to the apartment. The act of grocery shopping had been, as it always was, depressing. It implied a domesticity he didn't feel. He really didn't live anywhere, and the fact that he had to go on eating, that he had to go on performing these stupid little duties just to survive irritated him, like back-rubbing the fur of a cat.

Survival.

There was that word again, Burke thought. But the truth was that he really did want to survive. He didn't want to want to, but he did. He had discovered that he couldn't change that aspect of human nature anymore than... anymore than a man could change basic physical needs. He again held the subject of sexuality at arm's length and forced his mind back to the topic of survival.

Because he had wanted to survive, he'd spent the rest of the afternoon and early evening working on the *Stroker* case. When he'd exhausted that, and himself, he'd tried to watch TV... but failed. Finally, the emptiness of the apartment had driven him back onto the streets. He'd run and run and run and, when his body had refused to go a step farther, he'd returned to the apartment. There, he'd showered and tumbled into bed. And proceeded to be restlessly awake.

He should have accepted Jill's offer.

Jill.

A slight smile curved his lips. She could always make him smile. She was a small bundle of irrepressible energy. Small... She was smaller than he'd remembered. Burke shifted and nuzzled his head into the softness of the pillow. He gave a quiet sigh as sleep stepped closer. She was small, but... womanly. His eyelids shut. And her hair was like a blaze of scarlet fire in a yellow summer sun. Her eyes... they were a man-tempting blue... blue... blue... Sleep danced around him with its foggy reality until thoughts were nothing but a surreal jumble.

Contacts...

Glasses... glasses... intelligent looking in glasses...

Jill... Jill... Ji—

Burke's breathing filled the room with its soft, contented cadence. For the first time in eighteen months, he had fallen asleep thinking of something, someone, other than his dead wife.

CHAPTER THREE

MARY MCCLAIN came down with a cold.

That fact greatly relieved Jill and persuaded her that her imagination had been overly vivid. The phone call on Saturday night had obviously been exactly what Mary had said: a wrong number. That issue settled in her mind, Jill was free to turn her full attention to the impending *Stroker* case. And she did, with Burke at her side, Monday night, until the wearying, wee-morning hour of one o'clock. They both had then crawled home to beds that, despite their fatigue, had seemed large and lonely.

Tuesday they again met with their client, Alysia Stroker, a women of tremendous integrity, average intelligence and minimal beauty. She had, however, a combination of attributes that blended into an attractive and compelling dignity. Jill wasn't surprised Wednesday morning to see the socialite's name once more splashed across the front page of the *Boston Herald*. She was surprised, however, to see that both she and Burke, as her lawyers, had been given inches of copy in the article. Apparently, anyone associated with the case was deemed newsworthy.

When Jill arrived at work later that morning, she found Burke in a quiet mood. She wondered if it had anything to do with the fact that the article had briefly, and tactlessly, she thought, mentioned Nicole Rawlins's accident. She didn't inquire, and Burke didn't offer to share.

"Don't tell me you two are working late again," Andrew Rawlins called from the doorway of Burke's office. It was a quarter to seven Wednesday evening, and two pairs of bleary eyes immediately glanced upward. As she had a countless number of times in the past hour, Jill blinked over sandy-feeling contacts.

"Hi, Dad. What're you doing here this late?"

"Finishing up some paperwork," the elder Rawlins said, stepping into the room and seating himself in the chair beside Jill.

She watched him cross one leg over the other in a way that ran the risk of being termed effeminate, but fell far short of it and into an area simply called grandly elegant. In truth, Andrew Rawlins, with his snow-white hair and Brooks Brothers suit, looked like a male model in search of a camera. As did his son, Jill thought, her eyes coasting to the man behind the desk. With Burke, however, the pose was altogether different. He sat negligently back in the leather chair with his right foot wedged in the space created between the desk and an open top drawer. His leg was bent at the knee and leaned masculinely outward, allowing a clear view of the taut muscles that resided beneath the oxford-gray pants. His sleeves were rolled up to reveal a dark dusting of hair, a replica of the brown coils spilling from the vee of his unbuttoned shirt. He looked both athletically fit and superbly attractive. And sexy?

Jill deliberately let her attention be swallowed up by the conversation.

"You look tired," the older man was saying. "I'd prefer you two not to be comatose when you try the case."

Burke's lips worked ever-so-slowly into a slight smile. "Jill and I are going to take turns being conscious in court."

The smile, the late-day teasing resulting from fatigue, was infectious. "To be honest," Jill said, "I'm praying hard to get fired."

"Never, Ms McClain, have your chances been so unlikely," Andrew Rawlins teased back. "How is it going?" he asked, his tone suddenly serious.

"Okay. Fine," came the two answers that managed to merge into one. Briefly, blue eyes met with green.

He does look tired, she thought.

Her eyes look glazed, Burke thought. *And she keeps rubbing her left one. It must hurt. Are the contacts...*

"Have you settled on a strategy yet?" the senior Rawlins asked.

Burke dropped his gaze from Jill's face at the same time he unwedged his foot and dropped it to the floor. Looking outside, he noted that the first star of evening was born in a blaze of silvered fury. He straightened and tossed the legal pad in his lap onto the desk. "We're going to take full advantage of the fact that Massachusetts allows the prosecution of husbands who rape their wives."

Andrew Rawlins nodded approval. "And can you win with that tactic?"

"There's no question in our minds," Jill said, "that Stroker raped his wife, if you define rape as sexual intercourse without consent. We'll also charge that his obsession for an heir took the form of other physical and emotional abuse."

"The rape is her word against his," Burke added, "but we have plenty of corroborative evidence concerning physical and emotional abuse—friends, servants, whose depositions we're getting."

"I repeat," Andrew Rawlins persisted, "can you win with that tactic?"

"I think so," Burke replied. "Especially since our client is seeking a fair settlement rather than the imprisonment of her husband."

"I think we have a better-than-fighting chance," Jill agreed.

Andrew Rawlins nodded again. "How does *Rideout* versus *Rideout* help you?" he asked, referring to a well-known rape-within-marriage case.

"Not at all," Jill said. "The verdict was in favor of the husband. Their cohabitation at the time of the rape was the determining factor."

"Mrs. Stroker claims she and her husband were estranged at the time of one of the rapes," Burke supplied.

"And there's a New Jersey man serving time right now for raping his estranged wife."

"Excellent," the senior Rawlins said. "By the way, rumor has it that Judge O'Halleron's going to preside."

Both Jill and Burke groaned.

"Ole Banging Judge O'Halleron, huh?" Burke commented. "You'd think he'd retire."

Judge Timothy O'Halleron, baldheaded, full bearded, and florid faced, had the reputation of being the oldest, the most conservative and the most no-nonsense judge seated on any Massachusetts bench. So strict was he that his gavel was always in a state of motion, which had earned him the title "banging judge."

"I also hear that the mother of the illegitimate child will be bringing her own suit on behalf of the daughter later," the silver-haired Rawlins added, asking on the heels of the remark, "What about a court date?"

"Nothing's been set," Jill answered.

"Speaking of calendar dates," Andrew Rawlins said, now pointedly addressing his son, "have you made plans to attend the Bar Association dinner?"

Jill could feel the web-fine tension that suddenly wove around Burke.

"I really don't think I'm ready—"

"It's for a worthwhile charity," his father interrupted. "The Cancer Society—"

"I have no quarrel with the cause," Burke, too, interrupted. "I just don't want to—"

"You really ought to go, Burke." There was a paternal command in the older man's voice, along with an understanding look in his eyes that said, "Trust me in this, Son. There's never going to be a good time to pick up the threads of your life."

In the short interim filled with the two men's stares, Jill wished that she wasn't privy to such a private conversation. She also wondered what Burke's decision would be. And, if he went, would he take some—

"Why don't you two go together?" Andrew Rawlins said, machete-slashing through Jill's thoughts.

Her eyes flew to Burke's. Nothing there gave any hint as to what he was feeling.

"Or am I being too presumptuous to think you don't already have plans?" the elder Rawlins asked Jill.

She dragged her eyes from Burke to the man beside her. "No . . . no, sir. No plans other than attending the dinner." Though the event was still two weeks off, she'd had her ticket for months, had even already turned down, politely, of course, Charles Evans's offer to take her.

"You two are already linked together on the case—you can thank the ever-scavenging press for that. It would be perfectly natural to show up at the dinner together."

Jill knew what Andrew Rawlins was trying to do. He was trying to assure Burke that no one would misunderstand his being seen with his law partner. Which was true, of course. Only it strangely hurt to be considered a safe nonentity. Or did it just hurt to be considered a safe nonentity in Burke's life? Not wanting to answer that question, she glanced back at Burke . . . and waited patiently for him to say something. He didn't. He just stared at her. In the end, social decorum demanded Jill answer. "It's all right with me. Why don't I swing by and pick you up?"

Still Burke said nothing.

It was Andrew Rawlins who did. "Good. Then it's settled." With that, he stood. "I'm heading home. Why don't you two do the same?"

"Yes, sir," Jill said.

"Good night," Burke called after his father.

For a solid quarter-minute after the door closed, neither spoke. Except with work-tired eyes.

"I'm sorry Dad boxed you into a corner."

"He didn't."

"He did."

"He didn't!"

"McClain, you're in a corner."

"Rawlins," she said, gesturing around, "it looks like I'm in the middle of the room."

"You're in a corner. Daddy insisted that you take his little boy to the prom."

Both were now grinning. The masculine smile faded, however.

"I'm giving you a chance to back out."

The feminine smile faded as well, as she realized the truth of her reply: "I don't want to back out."

"There isn't some great guy waiting for your yes?"

"Actually, the only guy that asked me I said no to. Charles Evans."

"Evans? Is he your type?"

"Obviously not. I turned him down."

Burke gave a facial expression that indicated the logic of her answer. "Okay, this is your next-to-the-last chance to tell me to get lost."

"Next-to-the-last?"

"Now it's your last."

"I'll pick you up about seven-thirty, Rawlins. Now, what do you say let's finish up here and get eight hours of sleep like the rest of the world?"

"Suits me." He reached for his pad; she reached for a book. "Hey, McClain?"

She glanced up. "Yeah?"

"You getting me a corsage?"

A playful pencil sailed across the desk.

A few minutes later, and in regard to the last thing on the day's agenda, Burke asked, "You want to give the opening or closing remarks?"

"Opening," Jill said, blinking her left eye and automatically sending fingers up to rub it. "No, closing. No, opening." She blinked, rubbed, blinked again.

"With that kind of decisiveness, I'm certain our opposition is sleeping nights," Burke said, adding with a frown, "Is something wrong with your eye?"

"What?"

"Your eye. You keep blinking it."

"I think my contact's slipping."

"Slipping? They do that?"

"Uh-huh. You want to hand me the compact out of my handbag?"

"Where's your handbag?"

"On the floor. Over there. By the desk."

Burke reached for the rectangular piece of black leather and started rummaging through its contents in a way that was intimately familiar, though neither seemed aware of the fact.

"You want to hurry?" she asked, her eye now entirely closed and pain pinching her face.

Burke glanced up, his hands continuing to search for something round, something compacty feeling. "What's wrong?"

"It just slid into my forehead."

"Your forehead!" he said in a tone very much as the *Titanic*'s captain said "Iceberg!"

"Don't panic, Rawlins. Just get me a mirror."

Mumbling something crude, he simultaneously plunged into panic and through the purse's contents—a tube of lipstick, a wallet, Clorets and a chain full of jangling keys. "Well, I've at least solved the mystery of the missing continent of Atlantis. It's in this damned purse!"

"You're panicking," Jill accused, then moaned as the lens slid even deeper under her eyelid. "Hurry."

"Why in the world anyone would want to wear contacts is beyond me." He flipped over a checkbook and riffled through torn tickets to the Boston Philharmonic. "Why anyone wants to poke things in her eyes, why anyone..."

"Shut up."

"Here."

"Thanks. Can you hold it? There. No, up more. There."

Burke now stood between her and the desk, his hands trying to hold the oval of glass still. Jill, her eyelid pulled upward, was touching the visible edge of the contact with a tentative tip. The bulk of the lens did, indeed, appear to have drifted into her forehead.

"Does it hurt?" Burke asked, mimicking her grimace.

Jill gave him a withering look out of her good eye.

"Okay. Stupid question. My God," he said as she stretched the eyelid farther to reveal raw, pink tissue, "I've seen surgeries that involved less!"

"Got it," Jill said, sighing and withdrawing the culprit on the end of her index finger. She stored it in its case and glanced back up at Burke. He was still standing before her, still watching her.

"Your eye looks awful."

"It feels awful."

"Here, let me see." As naturally as the sky outside was darkening for evening, Burke slipped his finger to Jill's chin and tilted her head upward. "You ought to use some dro—" Their eyes met. His warm breath flooded across her cheek; her warm skin penetrated the layers of his loneliness to reach his starving senses.

Warm breath.

Warm skin.

Warm feelings.

Feelings that were too warm.

Burke was suddenly very much aware that he was man, and she a woman. It was the same basic realization that Jill had just made.

Dropping his eyes, he jerked away his finger as though her chin burned hot. He stepped back and cleared his husky throat. "You ought to use some drops when you get home."

He would have denied that something had happened between them, but denying the fact would have given the moment, the issue, more substance than he could deal with.

The removal of his hand from her chin left Jill with a feeling of abandonment. The reason why was inexplicable. And totally unexpected. It was also disturbing. As was the strange way her body had felt at his touch—as if everything feminine within her had awakened from a long sleep. "I will," she said, hastily stuffing compact and contact case back into her handbag. Refusing to look his way, she stood. "Well, I'm headed home."

Minutes later, as she walked alone from the building—Burke had insisted on finishing something she thought had already been finished—Jill felt it necessary to deny that anything had just happened between her and Burke. She couldn't help but secretly wonder, though, if for the first time in her life, honest Jill McClain wasn't lying to herself.

Lies.

As Jill left the office, Mary McClain sat staring at Jill's name in the paper and pondering the insidious power of lies. They were always such fragile untruths in the beginning, she thought, but as the years honed and tempered them, they took on a strength, mantled themselves in a force that quite literally gave them a life of their own. A dark life that instinctively fought to survive by refusing to let itself be destroyed in the act of revelation.

It had been her intention from the very beginning to tell Jill the truth. When she was old enough to understand. When she had lived long enough to know that right and wrong never dressed solely in the blunt shades of black and white. But each day had passed, the lie still intact, until it had been too late. The lie had begun to breathe life. And even if it had not, how could you tell the most innately honest person you knew that her life had always been a lie?

You didn't, Mary thought. Instead, you buried the secret deep, sharing it with no one but the night.

No one.

Yet somehow someone knew. Some strange male voice on the telephone knew. Someone knew her secret!

Mary forced her breath to a more even pace, forced herself to desert questions of who and why. Instead, she clung to the hope, feeble as it was, that the man wouldn't call again. He hadn't but that one time. Maybe if she wished hard enough, prayed hard enough...

The phone rang. Mary jumped. Stared. Listened to the loud, incessant intrusion.

Ring... ring... ring...

Please, Mary silently pleaded as she reached for the phone.

"Hello?" Her heart was beating so furiously that it roared in her ears, a roaring so loud that the male voice sounded like a whisper on the far side of a storm.

"Mary?"

Realization dawned, buckling her knees with relief. "Rob?"

"Who were you expecting, babe?"

"No one," she lied, closing her eyes and thinking on a wave of guilt that lying was the one thing she did well.

"YOU WANT A CUP of Charles River sludge?" Burke asked Friday afternoon as the hands on the clock crawled their way from four to four-thirty.

Jill glanced up and grinned. "Yeah," she said, slipping the tortoiseshell-framed glasses from her face and tossing them onto Burke's desk. She had worn glasses in lieu of contacts since Wednesday. She had no idea why, except that if pushed for an answer, she'd have to admit that it had something to do with what had happened Wednesday—not the contact getting stuck, but the feel of Burke's hand on her chin, the feel of his moist breath against her cheek, the hot feel of sexual sensations vibrating over her body. "May I use your phone?" she asked, once more ignoring what she really didn't want to deal with.

"Sure."

Quickly, Jill punched in her sister's number and sat back to listen to the long string of rings. She was on the verge of hanging up when Mary answered.

"Hello?"

"Hi. Did I drag you from outside?"

There was the briefest of hesitations. "No. I, uh ... I was in the back of the house."

"I was just calling to see if we're still on for tomorrow night." Jill smiled a silent thanks as Burke set a foam cup of thick, raven-black liquid before her. He moved toward the wall of windows where he stood sipping coffee and gazing out. Jill's eyes followed him before deliberately looking away.

"Certainly," Mary said with unfaked enthusiasm. In a world that had suddenly become unstable, the simple act of being with family was in and of itself stabilizing. Then, too, there'd been no other phone calls. That was cause aplenty for celebration. "I thought we'd broil steaks outside."

"Sounds like a great way to spend Saturday evening," Jill commented, and promised to bring a sinful chocolate dessert from her favorite bakery.

Saturday evening.

The two words echoed in Burke's mind with the overpowering force of a well-remembered and greatly-respected enemy. *My God,* he thought, *how am I going to get through another Saturday night? Another lonely Saturday night?* It had been bad enough when he could run wild and free on the shores of the Atlantic, but here in the city the misery was amplified. He was like a beast in hateful captivity. And the four walls of that apartment, the four shrinking walls of that apartment, were like a cage. With his guilt the restraining iron bars, his bitterness the...

"Burke? Burke?"

The word penetrated his misery, and he meshed his eyes with Jill's.

"Mary wants to know if you'd like to come to dinner tomorrow night." Jill's palm spread across the receiver to insure privacy. "There's no pressure. If you don't want..."

"Yes."

Surprise flickered across blue irises. A little surprise even flickered across green. Jill's eyes still on Burke's, she spoke into the phone. "He said yes. Right. I'll tell him." After a proper goodbye, she replaced the receiver. Seconds crept by. "I'll pick you up about six."

"Six o'clock," he repeated.

"Oh, Mary said to dress casual."

He nodded. "Casual."

She nodded and stupidly repeated, "Casual."

Why had things suddenly turned so awkward? As if the two of them weren't good friends? As if the two of them didn't spend almost all their time together anyway? As if either one of them could possibly misconstrue the evening as a date?

"Why don't I dress casual?" he asked, covering the awkwardness with humor.

Jill grinned, suppressing her discomfort in the same manner. "Suit yourself. I'm gonna dress casual."

HE DRESSED CASUAL.

Jill noted the fact the moment Burke pushed from the side of the apartment building and sprinted toward the car she was pulling alongside the curb. She noted it as he eased in beside her, noted it as she negotiated Saturday-evening traffic, noted it as he unfolded his long frame from the car and started up the sidewalk, she at his side, toward Mary McClain's little yellow house.

As his joggers shuffled up the steps, Jill remembered once speculating that Burke probably looked sensational in jeans. Probability had now moved into the realm of certainty in a way that would have pleased Levi Strauss. To say nothing of Mrs. Strauss's pleasure. Even the ordinary red sweatshirt, its long sleeves pushed to the middle of Burke's hairy arms, molded his chest and shoulders in a way that was arresting.

"Am I dressed too casual?" Burke asked under his breath.

"What?"

"Did I overdo the casual?" His eyes made a quick assessment of her pertly creased navy slacks, plaid shirt and white sweater carelessly but stylishly tied around her neck.

"No. You look...great." *And sexy,* some part of her mind tossed in just for the perverse heck of it.

She pulled open the screen door and motioned him into the cool, shadowy interior of the house. They were immediately met by Rob Sheffield.

"Hey, Blue Eyes," he said, swooping to plant a kiss on Jill's cheek. Without waiting for a proper introduction, he swiped his hand down his jeans leg and extended it to Burke, who had to juggle Jill's cake and his bottle of wine to reciprocate. "Hi. You must be Burke."

"Guilty," Burke replied. "And you're Rob."

"Equally guilty."

"Sorry about the hand. I've been playing in the charcoal. By the way, how do you like your steak cooked?"

"Medium obliterated," Burke replied. All three smiled.

"Hi," singsonged a low and throaty feminine voice.

"Hi," Jill called back and watched her sister advance wearing an apron that read Kiss the Cook. "Mary, I'd like you to meet Burke. Burke, Mary."

Mary McClain likewise extended her freckle-sprinkled hand, accompanied by a sincere smile. "I'm so glad you could come."

"Thank you for the invitation." Burke's lips tilted upward. "I confess you're nothing like what I was expecting. I thought you'd be..." He stalled.

"In need of Wheaties like me?" Jill supplied.

"Petite," Burke substituted with a teasing look in Jill's direction.

"I'm the only small fry in the family," Jill said. "At least as far back as the family photo albums go. Makes you wonder about genetics, doesn't it? Here, give me that," she said, taking the cake box out of Burke's arms and missing the look that sprang into Mary's eyes. "The wine's Burke's," she called out, heading for the cabinet.

There was a moment's hesitation in which Rob waited for his fiancée to take the wine bottle being offered. When she didn't, he did. "Great. We were just wondering if we had enough."

The simple movement snagged Mary's attention. She glanced up quickly, guiltily, at Rob, who was watching her with thinly disguised interest. Suddenly, she smiled as if nothing in the world could possibly be wrong and waved behind her. "Why don't we go into the backyard?"

The backyard was very much like the house: small and unpretentious, but immaculately kept. At that hour of evening, the golden sun was bidding farewell to a fair sky, and the late-March air was chilling to a pleasant nip. Charcoal squares glowed gray and red in a grill, and the refreshing sound of a tin can being drawn from chunks of ice filled the silence along with the musical chords of an eager cicada.

"Want a beer?" Rob called to Burke from the cooler.

"Yeah."

"Jill?" Rob asked.

"Later," she answered, automatically starting to help Mary with the few things that needed doing.

Although the weather was cool, they decided to eat outdoors. A red-and-white checkered cloth was draped over the redwood table, and plastic plates in assorted bright colors were laid out. As Jill wrapped corn on the cob in foil, Mary readied the steaks and put the finishing touch to a potato-and-cheese dish.

"He's nice," Mary whispered over the sound of crinkling foil.

"Uh-huh. Very."

"He's also nice looking."

Jill glanced up at her sister, then across the yard to where Burke, beer can in hand, stood talking to Rob. At that precise moment, Burke smiled at something the other man said. He also ran a hand into the back pocket of his jeans, drawing attention to the masculine curve of his hips. The gorgeous, sexy, wake-up-every-female-in-the-area curve of his hips. "Yes, he is," she admitted honestly, adding, just as candidly and for the benefit of the gleam in Mary's eyes, "We work together. Nothing more. So don't go indulging in sisterly matchmaking."

"Sometimes people who work together..."

"He's married," Jill interrupted, her gaze once more finding Burke. As he tipped the can of beer to his lips, the gold band on his finger glinted mockingly in the day's fading light. "His wife's dead, but he's still very much married." The realization hurt. She didn't ask herself why.

"And if he weren't?" Mary asked.

Jill's eyes lowered from Burke to her sister. "We're friends. We're co-workers. Nothing more." It was the truth. Totally. Completely. Wasn't it?

Seconds later, Mary carried the potato-cheese casserole into the kitchen, leaving her question behind to nag Jill. It was still nagging—what *if* Burke wasn't grieving over his wife?—when she heard a familiar male voice at her side.

"Hi."

"Hi."

"Looks good," he said of the four-layer cast-calories-to-the-wind chocolate cake that now presided in all its fattening glory from the middle of the table. He stretched, scooped a dash of chocolate icing that the baker had let drip onto the paper doily decorating the cardboard bottom, and licked it from his index finger.

Jill watched as his lips closed over the pad of his finger and sucked at the icing. She briefly saw the tip of his tongue. The sight ignited a warmth and slow-spread it throughout her body. Instantly, as if seeking sanctuary, she raised her gaze to his eyes. In the sophisticated denial pattern of human beings, she ignored what she'd just felt.

"Chocolate and beer?" she asked with an appropriate face.

"Nicole always said . . ." He stopped.

Curiously, so did Jill's heart. Just a little bit. Nicole's name was as sobering as a splash of cold water to the spirited question she'd just been entertaining. What if Burke wasn't grieving over his wife? The answer was simple: Forget it, because he is. With logical precision, everything fell back into proper perspective.

Jill smiled, understandingly, encouragingly. "What did Nicole always say?"

Burke studied the blue eyes behind the glasses. The kind, comforting blue eyes. The blue eyes he'd so closely looked into the night her contact slipped. He let the thought drift away because there was something decidedly disturbing about remembering that night. "She said my stomach had all the delicacy of a garbage disposal."

Jill's smile spread. "And here I though you athletes watched what you ate."

"Athlete? You've got to be kidding. I run purely for therapy. Usually right after I've devoured a ton of junk food."

"You don't enjoy running?"

He gave the question serious consideration. Finally, he shrugged. "Yeah, I guess I do."

"But not enough to enter the Boston Marathon next month?" she teased.

He laughed—a low, all-male sound that reminded Jill of thunder on a still, summer day. "Not on your life. I'd get trampled before the first watering hole."

"Me too."

"You run?" he asked, again bringing the beer can to his lips.

She shook her head, swaying the ponytail she'd opted for that evening. "Not really. Sometimes I feel guilty about not exercising, usually right after a TV commercial where the woman is shadow-thin and exists on crunchy cereal and workouts. Then I'll jog or run or walk for a couple of days."

"We'll run together sometime," he said.

It was a simple statement, with no underlying meaning, and yet Jill's stomach somersaulted. She told herself she was hungry. "Yeah, right out of town if we lose the *Stroker* case," she teased.

He grinned down at her. "We won't."

She grinned up at him. "You sound confident, counselor."

"I am. I'm working with the best lawyer in the city."

"Thanks," she said, pleased that Burke respected her professional capabilities.

The compliment curiously slowed time.

His eyes were a remarkable shade of green, she thought. The kind of green that probably darkened in moments of passion. And his mouth... She dragged her eyes away. "I think I'll get a beer too," she said, glancing over toward the cooler. At the sight of Mary and Rob seriously engaged in interpreting the message on her sister's apron, Jill added, "Then again, maybe I'll wait."

Burke's gaze followed Jill's, and both watched as Rob's lips moved over Mary's in a slow rhythm. When their lips disengaged, he whispered a question to which Mary shook her head a reassuring no. He then grazed her cheek with a knuckle before lowering his mouth once more to hers. Even at a distance, one could see that the kiss was gentle and sensual and begging for closer intimacy.

A longing, knife-sharp and strong, speared both Burke's and Jill's bodies. The scene reminded Burke of what he'd lost, Jill of what she'd never had. Instinctively, neither able to help it, their eyes met. But held for only seconds. Because looking into each other's eyes only seemed to intensify the painful longing.

Without any real thought to the act, Burke shoved his can of beer forward, indicating for Jill to take it. She did. And took a swallow. At the exact spot where his lips had been. The spot was warm. And malty-tasting. Like his mouth? Jill again banished the thought of his mouth, handed the can back with thanks, and leaned against the edge of the redwood table. Burke joined her. Together, they watched the stars appear in the sky.

Neither spoke for a long while.

In the deep silence, a siren wailed. Burke automatically searched out the guilt in his heart. He found it, crouching and ready to spring as always. But tonight it didn't. For once. The beauty of the night, the tranquility of the night, had momentarily diluted its power. As had the friend at his side.

"I'm glad I came tonight," he said softly.

Jill's eyes met his. Blue and green. Sincerity and sincerity. "I'm glad you did, too."

JILL'S GLASSES LAY ABANDONED on the redwood table. Fine wisps of reddish-blond hair escaped from her ponytail and wafted about her ears and neck, and her shirttail was pulled from pants that had lost their crease. Even with the chill in the evening air, even with the white sweater now encasing her arms, a thin dotting of perspiration lay across her upper lip.

Burke's hair, more golden than brown in the outside lights, slashed across his sweat-damp forehead, while his breathing was a husky rasp that sent his chest heaving in and out. A smile, which would have measured somewhere between that of a boy's and a man's, tugged at the corners of his mouth.

"So you want to play dirty, huh?" he asked.

"That's the problem, Rawlins," Jill taunted, rubbing her grass-stained palms down her pant legs. "You and Mary are playing, while Rob and I are dead serious."

That comment brought instant disagreement from Mary, instant agreement from Rob. It brought laughter from everyone.

After dinner, someone—none of the four would take credit for the idea now—had suggested touch football. As the game progressed and the close competition became heated, the mild rules of touch football had given way to a more rambunctious form of the game. In fact, Jill had just tried to trip Burke as he'd spectacularly caught Mary's pass in midair.

"C'mon, let's get down and get dirty," Jill said, adding, "This is the tiebreaker, right?"

"Right," a trio of determined voices answered.

The two teams broke into huddles, Burke and Mary whispering low, Jill and Rob gesturing in secret ways.

"Let's play ball!" Rob called, clapping his hands together.

Burke and Mary gave one more whispered exchange before getting into position.

Jill made hunkering preparations to hand the ball off to Rob, who stood behind her. Her and Burke's eyes collided, head-on and with a smiling threat.

"Ninety-two, forty-seven, hike . . ." Rob called out, only to be interrupted by the muted ringing of the telephone within the house. He straightened. "I'll get . . ."

"No!" Mary cried. Three pairs of eyes swerved toward her. The panicked electricity in the air could have made hair stand on forearms. "I mean, let it ring. If it's important, they'll call back." Seconds passed slowly. The look on Mary's face was one of pleading.

Jill and Rob exchanged quick glances, but it was as though neither could settle on an opinion. Even Burke had a look of uncertainty.

The phone rang again and again. Then it stopped.

As if on cue, as if deeply relieved, Mary smiled. "C'mon, let's play," she said, falling back into a bent position with the fingers of one hand resting on the grass.

Jill, Rob and Burke hesitated, then one by one slipped back into place. Moments later, the game was in progress and all but the score forgotten.

Jill handed off to Rob. Rob ran to the right. Jill circled to the left, right in front of Burke. He segued at the last moment and zeroed in on the ball headed straight for Jill's tummy. Her hands grabbed it. His hands grabbed it. Their feet became tangled, their legs laced.

Shrieking and giggling, Jill fell to the grass.

Laughter rumbling in his chest, Burke followed.

And in the exact time that it took the unexpected to happen, one large male body sprawled across one petite feminine form.

CHAPTER FOUR

JILL'S SENSES STUNG with awareness.

The heaviness of Burke's body. The damp, clingy feel of his sweatshirt. His heartbeat shattering against her own. She was also assailed by the sudden invasion of smells—that of crushed, spring grass merging with a masculine cologne and the more masculine fragrance of sweat. Sweat. She could almost taste—her tongue moved restlessly behind her lips—the salt in the perspiration slicking his forehead. She even fantasized that she could hear the sound of the moist bead that dripped from his temple onto her cotton shirt. Without question, she felt it, even as she felt the lower portion of his stomach laid bare against hers, even as she felt the snap of his jeans pressed against the slight mound of her womanhood.

Even as she felt the exquisite proof that he was a man.

Woman. The message registered in Burke's mind with all the speed of rain-chased lightning. He felt curves and hollows that were indisputably feminine, curves and hollows and rounded breasts that he hadn't felt against his body in so long that he had almost forgotten the feel. Almost. He also smelled perfume, something light and airy and as elementally honest as its wearer, and he heard the smothered, rushing sound of breathing. His? Hers? He didn't know. Perhaps it was a combination of both.

Realization slowly dawned that they were staring into each other's eyes, and for the briefest of unguarded moments his gaze plunged deeply into hers. She was startled by the raw, hungry need she saw in him. And by the raw, hungry need unleashed in herself. So startled that her reaction was uncensored. She wanted, more than the next beat of her heart, to shift her legs, to spread them, to welcome him between them as woman was meant to welcome man. Only some innate sense of propriety stopped her. That and the fact that she'd never felt any need so strongly, so strongly that it was frightening. And stunning. And a thousand other baffling emotions.

"Hey, are you two all right?" Rob called out in concern as he jogged toward them.

Reality slapped them with its cold hand.

Burke blinked, Jill's gaze shifted to Rob Sheffield, and, when she looked back, a curtain had fallen across Burke's eyes. They were now neutral, impersonal, blank. Hers turned a pale shade of confusion. Had she only imagined the desire in his eyes?

Pulling to his feet, and without making eye contact, Burke reached out his hand. Automatically, Jill took it. He tugged. His hand was warm—and trembly?—touching hers so briefly that she almost stumbled when he let go.

Somehow he'd managed to hold on to the football, which he now tossed to Rob.

"Your point," Burke said in a voice that sounded foggy and thick.

"Okay!" Rob hollered, spiking the ball and grabbing Jill around the waist for a crush-your-ribs hug. "Guess we showed 'em, huh, Blue Eyes?"

"Yeah," Jill said with a forced smile. Her eyes sought out Burke. He wasn't looking at her. In fact, he seemed determined not to look at her.

"You two want to play a catch-up game?" Rob asked Burke and Mary. It was Burke and Jill who answered, however.

"I don't think..."

"It's getting kinda..."

Burke's and Jill's eyes met. Fully. For just a second.

"It's getting kinda late," Jill repeated.

"C'mon, guys. It's only a little after ten," Rob pointed out.

"We've been putting in long hours at the office," Jill explained.

After a couple more protests from Rob—Jill was later to realize that Mary had seemed so distracted that she'd never once insisted they stay—they were allowed a gracious departure. Jill had promised to call soon. Burke had promised to visit again. Jill had thought his voice lacked sincerity.

The drive back possessed all the silence of eternity. Burke sat stonily, rarely glancing Jill's way. She, on the other hand, felt as fidgety as an expectant father. On the rare occasion when they did speak, there was an awkwardness in the exchange.

As they passed by the Boston Common, which by day was filled with crisp activity but by night was as quiet and still as the inside of the car, Burke said, "Your family's nice." As he spoke, a renegade image flashed through his mind. It was the image of a small, sensual woman trapped beneath him. He instantly fought the memory.

Jill gave him a quick glance. He sat, ankle squared to knee, staring straight ahead. "Yes." Firm, she thought, his body had felt firm and strong against hers.

Minutes later, as the Boston Public Garden came into and out of view, he added, "When are they getting married?" Burke remembered beautiful blue eyes drowning in his... and shook his head.

"May," Jill answered, remembering the feel of his stomach rubbing against hers, the feel of his manhood nestled snugly, promisingly, against her.

"I, uh...I appreciate the invitation tonight." He recalled soft, tempting lips resting so near his own...and breathed deeply, shattering the unwanted vision.

"Did you get enough to eat?" she asked, blatantly wondering what it would be like to kiss him.

"Are you kidding?" This time he did look at her, briefly, and grinned, slightly.

She dragged her eyes from his mouth. "Good." Which probably described the way he kissed.

"I liked the cake." *...and the way you smell...*

"I got it at this great little bakery on Newbury Street." *Would he be a tender lover? A demanding one?*

"I'll have to get the name of it. The bakery, I mean. Sometime when the old chocolate tooth is aching." *Ache, ache... God, he ached!*

"Sure. Just let me know."

"Okay."

"Okay."

End of subject. End of stupid subject.

Didn't you feel what I did! she suddenly wanted to scream. Doesn't your body still tingle with need? Sweet heaven, what's happening to me?

God, what's happening to me? Burke questioned frantically. He forced thoughts of Nicole into his mind, thoughts of Nicole's laughter, thoughts of Nicole's beauty, thoughts of Nicole making love to him.

"Burke?"

He glanced up sharply. And noticed that they were pulled alongside the curb in front of his apartment building. He noticed also that Jill was staring at his hands. He glanced down... and to the sight of his fingers turning, turning, turning, the gold wedding band. Abruptly, his fingers stilled. His eyes found hers. Even in the night's shadow and shade, she could tell that his irises darkened.

"I, uh... I enjoyed the evening," he said.

"Me too."

"Thank Mary again for me."

"I will."

Hesitation.

"Well, good night," he said, throwing open the door.

"Good night," she called after him.

Once on the outside, he hesitated again and, bracing his arm across the top of the car, leaned down to stare into the open window. Before he could analyze why it seemed so necessary to say so, he said, "Drive carefully."

Cars passed. Somewhere there was the muted chatter of people. The light at the corner turned from red to green and back to red again without Jill or Burke realizing the passage of time.

"Well, good night," he said again, this time pushing from the car.

Jill watched as he walked toward the entrance of the multistory, chic complex of apartments. She watched as he jogged the last few steps and disappeared inside the building without even a backward glance. She watched the suddenly empty doorway.

In that moment, she cursed her own honesty because it forced her to painfully lay the cards on the table. She was attracted to Burke Rawlins. Strongly. The admission instantly brought to mind the lyrics of an old song that asked the question: How long has this been going on? She had no idea how long, had no idea whether it had begun his first day back, whether it had begun at some point during the long hours they'd worked, and laughed, together; whether it had begun the night her contact lens had slipped, or whether it had started only a half hour before, when his body had lain intimately against hers. Perhaps it had always been there, just waiting for the proper catalyst to spark it to life. She couldn't honestly pinpoint its inception. She just knew that, at this moment, she recognized the attraction. She thought she even sensed Burke's attraction to her, but couldn't be sure she hadn't fancifully imagined it. One thing was certain; if it was real, he was denying it. Vehemently. Completely. With every ounce of strength he had. Either way, it translated to the same stark reality. She had just entered into a one-sided relationship.

HAD SHE OR HADN'T SHE?

The question became a litany during the next week. Each time Jill asked it, however, she came no closer to an answer. One minute she did indeed believe she had imagined, out of wishful thinking, the flicker of desire in Burke's eyes, while the next minute she was certain she'd seen it. If something mutual hadn't happened that few seconds he'd had her pinned to the ground, why had he participated in the virtual silence that had prevailed on the drive back?

Simple, she'd taunted herself. Maybe he had sensed her desire and felt awkward about being its cause without being able to be its cure. Maybe he'd felt something all right. Maybe, sprawled atop her, he'd been reminded of Nicole and how much he loved and missed her. Maybe... Jill conceded that there may be a thousand, nerve-shattering maybes.

The atmosphere around the office gave no clue as to Burke's feelings, though Jill sensed a subtle change in him and their relationship. While they still worked together as compatibly as ever, Burke seemed quiet, moody even, and less willing to engage in the teasing she had been getting so accustomed to. He seemed all business, though that business no longer involved working late. In fact, he'd made lame excuses both times she'd suggested it.

But if Jill sensed a change in Burke, she likewise sensed a change in herself. Though it was as delicate and slight as a mist of warm rain, it was still present. She felt somehow...different after her bold response to his body on hers. Almost as if she no longer knew herself. Her reaction had been stronger than any she'd ever experienced with a man. With no questions asked, no holds barred, she had been willing to make love to him. And what's more, it had seemed the perfectly natural thing to do. All of this was now demanding a new perception of a man she'd such a short time before considered only a friend. The adjustment made her feel strange. Especially around him. Which only added to the disquieting feeling of change.

Change. It seemed to be in the air. Even Mary seemed different—again, in a way too subtle to pinpoint. She had become edgy, jumpy—traits she'd never exhibited before. Most of the time Jill passed the change off as premarriage jitters. Occasionally, when worry insisted on having its due, she wondered if it could be something more. Though what that "more" could possibly be, she had no idea.

When Friday rolled around, Jill was relieved. She badly needed some rest from the emotionally draining week. As she was leaving her office for the day, she ran into Burke and his father. The two of them were planning dinner together. Jill had shown them her dinner companion, a book on rape, which she wanted to read in hopes of gaining some insights into the case she and Burke would be defending. They'd parted in the main lobby of the building, and as Jill had walked alone to the underground garage, she'd had the unsettling feeling that Burke was watching her. She hadn't had the courage, however, to turn around to confirm or deny her hunch. She didn't know whether she was more afraid to learn that he was or that he wasn't.

By seven o'clock, she had eaten a sandwich, bathed, and settled in bed with a law book. She adamantly refused to think of Burke Rawlins. At a quarter to ten, tired from reading and weary from constantly shoving Burke out of her mind, she reached for the phone and dialed her sister's number. She got a busy signal.

"WHO IS THIS? What do you want?" Mary whispered, cold sweat blistering her forehead at the sound of the strange male voice. It was only the second time she'd heard it, though it was the thousandth time she'd imagined the call. She'd prayed that she wouldn't hear from him again, but she'd known in her heart that she would.

"It don't matter who I am," the low, slow, gravelly voice replied. "It's what I want that counts." He allowed a meaningful pause. "I want money. Five thousand dollars in small bills..."

"I don't have that kind of money!" she cried.

"Sure you do," the voice said so softly, so soothingly, that that in and of itself leant an air of malignancy to the conversation. "If you don't, lawyer Jill does. Or maybe that fiancé of yours..."

"How do you know about..."

"About Rob? Oh, I know everything about you. Everything important. Like that little secret of yours. C'mon, Mary, five thousand and I'll forget all about your past."

"Don't...please..."

The voice became firm. "Five thousand by Friday. Leave it on a bench in the Public Garden." The stranger spent the next few minutes identifying exactly which bench in exactly which section of the park. And exactly when to leave the money. "You will show, won't you, Mary? 'Cause if you don't, I'll have to talk to Jill. And I don't think you'd like that." The phone went dead.

"Wait!"

The dial tone hummed a loud, irritating tune.

"Wait," she whispered. "Please wait." Tears sprang into her eyes as she eased onto the sofa. The receiver slid forgotten from her hand. Within seconds, the tears turned to soft weeping, which quickly gave way to a deluge, a deluge spawned by guilt and regret. All the while, the phone dangled . . . and whined its monotonous message.

At 10:15 p.m., the busy signal still beep-beeped in Jill's ear. She smiled. Rob. It had to be Rob. The smile faded, leaving behind an undisguised look of longing. She suddenly felt singular in a coupled world. The thought inevitably led to thoughts of Burke and to the groove-worn litany. Had she imagined his desire or had it been the real thing? And how many kinds of a fool was she for asking the same question over and over?

Over and over, footsteps pounded the sidewalk, jarring the night's silence and replacing it with the huffing sound of breath being sucked in and out of a deep chest. Racing against the wind, Burke emptied his mind the way he'd tried to keep it empty all week except for selected thoughts and memories. Right now, he registered nothing but the feeling of exhaustion—how many miles had he run? Ten, twelve, fifteen?—and the torment of unrelenting pain, pain in his chest, pain in his legs, pain in every inch of his body. Good pain. Desired pain. Because pain allowed nothing, no unwanted thoughts, to share its spotlight.

He had no idea how many hours he'd run that week, nor how many miles he'd logged. He knew only that every evening after dinner, he'd taken to the streets. Those hours when he wasn't running, he had deliberately hugged thoughts of Nicole to himself. He'd forced himself to remember every minute of the nearly five years they'd shared together—the first time he'd seen her, the first time he'd kissed her, their wedding day, that first night they'd spent together as man and wife, the accident. *The accident.* He relived that memory again and again because it was the most potent, the most powerful, the most punishing. And he felt the need to be punished. He could never clearly define why, though he knew it had everything to do with Saturday night.

He slowed his pace, from running to jogging to walking to finally collapsing against the side of a brick building. With eyes closed, he bent at the waist and planted his hands just above his knees. His breath was fast and short and agonized. Long moments passed while he steadied it to a slower, more even rhythm. At last he opened his eyes. His gaze fell to the wedding ring. But it wasn't an image of his wife that filled his mind. It was an image of Jill—and how good she'd felt beneath him.

In punishment of the betraying thought, he ran another mile.

MILES AWAY, on the sleazy side of Boston, in a two-room efficiency apartment that had rust stains in the chipped porcelain sink and cracks in the Naugahyde sofa bed, a man sat staring at a photo. The man in the picture was of short stature, had a youthful face and was wearing a newly issued, crisply creased khaki uniform. Across the back of the photo, written in a woman's small neat script was: "May 2, 1951—Tommy, leaving for Korea."

"That's wonderful, Tommy, you made straight A's again."

"Lenny, did you hear that your cousin made the swimming team?"

"He's never been a minute's trouble since we took him under our roof."

"It was like losing a son. He was such a fine boy. So proud to be going off to war. He was going to go to law school, you know."

The man in the two-room efficiency apartment shook his head, ending the intrusive, shoutingly silent dialogue. With a careless flick of his thick wrist, he tossed the snapshot into a cardboard box that held all the worldly possessions of his recently deceased mother. He gave a snort of laughter. A cardboard box. It wasn't a whole helluva lot to show for seventy-two years. But then, Maude Larimer hadn't been a worldly woman. She'd been a woman of principle and good deeds. Good to everyone but her own son.

Anger coiled inside the man's stomach, and he rummaged more persistently through the cardboard box. He'd probably been through the contents a hundred times since the nursing home had signed them over to him, but there was something therapeutic about touching the left-behind mementos. The touching was a validation that he was alive. His mother was dead. Straight-A, fine-boy, perfect Tommy was dead. But he, Lenny, was alive.

He shoved aside a small, worn book of poetry and rifled through the bundle of letters, held together with a time-cracked rubber band, that he'd sent her over the years, most asking for money, which she'd never sent. There was even the childish valentine, with his crudely written young name, that he'd given her in the second grade. That was the first year he'd flunked school, and he could still remember the licking he'd gotten. From both her and Poppa. But somehow hers always hurt worse because it was his momma that he'd wanted to please. Because pleasing Momma had been impossible for him to do from the day he was born.

His fingers stopped at the brown-tinged obituary dating back to 1951. He knew what it said. He'd read it a dozen times. He read it once more.

Private Thomas Jacob Wilson, son of the late June and John Wilson, was killed June 1, 1951, in the service of his country. For valorous actions which resulted in his death...

"...He was posthumously awarded the Medal of Honor. Interment was in Arlington National Cemetery," the man said aloud by rote, even though he'd already tossed the column back into the box.

He lived perfect. He died perfect. He was just goddamned perfect!

"Don't you talk that way about your dead cousin. And don't you swear in this house, Leonard Larimer," he heard his mother's voice saying as clearly as if it had been thirty years before.

"I'll say any damn thing about Tommy that..."

The crack of a remembered slap had silenced him.

"If perfection means having a sense of decency, then Tommy was perfect."

Perfect

The man laughed hollowly. As it turned out, Thomas Jacob Wilson was as human as any man.

Reaching for the one dog-eared letter that he'd found at the very bottom of the cardboard box, a letter postmarked Boston, he opened it. A strange handwriting confronted him. The letter was dated January 13, 1952. It began:

Dear Maude,
The child was born yesterday. It's a girl. I think she's going to have Tommy's eyes...

Leonard Larimer stared for a long while at the letter. He stared and wondered and brooded over why he'd been allowed to live his life thinking that Thomas Jacob Wilson had been perfect.

BURKE FLEW to New York the following Monday morning. He remained there all week. The trip was unexpected and had to do with another case that the firm was handling. Burke had volunteered to do the footwork on this second case while juggling the ongoing *Stroker* case, which as yet had not been scheduled for trial.

The fact that he had volunteered for the trip so readily led Jill to a bold conclusion. She had been right in believing that he had responded to her that Saturday night at Mary's house—something that Burke was literally running away from. She faced one other fact as well. It really didn't matter that she had seen a seed of desire in his eyes, because he was in no way emotionally fit to deal with it. He was a man married to a dead woman, and a dead woman was a far more formidable opponent than a live one. In fact, so formidable that Jill had no intention of entering into competition. She'd never played at no-win games, and she didn't intend to start now.

Furthermore, she told herself, it was important to her to keep the old Burke in her life. He was her friend and co-worker, and she didn't want to complicate a simple issue. She would just file that Saturday night under the heading What Might Have Been Had Things Been Different. She didn't bother to file the feeling of unfairness she felt.

The Bar Association dinner was at eight o'clock Friday night, and Burke's plane taxied to a stop at exactly two minutes of seven. With his briefcase in one hand and a garment bag in the other, he rushed through the corridors of Logan Airport and grabbed the first phone he saw. He shoved a coin into the slot and dialed Jill's number. As he waited, he wished for the dozenth time that he hadn't committed himself to the dinner. Or was it that he wished that he hadn't committed himself to the dinner with Jill? Some secret part of his heart asked, and in so doing, declared the week away a dismal failure.

Jill had just stepped from the tub and into the warmth of a terry bath sheet that swallowed her whole when the phone rang. The jingling cut short the thought that had flitted in and out of her mind all day. She wished she wasn't going to the dinner. She wished even more vehemently that she wasn't going with Burke. She didn't bother to analyze that this was contradictory to the new attitude she'd adopted.

"Hello?"

Her voice was warm and womanly and not a damned thing like he'd remembered. It was a thousand times better, ten thousand times better, a hundred thousand...

"I'm running late," he said, his voice somewhere between choked and husky.

Jill's hand slid to her stomach where it splayed against the sudden hollow feeling. It seemed like forever since she'd talked to him. "Hi," she said, her tone softening.

"Hi. Look," he said, turning his back to the man dialing the phone beside him, "the plane just got in, and I'm still at the airport."

"Want me to pick you up later than planned?"

"Yeah. What about eight-fifteen?"

"Fine. It doesn't matter if we arrive late."

"Come on up instead of waiting for me at the curb. There's parking in the back."

"That's all right. I'll just wait..."

"I don't know how long it'll take me to get a cab. Then I've got to shower and shave and dress. Come on up."

The mention of showering and shaving and dressing brought to mind images that deepened the hollow feeling in Jill's stomach to cave proportions. She felt a rush of warmth, but ignored it.

"Okay," she said, forcefully holding on to the resolve she'd made that week. "See you at eight-fifteen." She paused. "How did everything go in New York?"

"Fine. How's everything here?"

"Quiet. We sent our troublemaker to New York."

One side of Burke's mouth tilted upward. It was the first time he'd smiled in a week. It was funny, but Jill McClain was fast becoming the guardian of his good mood.

"See you later," he said.

"Right. Oh, Rawlins... what's your apartment number?"

She could tell he was still smiling. "After that comment about troublemaker, I ought to make you look for it."

"Troublemaker," she reaffirmed.

"Five-eighteen," he said, and hung up.

Her own lips curved into a smile. The smile slowly faded. God help her, she couldn't wait to see him again.

As Jill was piling her hair into a loose knot atop her head and applying frosted shadow to her lids, Mary McClain was boarding the subway. She carried a large tapestry bag that had a plain grocery sack inside it. She was frightened.

As Jill patted glittery gold dust on her bare shoulders, Mary exited the subway and walked toward the Boston Public Garden. Evening shadows were falling, painting the sculpted landscape in watercolor shades of gray and lavender. Mary's heart quickened, and she asked herself why she just didn't tell Jill the truth, instead of emptying her savings account and perpetuating the lie in a way that made her sick to her stomach. The answer was immediate. Jill would never forgive her for not telling her in the beginning, and if a note of this sordid song leaked to the press, they'd have a heyday, especially with Jill already getting coverage because of the trial. No, she thought, she had no choice. She'd forfeited that luxury years before.

As Jill slipped her dress over softly curved hips, Mary searched for a wooden bench under a crooked elm tree bordered by pansies and tulips.

As Jill donned gold sandals with three-inch heels, grabbed her gold filigree clutch and headed out of the apartment, Mary glanced quickly about her and practically threw the grocery bag onto the bench. She knew he was watching. She could feel him—like a tainted, unclean mist rising off stagnant water. She walked, walked, ran—she couldn't stop herself—until she emerged back onto the street. Gasping for breath, she slowed her pace and smiled nervously at the couple coming toward her.

As Jill parked the car and started for Burke's apartment building, Mary turned the key in the lock of her front door. Stepping inside, she closed the door behind her and leaned back against it. She sighed and closed her eyes. Thank God it was over!

Jill ran her eyes over the metal numbers tacked to the doors. Five-eighteen. She stopped, hesitated, then rang the doorbell. A swarm of butterflies launched into flight in her stomach.

"It's open!" a voice shouted from within.

Turning the knob, Jill pushed the door inward. She stepped inside. And told the butterflies to settle down.

"Be with you in a minute!" The voice came from what Jill surmised to be the bedroom.

"Don't you know you shouldn't leave your door unlocked?" she asked, looking around her. Her immediate impression was that of a small, but expensively nice, apartment in a neutral color scheme unquestionably chosen to please a great many tastes rather than express any individual one.

"Yeah, well, I was kinda hoping someone would break in and steal this damned tux! Look, fix yourself a drink if you like. The bar's in the kitchen."

Jill's eyes automatically drifted in that direction. She saw a couple of nearly full bottles of liquor and a garment bag haphazardly thrown across the width of the bar. A briefcase sat on the floor. The abandonment of bag and case suggested haste.

"No, thanks," she called back. "I'm fine."

"Make yourself at home."

"Right," she said, but stood exactly where she was, somewhere between the kitchen and the back of the sofa, somewhere between wanting to see him and not wanting to see him.

Her eyes, however, continued to scan the room, and she made brief, almost disjointed, observations. Cream-colored carpeting. Sage-green furniture in plaids and paisleys that decorously blended. Dark wood, fireplace, burgundy accents, a photograph of... Nicole. Pretty. God, she was so pretty! In a classic kind of way. Jill suddenly felt so... ordinary. So little, so drab and ordinary. So unable to compete in a competition she'd already sworn she wouldn't involve herself in.

"Damn!" Burke swore.

Jill's eyes shifted to the bedroom door.

"Do you know anything about cuff—" their eyes met, solidly and as thirsting men drink water "—links?" The last word was nothing more than a sibilation of sound.

Burke felt as if some giant fist had just walloped him in the stomach, while Jill felt as if someone had just carved out her insides and carelessly tossed them aside. Both would have sworn that the room's oxygen supply had dwindled. Dwindled dangerously.

Jill McClain was stunningly beautiful. The thought raced through Burke's mind with the intensity and speed of high-voltage electricity. Even as he thought it, his eyes began a slow perusal just to confirm the fact. Golden-red hair, which strangely reminded him of the color of the tea roses his mother used to grow, swirled on top of her head with dangling wisps falling at brow and ear and neck, while her cheekbones rode high with a natural grace that shamed the artifice of apricot blush. Her eyes sparkled the blue of a sky just washed clean by rain—she was wearing contacts, he noted—and her lips gleamed a bronzy color that blended with her dress. Her dress. Burke's eyes slid over the glittery gold-lamé dress, from its high cowl neck to its long sleeves to its belted waist to its straight, floor-length skirt. A slit ran provocatively up one side. Once he'd finished the journey, he confirmed his original finding. She was beautiful. Stunningly beautiful.

Handsome, Jill thought as her eyes roamed over the man before her. His sandy-brown hair shone with healthy highlights, his cheeks with the gloss of newly shaved skin. His eyes were a deep dark green that in that moment suggested a forest, a primeval forest. He wore a black tux and a pristine white shirt that made a boldly attractive color contrast, a contrast that somehow lent strength and authority and . . . sensuality to the man wearing it.

She had missed him, she admitted honestly.

It had been a long, lonely, smileless week, Burke admitted, even though the realization caused him a painful pang of guilt.

The silence had lengthened until it was now almost embarrassing.

Jill forced her eyes to Burke's wrist. His other hand was holding the folds of the shirtsleeve together. "Do you need—" she cleared her throat "—some help?"

Burke lowered his eyes. He seemed genuinely surprised at the difficulty he was experiencing with the cuff link. "Yeah," he managed to say.

Laying her handbag on the bar, Jill stepped forward with a gentle sway of her hips. The motion didn't escape Burke's attention. "What's the problem?"

"The, uh . . . the cuff link. I got one, but . . ."

The words trailed off as Jill's fingers started to fumble at his wrist. With a skill that defied trembling, she took the onyx-and-gold cuff link he offered—their fingers touched, scoring two bodies with hot, sizzling feelings—and penetrated the slit of the highly starched cuff. In so doing, she inserted her finger under the cuff's edge.

She felt the prickly feel of pasty starch and the warm feel of skin. Skin covered in a mat of hair that stimulatingly felt between silky and crisp. She even felt a raised vein on the back of his hand.

Burke experienced the feel of warm, warm skin and the feel of her nail lightly scraping back and forth. When she bent her head to fasten the cuff-link clasp, a tendril of hair, which curled just at her ear, brushed against the back of his hand. The gentle abrasion had all the subtlety of a ton of bricks tumbling onto his senses. He had the sudden need for exercise. Like running around the world.

"There," she said, her breath washing across his hand.

Like running around it twice, he amended.

She looked up into his eyes. He looked down into hers.

"Thank you." His voice was reed thin.

"You're welcome." Hers was soft like snowflakes on a velvet landscape.

Time dragged. Both forced breath into their lungs.

"Well, are you ready?" he asked, stepping back. With this distancing of his body from hers came the sudden feeling of more oxygen in the room. He experienced the heady feeling of optimism. The night was going to be okay.

"Sure," she said, turning and walking the few steps it took to retrieve her handbag.

Burke's eyes fell to Jill's back. Jill's bare back. The dress draped in a perfect and wide U that exposed every inch of skin from neck to waist. Every inch of beckoning skin. Burke realized his optimism had been premature.

Oh, God, he thought, *it's going to be a long evening.*

CHAPTER FIVE

THE CHAMPAGNE WAS EXPENSIVE and effervescent, the veal they'd been served at dinner had been cooked to a succulent perfection, and the orchestra was now playing the finest and purest of notes. Burke noticed none of this. Nor did he notice the rich appointments of the Copley Plaza Hotel—not the gilded ceiling, not the Waterford crystal chandelier, not the marble-top tables, nor the antique furniture.

In truth, his whole world had been reduced to a woman's back. Jill's back. Jill's smooth, cream-colored back, sprinkled with reddish-brown freckles and gold dust. The latter glittered provocatively in the right light.

Burke drew the glass to his lips and swallowed a portion of the chilled and tasteless champagne. Twenty-three, he mused sarcastically as he watched the man, a good-looking jock type from another law firm, brush Jill's back with his fingertips. That was the two-dozenth—give or take a feel—man to touch her. He'd never realized before just what open season it was on a woman's back. And all of the touching fell within the perimeters of propriety. It was the most natural thing in the world for a man to assist and guide a woman by placing his hand at any number of spots from neck to waist. In fact, hadn't he almost done it a half-dozen times himself? It was also apparently socially acceptable to lingeringly touch a woman for a fraction of a second during the course of conversation. As long as a man didn't salivate noticeably doing it.

Twenty-four. Burke watched as Charles Evans, dressed in a steel-gray tux and pink shirt, stepped to Jill's side and made the score an even twenty-four. Burke marked the event with another mouthful of champagne. Then checked his watch. He had been right. It had been a long evening. And it was growing longer by the minute.

"Cape Cod."

Burke inclined his head to the woman at his side, the woman he was supposed to be having a conversation with, though that presupposed that he was paying attention. Which he wasn't. "I beg your pardon?"

Harriet Cummings, a prominent corporation lawyer and an individual with the reputation of always knowing whom to call if you wanted to wade through the city hall's records at a run, pulled a gold case from her evening bag. "Do you mind?" she asked, indicating elegantly shaped cigarettes. Burke nodded that he didn't. "I said, I adore Cape Cod. Did you buy or rent a cottage there?"

"Rented," Burke said, his gaze once more magnet-drawn to Jill. She, too, glanced up. Their eyes grazed, then raced away as if they'd been caught in a naughty indiscretion.

"It's so nice to have you back practicing law."

"It's good to be back," Burke answered absently.

"I understand you and Jill McClain are involved..." Here, Harriet Cummings paused to light her cigarette. Burke's head jerked to attention. "...on the *Stroker* case." A curl of white smoke climbed upward through carnelian-red nails.

Burke felt foolish. "Yes. Yes, we are."

"It promises to be an interesting case. Every legal eye in Boston..."

Burke again tuned out the voice. And cast his legal eye once more on Jill. She stood in profile, but he could still see her back. It was then, as his eyes were traveling over the endless expanse of the ivory skin contained within the fashionable U, that the question came to him. What did a woman do for a bra when she wore a dress like that? Automatically his eyes lowered to the gentle swells thrusting against the gold-lamé fabric. Jill shifted her stance. Nothing. A woman did nothing. At the sudden realization of what he was thinking, a wave of self-disgust flooded him.

Cresting on the wave were droplets of guilt. My God, what was he doing? In answer to the question, he amended the score to twenty-five.

Burke drained his champagne.

Just as Jill drained hers.

Was it her imagination or had every woman in the room singled out Burke? Even as she asked the question, she saw Harriet Cummings stroll away, only to be replaced by yet another woman. This one Jill didn't know, though she was tall and willowy and gorgeous. Just like... She refused to acknowledge Nicole's name.

"He's yummy looking, isn't he?" Ellen said wistfully at Jill's elbow.

Jill was irrationally irritated. "Remind me to teach you a new word Monday," she said, and stalked away.

Ellen's surprised eyes were almost the size of her augmented chest.

The evening progressed. Strangely. One moment, Jill and Burke seemed to withdraw from each other, the way they had for the past couple of weeks. It was a discreet distancing, both physical and emotional. At those times, Jill sensed a sultry, smoke-thick tension in the air. Did he feel it too? Or was she simply projecting her own feelings? Then, at other times, the old Jill and Burke renewed their acquaintance, the old Jill and Burke who knew how to talk and tease and be friends.

It was during one of these latter periods that Jill, fresh from a talk with Judge O'Halleron, eased over to Burke's side and said, "I thought there would be nothing left of you by now."

One of Burke's brows hiked upward.

"If Ellen tells me one more time how yummy looking you are..." she said, leaving the threat unfinished. "She's been devouring you with her eyes."

The comment caught Burke entirely off guard. He laughed. The sound was one-hundred-percent male. Jill's one-hundred-percent feminine heart flopped over. She cursed herself for the weakness.

"She thinks anyone with matching chromosomes is 'yummy.'"

"That's a distinct possibility," Jill said.

"Has she been surgically augmented again?"

Jill shrugged offhandedly. "Can you buy anything bigger than a size forty-two?"

"Why do women do that?" he asked seriously.

"Naturally not every woman's reason is the same, but I think it's fair to conclude that a good many women do it to be more appealing to men."

"But breast size has little to do with being appealing. There are a lot of things about a woman that are sexier."

Like what? she had the sudden urge to ask.

Like a perfectly flawless back, he had the sudden urge to volunteer.

The mood had changed again, this time evolving into an intimacy that neither had expected, that neither knew quite how to handle. And for that matter, neither knew how to break eye contact. Nor did either want to. Except that staring at each other was becoming more and more awkward as the seconds ripened into a mature silence.

In the background the orchestra began a slow song. People two by two, migrated to the floor. As they did so, they passed by, and around, the couple standing and gazing into each other's eyes.

Casting caution to the wind, Jill allowed herself the luxury of imagining what it would be like to dance with Burke. She imagined the feel of his arms around her; she imagined the feel of his body only inches from hers; she imagined that for the span of a dance they were a couple. A normal couple. She knew, though, that they weren't. Normal or otherwise. And that he had no intention of asking her to dance. She told herself that she really didn't want him to. It was best in view of her noninvolvement policy. Yet she fantasized that she heard him ask her.

"Would you like to dance?"

She heard the words as clearly as bells ringing on a still day, though his lips made no movement. Fantasies were strange things, she was concluding when she heard the question again.

"Jilly, you wanna dance?"

The spell tumbled, wish over wish...and she looked up into the expectant eyes of Charles Evans.

"Wanna dance?"

"I, uh...sure," Jill said with a half smile. Her eyes briefly connected with Burke's. His blank eyes matched his expression. "Excuse me," she all but whispered.

Burke made no reply, but watched as Charles Evans guided Jill onto the dance floor. His hand caressed the middle of her back. It rested there as he took her into his arms. Burke had a flash sensation of what that hand must be feeling. Warm, smooth, soft skin. Skin soft like silk. Or intimate like whispers at midnight. He dismissed the thought. Just the way he shoved aside the thought that Jill, with her petite figure, and Charles Evans, with his medium height and athletically stocky build, made a nice-looking couple.

You could have asked her to dance, some part of his heart accused.

No, you couldn't, another part, presiding over emotional survival, answered.

Charles Evans stared down into Jill's face, said something, and she laughed.

Burke reached for another glass of champagne. His third. But who was counting? he sneered.

She danced well, he thought. Even at a distance he could tell that. The way her feet moved, the way her shoulders swayed, the way her hips... She danced well.

Evans's hand slid downward, to a spot just shy of the small of Jill's back. Exerting a pressure there—which Burke could almost feel—he turned her. As he did, the slit of her skirt parted. In that brief wink of fabric, Burke saw a shapely, silky leg.

He took another drink. A hefty belt. And went with the stream-of-consciousness thoughts bombarding his brain. *She'll marry a man like Evans someday—a bright, success-*

ful, handsome man—and have his kids. That's the way it should be. The way it should have been for me and . . . Did Evans hand shift lower? None of your business, Rawlins. None of your bus . . . Wonder what he just said to her. And what is she saying to him?

Burke took another drink.

Evans's hand, not crudely but in the tradition of man making a move on woman, glided onto the rounded fullness of Jill's hip.

Just moments before Burke had wanted Evans to get his hand off Jill's bare back. Now he wished he'd return it. He told himself he had no right to wish anything, but he did.

The music trailed off. The dancing couples halted. Charles Evans's hand gradually, reluctantly, fell away from Jill's body. They spoke briefly. Laughed. Evans spoke again. Burke could tell he'd made some comment about Jill's dress. A compliment, no doubt. She thanked him.

The music, once more a slow song punctuated by the weary wail of a saxophone, recommenced. Jill started away from the floor. Charles Evans gently grabbed her arm. He spoke, then jerked his head backward toward the already slow-swaying couples. He smiled enticingly, temptingly. Irresistibly?

Burke drained his champagne, set the glass on a nearby table, and stepped forward. He told himself not to be impulsive. He then ignored his own command.

"C'mon, Jilly," Charles Evans was saying, "one more." He was tugging at her arm as he spoke.

Burke had the irrational—and strong—urge to physically remove Evans's hand. But he didn't. Instead, he said, "How about that dance you promised me?"

Jill's eyes flew upward. And met Burke's. His were a shade somewhere between jade and jealousy. Hers simply registered a shade of surprise.

For a minute it looked as if the trio had been frozen in space and time.

Finally a grinning Charles Evans unwrapped his fingers from Jill's arm and spoke. "Hey, if the boss wants to pull rank, it's okay with me. Just make sure my file indicates my cooperativeness. Better yet, my paycheck.'' His grin widened and there was a sense of expectancy on his face as he waited for the other two to join in the humor. They didn't. They were still staring at each other, totally oblivious to the fact that the rest of the world was inhabited. Giving his blessing to something already decided, Charles Evans said, somewhat awkwardly, ''Yeah, sure. Go ahead. I'll catch you later, Jill.''

Jill never remembered stepping into Burke's arms. It was just that one moment she was standing alone, while the next she was swallowed up by the most incredible warmth. A massive warmth. A sheltering warmth. A warmth that spun itself around her in fiery, candent threads.

He was so tall!

She was so petite!

Jill's arm strained to reach his shoulder. Burke's hand strained to stay away from her back. Instead, he clung to her side where the fabric acted as a buffer between bare skin. It was a clumsy arrangement, but one he considered necessary—the way he considered air and water necessary.

''You lied,'' she said, her eyes finding his after a few seconds. ''You never asked me for a dance, so how could I have promised one?''

''So sue me for perjury.''

''Know a good lawyer?''

They smiled at each other. Genuinely. With no barriers between them.

Playfully, Jill thought that she might not know a good lawyer, but she knew a lawyer who looked good. And felt good. That observation was followed by the thought that, if she wanted to be good to herself, she'd stop thinking along those lines. Those counterproductive lines. To put backbone in the issue, she deliberately let her eyes find the hand entwined with hers . . . and the wedding ring encircling the third finger.

It was just a dance, she reminded herself. Nothing more. Why then did the hand holding hers, the warm hand, seem like so much more than a casual dance partner's? And why did she simply want to melt against, and into, his strong body?

"I see the cuff links are holding," she said, chasing the thought away.

He muttered something inflammatory about cuff links and their inventor.

This time they avoided each other's eyes, as if fearing they'd see reminders there of those unsettling few minutes at his apartment.

"Are you tired?" she asked moments later. The question was addressed to the smartly tied black bow of his tux. "I mean, you've had a rough day. What with New York this morning and Boston this evening."

"Yeah," he answered. "I am tired."

She looked up, past the tuck of his neck and the square of his cleanly shaven jaw. The smell of a richly scented, tempting cologne reached her nose. "We'll leave whenever you like."

Like. He tried to ignore it but he liked the color of her eyes. He liked the fresh sweet fragrance that he was beginning to associate with her. He liked the way her gold dress swished in a faint, teasing rhythm.

He cleared his head of the disturbing thoughts. "Whenever. I'm with you."

Perhaps it was the height difference, perhaps it was the fact that they were tired, but more probably it was the fact that they were staring more than dancing, whatever the cause, Jill missed a step.

"Oh!" she gasped, grabbing the lapel of his tux. In a totally spontaneous act, Burke's hand tightened, shifted, grazing the bare skin of her back.

Hot!

The touch was the ultimate definition of hot. It seared, scorched, burned until its reality lay as ashes at their feet. From the ashes rose hunger.

Burke's eyes deepened to the color of smoky emeralds. Jill's darkened to the hue of an ocean in the hush of night.

Each waited, breathing suspended on an airy, uneven note.

He told himself not to do it, not to lay his hand full on her back, but, sweet heaven, he couldn't help himself! It was what he'd wanted to do all evening. Denying all wisdom, defying his will, his fingertips brushed her skin, easing ahead like scouts on a daring mission. She shivered. Or did he? Slowly, slowly, his eyes still fastened to hers, he eased the length and breadth of his hand against her back. At a spot shy of shoulder and straddling spine.

There was an unwanted sigh. A shudder. A falling from control. For him. For her. For both.

Jill's eyes fluttered. Somehow their thighs connected, and the tips of unconfined breasts skimmed against a solid male chest. Hearts raced. And for one brief, breath-held second, he lowered his eyes from hers to her lips.

Lowered.

Held.

Wished for...

"Your wife."

The word chilled like a ruthless winter wind. Burke's eyes flew upward... to those of... He scoured his brain for a name. His brain responded with Ted. Yeah, yeah, Ted Something-or-other. He worked with Harriet Cummings. Burke's brain volunteered, mockingly, the fact that the music had stopped. He didn't dare ask it how long ago. Instead, his eyes raced once more to Jill's. Quickly, guiltily, he drew his hands from her and stepped backward. The hand that seconds before had held her, he jammed into his pocket. It still felt warm, Jill-warm.

"...sorry," Ted Something-or-other was saying.

"Thank you," Burke answered absently.

"Glad you're back."

"Yeah. Thanks."

The man and his dance partner moved on by, leaving Jill and Burke alone in a sea of people. Their eyes met.

Guilt. It flowed from every pore of his being. She could see it as clearly as if it were written across his still-smoky irises. And his eyes were smoky, smoky from a hunger he'd felt for her. That was what hurt the most. She now knew beyond a doubt that he was attracted to her, yet that attraction had only the power to cause guilt. Not joy. Not pleasure. Just guilt. Monumental, unadulterated guilt. And something more, something she saw bubbling to life. Anger. Unless she was very much mistaken, he was angry with himself...and angry with her. With himself, for wanting her; with her, for making him want her.

"Burke..."

"I'd like to go," he said with a steely softness. There was no doubt as to where. Home. Safe home. Home where he could wallow in guilt and assuage it with anger.

Jill didn't object. She suddenly wanted out, too; out where the night air could cool her fevered senses. With Burke behind her, she stepped from the dance floor and toward the door. She was through it and into the mosaic-tiled foyer of the hotel when she heard her name being called.

"Jilly?"

She stopped, almost colliding with Burke in the process.

"Hey, you two aren't leaving, are you?" Charles Evans asked. There was an incredulous look on his handsome face.

Both Jill and Burke exchanged glances.

"Yeah," she said. "It's, uh...it's been a long day."

"I'm tired," Burke said, then added something about New York and late planes.

"C'mon, you guys. It's early."

"No, really, we..."

"We'll see you Monday."

When it became obvious that the two were leaving, Charles Evans half skipped to Jill's side. "Look, I was going to ask you later, but...well, I have two tickets to the theater next week. I was wondering if..."

"Charles, I don't..." she said, still slowly heading for the door.

Sensing a rejection, the man added, "Why don't I call you about it tomorrow?"

"I don't . . ." Jill stopped—her words, not her steps. She couldn't turn him down so rudely. Charles was a nice man, and she didn't want to hurt his feelings. She even managed a smile. "Right. Call me."

Burke's hand snaked from behind and pushed open the entrance door. Jill had a quick glimpse of a starched white cuff against the black of tux and the tan of skin. Dark hair swirled at the sculpted wrist. She also caught a flash of a gold band. For the first time, the sight of it caused a ripple of anger. *Good grief,* she asked herself, *just how long is the man going to wear the damned thing?*

At the hotel entrance, Burke gave the parking attendant a description of the car. During the wait, neither spoke. Minutes later, Jill pulled the car into the flow of Saturday-night traffic. The drive from St. James Avenue to Burke's apartment was short and, just as it had been the night they'd returned from Mary's house, silent.

Jill would have paid a large sum of money to know what Burke was thinking. For that matter, she would have paid a lot to unscramble her own thoughts and feelings. One emotion she felt clearly was frustration. She was attracted to him. He was attracted to her. It should be simple, but it was everything but. A sudden thought occurred to her: surely he could no longer deny the attraction. Could he? She glanced over at the man hugging the far side of the car. His face was stern, his features set. She sighed. Not only could he deny it, he probably still was denying it—at least on some plane of thought. This realization shoved her once more in the direction of anger. How long was the man going to grieve? She admitted, grudgingly, that hers was an unfair, an insensitive, question.

She also admitted that it was unfair how good his hand had felt on her back. This pushed the anger button once more, so that when he finally spoke, she answered with an irritation that matched his.

"Jilly?" He said the word in an almost snide tone.

She threw a quick glance in his direction. His eyes were waiting for hers. "So he calls me Jilly?" Her tone said, "Make something of it, buster."

"Are you going out with him?"

She shrugged, when in fact she hadn't the least desire to date Charles Evans.

"He isn't your type."

"Who said?"

"You did."

Their eyes locked. Neither could read what lay in such secret depths.

"Oh," she said finally and sheepishly.

Neither spoke again until she pulled the car parallel to the curb in front of Burke's apartment building.

He reached for the door handle, then hesitated.

"I, uh—" he brought his eyes to hers "—I appreciate your coming by for me."

She nodded, sending wisps of pale hair into delicate motion. "No problem." A lifetime passed before she swallowed and added, "Burke..."

"No," he said, his voice, his eyes, full of pleading. "Please don't."

She wanted to say, "We need to talk. Can't you see what's happening between us? Can't you feel it?" In the end, however, she said nothing. She simply watched as his eyes withdrew from hers, and he opened the car door and got out. Though he walked tall and erect, she could see the guilt sitting squarely on his shoulders. In fact, it was beginning to make permanent grooves.

It was illogical, it was irrational, it was nothing of which she was proud, but in that moment she hated Nicole Rawlins. Why, why, wouldn't she let Burke go? The answer was simple. The answer hurt. Nicole Rawlins wasn't holding on to him. He was holding on to her. Because he loved her.

TEN MINUTES after Jill pulled away from the curb, Burke had changed into running gear and had hit the Boston sidewalks. With no real destination in mind, he found himself on Newbury Street, where he jogged past elegant boutiques and expensive specialty shops that had long ago closed for the evening. The buildings, most old brownstones that were once home to high society, looked out through dark, sleepy windows at the stranger in their midst. Some, their doorways curved into yawning arches, even seemed to smile, understandingly and with the wisdom of the ages, at the stranger's restlessness. At a quarter to one, tired, sweat dripping from brow and limb, Burke entered his apartment. He deliberately moved Nicole's picture from the living room to the bedroom, showered, then fell naked onto the bed. He was still awake, however, at three o'clock. Dammit, he wondered, why couldn't he forget the feel of Jill's warm skin?

As Burke was swearing, Jill was tossing. She floundered and flounced, her white cotton gown alternately caught at her ankles and riding her hips, until the pale-morning. At three minutes after the hour of five o'clock, she dozed off and slept until early afternoon, at which time she awoke with a throbbing headache. As she took two aspirins, muted the ring on the telephone and slipped back beneath the covers, Burke once more took to the streets. He ran until he pulled a groin muscle, then limped home to a hot shower and another restless day and sleepless night.

Both he and Jill awoke Monday morning with a powerful irritability.

JILL'S HEELS STRUCK the hallway of Rawlins, Rawlins, Nugent and Carson, with a force that sounded like bullets spewing from a gun. Her lips were sliced into a severe slit and anger fire-danced in her blue eyes.

"Hi," Ellen said as she passed by. "Wasn't Saturday night fun?"

"I tried to call you yesterday," Charles Evans said.

"Do you have change for the Coke machine?" the receptionist asked.

Jill answered no one. In fact, no one's remarks had registered. Her full attention was on the papers in her hand.

The red-pencil-corrected, words-marked-out, words-written-in, papers in her hand.

Without knocking, which was totally uncharacteristic, she threw open the door of Burke's office and stormed in. From his place behind the desk, where he sat scribbling notes with one hand and holding the phone to his ear with the other, he glanced up.

Angry. She was angry, he thought. On the heels of that came the realization she had never looked more beautiful. Her reddish-blond hair, in curls and held back from her face with turquoise-colored combs that matched her unstructured jacket, fairly bounced with energy as she moved, while her eyes shone a piercing, though pleasing, blue. Beneath the beige tailored blouse and beige skirt lay the back, the legs, the breasts that had been degrees of bare and braless Saturday night. The quick memory-image that Burke received in his brain led him to a silent curse.

It was a curse that Jill echoed. "What in hell is this?" She sailed the papers onto his desk. They fluttered, seemingly alive with their own irritation.

"Let me call you back," Burke said calmly into the phone. It was a calmness that piqued Jill's ire even more. With a twist of his wrist—his uncuff-linked wrist, Jill noted and hated herself for the memories that bombarded her—he replaced the receiver, stared briefly into Jill's flashing eyes, then down at the papers strewn across his desk. He recognized them for what they were: the only bit of work he'd done that weekend. "If I were guessing," he said, still in a voice that qualified as unemotional, "I'd say it's your opening speech to the jury."

"Wrong," Jill said in a frigid tone. "It's your opening speech to the jury. Oh, it used to be mine before your little red pencil went wild."

"You asked for my comments," he said, his own voice now slipping into the anger he'd nursed all weekend.

"I didn't ask you to rewrite it!"

"And I didn't re..."

"When did you do this?" she interrupted.

"What?"

"When did you 'give your comments'?"

"What has that got to do..."

"When, counselor?"

"Yesterday!"

A look of *I knew it* crossed Jill's face, and she sighed in utter disgust. "Oh, Burke, that's so contemptibly beneath you."

With that, she turned and marched from the room.

It took Burke exactly fifty-seven seconds to gather up the papers and limp into Jill's office. He found her standing and staring out the window.

"Are you implying what I think you're implying?" he asked, throwing the papers down on her desk. One sheet swooped to the floor like a glider coming in for a landing.

She whirled at the sound of his voice... and wondered if she was going to faint from the utter handsomeness of the man. His toasty-brown jacket, tan vest and brown slacks fit him to perfection, to heart-stopping perfection. With effort, Jill quelled her thoughts.

"And just what are you implying that I'm implying?"

"That I've allowed my private life to influence my professional life."

Jill saw her advantage... and, like a good lawyer, took it. "And just how is that possible? How could I be implying that your private life is influencing your professional one?"

"You know damned well what I'm talking about," he said, the fingers of one hand dipping inside his jacket to splay at his waist. "You're implying that what happened Friday night..." He stopped, realizing the corner he was trapped in, the corner he'd trapped himself in.

Jill moved in for the kill. "Just what did happen Friday night, Burke?"

She could feel the hurt the question caused, the guilt it stirred. For the briefest of seconds she felt sorry for him. But the second passed. Dammit, she was hurting, too!

He took an instinctive step backward. "Nothing," he said hoarsely. "Nothing happened."

"Liar," she accused, with a softness that took the sting from the accusation.

His face filled with a vulnerability that tugged at Jill's heart.

"Burke..."

"Don't!" he whispered. Turning, he walked—limped— from the room.

"Burke!" she called after him.

He didn't stop, he didn't answer, he simply fled. He had made it back to the safety of his office, but was only mid- way into the room, when the door burst open for the sec- ond time. He whirled around. Green eyes clashed with blue.

"I'm sorry, Burke," she said. "But you're not going to run away this time."

"What are you talking..."

"If you won't tell me what's going on..."

"Nothing's going..."

"...then I'll tell you."

"Jill, don't..."

"You're attracted to me," she said, her innate honesty refusing to let her speak less than the truth. "And you're eating yourself alive with guilt because of it."

The words hung in the air, as threateningly as gray clouds in a blue sky.

From where she stood, Jill could actually see Burke's Adam's apple bob in a slow swallow.

"You're wrong," he said, the denial barely audible.

"Am I?"

"I just said you were."

"Then prove it," she said, walking resolutely toward him.

"Wh-what do you mean?"

She now stood directly in front of him, all ninety-one pounds of her.

"Just what I said. Prove you're not attracted to me." Standing on tiptoe, she slipped her hand around the back of his neck. "All you have to do," she whispered, drawing his lips to hers, "is not respond."

CHAPTER SIX

SHE TOOK HIM by surprise.

The result was that soft, stunned flesh met hers before he could react in any way. There were milliseconds of pliancy, milliseconds of a warm intimacy, glimpsed promises of what Burke's kiss could be like, before she felt his resistance. His lips stiffened, yet, curiously, took on a blankness. Likewise his body tensed, yet donned a passivity. A willed passivity. A strong-willed passivity. He did not pull away, however, when he most assuredly could have. Did it mean anything? Jill responded as if it did.

Her mouth moved surely, purposefully, against his. Ignoring his nonparticipation, she parted her lips and slow-drove them into his. In a tempting, circular, relentless rhythm, she seduced him with every bit of expertise and feminine wile she knew.

Don't, don't, don't! Burke chanted, steeling himself against a reaction. He told himself that he didn't want this kiss, that he hadn't longed for it all weekend, that he hadn't longed for it maybe even longer than that. One part of him asked why he didn't pull away, while another part tried to conjure up an image of Nicole. Brown hair, blue eyes. No, no! Nicole's eyes were brown. The blue eyes belonged to...

Jill moved closer, meshing her body with his until her breasts flirted with the breadth of his chest. She placed her right hand against his cheek. It felt smooth and warm and angular. Her fingers at his chin, she tilted his face downward at a more convenient angle to hers. Opening her lips even more, she deepened the kiss. *No!* he cried silently, while Jill mercilessly sent the tip of her tongue to tasting the seam of his mouth.

Even with his mouth suctioned to hers, he gasped. It was a raw intake of air. His hands knotted into tight, painful fists at his sides.

"Kiss me," she ordered raggedly against his lips and slid her tongue forward until it met his. It was half command, half plea. It was wholly irresistible.

With a deep-throated groan, Burke surrendered. He grabbed her shoulders and hauled her against him. Her breasts flattened against his chest until he could feel every fiber of her jacket and a small, hard button of her blouse— or was that the hard nipple of her breast? The latter thought destroyed him. Splaying one hand across her back he tangled the other, fistlike, in the red-blond thickness of her hair. Primitively. Almost punishingly. His mouth opened, wide, wider, and assumed the control she'd only moments before been exerting.

He couldn't help himself. He didn't try to help himself. He simply felt. God, was it so wrong to feel again? Everything masculine about him cried *No, no!*

His tongue darted forward, curled with hers, then plunged deep inside the cavity of her mouth. There, he stroked and washed the walls in sensual designs.

He moaned.

She moaned.

She coiled her arms more tightly about his neck. And came closer at the very moment that he sought to draw her closer. His hands ran the length of her back and intimately slid onto her hips. The secret place between her thighs sweet-throbbed; his maleness blossomed against her stomach. Hard and noticeably.

Jill felt her head spinning, swirling. She felt everything in her opening up—her mouth, her arms, her womb, her heart—to receive the fullness of him. She felt . . . she felt . . . God, she didn't know how she felt! Out of control. Wonderfully out of control! And she could feel Burke's loss of control, too. His kiss had turned deep and savage—fire and windswept fury. And God, she liked it!

Alive...alive... The words blared in Burke's head. Dear God, she felt so warm, so womanly, so *alive*!

Heads tilted, lips ground together, tongues clashed and claimed.

In the end, the kiss didn't burn itself out. It simply got too hot to handle. Physically and emotionally.

In the middle of the most sweetness, the most sensuality either had ever known, Burke tore his mouth from hers. Gasping, chests heaving, astonished at the intensity of the emotions ravaging them, they just stared. Wide-eyed, moist lipped. With their hearts bare and vulnerable. Ultimately, he released her. She stepped backward. As if claiming the space, the distance, to gain some perspective.

Perspective. The need for it was settling about Burke's shoulders, like cold chunky flakes of a winter snow. Slowly, and all too predictably, the guilt straddled his back once more. It was now magnified. Tenfold. A hundredfold. The look on his face, the look of confusion and defeat and self-loathing, knifed at her heart. Sweet heaven, what had she done?

Her trembling fingers rose to her lips, her already swelling lips. She worked her mouth, but no words came out. She took another step backward, then another, and suddenly she was running from the room . . . and from her supreme folly.

JILL SHUT THE DOOR of her office and leaned back against the hard wood. She closed her eyes. Her heart was still pounding a too-quick cadence, her body still tingling from Burke's kiss, and she was still feeling like a fool. A first-class fool. She had confronted the situation with her customary honesty, but where had it gotten her? In one irrevocable step, she had destroyed the relationship she and Burke had . . . with no promise of a new one to replace it. And she had single-handedly caused Burke pain. She'd seen it in his eyes, seen it in the tortured paleness of his face.

Pushing from the door with hands that shook, she headed for the expanse of windows and stood staring down at a bright, midmorning Boston. From twelve stories up, the people in the streets looked tiny, unreal, doll-like. They looked devoid of the spectrum of human emotions. Yet they dreamed, wished, hurt, cried, loved... Loved. Was she falling in love with Burke? She had no idea. She knew only that what she'd felt minutes before she'd never felt in any other man's arms. In fact, she'd never even come close.

Her fingers trailed to her still-wet lips. They were... bruised. In exactly the way her emotions were.

She was standing, fingers on lips, heart in throat, when she heard the door open. Snatches of hallway conversation darted in before the loud symphony of silence resumed. She didn't turn around, but she knew that Burke stood behind her. She felt him. Felt also a requickening of her heartbeat, a reheating of her body's warmth.

"We have to talk," he said. The words sounded as if they'd been laid bare until they were raw; bone, blood raw.

Jill glanced over her shoulder... met his eyes, his hazy eyes... and realized that one side of her hair had tumbled loose. Running her fingers through the mass of curls, she groped for the anchoring comb, but couldn't find it. She'd lost it. Where, she had no idea. Maybe...

"Here," Burke said, handing her the comb.

Their eyes touched briefly before she reached for the turquoise adornment. They clumsily avoided contact. "Thank you."

Turning, she gazed back out the window. With unsteady fingers, she threaded the comb's teeth through her hair and secured the renegade tresses. Burke watched, fascinated against his will, before stepping to her side. He stared outside with her.

"You, uh...you have...lipstick..." she said after a few seconds.

Burke looked at her and when she didn't reciprocate, he ran a hand into a back pocket and pulled out a white handkerchief. He wiped it across his mouth—once, twice—before repocketing the cloth. He vaguely wondered if her mouth was as tender as his.

For long seconds, time was but a canvas on which was painted emotions—bold, red streaks of uncertainty and regret, splashed with the cooler colors of doubt and frustration. And dominating all were the myriad black shades of guilt.

"As a lawyer, I, uh . . . I've been trained to deal in facts," Burke finally said, never taking his eyes from some distant spot on the far horizon. "Facts substantiated by evidence." He nervously shifted his weight from one foot to the other. "All the evidence points to the fact that I find you—" he swallowed and amended roughly "—that I want you."

Jill said nothing. She didn't know what to say. She knew only what she was feeling: a sense of relief that he'd at last admitted to the attraction, yet a sense of pain that it was hurting him to do so.

Suddenly, his laugh bounced about the room in a sharp staccato burst of sound. "It's kinda hard to deny it when I practically threw you to the floor of my office." Anger once more informed his tone. Was it directed at him or her? Probably at them both.

"Burke, it was my fault. If I hadn't . . ."

"It wasn't your fault."

"Yes, it was."

"It wasn't."

"It was!"

His eyes caught hers in a blistering glare. "Dammit, Jill, you didn't force me to get hot and hard!" The words were blunt, to both sets of ears. He rammed his hands into his pant pockets. Jill wondered if the gesture was meant to hide any lingering evidence of his response. His voice was lower-pitched, though no more calm, when he added, "I could have pushed you away. I obviously chose not to."

Memories of minutes before assailed them. Jill remembered the way Burke's mouth had smothered hers, the way his tongue, with its velvety roughness, had caressed her own, the way his male body, hard and full of sensual strength, had pressed intimately, unashamedly, against hers.

Burke remembered the incredible feel of her soft body clinging to his, the way her lips were malleable, but masterful, the way she wasn't afraid, or embarrassed, to show her desire. She would be an aggressive lover—he knew that—and he found that fact... He stopped himself short of the word exciting. It was too late, though. Guilt was already slithering through his body.

"I, uh—" Burke raked his fingers through his brown hair "—I have to be honest."

"Please do."

"I'm... I'm not sure of the reason... I mean, I'm attracted to you, but I don't know..." He hesitated, unable to express himself.

"Don't know what?" she prompted.

"I don't know if it's because I haven't..." He stopped once more and this time he swore. "How can you always be so damned honest?" he asked, knowing that what he had to say would hurt her.

"What are you trying to say, Burke?"

His eyes grazed hers. "Jill, I..."

"Just say it."

"I haven't been with a woman since... Nicole."

Jill let the words sink in, along with their implication. "And you aren't certain that the attraction you feel for me isn't simply because you just need a woman."

He felt some innate need to protect her, even from himself, and fought against the desire to pull her back into his arms. "Yes," he whispered.

The admission caused a dull pain in Jill's heart. She accepted the pain, however, squarely and with dignity. "I suppose that's a possibility, isn't it?"

He saw the emotions tearing at her, witnessed the prideful tilt of her chin and the honest square of her shoulders—the square of her dainty though strong shoulders. In that moment he'd never respected anyone more. He also admitted what he guessed he'd known all along: Jill McClain was a woman of substance. A woman a man could walk with, trust in and lean on, as the inconsistencies of life dictated.

"Jill, I...I don't know what I'm feeling." He sighed, adding irritably, "I don't want to feel anything. I don't want to have..." He stopped.

"Needs?"

"Yes!" he answered, his voice harsh, ragged, impatient with the humanness of his body. "Yes," he repeated in a calmer tone, "but I can't seem to stop them. I wanted them to die with Nicole, but..."

"They keep insisting on reminding you that you're alive?" Jill offered, hoping she'd scored at least a shallow point.

She had. His eyes said so. They said, too, that he rejected the easy excuse.

Burke drew in a deep breath, knowing that there was one more thing he had to say. It was the only thing he could offer Jill. Admitting it, though, would add one more layer to his guilt. "I want you to know something," he began. "I said that I may be attracted to you only because I hadn't..." He paused, drawing in a richer lungful of air. "The truth is that no one else...I mean, no other woman...I haven't felt this way with anyone else."

The words warmed Jill's heart. Even more so because she knew how difficult it had been for him to say them. "Thank you for saying that."

They stared into each other's eyes, both feeling the other's pain, both wanting to ease that pain.

"Jill..." he began, but couldn't find the words to convey what was in his heart.

"I want you," she said with her typical frankness. "I want you in my life. For one simple reason. I care for you." She smiled, sending her lips into a subtle curve. "I don't know when it happened. I just know that it did, that right this moment it's fact."

Her honest admission disarmed him. "Jill, I...I have nothing to offer you. I'm still tied to the past. I'm caught somewhere between being dead and alive. I'm neither."

"Because you choose to be," she said bluntly.

"No. Because I deserve to be."

Her smooth brow wrinkled. "What does that mean?"

Burke glanced away, somewhere to a past that owned his soul. "I killed my wife. If it hadn't been for me . . ."

"You can't be serious," Jill interrupted. "My God, Burke, that's the oldest guilt trip in the world. Surely, you're too intelligent to believe . . ."

"It doesn't matter whether it's rationally true or not! It's what I feel. In the night. When I'm alone. When it's just me and those damned headlights that came out of nowhere! I should have done something, I should have seen it coming, I should have . . ."

"Died with her?"

Their eyes collided. "Yes, dammit! Yes!"

"That's the stupidest thing I've ever heard," Jill said, her own emotions string thin and quivering. "I never knew Nicole, but I can assure you she'd be livid to hear you say that! Love doesn't chain, Burke. It frees."

Long seconds passed, with the electricity of passions popping in the air.

"Can't you see that you're paying for a debt that you don't owe?" she asked at last. "Can't you see that you're cheating yourself?"

"That's better than cheating you." Their eyes lingered, neither knowing what to say or do. Finally Burke whispered, "I'm sorry."

He was already at the door when Jill spoke. "Burke?"

He turned.

"One of these days you're going to have to face the fact that Nicole's dead, that you're alive and that neither fact is your fault."

He said nothing. He simply stared at her for the span of an uneven heartbeat, then opened the door and disappeared.

THAT AFTERNOON, tired and in need of inspiration, seemingly every employee of Rawlins, Rawlins, Nugent and

Carson converged on the refreshment alcove at the same time.

"Sugar?"

"Yes, please."

"Could you hand me the creamer?"

"Yeah. Hey, where's the creamer? Anybody seen the creamer?"

"You're stepping on my foot!"

"This darned thing ate my quarter again!" Thud, thud, pound!—a fist walloped the Coke machine in the stomach.

Jill eased her way through the mob, headed for the coffeepot. "Hi," she said to Ida Tumbrello, who was just pouring out a cup of the murky liquid. "Any left?"

"Are you kidding? This stuff is so strong it reproduces itself."

"Still no one taking credit for making it?"

"Terrorist acts people will admit to; this coffee, no way."

Jill laughed and reached for a Styrofoam cup.

"See you later," the older woman said, forging a trail back through the crowd.

"Right," Jill answered, smiling at the ritual that she'd been told was almost ten years old. Every workday at four o'clock—not a minute before or after—since the death of Andrew Rawlins's wife, Ida Tumbrello had poured her boss a cup of coffee, carried it to him and had then spent the next ten minutes—not a minute more or less—discussing anything that came into their heads. Jill had often wondered if it was during these ten-minute sharings that Ida had fallen in love with Andrew Rawlins. Or had she always been in love with him? The question led her to thoughts of Burke. Had she always harbored these feelings—whatever they were—for him, but always kept them carefully hidden? Even from herself? She had no answer.

"Ooh, excuse me," Ellen said, now slinking through the crowd in a white sweater that looked as if she were packing a pair of Alps. "That soda looks yummy. Does anyone have a quarter I can borrow?"

All the men's hands rushed to their pockets.

All except one man's. Burke stood mesmerized at the sight of the woman pouring the coffee. He'd avoided Jill all day. Now he questioned the prudence of his decision. The impact of seeing her again after long hours had practically emptied his lungs of air. How had he worked beside her for so long and never realized how beautiful she was? How desirable?

As if sensing someone watching her, Jill glanced up. Her eyes instantly gravitated to Burke's. The solid ground beneath her feet seemed to shift.

"Will you pour me some coffee?" he asked, mouthing the words over the chaotic din. "I can't get through."

She nodded, poured another cup—were her hands trembling?—and wove her way through the throng. She almost collided with Charles Evans.

"Careful, Jilly!" Charles cautioned, his hand automatically grasping her shoulder. Burke's gaze shifted from her face to Charles Evans's hand. His stomach tightened.

"Sorry," she said, moving by. A few steps more and she stood before Burke. Handing him a cup, she said, "Be careful. It's—" their fingers brushed, causing their eyes to instantly meet "—hot." The word had all the consistency of vapor. As if choreographed to do so, eyes lowered to mouths.

Warm, she thought. She could still remember how warm his mouth had felt against hers. And how demanding. She wondered if it was her imagination or if his lips were a little swollen.

Soft, he thought. Silky soft and tasting of honey and passion. He wondered if it was his imagination or if her lips were swollen. My, God, had he kissed her that hard?

He forced his eyes back to hers. "How's the work going?"

She shrugged. "Okay. I just made some changes to my opening speech."

Her comment was just one more thing to make him feel like a heel. "It was fine. I shouldn't have . . ."

"No, you had several valid criticisms."

"Use what you want. Throw the rest out."

"Have we heard anything more about a court date?"

"No. Rumor has it, though, that we will soon."

"Good."

Charles Evans, a cup in his hand, stepped to Jill's side. He took a sip of his coffee and grimaced—whether from the taste or the tongue-searing heat wasn't quite clear. "I'll pick you up around seven-thirty."

Jill's eyes briefly met Burke's before shifting to the man beside her. "Fine," she answered with entirely no enthusiasm, though she did make a noble effort.

"What did you do to your leg, Rawlins?" Charles Evans asked.

No response followed. Burke's attention was fully on Jill. She sensed it and refused to look up.

The heat of Charles Evans's stare finally penetrated Burke's consciousness. He glanced over. "What?"

"I saw you limping. What did you do to your leg?"

"Pulled a muscle."

"Running?"

"Yeah."

"I did that once. Trying to get into shape for summer camp when I played college football." For the next couple of minutes, they listened to graphic details about Charles Evans's once-wrenched muscle. "Well, gotta get back to it," he finally said, strolling off...after a smile at Jill.

A silence descended.

"I, uh...I'm going to the theater with Charles."

What she didn't say was why. He had cornered her at noon, repeated his offer of the theater, and when it appeared she was going to turn him down, he asked if it was because of Burke. Jill had been stunned. What did he mean? He had shrugged, saying that it had crossed his mind that "the two of them might have something going." What with "leaving the dance early and all." The "and all" Jill was afraid to question. Had Charles Evans sensed an undercurrent? Not wanting a rumor started, she had agreed to go. She couldn't help but wonder if she had agreed for one other reason, as well. A human reason. A feminine reason. Had she hoped to make Burke jealous?

"When?" Burke now asked.

"Wednesday evening."

"I see." His voice didn't sound quite full. "Actually, that's good. I, uh . . . I hope you have fun." Their eyes held for seconds longer before Burke added, "Well, I've got some phone calls to make."

Jill watched as he walked—limped—off. Why hadn't she noticed the limp before? But then, the time she'd spent around him that morning had been occupied with either anger or. . .

"Burke?"

He turned.

"Does it hurt? Your leg, I mean."

"Yes," he answered. In some secret-dark corner of his mind, he admitted, however, that the pulled muscle hurt little compared to the knowledge that Jill would be spending Wednesday evening with another man.

WEDNESDAY NIGHT it rained—marblelike drops that splattered against the windows in a restless rhythm. Or was it just that he was restless? Burke mused.

Barefoot and bare chested, wearing only a pair of worn jeans, he forced himself to stop roaming the room. He plopped onto the sofa. Picking up the latest issue of *The New Yorker*, he paged through it, bypassing an article on the economy and one on foreign markets. With a deep, impatient sigh, he chucked the magazine back onto the coffee table. He reached for the remote-control panel of the TV.

Black brightened to color, silence to sound. A woman with shapely legs touted the miracle feel of a brand of panty hose. She was followed by a man selling microwave-oven popcorn. They were followed by a man from outer space who knew all about fabric softeners. Burke said something foul about commercials and silenced the TV. He rose and headed for the kitchen. There, he poured himself a bourbon and water, only the second he'd had since returning to Boston.

Slanting the glass, the amber liquid flowed over tinkling cubes of ice to reach his lips. It was smooth but strong. It was also ten-thirteen, he noticed, his eyes catching the hands of the watch on his uptilted wrist.

Was she home yet?

He downed the drink, trying to wash the question away. Shutting off the lights in the front of the apartment, he walked to the bedroom where he shucked his jeans and slipped into a hot shower. Minutes later, wet and warm, he stepped out of the frosted-glass stall, grabbed a towel and a bottle of liniment, and headed for the bed. Haphazardly drying his body, he threw the towel to the floor in a careless heap and dropped onto the mattress.

Bending his left leg at the knee, he uncapped the liniment and poured a puddle of white into his palm. He leaned against the headboard and spread his bent leg. With a firm pressure, he rubbed the lotion into his sore, but healing groin muscle, the moistness plastering the dark hair on his inner thigh into copious swirls. The pungent-smelling cream penetrated deeply, leaving behind a menthol-cool feel.

It felt good. Real good. Only one thing might feel better. A woman's hand—Jill's hand—doing the rubbing. The thought brought an instant reaction. His breath quickened. His heartbeat raced. His body became aroused. All of this was tailgated by a rush of guilt, which he tried to absolve himself of by deliberately focusing on the picture of Nicole that stood on the nightstand. It was his favorite picture of her, taken only months before she'd...died. It was her smile that made the picture so special. That so-full-of-life smile. She'd been happy. He knew he'd made her happy. He knew also that she'd loved him. That realization suddenly filled him with a satisfying warmth.

"Love doesn't chain. It frees."

The words reminded him of the woman who'd spoken them, and Burke glanced at the bedside clock. 10:33 p.m.

Was she home yet? Would Evans kiss her good-night? Was he at this moment tasting her lips? Was he . . .

Burke swore, rolled from the bed, and flung back the covers. Impatiently, he shut off the lamp and slid between the cool sheets. He planted his hands at the back of his head and dared himself to think an unwanted thought.

Darkness. Rain. Thunder. Lightning that ribboned across the tender sky. Ticktock . . . ticktock . . . ticktock . . . Burke angled his head toward the clock. 10:34 p.m. Only one minute had passed. One damned minute!

"I want you in my life. For one simple reason. I care for you."

"Jilly?"

"So he calls me Jilly?"

Jilly . . . Jilly . . . Jilly . . .

A vision of Charles Evans's mouth closing over Jill's jumped into Burke's mind. He swore again. Without turning on the lamp—somehow the darkness sanctioned the act—he yanked the phone from the hook.

Thunder growled a low, provocative sound just as the phone rang in Jill's bedroom. Not bothering to switch on the lamp, she stretched, searched for and finally found the receiver. Her gown, short and pale-yellow satin, rode upward to almost the middle of her stomach. She wore nothing beneath it.

"Hello?"

Her voice carried through the line like a breeze tiptoeing over the top of a lacey-leafed tree. Burke's stomach suddenly felt weightless. "Hi."

Jill's stomach jumped into her throat. "Burke?"

"I, uh . . . I'm not calling at a bad time, am I? I mean, Evans isn't still . . ."

"No. He's already gone."

Relief flooded Burke, but disappeared as quickly as it had come. Had Evans kissed her? Had they done more than kiss? Evans was a healthy, normal male . . . A thought crossed Burke's mind. With Evans's athletic build, and Jill's petite size, would he hurt her if they made love? A large man would have to be careful not to crush her with his weight. And at the moment his body fitted itself into hers . . . Burke deliberately fought the powerful thought. "I was just calling to tell you that we have a court date."

He told himself that the news could have waited till morning at the same time that disappointment claimed Jill. *Stupid, why did you think he was calling? Because he was jealous?*

"I got a call right after you left the office this afternoon."

"When are we scheduled?" she asked, trying to sound professional.

She didn't have to sound so damned businesslike, Burke thought, suddenly irrationally disappointed that her response hadn't been more that of a woman than a lawyer.

"Monday. Bright and early."

"That's good. We're ready."

"Yeah, we'll beat their socks off."

"Might even win the case while we're at it," Jill teased.

Burke's lips slanted into a smile, and he turned to his side. The sheet wrapped tightly around his hips. It hurt. But then the slightest pressure hurt these days. He ran his hand the length of his bare stomach and, tugging, loosened the sheet. "Yeah," he answered, but the word struggled to escape.

There was a sudden silence.

Was he in bed? He sounded all warm and mellow and stretched out.

Was she in bed? She sounded relaxed and sultrily lazy. He wondered what she slept in.

Burke cleared his throat and told himself to hang up. Instead, he asked, "How was the play?"

Jill pushed to her elbow, her hair fanning about her like a red and gold, delicately spun curtain. "Good. It was a musical comedy."

"One of those where the guy breaks into song just as he's about to kiss the girl?"

The question sent funny feelings scurrying over both bodies.

"Yeah."

There was another awkward pause filled with the sound of thunder.

"It's raining here," he said, still resisting hanging up.

"It's raining here."

Burke grinned. "What a coincidence, huh?"

Jill rolled once more onto her back and smiled, the corner of her mouth curling into the pillow. "Yeah." The silence pleaded that he wouldn't hang up just yet. "How's your leg?" she asked, assuring a few more seconds.

The question made him aware of the hot menthol still stinging his thigh. It also reminded him of what he'd earlier wished Jill's hand was doing—rubbing, stroking, caressing... He banished the thought to a hot spot in hell. "Almost well. I'll be running again by the weekend."

"Good. Where do you run?"

"Anywhere. I just start out."

There was another interlude of silken silence. This time it was too uncomfortable to tolerate, especially after the wayward turn of Burke's last thought. He also had the incredible urge to ask if Charles Evans had kissed her good-night. If he didn't hang up, he couldn't guarantee that he wouldn't.

"Well, I'll let you go. Just wanted to tell you about the date."

"Thanks. See you tomorrow."

"Yeah. Good night."

"Good night."

For a long time after Jill hung up, she lay quiet and still in the dark. One moment she told herself that what he'd called about could have kept till morning; the next, that she was just trying to give herself hope where none was really justified.

Burke, on the other hand, tossed and turned, relentlessly and in madman fashion. At a point near midnight, his anguished cry filled the room. It was the tortured sound of entrapment. He was caught somewhere between the cool, distant memories of Nicole and the warm, vibrant memories of Jill.

FOR THE REMAINDER of the week, the rain continued. Sunday morning, however, the sun rose with a brilliance that was dazzling. Bostonians thanked it by flocking out-of-doors.

Her hands still dirty from potting a blood-red geranium, Jill had just stepped from the patio and back into the kitchen when her doorbell rang.

"Coming," she called, wondering who it could be. She wasn't expecting anyone. And it was only—she glanced back at the clock on the kitchen wall—nine-thirty-five.

Opening the door the inch slit that the chain lock allowed, she peeked out. She saw a man, bare except for a pair of blue nylon running shorts and a pair of running shoes. The latter were even sans socks. Jill's immediate impression was of lots of tanned skin, a mass of dark chest hair and sweat everywhere.

The man peered back through the slit . . . and waited.

Jill unlatched the door and pulled it open. She looked up into Burke's moss-green eyes.

"Don't ask me what I'm doing here," he said. His breathing was still wild from running and, combined with the seriousness with which he spoke, made his delivery as eloquent as any ever exhibited by statesman or orator.

In truth, he had no idea why he was there. He had just started out running. Somewhere along the way, he'd realized he was running to instead of away from something. He was running to Jill. He didn't want to analyze why. He didn't want to make a big deal out of it. He didn't want to feel guilty because of it. He just wanted to see Jill. Surely there was nothing wrong in just wanting to see Jill . . . on a pretty Sunday morning . . . when he was feeling good.

"If I can't ask you what you're doing here, can I at least ask you to come in?" She was smiling. It was a smile that she felt all the way to her soul because, suddenly, the Sunday-morning sun shone brighter.

Burke grinned as he hiked both hands to his hips. "Yeah. You can ask me in." He stepped in as she stepped back. "I promise not to puddle on the floor," he said, referring to his sweat-drenched state. "I also promise to stay a safe distance from your nose."

"Did you run all the way from your apartment over here?" she asked in disbelief. Involuntarily, her eyes scanned his wide chest. It was glistening a bronzed color beneath the sheen of perspiration. The chest hair was wet and matted and almost begging her to touch it. The sight did curious things to her stomach, all of which she blamed on the small breakfast she'd had.

"No, I took a cab part of the way," he teased. "Of course, I ran it, McClain. It's only five, six miles."

"Only?"

"Piece of cake."

"Looks like a piece of coronary to me."

"Don't let the . . . gasping fool you," he said still gasping. "C'mon, let's go," he said, when he caught his breath.

"Go?"

"Come run with me."

"But I . . ."

"C'mon, you promised."

Jill remembered the discussion they'd had at Mary's. "I think that was sort of a loose arrangement along the lines of maybe someday we'll run together."

"Well, let's firm it up."

"I'm not dressed." But then, neither was he, she thought as her stomach did funny, turnover things.

"Go trade the jeans for shorts."

"I'm dirty," she protested, holding up a hand. "I was potting some flowers . . ."

"Trust me. You'll be dirtier."

She hesitated. "Burke, I . . ."

"I'll take it easy with you." The words had an intimacy that both chose to ignore. When she still stood riveted to the same spot, Burke ordered. "Go, woman! My muscles are cooling!"

Twenty minutes later, Jill thought she was going to die. Her breath felt like a knife slashing at her chest, and her legs felt like . . . her legs felt like nothing. They had gone from aching to paining to numb. Dead numb. Let's-bury-these-legs-and-get-it-over-with numb.

"I quit," she gasped, stopping, slouching her shoulders and heaving in place.

Burke, too, stopped. "Yeah, me, too," he agreed. "We'll walk back." As he spoke, he bent at the waist, hands to knees, held the position a moment, then raised himself and started walking in small cooling-down circles.

Jill noticed that he gave in to his left leg. "Did you hurt your leg again?"

He glanced up, sweat running off and down his forehead. "It's okay. Probably should have taken it a little easier the first time out, though."

"You're an idiot," she said.

"Flattery, McClain, will get you nowhere."

Both smiled into the glare of the sun.

Burke noticed that Jill's blouse clung to her sweat-dewed body. In fact, he could see the outline of her bra. He could also remember the feel of her breasts against his chest. They had felt good and no amount of wishing they hadn't could change that fact. Not even Nicole could change that fact.

Jill noticed that Burke's shorts were so wet across the back that they were plastered to his rear. In front, they were... She tried not to notice what they were in front. She could remember, however, and very vividly, what his front had felt like flush against her own. The words satisfyingly hard came to mind.

Burke kicked his feet.

Jill fiddled with her hair. Her damp hair. In fact, it was so damp that it was frizzed.

"I know now why you don't see runners with loose long hair," she said, trying to drag the moist strands from her face.

Without thinking, Burke reached out a finger and shoved back a wisp from her exercise-reddened cheek. Her skin was hot...sweet...soft. They both felt the touch as if it were the most intimate contact. Burke's eyes tumbled into hers. They were blue... deep... so deep a man could lose himself and never care. He swallowed... and lowered his eyes to her mouth. Her provocatively curved, woman's mouth. Which he suddenly longed to do all kinds of manly things to.

Time stopped. Bodies pulsated. The smell of desire and sweat permeated the air.

"Did he kiss you?" Burke heard himself asking and couldn't have been more stunned if he'd just asked someone to shoot him. Suddenly, the answer to that question mattered more than he could have ever believed possible.

"What?"

Burke's finger inched nearer her mouth, almost touching the corner now. "Evans. Did he kiss you?" he repeated hoarsely.

Jill's stomach felt gutted—at Burke's nearness, at the question. "No," she whispered, shaking her head. The action brushed his finger across her mouth. Both would have agreed that the touch was devastatingly sensual.

"But he tried, right?"

"Burke..."

"He tried, didn't he?"

"Yes."

The obvious question was, Why did you stop him? It was what was on the tip of Burke's tongue; it was what Jill expected. Both were, therefore, surprised when, after what seemed like an eternity's delay, he simply stepped back and asked, "Will you drive me back to my apartment?"

She did. On the drive, she settled on an answer as to why he hadn't asked the question. The answer was simple. He'd known the answer and didn't want to hear it. It was too uncomfortable for a man fighting to stay uninvolved.

"Burke?" she called softly after he'd thanked her and opened the car door.

He swiveled in the seat, his eyes meshing with hers.

"I didn't let him kiss me because he wasn't you."

The comment produced the anticipated reaction. "Jill, please..."

"I won't fight Nicole for you, Burke. But neither will I make it easy for you to turn your back on me."

The words hung in the air like a silken threat. Burke heard it, felt it. And couldn't honestly say that he wanted Jill to make it easy.

what he'd done to Mary McClain. He knew that. As a human being, he knew that. As the son of a saintly woman who'd more than once crammed conscience down his throat, he knew that. He knew, however, that, like one anesthetized to pain, he felt no guilt. Not even the tiniest bit. In fact, he could never remember feeling guilty about anything. All he'd ever felt, and in staggering proportions, was the unfairness of life. Beginning with a mother who'd never loved him, a cousin who'd taunted him with his perfection and a series of other life events whose sole purpose seemed to be to take the wind out of Lenny Larimer's sails.

"You bring on your own problems," he could hear Maude Larimer pronounce in that sanctimonious way she had. God, how he hated her when she said that!

Like it was his fault he wasn't smart and couldn't get good grades and go to law school. Like it was his fault he hadn't died a hero in some stupid war. Like it was his fault that once he'd finally made the police force, they'd kicked him out without even listening to his side of the story and forced him into one barely-make-ends-meet night-watchman job after another.

"It was your fault they fired you, Lenny. Your temper's too quick. You shouldn't be anywhere near a gun. Your fault ... your fault ..."

Leonard Larimer thought of the gun back in his cubbyhole apartment. His lips curled into a twisted semblance of a smile. His mother wouldn't approve of the gun. Which was just fine with him. He liked to do things she wouldn't approve of. And he knew for certain she wouldn't approve of what he'd done to Mary.

His mind scurried back to weeks before when he'd found the letter in the bottom of the box. His first reaction had been, Why hadn't she told him that Tommy wasn't perfect either? That reaction had soon given way to the need for revenge. He'd wanted to hurt his mother the same way she'd hurt him. All these long, lonely years. The only way he could do that was to hurt Tommy. Which meant he had to hurt something Tommy loved. And God, how he'd loved

Mary McClain! Because of that, he had to make her suffer. It wasn't his fault. She owed him. Tommy owed him. His mother owed him. Life owed him.

Hell, maybe even Tommy's little blue-eyed bastard owed him!

Leonard Larimer's attention was snagged by the words Jill was just then speaking, with such eloquence: "...You owe it to my client, you owe it to all women, you owe it to yourself, to listen openly and fair-mindedly to the evidence the plaintiff presents and then render your verdict intelligently, conscientiously." Her hands on the railing, she leaned forward. She paused for the proper effect. "That's all Alysia Wainwright Stroker asks of you, all the state of Massachusetts asks." Another dramatic pause and then she pushed from the railing and headed back to her seat.

A hush descended over the courtroom, as if no one wanted to sully what had just been said.

Finally, Judge O'Halleron broke the silence. "Since we're so near the hour of twelve, we'll break for lunch. Court will resume at 2:00 p.m. sharp."

A pound of the gavel, an "All rise," and the courtroom erupted into chatter.

"How about some lunch?" Burke asked, turning to Alysia Stroker and Jill. Both women agreed and, after Burke and Jill closed their briefcases, the trio started wading through the crush of people.

"Mr. Rawlins, what are your opinions on the trial so far?" asked a reporter as he stuffed a mike beneath Burke's nose.

"No comment," Burke replied, unruffled.

"Ms McClain, feel you've got a sympathetic jury?"

"No comment," she answered.

"You just addressed the jury," the reporter persisted. "What kind of vibes were you getting?"

"Please," Burke said nicely, but firmly, "could we pass by?" Jill felt Burke's hand at the small of her back as he nudged her and their client on through the throng. His hand felt wonderfully comforting, in a way that no man's hand ever had. It also evoked tingly sensations. "By the way, McClain," Burke added, leaning close to her ear, "your opening remarks were excellent."

She glanced up, ignoring the fact that he was so very near. Or at least giving it a good try. She smiled with a sudden impishness. "Thanks. I had some good input from a colleague."

Burke responded with a grin.

Then, as if both simultaneously remembered what had happened following their argument over her speech, their smiles faded. Their eyes lingered where those smiles had been. Briefly lingered. Before each pushed the past away in favor of the present.

Borne along by the sometimes shoulder-to-shoulder crowd, they were approaching the door of the courtroom when Jill felt the sharp jab of an elbow to her arm. She jerked her head upward...to a thick, square chin that could have used a shaving...to gray eyes that could have used softening. Jill had the immediate impression of cold. Ice-cold. A cold that marched like an army of icicles up and down her body.

"Excuse me," she said politely, not knowing whether it was he or she who should apologize.

"That's all right," he answered in a low, slow, gravelly voice. "Nobody's perfect."

Jill was never conscious of lowering her eyes from his—they were almost mesmerizing—but seconds later, she stood in the courthouse hallway, now swamped by news-craving reporters.

"Ms McClain, what do..."

"Mr. Rawlins, do you think..."

"Mrs. Stroker, are you pleased..."

"Ladies, gentlemen," Burke said, "could you let us through?"

With some pushing and shoving, the three finally emerged on the other side of the press crowd, which was now surging toward Mr. Stroker and his legal entourage with the same unending zeal.

"It's going to get worse before it gets better," Burke said of the press coverage.

Jill agreed. As she walked on down the hall, she threw a quick glance back over her shoulder. The man in the gray plaid shirt was gone. For some crazy reason, she felt relieved.

BY THE END of the week, Jill realized just how prophetic Burke's statement had been. And not only about the press. The entire trial apparently was going to get worse before it got better. Judge O'Halleron, in his ultraconservative posture, had banged his gavel so repeatedly, and had sustained so many of their opponent's objections, that the plantiff had not been allowed to introduce all of its evidence concerning the rape. The net result was that it was simply Mrs. Stroker's word against her husband's, and with the defense making David Gareth Stroker III out to be such a philanthropist, such an outstanding member of the community, it was hard, if not impossible, to accept him in such a brutal role.

"Damn!" Burke said Friday afternoon when O'Halleron's gavel had pounded the trial to a close for the weekend.

"Do we have problems?" Alysia Stroker asked.

"No, no!" both Jill and Burke assured. "None we can't handle," Jill added, placing a comforting hand on the woman's arm.

"You're paying us to worry," Burke said with a smile that melted Jill's heart if not their client's. "You just go have a restful weekend and be back here first thing Monday morning."

Minutes later, Burke and Jill watched their client walk away, surrounded as usual by a sea of reporters.

"Damn," Burke repeated. "I understand O'Halleron's position, but..."

"...Damn his position," Jill filled in.

"Exactly," Burke agreed, adding, at the sudden loss of Jill's attention, "What's wrong?" His eyes sought out the object of her interest. It was the Strokers' former servant, today in court without the child. The young woman's eyes looked fully into Jill's, then skittered away, almost nervously. Shouldering her handbag, and without glancing back, she started for the door. "What was that all about?"

"I don't know," Jill said, "but that's the second time today I've found her staring at me." Even as she spoke, Jill became aware of the man in the gray plaid shirt. He, too, was making his way toward the door. His eyes were cold-burning into hers. "Then again, maybe I'm just being paranoid."

"What do you mean?"

"The guy at the door, the one in the gray plaid shirt, he's been watching me all week, too."

Burke glanced across the room, but caught only a glimpse of a broad back as the man disappeared through the door. His eyes shifted back to Jill. Just as hers shifted back to him. Some carefully bridled emotion slipped its reins. "There's no mystery to that," he said, his voice lowering to a rumble. "Every man in court has been watching you."

The words bound her in a gentle captivity. "Have you?" The question was direct and typically Jill.

"Yes." The answer was direct and atypically Burke. Somewhere in the back of his mind, he told himself that he'd been spending too much time with her. Another part of his mind told him he wasn't spending enough time with her. Not in the intimate way he'd like. In the end, guilt rained down, but more in a shower than the deluge he'd come to expect. The guilt he did feel was offset by the relief he felt at speaking the truth.

Jill simply felt the strong need to be kissed. Because of that, she unconsciously moistened her bottom lip with the tip of her tongue.

Burke's eyes heated and hazed.

"At least O'Halleron's consistent." A voice cut through the sultry moment.

Jill and Burke jerked their heads around. Strangely, both were grateful for Andrew Rawlins's intrusion. Their attention quickly reverted to the trial. It was only later, as Jill drove home alone, that she allowed Burke's remark, and the look in his eyes, to penetrate her thoughts. The memories brought an afterglow that hugged her body in its rich, golden arms. Small though it was, she had scored a victory. If Burke walked away from her, he wouldn't do so totally unscathed.

FRIDAY NIGHT, all day Saturday and well into Saturday night, Jill studied trial transcripts, looking for any way to get the edge over their opposition. She and Burke spoke once by phone, but the conversation stayed well within the perimeters of business, possibly because Andrew Rawlins was present at Burke's end, possibly because Burke wished it so. The latter thought depressed her.

By Sunday afternoon, Jill needed a break, both from the case and from thoughts of Burke. She decided to check on Mary whom she'd called several times during the week only to get no answer. One thirty-minute drive and several ringings of the doorbell later, she used her own key and entered the house. She found Mary in the attic, knee-deep in boxes and dust and memories. A musty smell of the past filled the air.

"Let me guess. You're having the world's biggest junk sale," Jill said, bracing herself on the skinny stairway and poking her head through the opening in the floor.

Mary jumped, sighed in relief, and smiled. "Hi," she said, feeling love and pride in equal proportions the way she always did at the sight of Jill. "And I'll have you know, this is not junk," she said with a careless swipe of her hand that left a sooty smudge on the end of her nose. "It's first-class memorabilia. That's why I'm carefully boxing it and moving it over to Rob's."

Jill slipped through the hole and into the small room that was used solely for storage. "You mean your possessions can live with him without benefit of marriage, but you can't?"

"Don't start on me," Mary teased with an ear-to-ear grin.

Jill returned the smile. "You look wonderful," she said, adding, "I've been worried about you."

Mary gave an uncomfortable laugh. "C'mon, you know I always go a little crazy toward the end of school."

"That isn't for quite a while," Jill pointed out.

"So I got a head start this year." Eager to drop the subject, she said, "I'm feeling wonderful. Really, I am." Now that the nightmare is over, she added to herself. She tried not to let her thoughts travel in that direction, though she couldn't help but wonder where her hard-earned five thousand dollars was . . . and what kind of person would be so inhumanly cruel. She also wondered how he'd found out something that she, and her parents, had worked so hard to keep a secret. But the whole ugly mess was over. She was packing it, and the past, up just as she was packing up her things and transferring them to Rob's house. Only she wouldn't take the malignant part of the past with her. The move, the marriage, was going to be a new beginning, and she refused to give voice to the niggling worry that blackmailers—God, what an ugly word!—were notoriously greedy people. "I'm feeling wonderful," she repeated, because it felt good to say so and because saying so kept dark thoughts at bay.

"Want some help?" Jill asked, folding her jean-clad legs onto the floor in an Indian-style position.

"Do I look stupid? Of course, I want some help." She pushed an empty box forward with her foot and nodded toward the columns of old paperback books. "Here, start with these and then you can sort that junk—that memorabilia—behind you."

Both women giggled.

"I tried to call you this week."

"I've spent a good part of it over at Rob's."

"That's what I figured." Jill frowned and blew the dust off a yellowed mystery novel. "Do you ever throw anything away?"

"Sure. Those little wires that you tie the bread wrapper with. I can't figure out anything to do with them."

"And you can this antiquated copy of *Murder at Midnight*?"

"Have you ever seen another copy of it?"

"No, but . . ."

"I rest my case." On the heels of that, and with an enthusiasm that bubbled like champagne in her veins, she added, "You want to go shopping for a wedding dress with me next Saturday? I thought maybe just a knee-length dress, a chiffon or a silk, in a pastel color. Do you think I'd look better in pink or blue?"

When there was no answer, Mary glanced up from the bric-a-brac she was packing. Her eyes met the tear-glassed eyes of Jill.

"I love you," Jill said, smiling sheepishly at her own sentimentality. "I don't think I've said that in a long time."

Mary's heart constricted into a tight knot. "Why now?" she asked in a voice grown husky. She remembered exactly the last time Jill had told her she loved her. Just the way she remembered every time she had.

Jill shrugged. "I don't know. It just seemed real for the first time—that you and Rob are getting married, I mean." She looked embarrassed, but was too honest not to add, "I have these crazy, mixed feelings all of a sudden."

"What do you mean?"

"I want you and Rob to be happy, you know that, but it suddenly seems as if I'm losing you. It's just been us for so long." She wiped her hand across her runny nose. "This sounds like I'm not happy for you, Mary, and I really am. I swear it," she added, as if genuinely perplexed by her emotions.

Mary leaned forward and placed her palm against Jill's cheek. It felt warm, and a single tear ran beneath her fingers. She fought the urge to take her in her arms and comfort her like a moth . . . She stopped. She had never allowed herself to acknowledge the word. Silently or aloud. It was part of the bargain she'd made. "I love you, too. And you're not losing me."

As Mary knelt looking into Jill's sea-blue eyes, her own eyes glistened. She'd fight every devil in hell if need be to keep her secret safe. Nothing, no one, must ever be allowed to destroy Jill's feelings for her. And if Jill knew the truth...

"Sisters forever?" Jill asked with a tentative smile.

"Sisters—" the word was always comparable to cutting out her heart with a rusty knife "—forever." Mary forced her hand from Jill's cheek. Deliberately she went back to packing. "Now, are you going shopping with me?"

"Yes," Jill answered, relieved to have the subject once more emotionally neutral. "I think you'd look pretty in blue. Maybe even a soft lavender. Or what about..."

They were lost to girl talk, clothes talk, wedding talk.

"How's the trial going?" Mary asked during the first lull in conversation. "By the way, I planned on going to the trial Friday after school, but a parent stopped by unexpectedly." Mary seldom ever attended Jill's court sessions—usually they conflicted with her own work schedule—but she had stayed away from this case primarily because of the illegitimacy issue... and because of the madness happening in her own life.

"I wish you could have, but I understand."

"I did see your picture in the paper. You looked annoyed."

"I was. The press was badgering my client. As to how the trial is going," Jill said as she continued stacking books into the box, "the answer is somewhere right next to nowhere."

"Problems?"

"Not if we could hide the judge's gavel. He won't let us introduce some valuable material about the rape. Alysia Stroker has a sister we want to testify, but the defense, and Judge O'Halleron, insist that anything she says is simply what Alysia Stroker said to her, which is true, but—" Jill sighed "—it's been a frustrating case. All the way around."

"How so?" Mary asked, starting to stuff another box with fruit jars.

"It's just that . . . it's just that it's reminded me how we human beings love to make things black and white, and how things never really are. You know what I mean?"

Mary's hands paused ever so slightly. "Yes. I know what you mean."

Jill gave another deep, reflective sigh. "I don't know, Mary. My heart goes out to Alysia Stroker and to the former servant . . . Paula Keszler, I think her name is. And the child. Here Rawlins, Rawlins, Nugent and Carson are defending Alysia Stroker and, if we win, she'll be awarded a huge settlement. But what about Paula Keszler? Doesn't she deserve something? After all, she did have the man's child. And what about the child?"

"What about her?" Mary asked, falsely busying herself with packing.

"She is the product of an unwed union . . ."

"You make it sound so sordid," Mary interrupted.

"It's certainly no social stigma to be illegitimate anymore, but it's bound to be something of a burden to carry. Plus, there's no question that the child's the product of a notorious trial. No, the child has her own set of problems now and deserves some kind of compensation."

"Surely all that'll be addressed in the next trial," Mary said, straining to keep her voice natural.

"Oh, yeah. I can't help but wonder, though, why Paula Keszler's waited this long to identify the father."

"Maybe she saw the money slipping away and . . ."

Jill frowned. "No, I don't think so. She doesn't look money hungry to me." Shrugging, she added, "Who knows? I wonder if she was eventually planning on telling the child who her father was."

"Maybe she didn't want her to know," Mary said, suddenly feeling the cloying heat in the attic. Why hadn't she noticed how hot it was up here before?

"Does a parent have the right to decide that? Surely the child should know who her mother and father are, if for no other reason than the genetic problems that can arise. I mean, what would happen if—'' Jill stopped at the sight of Mary's pale face ''—Mary, are you all right?''

Mary smiled faintly. "It's just a little warm up here. Aren't you a little warm?''

"No, but..."

"How about a soda?''

"Sure," Jill said, concerned. "You stay here and I'll go get us two.''

"No, I'll go..."

"Stay put. I can scramble down faster than you.''

"Is that a reference to my age?" Mary teased, feeling better now that the subject had changed.

"No, just a testimony to my shrimpy size.''

A few minutes later Jill returned, bearing canned drinks and an oscillating fan. Within a short time, giggles were once more filling the air.

"Well, I've gotta run," Jill said just as the sky was turning the gray of gloaming. "Want me to take my box down as I go?''

"Yeah, just set it anywhere downstairs.''

"Okay," she said, throwing in the last of the books, scrapbooks and photo albums that were piled behind her. As she did so, a black-and-white photograph, age worn and faded, fell onto the floor. Jill picked it up...and stared down at a young man, short in height, wide in smile, who was dressed in spanking-new military khakis. She turned the picture over. "Who's Tommy?''

The cola can clinked against the floor, and a brown puddle spread into a fizzing lake. Immediately the two women tried to contain it with old rags that had previously been used to fight the dust.

"I've got it," Mary said, her voice strong only because she willed it so.

"It's no big deal," Jill said, assuming that the tension in the air had to do with the spilled drink. "The cola didn't get on anything," she said as she sopped it up with her rag. "So who's Tommy?''

Mary forced herself to glance down at the snapshot. It was a snapshot she'd seen a thousand times, one she'd carried in her wallet for all the youthful years of her adult life. "Tommy... Wilson. He, uh... he used to be a neighbor in Shawsheen."

"I don't remember him."

"No... no, you wouldn't," she said, deliberately averting her eyes. "He died in Korea and his family, his aunt, moved away shortly afterward."

Satisfied completely with Mary's explanation, Jill negligently tossed the picture into the box with everything else and hoisted the cardboard monster into her arms. "Well, I'll phone you next week."

"Right," Mary answered, and watched as Jill negotiated the stairs.

"Bye," called Jill.

"Bye," Mary replied, closed her eyes and slumped back against the wall. Her heart was pounding so hard that it hurt. Or maybe the pain was nothing more than the accumulative effects of deception.

Downstairs, the phone was ringing. As fast as she could with the box in her hands, Jill hastened toward it, knowing that Mary wouldn't even hear it, let alone reach it in time. Bracing the box on the back of the sofa, she grabbed the receiver.

"Hello?" she said breathlessly.

There was a slight pause. "We need to talk about your daughter again," the low, slow, gravelly voice said.

"You have the wrong number," Jill said politely and recradled the phone. Fitting her hands once more beneath the box, she lifted it and sat it by the front door. She then opened the door and stepped out into the night. In no way did it cross her mind that she'd heard the caller's voice before.

LATER THAT NIGHT it rained, a slow, drizzling, lazy kind of rain that streaked windows in wet and wistful messages. Burke lay in bed trying not to think of Jill, Jill lay in bed trying not to think of Burke, while both their bodies betrayed them with heavy, aching needs. Rob sat pouring over some business reports that he'd promised himself he'd finish before calling Mary. Mary sat on the sofa staring down at the picture of Tommy Wilson. It had taken a long time, but the hurt of his loss had healed, leaving behind only a pleasant memory of a fine young man's love.

When the phone rang at a quarter to nine, she smiled, tossed the picture onto the coffee table and reached for the receiver.

"Hi, darling," she said without preamble, "did you finish the reports?" Whether it was the long pause or the raspy breathing that first alerted her, Mary didn't know. She knew only that a black, cold fear crawled up her spine. She swallowed, low and hard, and tried to speak. "Who...who is this?"

"I saw her, Mary," the low, slow gravelly voice said. "I even spoke to her at the courthouse."

The fear changed pace. It now chased up and down her spine.

"No," she whispered, suddenly sick at her stomach to think he might have been near Jill. Not her Jill near something so...vile.

"It'd be so easy to tell her."

"You promised," Mary pleaded, knowing full well he'd never made any such promise. Had he intended to play this game all along?

"I've been thinking. I don't think five thousand's enough. I want another two, Mary."

"I don't have another two thousand!" she shrieked. She felt the ugly, jagged petals of hysteria blossoming into a dark flower. "I gave you all I had!"

"Get it," he said curtly. "By Friday."

"I can't..."

"Then I'll just arrange a little talk with Jill."

"Listen," Mary said, her mind whirling for a solution, "I, uh...I'm selling my house. If you could wait..."

"I've waited a lifetime, Mary. Friday. Same place. By three."

"No, listen," she pleaded, grasping the phone until her knuckles turned white, "I could give you more..."

Click. The dial tone whirred in Mary's head. It was joined by the heavy pound-pound of her heart that echoed sharply in her ears.

This time, there were no tears. Calmly, she replaced the receiver and stared vacuously into space. Finally she quietly lay down on the sofa and drew her knees to her chin in a fetal position. Slowly, she began a monotonous, chilling, rocking motion. There she lay, long after the rain stopped, long after the phone rang and rang and rang Rob's call, long after the nausea in her stomach had eased to a dull pain in her head.

THE NOTE CAME at the eleventh hour of the trial and as Jill was feeling more helpless than she'd ever felt in her life. All week the trial had gone badly for the plantiff, and Thursday afternoon, with only both sides' closing remarks left, Jill had been reduced to her last legal option. She was praying for a miracle. It came in the form of a slip of paper handed her by the bailiff. With a frown, she glanced behind her. Her eyes met those of Paula Keszler.

Giving her attention once more to the paper in her hand, she unfolded it and read the message. Jill's heart leapt. She forced herself to read the message again, more slowly, just to make certain she hadn't misread it. She hadn't. Looking over at Burke, who wore a quizzical expression, she passed him the note and, scraping back her chair, stood.

"Your Honor, the plantiff would like to call one last witness."

Judge Timothy O'Halleron, with his stern brown eyes, his long, pointed, russet-colored beard and his black judicial robes, looked more like an eighteenth-century Quaker than an instrument of the law. "Your request is highly irregular, Ms McClain."

"Yes, sir. The plantiff appreciates that fact, but something vital has just come to our attention."

"Is the witness you want to call in court?"

"Yes, sir."

Every eye in the courtroom, especially those of the defense, began scanning the sea of spectator faces.

"Your Honor, the defense objects."

Jill's eyes sought Burke's. His prayer entwined with hers as they awaited the judge's ruling.

It came after a long, contemplative silence. "Overruled."

Both Jill and Burke let out an audible sigh.

"Call your witness, Ms McClain."

"Your Honor, the prosecution calls Paula Keszler to the stand."

Low murmurs undulated like sea waves across the room. Moments later, Paula Keszler, her eyes wide, her hands trembling, sat in the witness chair.

Jill walked slowly toward the young woman, smiled her most reassuring smile and said, "Ms Keszler, I want to ask you only two questions. Is David Gareth Stroker III the father of your child?"

"Yes," came the hushed reply.

"Speak up, Ms Keszler," the judge admonished.

Paula Keszler quickly glanced in the direction of the man giving the steely-timbred command. Her gaze returned to Jill. "Yes," she said in roughly raised compliance.

"Ms Keszler," Jill said, choosing her words carefully, "were you and David Gareth Stroker III . . . lovers?"

Silence. Followed by a "No."

"Ms Keszler, please speak . . ." Judge O'Halleron began.

"No!" she cried, then lowered her voice. "No, we were not lovers."

"I'm afraid I don't understand," Jill said, understanding exactly what she was doing. "You say your child is his and yet you say that the two of you weren't lovers. How can that be?"

The courtroom was dead silent; everyone awaited the answer.

Paula Keszler looked up and over at the socially prominent, the personally powerful, defendant. Fear danced across the irises of her gray eyes. Then, proudly, fearlessly and in a voice that carried the width and breadth of the room, she said, "He raped me."

The courtroom burst into chatter. Judge O'Halleron hammered his gavel.

"Ms Keszler, I'm curious," Jill asked. "Why haven't you come forward before now?"

This time there was no hesitation. "Because he threatened me."

The courtroom went wild again. Judge O'Halleron went wild with his gavel.

Exactly forty-nine minutes later, at three minutes of five o'clock, the jury returned its verdict. It found in favor of Alysia Wainwright Stroker. At the reading of the verdict, chaos reigned supreme. Reporters converged, family converged, lawyers, those connected with Rawlins, Rawlins, Nugent and Carson, and those not connected, converged. Hugging and handshaking became the order of the day.

In a matter of minutes, with laughter and talk and shouting engulfing them, Burke and Jill found themselves facing each other. They smiled.

"We took it right to the wire, counselor," Burke said.

"It was about to fall over the wire," Jill answered, her face radiant.

His smile widened, her smile widened, and suddenly she was in his arms, all sixty inches of her pressed tightly against all six-plus feet of him, his hands splayed across her back, her hands against the nape of his neck. Bodies blending, they hugged triumphantly. Pulling back, their eyes met. Like swimmers from high, treacherous cliffs, blue plunged into green, green into blue. Their smiles vanished.

Whether it was the exhilaration of their victory, the adrenaline speeding through their bodies, or simply feelings that had been too long suppressed and denied—whatever the reason, their senses heightened to an almost-unbearable state. Smells of cologne and perfume intoxicated to the point of faintness, eyes inhaled images of the other's face, ears devoured every shallow nuance of breathing. And bodies burned, blazed, raged with a passion that was so palpable it was almost a taste on the tongue.

Because of their surroundings, because he was burning to cinders, Burke slowly released her. Because of their surroundings, because liquid fire sizzled in her veins, she stepped from his arms. Neither, though, could break eye contact.

"Mr. Rawlins, how do you feel?" a member of the press asked.

The word horny sprang to Burke's mind.

"Ms McClain, were you surprised?"

"Yes," she answered weakly, adding to herself, *I had forgotten how wonderful his arms felt.*

"Do you think the verdict will have any effect on future rape-within-marriage cases?"

The seriousness of the question forced Jill and Burke to unlock their gazes.

"Uh, yes, as a matter of fact," Jill began to explain. Burke followed suit. Once again, their private life was placed on hold. And there it stayed for the next hour as they fielded questions from the press.

At 6:00 p.m., the two of them made their way to Jill's car, which had been parked in a nearby underground garage.

"You sure you don't mind giving me a lift?" Burke asked.

"No, of course not."

Both avoided looking at each other. Both walked discreet distances apart. Both bodies were taut with restraint. Burke felt on the sliver-thin edge of the explosion he'd sensed coming. Jill just felt Burke in every cell of her being. Along with need. And desire. And some warm feeling that kept ribboning in and out of her heart.

Within minutes, they were inside the car. Still without looking his way, she started the engine. She cupped her hand over the floor shift. Before she could slip it from Park to

Drive, Burke's hand covered hers. Quickly. Spontaneously. Without imprisoning thought. For long seconds, with her heart pounding a too-fast rhythm, Jill just stared at the hand blanketing hers—at the suntanned skin, at the dark hair curling over the cuff of the white shirt, at the vein almost visibly throbbing at his wrist. Slowly her eyes traveled the length of his navy jacket, over the width of his shoulder, up to his silvery-green eyes.

He, too, was staring. At her hair piled atop her head in a way that left her neck open and vulnerable. At the man-eating blue of her eyes. At the curve of her lips. At her incredibly soft-looking lips. Her lips that were beckoning, calling, pushing him over the explosive edge.

Suddenly he tumbled.

Groaning in abject defeat, Burke wrapped his hand around the back of her neck, pulled her forward and crushed her mouth with his.

CHAPTER EIGHT

AT LEAST ONCE in every human being's life is born the moment when thought is the captive of feeling. As Burke's lips met Jill's, his moment was born. God help him, Nicole forgive him, guilt be damned, he had to have Jill's mouth or die! With that elemental thought, he kissed her deeply and savagely.

His lips were commanding and desperately seeking. Caught off guard by the power of his kiss, Jill leaned forward and anchored her hand against his chest. She parted her lips beneath the persuasive pressure of his. Her immediate acquiescence fired his blood until it was a scalding liquid need pumping through his restless body. He felt the need gravitating to the most supremely male part of him. He hurt. He ached. He wanted her. As always, and out of habit, he cursed his reaction, and yet, curiously and for the first time in a long while, he also treasured it.

Placing both hands on the satin skin of her neck, he pulled her closer. Her breasts were soft orbs plumped against his chest. Her nipples peaked impertinently. His chest was a solid hard wall that strained against her.

Fast and furiously, slow and leisurely, he took her sweetness and, when he took all that he thought he could without bruising her lips or causing his body to explode with desire, he took more because there had been altogether too many long nights without knowing the infinite mystery of a woman.

Long, sensually quiet moments later, both Burke and Jill gasped for air. Their lips tore far enough apart that breathing was possible, yet touch was still maintained. At least between bottom lips. Eyes closed, Burke rested his forehead against Jill's. Both hearts pounded wildly, like stallions stampeding over dry, barren earth. At last, heartbeats slowed. Yet still they didn't pull apart.

"Burke..." she whispered against his lips, sending tickling, tingling shivers of motion purling across the flesh of his mouth. The sound also sent shivers of molten emotion lapping over his body. He shuddered.

"Shh..." he answered as he started to nibble and tease the tender skin of her lower lip. He pulled it inside his mouth and gently worried it with his teeth. He didn't want to talk, he didn't want to think, he just wanted to feel. He just wanted to kiss her.

His teeth bit and nipped. His tongue flicked across the fullness of her lips, imprinting them with a slick shiny wetness. The same tongue darted into the tight corner of her mouth before outlining the feminine curves of her upper lip.

His hand slid beneath her chin and tilted her head upward. Flirting with the seam of her lips, he eased his tongue forward. The tip of his met the tip of hers. The sensitive points touched, rubbed, stroked. The tip of hers danced with his; his curled around hers. She opened her mouth for him to come inside. Maddeningly, he didn't. Instead, he withdrew his tongue entirely and settled his lips back on hers. He kissed her softly, slowly, teasingly, until her head lolled back against the seat in abject surrender. Languidly, he pulled his mouth from hers and opened his eyes.

God, she was beautiful, he thought as he watched her tawny-lashed eyes slowly drift open, too. Her eyes were blue...and smoky with passion. In the split of a second, fully aware that the devil guilt might demand payment, he made the decision.

"Burke..." she tried again.

He interrupted her by placing his fingertips at her lips. "Let's celebrate our victory in court."

She hesitated before nodding. "Okay," she said finally, though it was obvious she'd rather have discussed the intimacy they had just shared. "What do you have in mind?"

"Steaks and champagne." He paused, meaningfully, and as his eyes darkened to jade moons at midnight. "At your place."

HAD SHE MISUNDERSTOOD? she thought two hours later as they sat across from each other at her small table. Had she read into his suggestion of dining at her place more than he'd intended? When she remembered the sultry look in his eyes on first seeing her when she'd walked back into the kitchen after releasing her hair from its topknot, she thought no. She thought no again when she remembered the moment they'd accidentally bumped into each other while preparing the meal. The blatant desire that had shimmied across bodies and stabbed deep into irises had been obvious. At least she'd thought it had been. Now she didn't know. Maybe she was the only one who'd grown so weak she could hardly stand. How else could she explain the fact that Burke had made no further attempt to touch her in any way?

"Would, uh...would you like something else?" Jill asked, laying her fork on the side of the almost untouched plate of food. The action produced a clatter that jarred her dancing-on-edge nerves. "I think there's more..."

"No. No, thank you," Burke answered, swallowing the last bite of his steak. It had been a hard-won battle of man over beef, but finally he'd gotten it down a throat that seemed to grow tighter by the minute. Just the way another part of his body was growing tighter and tighter and... "Everything was good," he said in a cloudy voice as he shifted in the chair.

"Yes," she agreed, running her finger up the stem of a champagne glass. An almost-empty champagne glass. The tiny sparkling bubbles, which she fancifully imagined were laughing at the adolescent awkwardness the two adults were exhibiting, had been about the only things she'd been able to choke down.

"You didn't eat much," he pointed out.

She shrugged and smiled. "I wasn't hungry. I guess the day was too emotional." Interestingly, the comment brought to mind thoughts of the kiss, not thoughts of the trial.

The same thoughts jumped into Burke's mind, where they played careless havoc and caused that part of his body already tight to grow even tighter. He swallowed. "Yeah."

"I, uh . . . I wish I had some dessert to offer you, but . . ."

"I don't need anything," he said, silently adding, except you. *God, do I need you!* He shifted in his chair again, trying once more to ease, or at least to accommodate, the escalating ache.

She laughed nervously. "I don't either. I'm gaining weight as it is."

The feel of her body drawn flush against his flooded his mind—rounded breasts a man could hold in his hands, a small waist that a man's hands could span, hips that flared in a pattern that kindled a man's imagination. "You're perfect." His voice was husky and as warm as sun-heated bourbon. The look in his eyes was as potent as a straight shot of the same drink.

Jill felt her body tremble. And burn wickedly hot in places she couldn't ignore. *God, Burke, say something, do something!*

Jill, help me! I don't know how to play these stupid dating games. I've been a married man, for God's sake!

Shoving back her chair, Jill said, "Why don't you go into the living room? I'll just set these dishes in the sink." *Hold me. Take this plate out of my hands and hold me until I stop trembling.*

Burke raked back his chair and stood. "I'll help you." *I want to hold you. So bad. God, I need to feel your body against mine!*

"No, I can do it," she said, her eyes traitorously going to his lips. *Kiss me. Until I'm senseless. Until you're senseless. Until tonight has turned into tomorrow.*

His eyes had traveled to her lips. "I don't mind helping." *I want to taste you again. And again. And then make love to you. Do you want me to kiss you? Make love to you?*

Make love. What would it be like to make love to a woman other than Nicole?

"No, really. I can do it. I'll only be a minute. Why don't you pour us the last of the champagne?"

Looking both reluctant and relieved, he did as she suggested.

A short time later, Jill entered the living room and found Burke staring out the window. One hand was buried in his pant pocket, the other nursed the champagne glass. His beige suit jacket lay discarded over the back of a white velvet chair, while his tie trailed across a matching white sofa. Everything else in the room was white, too, except for apricot-colored carpeting that complemented the strips in the acquamarine-apricot-white wallpaper. Jill felt as washed out as the snow-pale furniture and hastened toward her glass of champagne that sat bubbling and beckoning on the coffee table. She picked up the glass and downed a generous amount of the straw-yellow liquid.

Burke turned at her entry. Their eyes locked.

He once more had the feeling of having just stepped onto a narrow ledge of a very tall building. He also felt the blood thickening in his lower body. He briefly wondered if she could see the physical evidence of it. He decided that he didn't give a damn.

She once more felt the quickening of all her feminine senses. Dark hair taunted from the vee of his white shirt, along with a slice of tanned skin. His shirtsleeves were rolled negligently upward to reveal the same coiled, dark-brown hair. Suddenly she wanted his hair-dusted arms about her so badly that her eyes blurred with tears. She also felt her thinly held control toppling.

"What do you want from me, Burke?" she whispered, her body hot, her body cold, her body in need of his.

"What do you want from me?" he countered.

"That's a cop-out," she accused, stepping toward the alabaster mantel and presenting him her back. Her hair, gleaming a burnished gold in the room's light, flowed like a silken waterfall to her tiny waist. Burke had the strong urge to drown himself in it. "Besides," she added, taking another mouthful of champagne, "you know what I want."

"What?" The word was blunt, bold, yet braided with brittle threads of vulnerability.

Jill glanced back over her shoulder.

"Say it," he demanded roughly.

For endless seconds the only sound in the room was the fast-beating of two hearts. That and the tread of destiny.

"All right," Jill answered in a voice as subtle as the sunset that had splashed the April sky in color only hours before. She swallowed low in her throat and answered honestly. "I want you to take this glass out of my hands, tangle your fingers in my hair, kiss me silly and senseless, then carry me to the bedroom and..." She stopped. Simply because there wasn't air enough in her lungs to continue.

Time beat its trapped wings between hesitation and hope.

Slowly, his eyes never leaving hers, Burke pulled his hand from his pocket and, bending at the waist, set his glass on the coffee table. He started toward her, halting only when he stood over her. His height required her to bend her neck and look up. "And what?" he whispered in sensual challenge.

"...and make love to me." The words seemed nothing more than a mouthing of her lips. Her suddenly dry lips.

Burke watched the formation of the words, watched as her lips opened and closed, watched as her tongue moistened away the nervous dryness. Without a word, he slipped the glass from her still-curled fingers and set it on the mantel with a clunk. Turning back to her, he whispered, "Like that?"

"Yes," she sighed.

With infinite tenderness, he wove his fingers through the cascade of hair at her temples. "Like that?"

"Yes."

His thumbs at her cheeks, he tilted her chin. Slowly lowering his head, he brushed his mouth across hers. "Like that?"

"No."

His lips settled for a more committed, though still quick kiss. "Like..."

"No," she whispered, pulling his lips down onto hers.

This kiss he intended to be slow and melting. Instead, the sealing of their mouths ignited fires that neither could control. Groaning, he urgently clamped his mouth on hers. Burke's tongue rushed forward to join hers, filling her mouth the way he longed to fill her woman's body.

Standing on tiptoe, Jill wound her arms about his neck and simply hung on as white-hot heat blazed in every cell of her body.

"Jill...Jill...Jill..." he chanted as his mouth released, reclaimed and frenziedly explored hers over and over again. "I need you," he whispered against her mouth. "God, I need you so much." Tearing his lips from hers, he yanked her swiftly against the muscular length of his body. He buried his lips against the soft, fragrant column of her neck. His breath was moist and warm as it fell into the shell-like contour of her ear. "I'm afraid. Sweet God, I'm afraid." And there was fear in each honestly spoken syllable.

"Of what?" Jill asked, her breath penetrating the thin fabric of his shirt and heating his shoulder. Her heartbeat thudded a dissonant rhythm against his.

"Of needing anything this badly." His hands shook as they slid down her back and cupped her hips. He pulled her flush against his need. And rubbed the vee of her thighs back and forth against him. He groaned at this heightened torture...but didn't stop it. In truth, he couldn't stop it. "God, Jill, I hurt...so bad." The confession was ragged, rough, wrung from him in a way that tore at Jill's heart.

"I know," she said in a tattered tone as she slipped her hand between their bodies. It unerringly found its target.

"Oh, Jill!" Burke groaned as her hand spread over the thick, hard, swollen heat of his need. His hand clamped hers more tightly to him, while his body trembled under the weight of her caress.

In that moment she would have given him anything. She certainly intended to give him everything she had. And for it, she was asking nothing in return. She harbored no illusions. This was not to be a night of shared love, for they had not spoken of love. Only need. Burke had said only that he needed her. Not even that he wanted her, but that he needed her, as man needed woman. She'd be his woman. She'd give him what he needed—she would please him—because she needed him to need her, and because she needed him as badly as he needed her.

"Make love to me," she whispered, moving her hand to become the bold aggressor that no man, especially one who'd lived in abstinence for a year and a half, could resist.

Groaning, Burke lifted her into his arms.

It should have been clinical, Jill thought moments later as they stood by the side of her bed in the golden glow of the lamp. Each of them undressing in hasty preparation for going to bed and making love should have been sexually clinical. In her dreams, Burke had always meticulously undressed her, then himself. Or he'd encouraged her to undress him. But in reality, haste was in the air, bidding them to hurry, hurry. In a way that should have been clinical.

But it wasn't.

Because of the emerald heat in his eyes as he watched every move she made.

Because of the way he invited her to watch every move he made.

Because along with haste, there was something else in the air—some unnamed emotion neither wanted to consider.

Unbuttoning her blouse and rolling her shoulders from it, Jill tossed the garment to the floor. Matching her, Burke unbuttoned the shirt he wore, tugged it from his pants and slid his arms from the endlessly long sleeves. Jill watched as his chest lurched forward, wide, strong, matted in dark spirals of hair that she fiercely longed to forage her fingers through.

He waited until her skirt had been unfastened and lay, a navy-blue puddle on the carpet, before reaching for the buckle of his belt. She slid the pure-white satin straps of her slip over her shoulders and it, too, slithered to the floor at her feet. Her eyes lifting to his, she reached behind her and released the snap of her bra as he released the snap of his pants. The metal zipper rasped a sharp, sensual sound in the silent room. Both hesitated, then removed that article of clothing. Her breasts fell forward; he pulled his pants down hair-covered striated-muscled legs.

At the sight of her round, rosy-crested breasts, Burke's breathing shallowed until he felt faint. At the sight of his maleness straining against the cotton of his briefs, Jill's body flushed with a heat so profuse she felt it as bright pink color in her cheeks.

Deliberately, her actions those of consummate woman, she eased down her panty hose. The thin, lacy scrap of silk she called panties followed. When she glanced up, Burke was bare . . . naked . . . consummate man.

She saw plains of bronzed flesh, a forest of brown hair scoring chest and legs, hair that provided a triangular haven for his bold sex, his unsatisfied sex. Oh, God, she thought, she was going to die if he didn't love her soon!

As Burke stared at the ivory of her skin, the high thrust of her perfectly shaped breasts and the shadowed delta between her legs, he thought that he'd had about as much as a man could take. If he didn't love her soon, he . . .

She turned and reached for the lamp.

"No." The command was husky, as if fog had drifted into his throat.

Her hand stopped. Her eyes mated with his.

"Leave it on. I want to see you."

She inched her hand away, turned back the bed covers and lay down.

He came to her.

Instantly, bodies tangled in love.

His mouth was hot on hers, his touch fevered as his hands roamed her body. It was the kind of heated touch that be-

longed to a man who has long thirsted and now has his lips
at a cup. But like the sun-parched man drinking cool water
for the first time in a long while, there was an imposed restraint. Burke was desperately trying to love her slowly, to
love her completely, to love her until she, too, was ready and
satisfied. The hand moving over the curve of her hip shook
from the pressure of that restraint.

"God, you're so small," he breathed, running his hand
the length of her thigh. "So perfect," he whispered as his
mammoth hand eased upward to cup her dainty, but wom-
anly-full breast. "But so small. Jill, I don't want to hurt
you. I won't hurt you, will I?" he mumbled, almost inco-
herently, unquestionably deliriously, as his lips kissed her
neck, then greedily merged once more with her mouth. His
tongue plunged deeply, hungrily.

She moaned, whispered a half no around the kiss, and
shifted her legs beneath him. He fell into the loving vee. He
lay heated, hard, moist and ready to join them. But he
didn't. Instead, he gasped at the intimate contact and
popped beads of sweat across his brow. His face was twisted
and drawn with lines of agony. Determinedly, though, he
sought to arouse her first.

"Burke," she whispered, arching against him.

"No, wait," he pleaded, "let me..."

"No," she argued, taking charge. She slid her hand
downward. Past navel. Past whorls of crisp hair.

His hand tried to intercept hers. "Jill, wait...no...ah,
God!" he moaned when she closed her hand around him.
His head arched backward, just as his hips instinctively
arched forward. His breath dissolved into full-throated
shudders. She eased him forward and, parting the moist
sweetness of her body, took him into her. Slowly. Fully. His
breath ceased to be. Along with hers. Both were replaced
instead by long.low moans of exquisite pleasure.

Hot. She was blistering hot, he thought, painfully fighting to keep his body still until hers could grow used to him.

Hard. He was steel-hard, but smooth as satin. And she
longed to feel him moving inside her.

Soft. She was softer than a new-born kitten. And wet. God, he could drown in the creamy wetness surrounding him and never care.

"Oh, Jill," he whispered near her ear as he supported himself with his hands. The muscles in his arms bulged from the strain of his weight. "So good...feels so good...nothing ever felt so good..."

"I know," she said, feeling the pressure of his penetration as the perfect filling of the emptiness within her. But then, her heart said, why shouldn't he be the perfect filling of the emptiness he himself had created? She moved her hands down his slide-curved back and arched against him—again and again until he had no choice but to join in.

"...so good," he whispered as his hips met hers in a steady beat, "so good...so..." Suddenly Burke felt a surge of too-keen pleasure rip through his body, followed by a feeling that was far too premature. He stilled his hips. "No, wait...too good...wait!" He tried to anchor her hips with his hand.

But it was too late. Jill knew that the instant Burke did. She felt his body tighten, felt him fight the speedy conclusion, felt him lose.

Burke felt the inexorable rush of climax. It was strong like the wind that blew in his face as he ran. It was powerful like the muscles of his legs as he ate away the miles, powerful like the sinewy muscles that presently strained and pumped against sheet and mattress.

"Damn!" he moaned, frantically increasing the rhythm of his hips. Suddenly he gasped, gasped again, then emptied himself into her in slow, hard thrusts.

Her hands slid down his back and cupped his hips as they moved against her. His buttocks were concave at the sides, his thighs rock-hard from exercise. His whole body was sweat-damp. Jill cherished the feel of his warm, wet skin and cherished also the relief he spilled into her. She hugged him to her, strangely feeling that the other times she'd made love had been but fake and false imitations. Right this moment, she felt very much like a just-awakened virgin.

At last, depleted, his eyes shuttered closed, Burke eased to her side. He drew her with him.

She watched him. For long minutes, she just watched him. He looked as much a man as a man could look, yet there was a little-boy innocence in the way his brown lashes lay crescented against his cheeks, a little-boy innocence in the part of his lips and the wayward sweep of his hair. Sweat dewed his forehead and the dimpled spot above his upper lip. His breathing was shallow, but growing stronger—so strong that his chest, woven in a furry tapestry, moved in and out. In and out in a way that begged her to touch it. She did. It, too, felt damp. And hard. And incredibly sexy.

As the latter thought was weaving a warm magic through her unfulfilled body, Jill felt her hand surrounded by one much larger. She glanced upward into Burke's eyes. He said nothing. He just stared. Softly. But thoroughly. Slowly, he raised her hand to his lips and kissed the palm. It was the most endearing, the purest, yet the most sensual, kiss she'd ever had.

"I forgot to tell you I'm a lousy lover," he said, the words shattering against her palm.

A half smile lazed about his lips—one she couldn't help but match.

"That's your opinion," she answered.

His smile suddenly faded. "I'm sorry. It had just been too long since..." He trailed off, repeating, "I'm sorry."

"It doesn't matter."

"It does to me. I wanted it to last longer."

She smiled again. "You were keeping track of time?"

"Yeah. With the second hand of my watch."

Her smile widened. So did his. His fingers inched forward and trailed across the width of her smile. His slowly disappeared again. He was remembering the way, only minutes before, her body had surrounded his. And the way he'd repeatedly, uncontrollably thrust himself deep inside her. "Did I hurt you?"

She shook her head. "I won't break, Burke. Honest."
Even as she said the words, she wondered if they were the

truth. Oh, it was true enough that he wouldn't break her physically, but what about emotionally? Was she getting in over her head? Or more to the point, was she getting in over her heart?

Jill might have tried to find an answer to the question, but just as she would have begun her search, Burke shifted, lowered his head, and, murmuring something about her day in court, covered the rosy nipple of her breast with his mouth. She sighed, laced her fingers in his hair and gave in to the sweet, swelling, heavy feelings that sluiced across her stomach . . . and beyond.

If she had controlled the first phase of their lovemaking, he controlled this one. The timing was all his. He kissed, suckled her breasts until they hurt with a tightness she'd never known, and when she thought she could take no more, his tongue would minister to the hurt in soft, tender licks that left her whole nipple wet and longing to be kissed and suckled again.

As honest in her passion as in all of her life, Jill held nothing back. With no inhibitions, she let him please her. She even helped him please her. When his hand slid between her legs, between petals still love-moist, she moaned and boldly drew his thumb to the heat of her passion. She eased her hand downward to cover his.

"Oh, yes, show me how," he whispered, her participation fanning the embers of his passion until he felt himself once more responding in a hard, turgid way. "Oh, Jill, you're so sexy. You make me feel so sexy."

"Oh, Burke," she groaned as her neck arched into beautiful submission.

"There?" he whispered, caressing her in a provocative, circular motion.

"Yes. Oh, yes. There. Harder!"

Under the guidance of hers, his hand became wildly creative. "Give me your mouth," he breathed, bonding their lips. His tongue dove forward in the same rhythm as his divinely ruthless fingers.

Minutes later, she cried his name in abject ecstasy as cool ripples of pleasure washed gently against the shores of her heated body. Before she could do little more than gather her breath, Burke eased his body onto hers and sank himself deep within her. Disbelieving, both once more walked on sensual shores. This time, together.

A LONG WHILE LATER, as Jill slept, Burke stood staring out into the moonlit night. He, too, had been asleep, but had wakened suddenly, restlessly. His mind was in turmoil. Nothing in his life had prepared him for this moment—this moment when his wife slept in her grave and his lover in the nearby bed.

He wasn't certain how he was supposed to be feeling. He moaned silently. Forget how you're supposed to be feeling, Rawlins, he told himself. How do you feel? He let the rhythm of his body settle into quiet contemplation. He felt . . . tired. It had been a long, emotionally taxing day. He also felt . . . unsettled. Like a fragile leaf fluttering in a wind that wasn't strong enough to blow it away, but kept it in a constant motion. But he also felt satisfied, body satisfied, the kind of satisfaction a man felt after a good and thorough loving. Jill. Thoughts of her body entwined with his shadow-danced in his mind and led to the question, Was he sorry they had become lovers?

No.

He waited for the guilt to come.

It didn't.

This gave him the courage to push the issue further, to make a comparison that no gentleman ever made, but it wasn't a crass comparison. In fact, it was a very gentle, very loving, one. He had loved his wife, he had loved making love to her—nothing could ever change that—but . . . but Jill's lack of inhibitions aroused him in a way—He stopped, knowing that he might be dangerously courting guilt. Say it, Rawlins, he taunted. You owe it to Jill. He sighed in acquiescence. Jill's lack of inhibitions, her raw response, aroused him in a way no woman ever hand. Not even Nicole.

He waited for the guilt to come.

Again, it didn't.

He gave another sigh, this one deep and relieved. He also realized that just thinking about Jill's lovemaking was arousing him. Once with her hadn't been enough. He had truly thought it would be. Hadn't he felt at some core level that simple, physical need had possessed him and that once that need had been met, once... But once hadn't been enough. And considering the present state of his body, neither had twice. And furthermore, he had the feeling that, if he made love to her a hundred more times, he'd still need a hundred and one. There was also the growing suspicion that he needed more than what her body offered. He needed her smile, the warmth of her personality, that special quality that made her uniquely Jill.

And how did he feel about that?

Strangely he felt both panicked and at peace. And guilty? Maybe. A little. He had grown accustomed to feeling guilty about everything since Nicole... Nicole. He frowned at the sudden realization that staggered his mind: not once, not once as Jill had lain beneath him, had he thought of Nicole. Quicker than quick, he felt guilt's powerful demons beside him.

"Are you thinking about her?" The voice was husky and came from near his elbow.

Burke turned toward the sound. Even if he hadn't been able to see Jill's silhouette in the pale moonlight, even if he hadn't recognized the voice that had so freely expressed her pleasure at his touch, he would have known it was she. No one but Jill McClain would have the guts to ask such a frank question, one that had such potential to hurt her.

"Yes," he answered. He could almost feel her stepping back under the weight of his verbal assault. He unquestionably felt her pain in his own heart. He reached out a hand to leave a solacing caress at her cheek. "But not the way you think. Actually," he said, pulling her into his arms when he realized the simple touch wasn't enough, at least not for him, "I was thinking more of you."

Jill readily went into his arms, her bare body folded close against his equally bare body. He fitted his hands at the small of her back, just beneath the wayward tumble of her hair. He rested his cheek on the top of her head. His arousal fit snugly, unselfconsciously, against her stomach.

"What about me?"

Burke's lips twitched at her expected curiosity. "I was thinking about how you arouse me."

"Do I?"

"What's wrong, lady? Can't you tell?"

He felt her smile curve into the hair on his chest. It tickled. He had the sudden urge to smother her in his arms, which tightened about her until her breasts flattened against him.

"What else were you thinking?"

He hesitated, then realized he'd been around her long enough that her honesty was rubbing off. "That you excite me," he said in a soft-rough voice, "in a way no one else ever has."

The admission was like sustenance to a starving woman. Jill hadn't even realized that she'd been hungry. She pulled back, her eyes finding his in the night. Nicole's name was never mentioned—Jill wouldn't have been that crude, nor Burke that treasonous—but her unspoken name drifted toward him in question. His answer was the gentle brush of his lips against Jill's before pulling her back into his arms. Her body hot-melted into his.

The moon had risen higher, the night had grown older, before Burke spoke again. "The answer is no."

"And the question?"

"Another one that you won't ask," he said, making it obvious that he had, indeed, known the turn of her thoughts minutes before. "I did not pretend that you were Nicole." He sighed, as if he still couldn't quite believe what he was about to say. "I never once thought of her, Jill. Never once."

Jill's heart filled with her joy and his sorrow. "And that surprises you?"

"Yes."

"And makes you feel guilty?"

"Guilty as hell."

She too sighed. "Oh, Burke, you're so determined to feel guilty, aren't you? So determined to punish yourself."

"I deserve..."

"Don't ever say that to me again," she interrupted sharply, her eyes once more finding his through the ebony thickness of the night. She deliberately softened her tone. "Don't every say that again." Her hand eased to the side of his face, where it rested against a slightly stubbly cheek. "You deserve good things. Because you're good."

Burke had the sudden liberating feeling that maybe, just maybe, if Jill said it long enough, often enough, he might believe he did deserve something good. Like her? Like a future? Like happiness?

"Are you staying the night?"

Burke heard the vulnerability in her voice and hated himself for what he was about to say. He drew the hand at his cheek to his mouth and kissed her warm, tender palm. "Jill, I don't know. I need...I need to clear some cobwebs out of my mind. Can you understand that?"

She understood. It hurt, but she did understand. "Yes." She moistened her lips and hoped her voice sounded stable. "I, uh...I'm going back to bed. If you want me to take you home, just wake..."

"I'll call a cab."

This time she didn't trust her voice. She simply nodded her head. She pulled her hand from his and stepped back. "Will you lock the door behind you if..."

"Yes."

He watched her walk away, watched her crawl back into bed, and thought that maybe it was his destiny to always be caught between. He was caught between life and death, yesterday and today, Nicole and Jill. Sighing in frustration, he turned back to the window and hiked a hand to his naked hip.

How much time passed he couldn't have said. Nor could he really have labeled his thoughts into any pattern. He thought of Nicole and of a picnic they'd once gone on. He thought of one Christmas when she'd given him a teddy bear. Curiously, the image of Nicole was faded, like a sepia-brown photograph from another lifetime. The only thing sharp was her voice saying over and over that she loved him. On the heels of that came Jill's pronouncement that love doesn't chain, it frees. For the first time, he wondered if he were insulting Nicole by hanging on so tenaciously to his guilt, by refusing to go on with his life. Jill was offering him resurrection. It was an offer he both resented and cherished.

"You deserve good things."

Burke turned toward the bed, his eyes lighting on the small heap beneath the covers. He thought of the eager way Jill's mouth had sought his, the unselfish way she'd loved him, the peace he'd felt inside her. He might not deserve anything as good as Jill, but the truth was, he couldn't turn away from her. Not tonight. Not tonight when his needs were so great and his thoughts so jumbled.

Stepping to the bed, he tugged back the covers and eased in beside her. Neither caring whether she was awake or asleep, he urgently pulled her into his arms. She was awake. At his touch, her tears began.

"I thought you were..."

"Shh," he whispered, "I'm not leaving. I can't."

He gently, roughly, pushed her to her back and, his mouth meeting hers, entered his male body into her feminine one. The action was as natural as night, as natural as their heartbeats mingling, as natural as the fact that grief, if given time, heals itself. With or without the griever's permission.

CHAPTER NINE

THE BUTTER-YELLOW SUN peered cheerfully through the sheer embroidered drapes. Jill stirred as sleep lazily, reluctantly fell away. Weight. What was the delicious weight at her waist? She sent her hand on a groggy reconnaissance mission. It reported that it felt an arm. A man's arm. Burke's arm.

Burke.

Jill's eyelids fluttered to slumbery slits. At the sight that greeted her, a smile tiptoed across her lips. He was...so thoroughly male, she thought as she studied the man sleeping beside her. He lay on his stomach, his right arm flung haphazardly, yet possessively, about her waist, while his left arm arched high on the pillow above his head. Almost like a halo. The thought broadened Jill's smile. No. There was nothing even remotely angelic about Burke in bed. He was pure man. Fourteen-karat and flawless.

Because she couldn't help herself, her eyes traveled over the wide expanse of his bare, bronzed, muscle-rippled back and up to his face, where thick, dusky lashes fanned his cheeks and lips whispered slow breaths. From there, her eyes shifted to his left arm. She saw a coiled biceps, she saw hair that began about the elbow and spread like wildfire down his arm, she saw a watch at his wrist, she saw a—

—gold wedding band on his finger.

An ache, as dull and gray as an autumn morning, folded itself over her like a suffocating blanket. No, she thought, her heart denying what she saw; yes, her mind confirmed. Tears sprang to her eyes. While he'd been whispering intimacies, he'd been wearing his wedding ring. While he'd been performing those intimacies, intimacies that had never felt right with any other man, he'd been wearing his wedding ring.

On the heels of this discovery came another. This one took her breath away and flung it alongside the scattered clouds peacefully dotting the morning sky. She was in love with Burke. Nothing short of love could have felt so good last night or could hurt so badly this morning.

But what about last night? Had it meant nothing to him except the release of pent-up needs? Probably not, Jill forced herself to admit. His body had needed hers, but his heart hadn't been involved. Because his heart belonged to someone else.

But hadn't he said last night that he'd never once thought of Nicole while making love to her? Hadn't he ultimately decided to stay the night? Hadn't he then made love to her with a tender fierceness that had paled anything she had previously known about making love? Jill's heart soared, then plummeted. Wasn't he still wearing the ring that bound him to another woman?

Suddenly the thought of the thin gold band was more than Jill could bear. Slipping carefully from beneath his arm—he moaned and shifted before settling back into sleep—she eased from the bed. She headed for the bathroom, where she forced herself to be practical. Today was Friday, a workday. Therefore, she had to shower, put on makeup and dress. Shelving personal thoughts as best she could, she managed the first two tasks as well as putting in her contacts. But when it was time to dress, she slid into her yellow satin robe instead. Jill padded back into the bedroom. Burke was still sound asleep. She'd just let him sleep a few more minutes, she told herself, adding that he needed the rest. She ignored the real reason that she didn't disturb him. She wouldn't know what to say to him when he would finally awake. And how could she possibly hide what was in her heart?

Grabbing his shirt from floor, she walked to the kitchen. She leveled the ironing board from its built-in nook in the wall, set the iron to heat and measured out some dark-roasted coffee granules. Soon the room was filled with the smell of brewing coffee and heated fabric. There was also the faint smell of Burke's cologne as the hot steam released the scent from the cotton cloth. It reminded Jill of Burke's body. Moving over hers.

Somewhere between sleeve and shirttail, Burke's arm curved around her waist. In that moment when his warm touch represented cold reality, Jill asked herself if she regretted last night. No, she hastily answered. She couldn't regret their lovemaking, regardless of how the relationship turned out; but dear heaven, right this moment how it hurt! Because it hurt so badly, because self-preservation is a powerful instinct, she steeled herself not to react to Burke's nearness.

She might have succeeded had not he pulled her back against his recently showered and still-bare chest. She still had a fighting chance when his right hand cupped her chin. She was lost completely, however, when his lips nuzzled hers until they had no choice but to part and allow him good-morning liberties that seemed more appropriate in the sexually pagan night.

"You don't have to do that," he whispered against her mouth, his breath warm, his lips hot.

Like heck she didn't, she thought in lazy panic, realizing seconds later that he hadn't been referring to her reaction to his kiss, but rather to her ironing his shirt. "Yes, I do," she whispered, "if you're going to wear it to work. It looks like..." She stopped, not quite willing to say what it did look like.

"Like I'd hastily thrown it off to make love?" he asked, his lips teasing hers by hovering near but not touching.

"Yes," she breathed, praying he'd kiss her and damning herself for the prayer.

When Burke did answer it, she forgot everything but the taste of his mouth; the inviting, taunting taste of his mouth. She forgot everything except how his tongue felt stroking hers, how that same tongue could flick and curl and tease so sinfully that it should be outlawed. She forgot everything except the feel of his smooth, soapy-smelling cheek—he'd obviously used her razor—rubbing up against hers like a male feline mating.

Get hold of yourself, Jill. Remember that this isn't a perfect relationship, and you're on the verge of getting hurt. Badly hurt.

She forced her mouth from his—God, the willpower it took!—and dragged her attention back to the shirt stretched out on the board. The hand that now guided the iron trembled. "I, uh...I need to get this done or we're going to be late."

Burke didn't seem to notice the restraint she was valiantly trying to hold on to. But then, he didn't seem to notice anything but her neck, which he'd exposed by taking his finger and drawing back the long flow of her hair. He was presently delivering tiny, nibbling kisses to the ivory column that seemed determined to arch, against its owner's will, so that he could deliver those kisses all the better, and move to bite, mouth, tongue the lobe of her ear.

Hot steam billowed upward. Jill wondered if it was coming from the idle iron or her body. Fighting back the moan of pleasure she wanted to give, she forced herself to pick up the iron once more. She whisked it across the last wrinkled section of the garment.

"Thank you," Burke whispered.

"You're welcome," Jill answered, shutting off the iron.

"Not the shirt," he said, now rooting his nose against the collar of her robe and planting kisses on her shoulder, "but, thank you for that, too."

Jill's hand hesitated in pulling the shirt from the board. Her veins suddenly ran cold with ice water. Surely he wouldn't thank her for...

"For what, then?"

"For last night," Burke answered as innocently as a lamb going to slaughter.

Jill recognized with some rational part of her brain that she was just looking for something to get angry about, something to offset the vulnerability she was feeling, and the hurt. If it wasn't this, it would be something else, because she needed to release the pressure building around her heart. Rationality damned, she whirled around, her flashing blue eyes meeting his.

"Don't you dare thank me for last night, Burke Rawlins! Just don't you dare sashay in here this morning thanking me as if... as if..." She vacuously waved her hand in the air. "Just don't you dare!"

Yanking up the shirt, the tails of her robe flapping in the air, she slap-slapped her bare feet across the kitchen tile toward the bedroom.

Having gone from warm neck to frigid-cold words in a matter of seconds, it took Burke several heartbeats to find his voice.

"Jill!" he cried out, following her. He found her standing in front of the dresser mirror heedlessly tearing the hairbrush through her long hair.

"What in hell..." he began, his hands plumped at his waist, then changed his tack. "What do you mean, don't thank you as if...? As if what?" His own voice had undergone a thunderous change.

Jill found his eyes in the mirror. His expectant, brooding eyes. She also found his bare chest. And the unbuttoned waistband of his pants. She tried to concentrate not on what she knew lay within those pants, not on the wisp of hair swirling in the tiny vee of the waistband, but on her anger. Her self-fabricated, self-perpetuating anger. "Don't you dare come in here thanking me as if I provide a service for sexually needy men. Got a hard-on, see Jill. Need sexual relief, see..."

Burke grabbed her wrist and hurled her around. The look in his eyes effectively silenced anything else she might have said. Time stood still as chests heaved, eyes battled. Jill mentally noted that he looked madder than hell—and that she hurt way down deep inside worse than that devil-owned place.

"I didn't know you gave me anything that I needed to thank you for," he said, his words deceptively soft as they slid between a thinned mouth. "I thought what happened between us was something that we shared. I thought I gave back everything I took. I didn't know either one of us was providing a service. Is that how you viewed it, Jill?"

The look on his face was one of anger, but also hurt, such sterling hurt that her eyes misted. She longed to throw herself into his arms and apologize . . . and beg him to love her the way he loved his wife, the way she, Jill, loved him. "No," she said, shaking her head. "No, I . . . Burke, I . . ."

"I was going to thank you," he interrupted, "for being so understanding last night. For giving me time to sort through my thoughts without pressuring me to stay. I know that wasn't easy. It wouldn't be for any woman. Or any man. Not after what we'd just . . ." He paused meaningfully. "What we shared."

A plethora of emotions swamped her. She felt unworthy of the praise he'd just bestowed on her. She also felt hurt, anger, fear—fear that he'd walk out of her life, fear that he wouldn't walk out of it until she loved him so much that she couldn't survive without him. But mostly, she just felt like a woman. She knew she couldn't stop herself from saying what she was about to. She knew it had been ordained the moment she'd seen the thin gold band on his finger.

"And did you sort through your thoughts, Burke?"

"Yes. I settled some issues."

"How about the issue of your wedding ring?"

For the briefest of seconds it appeared that Burke simply had no idea what she was talking about. At last, his eyes drifted to the hand still holding her wrist . . . and to the ring under dark discussion. Suddenly everything came into focus like a camera that's just been adjusted. Suddenly the argument made sense. Suddenly the anger in Jill's eyes looked more like hurt than anger.

"You never even said you wanted me, just that you needed me," she said in a broken, defeated tone that somehow made her look smaller than ever.

Crush-her-in-your-arms small, Burke thought.

"All the time you were making love to me, you were wearing..." She stopped, unable to go on because of the tears beginning to pool in her eyes.

Burke slowly released her wrist. The brush fell from her hand and thudded against the floor. Neither noticed. Without a word, he walked to the window and, leaning his hand against the frame, stared out at the mockingly carefree morning. As he watched a robin search out its breakfast, he thought how easy it was to screw things up. He also thought of the distant look in Jill's eyes and the hurt that trembled in the corners of her mouth. Suddenly, he cursed. Vilely.

"Jill, I..." He straightened and turned, his eyes melding with hers. "Jill, I'm sorry. I don't know what else to say. It was grossly insensitive of me. It was unforgivable. My only excuse is that...is that I've worn it so long, it's become such a part of me, that I simply didn't think about taking it off. I didn't take my watch off either," he said, holding up his arm to show her and pleading with her to understand. In three slow steps, he stood before her. And brushed the pad of his thumb across a silently fleeing tear. "I'm sorry. I'm sorry I hurt you," he whispered.

"It's all ri..." she tried to say.

"No, it isn't. It isn't all right at all. And I'm going to try very hard to make it up to you." The fingers of his right hand went to the ring on his left. "Beginning right..."

"No!" she said, her fingers stopping his. "Don't," she whispered, her eyes burning into his. "Unless... unless last night meant more than..." She hesitated, searching for the words that were in her heart.

It was Burke who found the words. "Unless last night meant more than my body needing yours?"

"Yes."

He smiled, sadly, self-derisively, and ran a knuckle across her cheek. "I haven't given you any reason to believe anything other than that, have I? I even told you from the very beginning that maybe all I felt for you was a physical attraction. I didn't want to mislead you, Jill, and I did believe it possible that I simply needed..." He paused, not liking the sound of the blunt admission.

"A woman?"

"Yes. I believed it until—" he swallowed "—until last night."

Their eyes said all kinds of things that words never seem capable of expressing. Beneath her hand, Burke's moved. Slowly, never taking his eyes from hers, he slid the ring from his finger. Jill, her heart pounding, stared at the white band it left behind, symbolic that something had changed, but that time was still needed to heal all wounds. His eyes still on hers, Burke pocketed the ring.

"And now, Jill McClain, there's something that I need to make very clear to you." His hands closed around her upper arms, and he pulled her to him. "It's something I should have made clear last night. Something I would have made clear if I hadn't been such a jerk." He took both her hands in his. One he nestled in a patch of hair dusting the spot over his fast-strumming heart, the other, he boldly settled against his sex. He was hard. Impressively so, considering it was early morning following a late night of loving. "I need you." He rubbed her hand up and down, down and up, the length of him, then slowly unzipped his pants and eased her hand onto his warm bare fullness. His breath escaped in a trickle, and his heartbeat accelerated. "I've made love to you three times," he whispered, his voice strained from her touch, "but I need you again. I need to be inside you. I need to feel you wet and warm around me. I need to feel your body moving beneath mine. I need to feel your body swallowing this ache." He pressed her hand hard against him for emphasis. "Need, Jill, need. Do you feel the need?"

"Yes," she answered, her voice strained every bit as much as his.

Burke's hands abandoned hers to their gentle witchery and moved to cup her face. "Now let me tell you what you can't feel. It's what's in my heart. I want you. I want you in a way I never believed I could want a woman again. I want to need you. I want you to need me. I want you to want me . . . as badly as I want you. I want, Jill, want. But most of all what I want," he said, lowering and inclining his head, "is for us to stop this conversation, stop arguing and make love."

His mouth took hers roughly, reeling her senses even as her head reeled backward to accept his kiss. As his lips worked over hers, his hands left her face and deftly untied her robe. Without hesitation, yet without haste, he eased the satin fabric from her shoulders. It darted to the floor like a slice of sunshine. His tongue piercing, probing, promising, his hands smoothed across her naked back and hips and tugged her tightly against him.

"We're going . . . to be . . . late for . . . work," she tried to say around his ravaging mouth.

"Do you really care?" he whispered, scooping her into his arms and starting for the bed without even once fully releasing her lips.

Her arms curled around his neck just as primitive need curled deep inside her woman's body. "No," she whispered, wantonly, wantingly. She threaded her fingers through his slightly damp hair and proceeded for the next hour to do everything she could to guarantee their tardiness.

THEY WERE LATE.

It was a fact no less than three people pointed out before they'd hardly pushed through the front door.

"You're late," the receptionist said as she kicked the soft-drink machine into submission.

"What didya do? Oversleep?" Ellen said, her pink sweater clinging to her full figure the way its image clung to a man's mind.

"Well, well. Look who finally decided to come in this morning," Charles Evans teased. "Guess being the two most famous lawyers in Boston has privileges, huh? Hey listen, you guys," he said, turning serious, "congrats. You did a great job in court. I was proud to be a colleague."

Jill and Burke slowed their pace, but didn't stop. Both smiled. "Thanks," they said in tandem.

As they walked by, Charles Evans couldn't resist one last lob. "If you two hurry up, you might get ten, fifteen minutes of work in before lunch."

"Stuff it, Evans," Burke replied, feeling inordinately happy for a man who'd had only a nodding acquaintance with sleep during the past twenty-four hours. The other man laughed. Jill and Burke walked on toward their offices. "Will you wipe the guilty look off your face, McClain?" he whispered out of the corner of his mouth.

"We should have staggered our arrivals," Jill said, smiling and saying good-morning to one of the secretaries.

"They'll think we met in the lobby."

"You should have gone by your apartment and changed suits."

"They'll think I'm not clothes conscious."

"They'll think your shirt is wrinkled . . . which it is, Rawlins," she said out of the side of her mouth.

Both nodded another round of good-mornings.

"It wouldn't have been wrinkled if you hadn't laid it on the bed after you ironed it," he accused.

"It wouldn't have been wrinkled if you'd watched where you laid me." At the realization of what she'd said, she glanced up sharply and blushed profusely. "I mean, where you put me, placed me, arranged me . . ." she stuttered.

Burke smiled wickedly. "I liked what you said first."

"You would," she answered, turning embarrassment into another instant smile and a "Good morning" for someone passing by.

"Good morning," Burke echoed.

"There you two are," Ida Tumbrello said as they approached her desk. She communicated with her usual efficiency. "Andrew wants to see you first thing, and you have tons of phone messages which I put on your respective desks."

"Thanks, Ida," Jill said.

"Congratulations," the older woman offered, her fawn-brown eyes beaming from her heart-shaped face.

Both Burke and Jill smiled.

"Thanks."

"Thanks."

"Is he in?" Burke asked, motioning toward the frosted-glass door with a nod of his head.

"Yeah," Ida said.

In the few steps from desk to door, Jill whispered, "Great. He's going to fire us right off."

"He can't. I own part of the firm. Besides, he's my father."

"Is it supposed to cheer me that I'll be looking for a job alone?"

"Don't worry, McClain," Burke said, tapping on the door with one knuckle and opening it. "I'll give you a reference. An excellent reference."

At the unladylike word she whispered as they stepped into the spacious, scarlet-carpeted office, a huge smile spread across Burke's face.

It was his son's smile that Andrew Rawlins saw first. He reacted like any father. With a silent prayer of gratitude for whatever—or whoever?—had put it there. His wise eyes roved to the woman beside his son.

"Good morning," Andrew Rawlins said with a smile of his own.

As always when confronting the senior member of the firm, the word distinguished came to Jill's mind. "Good morning, sir."

"Good morning, Dad. Sorry we're late. We had something we needed, wanted," Burke added, his eye catching Jill's, "to do."

Despite the inappropriateness of their surroundings, despite the numerous times they'd made love, Jill felt a tremor of renewed excitement course through her. She also felt unqualified love for this man. She was certain he saw her desire. Did he also see her love?

"No problem," Andrew Rawlins said, motioning for them to be seated. "You two earned a slow morning. By the way, I'm not sure I ever congratulated you yesterday, what with all the circuslike atmosphere toward the end. You did a fine job."

Burke and Jill nodded their appreciation.

"I was a little disappointed, though," Jill said, "that the verdict rested so much on outside intervention rather than on our legal cleverness."

"I have to confess to a little disappointment too," Burke said.

"I certainly understand what you're saying," Andrew Rawlins agreed, "but when you've been at this game as long as I have, you learn to gratefully accept help from any quarter. And I totally disagree," he said around a pair of steepled hands, "that your legal cleverness was lacking. You couldn't possibly have known what secret Paula Keszler was living with. The only thing you could do was present the case and create an atmosphere in which the woman wanted to come forward to help your client. You two did that. Obviously." The silver-haired man shifted in his chair and reached for a note. "All of which brings me to what I wanted to speak to you about. Mrs. Stroker called for you earlier and, when she couldn't get you, I talked with her. It seems she wants to make some fair settlement with regard to Ms Keszler and her daughter."

"Classy lady," Burke commented.

"I agree," his father replied, handing over the slip of paper.

Burke reached for it...with his left hand. There was only a brief hesitation, only a fraction of a second in which Andrew Rawlins's eyes fell to the pale circle of skin that indicated the absence of a ring. A long-worn ring. His eyes jumped to his son's and held for a meaningful moment. Gentleman that he was, he never glanced at Jill—she knew this was deliberate—and never missed a beat in the conversation. "This is where Mrs. Stroker said you could reach her."

"Thanks," Burke said, rising and picking up his brief-case.

Jill, too, stood and collected her case. She felt very much as if she were naked on a stage. Seconds later, as she and Burke were once more walking down the hall toward their offices, she said, "He knows."

"He approves. And even if he didn't..." Burke said, stopping in front of her office. The sentence was never finished because the two stood staring at each other like starry-eyed, high-school lovers walking each other to class and trying hard to get up the courage to say goodbye. "How in hell am I going to work, with you across the hall?" Burke asked, his voice husky and deep.

"The same way I am, Rawlins. With exemplary self-discipline."

"I don't seem to be real high on that commodity of late," he said, reminding her with the darkening of his eyes just how little self-discipline he'd had the past few hours.

Slowly those dark eyes lowered from her heaven-blue eyes to her moist, pink lips. It was a natural journey for what was on his mind.

Jill felt her whole stomach cave in. "Don't," she whispered.

"God, I want to," he whispered, his eyes brazenly meandering about her mouth before trailing upward. Blue and green eyes burned in a rainbow fire. "Shall I call Mrs. Stroker in lieu of a cold shower?" he asked finally.

She smiled. "Good idea, counselor."

"Right. Good idea." Burke took a step backward, then another, then turned and walked toward his office. Jill turned to enter hers.

"Jill?" he called out.

She turned back.

His face wore a haunted, vulnerable expression that bespoke long months spent alone. "I just wanted to see if it was true. That someone would be there if I called."

It was the hardest thing Jill ever did, but she somehow managed not to take him in her arms.

CONTRARY TO EXPECTATIONS, Jill did get some work done, primarily because the recent trial had knocked everything else into second place, a second place that now demanded attention. The list of that morning's return calls alone was staggering. Included in the list was a message for Jill to call Rob Sheffield. At first seeing the note, a frown had claimed her lips. Rob had never called her at work before. Was something wrong? Jill immediately thought of Mary, but told herself not to worry when she remembered the wonderful mood she'd found her sister in Sunday afternoon. Curiosity replacing concern, Jill had dialed Rob's number . . . only to be told that he was out and would call her back.

When lunchtime came, Burke and Jill found themselves committed to separate engagements. Both loathed the idea, though both agreed it was probably for the best. When Burke stuck his head in her door for a quick "See you later," the farewell turned out to be less than quick. Seeing the same need in her eyes that he felt, he had closed the door behind him and took her in his arms. The kiss ended only when it became necessary to end it or carry it to the natural conclusion. Both had endured frustrating lunches that in no way appeased the real hunger gnawing at their bodies. When Jill returned from lunch, she found another note saying Rob had called. She immediately phoned him back. He was once more out of the office.

If possible, the afternoon was busier than the morning. Jill heard Burke in the hall a couple of times, but he didn't stop in. She was and wasn't glad. When a light tap sounded on her door at a quarter to four, however, she half expected and wholly hoped it would be Burke.

It wasn't.

"Rob!" she said in surprise.

"Am I interrupting anything?"

"No, no. C'mon in." She stood and rounded the desk as her future brother-in-law closed the door behind him. "I tried to call you . . ."

"I know. I've been working in the field off and on today. I, uh . . . I was near here and thought I'd just stop in."

As he walked toward her, Jill's worry was reborn. Never had she seen his coffee-brown eyes without a smiling twinkle, never had she seen his face gaunt and haggard. He suddenly looked far older than his fifty-one years. He also looked scared.

"What is it?" she asked, indicating a chair and taking the one across from it. "What's wrong?"

"When did you last talk to Mary?"

Jill's heart accelerated. She had intuitively known what the topic would be. "Sunday. She seemed fine, though. Better than she has in a long while."

"What time, Sunday?"

"Afternoon. I probably left about six or seven. I left her in the attic packing. Why?"

"I called Sunday night about ten and got no answer. By eleven I still had no answer. I was frantic, so I went over, used my key and let myself in. I found her in a fetal position on the sofa." Here, his hand raked through his sun-bleached blond hair. "Jill, she was almost catatonic. She was in a world all her own. For a minute I don't think she even knew who I was." He paused, then added, "When she finally came around enough to be coherent, she said she was sick."

"Maybe she was," Jill said, grasping for straws.

"No," he said with finality. "She was lying. I know it. I could feel it." Restlessly, he stood and paced about the room. "She's been . . . I don't know, jittery, nervous, all week. The kicker came this morning." He sat back down as if he didn't realize he'd just gotten up from the same chair. "She called me about seven o'clock. She wanted to borrow two thousand dollars. Said it was for school, but I don't believe it. She was lying again."

The idea of Mary borrowing money was so foreign to Jill's thinking that it took a moment for Rob's words to register. "Mary borrow money?"

"Yeah. That's how it struck me, too." He was suddenly angry, the kind of anger that came from fear. "I don't care about the damned money, or what she's going to use it for—hell, she can have every dime I've got and burn it to cinders—but something's wrong. Badly wrong. And she won't tell me what it is . . . She won't trust me." The last remark revealed clearly that he wasn't only worried, he was also hurt.

"Rob, she loves you more than . . ."

"Will you talk to her?" he interrupted. "Maybe she'll tell you." His eyes turned glassy, and he fought to hold in check the strong emotions swamping him. "I'm losing her, Jill. To something. I don't even know what it is."

"Losing her. . . .losing her . . . I'm losing her . . ."

The thought wormed its way in and out of Jill's mind a thousand times after Rob left the office, and she started trying to reach Mary by phone. She tried every ten minutes until it was way beyond the hour Mary should have returned home from school. With each continued ring of the phone, Jill's own anxiety increased. Was something going on? And if so, what? And where the devil, Jill thought as she sat listening to yet another unanswered ring, was Mary?

MARY MCCLAIN STOOD in the Boston Public Garden. She was as close to panicking as she'd ever been in her life. She was supposed to have made the drop by four o'clock. It was now five-thirty, and the wooden bench under the crooked elm tree still held the sprawled figures of some of Boston's misfit youth. Punk hairstyles in flaming shades of purple and orange stood out against black leather worn so tight it was a miracle that it didn't restrict circulation. A safety pin pierced the ear of one young woman, while one young man wore a tattoo on his muscle-bulging arm that did more than suggest doing some obscenity to the world. What passed for music blared from a radio at such an obnoxious level that the pansies and tulips seemed to droop beneath its silence-shattering beat.

Two things were obvious: the punkers weren't leaving and she couldn't leave the money until they did. And furthermore, though she'd tried to be discreet, they were beginning to eye her suspiciously. Perhaps even maliciously.

Was he around? Could he see her dilemma? Or would he only think she hadn't complied?

"Hey, you!" the kid with the tattoo yelled.

"Hey, Momma, wanna party?" another hollered out and started toward her with an outstretched joint. The others laughed and jeered.

Fear, ugly and serpentine, slithered an acid streak through her stomach, causing adrenaline to spurt in her limbs. She started to run. Clutching the tapestry bag to her chest, she ran and ran, never once stopping, never once catching her breath. She ran from the ugliness in the park, she ran from the ugliness in the world, she ran with a prayer on her wind-chafed lips. *Please, please, let him call again! Please, please give me the chance to tell him it wasn't my fault!*

CHAPTER TEN

"WHY DON'T YOU try her again?"

Burke asked the question that Friday evening as he stood in the middle of Jill's kitchen. When he'd stopped by her office at five o'clock—the first time he'd seen her all afternoon—he'd been surprised to find her upset. He had immediately demanded to know what the problem was. She had immediately told him of Rob's visit and of the on-again, off-again worrying she herself had done over Mary the past few weeks. In a way neither thought to question, it was taken for granted that Burke would share her problem, just as it was taken for granted that they would share dinner.

"What time is it?" she asked. Glasses had replaced her contacts, jeans the dress she'd worn to work. Nothing had replaced the anxious look in her eyes.

"A quarter till seven."

"Where in hell could she be?" Jill said, her concern crossing over that thin line into anger as she snatched the phone from its hook and dialed. She leaned back against the wall. Even with her mind preoccupied, she couldn't help but notice, and react to, the truly fine way Burke's jeans fit across his derrière, stomach and thighs. After work, they had made a mad dash to his apartment so he could change clothes. They had then gone by a Chinese restaurant for take-out food. Burke had suggested the latter in lieu of dining out because it would keep Jill close to the phone. His sensitivity made her fall in love with him just a little more. She told herself she was possibly just that little bit more a fool.

"Do you want any more of this?" Burke asked, starting to clear the white cardboard cartons of egg rolls and shrimp-fried rice from the table.

Jill shook her head as the phone began to ring. She was already preparing herself for a long series of unanswered peals when Mary's voice came on the line before the first ring had even been fully completed.

"Hello?" There was a frenetic anticipation in the one word.

Followed by overwhelming relief in Jill's reply. "Mary?"

There was a pause. Then a deflated "Jill."

At that moment, Mary's disappointment eluded Jill. "Where have you been?" she asked in a lovingly fussy way. "I've been trying to get you for hours."

"I, uh . . . I had an errand to run after school."

Jill waited for an elaboration of said errand. When it was obvious that none was forthcoming, she asked point-blank, "Are you okay?"

"Of course I'm okay," Mary answered quickly—too quickly. "Why would you think I'm not?"

It crossed Jill's mind that she conservatively could give a score of replies to that single question. She settled on the response that first came to mind. It was also straightforward enough to be in tune with her personality. "Rob stopped by the office today. He's worried about you."

If the cold vibrations of surprise could carry through the phone lines, Jill's ear would have been frostbitten. "He did what?"

"He stopped by the office. Mary, he's half out of his mind with worry. He thinks something's bothering you." She didn't think it necessary to add that she herself shared the same concern.

"I . . . I . . ." Mary laughed nervously. "That's absurd. There's nothing bothering me. The last weeks of school are always hectic, you know that, and I'm trying to plan a wedding, for heaven's sake. I just wish the two of you would stop . . ." An uncharacteristic irritability had crept into

Mary's voice. She deliberately deleted it when she added, "Nothing's wrong. What more do you want me to say?"

I want you to tell me about the two thousand dollars you borrowed from Rob, Jill thought, but decided to wait until she was face to face to broach that subject. She consoled herself that she'd only have to wait overnight. Forcing lightness, she said, "What I want you to say is what time you want me to pick you up in the morning."

"Pick me up?"

"Yes. As in going shopping for a wedding dress. Remember?"

No, Mary hadn't remembered. Obviously. As the mile-thick silence attested to.

Jill's stomach retied itself in worry knots. "You are going, aren't you?"

"Ah... actually, Jill, I can't. Not tomorrow."

The knots tightened. "Why not?"

Silence stretched to the furthermost shores of frustration, where it crashed into bits of awkward flotsam. "Ah... Rob and I are going to the Berkshires for the weekend," she blurted out. "He thinks I ought to get away. In fact, we're leaving in a little while."

Jill first thought the answer was too fast, too pat, and too tidy, but then she remembered Rob's concern. It seemed well within the realm of probability to believe that with his protective personality he had persuaded Mary to go away for the weekend. But why hadn't he mentioned it that afternoon in her office? Maybe it had been spur of the moment. Yeah, that made sense. It also sounded like a good way to get Mary to open up to him. Which is probably what he had in mind.

"That sounds like fun."

"Yeah. I guess I have been working too hard."

"You'll be back Sunday?"

"Yeah. Most likely late."

"Then I'll talk to you Monday, huh?"

"Right." Silence. And more silence. "Look, I gotta run," Mary added, trying to keep her haste to get off the phone hidden.

"Sure." More silence, followed by Jill's sudden and strong need for reassurance. "Mary, everything is all right?"

"Everything is...great."

"Swear?"

Without the slightest hesitation, Mary answered, "I swear."

Even after both women had hung up, their hands reposed in contemplative stillness on the receivers. The phrase "I swear" echoed and reechoed in two minds.

SLOWLY, LIKE THE FIRST TREMORS of an earthquake, Mary's fingers began to tremble. Putting down the phone, she pressed them against her lips. Her lying lips. She'd never before lied to Jill. Never openly, never deliberately. The other had been a lie of omission; this was a blunt, purposeful distortion of the truth. And it had been so easy. Her mouth had so easily sworn to a falsehood; her mind had so easily conceived the lie about spending the weekend in the Berkshires with Rob.

Mary laughed—thin, tattered notes of a shallow hysteria that wove themselves in and out of shaking fingers. And what was worse, she was going to lie again. Now that the idea had occurred to her—the idea of making Jill and Rob believe she was spending the weekend with the other—she'd lie to Rob, too. Her future husband would call soon and, when he did, she'd lie. Easily. And necessarily. Because she had to have time and solitude. She had to wait right here by the phone until the blackmailer called. She had to make him understand that she had tried to deliver the money. She had to keep her secret safe from Jill.

Jill. Mary's eyes stung with salty tears. She had become the one thing Jill detested most. Or, perhaps, she'd been thus all along. Deceiver. Perjurer. Liar *extraordinaire*.

"WHAT'D SHE SAY?"

Jill slowly released the receiver and focused her eyes on the inquiring green of Burke's.

"That she'd run an errand after school. She said everything was all right. Even swore it."

"Do you believe her?"

Jill considered, brushed back a wisp of hair that had fallen to her forehead, and said, "She's never lied to me before."

"Then maybe that's reason to believe her now?" The comment was more question than statement.

Jill shrugged . . . and eventually smiled. "There is some logic to that." The smile faded. "I don't know, Burke. It's been like riding a roller coaster for weeks. One minute I think everything's all right, the next . . ." She sighed in frustration. "And then there's the question of the money. Why did she borrow the two thousand?"

"Maybe, just maybe," Burke said, "there's a logical explanation for the money. Maybe it does have something to do with school."

"But she never borrows. Anything. Certainly nothing that big."

"It's not like she went to a stranger for it. She's going to marry the man in a matter of weeks. Which brings me to another point," Burke said, stepping forward and raking back the same reddish-blond swath of hair that had once more stubbornly tumbled forward. "Maybe the vibes the two of you are picking up on are nothing more than the fact that she's just a little jittery about the wedding. How old is she?"

His touch was warm and created feather-fluttery feelings that scrambled over her body. "Fifty," she said on the breathless cloud of air his caress inspired.

His eyes dropped to her sweet-sighing mouth, while his voice just dropped. "You don't reach the age of fifty, without ever having been married, and enter lightly into the institution. Maybe she's just a little spooked."

"Yeah. Maybe. The idea had sorta crossed my mind, too," Jill agreed, adding, "She and Rob are going to the

Berkshires for the weekend.'' She watched Burke's mouth as if it had become the most fascinating thing in the world. Her lips unconsciously parted.

Burke's eyes darkened at the unspoken invitation. ''Good move. They can discuss whatever's wrong intimately.''

''Intimately,'' Jill repeated.

To both the word suddenly sounded very... very intimate. And the kiss they'd shared at lunch suddenly seemed like a very long time ago.

''There's probably nothing wrong that Rob can't fix with a few reassuring words,'' Burke said, his voice growing shallow, his body needy and hard.

''You may be right,'' Jill agreed, feeling that he might be right... and also feeling very soft and tingly in some very feminine places.

''A few caresses...'' His hand moved from the stray hair to her cheek.

''A few caresses...'' she repeated, her cheek nuzzling into his palm. Greedily nuzzling.

''...A few kisses...'' His thumb slid across her lower lip.

''...A few kisses...''

''...And he can probably get to the bottom of this,'' he whispered, his voice no longer substantial.

''And he can probably get to the bottom of this,'' she echoed, as though she had just enough breath to repeat this.

''There's no need to worry until you know you have something to worry about.''

''No... no need to worry... until...''

Jill's eyes closed. She sighed and swayed into the welcoming warmth of him, her fingers hooking into his belt loops for support. She felt weak from the ravages of worry and anxiety, weak from a day's worth, a lifetime's worth, of needing and wanting.

Burke's massive, comforting arms closed around her. As if he wanted to protect her from all troublesome things. As if he, too, were weak from needing the feel of her body against his.

"Don't leave me," she whispered in desperation. Tonight, tomorrow night, or a thousand nights from now, she pleaded silently.

"No," he whispered back.

Jill had no idea what he was promising temporally. And didn't really care. Right that moment she was in his arms. Right that moment his nearness overshadowed any lingering anxiety over Mary. Right that moment her love for him was greater than anything she'd ever known.

"...OH, BURKE..."

"Does that feel as good to you as..."

"Yes! Yes!"

"I'm so deep inside...are you sure I'm not hurting you?"

"You're not hurting me."

"But I'm so deep."

"You're not hurting me."

"I've wanted to be inside you all...oh, God, yes, do that..."

"Like that?"

"Yes! Oh, yes...ohh...ohh...oh, Jill!"

"Burke!"

"YOU HAVE THE SEXIEST BACK."

"Do I?"

"Yes. Remind me to tell you sometime how it once almost drove me crazy."

"Speaking of driving someone crazy, what are you doing?"

"Will you just lie still?"

"What are you doing?"

"I'm kissing this patch of freckles...and every, every, every vertebra of your spine...and..."

"That's not my spine. That's not even my back."

"Did you know you have a dimple on your tush?"

"Not until your tongue... What are you doing?"

"Rolling you over...and kissing your tummy... Did you know you had a dimple on your tummy?"

"That's my navel, idiot...and your tongue tickles... it.... Oh!"

"Oh, God, Jill, you taste so sweet. Like flowers and honey and Milky Way starlight."

"Burke!"

"Easy, love, easy. Just open up to me."

"Ah...ah...oh, yes..."

"I ALWAYS HATED BEING SMALL."

"Why?"

"Small isn't sexy."

"Wanna bet?"

"Will you keep you hand still? You're diverting me, and I'm trying to pour my soul out to you."

"Can I help it if your breast begs to be touched?"

"I don't hear it begging."

"You're too busy talking. Trust me, it's begging. So pour out your soul."

"Well, I always had these freckles..."

"I love freckles."

"...and I've worn glasses since I was five."

"I love glasses. They remind me of Sandi Turner."

"Who's Sandi Turner?"

"She was champion of the sixth-grade spelling bee. She had braids and braces and a pair of inch-thick glasses. That was when I first realized I was turned on by brains. By the way, McClain, you have a great pair of IQs."

"You're crazy."

"About your IQs. Incidentally, my IQ is not at zero, which is fortunate for you since it enables me to see the real gist of this conversation. You're asking me—in a round-about way, of course—if I think you're pretty."

"I am not!"

"Yes, you are."

"I am not that insecure a person. I am not that desperate for approval. I am not... So do you think I'm pretty? Don't laugh at me."

"That's not a laugh. That's an indulgent smile. And no, I do not think you're pretty."

"No?"

"No. I think you're absolutely beautiful. Here and here and here and . . ."

"Mmm . . . You kiss good."

"Pusillanimity."

"What?"

"The word Sandi won my heart with."

"Bet you can't spell it."

"H-o-r-n-y?"

"Close enough."

"DID YOU ALWAYS WANT to be a lawyer?"

"Yeah, Even when I was a little girl. It was sorta like it was programmed into me. I was hooked the moment I saw a *Perry Mason* episode. How about you? Did you always want to be a lawyer?"

"Nope. At five, I wanted to be a fireman. At ten, I wanted to be a policeman. At fifteen, I wanted to be a rock singer and have all the girls at my feet. At sixteen, as I recall, I wanted only two things: for my complexion to clear up and to get cheerleader Chrissie Newcomb in bed."

"Well?"

"Yeah, the complexion finally cleared up. Ouch! The hair on my chest is attached, McClain!"

"Not necessarily an unalterable fact, Rawlins. Give. What about Chrissie Newcomb?"

"By the time my complexion cleared up, she was going with Mean Tom Henderson. Tackle on the football team. There weren't no way I was messin' with him."

"So when did you decide on law?"

"My junior year of college. When Dad threatened to stop the money if I didn't major in something other than good times. But I loved law the moment I settled in with it."

"You're a good lawyer."

"I want to be better."

"Yeah. Me too."

"Why haven't you ever married?"

"That was an abrupt change of subjects, counselor."

"Not really. It's been on my mind for a long time."

"I don't know why I never married. I never wanted to be alone. I always saw myself with a house in suburbia, a station wagon, a dog with floppy ears and 2.5 kids, but it just never worked out. Oh, there were a few times it looked promising, but...I guess I was just too busy with my law studies. Sometimes lately, though..."

"Sometimes lately what?"

"I don't know, Burke. It's just that sometimes my life seems so empty. And at night. God, the night's are so long and...and..."

"And it seems that there's this big crack that you're falling through?"

"Yes. That's it exactly. And you're falling all alone...with nobody to give a damn that you're falling. Burke?"

"Hmm?"

"Do you still miss her so terribly?"

"That's funny. A week ago, I would have unequivocally said yes, but now..."

"But now?"

"Now I feel a hand pulling me out of the crack in the night."

"Burke?"

"Uh-huh?"

"You have hair on your chest..."

"Oh, my God, when did that happen?"

"...and I can find but one word to accurately describe it."

"Dare I ask what..."

"You dare. The word is yummy."

"Yummy?"

"Ellen was right all along. You are yummy...all over yummy...you're..."

"You're obviously giddy from no sleep."

"I told you my brain shuts off at 4:00 a.m."

"Do you want to go to sleep?"

"No. Do you?"

"No."

"So what do you want to do? Raid the refrigerator? Watch the late, late, late show? Hey, what are you doing?"

"Showing you what I want to do. Damn, McClain, you don't weight ten good pounds. Here, put your leg on this side...that one there...now, straddle me just like that...and let me look at you. Ah, Jill, you're so beautiful."

"Am I?"

"Yes, you am."

"Then why are you frowning?"

"I've kissed you too much. You're lips are swollen. Don't do that. Don't part your mouth that way or..."

"Or what?"

"Or I'm just going to have to kiss you again. Dammit, Jill, you did that on purpose."

"You're right. I...mmm..."

"Mmm yourself."

"Your lips are soft."

"So are your breasts. They feel so soft and full."

"Kiss them."

"Come here."

"Oh...oh, Burke...I love it when your tongue..."

"God, all I have to do is touch you and your nipple hardens. Look. See?"

"Yes...umm...oh, Burke, they hurt..."

"Funny, so do I. Slide your hips down."

"You're hard."

"You're dewy."

"You're hot."

"So are you."

"Oh, Burke, I..."

"Put me inside you. Ohh... God, Jill, what you do to me is criminal!"

"So try me in court, counselor."

"I'd rather try you right here in bed!"

JILL AND BURKE AWOKE in the middle of the day just as the sun was climbing to its highest, hottest point. They toyed with the idea of feeling guilty about still being in bed at such a decadent hour, but both decided that guilt could go take a flying leap. So fainéant and indulgent did they become, that they breakfasted in bed, read the morning paper in bed, then crawled into the shower—together—for a sinfully slow soaping and nothing even resembling a rapid rinse. That completed, they once more found themselves in bed—toweling each other off amid giggles and tumbling play.

They forced themselves to reenter the world of responsibilities at three-thirty. But even then they fudged. Though they made the most valiant of efforts to keep their minds on the task before them and their hands off one another as they negotiated the grocery basket, their efforts met with failure. Somewhere between floor wax and furniture polish, Burke pulled her into his arms and kissed her as soundly as both products promised to perform. Later, as he carried their sacks to the car, he realized it was the first time in months that buying groceries hadn't depressed him. In fact, he felt downright happy.

After shopping, Jill dropped Burke off at his apartment. Their plans were simple. She would pick him up again at seven o'clock, they would go to dinner and she'd spend the night at his apartment. What wasn't simple was how each would manage until seven o'clock. The prospect of a few hours apart seemed unbearable.

Jill spent the time doing the laundry and her nails and fighting niggling thoughts of Mary. She consoled herself with the fact that Mary was with Rob. Which was exactly where her sister needed to be, right? And hadn't he probably by now righted whatever the wrong had been? The truth was, she thought, as she stroked the frosted white enamel the length of her nail, there wasn't anything she could do about the real or imagined problem until Monday. That being the case, she considered a happier topic: Burke.

In regard to him, she allowed herself to feel a cautious optimism. She knew that she made him happy in a way he hadn't been in a long, lonely while. She knew that slowly she was tearing down self-imposed walls, walls erected with the concrete substance of regret and bitterness and held together with the mortar of guilt. She knew also that she needed desperately to tell him of her love—it was a heavy, smothering burden on her heart—but she was afraid to. Would it draw him nearer? Or distance him? It was a question for which she had no answer.

No more than Burke had an answer to his question. How had his life taken such a drastic turn in less than forty-eight hours? He didn't know. He knew only that it had. He knew only that he felt a soul-trembling jubilation—that kind of euphoric exultation that comes only from finding yourself alive after having already given yourself up for dead. It was the kind of rescue that heightened one's senses. As he dressed for the evening, the shower stung his skin with greater force, the cologne he splashed over his chest smelled richer, more fragrant, the cloth he wore felt stimulating to every newly awakened skin cell. Life suddenly seemed real, not merely pretended. And furthermore, it suddenly felt good—good, do you hear it, world?—to be alive.

Adjusting the silk tie, Burke turned and reached for his jacket. In midstretch, his eyes connected with the photo that stood a silent vigil at his bedside. He stopped, straightened and stepped toward the picture. He lifted it. And stared down into the face of the woman who'd been wife and lover to him. She smiled back in an eternal pose of joy. And understanding?

Burke made no attempt to classify his feelings, nor censor them, nor punish himself for them. He simply let them be, like mountains and night and silvery moonlight. Love. He had loved Nicole; he still loved her in a way that would always be real. In that way, he would be ever-faithful to her. But she was now a misty shadow-siren moving over the landscape of his sweet memories. She was yesterday. And things he could not change. Because mortal man had not the power. She was part of him, soul of him, heart of him; yet dead to him. She could never again call his name, never hold his hand, never dream life-dreams with him. She could not save him from the crack in the night. Only Jill could do that. Jill, who was becoming part of him, soul of him, heart of him. Jill, who was today and tomorrow and, in her own way, things he could not change, for he could not change what was growing in his heart.

Raising his hand, Burke brushed his fingertips across the zenith of a flawless cheek. He felt the dead-coldness of the glass, the live-warmth of his memories. He felt free. Free at last. Sighing her name in loving farewell, he stood, walked to the dresser and stored the picture of Nicole Lynch Rawlins in an empty drawer. Next to an abandoned circle of gold. Never looking back, Burke grabbed his jacket, turned out the light and walked from the room . . . and yesterday.

THE CHARLES RESTAURANT on Chestnut Street in historic Beacon Hill was a cozy little Italian hideaway. Nestled among town houses, it had a bay-windowed front and a brown-and-white canopy that umbrellaed over the entrance like a giant, benevolent caterpillar. Inside were chocolate-brown walls accented by white latticework and candelabras that gleamed with golden light.

At a back table, a sumptuous meal of chicken with fontina cheese and mushroom sauce behind them, Burke sat unabashedly adoring the woman before him.

"The breast of chicken was wonderful," Jill said, her chin resting on her steepled hands.

"Yes," he replied, his eyes drinking in the way curls dipped and plunged in wayward, drunken fashion from the silken knot secured atop her head. Though the strawberry-blond mass of hair looked beautiful in the severe style, Burke longed to free the pins from their imprisoning duties and let the hair flow through his fingers. He longed to feel it wrapped around his body with its fragrance tempting and teasing his senses.

"The wine was exquisite," Jill added.

"Yes," Burke agreed as his eyes delved into and sensuously swam in the deep, ocean blue of hers.

"The spumoni was great."

"Yes," Burke answered, his eyes roving from her soft, bronze tinted lips to the dusky peach of her skin. She wore an ivory knit sweater with a turquoise-and-gold snake choker coiled around her neck. Matching turquoise and gold studded her ears.

"There's a three-headed green monster sitting on your shoulder."

"Yes," he said, his eyes roaming over the gentle swell of her breasts, then roving upward to join once more with hers.

Jill's lips twitched. "You're not listening to me."

Burke's lips sliced into a slow grin. "Yes, I am. I have a three-headed green monster sitting on my shoulder." Without missing a beat, he added, "Have I mentioned to you tonight how beautiful you are?"

"Twice in the car, once as we were walking into the restaurant and once—or was that twice?—as we ate. But I have no objections to hearing it again."

"Greedy."

"Insatiably so."

"You're—" his hand stretched forward and his fingertips grazed her cheek "—gloriously beautiful. So very beautiful."

Unsteepling her hands, she placed her palm atop the warm hand at her cheek. For seemingly endless, for outrageously sensuous seconds, they simply stared at each other. Fiery vibrations flashed across the short distance separating them.

"Do you have any idea the restraint I'm exercising?" he whispered as he turned his hand over and meshed his fingers with hers. Drawing her hand to the table, he held it tightly, possessively, in a way that left no doubt as to the restraint he spoke of.

"You don't need to on my account," she taunted in a soft, seductive, steal-away-your-control voice.

Burke's eyes darkened in response. "Oh, but I do. I couldn't possibly do to you here what I want to. Not and stay out of jail tonight."

"What do you want to do to me?" They were playing games, lovers' games.

"You're playing with fire, McClain," he warned.

"A little heat never hurt."

"How about a lot of heat?"

"How about burning together?"

Leaning forward, speaking low, with his eyes and his lips, Burke answered her question of what he'd like to do to her—boldly, frankly and in minute and sensual detail. The intimacy was somehow made all that much greater by the crowd of people around them.

Jill felt her body go all steamy and smoldery. Burke felt his grow impossibly tight.

"You're right," she said with a sudden breathlessness, "you'd most definitely spend a couple of hours in jail over that."

"Would you bail me out?"

"Maybe," she said. Her free hand made daring little circles on the hand that held hers. "If you'd promise to do what you suggested to me again."

Slowly, suddenly, surely, the world receded. There were only two people in the room, two people with bodies aflame, two people with the need simply to be alone. Burke swallowed low; Jill sang a small sigh between provocatively parted lips.

"Let's go," he whispered roughly.

Settling the bill was torture, waiting for the valet to bring around the car a punishment that neither Jill nor Burke wanted to endure. A gentle rain had begun to fall, making a pattering, peppery noise on the overhead canopy. Somehow the tapping sound of the rain, its fresh, cool, earthy smell, only added to the sensuality of the moment.

Burke's hand rested at the small of Jill's back, where it burned...burned...burned. As did their eyes, each melting into the other's. The night had grown thick with longing.

Thighs brushed. Bodies begged. Breath halted.

"Burke..." she whispered, having no idea what words were to follow, knowing only that she had to say his name.

He groaned, circled his arm about her waist and blatantly hauled her to him. Before the night, before all of Boston, his mouth took hers. His lips had but sealed with hers, his tongue had but pierced the sweetness of her mouth, when the moment was shattered by—

"Burke?"

Their mouths fell apart. Burke's head jerked upward and around. His eyes met the fog-gray eyes of the man who'd called his name. His eyes then went to the brown eyes of the woman beside the man. Familiar brown eyes.

"Frank...Marlene..." Burke said in a tone that underscored his surprise.

The woman's brown eyes shifted, slowly, subtly, to the woman still partially in Burke's embrace. The gray eyes followed. Both pairs of eyes glazed with hurt; the gray filled with censure. In an instinctual move, Burke's hand slid from Jill's waist, leaving her with the sudden feeling of dread. No one spoke. For an embarrassingly long time.

At last coming to himself, Burke said, "I'm sorry. I'd like you to meet Jill McClain. Jill, Marlene and Frank Lynch." There was a hesitation, as if Burke were pulling the next words from deep within himself. He then added, with lips that still tasted of Jill, "Nicole's parents."

CHAPTER ELEVEN

SHE HAD KNOWN.

In an inexplicable way, Jill had known the couple were Burke's parents-in-law. Maybe it was because the brown eyes staring softly, sadly, at her were an exact replica of those in the picture in Burke's apartment. Maybe it was the disapproval imprisoned in the gray eyes. Maybe it was the way Burke's arm had slipped from her waist as if he'd been caught in some compromising situation. Whatever—she had known.

Just as she knew she had to respond in some way. "How do you do?" she answered, nodding and praying that the words hadn't sounded as stiff to them as they had to her. She also longed to wipe the incriminating wetness of Burke's mouth from her own. Contrarily, she longed to step back into his protective arms.

To her greeting, Frank and Marlene Lynch mumbled socially correct responses. Marlene even managed an awkward, insincere smile.

"Jill and I . . . we work together," Burke said.

And do a whole lot more together, the following silence accused.

Burke looked at his parents-in-law, the Lynches looked at their son-in-law and the woman who'd usurped their daughter, while Jill glanced up at Burke. His jaw was rigidly squared, with just a hint of a muscle twitching at the corner of his mouth. He didn't look at her. Whether it was deliberate or not, she didn't know.

Finally, and curiously, it was Marlene Lynch who tried to save the moment. "I saw your picture in the paper," she said to Jill. "You and Burke worked together on that trial."

"Yes," Jill answered, feeling that the woman was hurting desperately, but trying, just as desperately, to be fair. That attempt at fairness stabbed at Jill's heart and made it bleed with empathy. It also made her feel a guilt she knew that logically she didn't deserve to feel. Her reaction went a step further in making her realize the irrational guilt that had paralyzed Burke all these many months.

"Congratulations," Marlene Lynch said.

Jill tried to concentrate on the conversation, caught the word, and realized that the woman was speaking once more of the trial. "Thank you," she answered.

Another silence descended. The two men eyed each other and, though there was keen disapproval in the gray gaze of Frank Lynch, he eventually did say, almost resentfully, Jill thought, "You're looking well."

"I'm feeling well," Burke replied. "How have you been?"

"Not worth a damn."

"Don't you think we ought to go in?" Marlene Lynch interrupted, looping her arm through her husband's. "Our reservation is for nine o'clock." The look she gave the man beside her was pleading.

Another crisp, tart silence ensued. The moment, the people, seemed poised on an emotional precipice.

"Yeah," Frank Lynch said at last, adding in curt dismissal, "Burke."

Though Frank Lynch never once glanced back at Jill, Marlene gave a small, embarrassed smile that seemed to encompass both her and Burke. The woman had taken only a few steps when she stopped and briefly, so briefly, laid her hand on Burke's arm. "Keep in touch," she whispered. The couple then disappeared inside the restaurant.

The night grew darker. The rain pummeled harder. The car awaited them at the curb. Burke and Jill stood in place as if too war-weary to move. At last Burke gave a heavy, emotion-laden sigh. Jill turned toward him, wanting from him—as she wanted to give to him—some solace and comfort, some assurance that everything was all right even though the world at present seemed crazily tilted off its axis. Seeking, wanting, needing, her eyes climbed to his. Her heart stopped cold at the emotion she saw clouding the green irises. Anger. In all its chilling presence.

"Burke..." she whispered, confused and suddenly feeling as though she had washed ashore on a lone, deserted island. She reached out her hand to touch him. He rebuffed it by turning away.

"Let's get the hell out of here," he growled, and started for the car.

Jill's heart fell at her feet.

The drive back to his apartment was bleakly quiet except for the rhythm of windshield wipers. Jill negotiated the streets of Boston, while Burke seemed to negotiate those of hell. Staring straight ahead, never once looking at her, he seemed lost. Which was exactly how she would have described herself.

Why? she wanted to scream. Why had they had to run into Nicole's parents now? Why did they have to open wounds that had begun to heal? Why did they have to awaken a guilt that had begun to sleep? She understood with the clarity of a lover's paranoia that Burke's anger was directed at her, probably even at himself. It was the kind of anger that accompanied resentment and regret. Regret. Oh, God, she thought, as she remembered the way his arm had slid from her waist, the way his eyes had not met hers, the way he'd deliberately avoided her touch: he regretted their relationship!

Not a word was spoken as she parked the car in the lot behind Burke's apartment building, not a word was spoken as they took the elevator to the fifth floor, not a word was spoken as Burke unlocked the door and threw it open wide. He walked directly to the bar in the kitchen and poured himself a stiff bourbon on the rocks.

"Help yourself," he said gruffly, throwing off his jacket, wrestling loose the knot of his tie and whipping open a couple of buttons of his shirt. He headed for the glass door of the balcony, slid it to the left and stepped out into the rainy night. An overhang protected all except the balcony's wrought-iron rail from the free-falling rain. It was to this rail that Burke walked and stood staring out into the moist darkness. He drew the drink to his lips.

From the light of a lone living-room lamp, Jill watched him. In shadow, his shoulders were mountain broad. And isolating? Yes, isolating. They had become a wall of flesh that he was, even as she watched, erecting between them. He was shutting her out. He was pulling once more into himself. He was running away from her.

Jill's stomach emptied, then filled with a fuliginous panic. On the heels of that came a fiery-eyed anger. How dare he discard so lightly what they'd shared together!

Burke turned at the sound of Jill's advancing footsteps as she came outside. Silhouette met silhouette. Each sought the other's eyes, but could not find them in the night blackness. Instead, both settled for the other's presence.

Jill felt her heart pumping a pace that threatened survival. Burke felt his heart swelling with an emotion so powerfully tender that it practically knocked him back against the rail.

"Jill, I'm sor. . ." he began in a choked voice.

"No," she interrupted sharply. "I won't let you say it."

Burke's eyes narrowed.

"I won't let you tell me it's over. I won't let you tell me you're sorry about what's happened between us." Unknowingly, she took a step forward. Just as unknowingly, her bottom lip began to tremble. "I told you once I wouldn't fight Nicole for you. Well, I've changed my mind. I'll fight her, I'll fight her parents, I'll fight you. . ." Jill's voice cracked. "I'll fight the devil himself, but I won't. . ." Plump tears plunged from her eyes and rolled down her cheeks. "I won't. . . let you walk away."

She stood in dewy-eyed defiance; Burke stood in speechless surprise.

Finally, he bent, set his unfinished drink on the glass table flanking the chaise lounge and closed the short distance to Jill. He roughly pulled her into his arms. The actions knocked her topknot askew and sent hair spilling over an ear. "Where in sweet hell," he said, smothering her with his nearness, "did you get the idea that I'm walking away?"

"You're angry with me," she whispered, her arms clinging in tight desperation. Her warm breath penetrated his shirt and heated his chest, just as her tears seeped through and dampened it.

Burke was again speechless. What she'd just said made no sense. It made no sense at all unless... Pushing her just that distance from him that allowed his eyes to peer down into her tear-ravaged face, he said, "Angry, yes. At you, no. Ah, Jill," he added, his voice sandpaper scratchy, "I'm angry with myself."

"For getting involved with me?"

"No. God, no! Is that what you think?" She didn't have to answer. It was written in the moistness of her dark eyes. It was written in the mascara smudges on her cheeks. It was written in the quivering silence that followed the question. He pulled her back into a fierce embrace that cascaded another section of her partially upswept hair. "For a smart lady, lady, you sure can arrive at some dumb conclusions."

Her arms folded about his muscle-corrugated back. "I thought...I thought...you pulled away from me," she added in a lover's accusation.

"I didn't deserve your touch."

"You're not angry with me?"

"No! No!"

Tears again filled her eyes. These tears, however, were tears of relief and release. They were the kind of tears a woman didn't have to explain because they were granted to her simply by being a woman.

Burke asked for no explanation as he scooped her small body into his arms and carried her to the chaise lounge.

Carefully, he lowered her to its padded depths, then stretched out beside her. Once more, his body swallowed hers in an embrace.

He was warm and safe and hers in this dark night.

She was warm and woman-sweet and his in this dark night.

"Oh, Jill," he whispered as his lips spoke near the curve of her ear. "I'm sorry about this evening. I'm sorry you had to go through that with Nicole's parents." His voice lowered to the sound of regret dragged through jagged gravel. "I'm sorry I betrayed you."

She turned her head until her face was full with his. Their noses brushed, their lips almost touched, their breaths twined and laced. "Betrayed me? I don't under—"

"What else can you call what I did?" he interrupted irritably. "I sacrificed you at the altar of Nicole's parents." His jaws clenched, along with every muscle in his body. "Why didn't I tell Frank to take his rude censure and go straight to hell?"

"Because you're a caring, sensitive man and you knew that he was hurting." Jill eased her hand to Burke's neck and rubbed. The muscles there felt like gnarled knots in a tree trunk.

"But I should have defended you, our relationship. I should have told them you're the only good thing that's happened to me in so long... Oh, Lord," he said with a haunted sigh, "why do we never say what we later wished we had?"

"Because we're human."

He sighed again, this time resting his forehead against hers. "It was so stupid, Jill, but I felt this instant guilt at being caught with a woman in my arms." His voice roughened. "I hated myself for it, but even as I was hating myself, I felt my arms pulling away from you." As if to somehow make up for that fact, his arms now tightened about her.

"I know, Burke. I felt the guilt, too."

He looked down into her face. "You did?"

"Yeah," she said with a soft smile. "Guess I've been hanging around you too long."

"I hope not," he said, his expression dead serious. Her expression sobered to match his. "Oh, Jill, I'm sorry if they hurt you. I'm sorry if I hurt you."

"The only way you can hurt me is if you regret..."

"No," he said, the pad of his thumb drying the last of the tears from her face. "Never. And you don't have to fight anyone for me."

With a sensual slowness, his thumb caressed the softness of her cheek. Jill closed her eyes and gloried in the feel of him, gloried in the feeling of belonging to him. And she did belong to him. In a way that she didn't even belong to herself. For nothing in her incomplete being could satisfy her need to be possessed by him.

"Oh, Jill," he whispered, his lips roaming over her ear, her temple, the cheek his thumb was lovingly tormenting. Guiding her head with the deft pressure of that thumb, his mouth dropped to hers.

Sweet. His lips were candy sweet and fire hot. Just the movement of them on her mouth made her breasts grow firm, her body soft with dewy want. Like a lover who knew her body as well as his own, he sensed her instant response and brought his hand to her breast. He cupped the fullness, kneading and stroking until her nipple peaked and her breath trickled between his lips. Smoothing his hand down her skirt, he molded the cleft between her legs. He could feel the passion-heat seeping through the layers of fabric. His thumb made intimate swirls on the outside of the cloth. She melted, moaned, arched closer to what he temptingly offered.

Around them the night sang. Of blackness. Of rain. Of man and woman engaged in the oldest of rituals.

Jill's senses were swollen with the moment—the woodsy smell of Burke's cologne, the flowery smell of spring, the musky smell of desire, the feel of occasional raindrops splattering on the rail and wetting her stockinged legs.

Burke, too, was lost to his senses—the porcelain-fragile feel of the woman in his arms, the honeyed taste of her lips, the shadowy sight of her as she lay beneath him... responding honestly to every move of his body.

"Burke..." her lips pleaded against his.

He slid his hand beneath her skirt and slowly, maddeningly, trailed it up her thigh. With agile movements, he found and unfastened the garters she wore. He peeled away the scrap of cloth masquerading as panties. Then, with slight, subtle, actually quite discreet adjustments of their clothing, he shifted his weight and entered her.

Jill's body opened to receive his, just as her heart opened wide and full.

"I love you," she whispered, her hands easing into the loosened waistband of his pants and splaying across hot bare flesh.

"I know," he whispered. "I know. It's all that saves me!"

He didn't say he loved her—which she desperately wanted him to do. She felt his love, though. She felt it in his touch. She felt it in the way his body made love to hers. She heard it in the sweet-calling of her name in the dark, damp night.

As JILL AND BURKE exercised the sacred rites of love, Lenny Larimer exercised the profane rites of hate. His unconsecrated mementos before him—the letter he'd read a thousand times, the obituary he'd read a thousand times a thousand—he sat by the phone. His fingers stroked the receiver's smooth black surface in an unholy caress. A smile misshaped his slender lips.

He was making Mary McClain wait. He was making her sweat. He had seen what had happened in the park Friday and knew that she would be frantic to hear from him. He'd call her... oh, yeah, he'd call her... but he'd call her in his own time. For once, Leonard Larimer was calling the shots. For once...

He jerked his head upward at the sound of his name. His eyes scrambled about the room for the source of his mother's voice.

"Leonard Larimer, have you no conscience?"

"No," he whispered in protest to the noises invading his head. The way they always did of late, they made his heart throb...throb...throb...until his chest felt as if a heavy weight were crushing his ribs from front to back. His breath grew thin and slack. His hand clutched, frenziedly, at the shirt collar of his security-guard uniform, trying to rearrange it so he could breathe better.

"Have you no human decency?"

"Stop it!"

"Aren't you even the slightest bit ashamed?"

"No! Go away!" he roared, drawing the gun from its holster.

The noises stopped. Instantly. As though they'd never been.

He waited, brandishing the gun in warning.

Slowly he reholstered it. All remained quiet. Except for the throbbing thrum of his heart. This time there had been a pain in his chest, but it was going now, easing, dissolving into the flesh of his body.

"No," he whispered one last time, chasing away the last of his she-demon mother. The hand on the receiver once more stroked back and forth in an unholy caress.

MARY MCCLAIN'S HAND slowly, limply fell from the phone that was tucked at her side. She slept. At last. Finally. And for the first time in days. Shifting her weight on the sofa, she dreamed—of Rob and weddings, of a tiny baby she'd named Jill and of a man named Tommy, a first love, an innocent love, a love of so very long ago.

SUNDAY MORNING at four-thirty, Jill and Burke made the prudent decision to spend Sunday night in their respective homes since it was apparent they weren't sleeping while together and since it was also apparent that they had jobs to hold down. That decision made, they sealed it by again making love. Exhausted, sated, entwined in each other's arms, they fell asleep a little after five o'clock. They slept all day and parted that afternoon at four. By the following morning, both were suffering from withdrawal symptoms and were desperately in need of just a glimpse of the other. Jill arrived at the office first. She'd hoped to find Burke already there. She found Rob Sheffield's phone message instead.

She immediately called him. "Rob?" A horrible feeling of déjà vu swept over her. Rob sounded as if a storm had swept over him, leaving him tossed and twisted inside out. "What's wrong?" In some hazy quadrant of her mind, she realized she had asked what was wrong, not if something was.

"I wish I knew. I called Mary last night when I thought she'd be home." The words didn't sound appropriate for a man who'd spent the weekend with Mary, but under the duress of the moment, Jill let this pass. "I couldn't get her. I couldn't get her early this morning, either. I called the school at eight—she's always there by then—and they said she'd called in sick. So I called the house again. She still didn't answer. Jill, what's going on?" he said, his voice suddenly sounding wind wild. "Where in hell is Mary?"

Jill's pulse rate had increased the second Rob had begun to speak. It now ticked with a rampant rhythm. She told herself to just stay calm and rational. In honor of both, she said, "If she's sick, maybe she's gone to a doctor."

"I thought of that. But why not call me to take her? Or you?"

The same thought occurred to Jill even as she was making the comment. She was searching for another calm and rational explanation when Rob asked, "Did she give any indication this weekend of what's been bothering her?"

The question bit at Jill's composure like a sharp-toothed serpent. "What?" she asked breathlessly.

"Did she say anything this weekend? I thought maybe just the two of you together, she'd tell . . ."

"You didn't go to the Berkshires." It wasn't even a question. In her heart Jill already knew the hideous answer.

"What?"

"She told me...she told me the two of you were going to the Berkshires."

The silence was complete as the implications settled.

When Rob finally spoke, his voice was disturbingly calm. "She told me you and she...that you were going to finalize the wedding plans...look for dresses and all that. She made it sound like it was a girl-stuff weekend at your place."

Jill turned an unlikely mixture of searing hot and freezing cold. In all of her life, she had never felt so scared or so helpless. She would have given anything for the shelter of Burke's arms.

"Ji-ll..."

She heard the voice of a strong man crack and knew that at the other end of the phone Rob Sheffield was coming apart. For his sake only, she forced herself to be strong. "Rob, listen to me. There's got to be an explanation for all of this, and we'll find out what it is. You're at work, aren't you?"

"Yes. I, uh...I have a couple of things I have to do around here." He had entered the numb, nonfeeling world of shock, and his words had a spaced-out quality. "A report on an experiment..."

"Rob, I'll start calling her the minute I hang up. If I get her, I'll call you. In the meantime you finish up there, and can you go by the house and wait there for her?"

"Yeah," he said. "I'll...I'll take the rest of the day off."

"Everything's going to be okay," she said, praying to God she was right.

"Yeah...yeah."

"I'll talk to you later, then."

"Right." As Jill was lowering the phone from her ear, she heard, in a tone that cut at her heart, "Jill? Where is she?"

"I don't know, Rob," she replied, her own voice breaking. "I don't know."

MARY MCCLAIN SAT huddled on her sofa, the tapestry bag of money clutched tightly to her chest. Beside her, the phone rang. She had lost count of how many times it had rung. A dozen? Two dozen? She didn't know, and it didn't matter. She wasn't going to answer it. He had called the night before and had told her to bring the money at noon today. That had been the only phone call she'd wanted to take. She didn't want to talk to Rob or Jill. Talking to them only made her feel guilty. She had lied to them. The only two people in the whole world she really loved and she'd lied to them. And she felt sick, sick at her heart, that she had.

The phone stopped.

She relaxed her hold on the bag.

And checked her watch.

Three hours and it would be over. Or would it? Was this only the beginning? Would this nightmare go on and on and on until money and truth had been bled from her? Was it destined that she be exposed for what she was?

The phone began another sharp peal.

Mary jumped.

And fought back the clawing fear that her world was about to shatter.

IT WAS PRECISELY 9:09 a.m. when Burke tapped on and pushed open the door of Jill's office. A smile was already traveling to his lips, and that light-headed feeling he always got when he saw her was already thinning his thoughts.

At the sound of the door opening, Jill turned from where she was standing at the window. The incessant ringing of an unanswered phone still echoed in her ears.

When his eyes found hers, Burke frowned, slowed, then stopped altogether. "What's wrong?" he asked, knowing immediately that she wasn't crying, but close to it.

Jill swallowed back the clotted knot in her throat. "Mary didn't spend the weekend in the Berkshires with Rob."

"What?" he asked, stepping forward and placing his briefcase on the edge of her desk. Hers, too, lay there, unopened. "I thought..."

"She told Rob she was spending the weekend with me." Jill inclined her head to meet the eyes of the man now standing before her. "Rob called earlier and said that she called in sick today. But there's no answer when we call the house. Oh, Burke,'' she whispered, allowing her composure to slip now that he was near enough to catch it, ''she's disappeared again.''

The despairing look on her face, the blue eyes glassy with crystalline tears, tore at his heart. He did the only thing he could to comfort her: he pulled her into his arms.

Hers wrapped about his waist fiercely, as if she were trying to push her body into his. ''Hold me,'' she pleaded. ''Please hold me!''

''I've got you,'' he said, fitting her so tightly to him that body angles and planes blended and melded. ''I've got you.'' His hand moved to cup the back of her head, burrowing her face deep into his shoulder.

''I don't understand,'' she whispered. ''I just don't understand what's happening.'' His suit jacket had come unfastened, and she stood with her cheek flush against his shirt. Her words were fluttery vapor that drifted to his ears. ''She lied, Burke. She's never lied to me before.'' Hurt was profoundly present in her voice.

''Maybe...'' he began, but didn't finish. There was no ready reassurance on the tip of his tongue. ''Have you tried to call her?''

Jill glanced up into his concerned face. ''Conservatively, a hundred times.''

''What's the number?'' he asked, slowly disengaging their bodies and picking up the phone. She told him. He dialed it. Spreading his hand inside his jacket and at his waist, he waited for the phone to ring. Which it did. Again and again.

Jill watched, hoping, praying this was the moment Mary would finally answer. Her eyes locked with Burke's, she waited. Waited. Waited.

''I hate that damned phone!'' she said when it was obvious Mary wasn't going to answer. ''That stupid wrong number was the beginning of Mary's strange behavior.''

''The call she got the night you had dinner with her and Rob?'' Burke asked, remembering Jill's mention of the call

Friday evening, when she'd first worried about a vanishing Mary.

Jill nodded, raking back her hair with a hand that looked none too steady.

"I will admit," he said, "that she acted a little peculiar the evening I ate there. When the phone rang while we were playing ball..." He stopped at the sudden look that flashed across Jill's face. "What is it?"

"I just remembered another phone call," she said, her eyes going hazy blank with her effort to uncover details that were buried deep within her mind.

"When?"

"A week ago Sunday when I dropped by the house, I left Mary in the attic packing. As I was leaving, the phone rang. I answered it, but thought it was a wrong number."

"What did the caller say?"

"It was a man, and he said..."

"What?"

"I can't remember exactly. Something about...something about needing to talk about your daughter again." She shrugged. "I don't really know why I thought of it now, except it's just one more phone incident. You don't think it could have anything to do with... What is it?" she asked, concerned by the look on his face.

"Nothing," he said, but in his heart he wasn't so sure the thought that had just crossed his mind was nothing. In fact, he thought it might be a very decided something. He had just made a murky association between Mary McClain's frantic need for money and a strange caller who'd talked about a daughter. The thought was wild, the thought was crazy, but, dammit, the thought made sense! Most particularly in view of everything that was happening.

"No, it is something," Jill accurately assessed, moving toward him. "What?"

His hands gripped her shoulders. "Let me do some checking..."

"What?"

"I may be wrong."

"Tell me!"

He didn't want to. God, he didn't want to! What if he was wrong? But, worse, what if he was right?

"Please," she whispered, her eyes, her touch, begging in a way he couldn't resist.

"Jill, think about it. The scenario is perfect for... for blackmail."

The word hung in the air. Blackmail. It was that sinister crime that happened occasionally in real life, but mostly in dramatic mystery movies or TV soap operas.

"That's absurd," she said. "What would Mary have in her life to be blackmailed about?"

"Let me check on something," Burke repeated, reluctant to add anything more without proof.

"If you know something, if you only suspect something, I want to know what it is."

Her voice had a steel edge. It was the same steel that ran down the back of her diminutive frame. She might be physically pint-size, but she was emotionally pounds-strong. *In many ways, she is stronger than me,* Burke thought.

"I think it's possible... What if Mary has a daughter? What if someone found out and is blackmailing her?" His words were blunt. But it was the truth the way he knew Jill would want it.

He watched as denial registered on Jill's face. He then saw her struggle to at least accept the possibility. That acceptance was not without a price, however. He felt her knees weaken. At the slackness, he eased her into the nearby chair and, pulling at his pant legs, hunched down before her. His palm splayed across her cheek. It felt chilled.

"I could be wrong, you know. Dead wrong."

"How... how can you verify it?"

"Do you want me to try?"

She swallowed, making her mouth form the hateful words. "You know I do."

Yes, he did know it. And in that moment he prayed harder than he'd ever prayed for anything that he was wrong. "Let me go to my office and make a few phone calls..."

"No!" she said, grabbing his hand in hers. "Make them here."

His eyes bore deeply into hers. Slowly, he brought her hand to his lips and tenderly kissed her knuckles. He then pulled his hand from hers and stood. Walking to her desk, he sat down in her chair and picked up the phone. The receptionist came on the line.

"Would you get Harriet Cummings for me?" he said, his eyes on Jill. At the mention of the corporate lawyer who had bureaucratic connections, Jill's blue irises glazed with a thin sheet of surprise. She said nothing, however. Seconds later, Burke spoke again, "Harriet, Burke Rawlins here. Fine, thanks. Listen, I want you to do something for me. Can you give me the name of someone in statistical records who can rush something through for me?" He listened. "Yes. Very important. Thanks. I owe you."

He hung up the phone and looked over at Jill. The usual color in her cheeks had faded to a white comparable to the shade of the ivory suit she wore. It took all of Burke's willpower not to get up and go to her.

"Is someone going to call you back?" she asked, wondering if the calm voice was really hers.

He nodded. They waited. For two long minutes. At last the phone rang. "Rawlins here. Yes, yes, I appreciate your calling, Susan. Listen, I, uh ... I need to confirm a birth. I know the mother's name, that the child was a girl, and I guesstimate it occurred about—" he remembered Jill's saying that Mary was fifty years old "—let's say thirty, thirty-five years ago." He frowned. "No way at all without the child's name?" He waited, listened. "That's great. Then let's try hospitals. Yes, I know they're a lot of hospitals in Massachusetts," he said semi-irritably. "For that matter, it could have been anywhere in the country. No, no, I know you can't check every hospital in the United States. Look, try the hospitals in Shawsheen under the name of Mary McClain. That's correct. M-c-C-l-a-i-n. Yes, I'll hold."

He looked up at Jill, who seemed even paler than before. The shock was receding and pain settling in.

"I'm waiting while she uses another line...something about a computer terminal." A seemingly endless period of time passed before he once more said into the phone, "Nothing?" He gave a disgruntled sigh.

"Try Massachusetts General," Jill said.

Burke glanced up. "I was born in Massachusetts General. Maybe Mother would have taken Mary...maybe Mary would have gone there to..." She stopped. "A large hospital away from home would have been more discreet for an...unwed mother."

Approving the logic, admiring the lady, he said, "Check Massachusetts General."

Time dragged. The clock ticked mockingly. Burke willed part of his strength to the woman who sat quietly waiting. Finally, "Yeah? Okay, give me that information," he added, picking up a pen and scribbling the notations on a pad. "Yeah. Yeah. When? Right. 1952." Abruptly, his hand stopped in midmotion. Along with his heart. He jerked his head toward Jill. "What did you say?" His voice was only a filmy pretense of speech. "Are you sure about the child's name? Well, dammit, be sure! I'm sorry. Please check again." His eyes darkened. "I see. Yes. Yes. I appreciate your help."

With nerveless fingers, Burke hung up the phone. A sick feeling snake-crawled through his stomach. Everything in him was screaming no! No, he couldn't be the one to tell her this. But, dear God, how could he trust this to anyone else?

Jill sensed Burke's sudden reticence. Her heart accelerated. "What is it? What did she say?" Her eyes pinned his, demanding an answer, an honest answer.

"Jill..."

"Just say it. Whatever it is."

But he couldn't. He couldn't!

"Dammit, Burke, what is it?" Jill asked, jumping from the chair and leaning across the desk to turn the notepad toward her. Burke's hand stopped hers. Her eyes warred with his. They also begged him to answer . . . and to somehow protect her from the ugly revelation she knew was coming.

"A Mary Elaine McClain gave birth to a daughter." He swallowed. "On January 12, 1952."

The fact that Mary McClain had, indeed, given birth to a daughter took precedence for a full cycle of wild heartbeats. When the date finally registered, Jill frowned. "But that's . . . that's my birthday." Still, the full implication of Burke's words had not dawned. Like a withering bolt out of the blue, it suddenly did. Her face blanched; her heart stopped. "What . . . what are you saying?" she asked, her string-thin voice a stranger to her own ears.

Slowly Burke stood, walked around the desk and took both of her hands in his. He felt them trembling even as he heard his own voice tremble. "She named the child . . . Jill Elizabeth."

CHAPTER TWELVE

"No. It's not true."

Jill heard the obligatory denial slip through her lips and thought how contradictory it was to what she was feeling in her heart. For there, in an intuitive way she couldn't explain, she believed totally, unequivocally, what Burke had just told her. She felt its truth. That truth, however, distorted her life as if she'd unexpectedly been shoved before a fun-house mirror.

No, Jill thought wildly, this newly revealed life was not the distortion. The old life, the old belief, the belief that Mary was her sister, that was unreal.

She realized vaguely that someone—Burke? Yes, Burke— was saying something to her. She tried to concentrate on what that something was.

"...right?"

"What?"

"Are you all right?"

She focused on his face and saw eyes that were bright with worry. She also noted that, while one of his hands still held one of hers, the other had slipped about her waist to offer a greater measure of support. She swayed into him and let his arm tighten. "Yes," she said, nodding. "I'm fine."

"Why don't you sit down?" Burke said, urging her toward a chair.

"I don't want..."

"Sit down," he said softly, but firmly. He exerted just enough pressure to force her onto the chair. "Stay right there," he ordered, trying to pull his hand from hers. Unconsciously, she held onto him, resisting abandonment.

"Jill, turn loose," he commanded, prying at her fingers. "I'll be right back." She let go of him ... or maybe he was just stronger than she. "Don't move. Do you hear me?"

Jill nodded again, her hair gently swaying about her shoulders.

With rapid steps, Burke crossed the room, opened the door and disappeared into the hall. Jill leaned back in the chair and closed her eyes. Her heart was hammering a swift rhythm that left a residue of smothered sound in her ears. Beyond it, she could hear the mocking repetition of her name: *Jill Elizabeth ... Jill Elizabeth ... Jill Elizabeth ...*

She thought back to the day in the attic when she'd felt such a sharp sense of separation at the thought of Mary marrying Rob. It was an almost too-keen feeling for a sibling relationship, but not for a child-parent one. Had some intuitive force been at work even then?

"Here." She opened her eyes—a shock-hazy fluttering of reddish-hued lashes. Burke was squatting before her and holding out a paper cup of water. She reached for it, took it, and they both watched as her hand trembled so badly the water almost sloshed over the edge.

"I'm shaking," she said in disbelief.

Burke placed his strong, steadying hand over hers. "Drink," he ordered in a tone that could only be described as a loving whisper.

The water tasted cool and moistened the stress-parched dryness of her mouth. With Burke's help, she took another sip, followed by another. She lowered the cup to her lap. Her eyes went to his. Subliminally, she realized he was worried about her. A warm feeling seeped through her. It was the kind of feeling people hold on to when the world is coming apart at the seams.

"Why?" she whispered. "Why let me believe all these years that Mary ... I don't understand. Why, Burke?"

His fingers tucked a truant wisp of hair back behind her ear. "I don't know, baby. I just don't know."

"What am I going to do?"

Her eyes shone wide, blue and with more vulnerability than Burke had ever seen in them. He longed to take her to bed, pull her next to him and shelter her with his body. And he would at some point because he needed to protect her the way she needed his protection. But right now, he said, "You're going to ask Mary the question you just asked me."

"Will you go with me?"

"Do you want me to?"

She reached for the hand at her cheek and threaded her fingers with his, a desperate lacing. "Yes. Please go with me."

He stood, drawing her up with him. "Let's wait for her at her house. Wherever she is, she'll go home eventually."

Within minutes, Burke had ordered all their appointments cancelled and was escorting Jill to her car. His arm at her waist was her only reality. There was a moment's silent apology as he held the door while she seated herself in front of the wheel. His look eloquently said that he should be driving and not she.

"I'm all right," she said. "Really I am."

And she did feel better. At least in some respects. There was something wonderfully comforting, something wonderfully normal, about stepping out into the sun-dappled spring morning. The world was still as it should be.

A thousand feelings—some she could catalog, some she couldn't—wandered in and out of her being as she drove the twenty-plus miles to the little yellow house that now had a poignant familiarity that was soul-painful. Shock, nature's kind, benevolent anesthetic, still numbed the outer edges of her consciousness, but deep within were churning the feelings of hurt and anger. How could *they*—she could not yet nominally distinguish between her mother and grandmother—betray her so? And why would they choose to?

"Do you have a birth certificate?" Burke asked, breaking into her musings.

She turned her eyes to him. "Yes." She knew what he was asking. "My parents are listed as Margaret and Edward

McClain." Somehow that planned deception, even from the moment of her birth, deepened the hurt.

Burke saw the pain. "Jill, give her a chance to explain. There may even be a chance we've misinterpreted..."

"Do you believe that?" she interrupted. When he didn't, couldn't, answer, she added, "Neither do I."

Slowly, she turned the car into Mary's driveway. The shades were pulled like lids over sleeping eyes, and the house looked lonely and vacant. Suddenly, Jill's heart filled with anxiety. Where was Mary? Was she in danger? Just as suddenly, her heart filled with a thick, loving emotion. It didn't matter what her biological tie was to the woman, it didn't matter about lies and deceptions and betrayals, she cared about her. She always had, she always would. It was the unbending, unending nature of love.

IT WOULD HAVE BEEN HARD to say who was the more surprised—Jill at unlocking the door and finding a missing Mary sitting on the sofa, or Mary, at finding an unexpected Jill standing before her.

"Mary!" Jill said, relief flash-dancing through her body.

"Jill!" The hands holding the tapestry bag tightened until the knuckles were bleached of color. Normally docile eyes were suddenly streaked in panic. "W-what are you doing here?"

"I've, we've, been trying to reach you all morning," Jill said, thinking that Mary looked awful, a sleepless and sallow-skin kind of awful.

"I... I was just on my way out." Her response was in no way an appropriate explanation of why she had been unreachable all morning, and all three people in the room knew it.

"Where are you going?" Jill asked, her eyes, along with Burke's, lowering to the bag being throttled to death in Mary's lap. Mary's eyes followed theirs. She forced herself to relax her grip. "I, uh... just out... an errand..."

"Out to meet a blackmailer?" Jill suggested, posing the question in her typically blunt fashion.

The room grew silent. Suck-in-a-breath silent. Mary McClain's face drained to a color so sheet-white that the freckles dotting her oval face seemed to turn pitch-black. The bag in her suddenly lifeless hands slid in slow motion, then fell from her lap and to the floor. In the stillness, the fall sounded like a deafening thunk, just as the fluttering of twenty-dollar bills escaping the bag sounded a great deal like the end of the world. Three pairs of eyes lowered to the incriminating green-and-white currency.

Burke sighed, momentarily closed his eyes and wished to God that he'd been wrong.

Mary prayed—foolishly, she knew—that Jill didn't know why she was being blackmailed.

Jill felt a wave of nausea. In spite of everything, she realized that she was still holding out hope that she and Burke had been wrong. But they hadn't been. Dear God, they hadn't been! And if they were right about the blackmail, they were right about...

Jill raised her eyes to meet those of the woman before her. What was to play out now was nothing more than a verbal ritual. Jill would ask the question, just as each knew she would, just as each knew she must. Mary would answer, in exactly the same way, for exactly the same reason. And the answer, both women already knew.

"Are you my mother?" Jill asked softly.

In an unconscious gesture of protection, Burke stepped closer to Jill. His hand touched the small of her back.

Mary McClain swallowed, deeply, and opened her mouth. No words emerged from her pallid lips. Ultimately, she pushed herself from the sofa and stood. Shaky, unsteady, she swayed. Instinctively, Burke grasped her upper arm to balance her. She glanced up at him and smiled. "Thank you," she whispered, then woodenly moved off toward the window. She stared out into the sun-drenched morning and thought about her first-graders who were probably at recess—playing ball and jumping rope and squealing in tag, doing all those innocent things that children do. Innocent. The opposite of guilty.

"Mary?" Jill pleaded in an I-need-to-hear-you-say-it tone.

Mary McClain turned, her autumn-brown eyes glistening with the tears of thirty-four years' worth of sorrow. She also felt a keen sense of resignation. She supposed she had always known this moment would come. It briefly crossed her mind to wonder how Jill had discovered the truth, but admitted that the how didn't really matter. Nothing mattered except the cleansing of guilt, the begging of forgiveness.

Mary again swallowed; this time she spoke. "Please believe me, Jill. I never intended for you not to know. I promised that to myself, and to you, the first time I ever held you in my arms."

Fine tremors had begun a wavy surge over Jill's body. "Then why?" Her voice was barely audible.

"I was waiting for the day when you were old enough to understand. I . . . I guess I didn't know how to judge that day." She smiled again, this time sadly and in accompaniment to a lone tear that slid down her cheek. "I kept thinking that tomorrow would be a better day to tell you. And then it was too late. Too many tomorrows had passed." She wiped at the tear with the heel of her hand. "And in a strange way I guess I had begun to believe the lie I had lived so long. Lies are like that. They deceive the liar as well as those lied to."

"But why lie at all?" Jill asked, not even attempting to hide her lack of understanding. "Why not from the beginning . . . ?"

"Don't you think I wanted to?" Mary asked, slicing through Jill's question with a voice harsh and rough and totally atypical. Fresh tears flooded her eyes, robbing her words of their stability. "Don't you think I wanted to claim you as my daughter?"

"Then why?" There was an equal roughness in Jill's voice, an impatience, a make-me-understand.

"Your grandparents!" Mary shouted before deliberately forcing her voice to a lower pitch. "Your grandparents wouldn't let me." Bitterness clung like cloying hands to each word as she added, "I don't think I've ever forgiven them for that. Or ever will."

The couple she'd always thought of as parents being referred to as her grandparents further disoriented Jill. She had the sudden urge to pinch herself awake from a bad dream. She also had the sudden need to be in Burke's arms. She settled for stepping closer into the hand still at her back. It splayed wide in a way that was comforting.

"I don't know," Mary said, "maybe I should have stood my ground. But I was only sixteen, Jill. Sixteen. And scared. And we'd already had a battle royal. When I told them I was pregnant, they insisted I give the baby up for adoption. I told them I'd never do that. Never. And I meant it. I also accused Mother of being more concerned about her social standing in Shawsheen than she was about me." Mary's face clouded with painful memories that the years had not been able to whitewash. "It was the only time Mother ever struck me. But it was true. God help me, it was true. She was more concerned about what her friends and neighbors would think than she was about what happened to me."

For the first time Mary's prejudice against small-town thinking made sense. What didn't make sense was the fact that never once had Jill suspected Mary's antagonism toward Margaret and Ed McClain. Perhaps it was to Mary's credit that she'd tried not to taint Jill's opinion of the couple.

"So they told you you could keep the baby, but that they'd raise it as their own," Jill offered, unable now, though, to keep a sense of bitterness at bay.

"Yes," Mary concurred quietly. "Oh, and they concocted an elaborate plan," she said with a mirthless laugh. She wiped futilely at the wetness on her cheek and sniffed. "Suddenly, and very conveniently, Mother had an aunt dying in Boston. Mind you, the aunt had already been dead three years when Mother moved to Boston to take care of her." An unaccustomed sarcasm laced Mary's words. "I went with her, of course. She told everyone I was transferring to a school there. Which wasn't true. I studied on my own. Anyway, Mother planted all kinds of clues before she left, like the fact she couldn't keep anything on her stomach in the mornings, so that when she wrote back that she was pregnant, everyone bought it—hook, line and sinker.'' The sarcasm was back when she added, ''And everyone thought it so wonderful that Margaret and Ed were having another child because they'd wanted another one for so long.'' Mary's eyes filled once more, and she turned back to the window. Her shoulders heaved in silent tears.

Jill longed to comfort her, but couldn't. Everything was so new, so changed, and she herself was hurting. So badly. ''So I became . . . your sister.''

Mary nodded and spoke in an uneven, moist voice. ''Yes. You were born in Massachusetts General, and somehow or other, Dad persuaded the records people to just list M. McClain as the mother.''

Jill frowned. ''But the birth certificate says Margaret.''

''You assumed it said Margaret. Just as the records people assumed the *M* stood for Mary. Oh, it was well planned,'' Mary said, ''down to the last detail and with the stipulation that . . . that the deception was never to be mentioned. Not even among ourselves. And that you were never to be called my daughter, nor I your mother. And I was never to care for you as a mother. I was never to do motherly things for you.'' Her voice broke again. ''We were all to play the game. And we did. I swear, I think that Mother actually grew to believe you were hers.'' Her shoulders heaved again, this time expelling great tears of great hurt. '' never—'' her voice sounded blubbery, quavery ''—I never found it that easy to play the game.''

Heartache. It filled the room like a tangible entity. Jill felt it undulating in cresting and ebbing waves, felt it welling and swelling in herself. Tears rushed to her own eyes.

Burke's arm slid about her waist. He simply held her to him as tightly as he could. He let her cry, knowing it was useless to try to stop her, knowing, too, that the release was therapeutic.

"Mary," Burke called softly when he thought the moment appropriate, "who's blackmailing you?"

She turned, assessed the intimate posture of Jill and Burke—on some faraway level she approved—and shook her head. "I don't know. Some man. He just started calling. He first asked for five thousand..."

"Did you pay it?" Burke asked.

She nodded. "I had to. I..." She broke off in deference to another scalding wash of tears.

"And he asked for more?" Burke rightly assumed.

"Yes. Two thousand more."

"You have no idea..."

She shook her head again. "No. Only the three of us knew—Mother, Dad and me."

"What about...the father?" Burke asked...and felt Jill's muscles stiffen.

Mary's eyes lowered from Burke's to her daughter's. "No," she whispered, "he never even knew I was going to have his baby." A tremendous sadness shaded Mary's eyes, leaving them the somber color of regret.

"Who is my father?" As she asked the question, Jill realized that she had been so caught up in the discovery that Mary was her mother that she had given only the most marginal consideration to her father. She now found herself waiting with bated breath.

"He's dead, Jill. He died in Korea.

"Oh."

Mary took a tentative step forward. "It was not...a tawdry affair. We were in love." She smiled again, plaintively. "Mother assured me it was only puppy love, that you couldn't experience the real thing at sixteen, but I knew better. I knew what I felt. I knew what he felt." She sniffed. And stepped closer. "He was a neighbor and two years older than me. We had known each other for a long time, then suddenly—" the look in her eyes became youthful as she relived happy memories "—suddenly everything clicked. We fell in love. We were going to be married." The happiness of yesteryear faded slightly though not fully. "He had just graduated from high school, with honors, and wanted to go to law school..."

Jill's eyes questioned.

Mary smiled, genuinely. "Yeah. I could hardly believe it when you told me you wanted to be a lawyer. It was like a little part of him lived ... that and your eyes. You have his eyes. His eyes were always so..." She again seemed lost in some bittersweet past that had draped a gauzy curtain about her. "Anyway," she said, continuing after a long pause, "he wanted to go to law school, but Korea broke out and..." She sighed, stepping closer. "He died a hero. They said that he saved five men's lives. He's buried in Arlington. They gave him... the Medal of Honor." Silent tears had begun again—both Mary's and Jill's. "He died before ... he never even knew that I... Oh, God," she said, crazily raking her fingers through her shorter-than-short hair, "he never even knew."

"The man in the picture," Jill said lowly.

"What?"

"The man in the picture was my father." *Don't ask me how I know,* she thought, *I just know.* It was the way she had felt the truth of Mary's relationship to her. Somehow, the hidden truth exposed, everything seemed right.

"Yes," Mary answered. "Tommy Wilson."

For a reason that made absolutely no sense, knowing that the man in the picture was her father increased Jill's sense of loss, personalized it in a way it hadn't been before. Jill's own heart ached at the callous unfairness of life. And, curiously, she felt an irreplaceable loss. She would never know the man who helped give her life. Suddenly that was very important. And supremely tragic.

Mary stood only inches from Jill. Tentatively, uncertainly, she reached out a hand. She hesitated, as if unsure she had the right, then brushed a strand of hair back from Jill's face. Her hand trembled. Jill felt the shaky motion at her temple. "Don't cry," Mary begged. "Please don't cry." It was a strange request, coming as it did from a woman who herself was crying.

Until that moment, Jill hadn't realized that she was crying. She sniffed and swiped at tears and ran a hand beneath a runny nose.

"He would have been so proud of you," Mary whispered, still stroking Jill's hair as if she couldn't stand the thought of drawing her hand away. "And he would have loved you—" her voice cracked into a million irreparable shards "—as much as I've always... They couldn't order me not to love you."

Burke had stepped away, leaving the two women to the private moment. He found his own eyes misty and his throat painfully constricted.

"Mary..." Jill began, to say heaven only knew what.

"Don't hate me," Mary interrupted. "Please don't hate me." Tears swelled and streamed. "I've already paid a price you can't possibly imagine. I paid it every time you called her mother, I paid it every time you ran to her with a scraped knee, I paid it every time you reached for her hand when you were scared."

Selfish. The word danced across Jill's conscience. She had been so concerned with her own feelings—her own feelings of confusion and betrayal—that she had quite forgotten she wasn't the only one suffering, that Mary had already done so, and would continue to do so, in ways that Jill could never equal. Mary had lost the man she'd loved and been denied her child. All in one fell swoop and at such a vulnerable age.

"I could never hate you," Jill said, now touching Mary's hair in a way that echoed Mary's last gesture. "I love you."

The declaration brought a fresh batch of tears from both women. Like intimate strangers, they just stood staring at each other, trying desperately to make the pieces of the world, the pieces of their lives, fit together.

"Sometimes at night when you were a baby," Mary said, her voice nothing but a wisp of sound, "I'd sneak into your room and...just hold you...just...just..." As if she had no will, she pulled Jill into her arms and cupped her hand at the back of her head. "I'd hold you." The words trailed into a mother's infinity. "Shh," she crooned as she gently stroked Jill's head, "it's all right. Everything's all right, baby...my sweet, sweet baby...everything's..."

Mary's eyes connected with those of the man standing only feet away. The abrupt, scissors-clipped silence drew both Jill's and Burke's immediate attention. Jill turned...and slowly stepped from Mary's embrace.

Rob Sheffield looked like a man shot and left for dead. That he'd been standing there long enough to piece a whole lot of facts together was more than obvious. It was also ob-vious that he was hurting.

"Why?" he asked gruffly, yet softly. "Why didn't you trust me?"

There seemed little emotion left in Mary, certainly no fight, no defense of herself. She answered honestly, tone-lessly, as if she were speaking for and of someone else. "Second chances in life are hard to come by. I didn't want to do anything to jeopardize mine."

"But surely I had a right..."

"I had loved Tommy very much," she interrupted. "So much that I spent years of my life mourning him. And then you came along. I couldn't believe I was falling in love again—and in a way that was much stronger than I'd ever loved before. I didn't deserve you—I knew that—but, God forgive me, I couldn't do anything that might drive you away. I reasoned that if Jill didn't know, why should any-one else?"

Rob worked his hand through his already finger-tangled hair. "Dammit, Mary, marriage is based on trust!"

A last light dimmed, then died in Mary's eyes. She smiled dejectedly, but with acceptance. "Yes, it is, isn't it?" she said, her eyes walking through the endless boundaries of his before dropping to the diamond on her left hand. It spar-kled beautifully, but mockingly. She had slipped the ring to her knuckle when Rob abruptly stopped her by shoving it back into place.

Her eyes flew upward.

"Don't you ever take that off," he barked tenderly, seconds before yanking her into his arms.

She went. Tears that she had believed to be cried out resurfaced. "I'm sorry," she sobbed into his shoulder. "Oh, Rob, I'm so sorry. I never meant to hurt . . . anyone."

"Shh, everything's all right . . . everything's all right . . ." he whispered over and over in the same litany that she, only minutes before, had chanted to Jill.

Jill's eyes filled again, and she glanced over at Burke.

His eyes sent her a heated, caring message before he stooped to pick up the money and stuff it back into the bag. That accomplished, he stood. "Mary?" She was still buried in Rob's embrace. "Mary?"

It was Rob's attention that he finally ensnared. Rob nudged the woman in his arms. She looked over at Burke

"When and where were you to deliver this?"

She told him.

The two men's eyes met and spoke. "Call the police," Burke said, "and tell them to meet me there."

He started for the door. Jill fell into step beside him.

"Where do you think you're going?" Burke asked, scowling.

"With you," she replied, stubbornly.

"Oh, no, you're not."

"Oh, yes, I am."

"Jill, this could be dangerous."

"I'm well aware of that."

"No."

"Yes."

"No! I won't . . ."

She grabbed his arm. "Burke, let me do this. Let me do it for Mary and . . . a man I'll never know." Time plodded by, an ceaseless patter of seconds. "Besides," she added, a slight smile curving her mouth, "who's gonna drive?"

The last question carried less weight than Burke would have thought possible days, weeks, months before. Jill's first statement, however, was another matter. It was something he simply did not have the right to deny her.

"Okay," he relented, "but you're going to stay in the car when we get there. You hear me?" They pushed through the front door—neither heard it slam—and out into the yard. Their steps briskly cut through grass and gravel. "Do you hear me, McClain?" he repeated, jerking open the car door and ducking his head inside. "Jill?"

"I hear, I hear!" she said, giving a final swipe to her nose and starting the engine.

It was high noon, and the hour of delivery, when Jill parked the car and silenced the motor. She immediately unlatched the door and swung it wide.

"Jill," Burke said, the one word a reminder of their agreement.

She got out and rounded the hood of the car.

"Jill!" he barked, throwing open his door.

Ignoring him, she headed off in the direction of the Boston Public Garden.

He grabbed her by the wrist, twirled her around, and pinned her against the car. "You promised me..."

"I said I heard you," she cut in, looking up into eyes that were caringly harsh. "I never said I'd stay in the car."

"We had a verbal contract based on a tacit implication."

Despite everything, maybe because of the pressure of everything, Jill smiled. "You sound like a lawyer."

Burke's lips curved into a slow smile. "Don't change the subject." His smile trailed away, and a fistful of knuckles grazed her chin. "If anything should happen to you, I..." He quite literally couldn't finish the sentence for the iceberg-cold feeling invading his heart. It threatened to frost the breath in his chest.

"Nothing's going to happen to me," she said in a sweet, silver-laced voice. "But that's why I have to go with you. I have to see that nothing happens to you. I'm not through loving you yet, Rawlins."

Her love words, the nearness of her body, thawed the glacial fingers choking his heart. That and the brilliant sun beating down on them. Nothing too tragic could happen on such a fair day to such a fair lady who did such unfair things to his heart. "Don't ever," he whispered, adding, "get through with loving me."

"No," she whispered with a shake of her head.

His eyes scanned her face. It bore the ravages of stress. Crying had puffed and reddened her eyes and had stripped mascara from lashes and left it in sooty lines on her lower lids. Her makeup had been streaked, her blusher eliminated entirely. It looked as though the color had been stolen from her lips and deposited at the end of her nose. In short, she should have looked awful. Burke thought she'd never looked more beautiful.

"You've had a bitch of a morning, haven't you?" he asked, his admiration growing with each moment he knew her.

"Yes. Why don't you kiss it and make it better?"

The set of knuckles beneath her chin exerted the pressure necessary to tilt her face up to his. His mouth lowered. His lips touched hers. At sublime contact the boundary between his and hers was obliterated. There was only the gentle working of mouths, each against the other. Slow and sure, familiar and intimate. In clingy reluctance, they parted.

"Please understand that I have to go with you," she whispered.

"All right," he agreed, "but will you stay out of sight and let me deliver the money?"

"No, let me drop it."

"Jill . . ."

"Burke, listen, he's expecting a woman. Seeing you might spook him."

"He's expecting Mary. And you don't look a thing like . . ."

"And you do look like her? Besides, he may not know what Mary looks like."

Burke hung his head in defeat, sighed and glanced back up. "Why don't we just wait for the police . . ."

"For the same reason you didn't want to wait just a second ago. It's time for the delivery now, and you know darned well we can't risk losing him. We have to at least give him the bait. And I'm the logical one to do that."

Burke hated himself for the admission, but there was a reasonableness to what she was suggesting. Surely there was safety in a public park in broad daylight. Surely the police were only seconds from arrival. Surely he must be half out of his mind to be agreeing. "Okay. But you put the bag on the bench and then walk away. Back toward me. Do you hear me, Jill? And I mean it this time. So help me, God, I'll come in after you." The look in his eyes left no doubt that he would.

"Okay."

"Promise."

"I will, I will. I promise. We have an explicit verbal contract."

"We better have," he said, a loving threat threading his words together. "This is one time, lady, I'll beat your fanny for breach."

"You have an intriguing concept of punishment, counselor," she said, taking the tapestry bag from him and moving off toward the garden.

Burke watched her go, allowing her to gain the distance necessary to make it appear that they weren't together. With each step that she took, she grew smaller and his fear greater. He told himself that the knot in his stomach was foolish. He told himself that nothing was going to happen. He told himself that it would all be over soon.

But stubbornly the fear persisted.

LENNY LARIMER KNEW the moment he saw the woman that she was Jill McClain. He knew also that something had gone wrong. His first reaction was to panic, to run. His second, was to conclude that everything might be all right after all. So Jill now knew about her birth? So what? Little Miss Hoity-toity Lawyer was obviously eager to keep her illegitimacy a secret. Otherwise, she wouldn't be delivering the money, would she?

He smiled and smeared nervous-damp hands along the length of his pants. He liked the idea of punishing Tommy's daughter personally. He liked the idea of her hurting, too. He liked the idea of her being under his control. Yeah, he liked it a whole lot. He also might like all that lawyer money she had.

She moved closer.

He stepped back into the shady shadows of the mammoth green-leafed oak. And waited. And watched. And willed his heart to stop its crazy, excited beat.

In the far distance the famed Swan Boats gently glided along the silver surface of the pond, giving visitors a scenic tour of the garden. Lenny's eyes darted to them, then to the man moving along the walkway. To the tall man in the business suit. For the briefest of moments, the man looked familiar, but the recognition fled under the pressure of the moment.

And he did feel stress, Lenny thought. Was that why his chest felt so heavy? Was that why his breath was short? Yeah, yeah. Maybe, though, he'd take some of the money and see a doctor. Maybe...

He watched as Jill looked about her—was she looking for him?—then she deposited the bag on the deserted bench. She hesitated, and looked about again, before starting back the way she had come. She glanced up at the man coming down the walkway. Even as far away as he stood, Lenny saw relief scoring the man's face. They knew each other! The fact slammed his heart into a rapid rhythm. It was a setup! He remembered now. The man was the lawyer he'd seen in court with her! It was a setup! It was...

Two uniformed police officers came into view.

Lenny Larimer's heart skipped a whole series of beats...

Right before the world went crazily out of control.

Jill saw the officers, Jill saw Burke pointing, Jill whirled. In the shadows of the tree, she felt the man. Then saw him. He was wearing a stricken look and a gray plaid shirt. Across the distance of yards and years, their eyes met. His were haunted, dull, the color of unrealized wants. They were also winter cold.

Her eyes, Lenny thought wildly, were exactly like Tommy's. Or were they like his mother's? Perfect... censuring... perfectly censuring... censuringly perfect...

"It's your own fault you've been found out." his mother's voice began to accuse in his head.

"No," he whimpered in protest.

"You always force people to hurt you."

"No!" he cried, the voice growing louder, more deafening. His heartbeat accelerated, pelting inside his chest at a thunderous speed. His heart felt as if it were a separate entity and threatened to split skin and sinew and spring forth in its own birth.

"I tried to love you, but you're sick, Lenny... sick... sick..."

"No!" he cried, covering his ears. The sound only increased. Now it was laughter. His mother's laughter. Tommy's laughter. The world's laughter.

Noises screeched in his head.

His chest hurt. Pain. Pain. Bad pain. Bad.

"You've been a bad boy... bad boy... bad boy..."

Lenny Larimer reached for the gun that he carried to work each night. He had tucked it into the waist of his jeans, beneath a sleeveless denim jacket. He aimed it at the woman, the woman with Tommy's eyes, the woman with his mother's laugh, the woman who represented everything that Lenny had always been denied.

And then, without the slightest bit of guilt, he pulled the trigger.

CHAPTER THIRTEEN

"Nooo!" Burke's voice rang out.

Helplessly, he listened as a shot pierced the park's peacefulness. Helplessly, he watched as Jill crumpled, without a sound and like a wireless puppet, to the ground.

An ice-death seized Burke, freezing him to the spot. Conversely, startled birds fast-fluttered a frenzied ascent. A millisecond and a thousand eternities passed. Suddenly, though his brain was still chilled, his legs began to thaw. He began to run. Instinctively. Desperately. In one mere stride, he outdistanced the policemen who were now in pursuit of the man running from the darkness of the oak tree. Another shot rang out—sharp, clear, sinister—this one discharged from a policeman's gun. Burke marginally noted that the blackmailer grabbed his leg and tumbled earthward. He heard the man muttering cries of pain.

Jill, on the other hand, was silent. Sickeningly silent. Frighteningly silent. Wearing her ivory suit and slumped on her stomach, she lay—a small white heap on the spring-green grass. She reminded Burke of a beautiful, peaceful dove shot from the sky by a callous hunter.

"Jill?" he whispered, dropping to his knees beside her. Deep inside him, the prayer had begun. *Please, God, please, don't let her be...* Even in the silence of his heart, he couldn't say the word.

His hand at her waist, he gently rolled her to her back within the framework of his arms. She was limp and pale and her eyelashes splashed thick and spiky against her colorless cheeks. A bright crimson stained her blouse in a visibly increasing circle.

Burke's heart stopped. "Jesus," he breathed, his finger-tips trailing across the sticky wetness of the scarlet puddle. "No...please...no..." It crossed his mind that he was diabolically caught in some eternal punishment of loving and always losing whomever he loved to the remorseless arms of death. His own arms tightened in resistance to the idea.

Jill's eyelashes fluttered and slowly rose.

Burke's heart began to beat again. "Jill?"

Shock had widened the irises of her eyes until they appeared bottomless pools of cool blue water. She attempted to smile, but it came across a pathetic, one-cornered affair. "Are you...going..."

"Shh, save your energy."

"...to beat my fanny...for breach?"

Burke's eyes stung. "You're damned right I am," he said in an unsteady voice.

"I...only stopped..."

"Shh, be quiet, Jill."

"...because you pointed..."

"Shh," he commanded again, running his hand into a back pocket of his pants for a handkerchief. Once produced, he laid it across the spot where he determined the bullet had entered her body. Somewhere near her breast, her incredibly beautiful breast. Somewhere near her life-necessary lungs and heart. Panic again cruised down the length of his spine.

"Burke?"

"What, honey?"

"I shouldn't...have stopped. He..."

She coughed and Burke heard a hateful gurgling sound. He heard voices to his left.

"Momma," came the less-than-lucid call of Lenny Larimer. "Momma...Momma..."

"His heartbeat's erratic," one of the policeman said.

The other answered, "I only clipped him in the leg."

"He's cold and clammy. Could be a heart attack."

"I'll call for an ambulance."

"Check on the woman."

"How is she?" an officer said, immediately appearing at Burke's side.

"She's shot." Burke swallowed. "A chest wound."

"I'll call for an ambulance."

"No, I can get her to the hospital faster." More than careful with the treasure he had, he gingerly lifted Jill into his arms. She moaned and cut out his heart with the sound. "Hang on, honey."

It seemed to Burke like a thousand years, but it could have been no more than three minutes before he was settling her in the front seat of the car. He knew she'd have been more comfortable in the back seat, but couldn't stand the thought of her being that far away from him. Stripping off his suit jacket, he bunched it into a pillow for her head. He then closed the door and ran around to the driver's side.

The inside of the car was stifling hot, and Burke plunged his hand into her purse for the key to start engine and air conditioning. When his fingers didn't readily find the keys, he cursed and emptied the purse's contents onto the car seat. The keys jingled out. Throwing everything back into the purse, he tossed it to the back and slipped behind the wheel. Never once did it cross his mind that he hadn't driven in eighteen months. All he knew was that he had to get Jill to the hospital . . . before she bled to death on the front seat of her car.

Turning the wheel sharply, he pulled out behind the police car now acting as escort. The car's siren began to wail, a menacing sound that parted the traffic like Moses parting the Red Sea.

"Am I . . . am I going to die?" Jill whispered halfway to Massachusetts General Hospital.

Burke's head jerked toward her. She was semipropped against the door. Her eyes were hazy, her skin pallid. "No!" he said gruffly. "Don't even think that!"

"If I do," she said, ignoring his command, "I want you to know . . ."

"Don't, Jill! You'll be all right!"

She swallowed and sought for a proper breath. "... that I love you more..."

"Jill, please!" he pleaded in a ragged whisper.

"...than I ever loved anything...or anybody." She smiled faintly, but strangely contentedly. "You made me happy."

It was the past tense of the verb that totally destroyed him. Burke fought to continue breathing and to keep the moisture from his eyes. *You can't drive if you can't see!* he screamed to himself. Break down later. Not now! Dammit, not now!

"You're going to be all right," he repeated, for his sake far more than for hers.

When she spoke again, her voice was thick, her words rambling toward incoherence. Her eyes were glazing over. "I thought it hurt... to be shot. But I don't—" she licked her lips "—feel ... anything."

"You're in shock," Burke said, refraining from pointing out that once the shock receded, she'd be screaming for something, anything, to ease the pain.

"I don't feel ... anything ... bleeding ... mmm ..." she moaned.

Burke threw her another glance. "Hang in, honey. Only a couple more blocks."

"Burke...feel anything...mmm." She moaned again and a grimace split wide her face.

"We're almost ..."

"Oh, God!" she groaned as a burning shaft tore through her body.

Burke drew the car to a screeching halt beside the entry-way. Killing the engine, he threw the door open and practically jumped the hood of the car. A stretcher, manned by two competent men in white, bolted through the hospital door just as Burke lifted Jill into his arms. She was crying, soft tears falling on gasps and moans.

"Burke ... it hurts. It ... Oh, God!" she cried, grasping his hand just as he laid her upon the sterile linen of the stretcher sheet. Her strength, even under the circumstances, threatened to stop the flow of blood in his fingers.

"Jill..." he began, running alongside the stretcher that had just entered the hospital. A horde of people in white descended.

"Sir, you're in the way. Sir..."

Someone, some well-meaning someone, wrenched apart the lovers' hands.

"Burke!" Jill cried in agonized desperation.

"Jill!" he answered, the word screaming from his very soul.

And then there was silence as the stretcher was rolled beyond swinging doors that read Emergency. Staff Only.

As he stood in the middle of the suddenly quiet room, a horrible feeling of déjà vu closed in around Burke. He remembered standing once before in almost exactly this same spot. He remembered the deafening silence. He remembered the overwhelming feeling of helplessness. He remembered the sickening feeling of fear.

EVERYTHING WAS THE SAME, Burke thought hours later as he impatiently waited for news from the operating room. The hospital reeked of the same sharp, antiseptic smells, and the same muted, muffled voices crawled down the hallways. Hope and hopelessness eternally sat side by side in waiting rooms, and everywhere there was the familiar surreal feeling that time had been suspended.

Restlessly, and for the thousandth time, Burke stood and walked to the window. He stared out at a late afternoon that seemed to have come from nowhere. Sunset had already brushed the sky in rainbow colors—bold indigo and shy lavender, bright tangerine and traces of vermilion red.

Red.

Like the dried blood on his white shirt. Like the rusty-red stains on his fingertips.

No, Burke suddenly thought, everything was not the same. Nicole had died with him at her side. If Jill died, she would die with strangers. And one other thing was different. She would die without ever hearing him say he loved her. Why had he never said he loved her? he asked himself

desperately. Why had he just assumed that he'd had all the
time in the world to come to terms with what he was feeling
for her?

"Burke?" came a soft voice at his side.

He glanced around and into the face of Mary McClain.
She was red-eyed and pale. That she was suffering was
etched in every line and crease of her face and, yet, as she
had been all afternoon she was sensitively aware of his pain.

"Why don't you go get some coffee?"

"No, I—"

"Why don't I go get you both some?" Rob said, laying a
comforting hand on Mary's shoulder. His fingers tightened
in reassurance before he stepped away and from the room.
Mary watched him go with a look of total adoration.

It was a look that increased Burke's pain. Would he ever
again see that look of love and devotion on Jill's face? He
glanced back out the window and did what he once said he'd
never do again. He prayed.

"How long has it been?" Mary asked.

Burke angled his wrist to look at his watch. "Four hours
and almost ten minutes." A lifetime, he thought miserably.
A damned lifetime! Or was that a deathtime? Were they all
just marking time until Jill... He made himself stop and
concentrate on what the nurse had said two hours before.
Updating them on the in-progress surgery, she'd said that
Jill was alive. He was going to hold on to that. With every
ounce of strength he had. He had to, because if he didn't,
he'd go absolutely mad.

"It's all my fault," he heard Mary say in a faltering voice.
"If I hadn't agreed to the blackmail, if I had just told the
truth from the beginning, if..."

"Don't," Burke demanded in a tone that instantly
brought her red eyes to his. "Don't do it to yourself. Take
it from someone who knows every subtlety of the word
guilt." He smiled faintly. "None of it was your fault, Mary.
None of it."

The way none of what happened to Nicole was my fault,
he silently added to himself. Neither her death, nor my sur-

vival. How perfectly clear it all seemed now. And how useless all the guilt, when everything that had happened had been nothing more than the fickle, accidental nature of life. And yet, maybe it was the capacity to feel guilt that indelibly marked one as a normal, and caring, human being.

"You're in love with her, aren't you?"

Burke's attention shifted back to Mary. "Yes," he answered, adding hoarsely, "but I've never told her."

"You will," Mary said.

It was a hope they both clung to.

Seconds later, at the sound of footsteps, Burke whirled around.

"Sorry," Rob said at the obvious expectation scoring Burke's face.

Burke sighed in disappointment and reached for a foam cup of steaming coffee. "Thanks," he said, drawing the cup to his lips and drinking. The coffee was scalding hot, and he relished the mini-diversion of his attention.

"One of the officers just told me that the blackmailer was DOA," Rob said. "They think he died of a coronary."

"Do they have any idea who he is…was?" Burke asked.

Rob shook his head. "They found in address in his wallet, but that was all. They're checking it out."

"I was hoping he'd live," Burke said.

"Yeah," Rob agreed.

The three also agreed that if they didn't hear something soon, they were all going to scream. But hear they didn't. At least not soon. Four-fifteen faded into four-thirty, which in turn gave way to four-forty-five and five o'clock, then six o'clock and beyond. Burke paced, sat, paced again. He sighed. He prayed. He rummaged fingers through his hair. He finally lost his patience.

"How the hell long can one surgery last?" he barked, jumping up and starting in on another pacing routine. "It's been almost—"

"Ms McClain?"

Burke's head, accompanied by two others, jerked toward the doorway. At the sight of the man still dressed in surgical-green attire—he carried a mask, and sweat stained the front of his shirt—Burke's heart slammed against his ribs.

"Yes," Mary whispered, rising. Rob instinctively moved to her side.

The doctor smiled wearily, reassuringly. "Your daughter's going to be all right."

Relief, more powerful than the adrenaline of concern, swept through Burke's body, leaving him weaker than had hours of anxiety.

"How...what kind of damage..." Burke stammered.

The doctor turned his attention to the man asking the fractured questions and obviously felt that the pallor of his skin entitled him to an answer. "The bullet entered the fleshy part of the right breast, angled downward, and lodged itself in her left side. Fortunately, it missed her lungs entirely. Unfortunately, it nicked the right ventricle of her heart."

The last words caused Burke's own heart to jump into an erratic rhythm. "But...that sounds serious," he managed to say.

"Not really. There was a lot of bleeding, which was one reason the surgery took so long, and then it also required some delicate suturing. Actually," the doctor said, still talking primarily to Burke, "she was lucky. If the bullet had been just an inch higher..." He left the remark unfinished.

Burke, however, silently filled in the missing words.

"Are you all right?" the doctor asked suddenly as Burke's complexion dimmed from pale to snow-white.

"Yes," he answered in a contradictory tone that barely rose above a whisper.

"I could get you some water—"

Burke cleared his throat, trying to clear his head of the hateful inch-higher theory. "No," he said gruffly, "I'm fine."

"She'll be all right," the physician repeated. "Barring complications, and given a proper period of convalescence."

"May I see her?" Mary asked.

The doctor was sympathetic but firm. "She'll be in recovery a while longer, then in intensive care for the rest of the night." He smiled. "Why don't the three of you get some sleep and come back tomorrow? I promise I'll let you see her then."

While none of the trio seemed inordinately pleased with the decision, all bowed to the doctor's superior judgment. Within minutes, they were stepping from the hospital and out into the April evening. Sunset had given way to a gloaming twilight that seemed to cover the city like a gray, gauzy canopy. First-stars friskily glimmered their arrival.

"Would you take her car home with you, Burke?" Mary asked, then remembered his aversion to driving. "Unless, of course . . ."

"I'll take it," he answered.

"Well, I . . . I guess I'll see you tomorrow."

"Right," Burke said. "Try to get some rest. Both of you." The two men exchanged a tired but friendly handshake. Burke then dropped a kiss on Mary's cheek. "Good night."

The farewell was echoed.

All the way home, Burke felt it building. Exactly what "it" was, he wasn't altogether sure, but by the time he'd pulled the car into a slot at his apartment complex and shut off the engine, he felt the acute symptoms of emotional distress.

He had almost lost her!

And in almost losing her had come the cold, stark reality that he was once again vulnerable. Love and the unpredictability of life had once more placed him on a high wire without a net.

"If the bullet had been just an inch higher . . ."

" . . . She would be dead," Burke whispered into the car's quiet listening interior. "Sweet Jesus, she would be . . ." He couldn't repeat the all-too-sobering word.

A fine, delayed trembling started in his hands, and he reached for his suit jacket that still lay crumpled on the far side of the car. He drew it close and inhaled the subtle, sweet smell emanating from where Jill's head had lain. He also saw the once-crimson, dark stain blotching fabric and memory.

"If the bullet had been just an inch higher..."

He closed his eyes and swallowed back the knot of fear that jumped into his throat and heart. It was the most all-consuming, all-debilitating feeling he'd ever known. It threatened his well-being. It threatened his very sanity. Suddenly it was crystal clear what he had to do.

He'd make her understand, he thought. Somehow he'd make her understand that he loved her and that, because he did, he had to banish her from his life.

CONSCIOUSNESS SLIPPED BACK in snatches of light and sound and pain. And in snippets of awareness that Burke sat at her bedside. Continuously, it seemed, for each time Jill rallied in the following days, a hazy though familiar figure was always only a smile away, a touch away. Sometimes she even imagined that Burke spoke to her, but it was of things she didn't understand, things about an inch higher, things about a high wire and no net, things about fear and cowardice and forgiveness.

On the fourth day after surgery, on a Friday afternoon that sang with a sprinkling rain, Jill opened her eyes. Really opened her eyes. She saw a white room. Heard the gentle patter of rain. Knew the smell of... roses? She inclined her head to the garnet-red blossoms spreading their petals in a fragrant fullness. The motion produced a silent grimace, and she eased her hand to her chest, her securely bandaged chest. She was on the verge of wondering where she was and what had happened when the past came flooding back. A shot. The park. Burke carrying her. Burke. Where was...? Her eyes shifted toward the miniscule sound of a magazine page turning.

He looked tired, she thought, as if he'd lost sleep and spent hours worrying. He also looked thin, gaunt even, and there were shadows lurking deep in the hollows of his cheeks. Even so, he had never looked better.

"Hi," she whispered, the word cutting her throat with its sharp edges.

Burke's gaze flew upward. The magazine slid to the floor. "Jill?"

"You got nothing better to do—" she stopped to corral her wispy breath "—than hang around . . . hospitals?"

He didn't answer. Instead, his concern evident, he stood and stepped to her side. "How do you feel?"

Jill smiled weakly. "I don't . . . know." She passed the tip of her tongue over her cracked lips. "Could I . . . have a drink?"

Burke poured water from the carafe and into a glass. Adding a straw, he brought it to her lips. She sipped. Good. It tasted good. And cool. And deliciously wet to a medicine-dry mouth.

"You want some more?"

She shook her head and, tired from the overexertion of drinking, snuggled back into the pillow. Burke returned the glass to the stand.

His eyes sank deeply into hers. "Do you hurt?"

She considered his question. "No," she said finally, shaking her head again. "Burke . . ."

"What, honey?"

". . . am I all right?"

"Yes, you're all right. The bullet nicked your heart . . ." At the sudden distraught look on her face, he hastened to add, "It sounds worse than it is. The doctor swears you're all right." Her face still wore a troubled expression. "I wouldn't lie to you."

The worry lines disappeared. "No," she said with a relieved smile, "you wouldn't."

"You want me to get you anything? Something to drink? Something to eat? Something . . ."

"No," she cut in, asking, "Did they get the man?" Before he could answer, she said, "He was the man I saw in court."

"He was DOA, Jill. He died of a coronary."

"Who was he?"

"His name was Leonard Larimer. He was a cousin of your father's." The relationship never ceased to surprise Burke, nor did his blinding hatred for the madman.

"A cousin? I don't understand. Why..."

"The police are still trying to figure out why. Don't worry about it now. Wait until you're stronger." His hand brushed back a lock of her hair as his eyes hungrily scanned her face, looking for every subtlety, every nuance, of her well-being.

"Don't look at me," she said, turning her face into the pillow. "I must look awful."

"No," he contradicted roughly as he gently brought her face back to his. "You've never looked more...beautiful." The word sailed between them on gossamer wings of feeling.

With his fingertips at her chin, with his eyes warm and soft, Jill would gladly have given part of her soul for Burke's kiss. That Burke was feeling the same need to kiss her she would have bet her life on. Yet, he didn't. She told herself it was out of deference to her condition.

"Who gave me the flowers?" she asked, noticing that the red roses were only the proverbial floral tip of an iceberg.

"The daisies are from the gang at work, the yellow roses are from Dad, the whatever-that-is," he said, pointing to a orange-blooming plant—

"Kalanchoe," she said with a half smile.

The other half of the smile slowly appeared on Burke's face. "The kalanchoe is from Mary and Rob."

"How is she?" Jill asked, suddenly serious.

"She's all right. She's been worried about you. She'll be back later this evening."

A strange blend of emotions bathed Jill's heart. On the one hand, she still thought of Mary as her sister—and always would. On the other hand, there was already growing a different kind of feeling: the feeling a child knows for her mother.

"What about the red roses?" she asked, letting the confusing subject of Mary rest until another time. "Who sent those?" Her eyes merged with Burke's as she awaited his answer.

"Just some guy who's been half out of his mind," he said unsteadily.

It suddenly seemed like a lifetime since she'd touched him. Which she had to to or simply die on the spot. Slowly, she inched her hand forward—it felt so heavy she could hardly lift it—and cupped the side of his face in her palm.

His jaw began a slow quiver beneath her touch, and his eyes burned with deep emotion. He covered her hand with his and drew her palm to his mouth, where he kissed the tender flesh. "I almost lost you," he whispered, burying his face in her hand as if she were silk and satin and all things sweet and soft. "I almost lost you. Oh, God, I almost lost you."

Jill stretched out her other hand and rested it on the crown of his bowed head. Neither spoke. She had the sudden and curious feeling that, despite what she'd been through, she was in far better shape than Burke.

It was the next evening, though, that she first suspected something was wrong. Burke had spent much of the day with her and, although everything appeared normal on the surface, there was an undercurrent that she couldn't quite interpret. He seemed to be... distancing her. Without question, he went out of his way not to touch her. And still he had not kissed her, although she had found his eyes on her lips more than once.

At eight o'clock sharp, the stout and stern night nurse ordered Burke from the room.

"I think she's hinting that I leave," he said, smiling as he stood by the side of the bed.

"Ms Subtlety," Jill teased back, though her crooked smile said she was tired.

Burke saw her fatigue and felt guilty. "You're exhausted. I should have gone earlier."

"No!"

Something in the passionate delivery of the one word created an instant intimacy. It was there between them, thick and vibrant and undeniable. Burke's eyes traitorously slid from her eyes to her lips. He swallowed. And fought against the urgent need to kiss her, to hold her.

"Well, good night," he said in a strangled voice.

"Burke?"

He hesitated, caught in the silken, silvery web she spun so effortlessly.

"Kiss me good-night."

Time stopped. Jill waited. Burke suffered. Finally, his head lowered and his lips swept across hers. It was an impersonal kiss, full of self-restraint that fairly shuddered through his suddenly taut body. It reminded her of the first time she'd kissed him. Then, however, she'd understood the restraint. Now, she didn't.

"Burke?" she whispered, her lips trembling beneath his as she pleaded for an explanation. Of necessity, the plea parted her lips and her breath flowed against Burke's mouth in a warm, moist wave. Their tongues met.

Burke was lost. Moaning, he widened his mouth over hers in a way that was very personal, most intimate, and totally without restraint. He kissed her deeply, hungrily. Slipping his arms beneath her shoulders, he smothered her body with the enormousness of his. In his touch was a gentle savagery, a wild desperation. In his touch was . . . fear. A fear that clearly transmitted itself to Jill's heart.

An indelicate cough at the doorway brought the kiss to an abrupt end. Burke left, shaken. Jill was confused.

THE NEXT MORNING, the first day of May, she asked the question. "What's wrong?"

Burke turned from where he'd been silently staring out the window. "What do you mean?"

"Something's wrong," she said from her position against newly fluffed pillows. "What is it?"

Burke's heart surged toward a scampering pulse. "Nothing's wr—"

"You don't lie to me, remember?" Jill interrupted.

She had been freshly bathed and wore a lacy pink gown that Mary had brought her the day before. Her hair was piled haphazardly but attractively atop her head and tied with a matching ribbon. Burke thought she looked like a child-woman, a child-woman who needed protection not hurt.

"I deserve to know the truth," she prompted.

The truth. What was that elusive substance? Burke thought. Was it the fact that he didn't have the courage to love her? Was it the fact that he was going to have to hurt her to save himself? Was it the fact that he was really doing her a favor because she deserved so much more than he could offer? He turned back to the window, shutting out the beauty of her face, the challenge in her sea-blue eyes.

"Burke?" she said, refusing to shelve the issue.

He didn't answer. He wanted to wait to tackle the subject of his leaving until she was stronger. Stronger. Maybe the elusive truth was that Jill, even flat on her back healing from a bullet wound, was stronger than he. For after all, he was nothing more than a coward.

"I'm taking another leave of absence from the firm," he heard himself saying.

The blood in Jill's veins chilled by degrees. In the long, long night, when she'd pondered over and over Burke's desperate, fear-laden kiss, an idea had occurred to her, but she had rejected it simply because it was too painful to even consider.

"Why?" she now whispered.

"I'm . . . I'm going back to the Cape."

The idea was back, swarming around Jill in all its hideous glory. "You're running away," she said flatly.

He whirled. "Yes!" he admitted bluntly, roughly, raking fingers through his neatly combed hair. "Yes, I'm running away." He stood a room away, a world away. Suddenly, he sighed. The sound was laced with self-hate. "Jill, I don't expect you to understand. I won't even ask you to."

"Make me understand," she said in a voice that both begged and demanded. "If you're walking out of my life, I have to understand why."

"Because I'm a coward," he said with no hesitation.

"I don't believe that."

"Believe it. It's true." Unknowingly, craving her nearness, he stepped closer. "When I..." He stopped, as if what he must say was so painful he could find neither breath nor words. "When I lost Nicole, I didn't think I was going to survive. For a long time I didn't want to. I never expected to...to love again. And then, you came into my life. You made me feel...alive. You made me feel..." His eyes glazed over with a film of moisture. "Oh, God, Jill, I love you so much," he whispered.

Jill's eyes, too, teared under the bittersweet irony of the moment. The words were what she had waited a "forever" length of time to hear. It was the timing that was wrong. All wrong!

"Then why leave me?" she asked, knowing the answer even before she heard it.

"Because I almost lost you," he said, the words refusing to slip easily through his tightened lips.

"If you leave, you lose me anyway."

"It's not the same thing."

"Isn't it?"

"No!" he hollered, then lowered his voice. "No," he repeated, "it's not the same. Jill," he pleaded, now desperate to make her understand, "I can't live through losing someone else. I can't bury..." These words would not pass through his lips. "I'm afraid," he confessed. He smiled self-derisively. "It's not very heroic, but it's the truth."

"So what are you going to do? Run away and conveniently forget you love me?"

"I'm going to try. I have to."

Green eyes and blue sparred in a silent, loving battle.

He looked so vulnerable, she thought, standing there with his heart on his sleeve and his past in his hand.

She looked so vulnerable, he thought, lying there pale and beautiful and bleeding from the barbs of his words.

"Don't ask me to stay," he begged in a whisper. "I would. I'd do anything you ask me to. But this time, it would only make us both miserable."

Miserable. Jill didn't see how she could be more miserable than she already was. Yet her love for Burke would not allow her to be the cause of his misery. If leaving her meant he'd be happier, she must set him free. Mustn't she? Why, then, did she want more than anything to beg him to stay? Slowly, faintly, tears held at bay, she smiled. "Love doesn't chain, Burke." Her voice cracked. "It frees."

The room was silent, a silence punctuated only by the sound of heartache. His heartache. Her heartache. Their heartache.

Walking to the bed, he entwined his fingers with hers and gently drew her knuckles to his mouth. He didn't kiss them. He just held them against the warmth of his lips. His trembling lips. His eyes closed in a savoring attitude, as if he were storing memories for lonely, black nights.

"You can't run away from love," Jill whispered at last. "You can run over every inch of the Cape, you can run through heaven and hell, but you can't run away from love."

He didn't argue the point. He looked long past arguing any point. He merely lowered her hand to the bed and slowly, and finally—oh, God, so finally she thought she would die!—unthreaded his fingers from hers. His tear-sheened eyes met hers briefly. Then, without a backward glance, he walked from the room . . . and from her life.

CHAPTER FOURTEEN

JILL DIDN'T CRY. She couldn't. She was too numb. She simply, and silently, succumbed to the pain in her heart that had nothing to do with the bullet's nick.

A single red rose was delivered that afternoon, along with a note that read: *Forgive me.* It was then she cried, tears that fell from her eyes and onto the velvet petals of the rose like giant drops of dew. She could take no comfort whatsoever in the fact that, had Burke loved her less, she would not now be alone.

Nor did the fact lend comfort in the endless days that followed. In truth, nothing lent comfort. Jill felt as if a hole had been carved in her heart, in her life, and that nothing would ever again fill it. At first she believed—possibly because she had to to survive—that Burke would eventually come to his senses, but when day followed day, and lonely night succeeded lonely night, she had to face the fact that he might never reconsider his decision. Oh, he might return to Boston—of that she had no doubt—but it grew daily more and more unlikely that he would return to her.

How could she live without him? she asked herself over and over.

By keeping busy, the survivor in her always replied.

To which she would respond, with a growing, surly impatience: How do you keep busy lying flat on your back in a hospital?

It was a toss-up who was the happier—Jill or the hospital staff—when she was discharged exactly three weeks to the day of the shooting. From the beginning, she abused her doctor's orders. She did not take things easy. She did con-

cede to staying in bed, possibly, probably, because Mary
took an early summer leave from school, moved into Jill's
apartment and threatened to tie her down. Of necessity,
Mary and Rob's wedding plans were postponed. Since it was
just one more thing for Jill to regret, she worked harder and
harder on the briefs that she had smuggled in from the office.

By the first of June, Jill had lost twelve pounds, had lost
enough sleep to qualify her as a bona fide insomniac, and
had lost her patience so many times that it was doubtful that
she'd ever find it again. And through it all, there was not
one minute of one hour of one day—or night—that she did
not wonder what Burke was doing. It was certainly the
question that kept her company that hot, sleepless, June-
first night.

FIFTY-SEVEN MILES south of Boston, in a small white beach
cottage, Burke stared at the glass of untouched bourbon and
water that temptingly sat on the kitchen table. Through the
open window, a warm summer breeze drifted in, swaying the
ruffled curtains and infusing the room with pine and salty-
sea scents. In also came the sound of the Atlantic tumbling
in rhythmic, and eternal, play. Burke, however, heard
nothing except the siren call of the bourbon and water...and the haunting words of Mary McClain. The latter
had been responsible for his pouring the former. The question now was: Who was stronger? Him or the liquor?

On returning to the Cape, he had vowed not to drown his
problems in a bottle. He would not make the mistake he'd
made once before. Until tonight, it had been a fairly easy
vow to keep. Until tonight, talking weekly with his father
had left the impression that Jill was coping. After all, she
was slowly integrating herself back into work by insisting
material be sent to the house. Tonight, however, for a reason he couldn't explain, he'd needed more reassurance. He'd
called Jill's house, hoping Mary would answer. She had.

"What do you want me to say, Burke?" Mary had asked
kindly, but with no punches pulled. *"That she's all right?*

Well, she's not. Oh, she's getting over the gunshot wound, but she's miserable. She won't eat, she's working herself to death despite the doctor's orders to the contrary, she's not sleeping, and though she tries hard not to cry in front of me, her eyes are always red.'' There had been a pause in the long-winded recital. *"Oh, Burke,"* she had said, her voice suddenly contrite, *"I'm sorry. I have no right..."*

''To remind me that I'm a son of a bitch?'' Burke whispered into the room's stillness. His eyes were still pinned to the glass. Inside the amber liquid, the ice cubes were beginning to melt.

The truth of the matter was, he mused, that he was in no better shape than Jill. Possibly he was in even worse shape. He was more miserable than he ever remembered being in his life. As for sleep and food, he'd had far too little of each. The only area in which she might be better off than he was was in the area of work. She at least had something to occupy her time. And she could at least cry. God, how he envied her that!

Yet, in all his pain, in all his guilt over her pain, he knew he'd done the right thing in leaving. In time, she would forget him. In time, he would forget her. And to help him forget tonight, and what he was doing to Jill, why didn't he just drink the ready solace that stood on the table?

His fingers slid up and down the cool, moist-growing glass, caressing it as if it were a cherished lover. His fingers closed around it. He lifted it. He brought it to his lips. But he didn't drink. Instead, he returned it to the table, roughly scraped back his chair, and headed for the door. He hit the beach at a run and didn't stop until beads of sweat bathed his body in exactly the same way that beads of condensate bathed the warming, untouched glass of bourbon.

For tonight, Burke had been stronger than temptation.

The only thing stronger was his memory of Jill.

In the second week of June, on a summer-warm Thursday afternoon, a double-chinned, jovial-eyed police officer brought a cardboard box to Jill. Inside were the effects of the late Leonard Larimer, who left behind no relatives, except the obscure, and ironic, one of Jill McClain.

With imagination, it was possible to piece together what had happened. The letter from Margaret McClain to Maude Larimer set the stage, and, though it would never be known with certainty how Maude Larimer had discovered the truth of Mary's pregnancy—had Margaret told her? Had Maude astutely guessed?—it was obvious that the woman had asked to be informed of the birth of her nephew's child. There was also a between-the-lines hint that the woman never meant to interfere in the mother's or child's life, which, of course, she never had. Not so, however, Leonard Larimer. While the motivation behind the blackmail was murky, it was still visible. Disjointed notes written in the margins of the letter and on a newspaper obituary column spoke powerfully of Leonard Larimer's love-hate relationship with his mother. And of his obsession with Tommy Wilson's perfection. It was a logical surmise that Mary and Jill, simply because of their relationship to Tommy, had been chosen to receive the brunt of that hate and obsession. Through them, Leonard Larimer would avenge himself. Regrettably, but perhaps just as importantly, Jill didn't know every nuance of the demented man's motivation and knew that she never would.

One thing she did know was that almost the entire sum of blackmail money had been recovered. She knew one other thing as well. She got a warm, goose-bumpy feeling when she held the Medal of Honor that had been found in a worn case in the bottom of the box. It was the only link she had with her father. It was the only link she would ever have. And yet, it was enough. It spoke to her of love, devotion, courage.

Courage.

Cowardice.

Burke believed himself a coward. She knew better than that, but there was no way that she could convince him of it. She also knew with a clarity that belied any contradiction that he should be there with her, sharing the night, sharing life. A familiar ache settled in her chest, and equally familiar tears filled her eyes. Would the pain ever end? Would she ever feel whole again?

At the sound of Mary at the bedroom door, Jill quickly sniffed and plastered a too-bright smile at her lips. "Hi," she said, laying the medal on the bedside table.

Mary hesitated, then crossed the room and sat by the side of the bed. Her eyes automatically went to the medal. She said what she always did when reminded of what Jill had endured...all at the hands of a distant relation. The fact that it had been a relative who had tried to take her life not only angered Mary, but also made her feel a sense of guilt she couldn't explain even to herself. "I'm so sorry that Leonard..."

"It isn't your fault. You're not to blame for Leonard Larimer's actions."

"I know, but..."

Jill reached out and took Mary's hand. "But what? If you hadn't fallen in love at sixteen? If the man you'd loved hadn't had a cousin?" She tightened her hands around Mary's. "It isn't your fault." She gave a small laugh. "And I guess in a way it wasn't even his. No court would have considered him sane enough to stand trial."

"I'm glad he's dead," Mary said simply. "Is that an awful thing to say?"

"It's an understandable thing." Jill didn't know how she felt about the man who'd tried to take her life. Whatever the emotion it wasn't hate. It was closer to pity. And in a strange way she was grateful for a lesson the stranger had taught her at a time in her life when she'd needed to understand the lesson most. She had learned how precious it was that she had first come to know her mother through friendship and love. Even though the sands of their relationship had shifted, demanding readjustments in thinking and attitude, there would never be hate such as Leonard Larimer had felt for his mother. She wanted to tell Mary all this, to share all that was in her heart, but the time didn't seem quite right yet, though Jill knew without a doubt that it was very near.

"Mary," she said, glancing once more at the medal on the table, "if you'd like to have the medal . . ."

"No," Mary said quickly. "I want you to have it. Your father would want you to have it." The moment grew heavy with emotion, the way it always did when Jill's parentage was mentioned. To ease that heaviness, Mary changed the subject. "You're sure you're going to be all right if I go home tomorrow?"

"I'm positive. Didn't the doctor say I could resume my activities?"

"He said you could resume some of them," Mary corrected.

"Go home," Jill said, a real smile working at the corners of her mouth.

"Trying to get rid of me, huh?" Mary teased.

"Yeah."

Mary's smile faded. "You've been crying."

"You're not supposed to notice."

"But I do." She didn't add that it was something mothers automatically did with their children, because it was still hard to talk about their new relationship. But the time would come when they could, and would, talk. Mary knew that.

"I'm fine, Mary," she said. "Really, I—" the tears started as if responding to some perverse cue "—am." Long weeks of heartache, and restraint, had reached their end. Long weeks of loving Burke without him at her side, and the hurtful, unchangeable knowledge that he never would be there, had taken their toll.

Mary pulled her daughter close. Jill went willingly, needing to feel a pair of comforting arms about her. "Shh," Mary whispered as she rocked Jill back and forth.

"It hurts. It hurts so bad."

"I know."

"I . . . I love him so much."

"He loves you."

"But not enough. Not enough."

Jill cried, Mary consoled, and over and over Jill babbled about love and hurt.

HURT.

Burke's whole body hurt from the exhaustion of running. His chest hurt, his legs hurt, even the rugged beard bristling his face seemed to hurt. But he ran on. To the murmuring ocean, he pleaded for help in forgetting Jill's smile. To the ebony night, he prayed to forget the taste of Jill's lips. To the moon, round and full and burning the sky in platinum, he begged to forget the feel of Jill in his arms.

But forgetfulness eluded him, just as pain consumed him.

What was she doing?

What was she thinking?

Had she forgotten him?

"You can't run away from love..."

Yes. Yes, he could. He had to!

Digging his feet into the moist beach, he sprinted forward, driving, pushing his body to the limit of endurance. Just as he was driving, pushing his heartache to its limit.

An image of Jill all soft eyed and dewy mouthed from loving him rushed through his mind. It was followed by an image of her laughing, an image of her combing her hair in sultry strokes, an image of her crying. He saw her standing in the shower, he saw her standing at the kitchen cabinet, he saw her ready to stand by his side forever. His heart ached, unbearably and in full measure, for the mere sight of her.

"Jill!" he cried, stumbling, then falling to his knees like the broken man he was. His heart pounded an absent lover's rhythm, and he searched deep in his lungs for another lonely breath. Briny tears stung his eyes before spilling over and heedlessly streaming down his hair-roughened cheeks.

Damp gritty sand beneath him, the moon shining over him, he wept. From his heart. From his soul. For the first time since he'd left her. In the cool, salt wind whispering against his face, he heard the mocking refrain of Jill's song: "You can't run from love, you can't run from love..."

When the tears and the darkest of the night were over, when his soul lay gutted at his feet, when he cared not for that day's sunset nor the morrow's dawn, Burke made a startling revelation. He had survived. Again.

LATE SATURDAY AFTERNOON, in a church filled with friends and flowers, Mary and Rob were married.

Wearing the palest of pale-blue chiffon, carrying a bouquet of pink-throated white orchids, Mary walked half of the church's long aisle alone, where she was met by Rob, who was symbolically pledging that he would always meet her halfway. Then, his love so obvious it warmed the hearts of all there, he escorted his bride to the hand-carved mahogany railing of the two-hundred-year-old church. Mary slid in beside a smiling Jill; Rob, in beside a nervous best man—his nineteen-year-old son.

After an appropriate preamble of welcome, the minister's deep baritone voice echoed the vows throughout the cavernous church.

"Do you, Robert Donald Sheffield, take Mary Elaine McClain to be your lawfully wedded wife..."

Rob's eyes plunged deeply, lovingly, into those of the woman beside him...and Jill's heart turned over in bittersweet remembrance. How many times had Burke looked at her in just that way? How many times had his body told hers what he had not verbally been able to say until the very last—the very last when it had been too late? What was he doing at this very minute? What was he thinking? Was he all right? Please, God, let him be all right...

"Do you, Mary Elaine McClain, take Robert Donald Sheffield to be your lawfully wedded husband..."

Jill studied the rapt expression captured in the love-softened features of the older woman's face and thought how perfectly deserved her happiness was. It was a happiness reflected in Mary's tear-glittery brown eyes. Jill felt her own eyes clouding beneath her contact lenses. She shed tears of both happiness and unhappiness. She was happy for Mary's sake, undeniably so, but unhappy for her own. She knew that she would never be sharing these sacred vows with the man she loved.

"May I have the ring?"

Jill shifted her divided attention back to the ceremony...just in time to take the bridal bouquet Mary handed her. For a brief moment, Mary's eyes scanned her daughter's face, looking for signs of fatigue. Jill smiled reassuringly.

At the same time a wave of semisuppressed but infectious titters spread through the guests as the best man dealt with that mandatory moment of panic when he couldn't find the ring. Instinctively, Jill glanced toward the laughter and added her broadened smile to it. Far at the back of the sanctuary, well beyond the scattering of people seated on the front pews, Jill saw a man enter the church and take a seat in the last row. She made the mental notation that he was probably a late guest. Seconds later, the ring being produced from the pant pocket of a red-faced best man restored solemnity once more and drew Jill's attention back to the front of the church.

"The ring is the outward symbol of an inner commitment..."

But her wayward attention wouldn't be tamed so easily. She would never wear Burke's ring, Jill couldn't help but think. She would never again sleep beside him. She would never have his children. She would never... Stop it! she silently shouted. Why keep punishing yourself?

"By the power vested in me, I now pronounce you husband and wife. What God has joined together, let no man put asunder. You may kiss your bride."

Jill watched as an almost-disbelieving Rob lowered his head to kiss his wife. She watched as their lips connected. Sweet feelings burst to life in her own body as she remembered the feel of Burke's lips on hers. It was a magic she could never forget.

Rob eased his mouth from Mary's, leaving her breathless and blushing. In one fluid motion, Mary turned toward Jill, and Jill handed back the bouquet. Stretching, she placed a kiss on Mary's cheek.

"Be happy," Jill whispered.

"We will," Mary answered, giving her daughter a quick hug before taking her husband's arm and starting back down the long aisle.

Transferring her bouquet of white carnations and yellow rosebuds to her right hand, Jill took the arm the best man was offering her, and the two slowly moved into step behind the bride and groom. Suddenly Jill was grateful for the support of a strong arm. She had grown tired. Beneath the champagne-hued dress she wore, the scars were healing, but her stamina was still not back to normal. She wondered how much of that fact had to do with her emotional unrest.

As she passed by the third pew, she saw Andrew Rawlins sitting beside Ida Tumbrello. There was a sadness in the moss-green eyes that looked so like Burke's. She knew that he, too, was hurting, for his son and for her. They smiled, each offering the other what comfort they could. Jill noted that Ida patted his hand reassuringly, affectionately, and hoped that the rumor that the two were at last dating was true.

Passing down the length of the aisle, Jill pondered again her decision to resign from Rawlins, Rawlins, Nugent and Carson. Her mind was already made up, her resignation was already typed, and come Monday morning she was mailing it to Andrew Rawlins. The resignation was equally for her and Burke's sake. She couldn't work alongside him—not after what they'd shared—nor was he likely to return without the same misgivings.

She had accepted the fact—not gracefully, but necessarily—that she would never see Burke again. Except perhaps in a courtroom. Except perhaps at some legal social function. Except perhaps...

Suddenly the newly married couple slowed their pace as they neared the back of the church. Then they stopped, necessitating that Jill and the best man do so as well. Slowly Mary and Rob parted. Jill instinctively peered through at the object of their interest.

Her heart immediately erupted into a fast, discordant rhythm. Was she hallucinating? No, Rob and Mary saw him too. Why else were they exchanging knowing looks and stepping around her and back up the aisle, Rob dragging his confused son behind him? Why else were they meeting the guests and herding them out a side door? Why else were they leaving the figure on the back pew and her alone?

Slowly, uncertainly, Burke stood.

Jill watched as his body unfolded to its tall, lean height. He was all silver-gray suit, striped shirt and yellow tie. He was all longer-than-usual hair and recently shaved cheeks. He was all beautifully bronzed skin, all beautifully seductive male.

Burke's smoke-green eyes roamed from the froth of yellow flowers and lace in her free-flowing hair to the satin shoes on her small feet. In between, he drank in the sight of champagne-colored brocade and ivory skin, of shiny taupe-glossed lips and empyrean-blue eyes.

"You were right," he whispered in a husky voice that seemed swallowed alive by the large, hollow-sounding chamber.

"About what?" Her voice was delicate, as fragile as the rosebuds and carnations she was crushing to her.

"You can't run away from love." He smiled—a mocking, sarcastic slant of his mouth. "Though, God knows, I tried."

Jill's heartbeat accelerated, pumping blood at a pace that spun her head.

"I, uh . . . I ran over all three hundred miles of the Cape. Maybe twice over. But no matter how far I ran, you were always there. No matter where I tried to hide, you were always there. No matter . . ." His voice broke into fractured decibels; his eyes glazed. He visibly fought to keep from falling apart. He wanted to say that he'd heard her voice in the wind. He wanted to say that he'd heard her laughter in the ocean, seen her hair in the silver moonlight, felt the heat of her body in the golden sun, but he couldn't find the words. All he could find were simple words that came from the heart. "I . . . I love you, Jill," he whispered in a shredded voice. "I can't live without y—"

The sentence was never finished. The words were caught somewhere between two hungry mouths. The words were caught somewhere between two desperate bodies. The words were caught somewhere between two loving hearts.

CHAPTER FIFTEEN

"THAT'S FAR ENOUGH," Burke gasped, slacking his pace from jogging to a dead halt. Exactly two weeks and three days had passed since Mary and Rob had become husband and wife.

Jill sailed on past Burke, hollering something about the boulder in the near distance. As she spoke, a wave crashed against said boulder, causing a fine curtainy mist to arc toward the end-of-the-day sky. In the west a majestic sunset gathered around a dying ball of sun-fire, while overhead a whitish-gray sea gull shrilled an evensong.

"Jill!" Burke cried in reprimand. "The doctor said to ease into exercise. Ease, as in take it slowly." His voice rose an octave as Jill drew farther and farther away.

Dragging his hands to his hips, he watched in exasperation as his wife defied him and the doctor. He also watched the sway of lean hips—her too-lean hips, in white running shorts—and the rhythmic undulation of shoulders beneath a red T-shirt that read Rawlins, Rawlins, Nugent, Carson and Rawlins, across the back. The promotion had been his dad's wedding present to her, while Ida Tumbrello's had been a word of caution: Never let Burke make the coffee, because the inability to do so might run in the family. Burke couldn't keep a smile from his lips when he remembered Ida's revelation that it was Andrew who'd always been responsible for the horrible office coffee, and that she'd agreed to go out with him only if he'd turn the job over to her. The smile on Burke's lips slowly disappeared as Jill reached the boulder, then jogged right by it.

"Okay, lady, that does it," he said, his bare feet coming alive as he started in after her. With his long legs pumping powerfully beneath the blue nylon running shorts, he reached her in seconds and snatched her up into his arms in midrun.

Startled, Jill gasped and giggled and tried to feign irritation. "How am I ever going to get my 'tamina back..."

"Your what?" Burke teased, hugging her close to his chest with one arm at her waist, the other under her knees. He started back toward the spread beach blanket at a sedate walk. He carried her as if she were feather light and precious.

"Stamina, stamina, and if you'll...let me catch my breath...I'll say the darned word. How am I ever going to get my stamina back if you don't let me exercise?"

"I can think of far more rewarding exercise," he said, a salacious grin on his lips.

The twin of the grin danced on her mouth. "I'll just bet you can, counselor."

It was uncertain whose lips made the aggressive move. All that was important was that they were kissing—again. That, and other refined ways of making love, seemed to be the only thing they'd done the three days they'd been married and honeymooning at Cape Cod. Burke said that the two weeks she'd made him wait to marry her was all the restraint he ever intended to display. As if remembering that pledge, his lips now sealed hers more fervently. She tightened her arms about his neck and snuggled more deeply against his bare chest. She made a tiny little sound of complete contentment.

The next thing she knew she was slowly, gingerly, being laid flat on her back on the beach towel. With reluctance their lips parted. She stared up into the face only inches from her own. It was a face she knew every line and crease of. She knew also that she loved it more than any face in the world. At that very moment, Burke was thinking similar thoughts about the oval, freckle-dusted face before him.

"I love y—"

"I love y—" they both said together, and laughed at the timing. Legs and bodies, more nude than clothed, automatically entwined, and he dropped a light kiss on the end of her nose.

Sobering, he said, "You're still too thin."

"I'm gaining," she said defensively.

"You still have circles under your eyes."

"They're not near as dark as they were."

"You're still too pale."

Jill's lips twitched. "Is there anything you like about me?"

"Yeah," he said with a fat grin. "I like your name, Mrs. Rawlins."

"What a coincidence," she said. "So do I."

Grinning, Burke eased beside her and rolled to his back. He tugged her across his bare, sweaty, hair-sprigged chest. Her strawberry-blond hair fanned out from the confinement of the scarlet-red sweatband encircling her head. Perspiration dotted her upper lip and moisture-glazed her cheeks.

"How do you feel about children?" she asked suddenly, as her fingers played in the damp hair on his chest.

"Children in general or ours in particular?" he asked, tugging her T-shirt upward and spanning her waist with his hands. Beneath his palms, he could feel her skin moist and warm from running.

"Ours in particular."

"Talk it up."

"Well," she said, tracing the pad of her thumb across his nipple—it hardened and his breathing nosedived—"they're cute and cuddly when they're young."

"And?"

"And they're a comfort when you're old."

"And?"

"And—" she grinned "—they're a lot of fun to make."

The smile that stole across his lips was so devastating that Jill felt her heart beat an entirely different rhythm. "How much fun?'' he asked, slowly sliding his hands up her sweat-slick back.

"Lots," she purred, sprawling across his chest like a cat curling atop its master.

Their lips were mere inches apart.

Burke's lips lost their tease. "When you health's better, we'll talk about it seriously."

"We could name a boy Andrew Thomas, after his grandfathers, and we could name a girl Mary?" The sentence was more question than statement.

"We can name them anything you like...as long as you're healthy when you have them...and as long as you let me be their father." The hands at her back exerted the pressure necessary to meld her mouth with his.

"I promise you can be their father," she whispered as her mouth settled against his.

His kiss was instant seduction. Drugging her with promises she knew his body could fulfill, his lips worked gently, provocatively, against hers. His tongue teased—just the tip piercing the gates of her open mouth—then plunged inside deeply, erotically. Her mouth was smooth, his tongue deliciously rough and well-practiced.

"Oh, Burke," she moaned.

She angled her head so his nibbling mouth could nip and bite her ear and rousingly travel the column of her neck. Gently, lost in the feel of her, he rolled her to her back. His hands fit just beneath the slopes of her breasts, and his fingers swished back and forth, swelling and hardening her nipples.

"God, you feel so good," he whispered. "You feel so..." He stopped, his fingers grazing the inches-long scar on her chest. As always, the experience sobered. As always, there was a shudder that ran through his body before he could stop it. As always, Jill noticed. And worried. It was the only thing that marred the perfection of their marriage.

"Burke..."

His eyes found hers. They were hazy with the remembrance of the color red staining the color ivory. They were hazy with the remembrance of fear, a fear that had once driven him from her.

"...I have no guarantees, no warranties, no indemnities, concerning life and death. As much as I would like to, I can't promise you..."

"I know," he interrupted. "And I can't offer you guarantees, warranties, or indemnities. I can't promise you that I won't die before you. If I do, you'll survive. If you...die before me, I'll survive. It's what human beings do best."

Jill looked deeply into his eyes, searching for sincerity. She found it. Though it was mingled with fear, it was there. She thought back to the moment she first saw him when he'd returned to work following Nicole's death. She had seen pain in his eyes, she had seen the hell he'd walked through, but she'd also seen a strength. She had thought then that it may be a strength he didn't yet know he possessed. The man before her now knew. Somewhere on the beach of the Atlantic shore, somewhere in the eastern wind, somewhere in the solar sun, he'd learned a universal truth.

"Yes," she whispered, her hand cupping the side of his face, "human beings survive."

"I know. I learned it here on this beach...one night when I had nothing more to lose."

The dying sun splashed the seaside in gray and silver shadows. In the distance the ocean rumbled and rolled toward shore.

Burke's mouth eased once more to hers. It was a gentle kiss that moved her as profoundly as any they'd ever shared.

"Let's die together," she whispered.

"Let's live together," he whispered back.

"Agreed."

A slow grin once more claimed Burke's mouth. "How do you feel about making love on a beach?"

"It's illegal, Rawlins."

His smile widened. "Not if you don't get caught."

Instinctively, Jill glanced around her. The isolated beach was as deserted as it had been the entire three days they'd been there.

"Burke Rawlins, you're so bad," she said, unable to keep her body from responding to the thought of making love there by the ocean in the twilight.

Easing her T-shirt upward, his nose nuzzled the swollen softness of her breast before his lips kissed the rosy crest. His fingers worked their impatient way inside the leg of her shorts. Boldly, he touched her in a way that was familiar and intimate and loving.

"Umm. You're so bad, you're good," she amended on a half cry, half sigh as her hips arched into his talented fingers. She felt his lips smile around the tip of her breast. She heard him mumble that she tasted salty. And sexy. And that he wanted her more than any man had ever wanted any woman.

Minutes later, they lay naked. Hands entwined—his ring exactly matching hers—he slowly, greedily slipped inside her waiting, willing, woman's body.

"Oh, Burke," she whispered at the glorious feel of the deep masculine pressure. Tightening the mesh of their fingers, she brought her hips up and against his.

"I love you," he whispered, his lips blanketing hers.

"I love you," she answered.

There on a secluded, sparkling-white beach, vows were silently repeated, repeated in caresses, kisses and the sacred joining of bodies and souls. There on a beach washed clean by the ocean, two lovers vowed to love until parted by death.

They had nothing in common.
But evidence was mounting to support
the theory that opposites attract.

A LEGAL AFFAIR

Bobby Hutchinson

"SO YOU'RE A LAWYER, right? I wanna know, what are my constitutional rights, here? How come parking meters only take quarters? Tell me *why* I should hafta carry around a pocketful of quarters when I've got dimes and nickels?"

A dirty fist plunged into a trouser pocket and came up with several coins.

"Just because they don't fit in the stupid machines, it's not my fault, right? And then some jerk up and tows my car! Is that *fair*, lady?"

Jenny Lathrop frowned at the bald giant scowling at her as he leaned against the narrow table that served as her desk.

"I ast you a question, lady lawyer. Answer me. You think tha's fair?"

Jenny pushed her wire-framed glasses higher on her nose, wishing that Vancouver's finest had towed Mr. Obnoxious away, instead of his car.

Jenny was beginning to believe that she'd made a big mistake, wanting to practice law. Here she was, a third-year student, donating valuable hours of her time to help people who couldn't afford to pay a practicing lawyer, and her very first client turned out to be a nut case.

Parking meters? Constitutional rights over whether the damned things took nickels and dimes? This wasn't exactly what she thought Professor Moffat had meant about people needing her advice.

"Working in the Legal Clinic will be a great experience," he'd enthused. "You work one-on-one with clients just the way you'll be doing when you're out in the field. The clinic's open once a week, on Thursday evenings beginning at seven sharp. There's always a graduate lawyer in attendance to help you with any problems."

Well, Jenny was having a problem, all right. She shot a glance across the room, hoping she could catch the eye of the graduate lawyer and get him to come over.

Mr. Jones was tall and elegant looking in his fancy three-piece suit. Jenny figured he was maybe thirty-four, thirty-five. At this moment he was bent solicitously over blond and curvaceous Gloria Spencer, one of Jenny's classmates. He had the same mesmerized look on his face that most of the male professors had whenever they were within a ten-foot radius of Gloria.

She recalled a comment a cynical friend of hers had made about why young lawyers volunteered for this job as clinic adviser.

"Sixty percent of law students are now female. Volunteering at clinics is a good way for these guys to meet women who are easily impressed by graduate lawyers. It ain't altruism that attracts them, honey."

And it didn't look as if she was going to have any luck getting Mr. Jones's attention away from Gloria. Jenny stared down at her neat piles of supplies on the table, hoping for inspiration. There were waivers, divorce kits, the *Law Student's Legal Advice Manual,* even a package of tissues in case some poor client burst into tears.

The way things were going, she might need the tissues herself.

She allowed herself one last, panicked glance at the Interview Checklist, page 1, point A.

Instructions for opening the interview: Greet client, make him feel comfortable, establish rapport by small talk, seat client, stress that client should carefully read the waiver and sign it. . . .

The all-important waiver.

"Listen," she began again, raising her voice and trying to be patient. "I can't be of any help to you unless you sign this, Mr., uh, what did you say your name was?"

She leaned forward and shook the paper in an effort to get his attention, but quickly drew back. The smell of liquor on his breath was enough to give her a hangover.

"My name's none of your business. I'm here for legal advice, like the sign outside said, so don't you raise your voice to me. I got my rights. This here's the free legal-advice clinic, ain't it? So give me some free advice, Red."

Red wasn't exactly her favorite nickname. Being teased about her copper-colored hair always raised every hackle in Jenny's body.

Free clinic or not, she was a professional and expected to be treated like one. Furious, she got up from her chair and leveled her most lethal glare at him.

"You've had too much to drink, that's what I figure. And you won't listen to a single word I say. So if you're going to go on with this monologue, then I suggest you leave," she ordered in a shaky, high voice.

He sneered at her. "Well, hoity-toity, aren't we? Who the hell are you to order me around?"

"That's it. Out you go, right now. Get out. As far as I'm concerned, this interview is over."

He stuck out his bulldog jaw at her and gave her an evil grin.

"Is that so?" he snapped, and then smashed a meaty fist down on the table, sending neat papers flying in all directions. It was a wonder the table legs didn't collapse. The sound echoed through the large room, quieting the subdued buzz of the other nine law students and drawing horrified stares from their clients.

"Leave, huh? Well, we'll just see who the hell is leaving around here!" His voice filled the room.

Jenny flinched, her anger shifting to alarm. She suspected that this Neanderthal wouldn't hesitate to hit her next. What to do?

Her gaze slid past her client's massive bulk and noted that now help was on the way. The classily dressed Mr. Jones, Q.C., L.L.D., had finally noticed something was wrong. He was striding over to her desk, a frown on his face.

Relief spilled through her when he appeared at the giant's left shoulder.

He put a manicured hand on her client's forearm and inquired in a deep, cultured baritone, "What seems to be the problem here . . . ?"

As if it were happening in slow motion, Jenny saw the man's fist curl and a vicious snarl appear on his beefy red face. He swung at Jones and connected. Jones grunted and, staggering back, grabbed at a chair, missed, and fell heavily to the floor, as blood burst from his finely shaped nose.

Stunned, he lay still for a moment.

Several women screamed.

The giant guffawed.

Two male law students came rushing over and then hung back, apparently having second thoughts about tackling Jenny's burly client, who was now feinting with his fists like a prizefighter, his broad back toward her and his treelike legs braced against her table as if he planned to take on every man in the room.

Jones was struggling to get to his feet. He looked affronted, like a monarch who'd been slammed in the face by a common thug. More people were crowding around.

There were screams, and someone hollered, "Call the police!" But no one seemed to be doing anything practical.

Suddenly disgusted by the lack of positive action, Jenny grabbed the first heavy thing at hand. It happened to be her massive four-inch-thick, *University of British Columbia Law Student's Legal Advice Manual*. She stepped up on her chair and then onto the unsteady surface of the table. She raised the book as high over her head as she could, and brought it down on her client's bald pate with every ounce of strength in her slender body.

Though her tormentor's knees buckled, still he didn't go down. He grunted and looked slowly around and up at her with a comically amazed expression, and then swore loudly as three male students and two clients grabbed his arms and hustled him out the door. He didn't put up much resistance at all.

Jenny scrambled down from the tabletop.

Pandemonium reigned. Everyone talked at once.

"You gonna sue the guy, Mr. Jones?"

"You want us to call an ambulance? Does it feel like your nose is broken?"

"Hey, anybody manage to get that guy's name or an address?"

Three female students were hovering over Mr. Jones, who was now off the floor and sprawled on the chair in front of Jenny's desk, pressing a wad of bloody tissue to his nostrils.

As Jenny gaped at him, Jones's thick, dark eyebrows rose like haughty question marks over angry green eyes. He glared back at her. There was something so amusing about his outraged expression that Jenny had the urge to laugh.

She suppressed one hysterical giggle, and then another. She tried to look away from Mr. Jones but was unable to move an eyelash. She felt her face turning red and hot, and she just knew her freckles were standing out like beacons across her nose and on her cheeks.

Stop it, Jenny.

"What's your name?" His query was muffled by the tissues, but it was understandable.

She couldn't answer. Bubbles of laughter floated up in her like helium gas. His burning gaze impaled her. Well, he might as well make good use of his eyesight while it lasted. It would only be a matter of hours before both those disconcerting green eyes turned interesting shades of black and swelled almost shut—if her guess was worth anything.

Mr. Constitutional Rights had landed Jones a good one right on the button.

My, he certainly had long eyelashes for a man with such a livid stare. Long eyelashes, and a sort of . . . regal presence.

It's a wonder his blood isn't blue, she thought, as hysteria battled with good sense. If ever a man looked as if he ought to have blue blood, Jones did.

His wavy dark brown hair hung in disarray over his forehead, and the front of his vest and fancy pink shirt and his gray-and-blue striped silk tie were covered with large bloodstains. The impeccable light gray suit was rumpled and dusty, and his trouser knees were filthy.

"Mr. Jones, one of us will be glad to drive you to the hospital," a female student suggested, brushing reverently at the dirt on his sleeve.

He ignored the offer and the fussing. Instead, he steadily regarded Jenny's scarlet face.

"What . . . is your . . . name?"

She was going to have to answer.

"Jenny. Umm, Jenny Lathrop." She struggled for control, swallowed, shoved her glasses higher on her nose and managed to overcome her treacherous laughter. "I'm, umm, a third-year law student."

Now that she was up close to him, she saw that Jones wasn't any weakling. Even sitting down, she could tell he was tall—probably a good ten inches taller than her. And he had wide shoulders for a lawyer.

"Mind telling me what went on between you and our mutual friend?"

Jenny told herself not to be intimidated. He was only a man, after all. A good-looking man. Under other circumstances, he might even be . . . sexy?

Whacking that bum on the head must have affected her brain.

But he had a good shape for a lawyer—no denying that. No sign of spread or spillover in the parts that usually expanded when a guy got successful. And if that classy suit was any indication, Jones was doing fine in his practice.

Probably some nice, profitable, boring, safe, corporate specialty. The thought sobered her.

"Well . . . . Ms. . . . . Lathrop? I'm waiting for some sort of explanation."

There was every indication in his tone that she was trying what little patience he had left.

Jenny was well aware of that, and grew irritated. If he expected an apology, he was barking up the wrong tree. What had occurred here wasn't the result of a single thing she'd said or done. She was innocent.

"It . . . it certainly wasn't my fault, if that's what you're thinking," she said, her indignation causing her to stammer. "I, umm, he—that man—just wouldn't listen. He went on and on and wouldn't sign the waiver, and he insulted me, so I asked him to leave." She drew in a deep breath and pushed her glasses higher on her nose. "He was raving on about parking meters and constitutional rights and his car getting towed away." She paused and then frowned when it struck her that constitutional rights weren't covered in the legal-advice manual. "How come the rights aren't in the manual? I've never seen any sign of them, and I've read the blamed thing from front to back until I practically know it by heart."

Jones looked nonplussed, but only for a split second. "I have no idea, and it's irrelevant. Now, what else happened? In detail."

Trying to sound dignified through a wad of tissue was not easy, as Jones was discovering. Fresh blood was now seeping through the tissues, but he did pretty well under the circumstances.

Jenny spotted her own package of tissues on the floor near her feet and bent over to retrieve them. Then she yanked out a good dozen, walked around the desk and thrust them at Jones. He took them and smoothly replaced one set with the other without one word of thanks.

She could smell his after-shave, or cologne, or whatever it was he wore. It was clean and outdoorsy—a definite contrast to his disheveled state.

Boy, did he ever bleed! She'd hate to be around if he was really wounded.

"What exactly did you say to set him off, Ms. Lathrop?"

He certainly was persistent. And judgmental, as well. For pete's sake, he still seemed to think it was her fault.

Was she on trial here?

"How do I know what set him off? He was drunk, looking for a fight. When I told him that he ought to leave, he smashed his fist on the table. Then you came over, and he punched you out."

"I'm well aware of that segment of the incident." His voice dripped with sarcasm.

"Well, that's a relief."

She knew she sounded sharp, but darn it all, he'd asked for it. What did he expect—a full psychological workup on some crazed drunk?

Their gazes held in a silent battle of wills. Finally Jones became aware that clients and students were milling around in a general state of disorder, many of them eavesdropping on everything he and Jenny were saying.

"Okay, everybody, let's get back to work," he announced in an authoritative way, and to Jenny's surprise, people returned to their tables, clients took their places in chairs and soon the hum of quiet conversation again filled the room.

"You must be used to having the serfs obey." She was sorry the instant the words were out.

He ignored it, however, other than giving her one last, scathing look.

"I suggest you carry on, as well, Ms. Lathrop," he said after a long pause. "There're a lot of people waiting, and you've wasted a great deal of time already."

She'd wasted time? She got angry all over again, but it faded once Jones turned and headed for the door, probably to find the washroom.

Jenny felt a pang of sympathy as she watched him walk away. There was a huge dirt stain across the back of his jacket, and for some reason, he looked a lot more vulnerable from the back than he had from the front. He had a crazy cowlick at the crown of his head. And he also had a neat, tight bottom and strong, long legs.... Heat enveloped her and she suddenly felt weak in the knees. She collapsed onto her chair and drew in several deep breaths, wondering if there was a hope in hell that the rest of the evening was going to improve.

A FAT WOMAN wearing a cherry-red knitted hat pulled down tight over her ears must have been watching for Jenny to sit down before she came over. She looked forty or even fifty. Her brown raincoat was buttoned to the neck, and she sidled over and eased herself into the chair in front of Jenny's desk without removing either hat or coat.

Now, this time, let's get this right, Lathrop. Greet the client.

"Hello there. How are you this evening?" Jenny pasted a wide, phony smile on her stiff face, making a point of standing and holding her hand out in a welcoming way. The woman hesitated and then touched Jenny's hand with yellow nicotine-stained fingers and drew back as if the contact were electric. Her watery blue eyes didn't quite meet Jenny's gaze.

"I'm Jenny Lathrop, and . . . your name is . . . ?"

"Veronica. I'm Veronica Glickman, I been here lots before. I seen what you done to that bum just now, and I wanna say I think it was something. He was no gentleman, that's for sure. You know how to take care of yourself, and I like that in a woman. So I asked the girl at the door if I could come over to you." Her voice was rough and low-pitched, as if she smoked too much. There was an aura of toughness about her. There was also a pungent smell like rotting fruit.

Jenny instinctively wanted to move back out of the woman's immediate vicinity, but didn't. Instead she smiled, more naturally this time, and at last made eye contact with her client. Something in Veronica's eyes made her seem vulnerable.

"Well, Ms. . . . . Glickman, thank you. And I'm delighted to be your counselor. Now, before we talk about your reason for coming here tonight, I must explain the purpose of this waiver. . . ."

It wasn't a perfect production, but it was the best Jenny had to offer at the moment. It was a thousand times better than her first disaster; that was certain.

Ten minutes later—waiver signed and over with—Veronica began to relax. First, she tugged the knitted cap off, revealing a brownish-gray mass of short hair that looked as if it had been lopped off with garden shears. She was talking all the while, complaining in a disjointed fashion about the student she'd seen last time she'd come to the Legal Clinic.

"See, I told him, I said I need a lawyer, somebody smart, because the damn city is going to tear down my house. Says so right here on this paper. . . . Now, where'd I put it? But he didn't listen right, that boy didn't. Said there wasn't anything he could do. Where is that cussed paper, anyway?"

She launched a search through the pockets of her raincoat, clicking her tongue against her teeth when she didn't find what she was looking for.

Then, to Jenny's amazement, Veronica unbuttoned the raincoat and revealed another, heavier coat underneath—this one a bright wool plaid, with a mad assortment of junk in the pockets, but not the paper Veronica was looking for. She was becoming more and more agitated, muttering under her breath, and her hands were shaking.

More buttons were undone. Still another coat was revealed, blue this time, and under that a heavy sweater over a voluminous skirt. In the skirt pocket, Veronica at last located a crumbled, soiled and multifolded letter, which she triumphantly handed to Jenny. She was perspiring, and she accepted the tissue Jenny offered and mopped her face with it.

"Here. I knew I brought it."

Jenny took the paper, saddened at what she'd seen. Veronica wasn't fat at all. She was actually rather scrawny under her protective covering. And Jenny suspected that she was also mentally disturbed.

Jenny unfolded the letter, which smelled like Veronica, and quickly scanned it.

It was a formal notice from the city Health Department stating that a house located at 4905 Powell Street was in the process of being condemned for health reasons.

"This is where you live, Veronica?"

"It's my house. I own that house. They got no right to tear it down. It's mine." A tear leaked out of the corner of her eye and found a path down the wrinkles on her cheek. She sniffed noisily. "Can you do anything?"

Jenny thought about it. There wasn't any way to check on the ownership of the property tonight. And the Health Department wouldn't open till nine tomorrow, either.

"Ms. Glickman, I can't help you right this minute, but I promise I'll have answers for you by next Thursday. I promise I'll do whatever is possible to help you. Can you come back and see me again at that time? This card has my name on it. You tell the aide at the door that you have an appointment with me."

"Sure. Sure, I'll be here Thursday, and you call me Veronica." She slid Jenny's card into some pocket or other, and began the laborious process of buttoning, zipping and tying all her various garments together again while Jenny filled in necessary details in a file with Veronica's name on it.

When she was done, Veronica yanked her cap down over her ears, waved a hand at Jenny and shuffled away.

THE OTHER CLIENTS Jenny had were straightforward. She didn't have to refer to the legal-advice manual even once. Her confidence returned. Once again sure of herself, she was filled with enthusiasm for her career in law.

She was in control.

She was only subliminally aware that Mr. Jones had never reappeared.

But he surfaced in her dreams that night.

BRENDA PENNINGTON was at her desk when Zachary Jones strode into his office at eight-fifteen Friday morning.

"Morning, Mr. Jones. You're early." Brenda had never succumbed to the informality of calling the partners by their first names.

Her lush blond exterior was a cover-up for the managerial skills and iron will of a thirty-year-old Margaret Thatcher. She'd been hired four years before. The partners had taken one look at her delicate face, lavish bosom and valentine-shaped bottom, and agreed unanimously.

"Hi, Brenda," Zach mumbled, doing his best to hold the morning paper at an angle that would cover his matched set of black eyes and swollen nostrils.

He'd hoped that maybe by coming in forty-five minutes before his usual arrival time, he'd escape just the sort of intensive scrutiny Brenda was now giving him. He should have known better.

"You get yourself in another brawl, Mr. Jones?"

Brenda had no illusions about any of the partners. She hadn't fallen for a single one of the furtive, but ingenious, carnal propositions each had made to her at some point over the past years. She treated them as if they were slow children, and accepted no excuses whatsoever as far as their productivity was concerned.

"Brenda, that's unfair. You make it sound as if I go out looking for recreational fights." Zach was in no mood for insinuations. "The only other time I had a black eye was when I fell off my board wind-surfing and the damn thing bashed into me."

"There was that wedding eight months ago, Mr. Jones."

"I was severely provoked on that occasion, Brenda." He tried to speak as haughtily as possible, but not being able to breathe through his nose made him sound adenoidal instead.

Brenda went on eyeing him with morbid curiosity.

"Is it broken?"

Zach was about to shake his head when he remembered how movement of any kind made his head feel.

"The doctor said probably cracked, but not needing a splint or realignment."

"Well, that's positive, isn't it?"

Zach could tell she wasn't finished yet.

"So what happened this time? How'd you get a matched set instead of a single?"

"A certifiable lunatic at the law clinic last night went berserk and socked me one."

"You get his name? We could sue on the grounds that you're going to scare customers away, looking like that."

Zach tried to scowl at her, but he knew from the sight that had greeted him in the mirror that morning that scowling was just as impossible as smiling. His face was both painful and frozen into one set expression.

"Not much point in suing somebody who goes to a free legal clinic," he growled. "Waste of time."

"Well, I wondered why you volunteered at that clinic in the first place. Altruism really doesn't suit you, Mr. Jones."

Before he could think of an answer to that, Zach heard the door open and shut behind him, and Ken Meredith's cheerful voice yodeled a good-morning.

Zach attempted a fast getaway. He'd had it up to the teeth with questions already this morning. There'd been the elevator man in his apartment building, the news vendor, the parking attendant. . . and Brenda.

He hurried toward the stairs leading to his second-floor office, with Ken dogging his heels like a terrier.

"Zach? Hey, Zach, old buddy. So, did you score at that clinic last night like we figured? Was it worth the time invested? Any lovely ladies old uncle Ken might connect with? Zach? Whadda ya say, hotshot?"

Ken's voice was growing blessedly fainter. Zach took the stairs to his office two at a time, doing his best to ignore the bolts of pain that shot through his head with each jarring step.

He didn't need to be reminded that his motives in volunteering at the damned legal-aid thing were a lot less than honorable, and he was furious with Ken for airing them in front of Brenda. He could imagine the knowing looks she was aiming at his back right this minute.

"So what's with him, Brenda? He get up on the wrong side of the bed, or what? I only asked a friendly question."

From the top of the landing, Zach heard Brenda giving his partner a rundown on his black eyes and swollen nose.

"It's quite grotesque. He's disfigured," he heard her comment, and Ken was unfeeling enough to guffaw.

Safe at last in his spacious office, Zach closed the door and moved toward the wall-size window where he stared unseeingly out, reviewing the past evening's events for the fiftieth time.

The thing that galled him was getting knocked down without even raising his fists.

If he hadn't still been fantasizing about that gorgeous blonde named Gloria something or other, maybe he'd have reacted quicker when that bastard socked him.

He sure as hell hadn't come off looking like any hero. The guy had coldcocked him when he least expected it. His lips tightened, and he was filled with rage. He'd give a lot for a chance to even the score.

And why the hell should the image of that skinny woman with those outdated wire-framed glasses and wild hair like new copper pennies keep intruding into his battered brain?

Had the punch on his nose dislodged some part of his mind? He could barely remember what the tall blonde looked like this morning, but every damned freckle on the redhead was etched in his memory.

He'd always gone for tall blondes, he reminded himself.

This girl...this Jenny Lathrop... Hell, she wasn't his type at all.

Not physically. Tiny, kind of flat-chested, wiry.

Not his type emotionally, either. She didn't have a shred of human kindness in her.

Strong, though. He remembered the gratifying sound of the blow she'd dealt the Neanderthal. Gutsy, when even the men were hanging back like wimps, letting the Neanderthal control the scene.

She had a fast, wicked mouth. He remembered women like her from his student days—always quick with an answer. Defensive. Antagonistic. Smart. Aggressive.

Interesting?

He recalled dating one or two. They'd made a nice change, driven him temporarily nuts and made him doubly grateful for the compliant cheerleader types.

Like Annemarie.

Was he getting old or stale or what? Since Annemarie walked out on him two months ago, he'd been uncharacteristically slow at finding a replacement.

Well, it wasn't going to be the likes of this redhead!

What sort of woman was she, anyway? What sort of woman would laugh when a guy was grievously injured, for God's sake?

And yet... There'd been that unmistakable current of pure energy running between them. Sexual energy.

Get ahold of yourself, Jones. She's nothing but trouble.

Look what happened to you the very first moment you were in her vicinity. You got socked in the face for no good reason. Now, wouldn't that seem a less-than-gentle hint from fate to stay away from that woman forever?

And yet, he kept remembering the damnedest things about her, when he least expected it. That uncontrollable grin, for one thing. God, that grin had gotten under his skin.

Other things, too. Eyes so very, very blue. She had a sort of triangular face, high cheekbones and a small, determined chin; and her nose was tiny, so those ridiculous glasses kept slipping down and needing to be pushed up again. She pushed at them with one clumsy index finger like a little kid might, and he'd found the gesture oddly endearing.

Then, from his undignified position on the floor, and with her up on that stupid table, he'd been forced to notice that her legs under that short black skirt were far too long and shapely to suit the rest of her. And there'd been a flash of pristine white panty when she—

The memory brought an undeniable surge in his groin.

But you're a bosom man, he reminded himself.

His intercom buzzed, and he sighed and moved to answer it.

He should have called in sick today. He didn't feel one hundred percent—in body or in spirit. He felt rather irritable and edgy and sore all over, and his sense of humor had gone on holiday without him.

"Mr. Jones," Brenda intoned, "there's a Ms. Jenny Lathrop on line one, wanting to speak with you. Also, your nine o'clock appointment is here a bit early. Should I send him up?"

Zach would never admit that a simple light blinking insistently on his telephone could have anything to do with a general lightening of his spirits or a significant rise in his blood pressure.

Without a doubt, Ms. Jenny Lathrop was calling to apologize for her behavior the night before.

And well she should. He deserved an apology from her.

"Offer my nine o'clock coffee and hold on to him until line one is clear, would you, Brenda?"

He cleared his throat before he punched the correct button on his phone, and the stiffness in the muscles of his face yielded just enough to allow a small, satisfied grin.

"Zachary Jones here, Ms. Lathrop. Good morning."

2

JONES'S BUSINESSLIKE words echoed in Jenny's ear.

Hunched over her old-fashioned black telephone on its wobbly three-legged table, she came close to hanging up without saying a word. She scrunched up a handful of the long blue flannelette nightgown she wore and held on to it as if it were a security blanket.

She longed to hang up.

Except that he already knew it was her on the line, so she had to say something just to save face. Damn her impulsiveness! What the heck had she been thinking of, calling him first thing this morning?

Just what made her do it? It might have had something to do with the way his voice and presence invaded her dreams all night. She'd asked for one of his business cards from another aide at the clinic last night. The moment she got up this morning she'd headed for the phone as if she were hypnotized and had dialed the number.

Lord, she didn't even have a plan worked out!

"Good morning, Mr. Jones. I wanted to . . . Ah, I thought maybe I should… I wondered if maybe…" Disgusted, Jenny listened to herself stammer and stutter. She even felt herself blushing, for heaven's sake. She screwed her eyes shut, took a deep breath, and made a monumental effort at coherence. Inspiration struck at last.

"A problem came up last night with one of my clients at the Legal Clinic, and you'd already left. I felt it was important to ask your advice."

A moment of humming silence. Then: "Yes, of course. How can I help you?"

Was there more than a tinge of impatience in his tone now?

He sounded as if his nose was plugged. Well, it was probably swollen. His eyes would be puffed up, as well.

She tried to visualize him that way and failed, as she scrambled through the stack of papers from the night before and chose the notes she'd made about Veronica Glickman.

"Here it is." She outlined the scenario that Veronica had told her about yesterday, rattling off a half page of details from what she'd written down. She'd already more or less figured out what to do, but Zachary Jones wouldn't know that.

"Ms. Lathrop." The interruption was brisk and definite.

"Yes, Mr. Jones?"

"You did consider the possibility that this woman might be completely out to lunch? I mean, a bag lady, claiming to own valuable property in downtown Vancouver?"

"Mentally unstable, you mean? Veronica seemed quite rational to me," Jenny lied. "Just because she's older and poor and a bit . . . eccentric, is no reason to suspect . . ." Jenny's increasing feeling of outrage showed in her voice. "I find that attitude discriminatory and unfair, Mr. Jones. All I wanted to know was how to go about helping her with this."

Now there was obvious exasperation in his voice. "Without knowing all the details, it's difficult to make suggestions. And I have someone waiting to see me. I suggest you begin by checking the title of the property at the registry office."

"She's coming back next Thursday. Maybe we could discuss it before the clinic opens?"

The words were out of her mouth before Jenny realized that her question was the real reason for her phone call.

She needed to know right now, this very minute, at ten minutes to nine on a Friday morning, whether or not Zachary Jones would be there next Thursday evening when Jenny arrived at the legal-aid clinic.

There was a long pause. Jenny found herself holding her breath. She knew that most of the volunteer lawyers attended only one clinic each semester and considered their duty done. She had no evidence that it would be different with him—especially after last night.

"That would seem the logical thing to do," he finally said reluctantly. "I'll be there a few minutes early and we can discuss this matter then. Goodbye, Ms. Lathrop."

"Wait—" Jenny's heart hammered with excitement at the thought of seeing him again. "I just wondered . . . Did you go and see a doctor last night, Mr. Jones? Was your nose broken?"

"Yes, I did, and no, it wasn't."

"I'm glad. That is, I mean I'm happy it wasn't broken."

His voice was a sarcastic growl. "So am I. Ecstatic. In fact, I consider it one of the high points of my life. Goodbye again, Ms. Lathrop."

Dial tone.

Boy, he was grumpy as a bear!

Jenny plopped the receiver back in the cradle and collapsed on the sagging sofa. The satisfied smile on her face refused to go away, and she felt exhilarated for any number of reasons.

She had no classes until one o'clock. For the first time in two years she wasn't exhausted from waitressing to earn tuition fees, and had time to perk a pot of coffee and sit here and drink it at her leisure.

And there was the sun.

A lot of mornings, the basement suite she rented was so dark Jenny was forced to turn on the overhead bulb to have enough light to make toast.

Today, rays of cheerful sunshine filtered in, illuminating the undeniably shabby furnishings and worn old burgundy area rugs her Scots landlord, Amos Carradine, had grudgingly donated to furnish the place.

Amos was so tight he squeaked, and Jenny had a hunch he'd scrounged the furnishings from the Salvation Army. Still, the suite was home to her, and most important of all, the rent was low enough that even she could afford it.

Jenny whistled while she scrambled eggs for breakfast.

Zachary was one weird name. Did his friends call him Zachy? She giggled, and popped two slices of bread into the toaster.

Thursday was still six days away. It seemed a long time, but Jenny was philosophical.

She was accustomed to having to wait. She'd waited until she was twenty-six to enter law school, and that had taken years of penny-pinching and part-time jobs. She could wait six measly days to see Zachary Jones again. Couldn't she?

Not that there was any chance of a single thing happening between them. The idea was ludicrous. Jenny slapped margarine on her charred toast. As she munched on it, she tried to get a handle on Jones.

From all evidence, he was wealthy, arrogant, accustomed to having his own way—especially where women were concerned—as well as narrow-minded and bigoted when it came to social issues.

Yep. Zachary Jones epitomized everything Jenny abhorred in the male species. Look at that crack he'd made about poor Veronica!

He was no big deal, she assured herself, setting out her breakfast on the Formica-topped table she'd shoved under the window. She just wanted more time to figure out why she found him so intriguing, that was all.

THE FOLLOWING THURSDAY evening, Zach saw her right away.

True to his word, he'd arrived three quarters of an hour early, but Jenny Lathrop was still there before him.

She was completely absorbed in the documents she was reading. As he walked across the room toward her, her forefinger came up to shove her glasses higher on her nose in that vigorous, clumsy gesture he remembered.

Unexpectedly, all the irritation he'd harbored against her crumbled away and disappeared.

It was a wonder she hadn't put her eye out by now, doing that.

He hooked a chair with one hand and swung it into position so he could sit directly facing her. But then he changed his mind.

Yielding to impulse, he leaned on her desk with both hands and said in the roughest voice he could manufacture, "How come those meters out there won't take nickels and dimes, huh, lady?"

She jumped. Then she looked up at him and in slow motion, she grinned—that same mischievous grin that had so annoyed him the week before, and that emphasized the already upturned corners of her generous mouth.

She had kissable lips.

"Hi, Mr. Jones." She studied him with those astonishing blue eyes and gave a little nod of satisfaction.

"Your eyes look pretty good. The swelling's almost gone, and there's only a trace of purple and green at the inside corners. Your nose still looks fat, though."

He had to laugh.

"You sure know how to make a guy feel good, y'know that? What about the food stuck in my teeth? Aren't you going to mention that, as well?"

She gave him a look of mock innocence.

"Actually, I was going to let you find out for yourself. It's always a humbling experience, finding out you've got spinach in your smile."

Zach sat down, folding his arms across his chest and propping one leg on the other knee, and met her forthright gaze with his best businesslike expression.

"Okay, Ms. Lathrop. Enough frivolity. Let's get down to business, here."

She nodded, but she went on staring at him. "Are you going to be the consulting lawyer here for the rest of this term, or is this your last night?"

Her question was blunt, bordering on rude, and Zach hadn't a clue how to answer. He'd already come in for more than his share of flak from his partners about donating yet another valuable Thursday evening to the clinic. Specifically, they'd accused him of being into sadomasochistic behavior.

"Why do you want to know?" Being a lawyer made answering a question with a question easy.

She didn't even blink. "Because if you're going to stick around, I think you might as well call me Jenny. Ms. Lathrop makes me nervous."

"Fine with me . . . Jenny. But you'll have to get used to the formal mode of address with your clients, you know."

"Yeah, I do know, Zachary." He blinked, but she was scrabbling through a pile of loose papers and didn't notice. "I figure there's plenty of time for that—I'm just in my third year. Now, here are the notes I took when I talked with Veronica Glickman. And here are the details about that house. It's hers, all right. I checked at city hall. The way I see it . . ."

It didn't take five minutes to find out that the way she saw it was diametrically opposite to the way Zach would have viewed the matter. But these students were here to learn, and a large part of that learning, he reminded himself, was making decisions on their own. So he kept quiet and listened.

He reached for the notes she offered and let her run on, noticing her short, unpainted fingernails and the fact that she didn't wear any rings. He realized after a moment or two that she wore no jewelry at all. He'd always sort of figured women were born wearing at least a pair of small diamond studs in their ears. But Jenny had an inexpensive, utilitarian watch on her wrist, and that was it.

"What I did was get ahold of the health department. I got them to agree to back off until I can convince Social Services to send some volunteers over to the property and clean it up. I talked with a couple of social workers yesterday and . . ."

She rattled on and Zach nodded several times, paying more attention to the play of expression on her face than to her exact words.

"I mean, it seems logical to use common sense in a situation like this, don't you think?"

"I suppose that's as good a solution as any. But don't you see that the whole thing isn't a legal problem at all?" he asked. "It's a human problem, isn't it?"

As Jenny continued to talk, her intensity reached out and enveloped him. Despite her efforts at containing her curly hair in a clumsy roll at the back of her neck, it tumbled loose around her face and bounced with each enthusiastic movement of her head.

She didn't have the typical pink complexion he might have expected with copper hair, though. Her skin was tanned golden brown, and was scattered with freckles that also appeared in the V-neck of her blue cotton blouse.

He found himself speculating as to whether her small, high breasts would be a startling white in comparison to her tan.

If she wore a bikini, there'd be that captivating tiny band of white skin again, intersected by the startling color of her hair— His body surged alarmingly.

"Zachary? Do you think so or not?"

She'd obviously been asking him something—several times, by the note of impatience now evident in her voice.

"I do think so. Yes, definitely." Zach tried to sound knowledgeable and positive about God only knew what, hoping his erection would subside by the time he had to stand.

"Good, I'll carry on the way I'm going, then." She gave him a wide smile. "Well, that's settled. I appreciate your coming early to discuss this." She looked down at her notes and added in a rush, "I really am sorry about you getting socked last week. I shouldn't have laughed. I tend to react that way when I'm off balance."

Zach studied the way her hair refused to part in a straight line on top of her head.

"No problem," he said in a soft tone.

"Well." She looked up and gave him a blinding smile. "It's going to be another busy evening, too. There must be a dozen people out there already."

Zach was suddenly aware of other voices; of subdued commotion in the reception area as the other law students took their places at the tables and desks. He felt oddly let down.

He stood and from across the room, Gloria waved to him. He raised a hand to her in a sort of salute and heard himself say to Jenny, "How about having dinner with me after the clinic's over tonight?"

The words were out, and he hadn't given one moment's thought to them before they spilled from his mouth.

Her smile changed, became uncertain, and then faded altogether. She shoved at her glasses with a forceful motion and frowned up at him.

"Why?"

"What do you mean, why?" Zach felt irritation flood through him. Couldn't she just refuse, instead of putting him through some dumb inquisition?

Besides, his ego was involved here. He couldn't remember the last time a woman had refused a dinner invitation. "A guy asks you to dinner, and all you can do is ask why?"

"I need to know, so I'm asking." Her expression was earnest and questioning. "Why do you want to? Have dinner with me?"

"I don't believe this. Let's see, because you need advice about applying your skills in areas that will most benefit your career in law? Because you need to learn some finesse when it comes to questions and answers?" Talk about fast on his feet. Imagine coming up with that high-sounding crap when all the time he was still wondering about her bikini line and the color of—

He gave her what he hoped was an ingenuous grin.

"Because I enjoy talking with you and want to get to know you better?"

"Bullshit."

She said it as if it were an ordinary, everyday word, and she went right on frowning at him.

Zach couldn't help himself. He started to laugh, because she was outrageous and absolutely right.

"Okay. I don't have the foggiest clue why I want to take you to dinner. You're difficult and argumentative but I like your hair. So, do you want to eat with me or not?"

She hesitated, and then nodded her head a couple of times. "That's pretty honest. All right, I guess I'll come."

ALTHOUGH THE CLIENTS that Jenny saw during the next several hours had the benefit of her full attention, not for one moment did she stop thinking about the date she'd made with Zachary Jones.

In typical female fashion—most *un*typical for her—she worried about her clothes. Her plain blue blouse and calf-length patterned cotton skirt was one of her favorite outfits because it was comfortable and easy to move in. Still, beside Zachary's elegant suit, it looked exactly what it was: an ensemble bought from the racks of a secondhand clothing store.

That didn't bother her in the least. After all, most of her clothing came from thrift shops. It was just that at home she had a sea-green rayon dress, acquired for eleven dollars at a garage sale. She'd have worn it tonight if she'd known. She'd hesitated about buying the darned thing because she didn't think she would have an occasion to wear it. And here was the perfect occasion. But, damn! The dress was crosstown in her closet.

It was a wasted opportunity, especially since there wouldn't be any second date with Zachary when she could wear the green dress. Jenny hated waste.

He'd said himself that he thought he was out of his mind, asking her out at all.

And she sensed in him all the characteristics she wanted *most* to avoid when she became a practicing lawyer.

But going out with him would be a learning experience, she told herself. She could learn a whole lot about the type of man she *should* avoid like the plague. Even negative learning experiences were valuable. Weren't they?

She dismissed the fact that he had the most disturbing effect on her heart rate whenever he was nearby.

HE TOOK HER to a restaurant hidden in a residential district of Kerrisdale—an old stone house with a wooden sign outside that simply read Philomene's.

They were met at the door by an older woman with shining silver hair, wearing a black silk dress and an air of absolute dignity. She greeted Zachary by his first name, gave Jenny a frosty smile, then led them into a tiny, completely private dining area and seated them at a round oak table set for two.

"Suzanne will be with you shortly, Zach. I'll send Antony in to take your order."

Soft piano music came from an adjoining room, and Jenny thought there surely must be other patrons around somewhere, but there was little evidence of them. She felt uncomfortable, as if she'd bungled into a private home, expecting dinner from people she didn't know.

Zachary was quite relaxed, however. He and Antony seemed to be the best of friends.

"Get much sailing in this summer?" he asked Zach.

"Not as much as I'd like. How about you?"

Antony launched into an account of a month spent surfing on the north coast of Hawaii before he got around to asking what they'd like to drink. Zach ordered a Scotch and water, but Jenny, wanting to keep her head clear, ordered a diet cola.

"Wouldn't you prefer a glass of wine?" Zach asked. But she shook her head.

"Not even with dinner?" He raised his eyebrows.

She glared at him and said no, and he shrugged, accepting her decision without any more argument, for which Jenny was grateful.

The menus were hand lettered and there were no prices marked. Jenny ordered a seafood linguine with a salad, and Zach wanted steak.

When at last the ordering was over with and they were alone again, Jenny began to relax a little. The atmosphere was tranquil, the piano soft and soothing, and she liked the private little alcove where they were seated.

"Well, Jenny Lathrop who doesn't drink wine." Zach's voice was lazy and just a little teasing. "Tell me about yourself."

Jenny sipped her cola and looked at him, tilting her head a bit in order to see through her glasses, which were on their inevitable journey down her nose.

"What do you want to know?"

He pursed his lips and considered that. "Oh, why you wanted to be a lawyer, for instance."

She studied him for a long moment. Was he being a trifle condescending?

She decided he needed to hear the truth.

"Mostly because my husband was killed in an accident six years ago."

Zach looked shocked. He'd been about to take a drink, but instead he set the glass back on the table, giving his full attention to Jenny. Her voice was quiet and controlled, matter-of-fact, as if she'd related her story many times before.

"He was working on a nonunion construction job, and a sheet of plate glass collapsed. Nick and three other guys were underneath it. It was negligence on the part of the company, but they wouldn't admit to fault."

She sipped her cola and shrugged before she went on. "We didn't have any kids, Nick and I, but all the other men did. The families received no compensation at all, because of bungled legal advice on our side and smart lawyers on theirs. The other wives had to take menial jobs to support their kids and pay off the legal expenses we all incurred in our fight for a settlement."

Her eyes were focused now on a picture on the wall behind him. "When the whole mess was over, I was good and mad. I took what money I had from a small insurance policy Nick left me and used it to go back to school. I thought it wouldn't hurt to find out what the law was like from the other side of the fence, and then maybe help other people with cases like mine. It was slow. It took me a year of upgrading to pass my LSAT, because I took most of my early education by correspondence, but I finally made it." She met his gaze now, her intense blue eyes watchful of his reaction.

Zach was looking at her in a different way than he had before. The laughter in his eyes had disappeared, and when he spoke, the teasing undertones were gone. He sounded apologetic, as well as embarrassed. There was something else, too.

Tenderness?

"God, I'm sorry, Jenny. About your husband. About . . . I didn't mean to pry. I never dreamed . . . I mean, you look far too young to have had all that happen to you."

Jenny suspected that in Zach's social circle, death and poverty weren't discussed over dinner.

Maybe they weren't discussed at all. Maybe he didn't want to hear anything heavy.

Well, in her social circles, no one ate in places like this, so how was she to know what was discussed?

So tonight could be a learning experience for both of them, she reflected with a tight enigmatic smile.

"I'm twenty-nine, in case you're wondering. I guess that's not middle-aged, but I don't feel very young at all. See, I was married to Nick when I was seventeen. We'd already been together six years when he died." She gave a little shrug and smiled.

"Back where I grew up, girls married young." She saw his eyebrows go up in silent questioning and added, "It was twenty miles outside a little coal-mining town called Fernie, in the Rocky Mountains of southern British Columbia. Hardly anyone's ever heard of it." As an afterthought, she added, "I grew up poor."

Just then, the waitress arrived with their food, and for a while, Jenny was far too busy eating the remarkable meal to talk much.

She was hungry, and the dinner was absolute perfection. Her linguine was smothered in scallops, shrimp, lobster and crab, as well as a marvelous sauce; and the dressing on the salad was an expert combination of gentle herbs and spices—unlike anything she'd had before. Every bite was heaven.

She noticed that Zach, however, was eating his own dinner with a lot less enthusiasm and appetite than she was.

Well, he probably took food like this for granted.

The fact was, he was watching her more than he was eating, but for some reason it didn't make her uneasy. She savored each mouthful, and when she swallowed the last bite of crab, she looked straight at him and grinned.

"Bet you're not used to feeding starving women."

"I'm not, but it's fun," was all he said.

He had already finished his meal, and she laid down her fork and folded her arms across her middle with a contented sigh, trying to ignore the sensual responses he stirred in her.

"That was fabulous."

"I'm glad you enjoyed it." Feeling that she scared Zach off with her bluntness, Jenny sighed, expecting they were about to exchange social niceties for the rest of the evening.

She was wrong.

"Jenny," he said next—and there was a seriousness in his voice that hadn't been there before—"I get the impression you don't quite approve of me. Why is that?"

He was turning the tables on her, being as uncomfortably direct as she had been, and Jenny respected him for it. But she wasn't about to reveal her innermost feelings to him, either.

"I don't know you. So how can I approve or disapprove?"

He gave her that long, level look. "Well, then, let's get on with it. Get to know me, why don't you?" His gaze was challenging. She found herself admiring the firm lines of his mouth, the deep cleft in his chin. And his long-fingered hands. There was an elegance about them—she could imagine them stroking a path from her neck down to her breasts....

She shivered. *Careful, Jenny.*

"Well, Mr. Zachary Jones," she began in a playful tone, "you're right, of course. Turnabout is fair play. So tell me about yourself. Why did you decide to be a lawyer?"

"Would you like to order dessert before we get into this? They have a great cheesecake here. I've had it before."

His politeness touched her. She was tempted, but her waistband already felt tight. "I'm full, darn it all. How about just coffee?"

The waitress brought two china cups of strong, hot coffee, along with a silver carafe for refills, and then they were alone again.

"Okay, now make with the answers," Jenny ordered, mock tough.

He settled back in his chair. "Well, unlike you, I can't say I remember deciding to be a lawyer. It was just taken for granted from the time I was a boy. There'd been four generations of lawyers in my family, and it was assumed I'd be the fifth."

"Wow, four generations! That's a heavy legacy to have to pack around. But wasn't there ever a time when you rebelled, when you wanted to be—oh, a rock star or a plumber when you were growing up?"

He laughed. "I did have one short lapse when I was about fifteen, when I wanted to be a pro football player. I got my nose broken, my knees severely damaged and three ribs smashed before I gave up on that and decided I'd rather live a bit longer. After that, it was law all the way."

"And you find it interesting?"

Zach hesitated for a long moment. She felt pleased, understanding that he was doing his honest best at giving her straight answers.

"I figure it's as good a way as any to spend your working hours," he finally said. "I specialize in litigation work, so it's not as exciting as criminal law."

Litigation: two parties, seeking legal counsel to attain a settlement of a dispute. Litigation was one of the most lucrative branches of the legal profession, partly because ninety-five percent of civil litigation actions settled out of court.

If there was one branch of the law Jenny liked least, it was litigation.

Zach was still talking. "Two friends and I set up our own office some years ago, and we're doing well. That's gratifying."

It might be, but Jenny couldn't detect much excitement in his voice.

"Did you find the work load in university overpowering?" she asked next. "Sometimes I feel as if a day ought to have twenty more hours."

He shook his head. "I didn't have to struggle to get by, but of course I had to study hard. Everyone does."

"But you didn't have to hold down a job while you were in school?"

Again he shook his head.

"Did you have any problems getting in? The law faculty seems to reject more applicants than it accepts."

"I was lucky. My dad and grandfather are both graduates. They put in a good word for me. Mind you, I still had to get good grades on the entrance requirements."

It was enough. He didn't have to detail the route he'd followed to gain admittance to the Faculty of Law. There were students like Zach in Jenny's classes—graduates of elite private schools whose entry into the law faculty was ensured by an old boys' network of fathers and grandfathers who'd been generous contributors to the university over the years. She had to swallow a lump of disappointment.

She'd been hoping he'd surprise her, and he hadn't.

It was his turn to question again.

"Was anyone in your family a lawyer, Jenny?"

"Are you kidding? My mom and dad were hippies. I grew up on a farming commune."

He didn't comment, but his expression once more revealed his surprise. Shock, maybe? She wasn't certain.

Jenny had been feeling wonderful up to this point. The relaxed atmosphere and good food had lulled her into forgetting about the chasm that divided her and Zachary Jones.

Their worlds were far apart.

After tonight, they'd go their separate ways.

But then, her natural optimism came to the rescue. If this was to be the only time they'd share, she'd better make the best of it. She felt an urgent need to know about him, to find out all she could in the few hours they had together.

Jenny didn't ask herself why she should need to know about Zachary Jones. She only knew the feeling was there, and that it was powerful.

She shoved her glasses higher on her nose and leaned her elbows on the thick linen tablecloth.

"Tell me, when's your birthday, Zach? When were you born?"

Might as well begin at the beginning.

3

"MY BIRTHDAY?"

For one crazy moment, he couldn't remember. Then he said, "June 30. I'm thirty-five years and three months old. Why? Are you interested in astrology?"

"I'm interested in understanding you better." She was serious and intense. "The sign you're born under tells me a great deal about what sort of person you are."

His disbelieving grin told her what he thought of that. "Okay, lay it on me. What am I like, Jenny?"

"You're a Cancer, the sign of the crab, and you don't reveal yourself easily, which is why you feel threatened at the thought of my knowing about you from your birth sign. Let's see now. You can be moody, but underneath you're a romantic. At the same time, you're practical and sensible." She gave him a wicked, teasing grin. "And you can get good and cranky now and then, too. Downright mean-tempered at times. In fact, you're meanest when you're afraid of losing something, aren't you? You're good at making money, though."

Zach did his best to hide his surprise. Her assessment of his personality disturbed him because it was pretty accurate and not at all flattering.

He'd been mean as an injured skunk when his last lady had said goodbye. Not because he was in love with her; just because she'd made the decision to leave him instead of the other way around.

But, he consoled himself, at least he had the ability to recognize his own worst traits. That had to count for something, didn't it?

It was disconcerting to have a person he barely knew zero in on his imperfections with such apparent ease.

This Jenny was full of surprises. She made conversational left turns like this without signaling, catching him unprepared. He found himself trying to second-guess what unlikely thing she'd say next.

"I guess you study your horoscope in the paper each morning for hints on how to conduct your day, Jenny?" He was goading her. He couldn't resist finding out whether her temper would flare.

She shook her head in serene denial. "Not on your life. I think it's wrong to let anyone else tell you what your life should be. You shouldn't ever give away your own power, even to the extent of relying on daily horoscopes. Don't you agree?"

He'd never given it a lot of thought, believing himself to be his own man in every instance.

"Sounds right to me. But if that's the case, why is my birthday important?"

She looked at him as if he were a little slow. "Surely you realize that astrology is an ancient and accurate science. I didn't mean you should discount the knowledge. Only that you should come to your own truths about it."

"And have you? Come to your own truths?" He realized how much he liked looking at her. Her face changed all the time, and her intense blue eyes seemed to draw him into their depths, even while her glasses acted like a barrier. It was her contradictory mix of passion and coolness that excited him.

At what point would her control disappear? That coolness transform into uncontrolled desire?

"How did you start relying on things like birthdays in the first place to find out what people were like?"

She studied him for a moment, as if considering whether or not to go on revealing herself the way she had been. Then she said, "My mother was a self-proclaimed white witch. She studied all the occult sciences. I absorbed a fair amount while I was growing up. A lot of the hippies were into that sort of thing long before the New-Age people came along."

Jenny Lathrop grew more complicated the longer he talked with her. More desirable, more challenging.

"And is she still a practicing witch? Your mother?"

"She's dead. She died two years before my husband was killed."

It was a matter-of-fact statement, not calling for any response from Zach. But again, it roused his compassion. Jenny's family seemed to have died off at a disturbing rate. Zach could only remember one person dying in his family since he was a child, and that was a great-aunt who must have been about ninety-seven.

"And what about your father?" He was almost afraid to ask.

Jenny shrugged. "He's somewhere in Mexico. He went there after Mom died. I get a card at Christmas, but he moves around a lot."

Zach couldn't imagine how that felt—not knowing where your father was. He thought of his own father, in his offices in downtown Vancouver every day as regular as a digital clock. His healthy, staid family all still lived in the house his grandfather had built on Marine Drive long before Zach was born. Even the housekeeper, Eva, had been with them since he was a baby.

Zach now had his own apartment, but it was taken for granted he'd eventually move home again. Preferably with a wife and family.

Family was important to the Jones clan.

"You're pretty much alone in the world, then, Jenny?"

She nodded, with a gesture of her shoulders that told without words that she was used to being alone and didn't mind it in the least. It made Zach want to draw her into his arms and keep her safe, free her from ever having to be bravely alone again.

And yet . . .

"In a way, I envy you that," he said in a quiet voice, and it was her turn to be surprised. She'd anticipated the usual social words of sympathy, but Zach added, "Being alone affords a kind of freedom I've never had the chance to experience."

Jenny liked him even more for that insight.

After that, they talked about certain professors they both knew, and disagreed with a vengeance about which they preferred. They went on to disagree about certain legal cases they'd both been following in the newspapers, and about the tactics of the lawyers involved.

They moved on to books they'd read. She liked spy thrillers and he preferred satire.

He played tennis. She never had.

She loved softball. He hadn't picked up a bat since he was thirteen.

They lost track of time, and it was long after their waitress had brought silver-wrapped mints and an astronomical bill on a crystal plate that they finally realized perhaps it was time to go.

ZACH SHUT OFF THE ENGINE of the powerful car in front of Jenny's place and turned toward her. She was tiny, almost fragile, beside him.

"I had a great evening, Jenny. How are you for time tomorrow? Want to meet me for lunch?"

She'd convinced herself that this single dinner was it as far as she and Zach were concerned. All during the drive home, she'd steeled herself to say goodbye with a light and nonchalant note in her voice, despite the knot of longing in her stomach that she couldn't seem to get rid of.

One evening with him wasn't enough.

Now she had to reassess everything and figure out—

Hell. She wanted to see him again—more than she was willing to admit. Her heart was hammering with delight, so why try and intellectualize it?

But she didn't want to seem too eager, either.

"I don't have classes in the afternoon," she confessed after a few seconds' silence. She was too conscious of his scent, warm and arousing and male, mingled with the expensive-car smell of leather upholstery.

"Funny, I seem to remember from my own student days how the profs all like a long weekend. How about meeting me at the corner of the Student Union Building and we'll go to the Faculty Club for a sandwich?"

She'd never been inside the hallowed doors of the Faculty Club.

If anyone asked, she'd probably say she considered it elitist to belong to a club that limited its membership to a chosen few.

Still, she was curious about the place.

And she wanted—needed—to spend more time with Zach.

Proceed with caution, flashed the warning sign in her brain.

But there was still so much to learn about him, she rationalized. It was really like knowing one's enemy, she reassured herself. Like taking a course in pesticides because you wanted to be an organic gardener.

Like flying straight at a flame if you were a moth.

"Meet you about one?"

She ignored the warning signals. "Fine. And Zach...thank you for my dinner tonight. It was delicious." She was trying to open the door when his hand closed on her shoulder and then cupped her chin, turning her toward him. His hands were warm, strong and gentle on her face, and a tremor of pure, overwhelming wanting skittered through her body.

His mouth came down on hers—warm lips, gentle pressure, hard and soft and coaxing. He moved his lips, sensually teasing hers with the tip of his tongue, entreating.

Her lips parted, and her tongue met his, warm and wet.

He kissed as if he was sure of himself. He kissed as if she was fragile, but irresistible. He kissed as if this was the only thing in the world he wanted to do at this moment.

As if he wanted more, as if he were holding himself back with the greatest difficulty.

When at last they drew apart, her glasses were steamy and crooked, and she had to straighten them before she could get out of the car. He tried to help her, gently and clumsily looping them at the wrong angle behind her ears.

"We'll have to be sure to take them off next time so they don't get broken. Shall I walk you to the door?" There was a gruffness in his voice that signaled desire.

She was breathing hard. She shook her head no. She wasn't certain she could deal with another, longer kiss, standing up in his arms, touching him with other parts of her body. He'd said "next time," hadn't he?

"Night, then, Jenny. See you tomorrow. Sweet dreams."

He waited until she was safely inside before he drove away.

He caught a glimpse of himself in the rearview mirror when he stopped for a light. He was grinning like a total idiot!

BEFORE NOON THE NEXT DAY, Jenny was having horrendous second thoughts about her date with Zach.

Her morning lecture was on mental health and the intricacies of admitting patients to institutions. By eleven-thirty, Jenny was certain she qualified as a candidate for just such an admission.

One minute, she couldn't wait to see him again. The next, she was certain she was making the biggest mistake of her entire life even associating with him.

What, exactly, was it about a simple little lunch date that was making her hands shake and her head ache? What was making her feel out of control and panicked about this whole thing?

She'd had dates since Nick died. She'd even had one significant relationship. Moderately significant. Well, it might have become significant if she'd been a little more enthusiastic and he'd been a little smarter than a stump.

Anyway, she wasn't a vulnerable recent widow, was she? Ripe to fall for the first sympathetic man who crossed her path?

So, what was the big deal here?

She trotted out all the things about Zach that irritated her—his Yuppie style of dressing, his privileged background, his attitude toward the law and its application, and, most disturbing of all, the gut feeling she had that he could easily have been one of the lawyers who outsmarted her and the other survivors in the negligence suit against the construction company. He dealt with cases like it all the time. His speciality, litigation law, was reason enough to keep her distance from Zach.

It was plain crazy to see him again. They were born to be in opposing camps. Why play immovable object to his irresistible force? She was bound to end up sorry.

But she couldn't, even for a moment, rid herself of the memory of that kiss last night. There was this overwhelming physical attraction between them, regardless of what her brain tried to tell her. And he was fun to talk to. And just thinking about his fingers on her skin made goose bumps—

"So, Ms. Lathrop, will you outline for the class the factors to be taken into account by a client considering informal admission to an institution, please?"

For the first time in two years of classes, she was caught without a single clue as to what the answer could be.

Damn Zachary Jones. He was turning her brain to jelly and making her crazy into the bargain. And there were exactly thirty-seven minutes left before she'd see him again.

HE WAS THERE, waiting for her. She saw him a full block away, lounging against a light standard, creating a flurry of head-turning among the female students hurrying past.

He waved long before she thought he'd noticed her. She hurried up and stood in front of him, a little out of breath, flushed and disheveled and ridiculously happy. For a long moment they stood and grinned at each other without saying a word, like a pair of simpletons.

Then he reached out with one finger and touched her on the chin for a second.

"Hiya, Jenny." The low, intimate timbre of his voice sent shivers down her body.

"Hello, Zach." She smiled at him.

As usual, he was impeccably dressed: pin-striped suit, pale pink shirt, blue-and-burgundy patterned tie.

"You look . . . great," she said.

Didn't the man own a pair of jeans?

"So do you."

Jenny beamed. She was wearing an outfit she was proud of because she felt it made her look professional.

She'd found the small-size men's tweed jacket at the Salvation Army clothing store and had it dry-cleaned. She'd also bought the dress shirt there. The shirt had needed several strong bleachings to make it white again, and last night she'd struggled with spray starch, ironing it. She'd made the almost-ankle-length navy tube skirt from a length of remnant fabric, and as long as she didn't sit in it for longer than three hours, it didn't bottom out too much. She wore tights and her only pair of classic black pumps: a find for eight dollars at the Army and Navy shoe sale.

"Busy morning?" she asked.

Zach shook her head. "A couple of clients. Nothing heavy. You?"

"Nope. Just lectures." And she'd ended up acting like the class dunce, but she wasn't going to tell Zach that.

"I'm starving, are you?"

She nodded with vigor, and he laughed and said, "Let's go find some food before you collapse, then." He took her hand and tucked it into the crook of his arm, making her feel tiny and protected.

They strolled the few blocks to the gray stone building that housed the Faculty Club. There was a sharp-eyed woman at a desk just inside the doors, obviously on the lookout for gate-crashers. She beamed at Zach.

"Good afternoon, Mr. Jones."

"Hi, Margie. Nice day, isn't it?"

Zach led Jenny to a set of wide, curving stairs leading down into an immense room. On the left was a dining area and on the right was a grouping of leather sofas and deep armchairs flanked by coffee tables.

Two men in tweeds and sweaters, and smoking pipes, sat reading. How could they, Jenny wondered, with that wall of windows and the magnificent panorama at their elbows?

"Oh, wow, look at that view!" she murmured, and Zach grinned down at her as if he'd arranged it personally for her pleasure.

The wide area was fronted with floor-to-ceiling windows.

The haughty maître d', whom Zach addressed as Alvin, led them through the busy dining area to a small round window table in a quiet alcove, seating Jenny with far more flourish and pomp than necessary.

She hardly noticed. She was busy studying the people around her, the food in front of them. She was absorbing the rarefied atmosphere of the university's privileged population—professors and senior executives in administration, who dined here in splendor with their guests.

"Would you like something to drink, Jenny?"

"Just water, thanks."

"I'll have a beer, one of the local varieties," Zach decided, and Jenny changed her mind about the water.

"That sounds good. I'll have one, too."

She'd crossed some kind of footbridge with him. She trusted him about certain things today.

Some of the awkwardness Jenny had felt the night before was gone. She didn't need to stay as much on guard anymore. She knew a little about the man sitting across from her now—inconsequential things like the fact that he sprinkled pepper with liberal abandon over most of what he ate, and that he took cream but no sugar in coffee, and that he had a way of looking at her that made her feel like the only woman in the room.

He had a laugh that came seldom but was contagious when it did. The pleasure his laughter gave her inspired her to say outrageous things.

She knew that he managed details like ordering and paying the bill with an ease Nick would never have attained in a lifetime. It made being with him easy.

She suspected that Zach treated all serving staff everywhere as valued friends and she couldn't fault him for that. She'd been out once or twice with pathetic men who thought it made them macho to be rude to waiters. Jenny had given each a tongue-lashing they wouldn't soon forget, and neither had asked her out again. She wouldn't have gone, anyway.

She couldn't acknowledge just yet that Zach had a profound effect on her. He simply made her feel charged with a special, joyful energy. He made her want to see more of him.

They walked out of the Faculty Club two hours and forty minutes later. Zach was holding Jenny's hand, and she was liking it a lot.

"I shouldn't have had that second beer. Now it's made my head go fuzzy," she admitted, squinting up through her glasses at the brilliance of the fall afternoon and wishing that the time had gone more slowly.

He watched and waited for her to shove her glasses back up on her nose, and she did, right on cue. He grinned with delight and said, "Hey, I know just the cure for fuzzy heads. Let's go for a walk in the rose gardens. Did you know that breathing in the perfume from the roses will clear the toxins from the beer out of your system?"

"I didn't know that."

"Neither did I, until I made it up a second ago."

"Maybe you should have been a fiction writer instead of a lawyer."

He smiled and then shrugged. "There's not all that much difference between the two sometimes, is there?"

A tiny bit of the shine dulled for her when he said that. There it was again—that cynical attitude of his toward the career she'd chosen and planned to pursue with integrity and honesty.

She withdrew her hand from his with deliberate intent. "I don't agree with you," she stated, and tilted her chin at an aggressive angle. "That attitude toward bending the truth where the law is concerned is exactly the thing that's most despicable among certain branches of the law."

He gave her an appraising glance and shook his head.

"Jenny, would you stop jumping to conclusions? I didn't mean that I believe dishonesty is acceptable. I meant that there's room for a lot of creativity in the practice of law, just as there is in writing novels."

"Oh." It was too nice a day to stay mad.

He stopped for an instant and slipped his suit jacket off, looping it over one shoulder with a careless hand. His shoulders were broad and smoothly muscled underneath the crisp pink shirt.

A bit shyly, she slipped her hand back into his free one. He gave her fingers a welcoming squeeze, and everything was fine again.

The rose gardens were only a few minutes' walk from the Faculty Club, and they wandered in silence for a while, drinking in the heady scent of roses in full bloom.

"I read an article a while ago on the effect smell has on people," Jenny remarked. "Certain generic scents have universal meaning, like the smell of bacon, for instance."

Zach was watching her with a bemused expression. Who else but Jenny would start talking about bacon in a rose garden, he wondered?

"Bacon?" he prompted.

"Yep. Even if you're a vegetarian, apparently the smell of bacon makes you feel wealthy," she explained. "It goes back to thousands of years of tribal lifetimes, when fat represented wealth."

Zach laughed, and the sound gave her pleasure.

"Are you making this up?"

"Not on your life. This was a serious, scientific study on pheromones—smells that affect us at a subliminal level."

They'd wandered along a maze of pathways, and now roses surrounded them. A bench was nestled there, and he sat, spreading his jacket under them, then drawing Jenny down beside him, curving an arm around her shoulders so she was cuddled close against his side.

Not only subliminal smells affected people, she mused. Her heart was beating a rapid tattoo at being this close to Zach, and she was conscious of the scent of his freshly laundered shirt, the hint of clean male sweat, the faint, pleasant tinge of beer on his breath. He smelled good; he always smelled good.

She was aware, as well, of his heart pounding against his ribs just as hard as hers.

"Jenny, I can't be near you without wanting to kiss you."

His voice was deep and intimate-sounding; his mouth was close to her ear so that she could feel the words as much as hear them. If she turned her head the slightest bit, her burning cheek would rest on his chest. She could feel the warmth of his body enveloping her, pulsing around her.

Wordless, she turned her face up to his. With tender care, he unlooped the temples of her glasses from behind her ears and laid them on the bench at his side. He wrapped his arms around her and he kissed her, and Jenny knew with certainty that this was right. Nothing that felt this good could be wrong. It was as simple as that.

The more he explored her lips and tongue with his own, the more of him she wanted. She moved her fingers up his neck and through his hair, learning its texture, memorizing the shape of his head and his jaw. She moved her palm down and put it over his heart, and she could feel the thundering madness in him, the same tempo that filled her with heat and pulsing desire.

"Jenny..."

His voice was choked and guttural.

When his lips moved to her throat and then down to the flushed skin above the opening in her shirt, she wanted nothing more than to throw her clothing and his into the bushes and sink with him to the bed of moss that covered the earth beneath their feet.

The heavy, sweet scent of roses surrounded them.

Roses were the most primitive of scents, and until now, she hadn't fully understood their power. Roses were an aphrodisiac. They had to be. She wouldn't be melting in Zach' arms this way unless they'd cast a potent spell on her.

Would she?

4

"MR. DAVID SOLOMEN is here to see you, Mr. Jones." Brenda's crisp voice came over the intercom a few minutes before ten o'clock the following Monday morning, snapping Zach out of a daydream about Jenny.

He hastily swung his legs down from the top of his desk and opened a file folder at random, scattering a few printed sheets around, making it look as if he'd been working instead of fantasizing for the past hour.

"Send him up, Brenda."

The weekend had been spent sailing—a two-day trip Zach had planned with a male friend weeks before—and on Friday evening, when he'd again dropped Jenny at her door, he'd felt a trifle relieved that the next two days were booked solid. Otherwise, he knew beyond a doubt that he'd have invited her out to breakfast Saturday, stretched that into lunch, extended it to dinner... and who knew where it would have ended?

Yet, provocative images of Jenny, naked in his arms, were strong enough to shove the other, more rational considerations right out of his brain.

He remembered the way her stockings had swished when she crossed those long, curvy legs....

Zach made a conscious effort to banish Jenny and get his brain onto business when a tap sounded on his office door.

"Come right in," he called. The door opened, and a tall, dark man came hesitantly in, his shyness apparent in his face when he returned Zach's welcoming smile.

Pay attention here, Jones. Forget legs and think law.

Zach got to his feet and extended his hand in greeting.

"Mr. Solomen, good morning. I'm Zach Jones. Have a seat. Can I pour you a coffee?"

Solomen refused. "I'm afraid I don't drink coffee," he said apologetically.

He took the comfortable leather armchair Zach indicated. He wore casual clothing, and nothing about him telegraphed a money message. In fact, he looked as if he just might have problems paying the firm's hefty fee, but appearances could be deceiving.

"Now, Mr. Solomen, tell me a bit about yourself and how I can help you," Zach suggested, settling himself in his chair with what he hoped was an air of attentive interest.

Solomen cleared his throat. "I'm a businessman. I own three Organic Produce Marts—one on Granville Island, one in North Vancouver, one in Richmond. All three are heavily mortgaged, but after a lot of struggling, they're finally starting to pay their own way. I just landed a long-term contract to supply two of the largest local vegetarian restaurants with organic fruits and vegetables, which will make a tremendous difference to my finances. I figured I was finally seeing daylight, financially, and believe me, it's been a long, hard climb. Then I received this."

Solomen opened the briefcase he'd brought, drawing out several sheets and putting them down on the desk in front of Zach.

"It seems I'm being sued by this organization called the Safefood Society, headed by a man named Paul Jensen."

Zach had heard of Jensen. His name was in the papers often in connection with environmental issues.

"They say here they've conducted tests, and certain of my products have unacceptable levels of pesticide residue. They've enclosed test results, and I have to admit they're right. I ran some tests myself and came up with similar results, not on all my stuff, but some." There was a note of disgust in Solomen's voice, as if he was appalled by the finding. "I know about this Safefood Society. It's part of a larger organization called Earthcare. Jensen's involved in that, as well. It's nonprofit, North America-wide, and it carries a lot of weight with the kind of people who buy my stuff. They publish a magazine every month, and their mailing list is extensive. They can bankrupt me without too much trouble."

Solomen sounded desperate and Zach understood why as the big man went on with his story.

"My fruit and produce are purchased almost exclusively through the Northwest Growers' Association because they have, in writing, guaranteed that their products are certified organic. I also buy from certain private farmers I know and trust, but there's not much doubt that the samples tested came from NGA."

Zach studied the papers. "So you feel the NGA are selling you produce under false pretenses?"

Solomen snorted. "Damned right, they are. And they're charging me and everybody else top prices for it, which we pay, confident that the food is what they claim it to be, and that they test the soil conditions regularly." His eyes narrowed and his jaw tightened. "What burns me up is that the real losers here are my customers. People who buy organic foods are willing to pay more, just as I have to, to ensure they're getting a totally natural product. It's going to ruin my credibility and probably my business as well, when this appears in *Earthcare* magazine. And damn it all, it's not my fault. I'm the little guy in this."

Like an echo he couldn't avoid, Zach remembered Jenny, over dinner that first night, telling him with bitter certitude that the little guys were always the losers when it came to legal negotiations. It had made him uncomfortable, because he couldn't help but recognize there was some truth in what she claimed.

Solomen was saying much the same thing now.

"See, they're a powerful group, the Growers' Association. They've got expensive grants and lots of backing from the government. Me, I'm just an independent businessman trying to make a living here."

Zach's mind was exploring the probable arguments, bouncing possibilities back and forth.

"Have you considered going to this Paul Jensen and telling him exactly what you've just told me? It sounds as if he ought to be breathing down their necks instead of yours."

Solomen nodded. "I've already tried that. He wouldn't listen. He's pretty fanatical, and I get the feeling he wants to use this whole thing as a way of stirring up people's natural concerns about the environment. I think he figures I'm a more visible target than the NGA would be."

Zach was inclined to think Solomen was right. He asked more questions, and Solomen answered them in his quiet, intelligent way.

"There's one more thing, Mr. Jones." Solomen met Zach's inquiring gaze with forthright directness. "I don't have the money to get into an expensive lawsuit. I know your firm is the best around, that's why I came here first. But unless you agree to taking my case on a contingency basis, I'll have to go elsewhere."

Contingency meant that the law firm would foot the bill for all the expenses incurred in preparing the case, with the understanding that if they won, they'd receive thirty percent of the settlement. If they lost, they were out costs, as well as expenses.

Zach liked Solomen, and the situation interested him, but he had to be careful here. Contingency was a risky business at best. He and his partners had an agreement that in questionable cases, all three partners decided whether or not to take the case. And his guess was that this one would be questionable indeed.

Taking on a government-backed organization like the NGA was a major undertaking, and environmental issues were high profile and touchy. The case could attract a huge amount of media attention, especially if Paul Jensen was indeed using it to stir up publicity, which could be either a very good thing for the firm or a very bad one.

Zach made an effort to explain to Solomen what the problems were—the problems he could see right off. And there were bound to be dozens more he hadn't even thought of yet

He kept his voice carefully neutral the way he'd trained himself to do.

"I sympathize with you, Mr. Solomen, but you have to be aware that this could be a difficult case to prove, and expensive to prepare for trial. We're up against proving beyond a doubt that the contaminated material came from NGA. We also have to prove that the contamination didn't happen after you received the produce. As I see it, the only way we could go in with an airtight case against your suppliers would be to have these Safefood people or someone like them standing by, testing your produce as it arrives, until a sizable amount of it is proved to be nonorganic. We call it 'continuity of the contaminated exhibits.' Is there a possibility they'd agree to doing that?"

Solomen grimaced and shook his head. "I know they wouldn't. Like I said, Jensen's more interested in finding a scapegoat than in justice being served, in my opinion."

"We're looking at a private investigator's services, then." Zach didn't say so, but the expense of that could be astronomical.

Zach asked several more questions, and then the interview was at an end. Solomen got to his feet, briefcase in hand.

"So, what do you think? Will your firm take my case?" There was undisguised anxiety in his voice. "Because if not, I've got to find somebody else, fast."

"I can't answer that until I've discussed this with my colleagues and looked into the whole thing a bit more. Can you give me a couple of days, Mr. Solomen? I'll be back to you by the middle of the week."

Solomen agreed, but there was a dejected slump to the man's shoulders as he left.

Zach watched him go, knowing the chances of his partners' agreeing to take on the Solomen case were almost nonexistent. Ordinarily, Zach would be in full agreement with them.

But this morning, he was uncomfortable with the inevitable refusal. For some reason he could hear Jenny's voice in his head, talking about people who were vegetarian, who used their limited food money to buy produce they believed was free from sprays, and who were being victimized here just as much as Solomen was.

What the hell was going on here, anyway? Was Jenny turning him into a bleeding-heart liberal? Next thing, he'd be lying down in front of bulldozers, for God's sake.

Get ahold of yourself, Jones.

For all her definite appeal, Jenny was woefully impractical in her approach to the practice of law.

He'd do well to remember that.

And while she was on his mind like this, he might just as well phone and ask her out tonight. He'd cancel his weekly squash game with Ken. As far as cardiovascular fitness went, he breathed a lot harder around Jenny than he did smashing a ball in a squash court, anyhow.

That way, if he knew he'd be seeing her later, maybe he could get some work done this afternoon.

"JENNY? Hi, it's Zach."

"Zachary Jones?"

"What other Zach do you know?"

"Well, there's Zachary Smith, and Zachary Brown, and..."

The hint of laughter in her voice brought a smile to his lips.

"Look, Jenny, I wondered if you'd like to have dinner with me tonight."

"Dinner? Again?" There was a note of incredulity in her voice.

"Whaddaya mean, again? We only had dinner together once before."

"Twice. Thursday, and then again on Friday."

"So, what do you do? Only eat dinner once a week? Besides, Friday doesn't count as dinner. We ate take-out pizza, remember?"

They'd driven down to the beach and eaten it watching the sunset over English Bay. He'd kissed her, and he remembered how her lips had felt—soft, tasting a little of mushrooms and cheese. It made his groin ache, remembering.

"I thought tonight we could maybe have seafood. Ever been to the Wharf?"

"I can't tonight, Zach. Tonight's my Aquafit. I need the exercise."

"Aquafit? What the hell's Aquafit?" He was aware of sounding annoyed. After all, he was willing to give up his weekly squash game, and here she was, turning him down over some dumb exercise program.

Her voice developed a trace of frost. "It's my weekly workout, and it's important to me. We do swimming and aerobics and stuff. It's the pauper's version of a health club."

"Oh, a health club. I belong to one, too."

"This one's not exactly like yours, I don't think. It's just a swimming pool. We do water aerobics."

"Well, what time are you done? I could come by and pick you up afterward. We could go and have a late dinner somewhere casual. Save the Wharf for another time. How about it? Doesn't all that exercise make you hungry?"

He waited for her answer, almost holding his breath. There was a long pause, and then, sounding as if the words were being pulled out of her with pliers, she said, "I guess that would be okay."

Zach relaxed. "Great. Fine. What time are you finished? What's the address?"

"It's the old YMCA building on Burrard. We're usually done about eight."

"See you then." He hung up before she could change her mind. Water aerobics, huh? She'd be in the pool. In a bathing suit. If he got there a little early, he could see for himself how much of her was tanned. He could study the shape of her thighs, the exact curvature of her hips and breasts . . . He locked his hands behind his head and tipped his chair back, giving in to fantasy.

"WATER TO CHEST LEVEL, class, knees bent, arm swings begin. Swing and one and swing and two . . ." The instructor's abrasive voice reverberated inside her head.

Norma had a voice that would have done credit to a drill sergeant. It bounced off the ceiling and walls and echoed from each of the corners. "We'll do our arm raises and leg pull-ups now. Double time, hup, hup."

Jenny rubbed at the lenses of her glasses with her fingers, trying to clear the steam off so she could see across to the clock high on the wall at the far end of the pool.

It looked like seven twenty-five. Another five minutes and she was heading for the locker room whether the class was finished or not. Norma hollered at people who quit early, but to heck with her. For several reasons, Jenny wanted to be safely dry and fully dressed before Zach arrived.

The first was that she'd feel more in control with her clothes on, and around Zachary Jones, she needed all the control she could muster. The second, more urgent consideration was that her old one-piece black tank suit had a hole in the back the size of a dime, right in the middle of her left buttock. Well, it might just have expanded to more like a quarter tonight...or even larger; without thinking, she sat on the rough concrete at the edge of the pool and slid in, and she'd felt it get much bigger.

It wouldn't have bothered her normally. She was here for exercise; what was a little hole in the bum of a swimming suit, anyway? Some of the women here wore suits so small there wasn't enough fabric to sprout a hole, for gosh sakes.

She just didn't want Zach to see it, that was all.

"Choose a partner, everyone." Just as she was about to climb out, Jenny found herself trapped into a group exercise, and for another seven minutes, she tossed a rubber ball to the stout woman on her left. The class was definitely running late tonight.

The instant the ballgame ended, Jenny hoisted herself out of the water. She was starting toward the women's locker room when, through her spotted glasses, she saw Zach sauntering toward her from the main entrance area.

Her heart sank. He saw her right away and smiled and waved, hurrying over to where she was standing, dripping helplessly all over the cement and cursing herself for leaving her towel in the locker room. She felt dreadfully exposed, even though he couldn't see the hole in the backside of her suit as long as she was facing him.

"Hi there, Jenny. I came a bit early. I didn't want to keep you waiting." He looked at her and grinned and shook his head. "Your glasses are all streaked. Can you even tell it's me?"

Before she could answer, he reached out and unhooked them gently from behind her ears. "Let me clean them off for you." He reached into a pocket and drew out a pristine white handkerchief, carefully polishing the lenses before he handed them back to her.

"Thanks. The chlorine or something makes them smear like that."

"Do you always wear your glasses in the water?"

She nodded. "I can't see the instructor without them. Or the other side of the pool, for that matter." She was calculating how she could reach the locker room without ever turning her back to him when Norma's unmistakable voice boomed from right behind her, making Jenny start.

"Lathrop, is your friend interested in joining our class?" Norma probably was a female power-lifter when she wasn't teaching Aquafit. She had muscles where most women didn't have places, and she was at least six feet tall. She wore black tights that came to just below her knees and she bulged in unlikely areas. Over the black Lycra tights she wore a skimpy red exercise suit. Out of the top spilled amazing segments of milky white breasts.

Zach smiled at her politely and shook his head. "Afraid, not. I just came by to get Jenny."

Norma moved in closer, ignoring Jenny and holding out a large hand toward Zach.

"I'm Norma Kaiser. I teach other classes besides this one. Maybe one of the others would suit you better."

"Zachary Jones. Actually, I belong to a health club already, and my time's limited, so . . ." He politely took Norma's hand and she gave it a hearty shake, holding on longer than necessary.

"Which club d'you belong to? I know most of the instructors around town."

Jenny edged away. This could work to her advantage. She could sort of sidle across to the locker room without Zach noticing, if Norma kept it up— But Zach reached out and took her hand before she'd gotten more than a single step away, restraining her. His eyes traveled provocatively down her wet body and back up again, and Jenny shivered.

"You getting cold, Jen? Sorry, Norma, we'll have to be going. Talk to you again."

He looped an arm around Jenny's bare shoulders and steered her toward the women's locker room.

"You'll get your jacket all wet," she warned.

"Forget the jacket. Just get me away from that amazon!" he whispered in her ear in such a desperate tone that Jenny giggled. Near the women's locker room he paused, and Jenny was several steps away when she remembered the hole in her suit.

He must have noticed by now. Instinctively, she put her hand back to cover the hole, but strong fingers caught her wrist and pulled it away. She felt herself blushing as she turned and met his amused green eyes.

"The things those designers won't think of to get a guy's attention," he said softly. He gave her a huge wink and a pat on the bottom, squarely on the bare area. "I'll be waiting in the hallway when you're done."

HE WAS THERE, lounging against the wall when she emerged some time later. He smiled at her.

She reached up and self-consciously smoothed back her soaking-wet hair. The women's dryers had been broken since the first time she came here.

She was wearing jeans, well-worn, with a tear in the right knee, and she had her funky boots on.

"All ready?" Zach straightened and reached for her bag, an old and battered one that had belonged to her husband.

He gave her another wide, welcoming smile and shifted her bag to one hand, reaching out for her with the other and taking her hand in his, swinging it between them as they made their way along the halls to the elevator.

"I was worried I'd missed you," he said. "I had to hide in the men's locker room there for a while. Your friend Norma caught up with me again."

"She's determined to get you into one of her classes."

He turned and looked down at her, and laughter was dancing in his eyes. "Actually, she offered me private sessions at the pool in her apartment building. And also invited me over for a drink while she works out the details of my fitness program."

"She did that?" Jenny was flabbergasted. "That—Why, that old . . . barracuda!" Jenny scowled.

Zach touched Jenny's arm. "Hey, it's okay. I told her my red-haired lady was jealous and held a black belt in karate."

"Damn right," Jenny agreed in a mock growl, but her heart pounded double time at his casual reference to her as his "lady."

It wasn't at all true, but it sounded so nice.

"Hungry?" He lifted an eyebrow at her, looking so well scrubbed and handsome she forgave him the small designer logo on the rear pocket of his jeans.

"Famished. I always am after Aquafit."

He teased her as they waited for the only elevator that didn't have an Out Of Order sign on it.

"Norma's not at all shy, I'll say that for her. I started thinking I was going to have to holler at you for help. You could have landed her one like you did that big ox at legal clinic."

Jenny snorted. "Some hope. She's bigger than both of us put together, and I haven't got my legal-advice manual. Forget it. You're on your own with Norma."

He gave a protracted groan and they got on the elevator, laughing like fools.

In the underground parking garage, half the overhead lights were out and a stale smell of urine and gas fumes hung in the air. The assortment of other cars were mostly economy models. Zach's shiny red sports car looked out of place and even ostentatious in this company. He unlocked it and handed Jenny in, stowing her beat-up sports bag in the trunk.

When he got in behind the wheel, he didn't immediately start the engine, however. Instead, he turned toward Jenny and studied her in the dim light, a curious expression on his face.

"How come," he asked slowly, "whenever I'm with you I have a great time? Even defending my honor with Norma?"

His words touched her, but she didn't want him to know that.

"Obviously," she said with a little shrug of her shoulders and a superior expression, "it's because I invite you to such swanky places."

"Now, why didn't I figure that out?" He took her chin gently in his fingers and held it steady as he leaned across and kissed her—a light, lingering kiss that left her trembling nonetheless.

He slid a caressing hand down her cheek and then, reluctantly, let her go and started the engine. "It's your night to make these exciting decisions, solicitor. Where do you suggest we eat?"

Jenny didn't hesitate. "One of my favorite places is close to here, it's a cafeteria-style place where they give you tons of food for hardly any money. Ever been to Fresco's?"

"Never. But if you recommend it, I'm sure it's great."

Was he teasing her? Too late, she remembered that economy wasn't exactly Zach's major concern in life. Well, maybe it was time he got to know about places like Fresco's.

He was gunning the little car out of the garage and up onto the street, whistling a tune under his breath.

"It's not very fancy, this place," she added belatedly, and he gave her a knowing smile.

"Somehow I never doubted that for an instant. Just as long as you promise me Norma won't pop out of the next booth wearing spangled tights and a G-string, I guarantee I'll love it."

"I promise. Well, I can't be absolutely certain about Norma, but I've never seen her there before. And they have a dress code, you have to wear a shirt and shoes."

"We'll just have to take our chances, then, won't we?" He reached out and took her fingers in his, raising them to his lips and feathering kisses across each knuckle, then grazing his teeth across her palm before he released her hand again to tend to his driving.

It wasn't the desire for food that made her stomach contract and her throat go dry.

5

"I CAN'T BELIEVE you've never been here before. Fresco's is a Vancouver landmark. You've been leading a deprived life!"

Jenny extracted one of the fries from the mountain on her plate and dipped it carefully in vinegar, then in catsup, and popped it into her mouth. They were seated in a booth. Besides fries, Jenny had a large bowl of soup and a toasted sandwich, plus rice pudding and a fat carrot muffin. She was starving.

"I've driven past lots of times. I just never had a reason to come in," Zach explained. "The food's plentiful, just like you said."

"It's open twenty-four hours, which makes it handy if you work till two or three in the morning and feel like eating something besides pizza."

"Have you done that? Worked till early morning, I mean?"

"Sure. Most of last year and the one before." Jenny chewed another fry and swallowed. "I worked at a pizza place to put myself through law school. I ate here sometimes. Pizzamania, where I worked, isn't far away. This year I won a scholarship, which made life a whole lot simpler."

Simpler in some ways, but far more complex in others, she mused. Zach was definitely a complication in her life—one she wasn't at all certain what to do about. If only he weren't so damned attractive. She took a huge bite of her sandwich and realized he was watching her again, with that unfathomable look on his face.

She swallowed with difficulty. "It's hard to eat with you staring at me like that. Chewing isn't my best accomplishment," she complained. "What is it? Have I got catsup on my face?"

He shook his head. "I admire you, Jenny. You make me feel guilty for always having had things so easy," he said quietly. "I've never had to hold down two jobs or work half the night and then go to classes in the morning."

Guilt, or even admiration, wasn't exactly what she wanted him to feel at the moment, but she took advantage of it, anyway. "Good. That means that any day now, you'll give up this profitable litigation law and turn to something altruisic, right? You'll understand the error of your ways and turn your energies to helping your fellow man."

She was teasing, but he didn't smile right away. A thoughtful look passed over his features before he replied in a light tone, "Man cannot live by altruism alone, but sometimes it's tempting to give it a try." Then he told her about David Solomen and the predicament he was in.

"Of course, you're going to take the case?"

Zach studied the burger on his plate for a long moment. "I'd like to. But it depends on my partners' decision."

"I see." Jenny chewed reflectively, and her clear blue eyes said all the things Zach had known they would, about responsibility to his fellowman, about doing things for reasons other than money.

Her eyes made him uncomfortable, so he changed the subject.

"Speaking of altruism, how are you making out with that bag woman of yours—Glickman, wasn't that her name?"

Jenny shoved her glasses up and sat forward on the padded seat, excited about what she'd accomplished. "That's what I was working on today, actually. Remember her house was condemned by the city? Well, I got them to agree not to take action for a month on the house thing, I got the Downtown Residents' Association involved and they brought some pressure to bear on the city officials, which helped. And then today I got in touch with the Social Services Department. Veronica obviously needs their help, and they're going to send volunteers to clean the house up, inside and out. The next step is to get a cleaning service who'll go around on a regular basis and help Veronica keep order. I contacted several places today but it's hard to find the type she needs."

Zach had stopped eating and was staring at her again. This time, he looked more than a little horrified.

"I can't believe you got involved to this extent with a client, Jenny. You know all you're supposed to do is supply legal advice—not get mixed up with Social Services and the Downtown Residents' Association, for God's sake. To say nothing of cleaning companies."

She finished her sandwich and began to spoon up rice pudding, pretending nonchalance even though his words annoyed her. "I don't see why I shouldn't use whatever facilities are out there. That's the whole problem with the system. Nobody integrates the different services. And people like Veronica, who can't do it themselves, end up not getting the help they need."

His voice was quiet and she could tell he was deliberately being patient with her. "Jenny, there're social workers who are paid to do that. You're supposed to be a lawyer, remember?"

She shot him a dangerous look. She was close to losing her temper. "Yeah. Well, I'm a human being first, lawyer second. What do you expect me to do? Send her on her way with a list of suggestions she doesn't have the faintest idea what to do about?"

She could tell that's exactly what he thought she should do, all right. It made her blood boil. He didn't say anything for a moment, sipping his coffee in silence while the clatter of the busy restaurant went on around them.

Then he set his cup down and reached across the table, trapping her hand under his and holding on when she tried to pull away.

Having him touch her made it much harder to stay angry.

"Jenny, don't look at me as if I'm some kind of ax murderer, here." There was a pleading note in his voice she found hard to resist. "All I'm trying to get across is that people aren't always what they appear to be on the surface. Maybe this Glickman woman is genuinely a poor unfortunate soul. But even if she is, it's not up to you in your role as a lawyer to solve the world's problems."

"This has nothing to do with the entire world," she insisted, still annoyed with him but unable to resist the lure of his voice or the way he was stroking the back of her hand with his fingers. "It's a personal obligation I feel toward people like Veronica. A feeling that I'm capable and they're not. So somebody has to take care of them, right?"

How could he make her feel so . . . lustful, just by touching the back of her hand? Her mind was only half on Veronica Glickman. The other half was imagining him slowly taking off her clothes, conducting a full exploration of all her secret places.

"I admire your good intentions, but I don't want to see you get yourself in a jam." He put down the spoon he'd been toying with and rubbed a hand through his hair, still hanging on to her hand. "Damn it all, Jenny, how come every time we talk about work, we end up in an argument like this?"

She'd forgotten temporarily what they were arguing about. She was thinking that if his touch felt like this on her hand, for mercy's sake, what would it feel like if he stroked other, less public, areas of her body?

It was an image that had recurred more and more often the past few days. It made her insides turn hot and liquid, and she wondered—as she had with increasing regularity—when he'd get around to doing more than kissing her.

"I like to argue. That's why I like being a lawyer," she said distractedly, running her own thumb in a light caress across his palm and feeling a stab of pleasure when his eyes darkened and he swallowed hard.

ZACH WAS BURNING with desire. Ever since he'd seen her in that ridiculous bathing suit with the provocative hole in the bottom, he'd wanted nothing more than to find a horizontal surface and make wonderful use of it.

The problem was, for the first time in his adult life, he was trying to be a perfect gentleman. Each time he was with Jenny, he became more captivated by her, more intrigued—by her ideas, her opinions, her originality. Confrontational as she was, she made him think and react in a way he hadn't done before with a woman. He enjoyed being with her, and he wanted the friendship they had to continue—which meant that allowing sex to rear its lovely head would only complicate matters and perhaps wreck them altogether. He ought to know how that happened; he had a long history of bedding women first and talking to them later.

This time, he vowed, it was going to be different, even if it killed him—and at times, he wondered what the statistics were on death from sexual frustration. Especially, he pondered, at moments like this, when her blue eyes were sending him signals that set his body aflame.

His resolve weakened. She'd have to be unconscious not to know that she affected him physically. She must have felt the unmistakable hardness that signaled his need, every time he kissed her.

Maybe there was such a thing as being too much of a gentleman?

How the hell was he to know, when he'd never tried it before?

WHAT ON EARTH was holding him back, Jenny wondered? Reticence wasn't a problem she'd encountered with men; she'd always been the one saying no.

"Are you going to finish your food?" She jerked her chin at part of a burger and an almost-full cup of coffee on his tray.

It wasn't the first time since Nick's death that she'd ached for physical lovemaking. She was young, and she and Nick had loved passionately. But before, she'd been able to subjugate it with hard work, lots of exercise, and good doses of fantasy.

She knew that this time, none of those things were going to be enough.

She *wanted* Zach. The physical need weighed her down, making her body feel hot and heavy, making a pulse deep in her abdomen throb and ache.

"I've had enough to eat. How about you, Jenny?"

Food, yes, she longed to say. *Loving, no.*

"I'm full. Shall we go?"

My God, he was turning her into some kind of a sex junkie! She couldn't seem to keep her mind on what was going on. It was disturbing, because it was the first time that she'd fantasized like this about one particular, special man making love to her.

So what was the problem with him? She'd been out with him how many times—four now? And still he never got beyond heavy breathing and those kisses and touches that stirred every feminine response she owned.

He followed her out of the restaurant, courteously holding the door, taking her arm, settling her in the car. His manners were superb. And they irritated her beyond measure.

All she wanted him to do was act less like a gentleman and more like a hungry male animal.

"Want to take a drive around Stanley Park?" The car was poised at an intersection.

There wasn't a lousy thing they could do in this small sports car in Stanley Park. Didn't he realize that?

"I think I'd rather go home now."

She'd ask him in for a coffee. Wasn't that a euphemism any guy understood?

"Tired, Jenny?"

Lord, he was being thick. Was he going to dump her at the door and just drive away?

"Not bad. You?"

"Not at all. It's still quite early."

And surely, she pleaded silently, admiring his profile and casting surreptitious glances down at the outline of what she now knew were admirable thighs and awe-inspiring male equipment—surely, counselor, you can think of a great way for us to spend the next few hours? If you really use your imagination?

But she wasn't at all sure he was getting the message.

It came to her as they were threading their way through the narrow streets close to her apartment.

Zach just might have some kind of sexual dysfunction. She'd read that a lot of guys did these days. The professional in the article had said it had something to do with the changing roles of men and women and the new caution over choice of sexual partners.

Why, the poor guy! Her mind went over the list of problems in the article, wondering which particular one Zach suffered from.

Well, given an opportunity she was absolutely certain she could help him over it. After all, she was probably far more experienced than he was, given the fact that she'd been married and he never had. A warm, generous glow enveloped her, mixing pleasantly with the sensual yearning that had been growing inside her all evening.

The car purred to a stop, and before he could say a word about what a great time it had been and that he'd see her tomorrow, Jenny blurted out, "Care to come in for a coffee?"

Too late, she remembered the full cup of coffee he'd left behind only minutes before at the restaurant.

HIS HEART BEGAN to hammer when she asked.

He was almost at the limits of his endurance. The memory of her in that demure black tank suit with the provocative hole in the seat kept reappearing in his mind's eye; no matter how hard he tried, he couldn't subdue the aching need she roused in him. The silky black material had outlined her small, round breasts, clung to her tiny waist and emphasized the feminine cleft between her slender thighs.

But he'd made a decision about it, and he was a man who stuck to his decisions. Wasn't he?

If only she weren't so desirable.

She managed to be provocative without any of the trappings he was used to women wearing. She wore little makeup that he could detect, she smelled of soap instead of expensive perfume, her clothes were obviously designed for utility rather than seduction—and yet he wanted her more than he'd ever wanted anyone.

How the hell did that work, anyhow?

"Coffee sounds great."

He got her sports bag from the trunk and followed her around the side of the dark house to the steps leading down to her basement apartment, bending to help her when she fumbled and then dropped the door key on the cement; mindful of the warmth her body gave off, the smell of her hair, as she straightened and let him somehow find the keyhole and open her door in the darkness.

The basement was also pitch-black, even darker than outside.

"Wait here while I turn on the light. The switch is inside my door. Amos is an absolute fanatic about not leaving lights on. He comes down and unscrews the light bulb if I go out and forget to switch it off."

"Amos is your landlord?" Zach squinted around as the dim bulb in the entrance flicked on, revealing a cavernous area on one side, with an ancient furnace whose pipes twisted grotesquely along the ceiling.

"Amos Carradine, yes. He lives upstairs. He's a crotchety old Scot."

Cheap as dirt, too! Imagine sneaking around unscrewing light bulbs. Zach thought of Jenny coming home late at night to this absolute darkness, and it made him want to go up and throttle tightfisted old Amos.

Jenny unlocked a second door. "Come on in," she urged.

Zach had to duck his head under the low door frame, and even then his head seemed to barely clear the tiled ceiling. The living area was quite large, with a minuscule kitchen at one end and an open door at the other, obviously leading to a bedroom. Another door, closed, probably led to a bathroom.

It was generally homey and very clean. Jenny had used plants, homemade pillows and bright, colored throws to disguise the underlying shabbiness. Still, there was a large watermark down one wall that a travel poster of Mexico didn't quite cover, the ceiling tiles were badly stained, and it was obvious under the harsh overhead light that the whole place needed painting, and had for some time.

"Sit down. I'll put the water on for coffee. Or would you rather have perked? I've got a can of real coffee, if you'd prefer that?"

Her voice was unnaturally high and she seemed nervous, flitting here and there, patting cushions, turning on the only lamp in the room and switching off the overhead bulb so that shadows filled the corners. Her skin was flushed, her freckles stood out boldly. She shoved at her glasses several times with that one-fingered gesture he found so endearing.

"Instant's fine." Zach sat on the couch and found that the springs were gone. It sagged so much his rear ended up a scant four inches from the floor, which gave him a bit of a start.

Jenny noticed. "Sorry. That dumb couch! Amos rented me this place partially furnished and I swear he got the stuff from the dump. It made me sorry I hadn't kept the furniture Nick and I had. It was pretty junky, but it beat this by a country mile."

"You sold all your things when your husband died?"

Zach's curiosity about Jenny's husband overcame his natural tact. More and more, he found himself wondering at odd moments what the guy had been like.

Had Jenny loved him so much, no other man would compare? She'd been married six years. That was a long time. What had their love life been like?

And how the hell could he feel jealous of somebody who'd been long dead?

She was in the kitchen, fussing with the small gas range and a kettle.

"Yeah, I did sell everything eventually. It took me a long time to figure out what I should do."

Zach loved the way gleams of light caught in her shiny, undisciplined mop of copper hair. He'd touched it, kissing her, and found it incredibly soft, but resilient, as if it held a life of its own.

He wondered what that hair would feel like, spread across his chest, gently tickling his stomach.... God. He almost groaned aloud at the instant response in his groin—the deep, aching need she roused in him.

Jenny left the kettle on the stove and came in and sat down on the sofa beside him, at the other end. She'd taken her shoes off, and now she tucked one bare foot under her bottom.

"We'd been living in a rented place out in Abbotsford. After Nick was killed I got to hating it, and it was too far from the university for me to even think of commuting, plus our car was old and not very reliable. So I had a massive garage sale, sold everything I could, and moved into the city. I was lucky to find this place. The rent's low and it's close to the campus."

Zach couldn't imagine anyone feeling grateful about living in a place like this. He thought of his own ultramodern apartment, the window wall with the panoramic view of the city, the comfortable, overstuffed furnishings—things his mother had labeled not quite suitable any longer for the house.

"It's certainly... cosy, all right," he managed to say.

The kettle began to boil, and Jenny jumped up again.

He watched her hips move as she walked away from him. She was slim, but there was a lovely flare to her hips all the same. The lines of her bikini underpants showed under her worn jeans, and he wished he'd told her he didn't want any coffee. He was hot enough without it.

But she was back in a moment, with two steaming mugs balanced on a painted tray that advertised a local beer company.

"Cream, no sugar, right?"

"Right. Thanks."

This time, she sat down more in the middle of the couch, closer to him. She placed the tray and her own mug on a small table beside the couch and pulled her foot up again, this time letting her knee rest against his thigh.

Zach liked that a lot. In fact, being a gentleman had lost every bit of its appeal in the last few moments. He figured he'd take two sips of the coffee, abandon it on the floor, and then reach over and—

But she was up again, turning the knob on a small transistor radio, tuning in a love ballad from a local FM station.

And this time, she managed to sit back down right beside him, twisted a little toward him. Her small palm seemed to come to rest on his thigh quite by accident, and she started stroking back and forth in an absentminded gesture that had Zach nearly frantic in two seconds.

In the dim light her blue eyes were wide and unnaturally shiny as she smiled at him.

Then she cleared her throat, as if something were stuck there, and, in a voice barely above a whisper, she said, "It's awfully warm in here, isn't it? Would you like to take your jacket off, Zach?"

It *was* warm. In fact, he felt as if he might be on fire. But something was starting to dawn on him, and if he was right, he wouldn't ruin it for the world. Zach couldn't really think a whole lot, but it had begun to dawn on him that Jenny might just have a game plan here. Something was happening, and whatever it was, he didn't feel any need to analyze it.

She reached over a little hesitantly and begun easing the garment off his shoulders, resting one hand innocently on his chest for a moment while she slipped the jacket down his arms, following its slow journey with her hands in a manner that could only be described as incendiary.

God, he was right. This delicious, funny, wonderful girl was trying to seduce him. He'd had dreams about this, but he'd never for one moment thought they might come true.

"There now," she said soothingly, tossing his coat rather carelessly onto the couch behind her. "You'll be much more comfortable this way, don't you think? Why don't you slip your shoes off, as well?"

He slid his feet out of his loafers.

They were sitting very close now, and Jenny's hand was still on his chest, running back and forth in the same provocative way it had done on his thigh. He could feel his nipples tense each time her warm palm rubbed over them through the T-shirt. There was no disguising the fact that his jeans were becoming more and more uncomfortably tight.

"I'll just pull this out—" she was tugging on his T-shirt now, pulling it out of the waistband of his jeans with some difficulty.

Zach, mesmerized by what he now knew was about to become a full-scale seduction, did all he could to help without startling her, praying that she'd go on . . . and on. . . .

"—and slip my hands up under here. . . . Mmm, your skin feels so good, Zach."

Her breath caught in her throat and he could feel her shudder. She'd moved so that her breasts were pressing against his arm, rubbing against him the way a cat would rub, back and forth, in slow, sinuous movements. He could feel how hard her nipples were through the thin cotton.

His breathing was erratic. Nothing had ever aroused him more than this sweet, half-wanton, half-shy approach she was taking, and the last thing he wanted to do was to stop her. He exerted an iron will over his raging need and sat passively, letting her do whatever she wished as disjointed thoughts raced through his brain.

The fact was, he couldn't take much more of this. He'd been about thirteen the last time he'd climaxed with his pants on, but he was in grave danger right now of having it happen again.

Would she suddenly pull away if he turned the way he longed to and gathered her into his arms?

Carefully, he slid an arm around her, snuggling her even closer to him.

She moaned, and with clumsy precision, reached up and grasped his hair in her fingers, drawing his head down to hers, meeting his impatient lips with an eager, wet, openmouthed kiss that shattered the last shred of his composure.

His arms went around her and he expertly positioned their bodies so that she was against him. He took control of the kiss, savagely using lips and tongue to communicate to her his intense need.

But her glasses were in the way, so with one trembling hand he unhooked them from her ears. She didn't seem to care about the glasses or their fate. She was fully engaged in kissing him, nibbling all around his mouth, moaning moist, wordless promises in the vicinity of his ear, blindly pressing sweet, swollen lips fully on his and using her tongue in intriguing, somewhat clumsy stabbing motions.

He reached an arm out and dropped the glasses on what he hoped was the rug.

She used the moment to wriggle until she was lying fully on top of him, and the way her hips moved against his erection sent a fresh warning to his muddled brain. She was nibbling her way across his chest now, her hot, wet mouth accurately finding his erect male nipples through the T-shirt and gently tugging on them.

He fought for control. He had to slow this down, he had to get their clothes off, he needed to get them on some sort of a flat surface—the sofa slouched beneath them like a hammock.

"Jenny." His voice was rough and urgent, desperate. "Jenny, your bedroom . . ."

He interpreted the muffled sound she made against his chest as approval. He tried to get up with her in his arms, but the sagging sofa made it impossible, so he untangled her body for an instant, praying the spell would hold.

When he was on his feet, he reached down and scooped her up.

She was light and almost boneless in his embrace. It gave him the most incredible sense of power to hold her small frame in his arms. She put her arms trustingly around his neck, and went on kissing his throat and then his chin as he hurried them to the bedroom.

There was just enough light from the other room to make out the shape of the bed. He laid her gently on it, and in two practiced, easy motions, he stripped off his jeans, socks, T-shirt and briefs. There was a necessary item in his wallet, in the back pocket of his jeans, and he extracted it before he dropped the whole mess of clothing to the floor and sank down beside her.

JENNY COULDN'T HELP but feel a trifle smug about the success of her plan to entice Zach—when her brain let her think at all.

Mostly, she was just feeling—a wild and raging desire, a sense of exultation, along with intense, throbbing anticipation.

She waited impatiently while he took off his clothes. To save time, she sat up enough to tug off her own T-shirt, and she was struggling with the button on her jeans when strong hands covered hers.

"Let me." His whisper was smoky with an echo of her own passionate need.

Deftly, he undid her jeans and eased them down her hips, kneeling on the bed beside her, letting his hands trail along the naked skin as it was uncovered.

"Jenny. Lovely Jenny, you're so tiny, so soft...."

Only her bra and bikini panties remained. He ran a finger under the elastic at her leg, tantalizing her, finding a warm, moist spot that surged toward his finger when he touched it, tempting them both with the promise of release.

Jenny opened her eyes, wanting to see him, wanting to know what the hidden parts of his body looked like.

She couldn't get a clear picture without her glasses, but even in the dimly lit blur, she could tell that Zach was as magnificently constructed as she thought he would be. She wanted to reach out and take him intimately in her hand, but suddenly a wave of shyness came over her.

He was on the bed beside her. The plywood she'd put under the mattress made the surface extra firm, but a niggling concern came and went in her mind as the bed moved with his weight.

Would the block of wood she'd used to prop up the corner where the leg had fallen off hold up to their lovemaking?

But Zach was kissing her again, undoing the front catch on her wispy bra, exploring her breasts with tender fingers, letting his mouth trail cleverly down her neck, down...

"Jenny, you're so perfect, you fit exactly in my palm...."

A gasp caught in her throat as his hot mouth closed around her right nipple. His lips and tongue knew exactly what to do, and she writhed as the electric sensations he created inside her rippled down to her abdomen and caused bursts of fiery desire to explode between her thighs.

"Jenny, touch me. Put this on for me . . . for us. . . ."

He slid a tiny packet into her hand, and she forgot to be shy. She closed one hand inquiringly over his substantial arousal. With the other, she gently rolled the protection into place.

His fingers traveled down to the damp spot where fire was throbbing between her legs. Beyond control, beyond reason, she surged against his touch.

"Please, Zach. Oh, please, now . . ."

The feel of him in her hand combined with the knowing touch of his fingers brought her to the brink of climax, and in another instant, he'd slid inside her, infinitely gentle but pressing deeper and still deeper until she was filled with his heat and size and power.

He paused, murmuring love words to her, telling her how perfect she was. Then he moved, long and slow, and she was lost.

She stiffened and called his name while speech was still possible. She heard him make a deep, guttural sound in his throat, and he drove himself into her, arching his body with hers.

Their voices joined in a wild incantation, and the echo was still in the room when the block of wood gave way and the foot of the bed collapsed beneath them with an earsplitting crash.

6

"WHAT THE BLOODY HELL . . . !"

Zach held on to her, protecting her as well as he could, as they slid abruptly to the floor. They ended in a tangled heap of arms and legs, with Jenny sprawled on top of him, and it took several confused moments to sort themselves out and sit up.

Jarred from the heights of rapture to the depths of absurdity, Jenny began to giggle. They were sitting on a puddle of clothing, her underwear and his jeans tangled together in disarray. Pillows and sheets and blankets were flung all around them on the worn rug, with the rough sheet of plywood she'd inserted under the thin mattress in plain view.

"God almighty, we've gone and broken your damned bed!" Zach sounded so horrified and disgusted, Jenny couldn't stop laughing to explain. At last she got control of herself.

"Zach, I'm . . . I'm sorry. It's not us. This bed is really just a set of springs on iron legs. The springs were saggy and one of the legs came off shortly after I moved in. So I got this piece of plywood for under the mattress and I propped the broken leg up on that piece of wood. I'm normally a quiet sleeper and I don't weigh much, so it's never been a problem till now. It did cross my mind when we first . . . But things were so nice, and I just hoped . . . You're not mad, are you?"

She squinted at him in the semidarkness, trying to decipher the expression on his face.

He was silent for a long moment, and her heart sank. He was probably used to sipping wine on silk sheets after making love.

He reached out and ran a gentle finger down her cheek. "No, sweetheart, I'm not angry."

Sweetheart. He'd called her *sweetheart*.

"I'm sort of . . . flabbergasted," he went on in a deep rumble. "Quite apart from landing on the floor, what happened between us was pretty incredible." He cradled her head between his palms and rested his forehead on hers, then ran his fingers through her hair and caressed her ears, her neck, with sensitive fingers.

"Jenny, whether you know it or not, you're unique. I've never met anyone like you in my entire life."

She was very still, and she closed her eyes a moment to consider his words.

"Is . . . is that a good thing, Zach?" Her voice was soft and hesitant. "I mean, a person could take that different ways."

"It's the best," he said fervently. "Tonight is one of the best things that ever happened to me. Apart from the stupid bed, of course."

Right then, sitting on the floor naked amid the wreckage, she realized that she was in the process of making a fatal error. She was falling in love with Zachary Jones.

It was a frightening realization, and there didn't seem to be a lot she could do about it. It had crept up on her, and somewhere in her subconscious she'd known it was happening all along.

"Jenny?" His voice penetrated her reverie. The room was chilly and he was wrapping a blanket around her shoulders. His tone was uncertain. "Jenny, do you...uhh, is there some reason that you . . . well, that you'd rather take the initiative in lovemaking?"

"Take the—" For an instant, she couldn't figure out what he was talking about. Her seduction plan had been so successful, she'd forgotten about it halfway through. She snuggled into the soft blanket and shook her head. "Oh. That. No, of course not. I just figured because...well, you seemed kind of . . . reticent . . . and I thought you maybe had some kind of problem. I read this article that said a lot of men do, so . . ."

There was silence again, and then she could hear the astonishment and a hint of laughter in his voice when he said,

"You thought I had a problem? A sexual problem, like impotence, or—?"

Her defense came quickly. "Well, you never went beyond kissing. What was I supposed to think, for goodness' sake?"

There was laughter in his voice. "Jenny, for the first time in my entire life, I was trying my damnedest to be a gentleman."

That possibility had never occurred to her.

"Ohh," she said after a while, relieved that there wasn't enough light for him to see the flush creeping up her face.

"It was sweet of you to want to help me, though."

He got up from the floor and started rearranging her bedroom. He tossed their clothing onto the chair and gave the mattress a yank. It came off the lopsided frame altogether and landed on the floor. He propped the frame on end against the wall, and now there was room for the mattress on the rug. Her pink fitted sheet was still intact except for one corner, and he tucked that under and then grabbed the rest of the bedding and pillows, making them into a clumsy, tumbled nest on top of the mattress.

She was still sitting on the floor, bundled into her blanket. He reached over and drew her with him onto the mattress, snuggling them both into the cocoon he'd made.

"At least this way the damned thing can't fall anywhere," he muttered, loosening her blanket.

Her breath caught when her warm body encountered his cool nakedness. He enclosed her in his arms, wrapping himself around her. His hands skimmed her rib cage, cupped her breasts and slid with tantalizing slowness down to her thighs. She could feel his hardness pressing against her. She adored the texture of his chest hair tickling her breasts. It was intoxicating to be able to run her hands anywhere she chose, touching, learning the feel of his skin, stroking the most intimate places on his body, here . . . and here . . . and there. . . .

He made a sound deep in his throat—of pleasure and impatience.

"Now, my little therapist. About that sexual problem of mine . . ."

HOURS LATER, Jenny had her blue flannel nightgown and her glasses on, and she was cooking them eggs and toast. It was long after midnight.

Zach was seated at her little table, making it look ridiculously small and rickety. His feet were bare, his legs sprawled out in front of him. He'd pulled on his jeans and T-shirt, but his hair was all tousled, and his eyes had the same half-closed, satisfied look she'd seen in her own eyes in the bathroom mirror.

He looked good. She kept stealing glances at him as she buttered the toast and found catsup and strawberry jam for the table. It seemed both strange and somehow right, being with him like this.

"Thanks, Jenny." He eyed the plate of eggs, fried tomatoes and toast appreciatively and picked up his fork when she sat down across from him. "I didn't realize you could cook."

"This isn't exactly a four-course meal, but yeah, I do like cooking. The way I grew up, everyone had to take their turn in the kitchen, preparing food for others. It was a challenge. We mostly used the stuff we grew ourselves. How about you? You like cooking?"

Zach was attacking his eggs eagerly. He shook his head, smearing jam on a piece of toast. "I can get cereal into a bowl, and I open cans without too much trouble. But beyond that, I'm lost. We've always had a housekeeper, Eva, at home. She's a marvelous cook and hates anyone messing around in her kitchen. She used to make me anything I wanted. So I just never learned."

Of all things, servants! She should have guessed it. Once again, the differences between her and Zach were glaringly obvious.

She kept her tone light. "You really had an underprivileged childhood, you poor man. We all had to help with the huge garden in the summer. I was always in the kitchen, peeling vegetables or tearing lettuce for salads. We made tons of salads. Most of the commune was vegetarian."

He gave her a curious look. "You're not now, though? Vegetarian?"

She shook her head. "Not strictly, no. I just don't eat red meat, and I buy organic produce whenever I can."

"Like what Solomen sells. He says it's more expensive. Is it worth it?"

"It does cost a little more, but it's worth it. No pesticides or anything. Amos lets me plant a few zucchini, carrots and lettuce in the backyard here. I share the crop with him. When I'm rich, I'm going to have enough land to grow all my own vegetables."

He smiled at her, feeling both tender and amused.

"You're just a country kid at heart, Jenny."

"Darned right," she agreed.

IN HIS OFFICE the next morning, Zach kept hearing Jenny's voice, talking about gardening. He was having disturbing flashbacks of other segments of the evening, as well, but it was the damned organic vegetables that truly haunted him.

He should have known Jenny would be one of the people who spent what little money they had on organic produce— which was anything but organic, thanks to suppliers like Northwest Growers.

Over morning coffee, Ken and his other partner, Derek, had turned thumbs down on the Solomen case—just as he'd feared they would—using all the practical, hardheaded arguments he'd thought of himself.

Well. He'd better phone Solomen and give him the news. There was a lawyer Zach recommended at times like this—a man he'd graduated with who always seemed eager to get into dubious cases; a passionate, fiery sort of guy who wouldn't balk at contingency.

Zach picked up the phone, began to dial Solomen's number, then slammed down the receiver halfway through.

Damn it all. He wanted this case himself, and he was going to take it.

No, he corrected. The firm was going to take it.

His partners owed him a couple of favors when you came right down to it. There was that fiasco with Ken's uncle a couple years ago, a drunk driving charge. Zach had gone to

court with the older man himself as a personal favor to Ken—
and gotten a tongue-lashing from the judge, as well as losing
the case. Which was a blessing, considering the guy's driving record.

And that breach-of-promise thing Derek had gotten himself involved in with that real-estate woman. It had taken all
three of them to get him off the hook on that one.

He pushed the intercom. "Brenda, are Ken and Derek with
clients right now?"

"No, Mr. Jones. Mr. Meredith is on the phone, and Mr.
Hanover is in the washroom."

"Tell them both to meet me in Ken's office in five minutes,
would you?"

Zach had to forcefully remind his partners of their past
follies and endure their accusations about going soft in his old
age. Half an hour later, though, he was able to call David
Solomen and tell him Meredith, Hanover and Jones would
be happy to take his case, on contingency.

It was an exaggeration, of course. Jones was happy to take
the case. Meredith and Hanover were decidedly unhappy
about it.

"This whole thing could blow up in your face, Zach," Ken
warned. "It's going to cost a bundle, and even if you win, the
settlement isn't going to be that great, anyway."

Zach knew all that. But, for the first time in a long while,
he was filled with excitement about a case he was handling.
It meant something to him, quite apart from dollars and
cents.

THE OTHER ISSUE Zach had decided to deal with was a personal matter. He'd spent the hours after he left Jenny last night
figuring out a plan and drafting a written agreement.

He left the office at two-thirty. Jenny had told him she had
classes all afternoon, so he knew the coast was clear.

He drove to her neighborhood and parked in front of Amos
Carradine's house, marched up the walk, briefcase in hand,
and rang the bell.

Carradine was tall—the same height as Zach—and he looked to be in his sixties. He was white-haired, as thin as a cadaver, and the deep, disapproving lines on his face looked as if smiling might do him permanent damage. He opened the front door after Zach had rung three times.

"What d'ya want?"

"Mr. Carradine? My name is Zachary Jones. I'm a friend of Jenny Lathrop. I'd like a word with you."

The piercing bleached-blue eyes flicked from Zach's face to the red sports car parked at the curb, and he made a contemptuous noise in his throat.

"Friend, ya say? Friend, hah! Ye're the one was down there half the night. Don't think I don't know what's goin' on. No morals. That's what's wrong with you young people today."

Zach ignored the attack for the time being, even though it made his blood boil. There were more important things to settle first.

"Mr. Carradine, I'm a lawyer. I'm here in a professional capacity and I'm afraid I have a few unpleasant truths to discuss with you. Do you want to conduct this conversation out here—" Zach glanced pointedly at the avidly interested neighbor raking up leaves on her lawn "—or do you think I could step inside for a moment?"

Carradine's frown became ferocious, but he grudgingly moved back and allowed Zach just inside the door, keeping him standing in a dingy hallway.

"Mr. Carradine, I understand the suite you rent downstairs is not registered at city hall, and Jenny tells me she pays you her rent in cash."

It was an educated guess. Jenny had told him no such thing, but Carradine's suddenly wary expression confirmed Zach's suspicions.

"And what business is that of yours?" The growling voice was low and menacing, and the cool smile Zach gave the unpleasant man in return was a lethal warning.

"I'm making it my business. You understand you're facing a heavy fine if anyone complains," Zach went on smoothly. "And then there's the matter of income tax, as well. It's a serious thing, not claiming income, isn't it? Now, Mr. Carradine, I've seen the premises downstairs and I know what Jenny's paying you for them."

He'd asked her, and although the rent was low, it was far more than the place was worth, in his opinion. He told Carradine so. "Quite frankly, she could easily find something much better for the same money, but for some obscure reason, she actually likes living in your basement suite. So that means you're going to have to make some changes down there, doesn't it? Because that place isn't fit to rent out at all, the way it is. It wouldn't be hard to have it condemned."

"You dare come in here and tell me what I'm going to do? You . . . you . . . I ought to . . . Get off my property!"

Carradine had been growing more and more red-faced, and the final words were nothing short of a bellow, accompanied by a fist shaken in Zach's face.

Zach suspected Amos had intimidated quite a few people in his time. He certainly had the lungs for it. Zach kept his voice reasonable, although the urge to physically attack the cranky old miser was almost overwhelming.

"I wouldn't consider anything hasty if I were you, Carradine. As I told you, I'm a friend of Jenny's. A very good friend. And from what I saw down in that dungeon you call a suite, she needs a friend badly in her dealings with you. Now here's what you're going to do. Unless, of course, you'd rather I made a call to city hall. And the income-tax department. And maybe the health officials."

Zach outlined his conditions and opened his briefcase, producing the agreement he'd drawn up. "This stipulates that you won't raise Jenny's rent for the next year. In return, I'll pay for the paint and supply a new sofa and bed—but I want a good job done, repairs made where they're needed. You hire workmen. No slapping cheap paint over the whole mess. See to it everything's done right, or you'll answer to me."

The elderly man was purple in the face, but he had little choice except to sign the paper. Since Zach was paying for some of it, Carradine wouldn't be out of pocket a great amount—Zach didn't really know how well-off the old man was, when it came right down to it.

"There's no need for Jenny to know about this meeting, or the agreement, is there, Mr. Carradine? Let's do your reputation some good and let her think the whole thing was your idea." Zach handed Carradine a copy of the agreement. "Oh, and two more things." Zach abandoned his reasonable tone of voice, allowing his anger and disgust to show.

"The first is that damned light in the hallway. From now on, it stays on. She could break her neck down there in the dark. The second thing is, you don't seem to understand that a tenant like Jenny has a right to privacy. What goes on down in her suite is her business, and if I hear even a whisper of you saying things to her like the things you said to me when I arrived today, I won't just be phoning city hall and reporting you, Carradine. I'll be over here discussing it man to man. You understand what I'm saying?"

Carradine had enough sense to swallow hard and nod.

Zach whistled his way back down the walk, giving the interested neighbor a wide smile and a wink.

Back at the office again, he called his sister, Serena, to ask about where to buy a top-quality bed and a sofa. Serena knew about things like that, and she was willing to help.

"You redecorating, big brother?" she asked curiously.

"They're not for me, they're for a friend."

Serena listed three different stores, and then told him which one she considered the best.

After that, he focused all his attention on the Solomen case.

The first step was to find out who all of Northwest Growers' suppliers were, and name all of them as codefendants. The second step was to hire a private investigator who could work for Solomen as a truck driver. That would give Zach his independent expert reports about the source of the contamination. On the strength of that, he'd launch a hefty countersuit against Northwest Growers, and Safefood, as well, for maligning Solomen's business reputation.

They'd need a date for the examination of discovery.

He pushed the intercom, feeling more excited about work than he'd felt since his first week of articling.

"Brenda, get Ozzie King on the phone for me, would you?" Ozzie was an excellent investigator.

"Does this mean you've decided to defend Mr. Solomen, Mr. Jones?"

"It sure does, Brenda."

There was more warmth in her voice than he was accustomed to hearing. "Mr. Jones, I think that's such a wise decision. Mr. Solomen is such a nice man. I'll get King on the line for you right away, and if there's anything else I can do, just ask."

Zach stared at the intercom.

What the hell had come over Brenda?

HE'D TOLD JENNY he'd pick her up after her last class, which finished at six, and he barely made it. She was waiting outside the law building when he pulled up, and the warm, intimate smile she gave him when he stopped the car spoke of shared secrets.

He let his gaze wander over her.

She was wearing jeans and a shirt with a long green sweater over it. His gaze traveled down her body, knowing now the exact shape and feel of the firm, small breasts hidden under her blue shirt, and the enticing curve of waist and hip and thigh—only hinted at beneath the worn denim of her jeans.

He also knew how that soft, luxurious cloud of hair felt, spread across his naked chest.

Ahh, Jenny. My darling, sexy Jenny.

Desire swirled in him just looking at her. He couldn't remember ever being this turned-on by a woman before.

He got out and hurried over to her, taking her in his arms for a quick, thorough kiss before he led her back to the car.

"I thought of you all day," she confessed shyly, settling in the passenger seat. It pleased him to see the trace of color that rose in her skin when she told him that. But then she gave him a wicked sideways grin and added, "Mostly because I could hardly stay awake, and I figure it's at least half your fault. I've got to get to bed earlier than two if I'm going to be functional the next day."

He nodded in sober agreement. "Absolutely. I'll make sure you get to bed much earlier tonight." He growled deep in his throat. "In fact," he added hopefully, "if you're really tired, maybe we should skip dinner and go straight to bed now?"

Bright spots of color appeared in her cheeks. She gave him a long, considering look over the top of her glasses, but then she sat up a little straighter in the seat, shoved her frames farther up on her nose and shook her head, no, making wisps of bright hair tumble around her face. "Woman doesn't live by... bed alone. And I'm starving. I'd really like some food. Do you want me to make us something at my place?"

"At your place?" He thought of the mattress on the concrete floor, the sagging sofa, and bitter old Carradine with a stethoscope pressed against the upstairs floorboards.

"How about coming over to my apartment? You haven't seen it yet." It was the day his cleaning service came, so everything would be shining. And there was his own huge water bed on its secure frame.... Fantasies began forming.

"Do you have food there?"

Jenny definitely had a one-track mind when it came to food. He thought of his fridge, with its half quart of milk and seven cans of beer. "Not exactly, but we could pick up something on our way."

"Okay. But I need to go home first. I'd like to change. There was gum on the bench in the cafeteria this morning, and it's all over my jeans."

"How about I pick up some take-out Chinese food while you're changing?"

"Super. Get some of those big fat noodles, okay? I adore those. And lots of rice."

She was getting ready to slide out of the car the moment it stopped, but he held on to her arm. "Jenny."

"Yes, what?"

"Will you spend the night with me?"

She gave him that long, considering glance he was getting used to. "Yes," she said after a pause that nearly did him in. "I'd like that."

He let out the breath he'd been holding and gave her his best smile. "I'd like that, too." It was the understatement of the century. "And Jenny?"

"What?"

"Don't bother bringing pajamas."

She grinned and got out, trotting around the house to the basement door. The light was on in the basement, and she squinted up at it, feeling guilty. Surely she hadn't forgotten and left it on all day? She'd been in such a fog when she left this morning, it was possible. Funny, Amos hadn't come down and unscrewed the bulb, though. He was like a bird dog about lights left on.

Well, she'd turn it off as soon as she got the door open.

She'd just gotten her key in the lock, thinking she'd have time for a quick shower if she hurried, when Amos himself materialized like a wraith from the furnace area, giving her a start.

"Gosh, Amos, you scared me."

"I'd like a word with you."

Damn, just when she was in a hurry. An apprehensive knot clenched tight in her stomach. Undoubtedly he was going to lecture her about the light, and probably about Zach's car being parked in front of the house half the night, as well. He was such an old prude.

"Yes, Amos?"

She opened her door and stood blocking it, so maybe he'd have his say and get it over with fast. Maybe if she apologized. "I'm sorry about the light, Amos. I must have forgotten it this morning."

"I put in a new bulb, turned it on myself. Leave the derned thing be. Might as well leave it on all the time. Uses up more power turning it off and on, anyhow."

Well. Miracles actually happened, after all. They'd had more than enough discussions over that blasted light in the three years she'd lived here. And she'd used that very argument about turning it on and leaving it time and again herself with him, to no avail.

What was up with him today? He looked strange; his mouth was even more pinched in than usual. His voice was sour and abrupt, but his next words were astonishing. "There's painters coming Friday to do your apartment over."

"Painters?" It was about the last thing she expected, and she couldn't take it in all at once. "Painters? Like, walls and . . . and, my God, Amos, not just the bathroom . . . the whole thing?"

"That's what I said. And I'll be moving that chesterfield out. The bed, as well. I've . . . humph . . . decided to put in new ones."

"New ones?" She was sounding more and more like an echo, but she was dumbfounded by this.

Amos Carradine, who pinched every nickel three times, offering to upgrade her apartment to this extent? And put in new furniture? Something was not right here, however wonderful it sounded. The logical, horrible reason popped into her head, and she wailed, "Are you raising my rent, Amos? Because I told you, I can't afford to pay any more. I promised not to bug you about things, as long as—"

"Same rent. Count yourself lucky." The foul look he gave her didn't go along with his denial. He turned on his heel and stomped away before Jenny could say anything else.

In a daze, she went in and shut the door, leaning on it for a few minutes and looking around at the place where she'd lived for the past three years.

It was dingy, no doubt about that. Seeing it through Zach's eyes last night, it had looked pretty awful. It could have been depressing, but she'd never allowed it to be. But with a new coat of paint—would they fill the holes in the walls?

Amos had said painters, which meant he'd hired someone. Surely professionals would do something about the cracks and things.

She shook her head in amazement.

And the couch, that awful, saggy piece of furniture he glorified by calling a chesterfield. And the bed . . .

The bed. This had happened awfully soon after the bed collapsed with her and Zach in it.

On it. It was coincidental, Amos making these changes the day after that happened.

Could Zach have somehow . . . ? No, that was ridiculous, she reasoned, tearing off her clothes and racing into the shower. There wasn't any way she could think of that Zach might have been responsible. How could he have been?

Don't look a gift horse in the mouth, Jenny, she cautioned herself. *Don't start imagining things. He's not going to get involved in your living arrangements. Be sensible, here.*

She soaped and rinsed, careful not to wet her hair, which had been washed that morning.

Colors. Was there any way Amos would let her choose the colors for the paint? Or dare she push him that one step further?

She would. Images of bright, clear, primary colors and the pleasure they'd give her on rainy mornings danced in rainbow images as she dried off. Sloshing on extravagant quantities of her cologne, she then scrabbled through her underwear drawer for clean panties and a nice bra, her mind half on the coming evening with Zach, half on the miracle that was going to occur in her apartment.

She paused for a moment, wondering what to wear tonight.

It didn't matter a whole lot, because she knew from the look in Zach's eyes that it wouldn't be long at all until she was naked.

The thought of being naked, in Zach's arms, made her shiver with delight. Even paint couldn't compete. She found a skirt and sweater that would do for school tomorrow, and wriggled into a pair of tights.

Her life was changing. She paused a moment, staring at herself in the mirror as she dabbed some lip gloss on and brushed her hair.

The paint on her walls would be permanent, once it was done.

But Zach... A knot tied itself into a hurtful coil in her stomach. Zach was strictly temporary. She knew that, and she had to keep reminding herself all the time not to get too used to having him in her life.

It was going to hurt awfully bad when he left and she was alone again. Could she bear it?

She straightened her shoulders and looked past the glasses, into her own eyes. She'd just have to live through it, because there wasn't any alternative. Besides, she'd had lots of practice at living through unbearable events. Hadn't she?

There'd been her mother's death, her father's desertion, losing her husband. She'd lived through all of those.

And what was the point of spoiling today with worries over what the future held?

For the time being, she was going to pull a Scarlett O'Hara. She'd think about the consequences tomorrow.

Tonight... Tonight belonged to her and Zach.

His knock sounded on the door, and she grabbed her backpack and her purse and danced across to open it.

"Ready, Jen?"

The way he looked at her made her feel special, as if she was pretty and sexy. Irresistible, even.

The light was still on in the hallway, and it gave her real pleasure to leave it on as she closed and locked the door behind her.

"Ready," she said, smiling up at him.

HIS APARTMENT was at the top of a new glass-and-brick tower built to capture a view of the city and the bay, and it intimidated the life out of Jenny for the first hour.

One entire wall was window, and she felt as though she were looking down at a make-believe world. The city below looked small and manageable from up here; the view of the bay was like a picture-postcard scene created solely for this vista.

"You've got so much...stuff," she commented, turning from the window to gaze around the huge, lavishly furnished open area that encompassed living room, dining area, and at one end, a roomy, space-age kitchen.

There were brass lamps discreetly lighting expensively framed pictures, a huge oak desk against one wall, matching oak coffee tables conveniently placed, and not one but three overstuffed sofa units covered in brown corduroy, scattered with dozens of cushions in cream and softly muted shades of brown. Goose down, Jenny deduced when she poked one with a tentative finger.

"This place is so...big."

Zach seemed a trifle embarrassed. "Yeah. Well, I bought it as an investment, before construction had even started, so a unit didn't cost a third of what they cost now. And the furniture's mostly castoffs from home—things Mom had stored in the attics. I like old things—that was my great grandfather's desk. My sister, Serena, insisted I get the sofas recovered. They were in bad shape. And she came over and arranged things for me after I moved in. It wouldn't look like this if I'd had to do it. I don't know much about decorating."

"I didn't even know you had a sister." It was eerie, knowing that he had a mole just above his left buttock, yet not knowing that he had a sister. It brought home to her how much there was about him that she didn't have the foggiest clue about. "Do you have other sisters and brothers, as well?"

In so many ways they were strangers.

"No, just the two of us. Serena's four years younger than I am. She's freaking out at the thought of turning thirty next month—though she'd kill me if she knew I told anybody that."

She opened her mouth to ask when the birthday was, exactly, but before she could form the question, he answered it.

"November 15th." He walked over and tipped her chin up with a forefinger, planting a kiss on her lips. "And what does that tell you about Serena, Madam Astrologer?"

Her arms went around him automatically, and she drew in the wonderful smell of him—musky, male, with that touch of lemony deodorant or after-shave. As usual, he was wearing an impeccably tailored charcoal gray suit, soft blue-striped shirt, matching silk tie.

She tightened her arms around his midriff. It made her feel less strange, being held in the familiar security of his arms. She reached up and loosened his tie, then stood on tiptoe to kiss his chin.

"She's Scorpio. She's probably beautiful, proud and very confident."

He whistled and looked surprised. His arms tightened around her. "That pretty much describes Serena, all right. I'm beginning to think maybe there's something to this astrology business, after all."

Jenny gave him a small poke in the back for being condescending, but she didn't expand on her description of Serena.

"What does she do?"

"Serena?" He planted a kiss on her nose and stood back, shrugging out of his suit jacket, undoing the buttons on his sleeves and rolling the cuffs back so his strong forearms showed.

Funny, she'd never noticed with other men how sexy forearms could be, dusted with hair like that....

"She's a psychiatrist, just finishing her residency."

Formidable.

Jenny was profoundly relieved that the chances of her ever meeting Serena Jones were minimal. Psychiatrists always made her feel as if her head were transparent; and she'd bet this Serena would want to look in every hidden corner of her mind—especially if she knew Jenny had anything to do with her big brother.

Zach had her in his arms again, and if he went on kissing her this way...

She made a heroic effort and managed to move away enough so that reason could operate.

"Zach, all that food you bought..." she managed to say.

"Right. It's gonna get cold. Let's eat." His voice was as unsteady as hers.

Together they set plates and forks out on the small dining table, and he opened the assortment of bags Jenny had helped him carry up, lifting out carton after carton of steaming Chinese food.

"You bought enough for an army!"

"Well, you said you were hungry. And I figured we'd need some left over for breakfast."

It struck her then—the full impact of being here with him, knowing they'd make love tonight, knowing that for the first time, she'd wake up beside him in the morning, in this fancy apartment that felt absolutely foreign to her, with this man whose suit had probably cost more than her entire wardrobe. What the heck was she doing, thinking this was how it should be?

She didn't belong here.

Her throat closed and she couldn't swallow. "Y'know, this...this scares me a little, Zach," she said in a choked voice, setting down her fork with the mouthful of noodles she'd been about to devour.

He didn't pretend not to understand what she meant. He looked across at her and set his fork down, too.

"Being here with me, you mean?" His voice was gentle.

She nodded, avoiding his eyes. "It's just that...well, since Nick died...I haven't...gotten too involved with anyone."

"I sort of guessed that." He smiled at her. "When the bed collapsed, you said you'd always been a quiet sleeper. I couldn't help but figure..."

"Yeah, well." She was blushing. She hadn't meant to be that obvious. "The thing is, you're so...different. I mean, really different than anyone else I know."

"So are you, Jenny. Wonderfully different."

"But...but, doesn't it...scare you a little? I mean, if you think about it, what have we really got in common? This apartment—it's more luxurious than anything I've ever seen. It makes me aware of...of all the spaces between us. You saw where I live."

He stood and came around the table, lifting her into his arms.

"The only spaces between us are the ones we allow to be there, Jenny." He slid an arm under her knees, swung her up in his arms, and set off down a hallway to his bedroom. She was aware of more spaciousness, of more heavy, old furniture. The room smelled of wax and his after-shave. She felt the immense bed undulate as he laid her on it. It was covered in something deep blue and soft.

His hands were quick and sure on her clothing, stripping it away. He undid the buttons on his shirt, and within seconds, he was naked, kneeling beside her on the gently moving surface.

"Jenny, I look at you and I see an outrageous, delightful woman who makes me laugh, who makes me crazy with wanting her. All day today, I didn't want to eat, or sleep, or work, or do any damned thing except this. This is where spaces between people don't really matter. And with us, like this, there aren't any here."

His lips trailed across her shoulder, his tongue creating a hot, wet path that made her shudder. "I'll prove to you there aren't any." He took her nipple into his mouth, drawing it deep, using subtle, knowing movements of his lips, and the heat that tingled between her thighs intensified to flame.

She moaned softly and reached up, wanting to draw him down on her, but he resisted. "Last night, darling Jenny, you led the way. Now it's my turn."

She could feel the strength of his arousal pressing against her side, and the heat and hardness made her desperate for him. She moved her hips, inviting, but he resisted, caressing her instead with his fingers, knowing the places that needed his touch, slipping into her wetness and out again in a rhythm that brought instant response from the depths of her body.

His lips explored her breasts, then slowly dipped lower until she could feel him trailing kisses down her stomach, descending languorously to the mound at her thighs.

For a moment, uncertainty came between her and sensation, and she reached down to touch his head, to hold him back.

"Zach, I don't . . . I've never . . ."

"Good. Now you'll belong only to me." The rough, raw passion in his voice thrilled her, and in another instant, his mouth and tongue found hidden parts of her, and there wasn't room for reluctance.

Her body arched and the bubble of need he'd created inside her exploded. She soared, lost in ecstasy.

He held her until the shuddering stilled, and then he entered her, long and slow, as if there was no urgency, no goal beyond the pleasure of flesh touching flesh; but she was aware again of his need, of the terrible effort he was making to hold back, to please only her.

"Now you," she whispered, using her body to lure him on. "Now you, Zach." She ran her hands down his warm, wet back, sliding them around, touching his belly, caressing.

But he wouldn't be drawn. Eyes shut tight, he held her still, fighting for control. His voice was shaky and hoarse. "Now, together, my lovely Jen. No spaces, remember?"

Slowly, ever so slowly, he began to excite her anew, in long, smooth sliding movements that paused at the brink of fulfillment—tantalizing, beckoning—and drew away.

She was full of him; filled and yet needing more; needing the increasing power of the surging joy he was creating once more in the deepest reaches of her body. She closed her eyes and hung on, beginning to move with him, unconsciously matching her rhythm to his. The tempo increased; the long, slow thrusts became more shallow.

She opened her eyes and he was above her, breath rasping in his throat, sweat slick on his features, shoulders bunched with muscle, intensity making the clean lines of his face almost gaunt.

At last, she was poised on the edge of the place they were seeking, overcome by the powerful waves of desire he stirred inside her.

"Zach?" Her voice sounded faint and faraway.

He understood. "Now, sweetheart. With me."

As one, they moved; and their voices joined as their bodies melded tightly to each other, sharing the rapture that they'd created together.

It was just as he'd promised. There were no spaces.

AFTER THAT NIGHT, they were together every moment they could steal from work or from university. The passion between them was like a potent drug, and they spent a fair amount of their time together experimenting with it, drunk with the sensual explosions they stirred in one another, eager only to be together, and alone.

Jenny blossomed during the next several weeks and Zach watched her, captivated by the aura of happiness and excitement that seemed to radiate from every pore of her body.

He'd never known a woman quite as alive as Jenny. She seemed to give off sparks of vitality.

Her unease at being in his apartment soon disappeared, and they spent marvelous hours together there, laughing and talking, watching the newest videos, almost always making love at some point, but also enjoying quiet times. Zach would work at his desk while Jenny studied, curled into a ball on one of the sofas. Afterward they'd sit outside on his small deck and watch the stars come out.

Jenny's ecstatic delight in the renovations to her basement suite gave Zach a special, secret pleasure. Carradine had grudgingly had the holes in the walls repaired, and a plumber corrected the leaking pipes that had stained the ceiling and warped the bathroom tile.

Jenny convinced Amos to let her choose the colors for the repainting job, and even Zach was amazed at the results. At her instruction, most of the walls and all the ceilings were done a basic pale eggshell, which made the entire place seem much larger and brighter than before, but in each area, Jenny had also chosen a dramatic splash of primary color for one feature wall.

The area behind her small kitchen table was daffodil, so that it seemed the sun was shining in even on the dullest mornings. In the tiny bathroom, blush pink created a feeling of warmth and space on the wall opposite the shower. In the bedroom, cornflower blue covered the wall behind the new double bed.

Zach loved that bed. He'd chosen it and the navy blue sofa, and had had them delivered, as he'd told Carradine he would. He made certain the bed had the finest mattress money could buy; no more plywood and loose blocks for Jenny.

He'd wanted to get a queen size, but the room proved too small, and after spending several delicious nights on the double, he was glad it had worked out that way. Less space meant they had to stay closely locked in one another's arms, and that suited him just fine.

Most things suited him these days—except the disagreements he and Jenny got into over her clients from the legal-aid clinic.

Three times in a single week, they'd been making love in Jenny's bedroom when the telephone rang late at night. Jenny only had one phone, and it was in the other room.

The first time, Zach could only assume that it was bad news—someone dead or in an accident. He'd grabbed a blanket and taken it to wrap around her bare shoulders, holding her against his warm body for a long moment to

omfort her if he could. But Jenny didn't seem to be notice-
bly upset, so Zach finally went back to bed.

As Jenny told him half an hour later when she crawled back
nto bed and put her cold feet on his legs, the caller was Ve-
onica Glickman.

"Glickman?" Zach was astonished. "How the hell did she
et your home number?"

"Oh, I gave it to her when she was so worried about her
ouse being condemned," Jenny said serenely. "It's hard to
et in touch with her. She doesn't have a phone, so she had
o call me. There wasn't any other way to talk with her."

Zach was disturbed. "You shouldn't ever give those peo-
le your home number, Jen. It's not professional. What was
he emergency tonight with Glickman, calling you at this
our?"

Jenny snuggled close to him, her cold hands warming fast
n his thighs. "No emergency. She was just lonely and wanted
o talk. She was calling from the lobby of some hotel."

Some bar, Zach thought, but he didn't say it, because Jen-
y's hands were much warmer now, and they were stroking
part of him that responded instantly to being stroked. A
oment later, he'd entirely forgotten Veronica Glickman,
ecause Jenny had rolled on top of him and taken him inside
er warm, wet depths.

WO NIGHTS LATER, they were again involved in a crucial
aneuver when the phone began to ring. This time, they tried
o ignore the strident summons, but neither succeeded. At
st, Jenny staggered out of bed, located her glasses and hur-
ed into the other room.

Again, it was Veronica Glickman.

This time, Zach was more vocal about it. They had what
mounted to an argument; but it was hard to stay annoyed
ith one another when they were both naked. And the bed
asn't that big, so they couldn't really avoid touching.

The third time, however, they had an outright quarrel over
eronica's call. It came at two in the morning, startling them

both out of sleep. Jenny was half frozen when she came back to bed, and Zach was furious.

"You've got to tell that bloody woman to stop calling you here. Either that or get your number changed."

He hadn't expected Jenny to get angry, but she did. She'd been cuddled next to him, and she jerked away, as far as the bed allowed, her small body taut with outrage.

"That bloody woman, as you call her, happens to be lonely, and if she wants to call me, that's between her and me. You don't understand the first thing about loneliness. How could you—surrounded all the time by your family and your friends?"

This was true, he had to admit. He'd never been really lonely that he could remember. He apologized, and Jenny relented, but it left a residue of bad feeling between them because he still felt Jenny was making a huge mistake, encouraging Veronica.

THE TROUBLE WAS, Jenny treated all her clients as if they were her friends, and it was causing Zach untold problems at the Thursday-evening legal-advice clinic.

As usual, the area smelled of stale coffee, wet overcoats and cheap perfume when he arrived that Thursday evening.

Tonight must be the sixth clinic he'd supervised, Zach reflected wearily, and he wished to God he'd stopped while he was ahead and quit coming here after the first two. Not that he minded helping the students; he actually found it enjoyable.

It wasn't the questions or the decisions that bothered him. It was this whole thing with Jenny and her street people. It was getting out of control. It was driving the assistants crazy and irritating the hell out of the other students.

One of the assistants hurried over to him as he was taking off his raincoat. Jenny had already settled in at her assigned table, and was talking with someone.

The assistant motioned to the long line of people waiting to be seen, and she sounded annoyed. "At least half of these people only want to see Ms. Lathrop, Mr. Jones, and I don'

know how to handle it. If I tell them they have to see whoever they're assigned to, they simply say they'll wait till Miss
Jenny's free. That's what they call her—Miss Jenny. What
should I do about it, Mr. Jones?"

He was damned if he knew. Zach heard them himself, the
bag ladies and derelicts, all asking for Miss Jenny. To begin
with, it was totally unprofessional, letting these people call
her by her first name. He'd spoken to her about it several
times, reemphasizing the need for professionalism, for distancing oneself from the client. Obviously, he was going to
have to bring it up again.

He tried hard not to make any exceptions as far as the clinic
was concerned in his dealings with her, although from glances
and overheard remarks, he knew the other students had
guessed long ago that there was something going on between them.

Difficult as it was, Zach really tried to be as professional
as possible while he was here.

"Ask Ms. Lathrop to come over when she's free."

He found a comparatively quiet corner and waited. In a
few moments, Jenny hurried over, her hair ablaze and coming loose from its bun, glasses falling off her nose, prim black
shirt and calf-length printed skirt hiding her long legs. He
knew she was wearing pink lace panties under her dark panty
hose—panties he'd bought her.

He shouldn't watch her dress when they were coming here.
It made everything that much tougher. He wanted to run a
hand up under her skirt, tug the panty hose down— He felt
his body grow hard, and he forced himself to pay attention
to the business at hand.

"Ms. Lathrop, why are all these people calling you by your
first name? You understand the importance of a professional
approach. And the assistants are complaining because too
many people insist on seeing only you."

That sounded pedantic and accusatory and petty. But what
the hell? He was doing the best he could under impossible
circumstances. He studiously avoided looking at her legs, but
that left her breasts, and he also knew she wasn't wearing a

bra under the damned shirt. She'd asked him whether or not
her nipples showed before they left, and he'd assured her they
didn't.

Now he wished he'd made her wear long underwear.

Jenny shoved her glasses higher on her nose and glared at
him. "It's Veronica's fault they all want to talk to me. She sits
out there every Thursday night and goes on and on about me.
I hate it as much as everybody else. My caseload is killing me.
And I always start out professional with them. For gosh
sakes, Zach, take a look at these people. They need some
human contact. They already feel the whole world looks
down on them. If it makes them more comfortable to call me
Miss Jenny, I can't see what harm it does. At least they say
'Miss.'"

"But you know it's a mistake to become personally involved on any level with a client, Ms. Lathrop," Zach reit-
erated patiently, for what seemed like the twentieth time. "A
client is a problem with a rational solution. You can't allow
yourself to relate on any level except that one. The practice
of law is a legal affair, not an emotional issue."

She gave him a defiantly stubborn look—a look Zach had
come to recognize uncomfortably—and dread.

"That's bullshit, Zach. Maybe you can practice law from
an ivory tower, but I can't. To me, clients are people first,
problems second. That's what makes being a lawyer fun.
Why don't you try talking to some of these people for a
change? Try relating on a human level instead of categoriz-
ing them as problems. And for God's sake, stop calling me
Ms. Lathrop. You're the only person here who does, and it's
ridiculous."

She turned and hurried back to her table, leaving Zach with
an overwhelming urge to rush over and strangle her. She
managed to make him feel guilty and snobbish and simple-
minded all in one bundle.

The simple truth was, he raged to himself, he didn't want
to talk with Jenny's people. The particular type of clients she
attracted made him uneasy. He'd never in a million years ad

mit it to her, but he'd always privately called them the "window people."

Before Jenny, he used to sit in expensive restaurants and see them pass by, always through the window. He felt sorry for them, he gave generously to community fund-raising drives aimed at providing shelters and food. But they had their life, he had his; it was just the way things operated.

Now, because of Jenny, he was being introduced to them, being drawn into their problems, being awakened at night by their phone calls, consulted about impossible situations he really had no idea how to handle. Technically, the things they talked to Jenny about more often than not weren't legal problems with clear-cut solutions at all. Or if they were, they were cases Zach wouldn't touch with a ten-foot pole.

Like the case of Elias Redthorn, for example.

The clinic was more than half over that evening when Jenny waved Zach over to her table. Zach had noticed the small, rather repulsive man in the heavy body brace; he'd been the one having an impassioned discussion with Veronica Glickman during the entire first half of the clinic. Veronica was undoubtedly the reason he'd refused to see the student he was assigned to, choosing instead to wait over an hour until Jenny was free.

He was now sitting on the wooden client's chair in front of her desk, with what Zach could only describe as a hangdog look on his long face.

Jenny introduced Zach, and the little man struggled to his feet to shake hands. Zach noticed that besides the cumbersome body brace, Redthorn wore a heavy orthopedic shoe on one foot, which was built up at least six inches. He shook the soft, sweaty paw the man extended, feeling a surge of pity but also feeling irritated by the obsequious way Redthorn acted and spoke.

"I need a bit of advice, Zach," Jenny began in an animated voice. She'd obviously forgotten the earlier scene. "Elias has a complex problem here. His car—"

Redthorn interrupted her. "It's an '82 Oldsmobile," he said, rubbing his palms together and smacking his lips in a way that set Zach's teeth on edge. "Mint condition. At least, it was before the accident."

Jenny took up the story again. "Elias's car was stolen two weeks ago. The police recovered it after a couple of days, and returned it to Elias, but they neglected to check it mechanically, to make sure it hadn't sustained damage while it was stolen."

Again Elias interrupted, in a pitiful nasal whine. "I've had it two years, that car. Nary a scratch on it. I keep it covered when I'm not using it." He cast what was obviously intended to be an appealing, pathetic look at Zach. "Not easy for someone like me to afford a car, y'see, gov'ner. Born with my leg like this, I was. Never got much schooling. Hard to find a steady job when you're a cripple, gov'ner, don't you agree?"

Zach had no idea what the hell to say to a question like that. He was feeling more and more uncomfortable. He shot Jenny a pleading glance, and she hurriedly took up the tale again.

"Elias took the car out for a drive, and it went out of control, even though he was trying to use the brakes." She referred now to a printed sheet in front of her. "It ran into a parked vehicle and then a lamppost. This report says there was extensive damage to both vehicles, and the post was sheared off at the base." She looked up, her blue eyes filled with righteous outrage. "Elias's back was injured, and now he's forced to wear that brace, perhaps permanently. And the police are charging him with undue care and attention, as well as dangerous driving. Can you believe it?"

"Never had an accident before, gov'ner. Very particular about my driving, I am."

Zach wished he would shut up. His voice grated like nails on a blackboard.

Zach tried to forget Redthorn and consider the problem here. "It shouldn't be too difficult to have the charge dismissed, if the police did in fact return the vehicle without having it thoroughly checked," he suggested.

Jenny waved a hand, brushing that aside. "Absolutely. That's exactly what I intend to do. No problem there. I've already told Elias that. What I wanted to consult you about is whether or not Elias has a case against the police force. He feels—and I think he's right—that he should receive a substantial settlement because of the injury he's sustained."

It was beginning to dawn on Zach that there was more here than he wanted to deal with. He felt a peculiar sinking sensation in his stomach as the ramifications of the thing became clear.

He and Jenny both knew that because she was still a student, she couldn't handle cases involving personal injury. They also both knew that Zach's firm handled this sort of thing all the time. Therefore . . .

Zach knew without a shadow of a doubt that his partners would turn thumbs down on this one without any deliberation at all. The chances of winning were minimal, the time involved in preparation would be major, and the client was indigent, so the work would be *pro bono*. For free.

He already had them embroiled in the Solomen case, against their better judgment.

They'd never agree to taking on Redthorn. They'd likely have Zach committed to a mental institution if he even brought it up. It would take only two doctors to accomplish that and Ken Meredith played squash with all the residents from Vancouver General Hospital.

Zach opened his mouth to tell Jenny she was flogging a very dead horse, and closed it again because of Redthorn's presence.

"I told Elias I was sure your firm would consider this a matter of moral conscience," she added with her sweetest smile, giving her glasses a triumphant poke and Zach a wide-eyed, hopeful look.

Zach managed what he prayed was a noncommittal noise in his throat before he made his escape. He must be developing some psychic ability, because for the first time in his life he could see the immediate future.

It was black—excessively black—shot through with nasty streaks of angry red.

8

"I JUST CAN'T BELIEVE your firm could be this callous!" Jenny's voice was trembling with outrage and increasing in volume, and several heads turned their way. "It reminds me all over again of what happened when Nick was killed—how we were all treated like second-class citizens just because we didn't have money behind us!"

The quietly luxurious dining room at the William Tell wasn't exactly the place to have a disagreement, Zach realized. A soft violin concerto discreetly playing in the background didn't muffle anything except murmurs, and Jenny wasn't exactly murmuring.

"If you had a shred of feeling for those less fortunate than yourself, you wouldn't hesitate to take Elias's case."

"Look, I'm sick of hearing about Elias Redthorn, okay?"

Zach was also more than a little tired of hearing about Jenny's dead husband, when it came right down to it—although he didn't say so. How the hell could he hope to compete with a dead man, for cripes' sake?

Zach made a conscious effort to lower his voice. "Look, Jenny, you're suggesting my firm sue the Vancouver Police Department. That's a serious undertaking. The firm's always been on the best of terms with them—we rely on their cooperation."

She rolled her eyes, silently expressing her disgust with that attitude.

"You've got to admit, Jenny, it's not even an open-and-shut case. This Redthorn guy—"

The waiter, face impassive, appeared at Zach's shoulder and ceremoniously picked up the bottle of wine Zach had optimistically ordered. He refilled their glasses.

Jenny's was still full. Zach emptied his so as to give the guy something to do and the waiter filled it again, emptying the bottle.

"Another bottle, sir?"

"No. No, thanks, that's enough."

"Very good, sir."

Zach decided he was also disillusioned with the William Tell, a place he'd always enjoyed till tonight. He'd counted, maybe just a trifle callously, on these elite surroundings to help him out with this discussion with Jenny, assuming— wrongly, as it turned out—that she'd be too intimidated by the five waiters, two busboys, haughty wine steward and stiffly formal maître d' hovering over and around their table to create a major scene over the damned Redthorn affair.

Well, he'd been wrong before. He'd just never been quite this wrong, this publicly.

He tried sweet reason. "Jenny, I don't run the firm by myself. It's a partnership, and when both other partners decide against taking a case, there's not a hell of a lot I can do."

She gave him a fiery glare over the top of her glasses. "You could set an example. You could threaten to leave the firm, on principle. You could take the case independently of the firm."

He was trying to control his anger, but it put a hard edge in his voice. "For Christ's sake, Jenny, do you understand what you're suggesting? I helped found the firm, I'm a partner. I'm not about to leave. That's the most unreasonable thing I've ever heard."

She sniffed and then stared down at her dinner for several long moments and when she looked up at him again there was less anger in her face. "I guess it is unreasonable," she admitted. "But the whole thing seems so unfair to me. You saw Elias, in that horrible body cast, with his built-up shoe. And he's dirt-poor. That's what this is really about, isn't it? If Elias had money, you'd take the case, right?"

"Not necessarily, no." Zach had to admit to himself, reluctantly, that it might be a lot more probable, though. "Look, Jenny, unfortunately firms like ours are out there to make money. This is a competitive business. You know how many legal firms go under each year. We have to be hard-headed about what we do."

She toyed with her seafood salad. "Ruthless," she said after a while, and there was a sad, weary acceptance in her tone. "You have to be ruthless, and people like Elias Redthorn are always the innocent victims."

Zach was silent. He was worn-out from arguing with her, and still smarting from the scene with Ken and Derek that afternoon, when he'd rashly proposed the Redthorn case to them. It had been nothing short of humiliating.

They'd told him in no uncertain terms they figured he was flipping out. First the Solomen thing, and now this? They'd suggested a nice long holiday, preferably at a mental-health facility, just as he'd figured they would.

Although he'd been unusually reticent about Jenny, they said they'd already guessed there was something going on in his life that was affecting his brain, and they figured it had a lot to do with another part of his body. They reminded him that he'd canceled squash games, avoided the usual weekend pub crawl, turned down a date with Ken's cousin's cousin from Oakland—a real, live honest-to-God California girl, blond and buxom and reportedly mad about Vancouver lawyers. To say nothing of volunteering for the entire semester at the legal-advice clinic. Which just might, Zach, old buddy, old pal, old rascal, have something to do with this new attitude. Right?

Nudge, nudge. Wink, wink.

Zach had deflected their pointed remarks about female law students, which of course was a dead giveaway.

The strange thing was, he'd never had the slightest desire before to conceal his love life from them. It hadn't mattered one whit to him, having his friends know he was sleeping with a new lady.

So why did it matter like hell this time?

Because it was Jenny.

He looked across the table at her. She was wearing a green dress with a soft, open neckline—a dress that clung to her breasts, her waist, her hips, then flared out gracefully at the hem. Her beautiful, shining hair was caught up in a high knot on top of her head, with some cascading down her back and wisps trailing over her forehead and in front of her ears. Her blue eyes were huge behind her glasses, and her freckles looked like little golden dots across her nose and cheeks.

A rush of feeling swept over him—regret that they were fighting, a surge of the intense physical desire he always experienced when he was near her, and another emotion—a tender, protective combination of confused, exasperated responses he wasn't ready to explore right now.

The truth was, he no longer saw Jenny objectively, he realized. He saw a woman who captivated him, whose body he knew intimately and adored, whose mind he admired, but whose convictions made him want to shake her until her brains rattled.

Nope, he wasn't the least bit objective about her. That was certain.

What he felt for Jenny was different from anything he'd ever felt before about a woman. If one of his partners today had dared make a remark less than respectful about her, he'd have broken that partner's nose without hesitating, friend or no friend. Whatever this was between him and Jenny, he needed to sort it out by himself.

"Would you like some dessert, sir?"

The waiters had cleared away their half-eaten plates of food, and their coffee steamed untouched in china cups.

"Jenny? Dessert?"

"No, thanks. Nothing more. I think I'd like to go home now, Zach." She was subdued and formal—not at all her usual, fiery self.

He paid the bill and they went out into the soft, rainy night. The valet service already had his car waiting under the awning. Zach gave him a tip, and soon they were idling their way through the crowded Friday-night streets.

Jenny was quiet, and Zach's mind kept replaying parts of their conversation.

"Jenny, what was your husband like?" The question seemed to pop out of his mouth of its own accord.

She turned and gave him a puzzled glance. "Nick? You want to know what Nick was like? Why, Zach?"

He struggled for words. "I . . . I guess I feel as if he's there between us all the time, that you're . . . comparing me to him, or something."

And finding me wanting, he added silently.

She turned away from him and looked out the window. "That's crazy. I'd never do that. You're very different from him. There's no basis for comparison at all."

He waited, but she didn't say anything more, and the tension that had been growing between them all evening increased.

"You want to go to your place, or mine?"

"Mine, I think. I've got a ton of homework to do."

"It's Friday. You've got the whole damned weekend to do your homework." He knew he sounded grouchy, and he didn't give a damn. She was pushing him.

"I still want to go home."

Zach stepped hard on the gas, and the powerful little car surged ahead, darting between a bus and a delivery truck with an inch to spare on either side.

She wanted to go home, he'd take her home.

JENNY KNEW HE WAS MAD at her. It was obvious from his clenched jaw and the way he was driving. She knew she'd been less than pleasant company tonight, raging at him in that fancy restaurant.

C'mon. Be honest, Jenny. You were an out-and-out bitch, and you know it. And you also know it wasn't all because of Elias Redthorn.

It was herself she was really angry with. Why in God's name had she let herself get this involved with Zachary Jones? She'd known from the first moment she'd laid eyes on him, in the Legal Clinic that night, that Jenny Lathrop and Zachary Jones might as well inhabit different planets, for all they had in common.

And knowing that, what had she done? She'd ambled along like a sheep to a slaughter and let herself fall in love with him. Well, maybe not like a sheep, exactly. Vivid memories of her avid seduction attempt contradicted the sheep analogy. *Love* was the operative word here, with a capital letter *L*, because she wasn't just a little in love; this wasn't a passing fancy, a here-today-gone-tomorrow liaison.

Nope, she'd gone the whole nine yards here. She actually had fantasies about having his babies, growing old with him, arguing with him over legal affairs until they were both too senile to know a writ of habeas corpus from a subpoena. And there wasn't a snowball's chance in hell of that ever happening; she'd known that from the beginning. So how stupid could a smart woman get, anyway?

He pulled up in front of the house, and without a word got out and came around to help her out. He had impeccable manners, even when he was furious.

He stalked behind her to the basement door, picked up the key when she dropped it, and opened the lock. Her glasses were covered in raindrops and she couldn't see his face clearly, but she knew he wasn't going to come in with her.

Panic gripped her, even though her brain knew the best thing that could happen was for him to walk out of her life right now, before things got even worse.

Better? That was the whole point. She could deal with "worse"; she'd been dealing with it most of her life. It was "better" she couldn't handle.

"Jenny." His voice was businesslike, impersonal. He was standing just inside the basement entrance, not touching her, his elegant raincoat dripping on the cement. The light that was always on now shone down on his stern features.

"Yes, Zach?" She was proud of the way she kept her own voice under control.

He was about to say goodbye, it's been difficult knowing you. And surely she could get through the few minutes it took without bursting into tears or screaming and throwing herself on him or anything nutty like that. There'd be plenty of time for tears later. . . .

"I was talking to my mother today, and she'd like to meet you. She's asked us to come for dinner tomorrow."

JENNY KNEW SHE WAS wearing the wrong thing, but there was some consolation in realizing that not a single garment in her closet would have been right, anyway. As it was, she'd changed four times before settling on the blue corduroy skirt, navy tights and plain white shirt she was wearing. Catching sight of herself in a full-length mirror in the entrance hall a moment ago, she'd realized too late that she looked like a schoolgirl in uniform. She'd even braided her hair—a French braid that she'd taken out seven times before she got it right.

"I THINK IT'S WARM ENOUGH to sit out on the deck, don't you, Serena?" Zach's mother, Lucille Jones, wasn't at all what Jenny had expected.

She was short and rather plump, with beautiful, deep-set hazel eyes and silvery blond hair. She ushered Jenny through one elegantly decorated room after the other, then out through sliding-glass doors onto a ground-level cedar deck.

Jenny surveyed the backyard. The place was like a park, for God's sake. Nearby was a swimming pool and a cabana. Beyond that was a tennis court.

"Eva dried the chairs off this morning after all that rain. Now the sun's out, we might as well take advantage of it. Jenny, you have glorious hair, dear. I always longed for hair like yours."

"Thank you, Mrs. Jones."

"Heavens, call me Lucille. Mrs. Jones makes me feel quite ancient."

Jenny had only been around Lucille Jones for fifteen minutes, and she liked the older woman, despite her prejudices. It would have been difficult not to like her; she'd greeted Jenny with a warm hug and an easy, sincere welcome. It was apparent she adored her tall son; she tugged him down to her level to plant a huge, noisy kiss on his cheek.

Zach's sister, Serena, on the other hand, was everything Jenny had been afraid she would be. Tall and model-slim, with honey-blond hair drawn back in the kind of elegant knot Jenny could never seem to manage, Serena was poised and coolly beautiful. Her low, husky voice was perfectly modulated. Her green eyes, like Zach's in color only, seemed to bore into Jenny mercilessly. Like Jenny, she was wearing a simple skirt and blouse, but hers bore not the slightest resemblance to any kind of uniform. The dramatic scarlet silk shirt and matching wool skirt, the simple silver chains and oversize hoop earrings made a fashion statement Jenny wouldn't know how to begin to emulate—even if she could afford to.

And on top of all that, Serena was a psychiatrist. Jenny tried to swallow the dry, hard lump in her throat and reminded herself that she wasn't a weird hippie kid any longer. She was a lawyer. Well, she would be in a matter of months.

Eventually they were seated around a glass-topped table. Even having Zach sit next to her and take her hand firmly in his didn't help Jenny much.

Serena scared her silly. The size and opulence of this damned mansion scared her silly, when it came down to it. It was probably lucky Zach's father wasn't around yet, or he'd scare her silly, as well. She was ashamed of herself for being such a coward, but it didn't change how she felt. She actually could feel her knees trembling in their damned navy tights.

"You're a lawyer, Jenny?" Serena's polite question sounded like the beginning of an inquisition to Jenny.

"Not yet. I'm a third-year student."

"Oh? And have you decided yet where you'll be articling?"

"I've had interviews and offers from several firms. There's one firm out in New Westminster I think I'd like. They had toys for kids in the waiting room."

"Toys?" Serena's smooth brow wrinkled ever so slightly. "I'm afraid I don't see what toys have to do with articling."

"I figure a firm that cares about kids cares about people in general. That's what the law's really about, isn't it? People."

Serena was looking at her as if she were exhibiting signs of mental aberration.

A tall, angular woman came out the sliding doors and over to them. "You having drinks, or tea, or what, Ms. Lucille? Zachary, hello there. About time you came to see us. You need a haircut, young man."

Zach got to his feet and went over to give the woman an affectionate hug, leading her over to where Jenny was sitting. "Eva, I'd like you to meet Jenny Lathrop. Jenny, Eva Kramer."

Jenny got to her feet and shook hands. Eva's narrow dark eyes assessed her thoroughly, and then she smiled at her.

Jenny refused a drink, choosing tea instead, and Lucille went off with Eva to help bring a tray.

"Is your family from Vancouver, Jenny?" Serena was on the trail again, and Jenny drew in a deep breath. She might just as well lay out the facts about herself like playing cards, faceup, right now, and let Serena draw her own conclusions. It would stop all this verbal fencing, and she had nothing she needed to hide.

Zach had her hand again, and she felt the reassuring warmth of his strong fingers around her own. She turned slightly, meeting Serena's disconcerting gaze head on.

"My mother's dead," she began, "and my father's somewhere in Mexico, I don't know exactly where. I grew up on a farming commune...."

THEY WERE BACK in Jenny's apartment late that night, with the lights out, the door locked, and snuggled down amid the blankets.

Jenny traced the hard planes of Zach's face with her hand, loving the feel of his muscular arm beneath her head, the weight of his leg across her thighs. The loving had been tumultuous, and they lingered in its afterglow, feeling peaceful and lethargic.

"You look like your dad, but you're a lot more relaxed than he is. Is he always that dressed up, or was it just because I was there, Zach?"

His voice was slow, lazy and drugged with recent passion. "He's always like that. I used to wish when I was a kid that he'd come out and throw a football with me, like some of the other kids' dads did. But it's tough to play football in a three-piece suit. Dad's a lawyer, through and through. He doesn't know any other way to be. It was Eva's husband, Karl, who taught me things like how to throw a football and fix a bicycle." With a sad note in his voice, he added, "Karl died a few years ago. I still miss him."

"So Eva's been with your family for a long time?"

"Ever since I was a baby. Technically, she's our housekeeper, but she and Mom are also good friends. And she's like a second mother to Serena and me."

"I love your mom." Her fingers traced the outline of his ear. She hadn't expected it to happen; she'd been a wreck at the thought of meeting his mother. And then Lucille had charmed her, put her at ease. "She's the kind of mother everybody needs—so warm and approving and affectionate."

It was Serena and Theodore Jones she ought to have been apprehensive about.

Zach was like his mother, Jenny reflected. And Serena—Jenny snuggled deeper into the cave of blankets, feeling suddenly chilled. Serena was exactly like her father: stiff, formal, seemingly unable to show any trace of human emotion.

"What was your mom like, Jenny? You never really say what your parents were like, you know. You skip the details."

She realized that was true. He'd taken her home to meet his family; surely he deserved a closer look at hers?

"You want to see some pictures of them? I've got some somewhere." She wriggled out of his arms and turned on the bedside light, pulling a cheap black cardboard album out of a dresser drawer. He punched the pillows into shape behind them and wrapped a quilt around their shoulders against the nighttime chill of the room.

The pictures seemed old, like moments from long ago frozen in time.

"This was when Mom and Dad were married. They waited until I was four before they made it legal. I told you they were hippies. That's me, with the flowers."

It was taken in a grassy field. A young and beautiful woman, fragile in a flowing Indian-style dress, and wearing a beaded headband low on her forehead, stood looking up at the tall, thin man with the luxuriant beard standing beside her. Her thick hair fell in loose waves past her waist. They held hands—the man and woman.

The child who had been Jenny, bare-legged and chubby, clutched a fistful of wildflowers and leaned against her father's leg, somehow outside the invisible circle the other two had drawn. Her smile and her father's were identical.

"What're their names?"

"My mother was Clara. My dad's name's Jacob. Jacob Neilson."

"She's very beautiful, your mother. You look like her," Zach commented gallantly, but Jenny shook her head.

"Don't flatter me. I look more like my dad. It sounds weird, probably, but I never knew my mother all that well. She was always off in her own world, meditating or reading or teaching people about herbs and plants, or working out astrological charts. She was always busy, and she never seemed to want to be bothered with me much. People were attracted to her, because she was so pretty, and there were always friends around her. Somehow I got lost in the shuffle." She shrugged. "But living on a commune, there were other women around who took me under their wing, so I wasn't the least bit deprived."

"Were you closer to your father?" Zach was turning the album's pages, stopping at a picture of a smiling group of long-haired people, gathered around a rough-hewn table at Christmastime.

"Not really. He was a dreamer. He was trained as a typesetter, but all he really wanted to do was write poetry. The center of his universe was my mother. He loved her so much, there wasn't room for anyone else. He was brokenhearted when she died. I think that's why he stays in Mexico, because there's nothing there to remind him of her."

"Do you miss him?"

She met his eyes and nodded—a slow, silent acknowledgment that touched his soul. "I wish things were different between him and me. I used to wish I was part of a huge, close family instead of being an only child."

She pointed to the picture he was looking at. "These people were sort of like my family, I guess. They lived with us on the farm. Other people came and went over the years, but Mary, Sergio, Janet and Bob were always there while I was growing up. Janet's daughter and I were the same age. Her name's Ilona. They all live in New Zealand now. They emigrated and bought a sheep ranch. I still keep in touch with them. This is me, here, beside Uncle Bill." She pointed to a wizened little old man, bald, with huge ears and a crooked grin. Standing beside him, Jenny was gangly now, with glasses perched on her nose. The old man's arm was around her shoulders.

"He was Janet's uncle. She rescued him out of a state nursing home when he was seventy-two and brought him to live with us. You had Karl, I had Uncle Bill. He taught me how to cook. He was fabulous in the kitchen. He'd owned a delicatessen when he was young—lost it to a crooked partner. He lived to ninety-three."

Zach turned the pages, and Jenny saw herself through his eyes, turning from a little girl into a bespectacled teen, awkward and ill at ease. Toward the end of the album was her wedding picture.

Nick, not much taller than Jenny and looking uncomfortable in the new suit he'd bought for the wedding, smiled out at them shyly, holding Jenny's hand in his. She was wearing an Empire-waisted long white dress with embroidery around the hem.

"Nick was twenty-one here, I was seventeen. I can't believe how young we were. If I had kids, I'd never want them marrying that young," she said thoughtfully, staring down at the photo. "I mean, at that age I didn't even know what was possible yet. I didn't know how different I'd be when I got older. Back then, I'd never have dared to even dream of being a lawyer. Nick would have laughed if I'd suggested it."

"Wouldn't he have been supportive of you?"

She thought about it, then shook her head. "I don't think so. He came from a traditional family. His father worked, his mother raised the kids, and that's how he figured it should be. I always had some kind of job after we were married, but Nick was never very happy about it. We needed the money, though, because his jobs in construction weren't steady. But for me to have pursued a career as a lawyer . . ." She considered it, and smiled sadly. "He'd have fought it. It would have made him feel inferior." She looked up into his eyes. "He wasn't self-assured, the way you are, Zach. He was gentle and kind, but he didn't have much education, and he didn't read a lot, either."

She looked down again, at the album. "I've often thought that if Nick had lived, we'd probably have been divorced by now," she said sadly. "We weren't well suited at all. He was the first boyfriend I ever had. How did I know what to look for in a husband?"

"Do you now, Jenny?" His voice was low, and there was a strange catch in it.

Jenny's heart skipped a beat. All of a sudden, she realized she was on dangerous ground here. She'd been babbling away, not realizing where this conversation was leading.

"I'm not looking for one now," she managed to say lightly. "I enjoy being on my own. Besides, what kind of life would the poor guy have? You know yourself how little time there is when you're a student. And then articling—I've heard you only work ten or twelve hours a day, if you're lucky. He'd be stuck with all the cooking and cleaning. And in case you haven't noticed, I can get pretty bad-tempered at times."

He didn't say anything. She could feel his warm breath on the side of her neck, his leg touching hers under the covers.

Almost like a reprieve, the telephone began to ring in the next room. Jenny scrambled off the bed and dragged her flannelette gown on over her head, feeling absurdly relieved by the interruption.

"You go to sleep," she said, pulling his socks over her bare feet. "It's probably Veronica. She's the only one who ever calls me this late. I'll try to get rid of her, but it's liable to take a while."

She hoped fervently that when she was gone he'd forget what they'd been talking about.

Zach lay with his arms behind his head, hearing the low mumble of Jenny's voice from the other room. The album was closed, resting on her pillow, but the images were clear in his mind.

It had answered so many of his questions, that album; laid to rest a lot of things he'd wondered about. But there were other questions it hadn't answered fully.

The image of the little girl, leaning against her father's leg, came to him clearly, and compassion for that child filled him. Even in the picture, Clara and Jacob formed an inner circle that Jenny wasn't part of.

It was hard to imagine what her childhood had been like. He had only his own to compare it with—private schools, Karl picking him up every day, his mother and Eva loving him—spoiling him, when it came right down to it.

It sounded to him as if Jenny hadn't been spoiled at all; or even loved the way she ought to have been—the way he and Serena had been loved. Stiff as his father was, Zach had never doubted Theodore Jones's devotion to his children. His father was like a rock that the family rested upon: always there, always reliable.

Jenny had described her father as a dreamer. Dreamers were nice, but they weren't necessarily reliable.

And Nick Lathrop, the rather ordinary man whom Jenny had been married to for six long years . . .

In his mind, Zach had been gradually building Jenny's dead husband into a paragon of men, better at everything than Zach could ever be. The wedding picture and Jenny's blunt words had rectified that impression. As Jenny had said, there was nothing similar between Nick Lathrop and himself.

There was no basis for comparison, good or bad, because they were different people.

It was comforting knowing that, believing it.

Today had been a landmark day in many ways. Jenny was the first woman he'd deliberately taken home to meet his family. Not that he needed or wanted their approval; it was simply a way of letting Jenny get to know him better.

Why?

He frowned up at the newly painted ceiling. Why was it important to him that Jenny meet his family, understand his background, his roots?

The answer slid into his mind almost casually, as if it had been waiting in the wings for him to finally address the question.

He was going to marry Jenny Lathrop. He'd known it on a gut level for some time now without consciously admitting it to himself. And though there were any number of horrific problems to be overcome—not the least of which was Jenny's indifference to having a husband—he'd give her time.

He heard her now, saying goodbye at last. "See you tomorrow afternoon, then. Night, Veronica."

Tomorrow afternoon? Tomorrow was Sunday. He'd planned on taking Jenny out on his sailboat.

She tiptoed into the room, thinking he was asleep. When she saw he wasn't, she made a flying leap at the bed, scurrying under the covers and pressing her icy body against his warmth.

"I'm frozen! It's cold out there. Veronica asked me to meet her for a cup of tea downtown tomorrow. She sounds desperately lonely. You don't mind, do you, Zach?"

He was methodically taking off the flannel nightgown, pulling his socks off her feet, warming her bare flesh with his hands and his body.

"Mind? Why should I mind? I'm going to have to spend the afternoon working on the Solomen case anyhow, so I'll probably miss dinner. The examination for discovery went ahead with no problems, and the trial is scheduled for the first week in November."

So he'd have a wife who spent Sundays having tea with bag ladies. He had no doubt Jenny would end up inviting Veronica or someone like her to their home for a good meal, if it came down to it.

What the hell. He'd learn to live with that.

A wicked grin came and went as he felt her beginning to melt under his conscientious stroking.

Maybe they'd invite his father over for one of those eclectic meals.

Zach had a feeling the unflappable Theodore Jones might have an exciting few years ahead of him, getting to really know the future mother of his grandchildren.

9

SHE WAS NICE AND WARM again. In fact, a few moments ago in his arms, she'd been scalding hot. And the lovemaking had made him forget the awkward discussion they'd been having about marriage.

She was thinking of the phone call. "Zach, you'll never believe what Veronica was telling me just now."

"Probably not, but try me anyway." His voice sounded sleepy. She ought to let him rest. Why was it lovemaking made her talkative and him tired?

"Well, she was going on about some guy she's having a relationship with. It sounds like all they do is fight. She's always telling me about her boyfriends. It's sad, because I'm certain most of it's her imagination. Anyhow, tonight she suddenly started telling me this story about being married once, a long time ago, to some singer named Conroy Clark. She got mad at me because I'd never heard of him. She said he's made several records, and that he's well-known around town. You know anybody by that name?"

Zach was nearly asleep; she could tell by the way his words slurred together. "Yeah. Sings blues, good guitarist. G'night, honey." He yawned, snuggled her closer, cupped one large, gentle hand around her right breast, and began to snore gently.

Jenny lay coiled in the security of his arms, thinking about Veronica. As usual, the older woman had been drinking when she phoned. Jenny felt deeply sorry for her.

She had similar feelings for many of her clients at the Legal Clinic—even though she'd learned that some told her outright lies about their predicaments.

It irritated her; it was a big waste of time when people were dishonest. It was disillusioning, as well. She'd never admit it to Zach, but her compassion was coupled now with skepticism. Her clients were definitely poor and underprivileged, but sometimes it wasn't surprising to see how they'd ended up that way. They had trouble making good decisions, and a number had the idea that life owed them—despite their lack of initiative.

She went over her visit today with Zach's family. They were the other side of the coin: filthy rich by Jenny's standards; privileged members of the upper class. If it weren't for the man asleep at her side, she'd never have put herself in a social situation like the one she'd weathered today. Attending an intimate family dinner at the Jones mansion on Marine Drive wasn't exactly high on her list of priorities. It had been an ordeal, and more than anything else, it pointed out to her the chasm that separated herself from Zach.

Not that his family hadn't been nice to her; Zach's sister, Serena, had even suggested they have lunch together one day soon. Jenny had said something noncommittal, vowing silently that it would be a chilly day in hell before she willingly ruined a lunch hour by choosing to spend it with Serena Jones.

She could feel the fuzziness of sleep creeping over her. Her last coherent thought was that this wonderful man—this magic interlude in her life—couldn't possibly last much longer.

ANOTHER WEEK PASSED. Seven hectic days of hard work and seven nights far too short for the lovemaking that filled them. The Solomen case was due to go to trial soon, and Zach was buried under a mountain of paperwork.

It was late afternoon on Tuesday, and he'd waded through most of it when Brenda buzzed.

"Mr. Solomen on line two, Mr. Jones."

Zach picked up the receiver. "David, how are you, I'm just—"

"Zach, the Safefood people are picketing me. They're all around this building." David's quiet voice was tense. "They're handing out leaflets and hollering slogans and doing their best to stop people from coming inside. They've got these big signs with skulls and crossbones all over them, and my customers have slowed to a trickle."

"Well, that does it. I'll get an injunction, get them stopped. I need to know how many protestors are there, exactly what they're saying, if they're physically blocking entry . . ."

He asked questions and made notes. "Sit tight, David. I'll be over there with an injunction as soon as I can."

He briefed Brenda on what was going on as he hurried out. She was extremely interested in the Solomen case, and she'd been remarkably helpful in its preparation, staying late and helping Zach prepare his statement of defense.

It took time—far more time than Zach expected—to obtain the injunction. Judge Paisley was old and cautious, and he questioned and reread every form twenty-three times before he finally agreed to sign. By the time Zach hurried out of the courthouse and into his car, it was rush hour.

The trip across town was endless. When Zach finally arrived at the block of stores that included Solomen's Organic Produce Mart, it was dusk, and he half expected the protestors would have packed up and gone home.

Instead, there seemed to be a riot going on in front of David's store. Several police cars were drawn up on the curb, red lights flashing, and a large, noisy crowd had gathered on the periphery of the action.

Zach shouldered his way through—official document safe in his briefcase, and a sense of foreboding growing in his stomach as the angry voices of the crowd grew louder.

As he drew near, he could see that the large front window of Solomen's store had been shattered, and the bins under the awning that had held fruits and vegetables were overturned. Oranges, lettuce and grapefruits were scattered everywhere.

A mobile TV-news truck was on hand, as well as several reporters.

"Who's in charge here? I'm Mr. Solomen's lawyer and I have a court order barring these people from any further picketing." The young officer Zach questioned pointed toward a police car where another officer was standing. Zach walked over and explained to the burly sergeant about the court order, and then demanded, "What happened here?"

The sergeant shook his head. "Started out with just these protestors, but then a lady came along, real feisty, started telling them what to do with their signs, and the big tall guy over there, name of Paul Jensen, he hassled her, calling her a few names and crowding her some. He's the organizer of this whole thing. Anyhow, Solomen came charging out of the store and socked the guy a good one. They had a battle over there on the sidewalk, and the other protestors went right out of control."

The sergeant shook his head in disgust. "Somebody in the crowd threw a chunk of cement through the window, smashed it to smithereens, somebody else turned over the bins, the lady got in the act and kicked one of the protestors a good one. Don't usually see this kind of violence over somethin' like this. More often it's a strike where this happens. Never thought vegetarians were the violent sort. Anyhow, you got a court order, that's Paul Jensen over there you serve, the big guy with the bruise on his face and the bleeding nose. I'll just tail along, be sure he pays attention."

"Where's my client now? Mr. Solomen?" Zach half expected to hear that David had been taken to hospital.

"Inside the store, with the lady. This yo-yo Jensen's screamin' about pressin' charges, but with the window broken and all, I figure he's on thin ice there."

With the officer standing behind him, Zach read the court order and handed it to the sullen Jensen.

The officer, with the help of a loud-hailer, informed the protestors that either they disappeared or they faced arrest, and within minutes the area was cleared. Only the television people with their mobile cameras were left on the scene, and they came hurrying over to Zach.

"I understand you're Mr. Solomen's lawyer. Can you tell us what's going on here?"

As clearly and concisely as he could, Zach told a young woman reporter about the picketing and the injunction, avoiding any judgmental comments.

"Can you tell us more about the impending court case against Mr. Solomen? We understand he's selling contaminated produce...."

Zach walked away without further comment. A frightened young clerk unlocked the front door and let him into the store, and Zach headed up the stairs at the back to where he knew David's office was.

He opened the door, and found David Solomen with his arms around a curvaceous blond woman. They were kissing—a passionate kiss that broke off reluctantly when Zach cleared his throat. "Sorry to interrupt, but I need to know exactly what happened out there."

They turned toward him, and Zach could hardly believe his eyes.

The woman in David's arms was Brenda Pennington, and she had the beginnings of a spectacular black eye.

STILL GLEEFULLY PLANNING the conversation he would have with Brenda the following morning at the office, Zach drove to Jenny's. She'd offered to cook him dinner tonight, and he was good and late, but she'd understand when he explained what had happened.

He glanced at his watch. Damn, it was almost nine. He'd tried to phone from David's store, but there was no answer at the apartment, which bothered him a little.

Where was Jenny, anyhow?

The basement door was unlocked. Zach hurried in. The apartment was empty, but there was the smell of onions cooking, and a pot of potatoes by the sink. A bowl of apples, half peeled, lay abandoned on the table beside the phone. There was also a note.

Veronica in trouble. Gone to city jail to rescue her. Can you pick me up at her house, 4905 Powell? Will wait for you there.

J.

Feeling as if he'd taken up permanent residence in his car, Zach drove downtown. Veronica's address was in a rough area. Zach parked the car under a streetlamp and locked it. A gang of young toughs on the corner eyed the sports car and made remarks about Zach's suit. An old man staggered by, so drunk he was barely able to stay upright.

Feeling edgy, Zach hurried along the sidewalk, trying to read the numbers on the run-down buildings. The houses here were close together, their front doors only a few feet from the crumbling sidewalk. Most of them were in darkness. Halfway down the street, Zach found 4905 and stumbled his way up the rotting front steps to ring the bell.

There was no answer. There wasn't any light at the front of the house, either. He tried again and decided the bell wasn't working. The front door was locked.

What the hell was going on here, and where was Jenny?

There was a faint light and the muted sound of voices coming from the back, so he fumbled his way around the side of the house, muttering curses under his breath, when he tripped on something and almost fell.

There was a small porch with two steps. The door was half glass, and just before Zach raised his hand to knock he looked inside. His hand dropped.

The tableau was lit harshly by a naked bulb that dangled at the end of a cord hanging from the kitchen ceiling. Jenny was backed against a cupboard, and there was fear in her eyes. Veronica, with one arm doubled up behind her back, was being held by a short man with a huge stomach. His face was a deep bloodred, and Zach could hear Veronica's hysterical voice through the door.

"Nobody uses me for a mud slide! Get your filthy hands off me, Louie—"

Zach took a deep breath, gripped the doorknob, twisted, and threw it open violently. It smashed back and into the wall.

As loudly and forcefully as he could, Zach bellowed, "What's going on in here? Take your hands off that woman! What d'you think you're doing? Move away, just move away...."

Keeping up a steady stream of commands, he swiftly placed himself between the man and Jenny, watching for a knife or gun and feeling the adrenaline course through his veins. If the guy had a weapon, this could get ugly fast.

Veronica screamed at the top of her lungs when he burst in—a shocking, high-pitched siren of sound—and the man hollered, "Holy Jesus! It's the cops!" He dropped Veronica's arm and whirled so he was facing Zach.

Veronica immediately turned to the cupboard, picked up a plate, and smashed it over his bald head. He let out a roar of pain, and pieces of crockery flew everywhere. A bright spot of blood appeared on his shiny skull, and he reached a hand up to check for damages, staring at the blood in horror.

"Jesus, woman, you cut me! What the hell—"

"Asshole! Liar! Cheat!" Without a pause, Veronica grabbed a pot from the sink, full of oily water, and tossed it over the man, then raised the pot to hit him with it.

Greasy water dripping off his head and shirt, he raised his arms to protect himself, backing toward the door. "Whatsa matter with you? You crazy or somethin'? You're crazy, y'hear me?"

Veronica advanced, hollering, "Get out, you creep! I never want to see you again!"

The man reached the doorway, threw himself out and raced into the darkness. Veronica slammed the door behind him and locked it.

There was a moment of silence in the kitchen. Zach could feel the tension in his muscles gradually begin to ease. He turned toward Jenny and she collapsed in his arms. He could feel her body trembling.

"God, Zach, I've never been so glad to see anybody."

Zach held her tightly, aware as never before how fragile her body felt against his. He looked over her head at Veronica, who was now taking off several of her coats, although her red toque was still pulled down over her ears. She was muttering to herself under her breath.

"What the hell is going on here, Jenny? Mrs. Glickman, where's your phone? I'm calling the police."

Veronica looked at him as if he were demented. "What for?" she queried, using one foot to gather the pieces of glass into a careless pile. "That's just Louie. He figured he could stay here but I kicked him out. He won't be back. Anyhow, I don't have a phone. Wouldn't want to get Louie in trouble even if I had. I know that creep. He's just a coward. There's no point in getting the police involved." Her face drew into an angry grimace. "Two-timin' little snot, I oughta broke his head for him good." She moved around the kitchen, opening the oven door and taking out a kettle. "Lucky thing I can take care of myself. You and me both can. Right, Miss Jenny? You want some tea? Or maybe a drink. I know there's some rye around here somewhere, 'less that sponger drank it...." Muttering to herself, she began opening cupboard doors and poking in drawers.

Zach unhooked Jenny's arms from their death clasp on his rib cage and held her away from him. Her face was pale, every freckle standing out in bold relief.

"Jenny, will you tell me what the hell this is all about? What are you doing down here in the first place?"

Her glasses were crooked and she reached up and straightened them. She looked embarrassed as she explained.

"Veronica phoned a couple of hours ago from the city jail. She'd been picked up for causing a disturbance in a bar, and she was pretty upset. I only had money for taxi fare one way, so that's why I left you that note. Anyhow, they released her on my recognizance and we walked over here. That man, Louie, was here in the kitchen, waiting. It was him Veronica had the fight with in the bar. She says he's been living with her, and she caught him tonight with another woman, and she lost her temper. He seemed violent. I didn't know for sure what he'd do next, and each time I tried to get out the door to go for help, he came at me." She shuddered. "There's no phone, and I wasn't sure any of the neighbors would come and help, anyhow. It's a pretty strange neighborhood. I was really scared," she confessed in a small voice.

Zach could feel his tension turning to horror as he imagined all the atrocities that might have occurred. "Let's get the hell out of here."

Jenny nodded. Veronica was still searching aimlessly through cupboards, and Jenny went over to her and took her arm to get her attention. "Veronica, we're going now. You stay inside and keep the doors locked tonight. No more brawling in bars, either. You understand?"

Veronica nodded cheerfully. "You got a smoke? I'm clean out of cigarettes."

Jenny sighed. "You know I don't smoke. Now, you heard what I told you? No going out—not for cigarettes or anything else. If the police see you wandering around again tonight, they'll haul you in. You heard what they said. I promised them I'd bring you straight home and you'd stay here."

"And I will." Veronica sounded insulted. "I'm a woman of my word, you know that, Miss Jenny." She gave Zach a long, measuring look. "Don't I know you? Weren't you the one got smacked that night at the Legal Clinic? Good thing you had a smart lady to rescue you that time, huh?"

Zach didn't answer. He was doing his best to keep his temper in check, but it was a losing battle. He was tired, and he was hungry. He wanted nothing more than to get Jenny and himself out of here and he didn't need any smart-mouthing from Veronica. The past few hours had been far too full of tension, and he still wasn't sure they were out of the woods.

"C'mon." He took Jenny firmly by the arm and led her through the dark house to the front door, aware of the sweet, sickly smell of years of neglect that permeated the place. He stumbled over various pieces of furniture and random boxes of junk as he went.

He fumbled with the chain lock and opened the front door. He looked carefully up and down the street before he led Jenny down the steps to the sidewalk, hustling her along to where he'd parked his car, grateful that Louie seemed to have vanished. So had everyone else. The dingy street was deserted.

About to unlock the passenger door, he stared in horror at an inch-wide gouge etched into his paint job, stretching from the back bumper to the front fender. There was an identical scratch on the driver's side.

He looked up and down the street for whoever was responsible, but there wasn't a single person in sight. Even the gang on the corner had disappeared.

A slow rage began to build inside him. He climbed in and slammed the door, thrust the key in the ignition and as soon as the motor caught, roared away, his jaw clenched.

"Zach?" Jenny's voice was uncertain. "I'm sorry about the car."

He made a superhuman effort at controlling his anger and failed. Furious words—words of anger compounded by frustration and fear for her safety—spilled out.

"It's not just the damned car, Jenny. I can have the car repainted. All I can think of is what might have happened to you back there. Do you have any idea how it makes me feel, having you wandering around this area alone at night, ending up in situations like that one? What if I hadn't made it down here when I did?"

She was immediately defensive. "But Veronica's my client. I can't very well just ignore a call from her when she needs me, can I?"

Zach tried to curb his anger, tried to inject some reason into his tone. "Jenny, it wouldn't hurt to let her sit it out in jail for a couple of hours, to wait until I could go with you."

She immediately got huffy. "Veronica can't stand being locked up. She goes crazy. She has this phobia. Besides, I don't need a chaperon, Zach. I'm a grown woman. I'm a lawyer—or I will be in a few months."

What was left of his control snapped. "You've got a hell of a lot to learn before you call yourself a lawyer! You fall for every cock-and-bull, down-and-out story you're handed. You let yourself get sucked into downright dangerous situations like this one tonight."

"For heaven's sake, Zach, I made an error in judgment. Don't you ever make mistakes?"

"Not with clients. I do my homework. I don't fall for every sob story I hear. I check out the facts." He could hear himself, sounding as righteous as a television evangelist, and couldn't seem to stop. This whole thing had gone too far. Things that had been sore points for weeks were close to the surface now, ready to erupt like boils. His voice was thick with disgust. "People like Veronica and that…Louie…Damn it, Jenny! You go on believing they're victims, when it's really *you* who's the scapegoat in the whole thing. You don't even get paid for putting your life on the line this way, for God's sake."

As soon as he said it, he knew it was the wrong, the very worst thing he could say. His mouth just seemed to have clicked into automatic.

"So, really, you're furious with me because I don't get a nice fat fee for what I'm doing. Isn't that right?" Her voice was trembling. "With you, it always comes down to money in the end, doesn't it? This much time and effort and concern equals this much money. To hell with the human factor."

"Don't be ridiculous. Money has nothing to do with this, and you know it."

"Oh, but it has everything to do with it! If Veronica were rich, you'd probably take her on as a client yourself, eccentric or not. If—" her voice was going out of control, and he was sorry he'd ever started all this "—if Elias Redthorn had money, he'd at least have some compensation for having to wear that body brace the rest of his life."

Zach slammed a hand down on the steering wheel. "How in God's name did Elias bloody Redthorn get into this? Would you tell me that?"

She gulped and went straight on. "Because if he had money, your precious firm would have taken his case. If . . ." She sniffed hard and scrabbled through her purse for a tissue, without success.

Zach found one in his pocket and handed it to her, and she blew her nose hard. He knew exactly where this was heading, and he didn't want to hear about it tonight.

Before she could say anything, he heard himself snarl, "And I'm sick to death of hearing about how you and those other poor women were taken advantage of by big bad business lawyers when your husband was killed, so don't bother telling me all over again."

Even as he said it, he knew why. He was a jealous fool, and he didn't want to be reminded she'd had a husband she cared about.

"Stop this car right now." Her hand was on the latch, and she had the door open.

"Jesus, Jenny—"

He reached for her arm with one hand and pulled sharply to the curb with the other.

Jenny pried his hand off her arm and slid out. "If you're that tired of hearing what I have to say, then you don't have to listen anymore, because I never want to see you again, Zachary Jones." She slammed the door hard enough to wreck the hinges.

"Jenny, get back in this car—"

A bus pulled up beside him and the driver leaned on the horn, glaring down at him. He was in a bus zone. Zach cursed and pulled out, watching for a parking spot. He found one just in time to see Jenny get on the bus.

Fuming, he pulled out into traffic and stepped ferociously on the gas. He'd wait for her at her place, and they'd get this straightened out, once and for all. He was zigzagging at a reckless speed through traffic on Broadway when he heard the siren.

The policeman asked if he'd been drinking, then gave him a lecture and a sizable ticket. When the patrol car pulled away at last, Zach sat for a minute or two, breathing slowly in and out. This wasn't his night.

Carefully, he started his engine and drove to his apartment. There were times when a temporary retreat was in order, and this was one of them.

He had a full bottle of Scotch in the cupboard over the refrigerator, and he broke the seal and poured himself a water glass full, with two ice cubes, before he dialed Jenny's number.

The line was busy.

He spent the next three hours alternately waiting for Jenny to phone him, trying to call her, and drinking whiskey.

Each time he dialed, the line was busy.

He finally realized she'd unplugged the phone, and that enraged him so much he had two more drinks.

He'd go over and have this out with her first thing in the morning, by God. *Before* he went to work.

He fell asleep on the couch at quarter past three.

10

BRENDA CALLED the apartment at nine forty-five the next morning, dragging Zach out of a drugged sleep and into a world of pain.

After twenty rings, he finally managed to find the telephone, aware only that he was in agony. His head had been invaded by demons, his stomach was churning, and it was beginning to dawn on him that he'd had a serious disagreement with Jenny.

He lifted the receiver and managed to indicate that he was still alive. Barely.

"Mr. Jones, the investigator, Mr. King, is here. You had an appointment with him this morning to go over the reports on the Solomen case. And you have to file the Pattison documents with the court registrar at one. And then you have appointments with two clients, one of them is Mr. Tremone from Hart, Mason and Stewart. And, Mr. Jones?"

Zach cleared his throat and managed a hoarse, "Yes, Brenda?"

"I really need to talk to you, too, Mr. Jones." It was the first time in over four years he'd ever heard her sound vulnerable.

"How's that shiner this morning, Brenda?" He'd had a whole list of smart remarks to tease her with, but his own misery made them seem cruel. Pain was a great leveler.

"Awful. I'm wearing dark glasses, but I'm still liable to scare away clients." The words were meant to be an attempt at humor, but her voice quavered. "And there're pictures in the morning paper, and Mr. Meredith and Mr. Hanover saw the whole episode on the late news last night. They said your tie was crooked. They've been quite vocal about my eye, as well."

Zach just bet they were vocal. Brenda had given them all enough tongue-lashings over the years about their own escapades to make this seem a golden opportunity for getting even.

He couldn't really blame them; he'd been planning something of the sort himself last night.

"Never mind them, Brenda. They're green with jealousy, seeing you with David Solomen. Look, take it easy. I'll be in as soon as I can. Ask Ozzie if he can wait half an hour. Knowing him, he'll bill me for the time anyway."

The moment the phone was free, he dialed Jenny's number.

It rang fourteen times before he hung up. Obviously, she'd already left for classes.

It took heavy-duty pain-relief capsules and a boiling-hot shower to enable him to get as far as the office.

A genuinely subdued and bruised Brenda took one look at him and poured him a giant mug of freshly brewed black coffee.

"You look dreadful, Mr. Jones." She sounded truly concerned.

He squinted at the oversize dark glasses she wore and the pallor of her face under the careful application of makeup.

"Well, you don't look half bad, Brenda," he managed to lie gallantly. "Women must be tougher than men."

When it came right down to it, there was a lot of compensation to having a Brenda Pennington with a few human problems. Any other time, she'd have tormented him with righteous remarks about alcoholism and taken delight in feeding him lukewarm instant coffee.

"Mr. King is waiting up in your office."

Zach took two long swallows from his mug and struggled up the stairs.

"Mornin', young man." Investigator Ozzie King was in fine form, suit as rumpled as ever, bloodshot beagle eyes quick to take in Zach's condition. "Tied on a good one, did ya? Happens to the best of us, counselor. I brought in these surveillance reports." He gestured to an enormous stack of paper on Zach's desk. "I'll go over them with ya now. There's a few details I need to explain."

It took eons. Ozzie left nothing out—which was why the firm used him—but his insistence on covering every last bruise on every last grapefruit meant that Zach had to swallow two more painkillers and then skip lunch in order to get rid of Ozzie and still arrive at the registrar's office at one. When he was finished there, he tried to get hold of Jenny by calling the law faculty at UBC, but after an interminable wait he was told she couldn't be located.

He dragged himself back to the office and found Brenda waiting anxiously for him.

"I really need to talk with you, Mr. Jones. It's urgent." She looked as bad as it was possible for a ravishing blonde to look, which Zach figured was about one millionth as bad as he looked right about now.

"Unless we do it over some lunch, Brenda, it's going to have to wait until tomorrow. I haven't had anything to eat yet today, and I'm about to collapse. How long have we got before my next appointment?"

She consulted the diary. "Exactly forty-five minutes. But Mr. Tremone is usually about ten minutes late."

"Let's go."

Brenda's ironclad policy had always been not to accept so much as a ride from any of the partners. It was unfortunate that both Ken and Derek saw them leave the building and get into Zach's car, but their raised eyebrows, wolf whistles and smart remarks were way down on the list of things Zach felt like getting concerned about today.

He chose a restaurant nearby. The waitress brought him a steaming bowl of chicken soup to start, and Brenda ordered a large salad and herbal tea. "I've been a vegetarian for years," she explained when Zach urged her to join him in having a steak.

In four years of working with her every day, Zach hadn't known that. There were probably lots of things about Brenda he didn't know, and the thing was, now that he had Jenny, he wasn't even mildly curious. A few months ago, talking Brenda into having lunch with him would have been a major coup. Today, all he could think about was Jenny and the quarrel they'd had.

A feeling of depression overwhelmed him.

Brenda considerately waited until he was almost done spooning up the broth before she began.

"I wanted to talk to you about David Solomen," she said at last, and her lovely skin flushed a dusky rose beneath the dark glasses still hiding her eyes. She fidgeted with her cutlery and refolded the napkin she hadn't used.

"Now, why isn't that a surprise?" Zach was trying to make her smile, but it was hopeless. "You're in love with him, right?" he added in a much gentler tone. He knew all about being in love. It could hurt like hell.

"Yes, I am. He's—" Brenda flushed "—he's everything I ever wanted in a man. But we have problems that I need to discuss with you. There are things he hasn't told you."

Zach's stomach gurgled. "Omigod. He's contaminating his own vegetables? He's paying somebody off to do it? The whole case is a big fraud?"

He was only half joking. Today he had the feeling that anything was possible—as long as it was bad.

"Please, Mr. Jones, don't tease at a time like this." Brenda was visibly upset. "David is the most honorable man I've ever met. He would never do anything like that."

"Thank the powers that be for minor blessings." Zach slouched back in his seat. There was a limit today to how much he could deal with calmly.

The waitress arrived with his steak and Brenda's salad.

"You really shouldn't load your system with dead flesh, plus all that dairy," she admonished when he began loading on sour cream, chives and five packages of butter into his baked potato. "It clogs your arteries. You're not all that young anymore, Mr. Jones. If you must have the steak, you ought to just have salad with it. You shouldn't mix protein with heavy carbohydrates."

He gave her a long look, and she blushed and then kept quiet about his eating habits.

When he'd devoured a fair portion of his food, she blurted, "First of all, I wanted to thank you for taking David's case on contingency. I know you had a hard time getting Mr. Meredith and Mr. Hanover to agree. David was probably too proud to tell you why he doesn't have any money. Am I right?"

"He didn't go into detail, no." Zach took another bite of the steak. The food was gradually easing the sickness in his stomach, and he felt more alive than he had all day. He'd try Jenny at home in an hour or so. She'd be finished classes early today. He'd pick her up and maybe they'd go to his place. They could make up on his water bed. . . . He forced himself to pay attention to what Brenda was saying.

"A lot of David's profits go to helping support his younger brother Melvin and Melvin's family, you see. David and Melvin were partners in the produce business, but Melvin was badly hurt in a car accident two years ago. He can't work, and he needs expensive therapy if he's ever to walk again. The insurance company found him not at fault for the accident, but there wasn't any settlement because the other guy was driving an out-of-province car with no insurance."

Zach now had a premonition of what was coming, and his heart sank. Why was this happening to him over and over again? First Jenny, now Brenda. First Redthorn, now Melvin Solomen. He began to eat his baked potato, listening to the rest of the story, knowing what Brenda was going to ask him to do. Being Brenda, she was as thorough as possible about setting him up.

"See, Melvin has three kids—three young boys—and David is making sure they get things like hockey equipment and football uniforms. He makes certain Melvin has the equipment and care he needs for rehabilitation. It costs a lot of money. David has all his own expenses, as well. When the stores are doing well, he just manages to make ends meet."

She fidgeted with her sunglasses and then took them off. Her eye was swollen, but she'd done a good job of masking it with makeup.

"I've offered to help. I've got some money from a few investments I've made, but David won't hear of it. And neither will he agree to getting married." She met Zach's gaze with a forlorn look. "He feels the financial pressure would eventually cause us problems. And maybe he's right. But the truth is, I'm not getting any younger myself, Mr. Jones. And now that I've found the man I want, I'd like to get married and get started on a family of my own."

Did David Solomen know what he was getting into here? But then he looked at her face, and felt rotten for thinking that way.

Tears were slowly trickling down her cheeks. She sniffed and took a deep breath, dabbing at her eyes with a napkin. "Mr. Jones, I know it's asking a lot, but could you look at the circumstances surrounding Melvin's case and maybe do something about it? They've had some guy from Legal Aid supposedly working on it, but he hasn't made any headway. They need a high-powered lawyer like you, Mr. Jones, if they're ever going to get anywhere. Oh, Mr. Jones, it would mean so much to me."

And what would it mean to Zach? She didn't say so, but of course the case would be *pro bono*. He thought of the money the firm had already spent on Solomen—the investigative charges, the time invested in preparing a statement of defense, the hours and hours spent going over evidence; and it was going to take at least another two days in court when the case was heard.

The fees were on contingency, and if he lost, the firm would be out a sizable amount of money. And there were no guarantees this new problem would result in a positive verdict, either. Even if it did, he'd never bill for his services. Not under the circumstances.

He ought to simply say no to Brenda. A few months ago, he'd have done just that without any qualms; he'd have hidden behind the firm's policies, his partners' decisions, his own hardheaded assumptions about business.

That was before Jenny. The story Brenda told was all too reminiscent of Jenny, of the situations she described both from her own life and from the lives of people at the legal-aid clinic.

Jenny had changed him—changed the way he reacted to people. A few months ago, he'd have considered what Brenda had just told him unfortunate, but not a deciding influence in his business dealings with Solomen. Hell, if it hadn't been for Jenny, he probably wouldn't be dealing with Solomen at all.

Because of Jenny, he'd been forced to see people differently than he had before—as individuals with circumstances and destinies less fortunate than his. Destinies he might have the ability to change, if he cared to.

He could hear Jenny's voice clearly, accusing him of basing his decisions solely on whether or not people could pay a nice fat fee.

Still . . . "If I were the only one involved, I wouldn't hesitate to take on Melvin's case," he began slowly. "The problem is, just as you said, Ken and Derek weren't happy about taking the Solomen case on at all, and I have to consider their reactions to a second one."

Brenda bristled. "The publicity the firm got last night should be worth something in itself, shouldn't it, Mr. Jones? We could remind Mr. Meredith and Mr. Hanover that publicity is worth money."

"It wasn't altogether positive publicity, Brenda." Zach tried to be gentle, but there was no escaping the fact that the papers had blown her role completely out of context, and emphasized her connection with the firm defending Solomen in a derisive sort of way. Paul Jensen was clever at manipulating the press, all right. Zach figured he was using the case as a publicity stunt, just as David had said he might.

Which definitely put David in the role of innocent victim.

"Look, Brenda, let me get this case of David's out of the way, and then I promise I'll give this other thing serious consideration."

Even if he didn't take Melvin's case through the firm, the least he could do would be to review the facts and make some recommendations. Hell, he could get Jenny involved. She'd love working on something like this, and she'd never give up until they won a settlement for Melvin, either. His spirits rose at the thought of working with her on it.

Brenda leaned across and put her hand on his, giving it a grateful squeeze. "I don't know how to thank you, Mr. Jones."

"There's one thing you could do, Brenda."

"What's that?"

"You could please for the love of God start calling me Zach."

THEY HURRIED BACK to the office, and Mr. Tremone was waiting, not pleased at all about the delay.

Somehow, Zach made it through the rest of the afternoon. When his last client finally left, he drove to Jenny's, using every shortcut he knew. A sense of urgency had been building in him all afternoon—a desperate need to see her, to smooth away the harsh words and anger of the night before.

He knocked, and she opened the door. She didn't rush into his embrace as he'd half hoped she might, and his heart sank. It would be easy, if only he could touch her, hold her. When she was in his arms, they never fought.

"Hello, Zach. Come in." She sounded remote and cool. This was going to be tough.

She looked pale and drawn—her bright hair a startling flash of color against her skin. Her blue eyes were tired-looking behind her glasses, and he felt remorse. She'd probably not slept well, and it was partly his fault.

"Jenny, I..." he began, but she interrupted, holding a hand up toward him, palm out, warding him off and talking quickly in a flat tone of voice, as if she'd prepared an unpleasant speech and was determined to deliver it.

"I've been doing a lot of thinking since last night, Zach, and this isn't going to work between us at all. What happened is bound to happen again—our beliefs and ideals about the law are too different. *We're* too different," she added with such a note of sadness in her voice that he longed to take the three steps that separated them, sweep her into his arms, and use his mouth to smother the things she was saying.

"I think it's better if we stop seeing each other. Permanently."

"Jenny..."

What was she saying? He took two steps toward her, and she moved away. There was an aloofness about her that infuriated him—an invisible barrier she'd put up between them. Her words registered, but he couldn't believe she meant them. He wanted to pull her into his arms, take her to the bedroom, grind his flesh into hers and make her cry out, hot and sweet and eager for his loving, the way she had so many times before.

"Jenny, that's ridiculous. So we had a disagreement. That's not the end of the world. Everybody has them. Surely we can talk it out."

Her eyes were unrelenting. "We *have* talked. As far as I'm concerned, there's nothing more to say."

But there was. He needed to tell her that he loved her, that the thought of not seeing her again was intolerable to him.

"I can't respect someone who puts money ahead of everything else," she said in a cool tone. "I can't respect someone who won't fight for the underdog without first thinking about a fee."

The unfairness of the accusation hit him like a punch in the gut. Pride kept him from defending himself. "Is that truly what you believe about me, Jenny?"

She stared at him for a long moment, and then she shrugged.

"What else can I believe? You've never given me any reason to think otherwise."

Before he could say anything else, she walked to the door, skirting around him carefully so she wouldn't touch him. She opened it and stood there.

"I think you'd better go now," she said in a stony voice, not meeting his eyes.

He thought of all the denials he could make, and then he thought about all the arguments they'd already gone through. Words weren't going to solve this. He'd tried that.

He considered taking her in his arms and using his lips and hands and body to change her mind. He knew if he did, it would work for right now. The sensual bond between them was overwhelming. But the time would inevitably come when the whole issue reared its head all over again.

Somehow, he had to find a way to convince her, once and for all, that she was wrong about his motives. It hurt—her assessment of him.

It was going to take time, and right now he was far too weary and heartsick and hung over to figure out a way. And her words were making him angry all over again.

"If that's how you really feel, I think you're right. I will go. Goodbye, Jenny."

HOURS LATER, curled in a miserable heap on her bed, she finally ran out of tears. She'd known all along it had to end; it was better to get it over with now, wasn't it? Before . . . before what? some remorseless voice interrupted.

Before she'd fallen hopelessly in love with him?

What a joke that was.

GOING TO THE LEGAL clinic the next night took every scrap of courage she possessed, but she needn't have been worried about it, because Zach didn't attend. An older lawyer, Mr. Humphreys, was there instead, and Jenny overhead one of the students asking him where Mr. Jones was.

"He won't be able to make it for a couple of weeks. He's tied up with a case that's taking all his time," Humphreys said.

Jenny felt a mixture of relief and wretched disappointment.

Some part of her had been hoping, in spite of everything, that Zach would be there.

And then what? He'd beg her to forgive him, she'd fall into his arms, and everything would be perfect forever?

Get real, Lathrop. Let him go. Don't humiliate yourself by chasing after what was only a dream.

But as day followed day, Jenny struggled with the almost-overwhelming urge to phone him, to grovel, to make any compromises with her conscience just to be able to be with him.

Like a blow to the chest that never stopped hurting, she came to understood at last the full extent of her feelings for Zach.

She loved him. In her entire life, she'd never loved a man this way; never loved any person with this degree of intensity. Every pore, every inch of her body, every sense longed for him, for the feel of his arms, the smell of his skin, the sound of his voice. When Nick was killed, she'd grieved for him, but not like this; not with this all-consuming physical and mental anguish. At times, she literally felt she'd die without him.

She couldn't sleep well. At first, food held no interest, and then she began to eat all the time, as if by filling her stomach, she'd fill the emptiness that losing him had left inside of her.

She was short-tempered with her clients at the Legal Clinic.

Ironically, now that Zach wasn't around to point it out, she could see clearly that for some of them the choices they'd made led directly to their problems. The more she became involved in their lives, the less she believed in an indifferent fate that penalized one person and allowed another to go free.

She began to see some of the self-destructive ways in which they created their own destiny.

Veronica was a case in point.

The second Thursday without Zach—which was how Jenny had begun to measure the days—Veronica was waiting for Jenny at the Legal Clinic just as she always was.

She didn't usually need legal advice; she considered Jenny her friend, and the clinic a social gathering.

"Hi, Miss Jenny. I brought you a doughnut for coffee break."

Jenny accepted the offering, wanly smiling her thanks, conscious as always of the pungent, moldy smell that emanated from Veronica's layers of clothing. Tonight she had at least four coats on, with the longest under the others. Crooked hemlines hung one below the other, one green, one dark brown, one beige, and the top one, black. She'd taken off her woolen toque, and her scarecrow hair stood up as if she'd suffered an electric shock. The inevitable cigarette dangled from one hand, unlit because the clinic was a non-smoking area.

Jenny wearily took her place behind her rickety table. She wondered how she was going to dispose of the doughnut without Veronica noticing. Small issues grew monumental now, and it seemed that life would never be full of laughter or wonder or joy again.

"Long and straight and dusty to the grave." Now, where had she read that? It certainly described her life without Zach.

Her first client, a lanky middle-aged man, ambled over and sat down. Jenny began the ritual of the waiver.

She glanced up from filling in the man's name and groaned aloud. Veronica had evaded the volunteer and was standing over Jenny's client, scowling down at him.

"No point even talkin' to him, honey," she announced in her rough voice, thrusting a finger under the man's nose. "He's nothin' but a con man. I know for a fact he gets Welfare under two different names. Probably wants you to figure out how he can set up a third, if I know him. You don't want to bother with the likes of that."

Naturally, Jenny's client objected to this, and it led to a loud argument between him and Veronica. Mr. Humphreys came hurrying over, and in a few moments, Veronica and the man were both assisted out the door, still shouting at one another.

Humphreys gave Jenny a mild lecture filled with advice about dealing with clients with mental problems, and Jenny was too despondent to even argue.

Veronica did have mental problems, and the truth was she was becoming a major nuisance.

Late that night, Jenny had just fallen into an exhausted doze when the phone rang. Heart thumping, knowing it couldn't be Zach but praying anyway, Jenny tumbled out of bed, ran blindly into the other room and picked up the receiver.

"Miss Jenny? Miss Jenny, I'm sorry for what happened tonight, but I was right. That man . . ."

Bitterly disappointed, tired to the bone, Jenny lost her patience and gave Veronica a tongue-lashing, adding that she didn't want Veronica phoning her at home again unless it was a true emergency.

Veronica started to cry, and Jenny felt like a heel. "I was just tryin' to help you out, one woman to another. I'm no bag lady, y'know," Veronica sniffled in her ear. "I got pride, I got friends, I got a house of my own. I don't hafta stay down here if I don't want to. I could sell for a bundle any time I like. And if I snap my fingers, old Conroy'll come back to me, too. See if he don't. He's playing at the Bayshore this week. You and that fancy boyfriend ought to go hear him. Conroy Clark's really somethin' to hear."

Jenny lost her temper all over again. "Veronica, that's all your imagination and you know it is. Now, get a grip on reality here. If you start bothering this Clark man, you're going to end up in jail, you hear me? And I won't be able to do a darned thing about it, either, so you—"

Veronica hung up in Jenny's ear.

TO FINISH a homework assignment a few days later, Jenny had to search a property claim at the Land Registry Office. When she had the information she needed, she looked up the tax information on Veronica's house, suspecting that her batty client was probably in serious arrears; but the taxes were paid up to date, always before they were due, always by check.

Payment was made—had been made for years—by a Mr. Conroy Clark.

SOMEONE WHO PUTS money ahead of all else.

Someone who won't fight for the underdog without first considering the fee.

Jenny's parting words had sliced into Zach like knife wounds. For the first few days, he felt lacerated, sliced open by her opinion of him, mortally wounded by the woman he loved.

Then he took refuge in cold, bitter anger. How could she believe he was heartless? How dare she accuse him of being a money-grubbing, selfish person? Didn't she know him better than that by now? He worked himself into a fury and told himself he was well rid of her.

At work, he was dangerously short-tempered. Ken and Derek began to avoid him.

Brenda couldn't. And one morning, after he'd snapped at her over the intercom again for very little reason, Zach looked up from some documents he couldn't make sense of to find her in his office.

He scowled. "What is it, Brenda? Surely you can see I'm busy."

Her bruised eye had healed, and she was giving him a look that might have made lesser men shiver in their Italian loafers.

"Look here, Mr—Zach." She shoved the door shut behind her and advanced toward his desk. "I'm sick and tired of having you suffer in silence and take out your foul temper on me." She plumped herself down in the leather client's chair and crossed her legs, causing her leather miniskirt to ride dangerously high on her thighs.

Zach didn't even notice.

"I came to you when I needed someone to talk to. Surely you could do the same with me. Your lady's dumped you, right?"

Zach gave her a look that ought to have shut her up forever, but Brenda was entirely unaffected. "Don't forget, Zachary, I've come to know you rather well in the years I've worked here. You've been foul-tempered before, but it's never lasted this long, and you've never been quite this . . . mean." She gave him a level look. "Are you in love with this Jenny

Lathrop? You've certainly changed since you've been seeing her, and I had thought for the better."

There wasn't much point in asking how Brenda knew about Jenny, or how much she knew. Zach figured she probably had meticulous files on every woman the three partners had dated for the past four years. He wondered for a moment if Interpol had any inkling what they'd slipped up on by not hiring Brenda Pennington.

He considered ordering her out of his office, but the anger that had sustained him for days was wearing thin enough to allow for a semblance of clear thinking.

What came through was the truth.

He slumped down in his chair and closed his eyes. Images of a redheaded vixen was there, waiting to taunt him.

"Yeah, I do. I do love Jenny Lathrop." It felt good to admit it.

"And she *has* dumped you?"

"For God's sake, Brenda, why don't you mind your own . . ." Zach glared at her.

Brenda didn't even blink.

Zach slumped again and sighed. "Yeah, she has. Irreconcilable differences having arisen, and all that."

Brenda stood and brushed her skirt into place with the air of someone who'd gotten to the root of a problem. "Well, then, Zachary, instead of acting like a bear with a sore head, I suggest you apply your fine mind to getting her back. You are a lawyer, after all. Lawyers are supposed to be good at logic, aren't they?"

She marched out.

Zach abandoned the file folders and did what Brenda had suggested. By noon, he'd arrived at several conclusions.

The first was that in spite of everything—and there was a lot of everything to consider here; it was Jenny he was dealing with—he loved her passionately, and he wasn't about to lose her. In fact, he was going to marry her, even if he had to carry her kicking and screaming to the altar.

That decision consoled him momentarily, and he considered ways and means of putting it into effect immediately.

But reason told him that if he went back and confronted her now, the way he longed to do, nothing between them would really have changed. Within days—hours, probably—the same old conflicts would surface all over again.

So, what were the sources of that conflict? And how could he best resolve them?

He tried to pinpoint the things that seemed to cause them the most trouble, and what he came back to repeatedly was Elias Redthorn.

Before that particular issue, they had argued; and he suspected that he and Jenny would always argue—with the same fervor they made love. But for some reason, the arguments had become bitter, and it had all started with Elias Redthorn. That case had devolved into a major sore point between them, probably because it seemed to symbolize to Jenny all the injustices she saw in the legal system.

The case had nagged at Zach, as well, even though he was far too proud to admit it to Jenny. The crippled man haunted him, and more than once he'd wished his partners had thought differently about the firm's taking it on.

The logical conclusion, therefore, was for Zach to do something about Elias Redthorn, damn his whiny little hide!

He was snowed under with the final preparations on the Solomen case—it went to court in exactly two days and four hours—but after that was out of the way, Zach vowed grimly, after that, it was Elias Redthorn all the way.

He pushed the button on the intercom.

"Yes, Mr—Zach?"

"Brenda, I'm going to need your help here. I need some files, from the legal-aid clinic. Could you please—"

"Would this have anything to do with Ms. Lathrop, Mr. Jones?"

Zach sighed. "Yes, Brenda. Yes, it would."

"No problem. I'll get you whatever you need. Nice to have you back, Zach."

There was such a thing as being too informal, and Brenda was on the verge. But he realized he was smiling for the first time in days.

11

THE SOLOMEN TRIAL took three days, and Zach had never been as emotionally involved in a case in his entire career. He did his absolute best, keeping a cool and contained persona both in court and outside, where he and the other people involved were besieged by the media.

Judge Munroe handed down his decision late on the afternoon of the third day.

"This court finds in favor of David Solomen."

They'd won. By God, they'd won! Zach felt a tidal wave of relief wash over him, mixed with heady elation. He gripped David's shoulder as the judge went on. "In the matter of Solomen versus Northwest Growers' Association, I award damages in the amount of $100,000 for loss of revenue and loss of opportunity.

"In the matter of *Solomen* versus *Safefood,* I award damages in the amount of $50,000 for damaging the reputation of Solomen Organic Produce Marts as suppliers in good faith of organically grown fruits and vegetables."

Zach turned to look at David. There were tears slowly rolling down the big, gentle man's cheeks, and he was making no effort to wipe them away.

"This court also directs that all of the costs in this action, plus legal fees, are to be borne by Safefood, who initiated these proceedings. The courts are not intended as a public forum. This matter could have been settled without the amount of publicity and public fanfare generated by a court action."

Afterward, David insisted on buying dinner for everyone at a vegetarian restaurant. Over glasses of apple juice, he announced that he and Brenda were engaged.

Brenda caught Zach's eye and held her glass up to him in a silent toast.

ALONE AT LAST, late that night, Zach sat in front of the television staring blindly at the screen. A talk-show host was holding forth, but earlier, the Solomen trial and the verdict had made the local news. Zach had squirmed at the sight of his own face and voice on the screen.

Ken and Derek had both phoned right after the broadcast, exuberant about his victory but also delighted with the amount of money and publicity the firm would receive from the case.

All in all, it *was* a marvelous victory, and Brenda had been right: The publicity was worth its weight in gold. So was winning a battle that he'd felt was morally right.

The one factor that made the whole thing bittersweet was not being able to share it with Jenny.

Each time the phone rang, his heart beat a little faster, as he hoped it might be her. But she hadn't called.

His mother did, bursting with excitement and pride, and even his father had come on the line. "Good work, son," was all he'd said, but Zach could count on one hand the number of times Theodore had said that to him.

Then Serena called, obviously proud of him, too; but like Theodore, she was very cool and reserved about it all.

"I thought I'd ask that young woman of yours, Jenny, to have lunch with me sometime soon," she remarked before she hung up. "Is she there with you, by any chance?"

How Zach wished he could say yes. "No, she's not," he admitted. "We had a blowup a couple of weeks ago. I haven't seen her since," he told Serena truthfully.

"And how do you feel about that?"

"Jesus, Serena, drop the analyst jargon, okay? If you really want to know, I feel suicidal, I feel brokenhearted, I feel devastated. But I've got a game plan here, and I'm going to get her back."

There was a long moment of silence, and then his sister's cool voice said, "I hope you're successful, big brother. I rather got the impression she wasn't one of your usual bimbos."

"Damned right, she isn't. I intend to marry Jenny." He almost added, "Whether she likes it or not."

There was another silence, longer this time. "I see. Well, if there's anything I can do to help . . ."

He got up after that call and poured himself another glass of the natural apple juice he'd bought on his way home. There was a lot to be said for the stuff. It wasn't Scotch by any stretch of the imagination, but it was wet, it filled the need to hold a glass in his hand at a time like this, and it wasn't going to give him a hangover in the morning.

He tried to imagine what Jenny was doing right at that moment. He figured probably sleeping, on her side the way she usually did, knees folded, arm beneath her head, hair tumbled all across the pillow.

He wistfully traced the shape and feel of her slight, warm body—the small, firm breasts, the rounded hips.

He became hard at the image.

Sighing, he chugged the apple juice down and planned his strategy in the matter of *Elias Redthorn* versus *the City of Vancouver*.

He'd begin the next morning using his success in the *Solomen* case as blackmail with Ken and Derek, to get them to agree to his taking on Redthorn.

He'd work his ass off and push for an early trial date on the thing—the sooner the better.

Because the sooner he got a sizable settlement for Elias Redthorn, the sooner he'd have Jenny back again.

HUNCHED ON HER new navy blue couch, Jenny sat bundled in her old flannelette nightgown, eating a bowl of cold cereal and watching Zach on television.

He was wearing his charcoal-gray suit with a pristine white shirt and the burgundy silk tie she'd undone numerous times. Seeing him made her tremble, and she set the cereal down on the floor, unfinished.

The attractive female news announcer sounded just the slightest bit breathless. "Give us your reaction to winning the *Solomen* case, Mr. Jones."

He smiled into the camera, and Jenny started to cry. That smile had been the first blurry thing she'd seen in the morning, when Zach was with her. She'd open her eyes, and he'd be smiling just like that, propped on an elbow, watching her struggle to wake up.

That memory intensified the loneliness that had grown intolerable these past weeks.

"It reassures me that justice is alive and well and living in Vancouver," he said. It was the perfect thing to say, Jenny thought as she blew her nose on a paper serviette; not preachy or boastful, just dignified and rather . . . honorable.

She was so proud of him she could hardly stand it.

"That was Zachary Jones, counsel for the defense in the case of *Safefood* versus *Solomen*. Judge Monroe handed down a landmark decision this afternoon, chastising the environmental group and penalizing them financially for what he terms the misuse of the judicial system. I'm Karen Baher, reporting from the courthouse."

Jenny blew her nose again, and thought uncomfortably of all the things she'd accused Zach of in that final, dreadful quarrel.

She'd known he was defending Solomen, and that the case was anything but a typical lucrative litigation case. He'd told her Solomen didn't have a lot of money, that he was fighting it on contingency. But she'd chosen to ignore that side of him.

Why hadn't she been willing to talk with him, discuss the things that were bothering both of them that night? Why had she forced the issue, said things that she knew would hurt him?

She'd been the one who ended it, not Zach. She'd asked him to leave. Why? Why wreck the one relationship in her life that truly was remarkable?

Because she was running scared.

Because her whole life had been a series of failures at loving, she'd been afraid to let herself believe that this time could be different. She'd been scared he would leave her, the way her mother had, her father, Nick—everyone she'd ever cared about. So she had engineered the final parting herself.

If I do it, you won't have a chance to. It won't hurt as much if I do it myself.

Oh, Zach, my beloved. What have I done to us?

She brought her knees up to her chest and held on tight as the bitter recognition spread through her.

The phone rang a long time later, and Jenny's heart leaped, just the way it always did before she could assure herself it wouldn't be Zach.

It wasn't him, of course. But it was his sister, Serena.

Jenny felt every nerve ending stand to wary attention. She fervently hoped that she didn't sound as if she'd been crying.

They went through a series of stilted formalities, and then Serena said, "Jenny, I thought it would be fun for us to get together for lunch one day this week. I just saw Zach on television. Wasn't he superb?"

Jenny wholeheartedly agreed.

"It reminded me that I haven't been in touch the way I promised. How about tomorrow? Are you free? I'll be on campus. We could meet at that little sandwich shop in the village."

God, she'd rather be guillotined than have to spend a lunch hour with Serena, Jenny thought in a panic. She couldn't keep up a facade of lighthearted chatter. She was far too vulnerable these days to be able to hide her misery for very long. Obviously, Serena had no idea Jenny and Zach had broken up. She wouldn't be wasting her time, taking Jenny's head apart to see what made it tick, if she knew Jenny was no longer a threat to the Jones dynasty.

Well, she wasn't about to enlighten her, Jenny decided. But she certainly wasn't about to strain her already shattered nervous system over a lunch with Serena Jones, either.

"I'm sorry, I can't possibly make it tomorrow." No explanation, no excuses. Who was it who said, Never apologize, never explain?

Silence for a long moment, and then, "What a shame. I was hoping . . . Well, perhaps another time soon. Give me a call. You can reach me either at home or at the Health Sciences psych unit on campus. Bye now."

Hands trembling, Jenny hung up.

THE FOLLOWING AFTERNOON, she was called out of her final class of the day to answer the phone. It was an emergency, the caller had insisted.

It was Veronica.

She was in jail again, charged with shoplifting.

"Shoplifting? Shoplifting. Jeez, Veronica, what did you go and do that for?" Jenny was thoroughly out of patience with her.

Weeping and stammering, Veronica begged Jenny to come and get her out. The recollection of the last time she'd rescued Veronica was all too fresh in Jenny's mind, and she hesitated.

"Please, oh, please, Miss Jenny. I can't stand being locked up. You know I can't. Please?"

Jenny sighed. She'd have to go. Her conscience wouldn't let her do anything else.

"All right, Veronica, I'll come down. But I have to take the bus, so it's going to be a while."

THIS TIME, getting Veronica released wasn't at all the simple matter it had been before.

The justice of the peace gave Jenny a scornful look and pulled out a file of legal documents. He consulted the computer and drew up Veronica's file. "This is a summary conviction offense, and Mrs. Glickman does have a permanent address and a history of appearing for court, but she also has a history of previous convictions for the same offense—eight of them. Under the circumstances, the crown will unquestionably be seeking a jail term. For this reason, I'm insisting that someone other than her counsel act as surety."

Jenny's heart sank. "But there's no one else but me. Couldn't you allow it just this once?"

The JP was unmoved. "Sorry." He turned away from the counter and picked up a cup of coffee he'd been drinking.

"Could I see my client then, please?"

Jenny rode the elevator to the top floor where the jail cells were. Veronica was brought into the cell set aside for interviews. She was a sad, disgusting mess. Her hair was a rat's nest, her eyes swollen from crying, and her layers of coats dirtier than usual. She was wringing her hands, obviously distraught.

"Miss Jenny, I'm so glad you're here. You can get me out, can't you?"

Jenny explained the predicament. Veronica, her watery blue eyes wild, became still more agitated. "What you've got to do, Miss Jenny, is call Conroy. He'll come and get me out. He's done it before. Go call him. His number's in the phone book—I can't ever remember it."

Exasperated, Jenny stared at her hapless client. Was Veronica hallucinating again, or was she relating facts? Jenny remembered the property taxes, the checks from a Mr. Clark. She sighed and shook her head. "I'll give it a try, Veronica, but I have the feeling you're about to have me make a gigantic fool of myself."

Downstairs again, she began searching the phone directory.

There were two or three pages of Clarks. But there, between Colin Clark and Cornelius Clark, was Conroy.

Dubious, she tried the number.

"Hello?" The man's voice was low-pitched and gentle.

"Mr. Clark, my name is Jenny Lathrop, I'm a law student, acting as counsel for Veronica Glickman. She's in some difficulty, and she seems to think—"

"Where is she?"

"At 312 Main Street. The city jail."

He sighed. "Again, huh? I'll be right down. Good thing you caught me on my day off."

Dumbfounded, Jenny slowly hung up.

CLARK WAS A TALL, thin man in his fifties, casually but expensively dressed in cords and a sheepskin-lined brown leather jacket. He was obviously familiar with the procedure that released Veronica. He posted bond, and announced that he'd drive Veronica, subdued and exhausted, over to her house.

"Do you have a car, Ms. Lathrop?" There was nothing dynamic about him, but he was quietly capable.

"I came by bus, I can easily—"

"Not at all. Come along with us."

Veronica had regained some of her usual bombastic aplomb by the time they were seated in Clark's elegant black Lincoln sedan. She insisted on getting in the front beside him. She demanded a cigarette and then, drawing deeply on it, regaled the other two with a convoluted tale of how she'd been framed and wrongfully charged. But by the time they reached her house, she was silent again, obviously worn-out.

Clark didn't lecture her, and neither did he flinch when she leaned over and kissed his cheek before she got out of the car. He patted her arm and gave her a weary smile.

"Goodbye, Veronica."

"If you want to come in, I'll buy you both a drink," Veronica offered with a final show of bravado.

Clark gently refused. Leaving the motor idling, he waited until Veronica had unlocked her front door and gone inside.

"Why not move up front, Ms. Lathrop?" His faint, weary smile came and went again. "It makes me feel less like a chauffeur."

Jenny did. Veronica's pungent aroma and the smell of her cigarette filled the car, and he pushed a button that rolled the windows down. He asked her address, and they drove through the evening streets of the downtown city almost in silence. There were a million questions Jenny wanted to ask, but Clark seemed lost in a reverie, driving competently without really thinking about what he was doing.

At a stoplight on Granville, he suddenly asked, "How did you meet Veronica, Ms. Lathrop?"

Jenny explained about the Legal Clinic and the problems with Veronica's house being condemned by the city. She wanted to ask him the same question, but she couldn't bring herself to do it.

Clark nodded at her answer. A moment later, he asked abruptly, "Have you had dinner, Ms. Lathrop?"

Jenny couldn't even remember having lunch.

"Would you consider having dinner with me? I hate eating alone, and there's a place near here where I often go."

He took her to a small Italian restaurant where the management obviously knew and liked him.

Although he was reticent at first, gradually over the delectable pasta and Caesar salad, he began to relax. He asked questions about law school and listened to Jenny's answers attentively. He ordered wine, and Jenny had a small glassful. It gave her courage to ask him the questions that had been haunting her all evening.

How did he know Veronica? What was his connection with the sad woman? What had made Veronica the way she was today?

"Veronica and I were married for seven years, a long time ago, when we both were young," he began slowly. He looked across the table at her for several long moments of silence, as if deliberating, and then he said, "Tell me, Ms. Lathrop, where did you grow up? What was your childhood like?"

"My name's Jenny," she insisted before she launched into an abbreviated version of her childhood. He listened closely. When she finished, he looked at her and nodded.

"Your own background might make it easier to understand what happened to us," he responded at last. "I grew up not far from where Veronica's house is situated now, in the Vancouver slums. My mother raised me. I never knew my father. An old guy sold me a beat-up guitar for five bucks I'd earned shoveling coal out of boxcars when I was thirteen, and by the time I was sixteen, I was singing on street corners."

A smile played across his mouth as he remembered. "I got in some trouble that year, spent six months in a juvenile detention home for breaking and entering. One of the supervisors there took an interest in me, arranged for me to have a few music lessons, and when I got out, a couple of coffee houses hired me to play and sing on weekends for their clientele, and that's how I met Veronica. I was nineteen by then, and so was she, and that's about all we had in common. She was the only child of a wealthy and prominent family. Her father was a liquor importer. She'd had a private-school education and a trip to Europe to celebrate her eighteenth birthday. She was the focus of her parents' lives, and she resented it. Even then, Veronica hated control of any sort. She needed to be a free spirit."

Jenny was fascinated. She didn't want to interrupt him even for a second, and she resented the arrival of the waiter with cups of hot, strong coffee. When he moved away, Clark took up the story where he'd left off.

"We fell in love. You might not think so now, but she was beautiful then. She symbolized all the things I'd never had, I guess."

He gazed down into his coffee cup and gave a small shrug.

"I got her pregnant. We eloped, drove down into the States and got married. Well, all hell broke loose when her family found out. Her father dredged up my conviction. They threatened to disown her unless she had the marriage annulled. When that didn't work, they tried to bribe her, with a car and a trip to Hawaii. Old man Glickman managed to have me fired from the gigs I'd gotten—he knew everybody around town. And of course, I came to hate him and his wife. I hated their money, their efforts to use it to control Veronica and me."

Lost in old, painful memories, Clark sat in silence, his coffee forgotten. Just when Jenny thought he'd forgotten all about her, too, he took up the tale again. "When our son, Derek, was born, they tried to make peace. They desperately wanted a part of their grandson."

He looked into Jenny's eyes and his voice was sardonic. "Now it was my turn to be snotty. I wouldn't let them near him. I had power at last, and I used it. Veronica adored her baby. She asked me to let her parents come and see him. But

I wouldn't give in, even when we found out Derek had a serious medical problem. His heart was damaged, and the surgery he needed wasn't available in Canada, which meant it would cost a huge amount of money. There was only a slim chance it would work, anyhow. Veronica told her father, and Glickman offered to pay, but there were conditions—about the boy's upbringing, his schooling. Veronica begged me to go along with it, but I swore I'd raise the money myself, steal it if I had to. Her parents pressured her, insisting she leave me and let them take over Derek's care."

The waiter came and poured them fresh coffee. Clark's hands trembled when he lifted his cup and took a long drink.

"See, she was in the middle. She loved me, she loved Derek, and she didn't want to lose either of us. But she wasn't emotionally strong like I was. She'd been pampered all her life, and her parents were her parents. She begged me, over and over, to accept their help, to bend just a little. But I went right on being stubborn."

He was quiet for so long Jenny began to wonder if he'd say anything more. When he did, his voice was filled with pain.

"Derek died early one morning. The doctors insisted nothing could have saved him, but Veronica went into a deep depression. She blamed all of us—me, her parents. But probably herself most of all."

A cold shiver went down Jenny's back, at the awful tragedy of the situation he was describing.

"It was ironic, but just when my personal life was falling apart, my career started to take off, and I had to be away from home a lot. I wasn't there when she needed me. She started roaming the streets, drinking too much. Eventually she had to go into a clinic. She spent a lot of time over the years in different facilities. That's why she has this horror of being locked up. But each time she was released, she'd gradually slide into the sort of life she lives now—wandering around, fighting, drinking, getting into trouble and out of it again. I tried for years, but she was lost, and eventually I divorced her. I couldn't handle the problems she created."

He was quiet again, and Jenny's heart ached for him.

"Before her father died, he bought her the house. He also left a trust fund for her. She gets money from it every month and will for the rest of her life. Far as I know, she gives most of it away or spends it on booze."

He didn't say anything about paying the property taxes and bailing Veronica out at times like this, and Jenny didn't mention it. Was it some remnant of affection for that young and beautiful Veronica that made him go on taking care of her? Or was it guilt?

Only Conroy Clark knew the answer, and Jenny thought his reasons didn't really matter. The thing was simply that he did it.

"Did you ever remarry?"

He smiled wistfully and shook his head, looking down at his coffee cup. "My job keeps me busy. I'm on the road a lot of the time—I don't really meet the marrying kind of woman." Then he met her gaze and said in a flat tone, "That's not entirely true. There was a lady, a few years back. I should've married her, but I didn't. Simple truth is, I lost my nerve somewhere along the line. You married, Jenny?"

"I was. He died."

"Well, try again. Don't get stuck in the past the way I did."

He drove her home soon afterward, and she thanked him for dinner and watched as the big, luxurious car slid silently away into the night.

Money didn't buy happiness, that was certain.

Later that night, she couldn't sleep.

She kept going over the tragic story Clark had told her, and thinking of herself and Zach.

Clark had, by his own admission, been unforgiving—just as judgmental in his own way as the Glickmans. Prejudice obviously wasn't limited to the Glickmans of the world. Clark's stiff-necked pride had been the cause of a lot of heartache.

How different were her own attitudes, when it came right down to it? From the very beginning she'd held Zach's privileged background against him. She'd been prepared not to like his family, just because they were wealthy. Why, only a few days ago, she'd assumed his sister was patronizing her with the offer of lunch.

What if Serena was offering friendship instead?

Jenny would never know.

Clark was alone, heading into old age sorry for the things he had and hadn't done, yet unable to muster the courage to try again.

Was that what she wanted her own future to hold?

And what if it was already too late? What if Zach didn't want her anymore? She'd been scathing. She'd said unforgivable things.

In the early hours of the morning, she decided to call Serena within the next few days and ask her to lunch. Maybe, after she'd made friends with Serena, she'd even work up enough courage to call Zach.

A person had to start somewhere.

By PULLING STRINGS and begging favors, Zach managed to arrange an early date for the Redthorn examination of discovery through the court registrar's office—too early, perhaps. He'd only have a little more than a week to prepare, but if he worked day and night, he might just make it.

Ken and Derek weren't exactly enthusiastic about his taking Redthorn on, and certainly not on a *pro bono* basis. At first they made a lot of negative noises but because of the Solomen triumph, they didn't object all that strenuously.

Zach was the hero of the moment, after all, and he attacked the Redthorn matter with puritanical zeal. He wanted to present Jenny with a happy ending to Redthorn's plight; he needed to hand her the victory as if it were a symbolic bunch of long-stemmed roses.

Zach had Brenda track down Elias Redthorn. The little man was overjoyed at Zach's decision to take on his case, and as Zach listened to him reiterate the details of how he came to be trapped inside the cumbersome body brace, he began to see Redthorn as the epitome of a man treated unfairly by a callous legal system.

Redthorn could hardly get around well enough to take care of his own needs.

Zach understood now why Jenny had been outraged at the situation.

The only real problem Zach had was the fact that he found his client just as repulsive as he had the first time he'd met him, at the Legal Clinic, and the more he saw of him, the stronger the feeling became.

Redthorn whined, fawned and groveled, dragging himself over to the overstuffed leather armchair in Zach's office and collapsing into it with a pathetic sigh.

"Lovely chair, governor, lovely. Wish you could see what I've got fer a chair at my place. Nothin' fancy like this, I can tell you. You're a lucky man, governor, able to afford a chair like this one. Eases me back, this does." He'd lean his head back and close his eyes, his stiff body brace jutting out from under his ill-fitting suit coat, his built-up shoe not quite touching the carpet.

By Redthorn's third visit, Zach was more than ready to donate the damned chair to the pathetic little man, just so he wouldn't have to watch the performance one more time.

But there wasn't time to dwell on personal feelings.

Zach put all his energy, all his waking hours and a substantial amount of the firm's money into preparing his case against the city's Police Department and Constable Marvin Scott, who'd recovered the car and then released it to Redthorn.

At great expense, he hired an engineering reconstructionist to go over Redthorn's car and present a crystal-clear picture of why it went out of control when Elias drove it after the theft. He interviewed all the policemen involved in the matter and subpoenaed them as witnesses. Elias supplied him with a detailed report from his doctor describing the injuries to his back.

When Thursday and the examination for discovery rolled around in the matter of *Redthorn* versus *Vancouver City Police*, Zach was ready. He put on his navy pin-striped suit and walked proudly into the hearing room, deliberately shortening his stride to keep pace with Elias, who was limping along bravely beside him.

Usually, there was a little anxiety about this procedure, a feeling of apprehension about the outcome of these rather formal, pretrial proceedings.

This morning, Zach was free of any misgivings about the action. He had absolute confidence in the essential rightness of this case, and consequently in his ability to eventually win a sizable settlement for Redthorn.

He'd never felt as assured or as philanthropic about anything in his entire life.

He'd never wanted a trial to proceed more than he did now.

He wanted to get this formality over with and have a trial date set, the sooner the better—because the sooner he won, the sooner he could convince the woman he loved to marry him.

The registrar, Mr. John Seaton, who happened to be an old friend of Zach's father, was a dignified and stately man. Conscious of propriety, he met Zach's gaze and gave an almost-imperceptible nod of recognition.

"In the matter of *Redthorn* versus *Vancouver City Police*, Mr. Jones, would you like to present your evidence?"

Feeling righteous, Zach began.

12

SERENA HAD SUGGESTED Thursday as a good day for lunch, and Jenny was waiting, more than a little nervous and annoyed, when Zach's sister hurried into the cozy restaurant long past the one o'clock they'd agreed on. Jenny had spent the time checking the menu prices and adding up the money in her wallet. She'd invited Serena, and she was determined she was paying for lunch. It gave her some obscure feeling of power and control.

"Sorry I'm late. There's always an emergency just when you're in a hurry. You're so fortunate to still be a student and not have to deal with the realities of the work world."

Jenny, even though she tried not to, felt a small stab of resentment at that. She thought of her trips down to the city jail to spring Veronica, and the fact that she'd cut an important lecture just to accommodate this luncheon. Now, because Serena was late, she'd miss the next one, as well. What the hell did this woman, in her expensive wool suit, know about reality?

She bit her tongue. She was going to be open and warm and friendly and nonjudgmental. Even if it strangled her.

But talking with Serena, one on one, was no easier than it had been with Zach beside her. She was so cool and utterly poised that Jenny felt like an awkward thirteen-year-old being subjected to an IQ test. A not-quite-bright thirteen-year-old.

After several eons had passed as they remarked on how nice the café was, the waitress finally came, and they ordered.

They discussed the weather as Serena nibbled at her salad and Jenny hungrily attacked her toasted tomato sandwich and double order of fries.

Serena hoped it would snow so she could go up to the condo at Whistler and get some skiing in.

Jenny prayed it wouldn't. Snow meant the city buses might not run, so transportation became a major pain, and her basement suite turned three degrees colder than an igloo.

Serena tactfully changed the subject to clothes. Did Jenny know that Elle, the smart little designer boutique in Granville, was having a sale?

Jenny knew the store. It was half a block from New To You, where she'd found some of her best bargains.

Stalemate.

Serena rallied, mentioning the latest prank the engineering students had pulled on campus. A hundred-foot-high balloon, shaped like a condom, was somehow attached to the top of the clock tower, with a fan inside that kept the thing constantly inflated.

Serena thought it was an outrage. Jenny had found it pretty funny.

Jenny ordered a hot-fudge sundae for dessert. Serena had tea—no cream or sugar. Jenny felt like a glutton, and didn't care.

She had her mouth full when Serena set her teacup down and cleared her throat. Her piercing green eyes boring into Jenny, she said, "I understand you and Zach are having some problems. I'm quite good at counseling, if you'd care to talk about it. It's the difference in your backgrounds that's causing the trouble?"

Jenny choked and before she could get her napkin to her mouth, spatters of chocolate ice cream went flying across the table, and through streaming eyes she saw them land on Serena's white silk shirt. Tears ran down her face, taking with them the mascara she'd put on in Serena's honor.

"It's...it's...umm...it's a private matter," she finally managed to gasp, taking a huge gulp of water. And how in blazing hell did Serena know so much about it, anyway?

As if she'd read her mind, Serena went on, unperturbed. "I was talking to Zach, and I was concerned. He's rather fond of you, Jenny."

"Fond?" Had Zach said that, too. That he was rather fond of her? The very idea of Zach discussing their relationship with anyone made her furious. Discussing her with Serena and using a word like *fond*... Well, she'd kill him for it.

Fond, indeed! She remembered the passion they'd shared, the intensity of their loving, and a fine rage took the place of the empty, lost feeling she'd been trying to fill with food ever since she'd lost him. She wanted to shock this confident, patronizing Jones woman right out of her elegant black pumps.

"Did he tell you he was fond enough of me to break my bed one night, making love?" Jenny heard herself saying in a furious tone to her.

To her amazement, Serena smiled at that—her controlled, cool smile, which Jenny considered condescending.

"Oh, I know the two of you are sexually compatible," she remarked, glancing at her diamond-encrusted wristwatch. "Well, if you don't want to discuss it, I'm afraid I must fly. It's been fun. We'll do it again soon. Good luck with my big brother."

She scooped up the check, paid the cashier and swept out the door, leaving Jenny frustrated, furious, trembling, and feeling betrayed.

Serena could drive a saint to homicide.

And Zach... How could he actually confide in that woman, sister or not?

Gradually, rage overcame the other emotions Serena had generated.

Tonight was Legal Clinic, there were things she had to prepare, and the afternoon was almost shot. But after the clinic, she was going to do her best to track down Zachary Jones and give him a piece of her mind.

"ANOTHER REFILL, SIR?"

"Sure, why not?" Zach had been in the pub for over an hour now, ever since the examination for discovery had ended earlier that afternoon. The coffee he was drinking certainly wasn't doing anything to blur the scene in the registrar's office, but Zach doubted anything would accomplish that. He still had the uncontrollable urge to murder Elias Redthorn, but maybe that would go away, too. Eventually.

"Thanks."

"No problem." The bartender gave him an odd look. He probably thought Zach was weird, sitting in a pub and drinking coffee, but he didn't say anything.

Zach took a long gulp of the lukewarm liquid, oblivious to the way it tasted.

The entire fiasco kept replaying in his head.

The plaintiff customarily presented evidence first, and Zach had stood with supreme confidence, reading the depositions from witnesses, producing the corroborative evidence the engineering reconstructionist had come up with about the car, showing the statement Redthorn had given him from the doctor detailing the back injuries.

Zach had made a short, brilliantly impassioned speech about the difficulties of getting through life doubly handicapped as the result of a miscarriage of justice.

He hadn't had a moment's doubt about a damned thing until Ozzie King appeared, carrying a video and apologizing to everyone for being late, then taking his place beside the lawyer for the defense.

When Zach sat down, the defense lawyer set up a video machine and from the moment it was switched on, Zach wished with all his heart that he'd become a football player instead of a lawyer.

The first frames were taken at Parker's Billiards, the day after Zach had agreed to take the case. Elias had obviously discarded the body brace and was bent over a snooker table, cue held expertly, a cigar in the corner of his lying little mouth.

In the next frames, Redthorn was drinking beer with his arm around a bosomy brunette in red tights. There was no sign of the body brace, and no indication that Elias was suffering any discomfort other than sexual turbulence.

The final shot was of Elias at the racetrack—again without the brace—limping over to collect his winnings from the ticket window, with a big grin on his devious face.

Mr. John Seaton had, of course, denied trial. He'd questioned Redthorn about the medical report and Elias admitted it was from a doctor he knew who would sign anything for fifty dollars.

Mr. Seaton then fixed Zach with his beady, judgmental eye and lectured him.

"Before you launch into an action of this nature, young man, you should delve deeper into the integrity of your client."

Zach humbly apologized for wasting everyone's time, feeling more a fool than he could ever remember.

He left the building with Redthorn plucking at his suit coat and whining about bad luck, and Ozzie King blaring out, "No hard feelings, right, counselor? A job's a job, right?"

It was to keep himself from shoving Redthorn into the path of an oncoming bus that Zach had taken refuge in the pub.

He'd started to order a drink, then changed it to coffee instead. He needed to get control of himself, and liquor wasn't the answer for that. The bartender refilled the mug twice, and it was almost empty again before the towering rage inside began to calm.

Another refill, and he gradually began to see the element of black humor in the whole thing.

He'd done exactly what he was always warning Jenny against doing. He'd taken Redthorn at face value; he'd believed his story because the man seemed so pathetic, so vulnerable. Why hadn't he checked him out minutely, the way he had Solomen, the way he did every other client he took on?

Zach admitted to himself that he'd decided to be a perfect hero in Jenny's eyes, and to hell with the facts. For the first time in his career, he'd let his heart rule his head.

It took a trip to the washroom and a hamburger platter to prevent caffeine poisoning before it dawned on him that maybe this whole thing wasn't so bad, after all.

Don't you ever make mistakes? Jenny had asked him.

Maybe being colossally wrong once in a while was the way to go with her. Maybe she'd appreciate a flawed hero more than a perfect one. You just never knew with Jenny.

Which was exactly why he loved her the way he did. She was the only woman in the entire world for him—except that he'd never told her that, had he?

Maybe he should go and tell her now. She'd be at the Legal Clinic for another hour.

And maybe he should have one little drink of something stronger than coffee, just to celebrate figuring all this out.

C'mon, Jones. If you're hell-bent on being honest, admit that you need the drink because you're scared. And that that's no good reason for having one.

WITH EACH PASSING HOUR, Jenny's decision to find Zach and have it all out with him became less resolute. The steady stream of people and problems wore her down, drained her, and each time she thought of the luncheon she'd endured with Serena, she felt exhausted and heartsick.

She'd come to the conclusion that the differences between her and Serena really weren't due to money or background. The two of them were simply opposites. They might as well have come from different planets, for all they had in common.

Was that true of her and Zach, as well? In between clients, she pondered it. Maybe she ought to just let well enough alone.

Most of the other students had finished with their clients and already gone home. Even Jenny's flood of troubled people had slowed to a trickle by now, and she decided it would be a relief to just go home herself.

Veronica was waiting until the end to talk with her, as usual, and the only other person waiting to see her was Mr. Travesano, a round, volatile little Italian whom Jenny had successfully defended for a traffic violation in small claims court several weeks before. Mr. Travesano had gotten himself into a mess with the Insurance Corporation, mostly because his English was sketchy at best, and when he was under duress, almost nonexistent. But Jenny had managed to sort it all out and get the charges against him dismissed. She'd noticed him waiting patiently in line again tonight and wondered what new difficulty brought him here.

He came over now and beamed at her, his dark eyes gleaming. "Missa Jenny, no problem. Just I come to say thank-you." He set a large brown paper bag on her table. "This is a wine for you, I make myself. I hope you like." He reached across to pump her hand up and down vigorously several times. "*Grazie*, Missa Jenny. If ever I need the lawyer again, I will come to you. *Grazie*."

"Why, Mr. Travesano, how kind of you! Thank you very much." Touched, Jenny smiled at him and came around from behind the table, whereupon Mr. Travesano moved closer to her, gripped her head between his sweating palms and kissed her—a huge, noisy smack on each cheek.

Jenny's delighted smile froze on her lips. Over Mr. Travesano's shoulder, she saw Zach coming toward her table, and he wasn't smiling at all. He had an overcoat slung over his shoulder, the top three buttons of his pale blue shirt were undone and his tie was loosened. His hair was tousled, his shirt sleeves were rolled up past his forearms, and there was a dangerous gleam in his green eyes.

"Ms. Lathrop, what seems to be the problem here? Is this man bothering you?" He leveled a malevolent look at poor Mr. Travesano. The little man began to back up, away from Zach.

"*Arrivederci*, Missa Jenny. *Arrivederci*. *Grazie*. No problem, no problem." Mr. Travesano turned on his heel and dashed for the door, where the volunteer was already shrugging into her raincoat. The large, echoing room was empty except for Veronica, who was now puffing her way across the room toward Jenny's desk.

"For heaven's sake, Zach, that man was my client. He brought me a bottle of wine..." Jenny's indignant voice trailed off as Zach took the final two steps that separated them and pulled her almost roughly into his arms.

"What the hell was he doing kissing you? That's what I'd like to know!" He glared down at her. "If anybody kisses you from here on in, they'll answer to me."

Veronica had arrived, and was all for protecting Jenny from Zach. She had ahold of one of Zach's arms and was doing her best to pull him away from Jenny.

"Hey, cut that out." Zach tried to shake her off, but she was tenacious, and much stronger than she looked. He shot Jenny a pleading look, still holding her close despite Veronica's best efforts to rip him bodily away.

"You want me to go call the cops, Miss Jenny?"

It was splendid being in his arms again, but it prevented her from thinking clearly. Distracted for a moment by Veronica, Jenny suddenly remembered what she'd been mad at him about. It almost killed her, but she struggled out of his embrace and scowled up at him.

"What I'd like to know is where you get off telling your sister, of all people, about us, Zachary Jones?" Jenny put her hands on her hips, remembering. "And what's with this 'fond' business? Did you actually tell Serena you were just fond of me?"

"What the hell are you talking about? Fond? I'm not fond of you, for cripes' sake." Zach was out of patience. He smacked his palm down on the tabletop, sending the box of tissues to the floor. "I love you, damn it all. I'm going to marry you. And I never told Serena a damned thing about us. Well, maybe I mentioned we'd had a fight and I was brokenhearted—"

"He's a raving loony! I'm going for the cops!" Veronica let go of Zach's sleeve and headed for the door.

"Jenny, would you do something about that woman?" Zach was watching Veronica struggling with the locked door.

He'd just said he loved her. He'd said he was going to marry her. Something like organ music was playing in Jenny's heart.

"She's going to have a squad car here any minute, and the Vancouver police aren't exactly amused by me today." Zach was sounding desperate.

"Veronica, it's all right," Jenny called out. "Mr. Jones is a friend of mine. He's harmless."

"Harmless? A friend?" Zach sounded as outraged as she'd been about "fond," and Jenny was delighted. She shoved her glasses higher up on her nose and grinned at him. Now that she knew the truth, she could maybe tease him just a little bit.

Veronica came back and took a stance two feet away from them, her arms crossed on her well-covered chest.

"That's what everybody thinks about serial killers, too, Miss Jenny. That they're harmless. I'm stayin' right here, don't you worry."

Zach gave her a malevolent look, and was reminded of Elias Redthorn.

He told Jenny about taking the case on, and what had happened at the examination for discovery. "Redthorn's a con man, and he made me look like a fool. You should have seen him at the horse races, spry as anything without his body brace."

"Why, that little creep!" Veronica was outraged. "Y'know, Miss Jenny, I never trusted that guy. I should never have sent him to you in the first place."

Jenny ignored Veronica. She was gazing up at Zach, her eyes suspiciously bright behind her glasses. "But you took the case on, after all. I can't believe you took the case. You did that for me, didn't you, Zach? And I was so proud of you over the Solomen victory. You were marvelous!" She walked over to him and reached up, putting her arms around his neck. "Oh, Zach, I'm sorry for all those things I said to you. I was scared of losing you, because I love you, too. I've loved you for so long...."

Veronica made a rude noise. "Don't fall for the likes of him, Miss Jenny. Be an independent woman, here. He'll just up and use you for a mud slide, and he's a lawyer into the bargain. You can't trust lawyers—I mean, apart from you. I know. I had trouble like you wouldn't believe with some of 'em. Take it from one who's been there...."

In unspoken and perfect agreement, Jenny and Zach each took Veronica gently by an arm. They quick-marched her over to the door. Zach wrestled the lock open, and they escorted her out.

"Veronica, we're both lawyers. There're things we have to discuss in private," Jenny told her quietly. "I'll see you next Thursday."

As they stepped back inside and closed the door, they could hear her grumbling about lawyers all the way down the steps. No personal feelings... All they cared about was the law....

Zach locked the door again and drew Jenny into his arms. "Now, counselor..."

He slipped her glasses off her nose and slid them into his pocket.

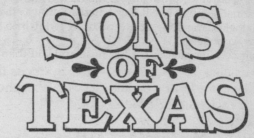

Your very favorite Silhouette miniseries
characters now have a BRAND-NEW story in

Brought to you by:

LINDA
HOWARD

DEBBIE
MACOMBER

LINDA
TURNER

A woman with a shocking secret.
A man without a past.
Together, their love could be nothing less than

Scandalous

The latest romantic adventure from

CANDACE CAMP

When a stranger suffering a loss of memory lands on Priscilla Hamilton's doorstep, her carefully guarded secret is threatened. Always a model of propriety, she knows that no one would believe the deep, dark desire that burns inside her at this stranger's touch.

As scandal and intrigue slowly close in on the lovers, will their attraction be strong enough to survive?

Find out this September at your favorite retail outlet.

MIRA **The brightest star in women's fiction**   MCCSC

Look us up on-line at:http://www.romance.net

National Bestselling Author

JoAnn Ross

Welcomes you to Raintree, Georgia—
steamy capital of sin, scandal and murder.

Southern Comforts

Chelsea Cassidy is the official biographer of
Roxanne Scarbrough—the Southern Queen of good
taste who's built an empire around the how-to's of
gracious living. It's clear to Chelsea that somebody
wants her employer dead.

As Chelsea explores the dark secrets of Roxanne's
life, the search leads Chelsea into the arms of
Cash Beaudine. And now her investigating becomes
personal with potentially fatal consequences.

Available this September wherever books are sold.

You're About to Become a *Privileged Woman*

Reap the rewards of fabulous free gifts and benefits with proofs-of-purchase from Harlequin and Silhouette books

Pages & Privileges™

It's our way of thanking you for buying our books at your favorite retail stores.

PROOF OF PURCHASE BR-PP171
Offer expires October 31, 1996

Pages & Privileges™

**Harlequin and Silhouette—
the most privileged readers in the world!**

For more information about Harlequin and Silhouette's PAGES & PRIVILEGES program call the Pages & Privileges Benefits Desk: 1-503-794-2499

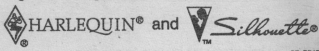
HARLEQUIN® and *Silhouette®*

BR-PP171